國語的句子與子句結構

SENTENCE AND CLAUSE STRUCTURE IN CHINESE:
A FUNCTIONAL PERSPECTIVE

曹逢甫著　　　　BY
　　　　　　FENG-FU TSAO

臺灣 學生書局 印行
Student Book Co., Ltd.
198, Ho-Ping East Road, 1st Section
Taipei, Taiwan, Republic of China 10610

曹逢甫 博士

著者簡介

　　曹逢甫，台灣省彰化縣人，民國三十一年生。民國五十三年畢業於國立台灣師範大學英語系。曾執教於台北建國中學、中山女高等校，五十九年至六十一年留學美國夏威夷大學，六十三年至六十五年又赴美國南加州大學研究語言學與語言教學，於六十六年八月獲博士學位。畢業後曾先後執教於師範大學、輔仁大學、香港大學、美國達慕斯大學以及匹茲堡大學。現執教於國立清華大學語言學研究所及外語系。著有「主題在國語中的功能研究(英文版)」一書及在國內外學術專刊發表之論文三十餘篇，並參與主編文馨當代英漢辭典以及文馨推理聽讀系列十冊等數種。

「現代語言學論叢」緣起

　　語言與文字是人類歷史上最偉大的發明。有了語言，人類才能超越一切禽獸成為萬物之靈。有了文字，祖先的文化遺產才能綿延不絕，相傳到現在。尤有進者，人的思維或推理都以語言為媒介，因此如能揭開語言之謎，對於人心之探求至少就可以獲得一半的解答。

　　中國對於語文的研究有一段悠久而輝煌的歷史，成為漢學中最受人重視的一環。為了繼承這光榮的傳統並且繼續予以發揚光大起見，我們準備刊行「現代語言學論叢」。在這論叢裏，我們有系統地介紹並討論現代語言學的理論與方法，同時運用這些理論與方法，從事國語語音、語法、語意各方面的分析與研究。論叢將分為兩大類：甲類用國文撰寫，乙類用英文撰寫。我們希望將來還能開闢第三類，以容納國內研究所學生的論文。

　　在人文科學普遍遭受歧視的今天，「現代語言學論叢」的出版可以說是一個相當勇敢的嘗試。我們除了感謝臺北學生書局提供這難得的機會以外，還虔誠地呼籲國內外從事漢語語言學研究的學者不斷給予支持與鼓勵。

湯　廷　池

民國六十五年九月二十九日於臺北

語文教學叢書緣起

　　現代語言學是行為科學的一環，當行為科學在我國逐漸受到重視的時候，現代語言學卻還停留在拓荒的階段。

　　為了在中國推展這門嶄新的學科，我們幾年前成立了「現代語言學論叢編輯委員會」，計畫有系統地介紹現代語言學的理論與方法，並利用這些理論與方法從事國語與其他語言有關語音、語法、語意、語用等各方面的分析與研究。經過這幾年來的努力耕耘，總算出版了幾本尚足稱道的書，逐漸受到中外學者與一般讀者的重視。

　　今天是羣策羣力、和衷共濟的時代，少數幾個人究竟難成「氣候」。為了開展語言學的領域，我們決定在「現代語言學論叢」之外，編印「語文教學叢書」，專門出版討論中外語文教學理論與實際應用的著作。我們竭誠歡迎對現代語言學與語文教學懷有熱忱的朋友共同來開拓這塊「新生地」。

語文教學叢書編輯委員會　謹誌

自 序

在我的博士論文:《國語主題的功能研究:邁向言談分析的第一步》裡我曾經寫到,當我初讀趙元任先生的創世紀大著《中國話的語法》時,我的確曾為裡頭許許多多有趣且詳盡精闢的分析而感到神迷。但當數年後我想用他的文法架構來從事言談分析時,又不能不感到失望,因為趙先生所界定的中文的句子往往不是實際言談中的一個完整獨立的單位。

從那時起已有許多人跟我提起說我把趙先生的大著單獨挑出來批評是不公平的,因為同樣的批評也適用於大多數已出版的中國文法。趙先生能看出主題一評論在中文中的重要已經是比一般文法家高明甚多了。這段對我的話的評論我想是相當公允的,其實我當時提出趙先生的大作只是想點明該書是促使我日後致力於尋找國語言談基本單位的原動力。

後來經數年不停的尋尋覓覓我終於發現要解開中文句子之謎非先徹底研究主題在句子結構中所起的作用不可。這一部分的研究成果就是我的博士論文。該論文寫就後兩年以單行本問世(台北學生書局,現代語言學論叢乙種第三冊)。 在該書中我曾多處提及主題串(一個以句首主題組與一個或數個有關於該主題的評論子句所串連而成的語言單位)為中國話的言談基本單位,惜當時因學力不足未能深究主題串中各種子句的結構以及它們和主題的關係。儘管如此,該書出版後仍在台灣、中國大陸和歐美的漢語學界引起相當大的迴響。除了歐美大學中文系採用為教材外,並曾在中國大陸出版的兩本漢語語法史中得到相當高的評價。這些好評當然加深了我的信心並促使我更加緊從主題串的觀點來探討中文句子和子句的結構。本書即是筆者最近十年來在這方面研究的集大成。因此本書也可以說是前提博士論文的延伸。

如前所言，本書在內容上採自筆者近十年來所發表之論文者甚多（詳見書後書目表），因此擬藉此再次向對這些論文有過幫助者提出誠摯的謝意。十年來，筆者也曾先後在台灣師範大學，國立清華大學，香港大學，美國達慕斯大學以及匹茲堡大學教授語法學，語意學以及漢語語言學，學生們的問題與討論一直是我寫作的泉源之一，對這些學生我也要說聲謝謝。前提論文中有數篇曾得到國科會的年度及優等獎助，有兩三篇也因得到國科會的補助而得以在國際研討會上發表。對國科會在這方面的獎勵，本人也擬藉此表達崇高的敬意。

本書在撰寫期間得清華大學語言研究所的林玉惠、蕭素英兩位助理甚多幫助，在輸入電腦以及編排方面也先後得張冬梅和樊菊英二位小姐的幫忙，筆者也要在此表達由衷的謝意。台北學生書局在用英文寫的語言學論文市場有限的情況下能慨允先把筆者的第一本書再版然後接著出版本書，筆者除了對他們在台灣文化界所做的奉獻表示敬意外，更當對他們的幫助表示無限的謝意。最後，我更要藉這個機會來謝謝內人蘇愛珠女士和我們的孩子－翠婷和煥之－他們除了在這段期間常有因為我工作忙碌不得不臨時取消旅遊計劃的失望之外，還得不時忍受我在研究遇到困難時所生的壞脾氣。沒有上述這麼多人的幫助、奉獻和忍耐，這部書是絕對出不來的。

曹逢甫 *1990年2月於清大文2202研究室*

PREFACE

In the preface to my Ph. D. dissertation, <u>A Functional Study of Topic in Chinese: The First Step Towards Discourse Analysis,</u> I stated that when I first read Chao's epoch-making volume, <u>A Grammar of Spoken Chinese</u>, soon after its publication in 1968, I was greatly impressed by its many interesting, and often detailed, observations and analyses about Chinese grammatical structure. However, a few years later, when I tried to apply his grammatical description to actual discourse analysis, I was disappointed, because what is identified by Chao as a sentence does not often function as a discourse unit.

It has since then been pointed out to me that I was rather unfair to single out Chao for that comment since the same comment was equally applicable to many published Chinese grammars. Anyway, fair or unfair, that was what set me off searching for a functional basic unit in Chinese discourse.

My quest has led me to the study of topic and the role it plays in the structure of Chinese. The result of this first stage of the search was presented in my dissertation, which, in its slightly revised version, was published by the Student Book Co., Taipei in 1979. In that book I suggested at various places without giving detailed arguments for it that topic chain, a stretch of discourse consisting of one or more clauses headed by a topic which is what each clause predicates of, is a basic discourse unit in Chinese. Despite this and other shortcomings, the book has since then been very well received, having been used as a textbook in a number of colleges and extensively reviewed and highly evaluated by two books on history of Chinese grammatical studies published in mainland China. This has considerably strengthened my conviction and prompted me to go into the study of Chinese sentence and clause structure from this perspective. I have since then done a number of studies about the most prominent clause types, ranging from the simplest SVO clause to the most complex such as the serial verb constructions and the so-called "*de* complement" constructions and the present volume is a composite result of those efforts. In this sense, this book is a continuation of my research presented in my dissertation.

In preparing this book, as I have just said, I have drawn heavily from many of the papers that I have published in the past ten years (please see the bibliography at the end for a complete list), I would, therefore, like to thank those who in one way or another have contributed to those papers. To all the students who took my Syntax, Semantics and Chinese Linguistics classes at National Taiwan Normal University, Fu Jen Catholic University, National Tsing Hua University, University of Hong Kong, Dartmouth College and University of Pittsburgh goes my deepest appreciation, for their questions and comments have helped shape many of the ideas presented here. My thanks also go to the National Science Council, ROC for providing several research awards and three travel grants to attend various conferences to present my papers that finally found their ways into this volume.

    I would like to take this opportunity to thank my assistants Y. H. Lin and S. Y. Hsiao at the Linguistics Institute, National Tsing Hua University for helping prepare the manuscript for publication and T. M. Chang and J. Y. Fan for keying-in and editing. Thanks are also due to the Student Book Co. for reprinting my first book and for printing the present volume. My greatest gratitude goes to wife, Ai-chu and two children, Patricia and David, who have had many occasions not only to bear with the disappointment of canceling promised outings but also to stand my bad temper when I met with difficulty in my research. Without the help and understanding of all those people, this book would never have become a reality.

F. F. T.

INTRODUCTION

In an interesting experiment, the 18 students in a Senior English Composition class at the National Taiwan Normal University were given the following four paragraphs, two in English and two in Chinese, to punctuate.

(1) 曾經是歷史最光輝的拳王阿里，近年來勝利後，總是說要退休，但總未退休，結果敗在初出道的史賓科斯手下，本來可以光榮退休的，卻不道落成這樣一個下場。[1]

(2) 而你不會相信那些傳說的，正像我也很難相信它一樣，因為我們全是有知識、有理性、有獨立思考能力的現代人，我們聽取了這一類的傳說立即會指陳它的荒謬，它的無稽來。但任何荒謬無稽的傳言都曾被一代一代裡更多的人們相信過，不然它不會像風一樣的衍傳，更不會傳到我們的耳中了。[2]

(3) At Dallas airport nearly 5000 people were waiting. The President in a dark—blue suit stepped from his plane smiling happily. He and Jackie were met by a committee that gave her a bouquet of red roses. Their car was ready to leave but Kennedy had to shake hands with some voters. Jackie, her roses cradled in her left arm, also touched the outstretched hands. After a few minutes she started to walk away, but noticing that her husband was still at it, smiled fondly and returned.[3]

(4) It seldom rains. The geography books credit this portion of Utah nine to ten inches of precipitation. Actual rainfall and snowfall vary widely from year to year. There are a few perennial springs hidden in secret places known only to the deer and coyotes, to myself and a few friends, but the water does not flow far before vanishing into the air and under the ground. Even the rain when it comes does not always fall to the

---

[1]The passage is cited from China Times, April 8, 1978, p.12.

[2]The passage is taken from *Luke yu Daoke* (Passers—by and Swordsmen), a collection of short stories by Sima Zhong—yuan, Huang—guan Magazine, Taipei, 1977, p. 51. Passages (1) and (2) in their Romanized form with English glosses appear in Appendix II.

[3](3) and (4) are taken from *Reader's Digest 50th Anniversary Treasury*, Reader's Digest Association Far East LTD., p.44 and 59 respectively.

ground, but can be seen evaporating halfway down—curtain of blue rain dangling out of reach, torture by tantalizing.

The result of their performance with regard to the use of full stops can be summarized in the following table.

Table I

	Chinese		English	
	1	2	3	4
Number of sentences in the original passage	1	2	6	5
Student's average number of sentences	2.53	3.82	5.49	4.94
Range	1–4	2–5	4–6	3–6
Number of Students who agree with the original author	1	1	8	6

This table clearly reveals, among other things, two interesting phenomena: First, while the 18 subjects are all native speakers of Chinese[4], they disagree considerably among themselves and with the original authors as to how many sentences there are in each of the two Chinese paragraphs. Second, while many of them are far from having a native command of English, their performance indicates considerably more agreement among themselves and with the original authors.

The first phenomenon, disconcerting though it is, has actually been repeatedly observed. In September and October, 1978, a number of short articles appeared in Central Daily News, Literary Supplement Section. Most of them deplore the fact that Chinese students and sometimes even well-known writers use far too many commas instead of full

---

[4] The eighteen speakers, of course, come from families that speak different Chinese dialects. However, as fas as written Chinese is concerned, the influence due to different native dialects is probably not significant and can be safely ignored.

stops, showing that they do not have a clear notion of what a sentence in Chinese is (see Ying, 1978; Chen, 1978 for example). Actually, the phenomenon had been observed by Wang (1955, p.403) and Yang (1982) before. Yang, who actually wrote a book entitled *A Study of the Chinese Punctuation System* mentioned in the Preface to the first edition (written in 1961) that when he was working as an editor of the *Chinese Student Weekly* in Hong Kong, he made a study of some 5,000 contributions mostly by middle school students from Hong Kong, Taiwan, Malaysia and Singapore. He found that 55% of them used commas throughout until they come to the end of a paragraph and only 5% of the contributors used the punctuation system correctly (1982:3).

However, current linguistic theory, to the extent that I am aware of, does not have much to offer in the way of explaining these phenomena. This is because almost all grammatical models have been designed by Indo—European grammarians on the basis of Indo—European languages. And most Chinese grammarians, since the completion of the first systematic Mandarin grammar, *Ma Shi Wen Tong* in 1898, have been working in these grammatical models. The most serious defect of writing a gammar of Mandarin Chinese in an Indo—European model is that a sentence thus defined does not actually function as a discourse unit in Chinese.

The present thesis, therefore, constitutes the first systematic attempt at discovering what such a unit is.[5] It is divided into three parts. Part One attempts to find out why Indo—European grammatical models, when applied to the Chinese data, failed to yield a functional discourse unit equivalent to the sentence in English. It then goes on to explore the notion of topic and its function in Chinese. At the end a preliminary conclusion is drawn that topic chain, a stretch of discourse headed by one or more topics, which are followed by one or more comment clauses, is a discourse unit equivalent to the English surface sentence.[6]

Part Two is then devoted to the exploration of various types of construction that can appear as a clause in a topic chain. Depending on the number and function of the topics contained in the clause, they can be further divided into: four types which are dealt with in each of the following four chapters respectively. The single topic clause, in cluding the presentative clause and the pre—telescopic clause is taken up in Chatper 3. The local double topic clause which includes the so—called 'double nominative' construction, and Topic—Adv.—V—(0) construction when the adverb (especially that of location and time) can

---

[5] Also see Shi (1989) for a more recent attempt.

[6] The notion of toipc chain will be further elucidated in Chapter 2.

be clearly identified as a secondary topic, is dealt with in Chapter 4. Chapter 5, on the other hand, takes care of other constructions involving two topics in which the secondary topic is in some sense, moved from a post-verbal position to a pre-verbal one. These constructions include the *ba* construction, the object-fronting construction, and the so-called "verb-copying" construction. In the last section of Part Two, we take up two special constructions which involve either the primary topic or both the primary and the secondary topics; namely, the *lian ... dou/ye* construction and the comparison construction (Chapter 6).

In Part Three we take up compound and complex sentences. Chapter 7 is devoted to the exploration of three kinds of topic chain, which form compound sentences in Chinese, namely the ordinary topic chain, the presentative topic chain and the telescopic topic chain. Chapter 8 then deals with complex sentences—more specifically, sentences containing a nominal clause, a relative clause or a so-called "complement" clause. It also features a long section on sentences containing raising predicates, which lie between simple and complex sentences.

However, before we actually begin our discussion, a few words about the data and the symbols and abbreviations used are in order. All the examples marked by F:X (where X stands for a number) are taken from a transcription made by myself of a telephone conversation between two friends. Other examples are either taken from other people's discussions or else are constructed by myself. Whenever possible, the sources are noted. All the Mandarin examples are given in the Pinyin system. The following abbreviations are used to indicate some frequently occurring function words.

ASP: aspect markers (*-le,* for perfective action[7]; *-zhe* for continuative aspect;

---

[7]There are two types of *le* in Mandarin. One indicates 'perfective action' and is here classified as an aspect marker. The other *le*, which indicates 'chang of state', is analyzed as a particle, because, unlike the perfective *-le*, which is suffixed to a verb, this *le* is an independent element occurring at the end of a sentence, as in the following example:
(i) wo xie-le   yi-fong   xin   le.
     I   write-ASP one-CL   letter PART
     'I wrote a letter.'
However, the two types of *le* cannot always be clearly distinguished. This is particularly true when a verb occurs at the end of a sentence. For example:
(ii) wo ba xin   ji   le.
     I BA letter send
     'I mailed the letter.'
(iii) tamen lai le
      they come
      'They have come.' or 'They are coming now.'
Le in (ii) and (iii) can be interpreted as a perfective aspect marker or as a combination of a perfective *-le* and a particle *le* with one of them deleted by haplology. As this is not our main concern here, a decision with no justification given is made in each

preverbal morpheme *zai* for progressive aspect; and *−guo* for 'indefinite past' and experiential aspect.

PART: pause particles *a (ya), ne, me,* and *ba*; sentence–final particles (e.g., *le, ba, a, me, ne*) and extent or degree particle *de*.

Rel. Mar.: relative clause marker *de*

POSS: possessive marker *−de*

CL: classifiers for nouns (e.g., *−ge, −zhang, −zhi*)

LOC: localizers for nouns (e.g., *−zhong, −shang, −qian*)

A list of all the symbols used in the transcription can be found in Appendix I.

---

individual case that is ambiguous.

TABLE OF CONTENTS

Preface (Chinese).. v
Preface (Engllish).. Vii
Introduction.. ix
Table of Contents... xv

PART ONE SENTENCE, CLAUSE, TOPIC AND SUBJECT
Chapter 1 Sentences in English and Chinese
  1. Sentence in English.. 1
    1.1 Nesfield's Definition..................................... 1
    1.2 Jespersen's Definition.................................... 2
    1.3 Chomsky's Characterization................................ 2
    1.4 Perceptual Strategies and Characterization of Sentence. 3
    1.5 Towards a Consensus....................................... 6
  2. Sentence in Chinese... 6
    2.1 Chao's Definition... 6
    2.2 Wang's Definition... 7
    2.3 Tang's Characterization................................... 7
    2.4 Teng's Characterization...................................11
  3. Concluding Remarks..17

Chapter 2 Subject, Topic and Topic Chain in Chinese
  1. Introductory..19
  2. Subject in Chinese..20
    2.1 Case Marking..20
    2.2 Position..21
    2.3 Referential Property......................................25
    2.4 Behavior and Control Properties...........................27
      2.4.1 Reflexivization and Imperativization................27
      2.4.2 Relativization and Conjunction Reduction...........29
      2.4.3 Coreferential NP Deletion..........................40
    2.5 Summary...53
  3. Topic in Chinese..53
    3.1 General Properties of Topic...............................53
    3.2 Properties of Topic in Chinese............................54
    3.3 Identifying Topic in Chinese..............................56
  4. Comparison of Subject and Topic...............................59
  5. Summary...63

PART TWO SIMPLE SENTENCES
Chapter 3 Basic Simple One—topic Sentences
  1. Introductory..67
  2. Types of Single Topic Sentences...............................68
    2.1 State Verbs v.s. Action Verbs.............................68
    2.2 Sentences with State Verbs................................70
      2.2.1 Adjectival Sentences...............................70
        2.2.1.1 Quality Verbs................................70
        2.2.1.2 Status Verbs.................................71
      2.2.2 Naming Sentences...................................73
      2.2.3 Possessive, Existential and Presentative Sentences.74
      2.2.4 Sentences of Emotive and Mental State..............78

    2.3 Sentences with Action Verbs..........................80
        2.3.1 Sentences with Intransitive Action Verbs..........87
            2.3.1.1 Verbs of Vocal Action........................88
            2.3.1.2 Verbs of Location............................89
            2.3.1.3 Verbs of Motion..............................90
        2.3.2 Sentences with Transitive Action Verbs............92
            2.3.2.1 Regular Transitive Action Verbs..............92
            2.3.2.2 Transitive Verbs of Location and Motion.......94
            2.3.2.3 Transitive Action Verbs That Take a Clause as
                    their Object................................94
            2.3.2.4 Telescopic, Transitive Action Verbs..........96
        2.3.3 Sentences with Ditransitive Verbs.................96
            2.3.3.1 Verbs of Transaction........................97
                2.3.3.1.1 "Give" Verbs..........................97
                2.3.3.1.2 "Take" Verbs..........................98
                2.3.3.1.3 "Rent" Verbs.........................101
            2.3.3.2 Verbs of Communication.....................102
    2.4 Passive Sentences....................................105
        2.4.1 The *Bei* Construction...........................106
        2.4.2 Sentences with Passive Verbs....................112
        2.4.3 The *Shi....De* Construction as a Passive Sentence..113
        2.4.4 Sentences with Transitive Verbs in the Middle Voice
             114
        2.4.5 Concluding Remarks Concerning Chinese Passive
              Sentences...................................116
3. Summary...117

Chapter 4 Sentences with Local Secondary Topics
1. Introductory...121
2. The So-called "Double Nominative" Construction............122
    2.1 Previous Analyses of the Construction................122
    2.2 The Proposed Analysis of the Double Nominative
        Construction..129
    2.3 Productive Double Nominative Constructions Versus
        Verbal Compounds....................................136
        2.3.1 Teng's View...................................136
        2.3.2 The Proposed Analysis.........................136
        2.3.3 The Further Development of Some Idiomatized
              Verbal Compounds.............................142
    2.4 The Origin of the Double Nominative Construction.....145
3. Non-sentence-initial Preverbal Locatives and Temperals as
   Topics..149
    3.1 General Remarks on Chinese Adverbs..................151
        3.1.1 The Problem of Identifying Chinese Adverbs.....151
        3.1.2 Placement of Multiple Adverbials..............154
    3.2 Temporals and Locatives as Non-primary Topics........155
        3.2.1 Placement of the Pause Particles..............156
        3.2.2 Definiteness in Reference.....................156
        3.2.3 The Contrastive Function......................158
        3.2.4 Placement of Adverbs *You* and *Ye*............159
        3.2.5 Domain and Control Properties.................161
        3.2.6 Similarities to Other Kinds of Secondary Topics...161
    3.3 Summary of Arguments and Ramifications...............163

Chapter 5 Sentences with Non-local Secondary Topics
1. The *Ba* Construction........................168
    1.1 The First Noun Phrase (NP$_1$)..................169
        1.1.1 The Properties of Subject in Chinese..............170
        1.1.2 The Properties of Topic in Chinese................170
        1.1.3 The First NP as Topic............................171
    1.2 The *Ba* NP (NP$_2$)........................172
        1.2.1 Arguments Against Regarding the *ba* NP as an Object
           172
        1.2.2 Semantic and Syntactic Properties of the *ba* NP....173
            1.2.2.1 The Referential Constraint of the *ba* NP.......173
            1.2.2.2 Separability by a Pause Particle..............174
            1.2.2.3 Heading a Topic Chain........................175
            1.2.2.4 Controlling the Pronominalization and
                    Coreferential NP Deletion Processes..........175
            1.2.2.5 The Properties of the *ba* NP and Those of the
                    Regular Topic NP Compared....................177
        1.2.3 Further Similarities Between the Primary Topic NP
              and the *ba* Topic NP...............................177
            1.2.3.1 The Relations That a Topic NP Bears to Some
                    Other Elements in the Same Clause............177
                1.2.3.1.1 As a Term of One of the Verbs in the
                          Clause...................................178
                1.2.3.1.2 As a Non-term of the Main Verb...........178
                1.2.3.1.3 Topics that Bear Some Semantic Relation-
                          ships to the Subject.....................179
                1.2.3.1.4 Summary..................................180
            1.2.3.2 The Relationships that a *ba* NP bears to Other
                    Elements in the Same Clause..................180
                1.2.3.2.1 As a Term of One of the Verbs in the Same
                          Clause...................................180
                1.2.3.2.2 As a Non-term of the Main Verb of the
                          Clause...................................182
                1.2.3.2.3 The ba NP that Bears Some Semantic
                          Relationships to the Direct Object of the
                          Clause...................................183
                1.2.3.2.4 Summary..................................185
            1.2.3.3 The Roles of the *ba* NP and Those of the
                    Primary Topic NP Compared....................185
            1.2.3.4 Three Additional Arguments for Treating the
                    ba NP as a Secondary Topic...................186
                1.2.3.4.1 Topical Ambiguity with Regard to the *ba* NP
                         186
                1.2.3.4.2 The Placement of Two Adverbs *You* and *Ye*..189
                1.2.3.4.3 The "Pseudo-transitive Verbs" and the *ba*
                          Construction.............................190
    1.3 The Meaning and Function of the *Ba* Construction.......197
        1.3.1 Wang's Theory of "Disposal"......................197
        1.3.2 Thompson's Analysis..............................200
2. The Object Fronting Construction........................205
    2.1 Topical Qualities of the Fronted Object...............206

   2.2 Additional Parallelism..................................209
      2.2.1 The Contrastive Function.........................210
      2.2.2 Relation with the Retained Object...............210
      2.2.3 Summary..211
   2.3 The Fronted Object and its Syntagmatic Relation.......212
      2.3.1 The Fronted Object and the Primary Topic.........212
      2.3.2 The Fronted Object and the Verb..................214
   2.4 The Fronted Object and its Paradigmatic Relation......218
      2.4.1 The Fronted Object and the *ba* NP................218
      2.4.2 The Fronted Object and the Second NP in the Double
          Nominative Construction..........................220
      2.4.3 The Fronted Object and the Non−S−initial Preverbal
          Locative and Temporal............................221
3. The VO−topicalization Construction..........................222
   3.1 The Traditional View of the Construction..............222
   3.2 Inadequacies of the Traditional Analysis..............225
   3.3 Evidence for the Deverbalization of V_1..............226
   3.4 Evidence in Support of the Analysis that $V_1 + NP_2$ Is a
      Topic NP..229
      3.4.1 The NP in Question and the Primary Topic NP
          Compared...229
      3.4.2 Two Additional Arguments for Treating $V_1 + NP_2$ as
          a Secondary Topic................................233
      3.4.3 Summary..236
   3.5 Differences between these Five Types of Secondary
      Topics..237
   3.6 The VO Topicalization and Its Syntagmatic Relation....239
   3.7 The Residual Problem..................................243

Chapter 6 Sentences with Special Topics
1. The *Lian...Dou/Ye* Construction............................249
   1.1 A Brief Review of Some Previous Analyses..............249
      1.1.1 Li and Thompson's Analysis......................250
      1.1.2 Paris' Analysis.................................253
      1.1.3 Tsao's Previous Analysis........................254
      1.1.4 Tang's Analysis.................................255
   1.2 The Nominal Nature of the *Lian* Constituent............256
   1.3 Arguments for Treating the *Lian* Constituent as a Topic
     264
      1.3.1 The Roles Played by the Primary Topic and Those
          Played by the *Lian* Constituent Compared..........264
      1.3.2 The Grammatical Qualities of the Primary Topic and
          Those of the *Lian* Constituent Compared...........268
      1.3.3 An Additional Argument..........................273
   1.4 The Function of *Dou* and *Ye* in this Construction......274
   1.5 The *Lian* Topic and Stress............................276
   1.6 Summary...277
2. The Comparative Constructions..............................278
   2.1 Introduction..278
   2.2 Li and Thompson's Analysis............................279
   2.3 The Proposal..282
      2.3.1 Topic Qualities of The Compared Constituent.....283

2.3.2 Parallelism between the Compared Constituent and
        the Primary Topic..................................288
  2.3.3 Parallelism between the Compared Constituent and
        the Secondary Topic................................289
 2.4 Principles of Compared Constituents Deletion..........297
  2.4.1 The Primary Principle...............................297
   2.4.1.1 Single-Topic Comparison.........................298
   2.4.1.2 Double-Topic Comparison.........................298
   2.4.1.3 Triple-Topic Comparison.........................300
  2.4.2 Deletion of Identical Elements in a Compared
        Constituent..302
  2.4.3 Two Minor Deletion Principles......................304
   2.4.3.1 Present-time Deletion Principle.................304
   2.4.3.2 The Second Compared Constituent Genitive
           Deletion Principle..............................305
 2.5 Summary and Implications..............................308
  2.5.1 Summary of Major Findings..........................308
  2.5.2 Theoretical Implications...........................309
   2.5.2.1 Are There Sentential Sources Underlying
           Comparison?.....................................309
   2.5.2.2 Topical Comparison vs. Sentential Comparison..309

PART THREE COMPOOUND AND COMPLEX SENTENCES
Chapter 7 Telescopic Sentences, Compound Sentences and Clause Connectives
1. The So-called "Serial Verb Constructions".................313
 1.1 Previous Treatments of Chinese Serial Verb
     Constructions...314
  1.1.1 Li and Thompson's Treatment........................314
   1.1.1.1 Two or More Separate Events.....................314
   1.1.1.2 The Pivotal Construction........................316
   1.1.1.3 Descriptive Clauses.............................316
    1.1.1.3.1 Realis Descriptive Clauses...................317
    1.1.1.3.2 Irrealis Descriptive Clauses.................317
   1.1.1.4 One VP/Clause Is the Subject or Direct Object
           of Another......................................318
  1.1.2 Chu's Treatment....................................319
   1.1.2.1 Loosely Bounded Clauses.........................319
   1.1.2.2 The Pivotal Construction........................319
   1.1.2.3 The "Elaborative" Clause........................321
  1.1.3 Summary and Comments...............................321
 1.2 The Proposed Analysis.................................324
  1.2.1 Type 1: The Plain Topic Chain......................324
  1.2.2 Type 2: Telescopic Construction....................327
  1.2.3 Type 3:..332
   1.2.3.1 Type 3A: Telescopic-Presentative Construction.332
   1.2.3.2 Type 3B: Telescopic-Descriptive Construction..337
 1.3 Summary and Implications..............................341
  1.3.1 Summary..341
  1.3.2 Implications for Universal Grammatical Theory......342
2. Compound Sentences And Clause Connectives................343
 2.1 Compound Sentences and Clause Connectives Defined.....343
 2.2 Traditional Classification of Clause Connectives......346

2.3 Clauses of Condition, Time, Concession and Reason as
    Topics..349
  2.3.1 Placement of Pause Particles.......................349
  2.3.2 Optional Occurrence of Some General Words as Head
    NP's..351
  2.3.3 The Position of the Clause in Question.............353
  2.3.4 Referential Constraint of the Clause in Question...354
  2.3.5 The Clause in Question as the *Ba* NP, *Lian* NP, and
    the Compared NP.......................................355
  2.3.6 Parallel between a Phrase Topic and the Clause in
    Question..357
  2.3.7 An Apparent Counterexample.........................358
2.4 Topic—Raising and the Placement of Clause Connectives.360
  2.4.1 Previous Discussion of the Placement of Clause
    Connectives...360
  2.4.2 The Rule of Topic—Raising..........................362
  2.4.3 Justifications for the Rule of Topic—Raising.......368
2.5 A Reclassification of Clause Connectives..............374

Chapter 8 Complex Sentences
1. Compound vs. Complex Sentences.........................377
2. Sentences with Raising Predicates......................377
  2.1 Two Classes of Raising Predicates...................377
  2.2 Modal Auxiliary Verbs...............................382
    2.2.1 The Semantics of Modal Auxiliaries..............383
      2.2.1.1 Epistemic Modality..........................383
      2.2.1.2 Deontic Modality............................384
      2.2.1.3 Dynamic Modality............................385
    2.2.2 The Syntax of Modal Auxiliaries.................387
    2.2.3 Summary...389
  2.3 *Shi* in the *Shi*...*De* Construction as a Raising Predicate
   390
    2.3.1 Different Uses of *Shi*.........................390
    2.3.2 The Meaning of *Shi* and *De* in the Cleft Sentence...396
    2.3.3 The Structure of the *Shi*...*De* Construction........399
    2.3.4 Summary...404
3. Sentences with Sentential Subjects and Objects.........405
  3.1 Sentential Subjects.................................405
    3.1.1 Verbs that Take Sentential Subjects.............405
    3.1.2 Raising vs. Non—raising Predicates..............406
  3.2 Sentential Objects..................................408
    3.2.1 The Form of the Sentential Object...............408
    3.2.2 Verbs that Take Sentential Objects..............413
      3.2.2.1 Major Classes of Matrix Verbs...............413
        3.2.2.1.1 Verbs of Location.......................413
        3.2.2.1.2 Verbs of Cognition......................414
        3.2.2.1.3 Verbs of Imagination....................414
        3.2.2.1.4 Verbs of Inquiry........................416
      3.2.2.2 The Interpretation of Sentential Object.....416
        3.2.2.2.1 Factive Sentential Objects.............416
        3.2.2.2.2 The Question of Direct vs. Indirect
          Interrogatives.................................418

```
        3.2.2.2.3 The Interpretation of Subject in a
                 Sentential Object........................423
4. Complex Sentences with Relative Clauses.................426
   4.1 Formal Characteristics..............................427
       4.1.1 Word Order....................................427
       4.1.2 Relative Pronouns.............................429
       4.1.3 Topicality....................................430
       4.1.4 Head NP's.....................................432
       4.1.5 Adverial Phrases within the Relative Clause...434
       4.1.6 Relative Clause Stacking......................436
   4.2 Functional Characteristics..........................437
       4.2.1 Uses of Relative Clause in English............437
       4.2.2 Uses of Relative Clauses in Chinese...........440
       4.2.3 Summary.......................................444
5. The So-called *De* Complement Construction..............445
   5.1 General Characteristics.............................445
   5.2 Two Different Analyses in the Past.................446
       5.2.1 The Final-Verb Hypothesis.....................446
       5.2.2 The Penultimate-Verb Hypothesis...............451
   5.3 Our Proposed Analysis...............................459
       5.3.1 Differences between The Two Types of Complement...459
       5.3.2 Deep Structures for the Descriptive and the
             Resultative Complements.......................464
   5.4 Residual Problems...................................466

Appendix I.................................................473
Appendix II................................................474
Bibliography...............................................476
Index......................................................492
```

PART I

SENTENCE, CLAUSE, TOPIC AND SUBJECT

CHAPTER ONE
SENTENCES IN ENGLISH AND CHINESE

1. Sentence in English

Grammarians of different schools in the past few centuries have given English sentence various definitions, which, judging from the surface, seem to be quite different. However, upon close examination, there turns out to be a close similarity. In what follows we would examine each representative definition very carefully, starting with Nesfield's, the traditional one.

1.1. Nesfield's Definition

Nesfield in his *Outline of English Grammar* (1961) classifies all English sentences into three types, namely, simple, multiple and complex. He further defines each type as follows:

> Simple sentence—A Simple sentence (Lat. simplex, single-fold) is one that has only one *Finite* verb expressed or understood (p. 128; the emphasis is in the original).
>
> Complex sentence—A Complex sentence consists of a Main clause (i.e. the clause containing the main *verb* of the sentence) with one or more Subordinate or dependent clauses (p. 129).
>
> Double or Multiple sentence—A Multiple sentence is one that is made up of two or more Co-ordinate sentences, any of which taken by itself may be either Simple or Complex (p. 150).

Early in the book, Nesfield defines a finite verb as a verb "which is limited or bounded to some subject" (p. 54). In other words, it is a verb that agrees with its subject in person and number and carries the tense, mood, and voice inflections of the sentence in which it occurs.

In these definitions, there are a few more terms that need to be defined. However, since these are terms used in school grammars, we will not go into them here. Suffice it to point out that even with these terms defined, there are still a number of inadequacies in the definitions. These inadequacies not withstanding, the definitions seem to work pretty well in defining sentences in English, as evidenced from the fact that traditional grammars like Nesfield's have been taught in school and have been used as writer's guide for a few centuries.

1.2. Jespersen's Definition

In the section on sentence in his *Philosophy of Grammar,* Jespersen (1958: 305) observes: "... though there is ... no consensus of theory, grammarians will generally be more apt to agree in practice, and when some concrete group of words is presented to them, will be in little doubt whether or not it should be recognized as a real sentence." This observation, if meant to cover all natural languages, then it seems to be inadequate, as we have seen from our previous discussion. However, if meant to cover only languages like English, then it seems to be true in general and is further confirmed by our experimental results reported in the introduction.

After some detailed discussion of general properties of sentence, Jespersen (op. cit. p. 307) finally concludes:

> A sentence is a (relatively) complete and independent human utterance— the completeness and independence being shown by its standing alone or its capacity of standing alone, i.e. of being uttered by itself.

Such a definition, no matter how general and watertight it is, is clearly of no help towards solving the problem that we have set for ourselves, namely, whether speakers of Chinese and those of English can be said to have a similar notion of what a sentence is in their respective language. In the final analysis, the judgment of completeness and independence will have to be obtained from native speakers. Since this is exactly what we want to find out, we cannot use the definition in answering the question without being circular.

Fortunately for our purpose, Jespersen in the same section also states (op. cit. p. 308):

> I do not even imitate those scholars who introduce the term "normal sentences" (normalsatz) for sentences containing a subject and a finite verb. Such sentences may be normal in quiet, easy–flowing, unemotional prose, but as soon as speech is affected by vivid emotion, an extensive use is made of sentences which fall outside this normal scheme and yet have every right to be considered natural and regular sentences.

To put it in a slightly different way, Jespersen, if I understand him correctly, is of the opinion that as long as we restrict ourselves to "quiet, easy–flowing, unemotional" writing, sentence in English can be defined as a stretch of discourse containing a subject and a predicate which, in turn, contains a finite verb phrase.

1.3. Chomsky's Characterization

In *Syntactic Structures,* Chomsky (1957) assumes without arguing for it that a sentence in its underlying form is made up of a noun phrase and a verb phrase, i.e. S – NP + VP, and that to the extent that they can be further characterized by rewriting rules and transformational rules, then the notion of sentence on the surface can be characterized.[1] Chomsky at this stage explicitly avoided the more traditional terms "subject" and "predicate" on the ground that the latter are functional units which play no role in transformations, which are to be stated in structural units only (for a completely different view see Postal, 1976). However, in *Aspects of the Theory of Syntax* (1965), for a number of reasons which do not concern us here, Chomsky modifies his position by allowing S to be rewritten as NP and Predicate— Phrase, even though he still refuses to grant the category subject any place in the deep structure. However, as Chomsky himself has demonstrated, the traditional category of subject can be defined as an NP that is immediately dominated by an S or that stands to the right of Predicate—Phrase in the deep–structure configuration (op. cit. 116–17).[2] It is also to be noted that in *Aspects of the Theory of Syntax* as well as in *Syntactic Structures,* subject and verb concord in English is to be taken care of by a transformational rule. If these observations are essentially correct, then it is not off the mark to say that Chomsky's definition of sentence in English on the surface, if he felt the need to give one, probably would not be very different from a traditional definition which makes use of the categories of subject and finite verb.

1.4. Perceptual Strategies and Characterization of Sentence

In an interesting paper entitled "A Dynamic Model of the Evolution of Language," Bever and Langendoen (1971) have demonstrated convincingly that there are two perceptual strategies in English which can be formally represented as (1).[3]

(1) a. $X_1 \quad \text{Nominal} \quad V_f \quad X_2 \rightarrow X_1 \quad _S[\text{Nominal} \quad V_f \quad X_2$

---

[1]Presumably, Chomsky is giving a universal definition of sentence by using English as an example. Without further confirmations from many other languages, this, however, remains a hypothesis. For our purpose, we would regard it as a way of defining sentence in English.

[2]Chomsky (1965:221) also mentions in a footnote how the grammatical relation topic—comment can be defined in his framework. This comment of his, however, is too sketchy to be worth commenting. For a more recent proposal, see Chomsky (1977). For a counterproposal within the same G–B framework, see Huang (1982). See also Chapter 7 and Chapter 9 for our comments on these two proposals.

[3]The version given in (1) is slightly different from the original one given by Bever and Langendoen.

b. $X_1 \ _S[\text{Nominal } V_f(\text{Nominal}) \ X_2 \rightarrow$
$X_1 \ _S[\text{Nominal } V_f(\text{Nominal})]_S \ X_2$

Informally put, strategy (a) says that when we come across a noun phrase followed by a finite verb phrase, then mark the noun phrase as the beginning of a sentence. Strategy (b) says that when the finite verb phrase in question is intransitive then mark it as the end of the sentence, and if it is transitive or if it is a linking verb phrase, then the noun phrase following the finite verb phrase will be the end of the sentence. An additional point needs to be mentioned in connection with (1): There are some optional elements such as adverbs of time, place, manner etc. which are not mentioned in the formula. It is simply assumed that native speakers of English know they can be there. (2) below shows the step—by—step application of (1).

(2) a. John believed that Bill was a fool.
 b. $_S$[John believed that $_S$[Bill was a fool.
 c. $_S$[John believed that $_S$[Bill was a fool]$_S$]$_S$.

That native speakers of English actually employ these strategies in comprehending sentences as demonstrated by the existence of many sentences in English in which they produce temporarily misleading analyses, thereby making the sentences hard to understand. In each of the following two examples, (a) sentence is hard to understand relative to (b).

(3) a. The umbrella the man sold *despite his wife is in the room.*
 b. The umbrella the man sold despite his relatives is in the room.

(4) a. *The horse raced past the barn* fell.
 b. The horse that was raced past the barn fell.

(3a) is difficult to comprehend because there is a noun—phrase—verb sequence present in the structure, namely, 'his wife is in the room' which may be assigned as a sentence according to (1), but native speakers of English also know that no sentence can occur in a position directly following a preposition, so his first approximation must be wrong. They, then, come back and re—parse the sentence into meaningful constituents. (3b), on the other hand, does not allow such an assignment because the finite verb, i.e., 'is' does not agree in number with the immediately preceding noun phrase. (4a) is difficult because the application of the perceptual strategies results in there being lexical material left over, namely, 'fell' which cannot be assigned to any meaningful structural cluster.[4]

In Bever and Langendeon's original paper, they also appealed to historical evidence. Consider:

(5) The doctor talked to the woman *that* John had married.
(6) The woman *that* John had married left the room.
(7) The doctor talked to the woman *that* was John's wife.
(8) The woman *that* was John's wife left the room.

In modern English, as we have pointed out, 'that' can be deleted from (5) and (6) but not from (7) and (8). In earlier forms of English, the facts were different. For several centuries, because of the requirement of case marking of all noun phrases, 'that' can be omitted from sentences equivalent to (7), but at no time in the history of English could 'that' be omitted from sentences equivalent to (8). These historical facts support their contention that strategies equivalent to (1) have been in force in English for quite some time and because of the considerable loss of case marking in modern English, they have become crucially important in our comprehension of English sentences (for an interesting discussion of many other similar strategies see Clark and Clark 1977, Chapter 2, and the bibliography cited there).

From the above discussion it is clear that a perceptual strategy is not a hard and fast grammatical rule. It is a probable rule used in performance which gives you quick result, as is required in actual communication, but the result is not always correct. However, it is generally agreed that a perceptual strategy should be based on a set of rules in a model of competence. To the extent that this is correct and that there are such perceptual strategies in English, then the notion of sentence seems to be able to be defined by a set of rules involving such notions as noun phrase (nominal) and finite verb phrase.

---

[4]In this connection, it is of special relevance to note that some subjects in the experiment cited in the Introduction, because of inadequate command of English, made a mistake (some of them later corrected themselves) by regarding 'waiting' in (3) of Introduction as a transitive verb. They, therefore, erred by placing a full stop after 'the President' rather than immediately after 'waiting', thus, showing the importance of the distinction between transitive and intransitive verbs in the demarkation of sentence boundaries and indirectly revealing the correctness of the strategies under discussion.

1.5. Towards a Consensus

Bever and Langendoen's discussion strongly indicates a need to characterize an English sentence in the surface. And if this is so, then from our previous discussion it seems clear that these linguists, who, at first glance, seem to disagree with each other widely on how to define an English sentence, have actually come quite close to having a common definition of sentence in English. At least, they seem to agree that an English sentence on the surface cannot be defined without recourse to categories such as subject and finite verb.

Actually a definition of an English sentence to that effect has been tacitly assumed in the field of pedagogical grammar for quite a long time. To cite just a recent example, in his *A Reference Grammar for Students of English*, published by Longman, R. A. Closs (1975) resorts to the notions of subject and finite verb in defining what a sentence is in English. This is quite clear from the following quotations from him.

> ... To be complete, a sentence needs at least one FINITE, INDEPENDENT CLAUSE. (p.1) While the subject of a clause is a noun phrase (NP), the predicate is a verb phrase (VP). Every finite clause has the following basic structure:
>
> NP(subject) + VP (predicate)
>
> in which VP consists sometimes of a FINITE VERB only ... but much more often of a group of words with a finite verb as its head.... (p. 9)

2. Sentence in Chinese

As we have pointed out, most Chinese linguists have adopted a grammatical model that has been designed by western linguists on the basis of Indo-European languages. Thus their definitions of the Chinese sentence all bear a close resemblance to definitions proposed by famous western linguists. This, in itself, is no criticism at all. The important point is whether the definitions work or not. In the following we will examine very closely some representative views on defining Chinese sentences.

2.1. Chao's Definition

Y. R. Chao (1968) defines a sentence as "a segment of speech bounded at both ends by pauses". He then hastens to observe that since in actual speech there may be interruptions or other factors that give rise to silence, pauses should be understood as "deliberate pauses made by the speaker and not simply as physical silence" (op. cit. p. 56).

Such a definition, despite the claim to the contrary, is not a grammatical definition but rather a physical characterization of an act of speech or an utterance. Harris (1951:14) has in fact defined an utterance as "any stretch of talk, by one person, before and after which there is a silence on the part of that person". Furthermore, such a definition, no matter how water-tight it is, tells us nothing about the constituent parts of the sentence and the distributional regularities of these constituents. It is on the basis of similar considerations that Lyons (1968: 179–180) argues to regard phonological criteria as secondary, i.e. criteria which are resorted to only when primary criteria based on grammatical distribution fail to yield a clear-cut result. Take for instance the following utterance: "*I saw him yesterday and I shall be seeing him again tomorrow*". By applying the primary criteria based on grammatical distribution, the utterance, according to Lyons (op. cit. 180), will be segmented as two sentences (the break coming between *yesterday* and *and*). It is only by applying the supplementary phonological criteria of potential pause and intonation that we know for sure whether the two consecutive sentences are to be taken as clauses in a single sentence or as independent sentences.

Elsewhere in the same book, Chao (1968:69) shows great insight by remarking that "the grammatical meaning of subject and predicate in Chinese is topic and comment, rather than actor and action". It is a pity that he stops short at this point without exploring further what this particular meaning relationship means for the analysis of Chinese sentences, as is evident from his preference for the terms subject and predicate.

2.2. Wang's Definition

Wang (1955:59–60) gives the following definition of the Chinese sentence, "A sentence is a complete and independent language unit." This is evidently a Chinese version of Jespersen's definition, which we commented on earlier. We would like to add, however, that the term "independent" is ambiguous. It can mean "physically independent" on the one hand, or "distributionally independent" on the other. If taken in the former sense, then our previous remarks on Chao's definition are also applicable. If taken in the latter sense, then it only tells us that the sentence is the largest unit of grammatical description. In other words, it tells us that the notion of distribution, which is based on substitutability, is simply not applicable to sentences. Again it tells us nothing about its constituent parts and their distributional limitations and dependencies. Since it is these distributional regularities that are of concern when we compare the notion of sentence across languages, we will simply dismiss this definition as irrelevant to our discussion.

2.3. Tang's Characterization

Most of the Chinese grammarians in the sixties and seventies have adopted Chomsky's model in doing Chinese grammatical analyses. Most of them accept Chomsky's assumption that a sentence in Chinese can be defined as: S → NP VP, together with a set of rewriting rules and transformational rules (see Huang, 1966; Hashimoto, 1971, for example). One of the most serious difficulties with this approach is that it fails to generate the so—called "double nominative" construction in Chinese, as exemplified in its simplest form by (9):

(9) ta tou teng.
he head ache
'He has a headache.'

Within the generative—transformational camp, only two serious attempts, as far as I know, have been made, one by Tang (1972, 1977) and the other by Teng (1974).

Tang, following Fillmore's suggestion (1968), posits a special type of case complement to the dative called 'adnominal dative.' This complement may be promoted as an independent case on a par with the original dative. When this happens, it can be topicalized. Thus (10), under this analysis, will have (11) as its source and is derived from it by applying Adnominal Dative Promotion and Topicalization.

(10) ta taitai hen piaoliang.
he wife very pretty
'He (topic), wife (is) very pretty.'

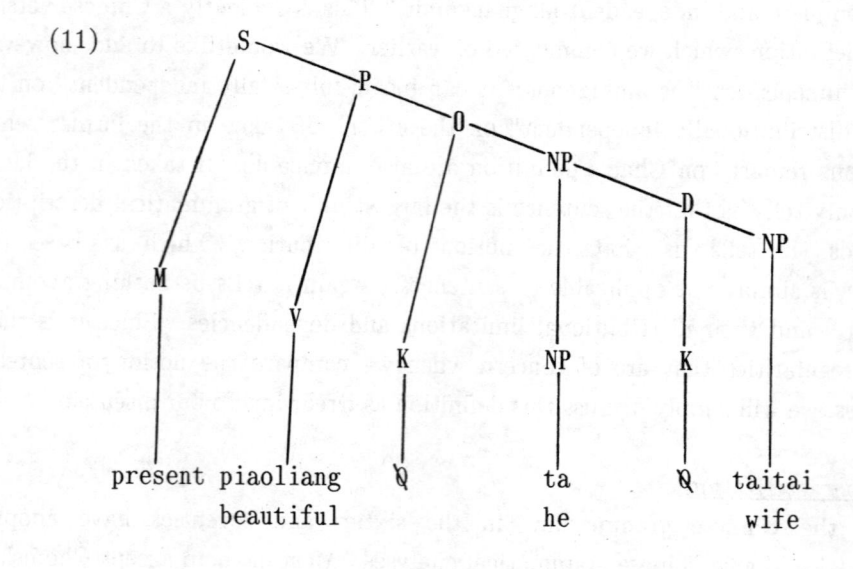

(11)

```
              S
              |
              P
              |
              0
             / \
           NP   D
                 \
                  NP
  M    V    K   NP   K   NP
  |    |    |    |   |    |
present piaoliang Q  ta  Q  taitai
        beautiful    he      wife
```

Tang also observes that the relationship between Dative and its complement seems to be restricted to that of inalienable possession (i.e., body parts and kinship).

Since Tang adopts Fillmore's case grammar and derives the first nominal in a double nominative construction by means of Adnominal Dative Promotion and Topicalization, his analysis encounters some problems that are inherent in the model. We will discuss some important ones in the following.

1. Tang's observation cited early, i.e., the relationship between Dative and its complement seems to be restricted to that of inalienable possession is far too restrictive. Counterexamples abound. To give just a few:

(12) zhei–ge ren xing–zi ji.
 this–Cl man temper quick
 'This man (topic), (his) temper (is) quick.'[5]

(13) Zhongguo di da, wubuo,
 Chinaland big resources comprehensive
 ren–kou duo.
 population great
 'China (topic), (its) land is big; (its) resources comprehensive; (and) (its) population great.'

(14) shi–ge li wu–ge lan–le, we–ge chi–le.
 ten–CL pear five–CL rot–ASP five–CL eat–ASP
 'The ten pears (topic), five rotted; (the other) five (were)eaten.'

(15) ta–men ni kan wo, wo kan ni.
 they you look–at me I look–at you
 'They looked at each other.'

Thus, while it is still possible to regard *xing–zi* 'temper' as an inalienable possession of

---

[5]In order to reflect the organization of the original Chinese sentences, many English translations of the examples are deliberately literal. Also elements that are required in English but are absent in the Chinese sentences are indicated by enclosing them in parentheses.

zhei-ge ren 'this man' by stretching the term a little, it is impossible to do so in the case of (13). *Di* 'land', *wu* 'resources' and *ren-kou* 'population' cannot be said to be an inalienable possession of *Zhongguo* 'China', at least not in the sense that Tang, following Fillmore (1968), is using it. In (14), the relationship between *wu-ge* 'five' and *shi-ge li* 'ten pears' is evidently that of 'part-whole.' Even though in this case a paraphrase with a possessive construction is possible as in (16), it is felt to be very unnatural:

(16) ? shi-ge li   li-tou-de   wu-ge   lan-le
      ten-CL pear among-POSS five-CL rot-ASP
      wu-ge   chi-le.
      five-CL eat-ASP
      'Of all the ten pears, five rotted;(the other) five(were) eaten.'

In the case of (15), however, a paraphrase with a possessive construction is impossible, as (17) is ungrammatical.

(17) * ta-men dang-zhong-de ni   kan   wo, wo kan
       they   among-POSS   you look-at me I look-at
       ni.
       you

2. However, the strongest objection we have against the treatment of the double-nominative construction in a case model is that the case model, like all the grammatical models before it, fails to recognize the fact that the first nominative, i.e., topic, is essentially a discourse element which may extend its domain over several clauses, although at the same time, it interacts with the syntactic organization of clauses under its domain in interesting ways. For illustration, examine (18):

(18) zhei-ke shu, hua   xiao yezi   da,
     this-CL tree flowers small leaves big
     zhen   nan-kan.
     really ugly
     'The tree (topic), (its) flowers (are) small,
     (its) leaves (are) big, (it) (is) really ugly.'

Why *zhei-ke shu* 'this tree' is chosen here as topic is something we cannot determine since no prior discourse is provided (for a discussion of some of the functions a topic plays with regard to the prior discourse, see Tsao, 1979 Chapter 6, and Sibley, 1980). However, once it is chosen, it may, and often does, extend its domain over several clauses as *zhei-ke shu* 'this tree' has its domain over three clauses, two of which have their own subjects. Unless this discourse nature of topic is appreciated, it is difficult to distinguish it from subject, and unless topic is properly differentiated from subject, one of the basic problems in the study of Chinese grammar will be difficult, if not impossible, to treat.

2.4. Teng's Characterization

Teng (1974) makes several claims concerning the double nominative construction in Chinese. Let us examine some of his claims one by one.

1. Teng argues that predicates can consist of an entire sentence; i.e., VP can be rewritten as S. Thus, a sentence containing a double nominative structure such as (19) will have an underlying structure such as (20) in his analysis.

(19) 'ta duzi   e.
       he stomach hungry
       '(Literally), he (topic), (his) stomach is hungry.'
       'He is hungry.'

(20)
```
              S
         /        \
       NP          VP
        |           |
        |           S
        |         /   \
        |        NP    VP
        |        |     |
        ta      duzi    e
        he    stomach hungry
```

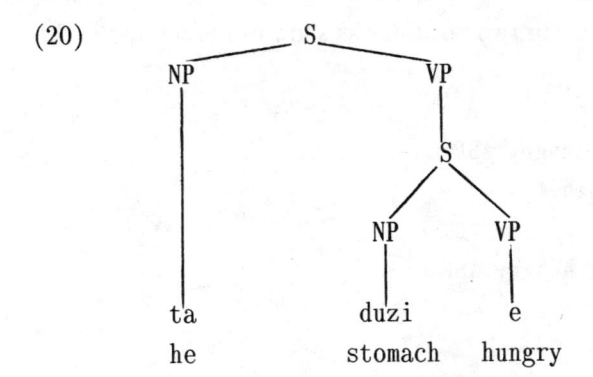

The same approach is posited by Wang (1956) and Chao (1968).[6] Our general comment about this approach is that it fails to distinguish between topic and subject. The discourse nature of the first nominative can be brought out very clearly if (19) is followed

---

[6]Chao and Wang, being non-generative-transformational grammarians, do not, of course, use such formalisms as rewriting rules.

by a possible discourse continuation as in (21):

    (21) ta duzi   e,   you zhao–bu–dao dongxi chi,
           he stomach hungry also couldn't–find things eat
           suo–yi tang zai chuang–shang shui–jiao
           so   lie in bed–LOC   sleep
           'He (topic), (his) stomach (was) hungry, (and) (he) couldn't find
           anything to eat, so (he) lay in bed sleeping.'

If we define topic as theme, as it is usually understood, (for a fuller discussion of the criteria for establishing topic in Chinese, see the next chapter), then the topic of these sentences is *ta* 'he' because it is the thing that each of the sentences is about. The subject of the first sentence is *duzi* 'stomach' and those of the second and the third, *ta* 'he', which are deleted by a process termed Topic–NP deletion to be discussed in the next chapter. Such an analysis not only agrees well with the general understanding that topic is what a sentence (or sentences) is (or are) about; it also accords well with the general agreement that subject, as a grammatical term, is always selectionally related to the verb (See E. L. Keenan, 1974, 1976a; Li and Thompson, 1976 for comments).

    There are more specific arguments in this claim of Teng's. Teng (op. cit,) argues that Chinese adverbs in general occur directly in front of verbs in the surface and yet, in double nominative sentences, they occur in two positions as shown in (22a) and (22b):

    (22) a. ta duzi   you   e   le.
              he stomach again hungry ASP
              'He is hungry again.'
         b. ta you   duzi e   le.
              he again   stomach hungry ASP
              'Same as (a).'

He then points out that if we regard *duzi e* 'stomach hungry' as a sentential predicate, then the rule of adverb–placing in Chinese can be simply stated as: Adverbs can occur before predicates. That this argument is very weak can be seen from the following two observations: First, not all adverbs can occur in the two positions just mentioned even with the same sentence. Thus, the most common adverb of frequency *hen* 'very' can occur only in one position:

(23) a. ta duzi hen e.
      he stomach very hungry
      'He is very hungry.'
   *b. ta hen duzi e.

Since no semantic incompatability is involved in (23), the fact that it is ungrammatical indicates that adverbs are far from a homogeneous class, and the rule of adverb placement cannot be simply stated (see Tsao, 1976 and Chapter 4 for discussion).

More seriously, not all the double nominative constructions exhibit these two possibilities with regard to the position of some adverbs such as *you* 'again' and *ye* 'also', as pointed out by T. C. Tang and Marie–Claude Paris cited by Li and Thompson (1976:487, footnote 9). Thus, in a sentence containing a double nominative construction like (24), only one position is allowed for *you* 'again'.

(24) a. zhei–ke shu, yeze you huang le.
        this–CL tree leaves again yellow ASP
        'This tree (topic), (its) leaves have turned yellow again.'
   *b. zhei–ke shu, you yezi huang le.
        this–CL tree again leaves yellow ASP.

Thus, the basic assumption of Teng is wrong. We have no strong evidence to show that what is posited by Teng as the 'sentential predicate' is actually a constituent dominated by a VP node.

2. Teng also claims that since in (22) the adverb *you* 'again' can occur in two positions while in (25) and (26) it cannot occur between two nominatives, (25) and (26) should not be analyzed as containing a double nominative construction.

(25) *ta you shou teng le.
      he again hand hurt ASP
      'His hand hurts again.'

(26) *ta ye duzi yuan.
      he also stomach round
      'His stomach is also round!'

We have already pointed out that whether *you* or *ye* can be placed at two different positions or not is not a valid test in distinghishing double nominative constructions from non—double nominative constructions.[7] From this observation alone we are convinced that Teng is wrong again in this claim. Our conviction, however, is further strengthened by the following two examples:

(27) ta shou teng de   hen, zhen   xiang qu kan yisheng.
     he hand hurt PART   very really want go see doctor
     'He (topic), (his)hand hurt badly;(he) really wanted to
     see a doctor.'

(28) ta duzi   hen yuan, tui you duan, zhen   nan—kan.
     he stomach very round legs also short really ugly
     'He (topic), (his) stomach is very round, and (his) legs are short;
     (he) is really ugly.'

(27) and (28) demonstrate clearly that given proper context, *shou* 'hand' in *shou teng* 'hand hurt' and *duzi* 'stomach' in *duzi yuan* 'stomach round' can occur as the second nominative in a double nominative construction.

3. Teng claims that (19) will be derived from an underlying structure like (20). (29) below also has the same underlying structure, the possessive marker *—de* being transformationally derived by a late rule called the 'pseudogenitive.'

(29) ta—de   duzi   e.
     he—POSS stomach hungry
     'His stomach is hungry.'

(30), on the other hand, will have (31) as its underlying structure.

(30) ta—de   duzi   hen yuan.
     he—POSS stomach very round
     'His stomach is round.'

---

[7]See Chapter 4 of this book where the proper relationship between the placement of *you* and *ye* and the double nominative construction is characterized.

(31)
```
              S
             / \
            NP  VP
           /\   /\
     ta-de duzi  hen yuan
     his stomach very round
```

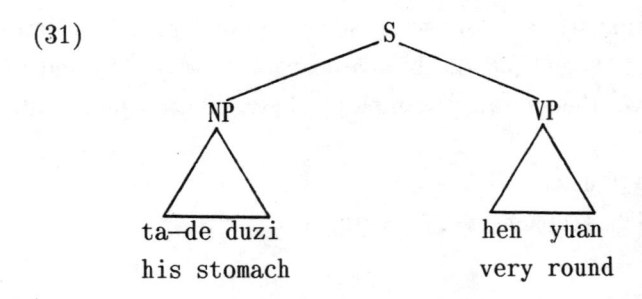

He gives the following evidence. First, he points out that a possessive sentence behaves differently from a pseudo-possessive sentence in conjunction reduction, as shown by (32) and (33) respectively.

(32) a. ta jie—le   Zhang San—de shu; wo jie—le
        he borrow—ASP Zhang San's book I borrow—ASP
        Li Si—de.
        Li Si's
        'He borrowed Zhang San's book; I borrowed Li Si's.'
     b. *ta jie—le Zhang San—de shu; wo jie—le Li Si.

(33) a. ta xue—le   yi—nian—de Zhongwen; wo xue—le
        he study—ASP one—year's Chinese   I study—ASP
        liang—nian.
        two—years
        'He studied Chinese for one year; I studied for two years.'
     b. *ta xue—le yi—nian—de Zhongwen; wo xue—le liang—nian—de.

This shows, according to Teng, that conjuction reduction follows the specification of the real possessive, but precedes the introduction of pseudo-possessive marker. The argument here is quite straighforward and convincing. However, it becomes very doubtful when Teng goes on to argue that this difference provides syntactic evidence for distinguishing the real possessive —de in (30) from the pseudo-possessive —de in (29). After all, the real possessive construction in (32) and the pseudo-possessive construction in (33) are semantically different. For one thing, the possessor in the former case is an animate noun while that in the latter is an inanimate one. But in the case of (29) and (30), the possessor in both cases refers to the same entity and so does the possessed. So if there should be any syntactic difference between (29) and (30), it could not be due to any semantic difference regarding the relation between the two nominatives. However, suspending our semantic objection for a while, let's examine whether (29) and (30) do behave in parallel with (32) and (33) in conjunction reduction. Teng gives the following examples and grammatical judgment:

(34) a. Zhang San–de duzi hen e;
Zhang San–POSS stomach very hungry
Li Si ye shi.
Li Si also is
'Zhang San's is very hungry; so is Li Si.'
b. *wo–de duzi hen e; ni–de ne?
my stomach very hungry yours PART
'I am hungry; are you?'
c. Zhang San–de duzi hen yuan; Li Si–de ye shi.
Zhang San's stomach very round Li Si's also is
'Zhang San's stomach is very round; so is Li Si's.'
d. *Zhang San–de duzi hen yuan; Li Si ye shi.
Zhang San's stomach very round Li Si also is
'Zhang San's stomach is very round; so is Li Si.'
(different meaning)

He goes on to explain that, at the stage of deleting identical elements, *de* in (a) is absent. This is supported by the ungrammaticality of (b), in which *de* appears. Since the genuine possessive marker is specified in the underlying structure, it must have been introduced by the stage of conjunction deletion and is not deletable, as indicated by the unacceptable (d).

This argument is extremely weak, as the grammaticality judgment on which the argument is based is far from firm. Speakers disagree with each other as to the grammaticality of the four sentences involved here.[8] That one should not base one's argument on such controversial sentences is self–evident. Besides, by positing (20) as the underlying structure of (19), Teng is ruling out the possibility that *ta–de duzi* 'his stomach' may become a topic when it is in construction with *e* 'hungry'. Actually, such a

---

[8]The thirty–one native speakers that I have asked gave the following judgments:
(34) a. G:19   b. G:18   c. G:23   d. G:13
      U:12   U:13   U: 8   U:18
As the results do not show any discernible pattern, I will not comment on them here. Suffice it to point out that even if we go by the rule of majority, most native speakers' grammaticality judgments in (b) still do not agree with Teng's.

possibility does exist. Witness the following example:

(35) ta-de duzi   yi e   jiu teng,
     his stomach once hungry then ache
     yiding you sheme maobing.
     must   have some trouble
     '(literally) His stomach (topic) as soon as (it) (is) hungry,
     (it) aches; (it) must have some trouble.'
     'As soon as his stomach is empty, it aches; there must be something
     wrong with it.'

Likewise, to posit an underlying structure such as (31) for (32) fails to account for sentences such as (28), in which the possessor is the topic instead of the whole possessive construction.

3. Concluding Remarks

Our previous discussion in the chapter has led us to the following conclusions.

1. Linguists of various schools have in the past attempted to define sentence in English. Their definitions, which appear to be quite different, have, upon close examination, turned out to have a close similarity. This common definition, however it is to be phrased, has to make use of such categories as subject and finite verb.

2. Chinese linguists, on the other hand, do not seem to have the luck. Chao's and Wang's definitions suffer from the fact that they are not strictly "grammatical" in the sense that they do not relate to the constituent parts of sentence and the distributional regularities of these constituents. Generative-transformational grammarians, on the other hand, suffer because their model fails to take care of the so-called "double-nominative" construction. Two noteworthy attempts to amend this defect in the generative-transformational model, have, upon close examination, also failed.

3. In the course of discussion we have seen that both topic and subject, rather than subject alone as in the case of English, seem to play a part in the grammatical organization of Chinese. Since these two important categories, due to the fact that such a distinction does not play an important role in the description of English and other Indo-European languages, are often mixed up, it is time to study their grammatical functions carefully in order to set them apart, a job we will turn to in the next chapter.

CHAPTER TWO
SUBJECT, TOPIC and TOPIC CHAIN IN CHINESE

1. Introductory

One of the conclusions we arrived at in the previous chapter is that both topic and subject seem to play a part in the grammar of Chinese and in order to see how Chinese sentence is organized we need to find the key to the question of whether topic and subject should be separated in the grammar of Chinese and if they should, how they can be identified. The present chapter, therefore, devotes itself to an in-depth exploration of this question.

The important distinction of subject and topic and the significance that this distinction has for the theory of grammar has been studied by Li and Thompson in a series of papers which culminated in "Subject and Topic: A New Typology of Languages" (1976).

In this final version, several important claims are made, the most important of which is: Chinese, together with Lisu and Lahu, two languages of the Lolo-Burmese family, is a topic-prominent language in direct contrast with English, which is a subject-prominent language. This contrast is further explained as:

> In Subject-prominent (Sp) languages, the structure of sentences favors a description in which the grammatical relation *subject-predicate* plays a major role; in topic-prominent (Tp) languages, the basic structure of sentences favors a description in which the grammatical relation *topic-comment* plays a major role. (Li and Thompson, op. cit. 459)

Tsao (1979) gave the following two comments on this position of theirs. First, although Li and Thompson admit that topic and subject both exist in Chinese, they do not describe how they are to be identified and differentiated, let alone give a full description of how the two notions interact in the grammar of Chinese. This neglect, Tsao points out, seriously biases the reader against the prominency of subject in Chinese. Second, although they realize that topic is a discourse notion, their discussion is still very much sentence-oriented, as can be seen from the quotation just cited as well as from the examples they give.

These two criticisms have been, for the most part, met in their more recent comprehensive grammar (1981). Thus, Mandarin Chinese has been re-characterized in the following terms:

One of the most striking features of Mandarin Chinese structure, and one that sets Mandarin apart from many other languages, is that in addition to the grammatical relations of "subject" and "direct object", the description of Mandarin must also include the element "topic". Because of the importance of "topic" in the grammar of Mandarin, it can be termed a topic-prominent language. (p. 15)

In addition to commenting on Li and Thompson's analysis, Tsao (1979) went into depth to discuss the properties of topic and subject, many of which were also mentioned by Li and Thompson (1976, 1981). Since we now, in general, agree with each other quite well, I will simply summarize the agreements and discuss the qualities they did not mention in more detail, incorporating at the same time recent findings by other researchers in the discussion.

For ease of discussion, we will begin with two generally held assumptions that topic is what a clause is about and that subject is an NP that has a "doing" or "being" relation with the verb in the sentence.

2. Subject in Chinese

E. L. Keenan (1976a) discusses thirty-odd qualities of subject, which he claims to be universally available, but not necessarily all utilized in a particular language. He also maintains a distinction between the basic sentences and non-basic sentences in a language. The subject of the former will have more subject qualities than that of the latter. In this section, we will examine actual Chinese data in the light of these qualities to see whether a certain NP in Chinese can be rightly called "basic subject".

2.1. Case Marking

Since in Chinese neither the noun nor the pronoun changes its form according to its case function in a clause, case marking in the traditional sense is irrelevant to the present discussion. However, if case marking is understood in Fillmore's sense (Fillmore, 1968), then Chinese does mark off its subject and direct object. When an NP is the surface subject or direct object, it is not marked by any preposition.

(1) ta <u>zai Dongjing</u> zuo jingchukou maoyi.
    he at Tokyo do import-export business
    'He does import-export business in Tokyo.'

(2) <u>Tongjing</u> you yi–qian–ba–bai–wan renkou.
    Tokyo   has eighteen–million   population
    'Tokyo has a population of eighteen million.'

(3) wo song yi–yang liwu <u>gei ta</u>.
    I give one–CL gift to him
    'I gave a gift to him.'

(4) <u>ta</u> mo–ming–qi–miao–de bei song–le yi–yang
    he puzzlingly   BEI give–ASP one–CL
    liwu.[1]
    gift
    'Much to his puzzlement, he was given a gift.'

If we compare (1) with (2), and (3) with (4), it is apparent that an NP in an oblique case is marked by a co–verb or preposition, but the same phrase is unmarked when it becomes the surface subject.[2]

2.2. Position

Except in presentative clauses, which will be discussed in detail in Chapter 5, subject in Chinese occurs preverbally. It can, however, be preceded by another NP identifiable as topic as in (5):

(5) <u>zhei–ge ren</u>   <u>wo</u> bu xihuan, <u>wo baba</u>   ye
    this–CL person I not like   my father also
    bu xihuan.
    not like
    'This person (topic), I don't like, (and) my father doesn't, either.'

---

[1]Many Chinese passive sentences can occur only in an unfavorable situation. That is the reason why *mo–ming–qi–miao–de* 'puzzlingly' has to be added here. For a discussion of this constraint in passivization see Tsao (1978), and Chu (1973, 1983).

[2]Whether these markers should be called co–verbs or prepositions is not our main concern here. For discussion related to this issue, see Li and Thompson (1981: 356–359), Chang (1977), and Yang (1982).

Here by the semantic properties that we have set up for topic and subject, we are able to determine that the singly underlined phrase is the topic because it is what each of the two clauses is about and those two doubly underlined phrases, namely *wo* and *wo baba* are the subject of each of the two clauses. For the time being, let us disregard the second clause, which we will argue later on that it also has, underlyingly, the same topic as the first clause but the topic is deleted by a process to be called Topic NP Deletion. Let us just concentrate on the first clause. Here clearly both topic and subject can occur preverbally and in that order.

There is one more complication. Objects can sometimes occur unmarked between a subject and a verb.[3]

(6) a. ta xie—wan   xin   le.
       he write—finish letter PART
       'He has finished the letter.'
    b. ta xin   xie—wan   le.
       he letter write—finish PART
       'He has finished the letter.'

By comparing (6a) with (6b), it is clear that the object in (6b) has been fronted to the preverbal position. The problem that arises is: Now we have two NPs, both unmarked,

---

[3]Objects can sometimes occur preverbally as in a *ba* or *bei* construction. Compare (a) and (b) sentences in (i) and (ii) below:
(i)   a. ta xie—wan   xin   le.
         he write—finish   letter   PART
         'He has written the letter.'
      b. ta ba xin   xie—wan   le.
         he BA letter   write—finish   PART
         'He has hed the letter written.'
(ii) a. ta tou—le   xin   le.
         he steal—ASP   letter   PART
         'He stole the letter.'
      b. xin   bei   ta tou   le.
         letter   BEI   he steal PART
         'The letter has been stolen by him.'

In the case of the *ba* construction, the preposed object is marked by *ba*, while the other case, the active subject is demoted and is marked by *bei*. In such cases no confusion of the roles of subject and object will ever arise. For further discussion of the interaction between topic, subject and object in the *ba* and *bei* construction, see Chapters 3 and 5.

occurring preverbally, how do we know which is which?

Here the notion of animateness comes to our rescue. It seems that in most cases only inanimate objects like *xin* 'letter' in (6a) can be fronted.[4] When an animate object is fronted as in (7b), ungrammaticality results.

(7) a. Wang xiansheng da–le   Li Xiaojie.
       Wang Mr.   hit–ASP Li Miss
       'Mr. Wang hit Miss Li.'
    b. *Wang xiansheng Li Xiaojie da–le.
        Wang Mr.   Li Miss   hit–ASP
       'Same as (a).'[5]

It is also due to the same constraint that when a noun phrase which taken in isolation can be either animate or inanimate, as *ji* 'chicken as a dish' or 'chicken as an animal', is placed in this position, it can only be interpreted as inanimate.

(8) wo ji   bu chi.
    I chicken not eat
    'I don't eat chicken.'
    *'I (topic), chickens don't eat (me).'

With this complication taken into account, we can now identify the surface subject in Chinese as the first unmarked animate NP to the left of the verb; otherwise, the unmarked NP immediately before the verb. This point is originally made by Y.C. Li (1972 and Li, et al. 1984), who intends it to be a syntactic way of identifying subject in the surface. This formulation is by and large correct except it doesn't take into account two facts. First, in a presentative sentence an indefinite subject occurs postverbally as we pointed out earlier.[6]

---

[4]The constraint, as it is stated, is too strong. We will give a more accurate reformulation in Chapter 5.

[5]This sentence can be grammatical if the initial NP, *Wang xiansheng* 'Mr. Wang' is interpreted as topic, meaning roughly 'Speaking of Mr. Wang, Miss Li hit (him).' See also further discussion of this matter in our analysis of the object–fronting construction in Chapter 5.

[6]Since the subject in a presentative clause lacks the quality of being definite and it occurs in a position where one normally finds an object but otherwise it has other subject qualities, it is arguable that it should be regarded as non–basic subject.

Second, subjects, especially when they are identical with the speaker or the hearer, or the topic NP can often be deleted (For a brief discussion of these deletion processes, see next section.) So, strictly speaking, this formulation is correct up to the point when these deletion processes take place.

With this understood, we can now apply this criterion to the identification of subject in the sentences we have discussed so far. Because of space limitation, we can only give a few examples (The subjects so identified are underlined):

(9) <u>shui</u> kai le.
    water boil PART
    'The water is boiling.'

(10) Wang Wu (a)   <u>Zhang San</u> bu renshi.
     Wang Wu (PART) Zhang San not know
     'Wang Wu (topic), Zhang San doesn't know (him).'

(11) <u>xuesheng—men</u> gongke   zuo—wan—le.
     students   homework do—finish—ASP
     'The students have finished their homework.'

(12) <u>qian</u> hua—wan—le.
     money use—up—ASP
     'The money (topic and subject) (was) used up.'

(13) qian _____ hua—wan—le.
     money   use—up—ASP
     'The money (topic) (some one) has used (it) up.'

Taken in isolation, (12) and (13) are exactly the same. Depending on whether or not an agent can be discovered in the previous discourse, it will be analyzed as (13) and (12) respectively.

Now examine the following longer stretches of discourse:

(14) <u>zhei—ge Yingwen juzi</u>   zhen   nan,   wo bu dong,
     this—CL English sentence really difficult I not understand

```
    ta ye  bu  dong.
    he also not understand
```
'This English sentence (topic), (it) is really difficult;
I don't understand (it); (and) he doesn't understand (it), either.'

(15) ta <u>duzi</u>   e,   ___ you zhao–bu–dao   dongxi chi,
     he stomach empty   also find–not–succeed thing eat
     suoyi ___ tang zai chuang–shang shuijiao.
     so   lie in bed–LOC   sleep
     'He (topic), (his) stomach was empty; (and) (he) couldn't find
     anything to eat; so (he) lay down on the bed to sleep.'

In (14) *zhei–ge Yingwen juzi* 'this English sentence' is the topic of the sentence since it is the subject matter under discussion. It is also the subject of the first clause, while the subject of the second is *wo* 'I' and that of the third is *ta* 'he'. In (15) *ta* 'he' is the topic of the sentence while *duzi* 'stomach' is the subject of the first clause and *ta* 'he' is the subject of the second and the third, which is in each case deleted by a process called Topic NP Deletion referred to earlier. This analysis, which has been arrived at independently on semantic grounds, can also be confirmed by using the coding properties of subject just discussed, namely, marking and position properties.

2.3. Referential Property

E. L. Keenan (1976a) states that the basic subject is more referential than the object or non–terms in a sentence. This is borne out by our examination of the basic subject in Chinese. Thus, in the majority of cases, the subject in Chinese has a definite reference while there is no such requirement for the object or non–terms in a sentence (In the case of topic the referential requirement is even more stringent, as will be discussed presently.). This point is first brought out by Millie (1932) and then discussed by Chao (1968) and Li and Thompson (1975). Since all these authors define subject and object somewhat differently, in the following we will discuss NPs which can be identified as subject in accordance with the subject properties discussed so far. Compare (a) and (b) sentences in the following:

(16) a. ta xihuan kan–shu.
         he like   read–book
         'He enjoys reading (books).'

b. shu shi wo—de.
   book is mine
   'The book is mine.'

(17) a. wo yao qing—ke.
        I want invite—guest
        'I want to give a party.'
     b. ke   lai—le.
        guest come—ASP
        'The guests have come.'

What we wish to illustrate here is a very general tendency in Chinese that the subject has a definite reference while the object does not. Quite a few objects have actually lost so much of their referential function that they blend with verbs to form verb—object compounds as those in (16a) and (17a) show.[7]

The object, of course, can be made definite with definite markers such as *zhe* 'this, these, the' and *nei* 'that, those, the' and very rarely, the subject can also be indefinite as in (18) cited from Chao (1968:76):[8]

(18) yi—ge mai—shuazi—de zai menkou.
     a—CL brush—peddler at door
     'A brush—peddler is at the door.'

However, even in such rare cases of indefinite subject, the object is still understood as referring to an object with that property while this does not seem to be the case with the objects in all the V—O compounds.

---

[7]Also related to this observation is the fact that objects in many verb compounds of this kind have also lost their inherent tones and assumed the neutral tone. See Chao (1968: 417) for discussion.

[8]Most native speakers that I asked do not regard (18) as fully grammatical though they would not rule out the possibility that some people may talk like that. All of them, however, prefer (i).
  (i) you   yi—ge   mai—shazi—de   zai   menkou.
       EXIST one—CL   brush—peddler   at   door
       'There is a brush—peddler at the door.'

2.4. Behavior and Control Properties

There are several pronominalization and deletion processes in Chinese which involve subject and/or topic as a controller or a victim. We will discuss some important ones in the following.

2.4.1 Reflexivization and Imperativization

Reflexivization may seem a straightforward process. In Tsao (1979) and Li and Thompson (1981), it is claimed that reflexivization is controlled by the subject, but not topic, of the same clause as the victim. This claim has been challenged by Huang (1984). Examine the following examples given by him:

(19)   Zhang San shuo Li Si zai zepei ziji.
         Zhang San say Li Si ASP blame self
   a.   i   j   i
   b.   i   j   j
   a.   'Zhang San said Li Si is blaming him.'
   b.   'Zhang San said Li Si is blaming himself.'

(20)   Zhang San zhidao Li Si bu xihuan ziji.
         Zhang San know   Li Si not like self
   a.   i   j   i
   b.   i   j   j
   a.   'Zhang San knows that Li Si doesn't like him.'
   b.   'Zhang San knows that Li Si doesn't like himself.'

The (a) interpretation of both (19) and (20), where *ziji* 'self' is coreferential with *Zhang San*, are counterexamples to the claim made by Tsao and Li and Thompson since the controller *Zhang San* does not occur in the same clause as the victim. Huang further points out, however, that when *Pro+ziji* form is used, the (a) interpretation is no longer possible. He concludes, on the basis of this and other evidences, that only *Pro+ziji* is a true reflexivization and that *Pro+ziji* and *ziji* should be posited separately in the deep structure rather than transformationally derive *ziji* through deleting *Pro,* as Li and Thompson (1981) claimed.

In view of these new findings, Tsao's (1979) position needs to be revised to refer to true reflexivization, rather than reflexivization alone, i.e., the type of reflexivization where *Pro+ziji* and *ziji* can both be used but not just *ziji* alone. The revised statement now reads:

In the true reflexivization process, the controller is always the subject, but not topic unless it is also the subject, of the same clause. The following examples demonstrate this statement.

(21)　Zhang San pian　(ta)—ziji.
　　　　　　　　cheat hi—self
　　'Zhang San cheats himself.'

(22)　*Zhang San, wo pian　ta—ziji.
　　　　　　　　I　cheat he—self
　　*'Zhang San (topic), I cheat himself.'

(23)　<u>Zhang San</u>, <u>baba</u>　zhi gu　　　<u>ta—ziji</u>.
　　　　　　　father only look—after he—self
　a.*　i　　　j　　　　　　　　　i
　b.　i　　　j　　　　　　　　　j
　a.* 'Zhang San (topic), (his) father only looks after himself.'
　b.　'Zhang San (topic), (his) father only looks after himself.'

(24)　*Zhang San zhidao wo bu　xihuan ta—ziji.
　　　　　　　　know　I not like　he—self
　　*'Zhang San knows that I don't like himself.'

Imperativization: Both Hashimoto (1971) and Li and Thompson (1981) give a detailed description of the imperative construction in Chinese. Imperatives can appear in the following three basic forms, as exemplified in (25), (26) and (27).

(25)　qu.
　　'Go.'

(26)　bie　qu.
　　'Don't go.'

(27)　bie　bu　qu.
　　don't not go
　　'(literally) Don't fail to go; Do go.'

Sometimes, a pronoun can appear in the initial position of an imperative sentence. The pro-forms are restricted to *ni* 'you', *ni-men* 'you, plural' and sometimes, *zan-men* 'we, inclusive'; in other words, a pronoun with a [+ second person] feature.[9] However, whether present or not one of these pronouns is always understood to be there semantically, a phenomenon also observed in many other languages in the world. Topic, however, cannot occur in an imperative sentence, as shown in (28).

(28) * ni, baba lai.
      you father come

(28) can only be interpreted as a statement, meaning, 'you (topic), (your)father came.' It cannot receive any interpretation as an imperative sentene.[10] As the NP involved always bears a "doing" relation to the verb, and as no topic can occur in the imperative construction, it is justified to say that in Chinese, as in many other languages in the world, the imperative sentence has an underlying subject that can be optionally deleted.[11]

2.4.2 Relativization and Conjunction Reduction

Keenan and Comrie (1977) have examined the relativization process in some fifty languages and come up with an interesting hierarchy which demonstrates that grammatical

---

[9]Most speakers in Taiwan do not maintain the distinction between *zan-men* 'we, inclusive' and *wo-men* 'we, exclusive'. They use *we-men* in all contexts. For these people, *wo-men* in the sense of 'we, inclusive' can be used here.

[10](28) in the interpretation of a topic followed by a comment may be similar in form to an imperative sentence preceded by a vocative, as in (i).
 (i) Xiao Ming, lai zheli.
     Xiao Ming come here
     'Xiao Ming, come here.'
In actual speech, the two are quite disinct. A vocative is usually said with a rising intonation and a pause after it is obligatory. A topic, on the other hand, is not said with a rising intonation and a pause after it is optional. This distinction is undoubtedly related to the functional difference of the two constructions. While the vocative is an attention-getting device, the topic is used for establishing or re-establishing given information.

[11]Later on we will generalize the notion of topic and show that in Chinese, at least, topic and subject do not belong to the same level of grammatical organization. Topic belongs to the sentential level and subject to the clausal level. So in the case of imperative sentences, the deleted NP is actually both topic and subject.

notions such as subject, direct object, etc., are universally utilized in the formation of relative clauses in these languages. They call this hierarchy the Accessibility Hierarchy (AH).

    Accessibility Hierarchy (AH)
       SU > DO > IO > OBL > GEN > OCOMP

Here ">" means 'is more accessible than'; SU stands for 'subject,' DO for 'direct object,' IO for 'indirect object,' OBL for 'major oblique case NP' (Nps that express arguments of the main predicate, as *the chest* in *John put the money in the chest* rather than ones having a more adverbial function like *Chicago* in *John lives in Chicago* or *that day* in *John left on that day*), GEN for 'genitive' (or 'possessor') NP (e.g., *the man* in *John took the man's hat*), and OCOMP for 'object of comparison' (e.g., *the man* in *John is taller than the man*).

Keenan and Comrie (op. cit.) further observe, on the basis of data provided by Sanders and Tai (1972),[12] that the pronominalization and deletion of the NP in a relative clause that is coreferential with the head NP in Chinese follows the hierarchy shown in TABLE 1. As can be seen, this hierarchy fits the AH very well.

TABLE 1

SU	DO	IO	OBL	GEN	OCOMP
−	+/−	+	+	+	+

Key: − means that no pronoun is retained;
       +/− means that in some cases the pronoun is retained and in others it is not;
       + means that pronoun retention is obligatory.

The AH is such a neat hierarchy that, if it were true of all languages in the world, it would be a good example for the universalists, especially a school that has come to be known as 'relational grammarians' (Gary and Keenan, 1977; Keenan, 1976a, 1976b; Johnson, 1974a, 1974b; Perlmutter and Postal, 1974, 1977; Perlmutter 1980). Unfortunately, this hierarchy doesn't hold true when Chinese relativization is carefully examined and the confounding factor seems to be topic.

Relativization in Chinese, as in Tagalog (Schachter, 1976), Japanese (Kuno, 1976),

---

[12]See Tang (1977) for some criticism of Sander and Tai's treatment of relativization in Chinese.

and Tok Pisin (Sankoff and Brown, 1976), seems to exhibit a close relation to the process of topicalization. Examine the following parallels between relativization and topicalization in Chinese.[13]

First, the conditions for the deletion or pronominalization of the relativized NP are nearly identical with those for the deletion or pronominalization of the topicalized NP. Compare the following sentences:

(29) a. <u>nei-ge xiaohaizi</u> hen xihuan ni. (Subject)
   that-CL child   very like you
   'The child likes you very much.'

b. <u>nei-ge xiaohaizi</u>, (ta) hen xihuan ni.
   that-CL child   he very like you
   'The child (topic), (he) likes you very much.'

c. ____ hen xihuan ni de   nei-ge <u>xiaohaizi</u> ...
        very like you Rel. Mar. that-CL child
   'the child who likes you very much ...'

d. ?<u>ta</u> hen xihuan ni de nei-ge xiaohaizi ...[14]
   '(Same as C)'

(30) a. zhei-ge nühai hen xihuan <u>nei-wei</u>
   this-CL girl very like   that-CL
   <u>xiansheng</u>. (DO)
   man
   'This girl likes that man very much.'

b. <u>nei-wei xiansheng</u>, zhei-ge nühai hen
   that-CL man   this-CL girl very
   xihuan (ta).
   like   (him)
   'That man (topic), this girl likes (him) very much.'

---

[13]A number of observations discussed in this section are originally due to Tang (1979b).

[14]This example, but not the grammatical judgment, was taken from Tang (1979b). But many native speakers, including myself, would regard it as slightly odd but not downright ungrammatical.

    c. zhei-ge nühai hen xihuan (ta) de
        this-CL girl very like (him) Rel. Mar.
        nei-wei xiansheng ...
        that-CL man
        'The man whom the girl likes very much ...'

In this connection, note that the constraint—a pronominal copy of a topic governed by *ba* or a preposition cannot be deleted—also applies in the deletion process of the relativized NP. Compare (31) with (32), and (33) with (34):

(31) a. <u>na-ge xiaohai</u>, wo shichang gen ta dajia.
       that-CL child I often with him fight
       'That child (topic), I often fight with him.'
   b. *<u>na-ge xiaohai</u>, wo shichang gen _____ dajia.

(32) a. wo shichang gen ta dajia de   <u>na-ge xiaohai</u> ...
       I often with him fight Rel. Mar. that-CL child
       'the child whom I often fight with ...'
   b. *wo shichang gen ____ daijia de <u>na-ge xiaohai</u> ...

(33) a. <u>nei-ben shu</u>, wo ba <u>ta</u> fang zai ni-de zhuozi-shang.
       that-CL book I <u>BA</u> it put on your desk-LOC
       'The book (topic), I put it on your desk.'
   b. *nei-ben shu, wo ba _____ fang zai ni-de zhuozi-shang.
       that-CL book I BA put at your desk-LOC

(34) a. wo ba <u>ta</u> fang zai ni-de zhuozi-shang de   nei-ben shu ....
       I BA it put at your desk-LOC Rel. Mar. that-CL book
       'the book that I put on your desk ....'
   b. *wo ba ____ fang zai ni-de zhuozi-shang de   nei-ben
       I BA put at your desk-LOC Rel. Mar. that-CL
       shu ....
       book
       'Same as (a).'

All the cases that we have discussed so far demonstrate the close relationship that exists between relativization and the process of topic formation. Most of them also agree with the hierarchy that Keenan and Comrie have posited for Chinese, however. One difficult case for them is (34), where relativization interacts with the *ba* construction. As we will argue in Chapter 6, the function of the *ba* construction is to move an NP, in most cases a direct object, to the preverbal position to mark it as a secondary topic of a special kind. The *ba* NP is therefore not an object NP, even though it might originate as one. In all the processes of pronominalization and NP deletion in which it is involved, it behaves like an NP governed by a co-verb or preposition. Thus, when the NP can be regarded as being moved out of its position as in relativization, a pronominal copy is always left in its place (Y. H. Li, 1980; C. Y. Li, 1985).

Second, the deletion of possesive NPs that are relativized is a complicated matter that has never, to the best of my knowledge, been fully studied. However, as far as we can determine, the general governing principle seems to be: if the possessive NP can become topic in a so-called "double nominative" construction, then it can also be relativized. For example, it has often been observed that only the possessing NP can become a topic, the possessed NP cannot. The same phenomenon is found with relativization; i.e., only the possessing NP can be relativized. Compare (35) with (36):

(35) a. nei—wei xiaojie yanjing hen piaoliang.
    that—CL lady eyes very beautiful
    'That lady (topic), (her) eyes are very beautiful.'

  b. *yanjing, nei—wei xiaojie hen piaoliang.[15]
    eyes that—CL lady very beautiful
    '(Her) eyes (topic), that lady is beautiful.'

(36) a. nei—wei yanjing hen piaoliang de xiaojie ....
    that—CL eyes very beautiful Rel. Mar. lady
    'the lady whose eyes are beautiful ....'

---

[15] As will be discussed in full in Chapter 4, the sentence can be grammatical if *yanjing* 'eyes' is taken in a generic sense, roughly paraphrasable in English as: 'Speaking of eyes, those of the lady are beautiful.'

b. *nei-wei xiaojie hen piaoliang de yanjing.[16]
   that-CL lady very beautiful Rel. Mar. eyes

When relativization does occur, the relativized possessive NP does not leave any pronominal copy behind as in the case of topicalization, as exemplified in (37).

(37) a. nei-ge nühai-de toufa hen chang.
        that-CL girl-POSS hair very long
        'The girl's hair (subject and topic) is very long.'
     b. *ta-de toufa hen chang de nei-ge nühai ....[17]
        she-POSS hair very long Rel. Mar. that-CL girl
        'the girl whose hair is very long ....'
     c. nei-ge nühai, toufa hen chang.
        that-CL girl hair very long
        'The girl (topic), (her) hair is very long.'
     d. toufa hen chang de nei-ge nühai ...
        hair very long Rel. Mar. that-CL girl
        'the girl whose hair is very long ...'

Furthermore, some so-called 'double nominative' constructions, as we have pointed out in Chapter 1, have no corresponding paraphrases with any sort of possessive construction and hence cannot be derived from the latter. These 'double nominative' constructions, however, can appear in relative clauses.

(38) a. na-qun   ren, ni kan   wo, wo kan
        that-group people you look-at me I look-at
        ni, yi-dian zhuyi ye meiyou.
        you a-CL   idea all not-have
        'The group of people (topic), they looked at each other,
        (and) had no idea at all.'

---

[16] This string is grammatical if it means 'those beautiful eyes of the lady ....' However, in such a case, there is no evidence that the string is an output of a relativization process.

[17] T. C. Tang (personal communication) has pointed out to me that according to his investigation, (37b) is ungrammatical unless *ta-de* 'her' is deleted as in (37d).

    b. ni kan wo, wo kan ni, yi-dian zhuyi
        you look-at me I look-at you a-CL idea
        ye meiyou de na-qun ren ...
        all not-have Rel. Mar. that-group people
        'the group of people that looked at each other (and)
        had no idea at all ...'

(39) a. nei-zhong zhi mei zhang yi-mao qian.
        that-kind paper every sheet ten-cents money
        'That kind of paper (topic), a sheet is worth ten cents.'
    b. mei zhang yi-mao qian de
        every sheet ten-cents money Rel. Mar.
        nei-zhong zhi ...
        that-kind paper
        'the kind of paper that is worth ten cents a sheet...'

The cases that we have discussed in this section have all shown that Keenan and Comrie's hierarchy is incorrect as far as the relativization of genitive NPs in Chinese is concerned. The hierarchy predicts that all cases of genitive NPs that are relativized should have a pronominal copy left in the relative clause. However, as (37) clearly shows, the opposite is actually the case. Just like the case of subject, a retained pronoun in the relative clause will result in an ungrammatical sentence. Furthermore, one of the Primary Relativization Constraints that go with the hierarchy states (op. cit.:68): "If a primary strategy in a given language can apply to a low position on the AH, then it can apply to all higher positions." Since GEN is very low in the hierarchy, the fact that it behaves like the subject sheds much doubt on the correctness of the hierarchy. On the other hand, we see that relativization seems to exhibit a very close tie to the process of topic formation. E. L. Keenan (personal communication) has recently claimed that he has some evidence for positing a separate hierarchy for genitive NPs, something like:

Genitive of SU > Genitive of DO > Genitive of IO

Even with this modification, the hierarchy cannot accommodate cases like (38) and (39) because the relativized NPs have no possessive sources.

    Third, predicate nominals after classificatory verbs may not become a topic, nor can they be relativized.

(40) a. ni hen xiang nei-ge nühai.
    you very like that-CL girl
    'You look very much like the girl.'
  b. *nei-ge nühai ni hen xiang.
    that-CL girl you very like
    'The girl (topic), you look very much like (her).'
  c. ?nei-ge nühai, ni hen xiang ta.
    that-CL girl you very like her
    'The girl (topic), you look very much like her.'
  d. *ni hen xiang de   nei-ge nühai . . .
    you very like Rel. Mar. that-CL girl
    'the girl whom you look like . . .'
  e. ?ni hen xiang <u>ta</u> de   nei-ge nühai . . .
    you very like her Rel. Mar. that-CL girl
    'the girl whom you look like . . .'

Finally, no noun phrases contained in a complex NP (see Ross, 1967 for a discussion of this notion) can be relativized or become a topic.

(41) a. wo renshi nei-ge shichang ma
    I know   the-CL often   scold
    Xiao Ming de   ren.
    Xiao Ming Rel. Mar. man
    'I know the man who often scolds Xiao Ming.'
  b. *nei-ge xiaohai, wo renshi nei-ge
    the-CL child   I know   the-CL
    shichang ma   de   ren.
    often   scold Rel. Mar. man
    *'The child (topic), I know the man who often scolds.'
  c. ?nei-ge xiaohai, wo renshi nei-ge
    the-CL child   I know   the-CL
    shichang ma   ta de   ren
    often   scold him Rel. Mar. man

?'The child (topic), I know the man who often scolds him.'
   d. *wo renshi nei–ge shichang ma   (ta)
      I know   the–CL   often   scold (him)
      de   ren de   nei–ge xiaohai.
      Rel. Mar. man Rel. Mar. that–CL child
      *'the child whom I know the man often scolds . . .'

All these parallels indicate that there is a close similarity between the topic construction and the relative clause.[18] After all, they both involve picking out an NP and saying something about it. However, the pragmatic functions of the two processes seem to be quite different (see Tsao, 1979, Chapters 6 and 7 and Chapter 8 of the present volume for some discussion of their respective functions). This can be inferred from the following cases where the two processes differ:

(42) a. yu   (a),   weiyu zui gui.
        fish (PART) tuna most expensive
        '(Speaking of) fish, tuna is the most expensive.'
     b. *weiyu zui gui   de   yu ..
        tuna most expensive Rel. Mar. fish
        *'fish that tuna is the most expensive ...'

(43) a. ta nei–ge dushengzi dai yangjing.
        he the–CL only–son wear glasses
        'His only son (topic and subject) wears glasses.'
     b. *ta nei–ge dai yanjing de   dushengzi ...[19]
        he the–CL wear glasses Rel. Mar. only–son
        *'His only son who wears glasses.'

If we assume that one of the basic functions of the relative clause is to provide some background information so that the hearer can identify the NP involved (Sankoff and

---

[18]What we are concerned with here is only the similarities between the two processes in a synchronic description of modern Chinese. For a discussion of how the relative clause in a number of languages actually developed through a stage in which a clause with a topic was loosely attached to the main clause, forming a kind of topic chain, please see Givon (1979).

[19]The relative clause in its nonrestrictive reading is grammatical.

Brown, 1976; Keenan and Schieffelin, 1976b) while the clause that follows a topic predicates something new about it, then it makes some sense that the (a) sentences are grammatical whereas the (b) sentences are not. (42b) is ungrammatical because it is impossible to identify all fish by talking about tuna alone. (43b) is ungrammatical in its restrictive reading because the relativized NP 'his only son' is in this context uniquely identifiable.

However, while it is true that "restrictive relative clauses are overwhelmingly background–presupposed information" (Givon, 1979a: 88), i.e., they have the identifying function, there are cases in English in which the relative clause does not represent background–presupposed information, as exemplified by (44) and (45):

(44) There was once a boy whose father died when he was three.
(45) He has a sister who is very fond of movies.

As we will argue in Chapter 8 by examining the Chinese equivalents of cases like (44) and (45) that the relative clause in these cases, though restrictive in form, is not background–presupposed information.[20] On the contrary, it presents new information while the main clause, contrary to what is usually supposed, only serves the purpose of introducing a topic, always indefinite in reference, into the discourse to be further commented upon by the relative clause. Interestingly, in these cases, as Chu (1983) correctly points out, Chinese uses a special type of serial verb construction, to be called "telescopic–presentative" construction in Chapter 7. This construction is exemplified here by (46) and (47), which are Chinese equivalents of (44) and (45) respectively.

(46) congqian you   yi–ge xiao–nan–hai, san–sui–de   shihou
     long–ago EXIST one–CL boy   3–year–old–POSS time
     baba   jiu   si–le.
     father (earlier–than–expected)   die–ASP
     'Same as (44).'

(47) ta you yi–ge meimei,   hen xihuan kan   dianying.
     he has one–CL younger sister very like   watch movie
     'Same as (45).'

---

[20]For a more detailed discussion of this phenomenon, see Tsao (1986).

This discussion of the relativization in Chinese is rather lengthy, but, unfortunately, still inconclusive. But at least we know that relativization and topic formation are in many respects closely related processes. Furthermore, as far as identifying topic and subject in Chinese is concerned, Keenan and Comrie's hierarchy cannot be relied upon.

Coordinate conjunction reduction: Tai (1969) observes in his dissertation that identity deletion in a coordinate structure is limited only to the subject in Chinese. It is not allowed in the object position. Compare (48) to (49):

(48) a. ta ti—le   qiu ta ye da—le   ren.
        he kick—ASP ball he also hit—ASP man
        'He kicked the ball and he hit the man.'
     b. ta ti—le   qiu ye da—le   ren.
        he kick—ASP ball also hit—ASP man
        'He kicked the ball and hit the man.'

(49) a. wo mai—le li, ni chi—le li.
        I buy—ASP pear you eat—ASP pear
        'I bought the pear; you ate the pear.'
     b. *wo mai—le, ni chi—le, li.
        I   buy—ASP you eat—ASP pear
        'I bought (and) you ate, the pear.'

Interestingly enough, however, if the identical object NP appears as the topic as in (49c), the sentence is grammatical.

(49) c. li, wo mai—le, ni chi—le.
        pear I buy—ASP you eat—ASP
        'The pear (topic), I bought (it) (and) you ate (it).'

If this fact is taken in conjunction with the previous observation that coordinate conjunction reduction is allowed only in the subject position (notice that in this case subject is, under this analysis, also topic), then it seems that coordinate conjunction reduction is allowed in Chinese only in the topic position, and it can be regarded as a subprocess of Topic–NP deletion, to be discussed presently.[21] The whole string of discourse thus forms a topic chain. Since this type of topic chain does not have any connective between any two clauses, we will call it the plain topic chain. More will be said about it in Chapter 7.

2.4.3. Coreferential NP Deletion

This is an overall term for at least four subprocesses, which will be termed Equi–NP deletion, Topic NP deletion, Discourse Theme deletion, and Speaker and Hearer deletion in this study. We will take them up one by one.

<u>Equi–NP deletion</u>: Many Chinese linguists have actually assumed the existence of such a rule of deletion without looking closely into it, so that its exact nature remains to be uncovered. However, there are at least two cases where it can be clearly demonstrated that subject is definitely involved. One case is the embedded subject of desiderative verbs such as *xiang* 'want' and the other case is the embedded subject of what Chao (1968) called "pivotal construction", originally derived through a direct request (for more detailed discussion of this latter construction, see Chapter 7 of the present study, and Li, 1985).

Let us begin with the desiderative verb construction. Take *xiang* 'want' for example.

---

[21]There is a slight complication here. Examine (i):

(i) Xiao Ming$_i$ baba$_j$ meitian dushu, ____$_j$
    Xiao Ming father every–day read
    xia–qi he ____$_j$ zuo–hua, mama ba
    play–chess and paint mother BA
    jiashi nong de haohao–de
    household–affairs manage PART well
    ta zhen xingfu.
    he really lucky.
'Xiao Ming (topic), (his) father reads, plays chess and paints every day; (his) mother manages the household afairs well; he is really lucky.'

It seems in this case what has just been defined as topic (i.e., Xiao Ming) does not control deletion in coordinate conjunction reduction. Instead, the subject (i.e., *baba* 'father') is in control here. Thus, it constitutes a counter–example to our claim. However, if we break down this big topic chain, we find that it consists of three small clauses; i.e., *baba meitian dushu, xia qi, he zuo–hua*; *mama ba jia–shi nong de haoaho–de*; and *ta zhen xingfu*. Each is an independent topic chain with its own topic. So, looking at (i) as a whole, perhaps it is not unjustifiable to claim that *baba*, *mama* and *ta* are functioning as subtopics here. In fact, we will present other strong arguments in a later chapter for treating the second nominal in a double nominative construction as a secondary topic capable of leading its own topic chain. The present slight revision has another advantage. It will enable us to state a generalizatiuon: Every subject is a topic, primary or otherwise.

It exhibits what has come to be known as "like-subject constraint," like *try* in English (Perlmutter, 1971) and the desiderative verb suffix *—tai* in Japanese (Kuno, 1973). Compare (50) with (51):

(51)   * Lao Zhang xiang Lao Li qu.
       Lao Zhang want Lao Li go
       'Lao Zhang wants Lao Li to go.'

(51)   Lao Zhang xiang qu.
       Lao Zhang want go
       'Lao Zhang wants to go.'

Since in (51) John is understood to be the one who is doing the action of wanting and going, there is adequate motivation to posit an underlying subject for *qu* 'go', which is deleted by the process of Equi—NP deletion. Furthermore, when an intensive subject (i.e., just *ziji* 'self' without being preceded by any personal pronoun) appears in the embedded sentence, it is understood to be coreferential with the subject of the matrix verb, as shown in (52).[22]

(52)   Lao Zhang bu xiang ziji qu.
       Lao Zhang not want self go
       'Lao Zhang doesn't want to go himself.'

Likewise, when the embedded sentence is a passive one, the deleted NP is again understood to be the derived subject, as in (53a):

(53) a.   Lao Zhang bu xiang bei ren qifu.
          Lao Zhang not want BEI people bully
          'Lao Zhang doesn't want to be bullied by people.'

---

[22]In Tsao (1979), this type of pronoun was called "reflexive", but, following T. C. Tang's suggestion, I have, on the basis of meaning, chosen to call it "intensive pronoun" here. However, regardless of whether *ziji* in (52) is reflexive or intensive, it can still be argued that (52) has (i) as its underlying source.
    (i)   Lao Zhang   bu xiang   ta—ziji   qu.
        Lao Zhang   not want   he—self   go
The rule of Equi—NP deletion can then apply as usual, deleting *ta* 'he' and leaving only *ziji* 'self'.

As can be expected, when the embedded passive sentence is put in the active form, the sentence becomes ungrammatical, as shown in (53b) and (53c):

(53) b. *Lao Zhang bu xiang ren   qifu   ta.
        Lao Zhang not want people bully him
        'Lao Zhang doesn't want people to bully him.'
     c. *Lao Zhang bu xiang ren   qifu.
        Lao Zhang not want people bully
        'Lao Zhang doesn't want people to bully (him).'

From the above examples, it is clear that the controller here is the subject of the matrix verb and the victim is the subject of the embedded verb, basic or derived. Topic, on the other hand, does not have this property.

(54) Lao Zhang$_i$ baba$_j$ xiang _____$*i;j$ qu.
     Lao Zhang   father   want   go
     'Lao Zhang (topic), (his) father wants to go.'

In (54) the deleted embedded subject can only be understood to be coreferential with the subject of the matrix verb, i.e., 'Lao Zhang's father' but not the topic, 'Lao Zhang'.

In a similar manner, there is a group of verbs, which is followed by an NP which plays double roles of being the object of the matrix verb and at the same time the subject of the embedded verb. This group includes *qing* 'invite, ask', *yaoqiu* 'request', *yao* 'want' and *mingling* 'order, command' etc.[23] Below are two examples.

(55) wo qing   Lao Zhang lai zheli.
     I invite Lao Zhang come here
     'I invited Lao Zhang to come here.'

(56) ta yaoqiu Lao Li mashang   likai.
     he request Lao Li immediately leave
     'He requested Lao Li to leave immediately.'

---

[23]Chao (1968) refers to this group of verbs as "pivotal" verbs and the construction involving this group of verbs as the "pivotal" construction. For a detailed discussion of this construction see Chao (1968) and Chapter 7 of the present volume.

Thus Lao Zhang in (55) and Lao Li in (56) are both understood to be the direct object of the first verb and the subject of the second verb in their respective clauses. Again, when the embedded clause is in the passive as in (57), the NP in question is understood to be the object of the first verb and the derived subject of the second verb as shown in the English translation.

(57) ta yaoqiu <u>fanren</u> bei chu sixing.
    he request criminal BEI judge death—sentence
    'He requested the criminal be given death sentence.'

The NP in question, furthermore, cannot be understood to be co-referential with the subject of the matrix verb, *ta* 'he'. Again when a topic which bears a relation other than that of subject appears in the place in question, the sentence is ungrammatical as is clear by comparing (58a) with (58b).

(58) a. Li Jiaoshou yao women mai na—ben shu.
        Li Professor want us   buy that—CL book
        'Professor Li wants us to buy that book.'
     b. *Li Jiaoshou yao na—ben shu women mai.
        Li Professor want that—CL book we buy

Therefore, we can safely conclude that in this construction the controller of the deletion process is the object of the matrix verb and the victim is the subject of the embedded verb. Topic, unless it is also the subject of the embedded verb, plays no part in this type of Equi—NP deletion process.

<u>Topic—NP deletion:</u> There is a special function of the topic construction called the Chaining Function (see Tsao, 1979, Chapter 6). We have come across several examples of topic in this function. When several sentences appear in a topic chain, the first topic acts as the controller and the topic in each of the subsequent clauses acts as the victim of this deletion process. Here is one more example from the spontaneous discourse data that I have collected:

(59)   F: 90
    c: zhei—bian,   yinwei limian
       this—side (house) because inside

```
jiu-jiu-zang-zang  ta shuo xiang
old-and-dirty      he said want
youqi-hao     ___  yihou zai
paint-finish       after then
mai     ___.
sell
```
'The house on this side (topic), because the inside is old and dirty he said (he) wanted to paint (it), (and) then (he) would sell (it).'

In this example, the speaker has some ideas about 'the house on this side,' so she starts out with that NP as topic and then in the subsequent clauses makes some comments on the same topic without repeating the topic referent. It is evident that the first topic is in control of the subsequent topic Nps deletion.

It may be argued that the subsequent NPs that get deleted may not be topics. That this is not the case can be seen from the following two pieces of supportive evidence. First, in Chinese, phrases denoting a period of time can often be put in the genitive form to modify another NP as in (60a):

(60) a. ta zhi jiao-le yi-ge xueqi-de   xuefei.
         he only pay-ASP a-CL semester-POSS tuition
         'He only paid tuition for a semester.'

However, the NP that is in construction with the time phrase can become a topic. When this is done, the possessive marker $-de$ is always deleted as is clear by comparing (b) with (c) in (60).

(60) b. xuefei, ta zhi jiao-le yi-ge xueqi.
         tuition he only pay-ASP a-CL semester
         '(As for) tuition (topic), he only pays for a semester.'
     c. *xuefei, ta zhi jiao-le yi-ge xueqi-de.

Now let's put (60 b and c) respectively as a second clause in a topic chain as in (61a) and (61b):

(61) a. xuefei   shizai tai gui   le,   suoyi ta
       tuition really too expensive PART so   he
       zhi   jiao—le yi—ge xueqi.
       only pay—ASP a—CL semester
       'The tuition is really high, so he only pays for a semester.'
   b. *xuefei shizai tai gui le, suoyi ta zhi jiao—le yi—ge xueqi—de.

By comparing the (a) and (b) sentences in (61), it is clear that *xuefei* 'tuition' in the second clause has become a topic before it is deleted by the first topic.

Second, as we pointed out in our previous discussion of relativization and topic formation, a predicate nominal after a classificatory verb cannot become a topic, as exemplified by (40b) and (40c). When we use them as the second clause in a topic chain as in (62a) and (62b), the results are also bad.

(62) a. *nei—ge nühai hen piaoliang, ni hen xiang.
        the—CL girl very beautiful you very like
        'The girl (topic), (she) is very beautiful;
        you look very much like (her).'
   b. ?nei—ge nühai hen piaoliang, ni hen xiang ta.

As we can detect no semantic incompatibility between the two clauses in the chain, the fact that (62a) and (62b) are both bad is probably due to a syntactic reason. We can explain their ungrammaticality if we assume that the predicate nominal occurring after *xiang* 'like' (i.e., *nei—ge nühai* 'the girl') has become a topic in violation of the constraint.

To sum up, it seems clear that the first topic in a topic chain is the controller of this deletion process while the subsequent topics are all victims. Seen in this light, the so—called coordinate conjunction reduction can then be considered as a special case of Topic—NP deletion. The former occurs when the controlling and the deleted Nps are topics which, at the same time, bear the same grammatical relations to their respective verbs i.e., they are both subjects or objects.

Li and Thompson in a paper titled "Third—person Pronouns and Zero—anaphora in Chinese Discourse" (1979) made an attempt to examine the deletion phenomenon in Chinese narrative discourse. However, while they, on the one hand, recognize the existence of the topic chain in Chinese, they deny the existence of the rule of topic NP deletion. This rather unusual position is best exemplified by the following stretch of discourse they cited from *Shui–Hu Zhuan,* a famous novel written in the vernacular in the late fourteenth century.

(63) a. Kong–Liang jiao–fu xiao–lou–lou yu–le Lu–Zhi–Sheng,
K–L   deliver soldiers   to–ASP L–Z–S
'K–L delivered the soldiers to L–Z–S,'

b. ϕ_1 zhi dai   yi–ge ban–dang,
only bring one–CL companion
'(he) only brought along one companion,'

c. ϕ_2 ban   zuo ke–shang,
disguise as merchant
'(he) disguised himself as a merchant.'

d. ϕ_3 xing–ye tou Liang–Shan–Bo lai.
quickly came L–S–B   to
'(he) quickly came to L–S–B.'

In their discussion of (63), they first point out that it looks like a typical case of topic chain in Chinese in that here are four comment clauses, represented by a, b, c and d respectively, which share a common topic, *Kong–Liang,* which occurs in the initial position of the first clause and is in control of the coreferential NP deletion of all other topics in the same chain. They, however, also claim that (63), in isolation, is "totally confusing to a native speaker of Chinese" in that a native speaker cannot decide whether ϕ_1, in (63b) should refer to K–L, or L–Z–S in (63a) or whether ϕ_2 in (63c) should refer to the 'companion' in (63b) or to the antecedent of ϕ_1. Thus, they conclude:

> This confusion on the part of the native speaker due to the ambiguity of ϕ_1 and ϕ_2 indicates that the principle of topic chain is not an inviolable rule governing referent interpretation of zero–pronouns. In other words, it does not have any special status among the native speaker's strategies for interpreting zero–pronouns in Chinese discourse (p.320).

This conclusion of theirs is called to doubt by the following observations. First, while in their discussion of the third person pronoun, they rely on the experimental results obtained by asking native speakers to supply a pronoun wherever they think necessary, the conclusion just cited is evidently not based on the same kind of evidence but rather on a native speaker's intuition. This is true of all their discussion of the phenomenon of zero–anaphora. However, if we follow the general assumption that co–referential NP deletion and coreferential pronominalization are closely related processes, then we have every reason to doubt the validity of the above conclusion when the two processes are approached in such different ways.

Second, such a conclusion does not seem to be compatible with the fact that the topic chain, even taken in its literal sense of containing more than two comment clauses headed by a common topic, occurs so frequently. Every Chinese example they cited, for instance, in both sections of the paper contains topic chains of various length. The argument here is that it is very unlikely that a process that occurs with such a high frequency in production should play no role in the native speaker's interpretation.

Finally, Topic NP deletion, as we will demonstrate later, interacts with other more general deletion processes such as Discourse Theme deletion. The topic chain is, therefore, not a self–contained unit impervious to other discourse processes. Also related to this is the observation that a topic chain, as we define it here, is a common topic followed by at least one comment clause. In other words, a topic chain, taken in isolation, may be perceived by some as one chain but by others as consisting of more than one chain, depending on the perceived meaning of the stretch of discourse in question. As a concrete example, let us return to (63). Native speakers who take ϕ_1 in (b) as referring to L–Z–S may actually regard (a) as a topic chain in itself while (b), (c) and (d) form another topic chain with L–Z–S as its common topic.

A position that is compatible with the above observations and one that is sufficiently different from Li and Thompson is to regard Topic NP deletion as a probable rule but nonetheless a rule that plays an important part in the native speaker's interpretation of zero–anaphora.[24] In other words, our contention is that native speakers tend to interpret the deleted topic NP as occurring in the subsequent comment clauses as coreferential with the first topic unless this is overridden by the meaning of the discourse or his knowledge of the world. Such a position is in agreement with the research findings by both Li (1985)

---

[24]In other words, rules of NP deletions should be differentiated into two types: the "must" rule and the "probable" rule. Equi–NP deletion, for example, is a must rule because whenever the condition is met, the rule will apply. Topic NP deletion, on the other hand, is a probable rule in that even when the condition is met the rule does not always apply.

and Tse (1986).

With this in mind, we can now go back to (63). By talking informally with some of the subjects who took the pretest, my suspicion was confirmed that the native speaker's confusion about the missing topic NPs in the chain was partly brought about by the fact that most educated native speakers know that Lu Zhi-Sheng is one of the "heroes" at Liang-Shan-Bo but they have no idea whether Kong-Liang is one of them or not.[25] So in the actual test, the positions of Lu-Zhi-Sheng and Kong-Liang were interchanged with the rest of the chain remaining intact. The result of the experiment is given below:

Interpretation for ϕ_1 ϕ_2 and ϕ_3	No. of subjects	Percentage
L-Z-S straight out	19	63
mixed	9	30
K-L straight out	2	7

The result confirms our hypothesis as stated above but is inconsistent with the interpretation that such a rule plays no significant part in the native speaker's interpretation of zero-anaphora.

How then is this process different from Equi-NP deletion? There are at least three important differences. First, Equi-NP deletion affects an NP in an embedded sentence while Topic-NP deletion affects NPs in conjoined sentences, although no over conjunction need be present. Second, while in the latter process, with the possible exception of the subprocess of coordinate conjunction reduction, the affected NP can sometimes leave a pronominal copy behind, it is not possible in the former process. Finally, while Equi-NP deletion is a "must" rule, in the sense explained in Note 24, Topic-NP deletion is a "probable" rule.

<u>Discourse Theme deletion</u>: In spontaneous discourse, the discourse theme can play an important role in controlling coreferential NP deletion. Although very little is known about this process, there seems to be a general principle: whenever a discourse theme is considered established, NPs that have to do with this general theme can be deleted. Typically, the NPs involved go through an intermediate stage of pronominalization before they are finally deleted through a stretch of discourse on the same theme. There are

---

[25]Most of my subjects are in-service high school English teachers in Taiwan, ranging in age from 26 to 45. They all speak Mandarin fluently and most of them read *Shui-Hu Zhuan* before they were twenty. For some reason, most of them remember Lu-Zhi-Sheng as one of the "heroes" at Liang-Shan-Bo, but very few remember Kong-Liang as one of them.

certain constraints, however. It seems that contrastiveness, emphasis, and change of turns may all constrain deletion, although the details have yet to be worked out. Now examine (64):

(64)
```
T:   shi   ya.  wo taitai  xie-xin       tongchang ye   dou shi ...
     right PART my wife    write-letter  usually   also is
     'Right. My wife usually starts writing letters also...'
C://ye   shi  zhe  yangzi a.
     also is   this way    PART
     'Is also in this manner?'
T:   shi-yi-er dian     cai  xie.  // ta
     11 or 12  o'clock  then write    she
     huilai       yihou, baitian ma,
     return-home then   daytime PART
     baba mama...
     Pa   Mom
     'Only after 11 or 12 does she write. After she returns home —
     during the daytime, Pa and Mom...'
C:   ã
     PART
T:   zai jia  kankan        xiaohai hen  xinku.
     at  home look-after    child   very laborious
     'do the laborious job of looking after the child at home.'
C:   ã
     PART
T:   ____ huilai dangran  ____   bu-hao-yi-si
          return of course        feel-uneasy
     zai   rang tamen dai
     again let  them  look after
     'So when (she) comes home, (she) feels uneasy to let them go
     on taking care of (the child).'
C:   dui. na  ta  shang-ban huilai = =
     right PART she work      return
     'That's right. So she returns from work...'
```

50

> T: == ___ shangban huilai yihou, ___ jiu
>   work   return after   then
>   kan   xiaohai.
>   look-after child
>   'After (she) returns from work, (she) then looks after the child.'
> C: oh!
>   PART
> T: ___ you-shihou deng ta
>   sometimes wait she (the child)
>   shui-le...
>   sleep-ASP
>   'Sometimes, (she) waits until she (the child) is asleep...'
> C: oh!
>   PART
> T: ___ cai   neng xiexin. ___ hen xinku.
>   only then can write-letters very hard
>   'only then can (she) write letters. It's really hard for (her).'

In this stretch of discourse, T is telling C about his wife's busy schedule. So we observe that the NP *wo taitai* 'my wife' is first pronominalized as *ta* 'she' and then is deleted in T's speech thereafter.

    An interesting question arises as to whether it is possible to regard Discourse Theme deletion as Topic-NP deletion across discourse. That is certainly an interesting area for researchers interested in discourse analysis to look into in the future. Right now we don't have enough data to prove it one way or the other. We tend to think that they are distinct processes on the ground that topic NPs, as they are defined in this study, often bear only indirect relation to the theme of the discourse (see Tsao, 1979, Chapter 6 and Sibley, 1980 for discussion of some important roles that topic NPs can play in discourse). For example, the general discourse theme may be the weather conditions of America, but in the discourse one may find a topic chain headed by 'California,' in which its geographical features and weather conditions are characterized. In a discourse like this, the NPs 'weather conditions' and 'America' will probably be in control of Discourse Theme deletion in the whole discourse while the NP 'California' will be in control of Topic-NP deletion in that particular topic chain.

    <u>Speaker and Hearer deletion</u>: In English, it is always possible to pronominalize the

speaker and the hearer (see Chafe, 1970 and 1974 for discussion). In Chinese, it is always possible to delete the speaker and the hearer. Just like the Discourse Theme deletion process, this process typically goes through an intermediate stage of pronominalization and is also subject to the same constraint as Discourse Theme deletion, as can be seen from the following example:

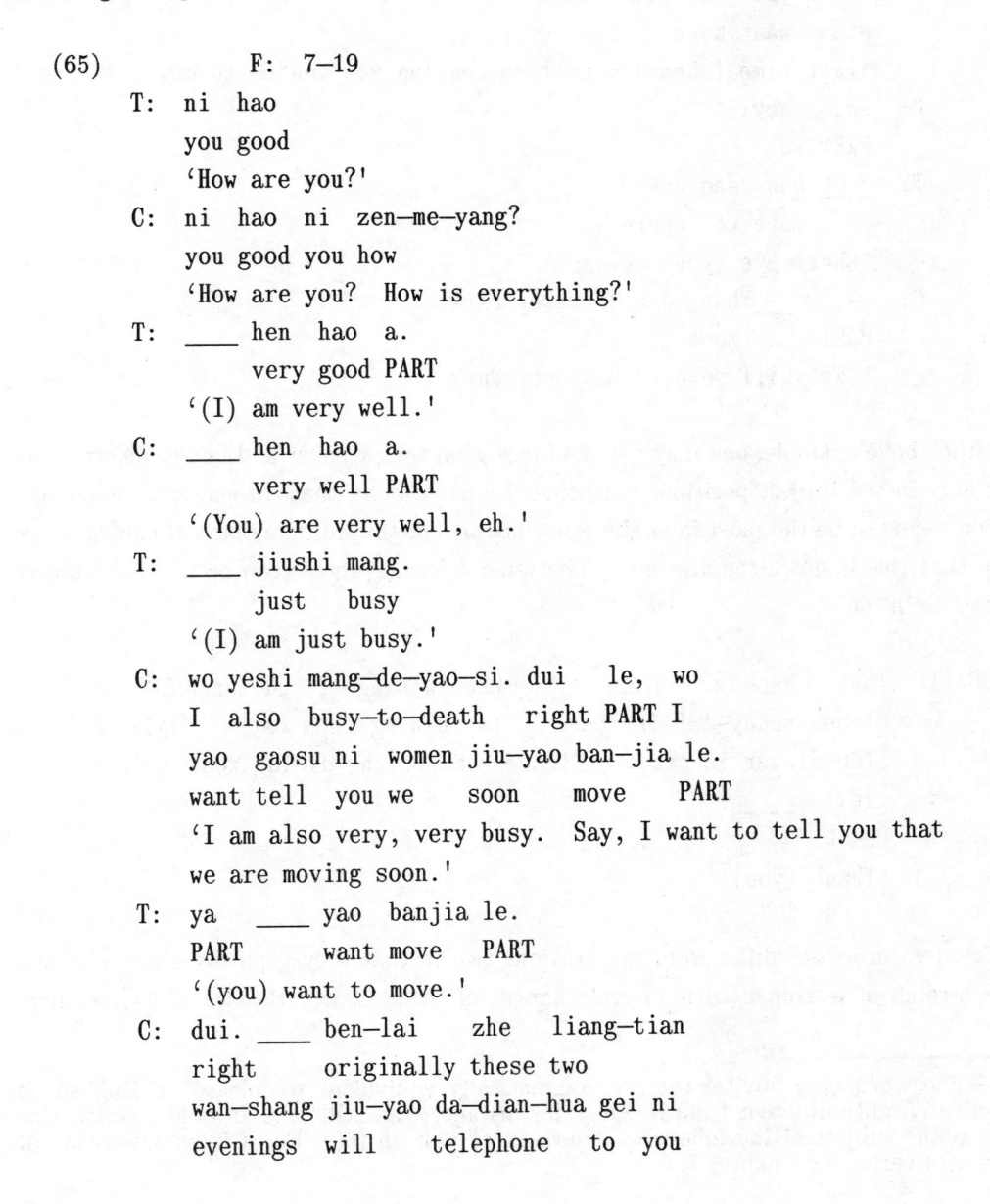

(65)   F: 7–19
   T: ni hao
       you good
       'How are you?'
   C: ni hao ni zen-me-yang?
       you good you how
       'How are you? How is everything?'
   T: ___ hen hao a.
           very good PART
       '(I) am very well.'
   C: ___ hen hao a.
           very well PART
       '(You) are very well, eh.'
   T: ___ jiushi mang.
           just busy
       '(I) am just busy.'
   C: wo yeshi mang-de-yao-si. dui le, wo
       I also busy-to-death right PART I
       yao gaosu ni women jiu-yao ban-jia le.
       want tell you we soon move PART
       'I am also very, very busy. Say, I want to tell you that we are moving soon.'
   T: ya ___ yao banjia le.
       PART   want move PART
       '(you) want to move.'
   C: dui. ___ ben-lai zhe liang-tian
       right   originally these two
       wan-shang jiu-yao da-dian-hua gei ni
       evenings will telephone to you

    'Right. Originally, (I) was going to call you one of these
    two evenings.'
  T: oh, wo shangci ting F jiang shuo
    PART I last—time heard F tell say
    nimen yao ban—jia shuoshi...
    you want move say
    'last time I heard F tell me, saying you wanted to move, saying.'
  C: en. suoyi
    PART so
  T: ____ ban dao na—li?
      move to where
    'Where are (you) moving?'
  C: ya. ____ ban dao Monterey Park.
    PART move to
    '(We) will move to Monterey Park.'

From the above example, one may get the impression that speaker and hearer deletion can occur only in the subject position. Although we have found that, in general, the subject position seems to be the most favorable spot for this deletion to take place, it can easily be shown that this is not a requirement. The same deletion process can occur in the object position, as in (66):

(66) A: fan hao—le. qing ____ dao fanting chifan ba.[26]
    dinner ready—ASP invite to dining—room eat PART
    'The dinner is ready. Please come to the dining room.'
  B: xiexie ____.
    thank
    'Thank (you).'

The last two processes differ from the previous two in that they typically operate over a longer stretch of discourse with several changes of turns in it. Besides, they are more

---

 [26]The word *qing* 'invite' though pragmatically equivalent to 'please' in English, is syntactically quite different from it. *Qing*, for instance, can still take an object which also serves as the subject of the following clause, as *ni* 'you' in (66). For a fuller discussion of this type of verbs, see Chapter 7.

subject to social linguistic factors such as the social distance between the speaker and the hearer and also discourse factors such as change of turns. They are, therefore, even more "probable" than Topic—NP deletion rule.

2.5. Summary

To sum up, we will give the following properties for subject in Chinese:

(67) a. Subject is always unmarked by preposition.
     b. In position, subject can be identified as the first animate NP to the left of the verb; otherwise, the NP immediately before the verb.
     c. Subject always bears some selectional relation to the main verb of a sentence.
     d. Subject tends to have a specific reference.
     e. Subject plays an important role in the following coreferential NP pronominalization or deletion processes: true reflexivization, imperativization, and Equi—NP deletion.

3. Topic in Chinese
3.1. General Properties of Topic

Li and Thompson (1976) give general properties of the topic as follows:

(68) a. Topic is always definite in the sense defined by Chafe (1976).
     b. Topic need not have any selectional relation with any verb in a sentence.
     c. Topic is not determined by the verb.
     d. The functional role of topic can be characterized as the 'center of attention.'
     e. Topic does not control verb agreement.
     f. Topic invariably occupies the S—initial position.
     g. Topic plays no role in such processes as reflexivization, passivization, Equi—NP deletion, and imperativization.

Li and Thompson claim these properties of topic to be universal, although they cite examples chiefly from Lahu, a Lolo—Burmese language, and Mandarin to support their claim. For lack of direct knowledge of Lahu, we will not have anything to say about it here. Rather, we will concentrate on Chinese and examine topic in Chinese in light of these properties.

3.2. Properties of Topic in Chinese

Except for the property mentioned in point d, which is too vague to be evaluated, the given properties, by and large, hold true when they are examined against Chinese data. Points a, b, c and d have been discussed at some length elsewhere (Tsao, 1979). Points e, f and g have also been examined in connection with the previous discussion of Chinese subject. We have found that points f and g, as they are stated, stand in need of revision.

Looking at point f again, we find that the term "sentence" (and its abbreviation S), as it is used here is ambiguous. It can refer to what is understood in the traditional grammar as a "clause" or a surface "sentence". We have, therefore, used "clause" and "sentence" to refer to them respectively. With this terminological distinction, we can now examine this property more closely.

Li and Thompson's chararterization here suffers because, as pointed out in our previous discussion, it fails to take care of the fact that topic may, and often does, extend its semantic domain over several clauses to form a topic chain and it is in control of what has been called Topic–NP deletion in the chain.

With this revision in mind, we propose that point f be further qualified as:

> f. Topic invariably occupies the clause–initial position unless it is deleted or pronominalized by the topic that appears at the first clause in the same chain.

In our previous discussion, we have found that some topics play double roles in being topic for a whole chain and subject in a particular clause in the same chain. We have also found that there are only three processes in which, subject, but not topic, plays an important part. They are true reflexivization, Equi–NP deletion and imperativization. On the basis of these two observations, point g needs to be further qualified as follows:

> g. Topic, except in clauses in which it is also subject, plays no role in such processes as reflexivization, Equi–NP deletion, and imperativization.

In addition, there is one specific topic property in Chinese that Li and Thompson do not discuss. The topic, where it overtly occurs, can be separated from the rest of the sentence by a pause or by one of the four pause particles, *a* (or its phonetic variant, *ya), ne, me,* and *ba.* Since Chao (1968) does not distinguish subject from topic in Chinese, he has mistakenly regarded this as a way of separating subject from predicate (1968:67). We have found this to be a reliable way of identifying topic in Chinese in difficult cases. Thus, under my analysis, an NP that will allow one of the particles to be inserted between it and the rest of the discourse will be regarded as a topic. Compare (69) to (70):

(69) a. zhei—ke shu de   yezi   a,   you xi   you chang,
       this—CL tree POSS leaves PART small and long
       zen   nan—kan.
       really ugly
       'The leaves of the tree (topic), (they) are long and small;
       (they) are ugly.'
    b. *zhei—ke shu de a, yezi you xi you chang, zhen nan—kan.

(70) a. *zhei—ke shu a,   yezi   you xi you chang,
       this—CL tree PART leaves small and long
       shugan you cu   you da, zhen   nan—kan,
       trunk   rough and big really ugly
       wo bu yao mai—le.
       I not want buy—ASP
       'This tree (topic), (its) leaves are small and long;
       (its) trunk is rough and big; (it) is really ugly;
       I don't want to buy (it).'
    b. *zhei—ke shu yezi a, you xi you chang,
       shugan you cu you da, zhen nan—kan,
       wo bu yao mai—le.

Since in (69), *zhei—ke shu de yezi* 'the leaves of the tree' is the thing under discussion, the pause particle *a* can only be placed immediately after it. It cannot be placed at other places. Likewise, in (70) the thing under discussion is *zhei—ke shu* 'this tree,' and the particle *a* can only be placed immediately after it. To place it at other points will result in ungrammatical sentences.

Summing up our discussion of topic so far, we give the following properties of Chinese topic:

(71) a. Topic invariably occupies the S-initial position of the first clause in a topic chain.
b. Topic can optionally be separated from the rest of the sentence in which it overtly occurs by one of the four pause particle *a (ya), ne, me*, and *ba*.
c. Topic is always definite.
d. Topic is a discourse notion; it may, and often does, extend its semantic domain to more than one clause.
e. Topic is in control of the pronominalization or deletion of all the coreferential NPs in a topic chain.
f. Topic, except in clauses in which it is also subject, plays no role in such processes as true reflexivization, Equi-NP deletion, and imperativization.

Using these properties, then, we can easily identify topics in Chinese.

3.3. Identifying Topic in Chinese

Utilizing the topic properties that we have set up, we can now identify a topic in each of the following stretches of discourse (the topic NPs are underlined):

(72) <u>Zhang San</u> (a), zuo-tian lai kan wo.
Zhang San (PART) yesterday came see me
'Zhang San (topic), (he) came to see me yesterday.'

(73) <u>Zhei-ben shu</u> (a), zhen nan.
this-CL book (PART) really difficult
'This book (topic), (it) is really difficult.'

(74) <u>zhei-ben shu</u> (a), wo yijing nian-le
this-CL book (PART) I already read-ASP
san-bian, haishi bu dong.
3-times still not understand
'This book (topic), I have already read (it) three times; still I don't understand (it).'

(75) <u>Li Si</u> (a), wo yijing song-le yi-fen li.
Li Si (PART) I already give-ASP a-CL gift
'Li Si (topic), I have already given (him) a present.'

(76) zhei—ben shu gen na—ben shu (a), wo dou yao mai.
    this—CL book and that—CL book (PART) I all want buy
    'This book and that book (topic), I want to buy both.'

(77) zuo—tian (a), Zhang San lai kan wo.
    yesterday (PART) Zhang San came see me
    'Yesterday (topic), Zhang San came to see me.'

(78) nei kuai tian (a) daozi zhang de hen
    that piece land (PART) rice grow PART very
    da, hen zhi—qian.
    big very worth (money)
    'That piece of land (topic), rice grows very big (in it);
    (it) is worth a lot of money.'

(79) Beijing (a), you ge Gu—gong.
    Peking (PART) exist a Old—Palace
    'Peking (topic), (there) exists a palace called Old Palace.'

(80) Beijingcheng—li (a), you ge Gu—Gong.
    Peking—city—inside (PART) exist a Old—Palace
    'Inside Peking city (topic), (there) exists a palace called
    Old Palace.'

(81) Zhe—li zhe—shi (a), lai—le yi—ge ren.
    this—place this—time (PART) come—ASP a—CL man
    'Here and now (topic), a man comes.'

(82) zhei—ge ren (a) tounao jiandan, si—zhi fada.
    this—CL man (PART) mind simple four—limbs well—developed
    'This man (topic), (his) mind is simple; (his) body well—developed.'

(83) Zhongguo (a), di da, wu buo,
    China (PART) land big resources comprehensive

renkou   duo.
population great
'China (topic), (its) land is big; (its) resources comprehensive; (its) population great.'

(84) <u>ta-de san-ge   haizi</u>   (a),   yi-ge
his   three-Class children (PART) one-Class
dang   lüshi, yi-ge hushi, haiyou
serve-as lawyer one-CL nurse still
yi-ge xue   jianzhu
one-CL study architecture
'His three children (topic), one works as a lawyer; another is a nurse; and the third studies architecture.'

(85) <u>sanshiliu ji</u>   (a),   zou
thirty-six alternative (PART) running-away
wei shang ji.
is best alternative
'(Of) the thirty-six alternatives, running-away is the best.'

(86) <u>yu</u>   (a),   wei-yu xianzai zui gui.
fish (PART) tuna   now   most expensive
'Fish (topic), tuna is now the most expensive.'

There are, however, cases where a bloc of discourse does not contain any topic. Examine the following examples:

(87) xia yu le. (topicless)
fall rain PART
'It is raining.'

(88) qi wu le. (topicless)
rise fog PART
'It becomes foggy.'

(89) lai–le   ren. (topicless)
      come–ASP people
      'Some people are coming.'

(90) you niao zai shu–shang. (topicless)
      exist bird on tree–LOC
      'There are birds on the tree.'

In (87) and (88) we have the typical cases of "weather" sentences. In (89) and (90) we have examples of what we call in this study 'existential' and 'presentative' sentences. It is apparent that there are no NPs qualified as topic in these sentences since the initial position of each is taken up by a verb, and with the possible exception of *shu–shang* 'tree–top,' which is preceded by *zai* 'at,' there are no definite NPs. Our next question will then be: Is there no subject in each of these sentences? The answer is 'yes' with qualification. There are no NPs in them that have all the subject properties that I have posited for Chinese. However, *yu* 'rain,' *wu* 'fog,' *niao* 'birds,' and *ren* 'people' are clearly selectionally related to the verbs *xia* 'fall,' *qi* 'rise,' *you* 'exist,' and *lai* 'come' in (87), (88), (89), and (90) respectively. (For a thorough discussion of the noun–verb relation involved in these examples, see Teng, 1972). Thus, strictly speaking, subjects so identified can only be regarded as non–basic in the sense defined by E. L. Keenan (1976a).

That this is by no means a far–fetched conclusion is further confirmed when the corresponding English sentences are examined against the subject properties of English. Among other things, a dummy subject is either necessary or possible in each of the corresponding English sentences, and a dummy subject, as its name implies, typically has less subjecthood than the regular subject.

4. Comparison of Subject and Topic

We have already found that both subject and topic can be identified in Chinese. In the course of our discussion, we have examined many processes involving either subject or topic. In re–examining these processes, we find further that they seem to fall into two groups, which is highly suggestive.

Group A: Processes in which subject plays an important role are true reflexivization, Equi–NP deletion and imperativization.

> **Group B:** Processes in which topic plays an important role are coordinate conjunction reduction, Topic—NP deletion, the former being a special case of the latter, relativization and relativized NP deletion.

Groups A and B seem to form natural classes. In Group A are processes that have to do with clause—internal mechanisms, and in Group B are processes that go beyond a single clause.[27]

This observation concerning these two groups ties in very well with the semantic domain of subject and topic respectively. Subject, as we have pointed out, is a syntactic notion and it has its domain over a VP node. It is, therefore, expected that it should play an important role in clause—internal grammatical processes. Topic, on the other hand, is a discourse notion and it may extend its domain over several clauses. It is not surprising that it should play an important part in all these processes involving more than one clause.

Also notice that subject is involved in true reflexivization, imperativization and NP deletion in some constructions involving action verbs. From this it seems clear that the essential function of subject in Chinese is agent in terms of case or actor in more general terms. This conclusion further confirms the working definition that we gave to subject before we start our investigation of properties that subject and topic have in Chinese.

Since in English topic and subject are usually not differentiated, one would expect that English subject to have all the qualities that we have found for subject and topic in Chinese. This is indeed the case.

Halliday, citing Sweet, distinguishes four functions of the subject (1970:164; see also Jespersen, 1924:145—154):

> The subject, in its traditional sense, is thus a complex of four distinct functions, three in the structure of the clause ...: 1. actor ('logical subject'): ideational; 2. modal subject ('grammatical subject'): interpersonal; 3. theme ('psychological subject1'): textual; together with a fourth function which is in the structure of the 'information unit': 4. given ('psychological subject2'): textual.

Withholding for a moment our comment on Halliday's claim that the third function should be included in the structure of the clause, we find that these four functions of English

---

[27]Many grammarians (see Thompson, 1971 and the references cited there) have argued that the relative clause should have extrasentential source.

subject are taken up by Chinese subject (1 and 2) and topic (3 and 4). Upon closer examination, we find further that the first two functions have to do with role-related clause-internal mechanisms while the remaining two functions are related to "text", or "discourse" as we call it in this study. This brings up the question of why Halliday, on the one hand, regards the third function as a "textual" function while, on the other hand, claims that it belongs to the structure of the clause. Perhaps he has in mind that English subject, while a constituent of a clause, plays, at the same time, a part in the organization of a text. If this is indeed the case, then this description fits English subject better than Chinese topic for the latter may not bear any direct syntactic relationship to the verb of a clause.

This minor difference aside, we find that these are perhaps the most important functions of subject/topic and languages differ as to the assignment of these functions to subject and topic. As far as Chinese is concerned, we have presented evidence to argue that there is indeed a division of functions along the line just proposed. This division, furthermore, accounts for a fact rather nicely. In the past, Chinese grammarians have failed to come to terms on the analysis of subject in Chinese. Some grammarians such as Chao (1968), Chang (1956) have defined subject as "theme", while others such as Wang (1956) and Lü (1949) have stressed the logical and grammatical function in their analyses of subject. Thus the two views agree well when these functions converge in the same constituent as in (91) but disagree widely while the functions diverge as in (92).

(91)　ta zuotian　lai-le.
　　　he yesterday come-ASP
　　　'He (topic and subject) came yesterday.'

(92)　zhe-ben shu, wo kan-guo san-bian　le.
　　　this-CL book I　read-ASP three-time PART
　　　'This book (topic), I (subject) have read (it) three times.'

If this division of roles between topic and subject is in general true, then it strongly suggests that perhaps we are not doing the right thing when we place topic and subject on the same plane and compare them. Allowing for cases of overlapping (i.e., sometimes an NP may be both topic and subject), they essentially belong to different levels of grammatical organization. A parallel can be found in phonology. Thus a certain segment may be treated differently depending on whether we are looking at it at the phonemic or morphophonemic level.[28] For example, in Mandarin it is generally agreed that there are four tone phonemes. To use Chao's five—point register, they can be represented as: 1. level tone (55), 2. rising tone (35), 3. falling—rising tone (214), and 4. falling tone (51). Due to tone sandhi, however, a word like *yi* 'one' may have any one of three tone phonemes according to three different environments:[29]

1. yi (55) if followed by a pause;
2. yi (35) if followed by a falling tone;
3. yi (51) if followed by tones other than the falling tone.

Thus, the word *yi* 'one' can only be treated as a word at the morphophonemic level. At the phonemic level, it has to be treated as three different entities. Likewise, a topic can be regarded as a topic only at the discourse level; at the clause level it may be regarded as several different things. If this is essentially correct, then given a Chinese sentence like (93), we can determine whether the S—initial NP is subject or topic, depending on where it occurs in a discourse and at what level we are looking at it:

(93) ta da wo.
      he hit me
      'He hit me.'

To clarify further what I mean, let us examine the following stretch of discourse:

(94) nei—ke shu   hua   xiao, ____   yezi   da,
      TOPIC   SUBJECT   TOPIC   SUBJECT
      that—CL tree flowers small   leaves big

      _____   hen nan—kan, suoyi _____
      TOPIC or SUB.   TOPIC or DIR. OBJ.
                 very ugly   so

---

[28]I do not wish to argue for the existence of a phenemic level here, as it is not our concern. For an interesting discussion of this level within the framework of generative phonology, refer to Shane (1971).

[29]The discussion is based on Chao (1968:45).

```
    wo mei mai.
    I  not buy
    'The tree (topic), (its) flowers are small.  (Its) leaves are big.
    (It) was ugly; so I didn't buy (it).'
```

The English translation is deliberately literal so that it can reflect the organization of the stretch of discourse in Chinese. The discourse is short and yet it is composed of a topic followed by four clauses, each with a subject (and object if the verb is transitive). The topic bears either syntactic or semantic relations to each of the clauses under its domain. For this reason, and for the reason that it extends its domain over several clauses, it should be regarded as a discourse element which interacts with the syntactic organization of the clauses under its domain.

5. Summary

To sum up, we have found in this chapter that it is not only necessary but also possible to distinguish topic from subject in the grammar of Chinese. Subject, as we have repeatedly shown, is a syntactic notion and it, therefore, should have its domain over a VP node. Topic, on the other hand, has its domain over a clause as well as a sentence.

We have also found that a sentence in Chinese can be roughly defined as a topic chain, which is a stretch of discourse composed of one or more comment clauses sharing a common topic, which heads the chain.[30] It follows that when a topic chain contains only one clause, that clause is then a simple sentence as (95) and (96) show.

```
(95)  niao  fei—zou   le.
      bird  fly—away  PART
      'The bird has flown away.'
```

---

[30]There are sentences which lack explicit topics such as (i) and (ii) below.
```
(i)   xia   yu    le.
      fall  rain  PART
      'It is raining now.'
(ii)  lai—le      san—ge     ren.
      come—ASP    three—CL   persons
      'There are three persons coming.'
```
These and other exceptional cases will be fully examined in our later discussion.

(96) nei—ben shu wo kan—wan   le.
　　　that—CL book I read—finish PART
　　　'(With regard to) the book, I've finished reading it.'

(95) and (96), though both simple sentences, differ in structure. In (95), *niao* 'bird' plays the dual role of being the topic and the subject while in (96) *nei—ben shu* 'the book' is the topic and *wo* 'I' is the subject.

    A topic chain, as its name implies, usually contains more than one clause. So if we add two more clauses sharing the same topic to (96) as in (97), we will have a topic chain of three clauses.

(97) <u>nei—ben shu</u>$_i$ wo kan—wan le, _____$_i$ ni
　　　TOPIC　　　　　　　　　　　　　TOPIC
　　　that—CL book I read—finish PART you
　　　xiang kan, _____$_i$ jiu na—qu   kan ba.
　　　　　　　　　TOPIC
　　　want read　　　then take—away read PART
　　　'(With regard to) the book, I've finished reading (it);
　　　if you want to read (it), you can take (it).'

(97) is a typical compound sentence in Chinese, where what is required of all the clauses is that they share the same topic.[31] In this connection, notice that there is no clause connective between C1 and C2, while there is one between C2 and C3, namely, *jiu* 'then'. So it seems clear that the presence of clause connective is not a requirement for the clauses to be "chain—mates".

    A topic chain can also become a noun clause in a certain sentence. (98) shows that (96) is transformed into a noun clause and serves as object of the verb *huaiyi* 'doubt'.

---

[31]As will be discussed in later chapters, sometimes the clauses in the chain can share more than one topic as shown in (i).
　(i)　<u>wo</u>$_i$　 <u>zuotian</u>$_j$　 yinwei　 sheng—bing　 suoyi　_____$_i$
　　　TOPIC1　TOPIC2　　　　　　　　　　　　　　　　　　　　　　 TOPIC1
　　　I　　　　yesterday　because　get—sick　　so
　　　_____$_j$ mei lai kai—hui.
　　　TOPIC2   not come attend—meeting
　　　'Because I was sick yesterday, I didn't attend the meeting.'

(98)　ta huaiyi nei—ben shu　wo kan—wan　　le.
　　　 he doubt that—CL book I　read—finish PART
　　　 'He doubted that I finished reading the book.'

In cases like (98) we will speak of complex sentences. Notice, in this connection, that when (96) occurs as an embedded noun clause in a complex sentence, it can still retain its topic, *nei—ben shu* 'the book'.

In Part Two we will examine closely various clause types that can occur in a simple sentence and in Part Three we will go into detail of various types of compound and complex sentences in Chinese.

PART II

SIMPLE SENTENCES

CHAPTER THREE
BASIC SIMPLE ONE–TOPIC SENTENCES

1. Introductory

Now that we have concluded that except in some rare cases where a sentence contains no topic (see section 3.3. in Chapter 2 for examples and discussion), topic chain is a functional basic unit in Chinese discourse, our next step is to characterize all the possible clause types that occur in a topic chain. For convenience of discussion, we will start with a topic chain of one clause, i.e. a simple sentence, in Part II.

Of all clause types that can occur in a simple sentence, the simplest is one where there is only one nominal occurring before the verb, i.e. only one topic, especially when this nominal can be identified as subject as well, as in (1) and (2).

(1) zhe–ge   Yingwen juzi   zhen   nan.
TOPIC and SUBJECT
this–CL   English sentence really difficult
'This English sentence is really difficult.'

(2) wo   bu   dong   zhe–ge Yingwen juzi.
TOPIC and SUBJECT
I   not understand this–CL English sentence
'I don't understand this English sentence.'

Since in this type of sentences there is only one topic in the sentence, we will refer to this type of sentences as single topic sentences.

As will be pointed out presently, this type of sentences certainly does not enjoy the privilege of occurrence in Chinese that its English counterpart does in English. In spite of the fact, we will still regard it as the canonical type in Chinese in the sense that it is closest to our mental representation of the verb–controlled clause patterns, i.e. one based exclusively on syntactic and semantic consideration without being tempered with by the informational and discoursal consideration. For this reason, we will first discuss the various types of construction that can occur in a clause like this in this chapter.

Since these clause types are all largely controlled by the verb, we will center our discussion on the interaction between the verb and the NPs that are associated with it.

2 Types of Single Topic Sentences
2.1 State Verbs vs. Action Verbs

Most grammarians in the past who have studied Chinese verbs extensively agree that adjectives in Chinese behave so much like verbs that they should be lumped together with verbs as one category. These grammarians, however, are divided in their opinion as to what is the single most important classificatory scheme for verbs in Chinese. Chao (1968), Li and Thompson (1981) and Tiee (1986) have followed the traditional way of dividing verbs into two categories: transitive and intransitive, while Tang (1975), Y. C. Li et al. (1984) and Chu (1983) take state vs. action as the most important division. The point of fact is that these two dividing schemes crosscut each other. As a result, there are verbs in each of the four categories provided by these two crosscutting sets as shown in (3).

(3)
	Transitive	Intransitive
Action	ti 'kick'	fei 'fly'
State	xihuan 'like'	gaoxing 'happy'

In view of this fact, it seems that one scheme is as good as the other. However, as we will point out presently, the distinction between state and action has more far-reaching effects on Chinese grammar. We will, therefore, make the first cut there.

An action verb indicates the action performed by a usually animate object. A state verb, on the other hand, denotes in most cases the state of affairs which something animate or inanimate is in. The grammatical correlates of the two categories can be summarized in (4).

(4) | | SV | AV |
|---|---|---|
| a. may occur in the imperative | No | Yes |
| b. may occur with the progressive zai or experiential guo | No | Yes |
| c. may occur with the durative zhe | No | Yes |
| d. may be modified by a degree adverb such as hen 'very' | Yes | No |
| e. may be modified by a manner adverb such as hao-hao-de 'appropriately, well' | No | Yes |

These grammatical correlates are exemplified by sentences (5) to (9), where (a) sentences are ones with a state verb and (b) sentences involve an action verb.

(5) a. * gao (An imperative sentence)
       tall
     * 'Be tall.'
    b. kan—zhe ta.
       see—ASP him
       'Keep an eye on him.'

(6) a. * ta zheng   zai zhidao zhe—jian
       he right:now ASP know   this—CL
       shi. (with **zai** progressive aspect)
       matter
     * 'He is knowing the matter.'
    b. ta zheng   zai xuexi.
       he right:now ASP learning
       'He is learning (it) now.'

(7) a. * ta zheng   piaoliang—zhe. (with **zhe** durative)
       she right:now beautiful—ASP
     * 'She is being beautiful.'
    b. ta zheng   da—zhe pai.
       she right:now play—ASP majiang
       'She is playing majiang now.'

(8) a. ta hen yonggong. (modified by a degree adverb)
       he very diligent
       'He is very diligent.'
    b. * ta hen chi fan
       he very eat meal

(9) a. * hao—hao—de   piaoliang.
       appropriately beautiful
     * 'Be appropriately beautiful.'

  b. hao—hao—de zuo.
    appropriately do
    'Do it well.'

2.2 Sentences with State Verbs

There are five types of state verbs, namely, (1) adjectival verbs, (2) naming verbs, (3) emotive verbs, (4) existential—presentative verbs and (5) modal auxiliary verbs. Corresponding to these five types of verbs we have five types of sentences to be called (1) adjectival sentences, (2) naming sentences, (3) emotive sentences, (4) existential—presentative sentences and (5) modal sentences. Except for the last type involving modal auxiliary verbs, some of which will be analyzed as a full verb taking a clause argument and they will therefore not be discussed until we come to complex sentences, all the remaining four will be taken up in some detail in the following.

2.2.1 Adjectival Sentences

An adjectival sentence contains what is traditionally an adjective as its main verb.[1] Adjectival verbs can be further divided into two types: quality adjectives and status adjectives.

2.2.1.1 Quality Verbs

A quality verb indicates a fairly lasting quality about a person or object. The following are some commonly found quality verbs.

(10) a. <u>hao</u> 'good' b. <u>huai</u> 'bad'
   c. <u>kuai</u> 'fast' d. <u>pang</u> 'fat'

---

[1]Some adjectives, however, under special circumstances may be "expediently" used as action verbs. Take *gaoxing* 'happy' for instance. As an adjective, it reduplicates in the form of AABB to show vividness as in sentence (i), but as sentence (ii) shows, it can have the reduplicated form of ABAB, just like an action verb, when it takes on the meaning of 'causing to be happy.'
(i) ta zou de shihou, hai shi gaogaoxingxing de.
  he go DE time   still SHI happy   DE
  'When he left, he was still very happy.'
(ii) jintian shi muqinjie,   wo dai Mama qu
   today   be Mother's Day I take Mom to
   ting geju, hao   rang ta gaoxinggaoxing.
   listen opera so:as:to let   her happy
   'Today is Mother's Day; I'm going to take Mom to an opera to cheer her up.'

e. <u>gao</u> 'high, tall'   f. <u>piaoliang</u> 'beautiful'
g. <u>nianqing</u> 'young'   h. <u>congming</u> 'clever, smart'
i. <u>youqian</u> 'rich'   j. <u>nenggan</u> 'competent'

As indicated by the gloss, they are translatable as adjectives in English. However, unlike their English counterparts, they are not preceded by any verb-to-be in their normal usage as shown in (11) and (12).

(11) ta bu hen congming.
he not very clever
'He is not very clever.'

(12) ta pang bu pang?
he fat not fat
'Is he fat?'

When *shi* 'be' is added to the sentence as in (13), it changes the meaning of the sentence by making it emphatic. Compare (13) with (11).

(13) ta shi bu hen congming.
he SHI not very clever
'He is really not very clever.'

2.2.1.2 Status Verbs

A status verb indicates a state or condition which a person or object is in for a while. The following are some common status verbs.

(14) a. <u>e</u> 'hungry'   b. <u>bao</u> 'full (of food)'
c. <u>zui</u> 'drunk'   d. <u>cui</u> 'crisp'
e. <u>fong</u> 'crazy'   f. <u>bing</u> 'sick'
g. <u>dong</u> 'frozen'   h. <u>xing</u> 'wake'
i. <u>zhong</u> 'swollen'   j. <u>ma</u> 'numbed'
k. <u>lei</u> 'tired'   l. <u>shiwang</u> 'disappointed'

Since this type of verbs indicate a relatively short state that a person or thing is in, sentences with a verb of this type often contains a sentence-final particle *le*, indicating a change of state, as (15) shows. Of course, if one's intention is just to describe a certain state that a person or thing is in, *le* is not there, as in (16).

(15) xiaohaizi xing le.
child awake PART
'The child is now awake.'

(16) ta hen e.
he very hungry
'He is very hungry.'

Since a quality verb attibutes a certain relatively long-lasting characteristic to a person or thing, a sentence having it as its main verb normally does not contain the sentence-final particle *le*. But even a long-lasting quality can change. When this happens, a sentence describing the situation will have *le* in it. Compare (a) with (b) in (17).

(17) a. Zhang Xiaojie hen piaoliang.
Zhang Miss very beautiful
'Miss Zhang is very beautiful.'
b. Zhang Xiaojie zuijin piaoliang duo le.
Zhang Miss recently beautiful much PART
'Miss Zhang has become a lot more beautiful recently.'

Again since whether the duration of a certain trait that one possesses is considered long or short can only be relative, it is to be expected that certain adjectival verbs are sometimes considered as expressing a quality and sometimes a status. Compare (a) and (b) in (18).

(18) a. zhe-tiao he-de shui hen zhuo. (quality)
this-CL river-POSS water very muddy
'The water of this river is very muddy.'
b. cai xia yihuir de yu, zhe-tiao
only fall a:while Rel. Mar. rain this-CL
he-de shui jiu zhuo le. (status)
river-POSS water then muddy PART

'After it rained for a short while, the water in the river has become muddy.'

2.2.2 Naming Sentences

A naming verb equates, defines or classifies the identity of a person or a thing. The naming verbs always occur in this pattern: S/T + V + N, where N is a subject complement. There are only a few naming verbs, all of which are listed in (19).

(19) a. shi 'be'
b. jiao (zuo) 'be called'
c. haocheng 'be spoken of as'
d. xing 'have the surname of'
e. zuo 'act as'
f. dang 'serve as'
g. xiang 'be like'
h. dengyu 'be equal (formal)'
i. xiangdangyu 'be equivalent (formal)'

Some examples follow.

(20) ta shi yisheng.
he be doctor
'He is a doctor.'

(21) ta jintian dang zhuxi.
he today serve:as chair—person
'She is serving as chair—person today.'

(22) a. ta jiao(zuo) Wang Ai—lian.
she call(as) Wang Ai—lian
'She is called Wang Ai—lian.'

Note that (22a) is related to two other constructions that we will take up in our later discussion. One of them is what we will call SVOC sentence, where C stands for complement. This is clear when we compare (22a) with (22c). The other construction to which it is more remotely related is what we will call "telescopic–transitive" sentence (see Section 2.3.2.4 of this chapter and Chapter 7 for more discussion). This becomes clear when we compare (22a) with (22b).

(22) b. women jiao ta zuo Wang Ai-lian.
         we   call her be Wang Ai-lian
         'We call her to be Wang Ai-lian.'
     c. women jiao ta (zuo) Wang Ai-lian
         we   call her (as) Wang Ai-lian
         'We call her Wang Ai-lian.'

Structurally speaking, *ta* 'she' in (22b) serves two functions. First, it is the object of the verb *jiao* 'call' in the first clause. At the same time, it is the topic/subject of the verb *zuo* 'be' in the second clause. However, later a reanalysis took place, triggered by the weakening of the second verb *zuo* 'be' to become a coverb meaning 'as'. Thus, what was originally a telescoped sentence of two clauses can be reanalyzed as a simple sentence with an object and an object complement in the form of a coverb phrase as shown in (22c).

At this stage, two things happened. First, the second verb, now reduced to a coverb, became optional. Second, the object became moveable (cf. the object in a transitive–telescopic construction, which can never be moved). Once the object is free to appear in the primary topic position and the agent is unexpressed as in (22a), then we have what we will later call a "middle–voice" sentence (see Section 2.4 of this chapter for discussion). This, incidentally, will also account for the passive reading we have in (22a), as reflected in the English translation.[2]

2.2.3 Possessive, Existential and Presentative Sentences

There is only one important possessive verb, namely *you* 'have'. *You* expresses possession in a broad sense of the word when the possessor appears as topic/subject and the possessed appears postverbally. The possessed NP can be definite as in (23a) or idenfinite as in (23b).

---

[2]Interested readers may want to compare the sentences in (22) with the following three English sentences.
    (i)   I consider him to be a student.
    (ii)   I consider him as a student.
    (iii) I consider him a student.

(23) a. wo you nei—ben shu.
      I have that—CL book
      'I have the book.'
   b. wo you yi—ge pengyou.
      I have one—CL friend
      'I have a friend.'

You, however, can have another important use, i.e. to indicate the existence of something or someone. In this use it is preceded by a place or sometimes a time expression and followed by an indefinite NP denoting something or someone.

(24) a. shan—shang you yi—jian wuzi.
        hill—LOC EXIST one—CL house
        'There is a house on the hill.'
   b. congqian you   yi—ge guowang.
      long:ago EXIST one—CL king
      'Long time ago there was a king.'

Sometimes when the place or time expression is understood from context or when it denotes immediate present, i.e. right now and here, it can be zero. When this happens, *you* 'EXIST' occurs at the beginning of a sentence, immediately followed by an indefinite noun, yielding the impression that it is an indefinite marker. Compare (a) and (b) in (25).

(25) a. qian—mian you   ren   lai le.
        front—LOC EXIST person come PART
        'There are some people coming in the front.'
   b. ____ you   ren   lai le.
           EXIST person come PART
        (i) 'There are some people coming.'
        (ii) 'Some people are coming.'

This must be the context that has led quite a few grammarians to analyze *you* as an indefinite marker rather than a verb. Although in such contexts as (25b), it does little harm to our understanding, this analysis is one that we will have to reject when we examine all the contexts that *you* can occur.

Another important existential verb is *shi* 'be', which occurs in the following pattern:

   Place Expression + Shi + Noun Phrase

Examine (26) and (27).

   (26) xuexiao-de zuo-bian shi yinhang.
        school-POSS left-LOC be bank
        'On the left of the school is a bank.'

   (27) fanguan-de dui-mian shi shudian.
        restaurant-POSS opposite-LOC be book-store
        'Opposite the restaurant is a book store.'

There are two differences between sentences with existential *shi* 'be' and those with *you* 'EXIST'. First, as an existential verb *shi* is more restricted than *you* in that the post-verbal noun can only denote a permenant structure while there is no such restriction in the case of *you*. Compare (28) with (29).

   (28) a. men wai-tou you liang-ge ren.
           door out-LOC EXIST two-CL person
           'There are two people outside the door.'
        b. men wai-tou you shan.
           door out-LOC EXIST mountain
           'There is a mountain outside the door.'

   (29) a. *men wai-tou shi liang-ge ren.
           door out-LOC be two-CL person
           ?'Outside the door are two people.'
        b. men wai-tou shi shan.
           door out-LOC be mountain
           'Outside the door is a mountain.'

Another difference is that the *shi* sentence implies exhaustiveness while the *you* sentence implies that there are other things besides the things mentioned. Thus, (28b) suggests that there are other things besides a mountain while (29b) implies that a mountain is the only thing outside the door.

There are two other classes of existential verbs, namely, verbs of location and verbs of motion. Listed in (30) and (31) are some important members of these two classes respectively.

(30)   Verbs of Location
   a. zuo 'sit'   b. tang 'lie'
   c. zhan 'stand'   d. ting 'stop'
   e. dun 'squat'   f. shui 'sleep'
   g. xie 'rest'   h. gua 'hang'
   i. gui 'kneel'   j. pa 'lie'

(31)   Verbs of Motion
   a. zou 'leave'   b. tao 'escape'
   c. chu 'exit'   d. qu 'go'
   e. dao 'arrive'   f. lai 'come'
   g. all other motion verbs taking lai or qu as its directional endings such as jin-lai 'come in (towards the speaker)' or zou-chuqu 'walk out (away from the speaker)'

Both verbs of position and verbs of motion have other uses, which we will take up in a later section. What makes them existential verbs is their ability to appear in the following pattern:

Place Expression + V_E + Indefinite NP

Sentences (32) to (35) show some of the verbs in this use.

(32)   waimian zhan-zhe yi-ge qigai.
       outside stand-ASP one-CL beggar
       'There is a beggar standing outside.'

(33)   qiang-shang gua-zhe yi-fu hua.
       wall-LOC   hang-ASP one-CL painting
       'There is a painting hanging on the wall.'

(34) shan–shang   qi   wu   le.
     mountain–LOC arise fog PART
     'There arose a fog in the mountain.'

(35) cong wuzi–li fei–chulai yi–zhi jian.
     from house–LOC fly–out   one–CL arrow
     'There flew out of the house an arrow.'

What all the existential sentences have in common is that there is a place expression (and in some cases with *you* 'EXIST' a time expression) and there is an indefinite NP occurring post– verbally. In terms of discourse function, the post–verbal NP is a presented topic, i.e. one whose existence has just been called into attention, often about which some more comments are intended, as shown in (36), which is a possible expansion of (33).

(36) qiang–shang qua–zhe   yi–fu hua,   shi
     wall–LOC   hang–ASP one–CL painting be
     Zhang Da–qian–de,   hen zhi–qian.
     Zhang Da–qian–POSS very worth–money
     'On the wall hung a painting; (it) is by Zhang Da–qian (and)
     is worth a great deal of money.'

(36) is a type of topic chain called "presentative topic chain", a special type of compound sentences to be discussed in detail in Chapter 7. The first clause in (36) is called an existential clause and when it appears as an independent sentence as in (33) then it is called an existential sentence.

2.2.4 Sentences of Emotive and Mental State

Verbs of Emotive and Mental State express the emotion, expectation and cognition of an animate being, usually a person. This class can be subdivided into three, namely, verbs of emotion, verbs of expectation and verbs of cognition. What they have in common is that they all take a noun or a clause as its object. Since in the latter case, we are dealing with a complex sentence, we will discuss it in Chapter 8. Here we will concentrate on the former case. But first, let us give some examples of this large class of verbs.

(37)   Verbs of Emotive and Mental State
     a. <u>ai</u> 'love'   b. <u>xin</u> 'believe'

      c. <u>xiangxin</u> 'believe in'   d. <u>tan</u> 'covet'
      e. <u>xiwang</u> 'hope'   f. <u>taoyan</u> 'dislike'
      g. <u>liaojie</u> 'understand' h. <u>xinshang</u> 'appreciate'
      i. <u>xuyao</u> 'need'

Some examplar sentences follow.

(38) ta hen taoyan ni.
      he very dislike you
      'He dislikes you very much.'

(39) zhe-ge ren bi ni geng tan qian.
      this-CL person COMP you more covet money
      'This man is even greedier for money than you.'

(40) zhe-ge xiaohai tai ai wan le.
      this-CL child too love play PART
      'This child is extremely fond of play.'

In Tang's (1975) analysis, what distinguishes this type of verbs from the regular transitive verbs such as *da* 'hit' and *chi* 'eat' is that in a sentence of emotive and mental state the subject is played by an Experiencer rather than an Agent. Teng (1975:66–67) argues against this analysis and claims, instead, that the subject is played by a Patient and the object by what he calls "Goal". As each analysis is couched in a particular version of case grammar, we will not go into detail of their differences. Suffice it to point out that the semantic relationships of the subject to its verb and the object to its verb in this case are quite different from those of a regular transitive verb. This difference accounts for the fact that (38) cannot be passivized (as is shown by the ungrammaticality of (38a)) despite the fact that the situation depicted is an unfavorable one, which is what most Chinese passive sentences are used for.

(38) a. * ni bei ta taoyan.
         you BEI him dislike
         'You are disliked by him.'

The difference also explains why the object in sentences of this type cannot occur as the *ba* object in the *ba* construction, as attested by (38b).

(38) b. * ta ba ni taoyan le.
      he BA you dislike PART
      'What he did to you is dislike you.'

The *ba* construction, as we will present argument to show, presupposes that transitivity relation holds between its subject and the *ba* NP. Since the relation between the subject and object of a sentence with a verb of emotive and mental state is incompatible with that presupposition, it cannot be put in a *ba* construction. (38b) is therefore ungrammatical.

2.3 Sentences with Action Verbs

An action verb is one that indicates the action performed by an animate subject. According to whether they can have an object or not, they can be further divided into intransitive and transitive action verbs. Some transitive verbs can take two, instead of one, objects. We will refer to these transitive verbs as ditransitive. The following discussion will be done according to this three—way distinction. However, before we take up the discussion of the transitivity relation, a word of warning is in order.

The scheme that we have proposed for discussion certainly strikes one as very common if not universal. After all, most English dictionaries, for instance, give this kind of information if the entry is a verb. However, in Chinese there are at least three complications.

First, in a number of frequently occurring constructions such as the primary topicalization (41), the object—fronting construction (42), the *ba* construction (43) and the so—called "verb—copying" construction (44), the object occurs preverbally.

(41) <u>fan</u>, ta chi le.
     meal he eat PART
     '(Speaking of) the meal, he has eaten (it).'

(42) ta <u>fan</u> chi le.
     he meal eat PART
     '(Speaking of) him and the meal, he has eaten (it).'

(43)   ta ba <u>fan</u>   chi le.
       he BA meal eat PART
       'He has eaten the meal.'

(44)   ta <u>chi-fan</u> chi-le san-ge   zhongtou.
       he eat-meal eat-ASP three-CL hour
       'Speaking of eating the meal, it took him three hours.'

To make the matter worse, when the object appears as the shared topic of a topic chain in a clause other than the first, it is often deleted. Examine (45), which is a topic chain of three clauses with *zhe-ge Yingwen juzi* 'this English sentence' as the common topic.

(45)   <u>zhe-ge Yingwen juzi</u>$_i$ zhen   nan,
       Topic and Subject
       this-CL English sentence really difficult

       _____$_i$ wo bu   dong,
       Topic and Object
                       I not understand

       _____$_i$ ta ye bu dong.
       Topic and Object
                       he also not understand
       'This English sentence is really difficult, I don't understand (it), and he doesn't, either.'

Notice that in the second and the third clause, the object is not only fronted it is deleted as well. These grammatical phenomena explain why SVO pattern in Chinese occurs far less frequently than the corresponding one in English does. We will return to this point when we take up the issue of whether Chinese should be regarded as an SVO language in our later discussion.

Second, in the evolution of the Chinese language, some objects have come to be so closely associated with their verbs that they form compounds of a kind. Examine the following examples.

(46) a. <u>shang-ke</u> 'attend-class = go to class'
b. <u>shang-fong</u> 'hurt-wing = catch cold'
c. <u>shui-jiao</u> 'sleep-sleep = take a nap, sleep'
d. <u>bi-ye</u> 'finish-instruction = graduate'
e. <u>xing-li</u> 'perform-salutation = salute'
f. <u>liu-bing</u> 'glide-ice = skate'
g. <u>sheng-qi</u> 'generate-anger = be angry'
h. <u>tiao-wu</u> 'jump-dance = dance'
i. <u>zhao-xiang</u> 'reflect-image = photograph'
j. <u>jie-hun</u> 'tie-marriage = marry'
k. <u>kai-wanxiao</u> 'crack-joke = joke with, make fun of'
l. <u>nian-shu</u> 'read-book = study'

Chao (1968:415) sets up three criteria for separating VO compounds from productive Verb + Object constituents. They are: (1) one or both of the constituents being bound morphemes; (2) idiomaticity of the meaning of the entire unit; and (3) inseparability or limited separability of the constituents. To this we may add, as we mentioned in Chapter 2, the loss or partial loss of referentiality of the object nominal.

As is already evident from the way that the criteria are set up, the association between the two constituents is a matter of degree. It is, therefore, impossible to draw any generalization that is applicable to all cases. As far as transitive-intransitive dichotomy is concerned, this group, therefore, poses some problems. First, while none of the object nominals function exactly like the full-fledged object, some behave more like the regular object than others. Compare sentences in (47), (48) and (49).

(47) a. ta kan-guo <u>nei-ben shu</u> le.
he read-ASP that-CL book PART
'He has read the book.'
b. ta <u>nei-ben shu</u> kan-guo le.
he that-CL book read-ASP PART
'(Speaking of) him and the book, (he) has read (it).'
c. <u>nei-ben shu</u> ta kan-guo le.
that-CL book he read-ASP PART
'(Speaking of) the book, he has read (it).'

(48) a. ta zhao–xiang   le.
       he take–picture PART
       'He has photographed (it).'
   b. ta <u>xiang</u>   zhao le.
       he picture take PART
       '(Speaking of) him and the picture, (he) has taken (it).'
   c. <u>xiang</u>   ta zhao le.
       picture he take PART
       '(Speaking of) the picture, he has taken (it).'

(49) a. ta sheng–<u>qi</u>   le.
       he generate–anger PART
       'He got angry.'
   b. *ta <u>qi</u>   sheng   le.
       he anger generate PART
       'Same as (a).'
   c. *<u>qi</u>   ta sheng   le.
       anger he generate PART
       'Same as (a).'

In (47a), *nei–ben shu* 'the book' is a regular object and as such it can be fronted to occur between the verb and the subject/topic as in (47b) or to become the primary topic as in (47c) if it is definite. However, while both *xiang* 'picture' in (48a) and *qi* 'anger' in (49a) are both the O constituent in a VO compound, *xiang* 'can be fronted like a regular object as shown by (48b and c) but *qi* 'anger' cannot, as both (49b) and (49c) are ungrammatical.

In addition, some VO compounds such as *jie–hun* 'marry' or *zhao–xiang* 'photograph' etc. are semantically transitive, i.e. one can talk about an object one marries or photographs, but because of the presence of O in a VO compound, they are never syntactically transitive. The object can only be added "obliquely". Take (46j) *jie–hun* 'tie–marriage = marry' for instance. The object of marriage can only be added as object of *gen,* a preposition meaning 'with', as shown in (50).

(50) a. ta jie–hun   le.
       he tie–marriage PART
       'He got married.'

  b. *ta jie—hun Zhang Xiejie le.
    he marry Zhang Miss PART
    'He married Miss Zhang.'
  c. ta gen Zhang Xiaojie jie—hun le.
    he with Zhang Miss marry PART
    'Same as (b).'

In the case of (46i), *zhao—xiang* 'reflect—image = photograph', the object of photographing can take the form of an object of a preposition *gei* 'for, on behalf of' or a modifier phrase of the second element in the compound as shown by (c) and (d) sentences in (51).

 (51) a. wo zhao—xiang le.
     I photograph PART
     'I have photographed.'
   b. *wo zhao—xiang ta le.
     I photograph him PART
     'I have photographed him.'
   c. wo gei ta zhao—xiang le.
     I for him photograph PART
     'Same as (b).'
   d. wo zhao ta—de xiang le.
     I reflect his image PART
     'Same as (b).'

  Third and finally, there are resultative verb compounds (RVC) and directional verb compounds (DVC). An RVC is a two—element combination in which the first element is an action verb, specifying the action involved and the second element is a verb indicating the result. Some examples are given in (52).

 (52) a. <u>da—po</u> 'hit—break = break by hitting'
   b. <u>qiao—kai</u> 'pry—open = open by prying'
   c. <u>kan—jian</u> 'look—perceive = see'
   d. <u>mai—dao</u> 'buy—obtain = succeed in buying'[3]

---

  [3]Many resultative compounds present serious problem for translation. Take *mai—dao* 'buy—attain' for instance. The attainment part of the meaning is often only implicit in the verb *buy* when it is in the past tense as shown in the English translation of (i). However,

e. <u>nian–shou</u> 'study–familiarize = become familiar through studying'

A DVC, on the other hand, is a two–element combination with the first element, a displacement verb, followed by a directional ending. The directional ending must be in one of the following forms: (1) either *lai* 'come = toward the speaker' or *qu* 'go = away from the speaker'; (2) one of the eight verbs of direction such as *shang* 'ascend = up', *jin* 'enter = in', *hui* 'return = back' and *guo* 'cross = over'; and (3) a directional verb followed by *lai* or *qu*. The three forms are exemplified by (a), (b) and (c) in (53) respectively.

(53) a. ta song–lai yi–ben shu.
he send–come one–CL book
'He sent over (toward the speaker) a book.'
b. ta tiao–jin he–li le.
he jump–enter river–LOC PART
'He jumped into the river.'
c. ta tiao–jin–qu le.
he jump–enter–go PART
'He jumped in (away from the speaker).'

Moreover, both types of compounds can occur in the potential mode, which is formed by inserting *de* 'can' or *bu* 'cannot' between the two elements in the compound, as exemplified by (54) and (55).

(54) a. ta zhao–de–dao nei–ge ren.
he look:for–can–attain that–CL person
'He can find the person.'
b. ta zhao–bu–dao nei–ge ren.
he look:for–can't–attain that–CL person

---

when the verb is in the present or future tense such part of meaning will have to be explicitly brought out as shown in the English translation of (ii).
(i) nei–gen shu wo zuotian mai–dao le.
that–CL book I yesterday buy–attain PART
'I bought the book yesterday.'
(ii) nei–ben shu wo mingtian hui mai–dao.
that–CL book I tomorrow will buy–attain
'I'll be able to buy the book tomorrow.'

'He can't find the person.'
(55) a. ta tiao—de—guo—qu.
he jump—can—cross—go
'He can jump over (away from the speaker).'
b. ta tiao—bu—guo—qu.
he jump—can't—cross—go
'He can't jump over (away from the speaker).'

As far as transitive—intransitive dichotomy is concerned, these compounds complicate the picture in two ways. First, even though whether or not the whole compound is transitive depends in most cases on the first verb, i.e. if it is transitive the whole compound is transitive and if not the compound is intransitive, there are cases where both elements are intransitive and yet the compound is transitive. (56) and (57) exemplify these exceptional cases.[4]

(56) ta ku—hong—le yanjing.
he cry—red—ASP eye
'He cried so much that his eyes became red.'

(57) ta xiao—wai—le zui.
he laugh—slant—ASP mouth
'He laughed so much that his mouth became twisted.'

Second, in the case of the DVC, when the directional ending contains either *lai* 'toward the speaker' or *qu* 'away from the speaker' i.e. either Type (1) or (3) and there is a post—verbal nominal (not necessarily an object, see previous discussion of existential and presenatative sentences), the nominal can occur in three positions if the ending is *lai* 'but only in two positions if the ending is *qu*. Compare (58) with (59).

(58) a. ta duan—le yi—wan tang shang—lai le.
he serve—ASP one—bowl soup ascend—come PART
'He served up a bowl of soup (toward the speaker).'

---

[4]See Chapter 5 for a discussion of the possible origin of these RVCs in connection with the *ba* construction.

    b. ta duan–shang <u>yi–wan tang</u> lai le.
       he serve–ascend one–bowl soup come PART
       'Same as (a).'
    c. ta duan–shang–lai <u>yi–wan tang</u> le.
       he serve–ascend–come one–bowl soup PART
       'Same as (a).'

(59) a. tamen gan–le <u>yi–ge yongren</u> chu–qu le.
       they chase–ASP one–CL servant exit–go PART
       'They have chased out a servant (away from the speaker).'
    b. *tamen gan–chu <u>yi–ge yongren</u> qu le.
       they chase–exit one–CL servant go PART
       'Same as (a).'
    c. tamen gan–chu–qu <u>yi–ge yongren</u> le.
       they chase–exit–go one–CL servant PART
       'Same as (a).'

In sum, we think it is fair to say that the distinction between transitive and intransitive vebs in Chinese is far less sharp than it is in English.

2.3.1 Sentences with Intransitive Action Verbs

The type of sentences we will discuss occurs in the pattern: Subject/Topic + V_A + (Complement). Since up to this point we haven't touched upon complement yet, we will take it up now. There are in Chinese four types of verbal complement, namely, (1) descriptive complements, (2) locative coverb phrases, (3) quantitative phrases and (4) resultative complements. They are exemplified by (60), (61), (62) and (63) respectively.

(60) ta pao <u>de hen man</u>.
    he run DE very slow
    'Roughly, he runs very slowly.'

(61) ta hen kuai–de pao <u>dao shichang</u>.
    he very quickly run to market
    'He ran to the market very quickly.'

(62) ta pao—le <u>wu   gongli</u>   le.
      he run—ASP five kilometer PART
      'He has run for five kilometers.'

(63) ta pao <u>de shang qi   bu jie   xia qi</u>.
      he run DE first breath not connect next breath
      'He ran so hard that he was out of breath.'

The complements in (60) and (63) are both introduced by *de*. As these two constructions have spawned very heated debate as to their correct analyses, we will examine them carefully and see how they fit into our framework in Chapter 8. For now our reference to verbal complements will be restricted to types (2) and (3).

Let us now turn our attention back to the intransitive action verb. Both Tang (1975) and Li et al. (1983) classify intransitive action verbs into three types, namely, verbs of vocal action, verbs of location and verbs of motion. We will take up each of them briefly.

2.3.1.1 Verbs of Vocal Action

(64) gives a list of important verbs of vocal action in Chinese. (65) and (66) illustrate how these verbs are used in sentences.

(64) a. <u>ku</u> 'cry, weep'   b. <u>xiao</u> 'laugh, smile'
      c. <u>jiao</u> 'call'   d. <u>rang</u> 'shout'
      e. <u>han</u> 'shout'

(65) ta xiao le.
      he smile PART
      'He smiled.'

(66) ta ku—le   san—ge   zhongtou.
      he cry—ASP three—CL hour
      'He cried for three hours.'

Notice that some of them such as *jiao* 'call' and *xiao* 'laugh' have transitive use as well, but in the case of *xiao,* when it is used transitively, it means 'laugh at' rather than 'laugh, or smile'. Compare (67) with (65).

(67) tamen zai xiao wo.
    they ASP laugh:at me
    'They are laughing at me.'

2.3.1.2 Verbs of Location

Some important verbs of location are given in (68).

(68) a. zuo 'sit'   b. zhan 'stand'
     c. dun 'squat'   d. ting 'stop'
     e. tang 'lie'   f. pa 'crawl'
     g. zhu 'live'   h. shui 'sleep'
     i. cang 'hide'   j. fu 'float'
     j. piao 'float, drift'

They are called verbs of location because semantically they always have a locative phrase associated with it. The locative phrase may show up postverbally as a complement as in (a) sentence or it may appear preverbally as in (b) sentence in (69).

(69) a. ta tang zai chuang-shang.
        he lie at bed-LOC
        'He is lying in bed.'
     b. ta zai chuang-shang tang-zhe.
        he at bed-LOC   lie-ASP
        '(Roughly) Same as (a).'

(69a) and (69b) are synonymous as far as cognitive meaning is concerned. This is the only type of verbs that has this property.

When the agent involved is indefinite in reference and hence unfit to be a topic, then the locative phrase assumes the function of one and the agent phrase ends up in the postverbal position as shown in (69c).

     c. (zai) chuang-shang tang-zhe yi-ge ren.
            at bed-LOC   lie-ASP one-CL person
        'There is a person lying in bed.'

Moreover, in our earlier discussion of existential verbs, we noted that verbs of location share with verbs of existence the same function of presenting a new topic and that once a topic is presented, one can go on adding comment clauses to it without having to repeat the topic NP even though it is indefinite. (69d) exemplifies a locative verb, here *tang* 'lie' in such a use.

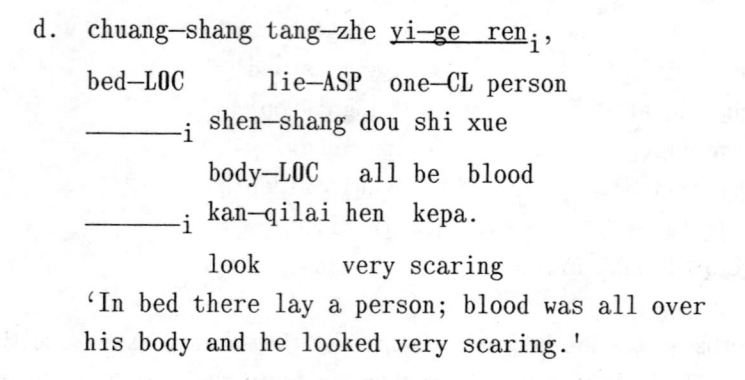

    d. chuang–shang tang–zhe yi-ge ren$_i$,
       bed–LOC   lie–ASP one–CL person

     _____$_i$ shen–shang dou shi xue
          body–LOC all be blood

     _____$_i$ kan–qilai hen kepa.
          look   very scaring

    'In bed there lay a person; blood was all over his body and he looked very scaring.'

When an intransitive verb of location appears in such a construction, it behaves like a state verb of existence and its function is to present a new topic. We will, therefore, speak of it as being used "presentatively".

2.3.1.3 Verbs of Motion

Important verbs of motion in Chinese are listed in (70).

(70) a. dao, daoda 'arrive'   b. lai 'come'
      c. qu 'go'   d. zou 'walk'
      e. pao 'run'   f. fei 'fly'
      g. kai 'sail, drive'   h. you 'swim'
      i. tiao 'jump'   j. gun 'roll'
      k. liu 'slip'   l. lüxing 'travel'

Sentences with verbs of motion, like those with verbs of location, may contain a locative phrase, but it is a locative phrase indicating goal. Examine (71a) and (72a).

(71) a. chezi kai dao Meiguo le.
        car   drive to America PART
        'The car has arrived at the U.S.'

(72) a. chezi kai wang Meiguo le.
        car drive for America PART
        'The car has left for the U.S.'

Please note that the use of *dao* 'to' in (71a) indicates that "the car has arrived" while the use of *wang* in (72a) only means that "the car is going in the direction of the U.S.". Also note that the *dao* phrase can only appear postverbally as a complement, as indicated by the ungrammaticality of (71b), where the *dao* 'to' phrase occurs preverbally. The *wang* 'for' phrase, on the other hand, can occur postverbally as well as preverbally, as attested by the grammaticality of both (72a) and (72b).

(71) b. *chezi dao Meiguo kai   le.
        car   to America drive PART
        'Same as (71a).'

(72) b. chezi wang Meiguo kai   le.
        car   for America drive PART
        'Same as (72a).'

Verbs of motion are often followed, appropriately, by directional verb endings to form directional verb compounds, as exemplified in (73a) and (73b).

(73) a. ta zou-jin-lai   le.
        he walk-enter-come PART
        'He has walked in (toward the speaker).'
     b. ta zou-chu-qu   le.
        he walk-exit-out PART
        'He has walked out (away from the speaker).'

Like verbs of location, verbs of motion can also be used "presentatively", as exemplified by the following sentences.

(74) (qian-mian) lai-le   san-ge   ren.
     front-LOC   come-ASP three-CL person
     'There are three people coming in the front.'

(75) zuotian zou—le <u>liang—wei keren</u>
yesterday leave—ASP two—CL guest
———_i shen—shang dou dai—zhe yi—ba qiang.
body—LOC all carry—ASP one—CL gun
'Yesterday two guests left, both carrying a gun with them.'

A few verbs of motion such as *xia* 'get off (a vehicle), *chu* 'leave (a place)', and *likai* 'go away (from)' take a source locative phrase as object, besides having a locative phrase as complement or modifier. Examine (76) and (77).

(76) wo <u>zai xia yi zhan</u> xia che.
I at next one station get:off car
'I'll get off the bus at the next station.'

(77) ta likai <u>Taiwan dao Riben</u> qu.
he leave Taiwan to Japan go
'He left Taiwan for Japan.'

2.3.2 Sentences with Transitive Action Verbs

This type of senteces all contain an action verb with an object and in some cases with an additional complement. In what follows we would like to discuss imortant classes of verbs that can occur in this pattern.

2.3.2.1 Regular Transitive Action Verbs

This is a very large class of verbs, some of which are given in (78).

(78) a. <u>na</u> 'take'   b. <u>die</u> 'fold'
      c. <u>nian</u> 'read'   d. <u>nong</u> 'do, play'
      e. <u>xiu</u> 'repair'   f. <u>da</u> 'beat'
      g. <u>mo</u> 'touch'   h. <u>ti</u> 'kick'
      i. <u>sha, sha—si</u> 'kill' j. <u>pai</u> 'tap'
      k. <u>qiao</u> 'knock'   l. <u>si</u> 'tear'
      m. <u>kai</u> 'open'   n. <u>da—kai</u> 'open'

o. <u>yang</u> 'raise, bring up'   p. <u>chi</u> 'eat'
q. <u>kan</u> 'look at'   r. <u>xie</u> 'write'

Some example sentences follow with DO underlined and complement, if any, double underlined.

(79) women yong kuaizi   chi <u>dongxi</u>.
     we   with chopsticks eat thing
     'We eat things with chopsticks.'

(80) ta ti—le   <u>wo</u> <u><u>liang jiao</u></u>.
     he kick—ASP me two   feet
     'He kicked me twice.'

(81) wo xiu—hao—le   <u>chezi</u> le.
     I repair—finish—ASP car   PART
     'I have finished repairing the car.'

Many generalizations can be drawn with regard to this class of verbs. Space permits us to make only three. First, many verbs in this class can also occur as the first element in a resultative verb compound. For example, *nian* 'read' can be followed by *hao* 'finish' or *wan* 'finish' to form *nian—hao* or *nian—wan,* both meaning 'finish reading' and *si* 'tear' can be combined with *huai* 'destroy' or *po* 'break' to form such RVCs as *si—huai* 'destroy by tearing' or *si—po* 'become broken as a result of tearing'. There are simply too many to be listed here. An important generalization to remember is that, as a rule of thumb, if the first verb is transitive, then the whole compound remains transitive after adding the resultative ending.

Second, many verbs of this class also form compounds with their frequently associated objects. Thus, *chi* 'eat' and *fan* 'meal' form a VO compound *chi—fan* 'eat meal' and *nian* 'read' and *shu* 'book' form another *nian—shu* 'study'. As we have discussed this type of compounds earlier, there is no need to repeat here. Suffice it to point out that as semi—frozen idiomatic expressions, these compounds constitute difficulty in many areas of gammatical description, especially those having to do with the object.

Third and finally, when the object is understood, either linguistically or extra—linguistically, then it is not said at all. At the beginning of this section we mentioned some linguistic contexts in which DO can be deleted. Here let us give some examples of situational omission. Imagine that you found your friend, Zhang San, reading a novel three hours ago. Then, three hours later, you can ask him whether he has finished reading it by using (82).

(82) nian—wan—le,   meiyou?
      read—finish—ASP not—have
      'Have you finished reading (it)?'

In a similar vein, if you visit your Chinese friend at around dinner time, your friend is likely to utter (83).

(83) chi—le, meiyou?
      eat—ASP not—have
      'Have you eaten (your dinner)?'

This being the case, the line between transitive and intransitive verbs in Chinese can only be drawn semantically. In other words, syntactically speaking, there are a great many transitive verbs in Chinese that can be used intransitively.

2.3.2.2 Transitive Verbs of Location and Motion

This class of verbs, important members of which are listed in (84), takes an object and a locational or directional complement.

(84) a. fang 'put'   b. gua 'hang'
     c. bai 'set'   d. pai 'arrange'
     e. tie 'post'   f. cha 'stick'
     g. shuai 'throw'   h. cang 'hide'
     i. tui 'push'   j. kai 'drive'
     k. ban 'move'   l. qian, yi 'move'

Verbs from (a) to (h) may take either the locational or the directional complement, as exemplified by (85a) and (85b). Verbs from (i) to (l) can only take the directional complement, as the addition of a locative complement will make this type of sentences ungrammatical. This is quite clear when we compare the grammatical (86a) with the ungrammatical (86b).

(85) a. ta gua yi-zhang hua <u>zai qiang-shang</u>.
     he hang one-CL painting at wall-LOC
     'He hung a painting on the wall.'
   b. ta gua yi-zhang hua <u>dao qiang-shang</u>.
     he hang one-CL painting onto wall-LOC
     'He hung a painting onto the wall.'
(86) a. ta kai chezi <u>dao Xianggang</u>.
     he drive car to Hong-Kong
     'He drove his car to Hong Kong.'
   b. *ta kai chezi <u>zai Xianggang</u>.[5]
     he drive car at Hong-Kong

By comparing this class of verbs with their intransitive counterparts (2.3.1.2 ; 2.3.1.3), we soon find that the major difference between the two is that transitive verbs of location and motion have an additional agent, which often appears as subject.

2.3.2.3 Transitive Action Verbs That Take a Clause as their Object

Transitive action verbs that take a clause as their object fall into two classes, namely, quatative verbs such as *shuo* 'say', *xuanbu* 'announce', *chengren* 'admit' and *tiyi* 'propose, suggest' and verbs of inception, termination, continuation and modality such as *kaishi* 'begin', *jixü* 'continue', *dasuan* 'intend' etc. As they necessarily involve embedding, we will take them up in detail when we come to complex sentences in Chapter 8.

In the context of the simple sentence, it is sufficient to point out that sometimes clauses can be reduced to nouns. When this happens, we are dealing with simple sentences with transitive action verbs. Compare (a), (b) and (c) in (87).

(87) a. ta chengren <u>ta tou-le dongxi</u>.
     he admit he steal-ASP thing
     'He admits that he has stolen things.'

---

[5]If what is meant is "He drives (a car) in Hong Kong", then the correct way of saying that is either (i) or (ii) in Chinese.
  (i)   ta zai Xianggang kai chezi.
        he at Hong:Kong drive car
  (ii) zai Xianggang ta kai chezi
        at Hong:Kong he drive car

> b. ta chengren <u>ta tou-le   dongxi na-jian shi</u>.
>   he admit   he steal-ASP thing   that-CL matter
>   'Same as (a).'
> c. ta chengren <u>na-jian shi</u>.
>   he admit   that-CL matter
>   'Same as (a).'

Thus, in (a) we have a noun clause embedded as object of *chengren* 'admit'. In (b) we have a noun clause followed by its appositive and in (c) only the appositive is left, turning a complex sentence into a simple one.

2.3.2.4 Telescopic, Transitive Action Verbs

To be distinguished from the previous class of verbs in a class which occurs in a construction similar to an existential (presentative) clause in that the verb is followed by a noun which serves as a telescopic link between two clauses. Take *ta* 'he' in (88) for example. It plays a role in both clauses, i.e. it is the object of *yao* 'want' in the first clause and at the same time it is the topic/subject of the following clause.

> (88) <u>wo yao ta</u> zou.
>   I want he go
>   'I want him to go.'

Verbs of this type fall into three sub-classes, with verbs of directive as the most important one. As they all involve at least two telescopic clauses, we will discuss them under compound sentences.

2.3.3 Sentences with Ditransitive Verbs

Tsao (1988c) finds that ditransitive verbs should be further divided into two types: verbs of transaction and verbs of communication. While the former can be classified into three subtypes according to the meaning of the verb and its syntactic interaction with the goal marker *gei* 'to', no such regularity is found in the case of verbs of communication, which pattern themselves after verbs of transaction in a way but only imperfectly. For this reason, the two types will be discussed separately.

2.3.3.1 Verbs of Transaction

In the following discussion, we will take *gei* 'to' as a goal marker and the NP marked by *gei* 'to' as the goal NP. In a similar manner the giving NP, which is often unmarked by a preposition, will be referred to as the "source NP" and the thing transacted will be called the "theme NP".

2.3.3.1.1 "Give" Verbs

The semantic direction of transaction with this type of verbs is "outward", i.e. from giver to receiver. Syntactically, a verb of this type can occur in either one of the following two patterns:

(i)   Source + V + Theme + Gei + Goal
(ii) Source + V + (Gei) + Goal + Theme

Depending on whether *gei* 'to' in (ii) is obligatory or optional, the "give" verbs can be further divided into two classes. Given in (89) are verbs that when they occur in Pattern (ii), the presence of *gei* 'to' is required, as exemplified by (90).

(89) a. <u>di</u> 'bring to'   b. <u>dai</u> 'bring to'
     c. <u>ji</u> 'mail'   d. <u>jiao</u> 'deliver, hand in'
     e. <u>mai</u> 'sell'   f. <u>ban</u> 'move'

(90) a. ta ji   yi–ben shu <u>gei wo</u>.
        he mail one–CL book to me
        'He mailed a book to me.'
     b. ta ji   <u>gei wo</u> yi–ben shu.
        he mail to me one–CL book
        'He mailed me a book.'
     c. *ta ji   wo yi–ben shu.
         he mail me one–CL book
         'Sames as (b).'

Those that do not require the presence of *gei* 'to' when occurring in Pattern (ii), on the other hand, are given in (91).

(91) a. <u>song</u> 'give'   b. <u>huan</u> 'return, give back'
     c. <u>shang</u> 'bestow'   d. <u>pei</u> 'compensate, pay back'
     e. <u>chuan</u> 'pass'   f. <u>fu</u> 'pay'
     g. <u>shu</u> 'lose'

Now compare (92) with (90).

(92) a. wo song yi-ben shu <u>gei ta</u>.
        I give one-CL book to him
        'I gave a book to him.'
     b. wo song <u>gei ta</u> yi-ben shu.
        I give to him one-CL book
        'I gave him a book.'
     c. wo song <u>ta</u> yi-ben shu.
        I give him one-CL book
        'Same as (b).'

2.3.3.1.2 "Take" Verbs

Semantically, the direction of transaction for this class of verbs is "inward", i.e. from receiver to giver. Syntactically, it appears in the pattern given in (i).

(i) Goal + V + Source + Theme

The important "take" verbs are given in (93), with some illustrative example sentences followed in (94).

(93) a. <u>tou</u> 'steal'   b. <u>ying</u> 'win'
     c. <u>qiang</u> 'rob'   d. <u>duo</u> 'snatch, take by force'
     e. <u>zhuan</u> 'earn'   f. <u>zhan</u> 'occupy'
     g. <u>pian</u> 'cheat, swindle' h. <u>fa</u> 'punish (by a fin)'
     i. <u>yao</u> 'ask (for)'

(94) a. ta tou-le   wo wu-kuai   qian.
        he steal-ASP me five-dollar money
        'He stole from me five dollars.'

b. *<u>gei ta</u> tou-le wo wu-kuai qian.
    to him steal-ASP me five-dollar money
    'Same as (a).'
c. *ta tou-le <u>gei wo</u> wu-kuai qian.
    he steal-ASP to me five-dollar money
    'Same as (a).'
d. *ta tou-le wu-kuai qian <u>gei wo</u>.[6]
    he steal-ASP five-dollar money to me
    'Same as (a).'
e. wo <u>gei ta</u> tou-le wu-kuai qian.
    I to-by him steal-ASP five-dollar money
    (i) 'Same as (a).'
    (ii) 'I was stolen five dollars by him.'
f. wo <u>bei ta</u> tou-le wu-kuai qian.
    I by him steal-ASP five-dollar money
    'Same as (eii).'
g. *<u>wu-kuai qian</u> bei ta cong wo tou le.
    five-dollar money BEI him from me steal PART
    'Five dollars were stolen from me by him'

Four important points are to be noted. First, since the goal NP ends up as subject in this type of sentences, it cannot be marked by any coverb or preposition and hence the (b) sentence, in which the subject *ta* 'he' is marked by *gei* 'to', is ungrammatical.

Second, as the subject position is taken up by the goal NP, the source NP ends up postverbally as an object. It, therefore, cannot be marked by *gei* 'to' for the obvious reason that it is not a goal NP. Hence (94c) is ungrammatical. Furthermore, as no coverb can occur before the source NP, it indicates that in Mandarin there is no marker for the source NP vis-a-vis *gei* 'to', the goal marker. There is, however, a marker for the source locative NP *cong* 'from', which can be used to express a similar meaning. Compare (94c) with (95a).

---

[6](94d) is grammatical if it means "He stole five dollars and gave it to me". But then, as shown in the English translation, it is no longer a simple sentence but rather a compound one. We will have more to say about this type of sentences in Chapter 7.

(95) a. ta <u>cong wo—nali</u> tou—le wu—kuai qian.
    he from I—LOC steal—ASP five—dollar money
    'He stole five dollars from me (as a location).'

Notice that in (95a) the *cong* 'from' phrase occurs in a position where a locative adverbial normally appears. Notice also that in order to be grammatical the object of the coverb *cong* 'from', *wo* 'I' has to be suffixed by *nali* 'there', a localizer whose function is to turn a regular NP into a locative. This latter point is attested by the ungrammatical (95b).

(95) b. *ta <u>cong wo</u> tou—le wu—kuai qian.
    he from we steal—ASP five—dollar money
    'Same as (a).'

Third, in this pattern the source NP always precedes the theme NP. If it doesn't, an ungrammatical sentence results, as attested by the ungrammatical (94d). This strongly indicates that in this pattern the source NP is the direct object while in other patterns involving a ditransitive verb, the theme NP is. This observation is affirmed by the fact that when (94a) is passivized as in (94f), the source NP becomes the topic/subject while a theme NP cannot, as attested by the ungrammaticality of (94g). A theme NP can be passivized only when the source NP appears as a locative, and hence not a proper candidate for the direct object position. Compare (94g) with (95c).

(95) c. <u>wu—kuai qian</u> bei ta <u>cong wo—nali</u>
    five—dollar money BEI him from I—LOC
    tou—qu le.
    steal—go PART
    'Five dollars were stolen by him from me (as a location).'

Fourth and finally, we find in (94e) that when the source NP becomes the topic/subject and the goal NP is demoted, *gei* 'to', the goal marker, re—surfaces. Furthermore, when we compare (94e) with (94f), we find that *gei* 'to', the goal marker, behaves in this case exactly like *bei* 'by', the most productive passive marker. Tsao (1988c) points out that this is exactly the context that gave rise to the passive marking function of *gei*.[7]

---

[7]In the same paper (Tsao,1988c), he also examines the origin of Taiwanese

2.3.3.1.3 "Rent" Verbs

Semantically this class of verbs can be characterized as bidirectional, i.e., it can be interpreted as either "inward" or "outward" in its direction of transaction. Syntactically, the Northern Mandarin takes the topic/subject to be the source NP, while the Southern Mandarin tends to do otherwise as demonstrated by (96).[8]

(96) a. wo jie   ni shi–kuai qian.
        I {borrow from} you ten–dollar money
         {lend to}
    (i) 'I'll borrow ten dollars from you.' (Northern)
    (ii) 'I'll lend ten dollars to you.' (Southern)

This ambiguity of direction, however, is revolved when *gei* 'to', the goal marker, is added. As (96b) and (96c) show, *jie* followed by *gei* 'to' can only mean 'lend'. Alternatively, other coverb phrases headed by *xiang* 'facing', indicating object of one's request' and *gen* 'with' can also be used to disambiguate the sentence, as shown in (96d).

  b. wo jie <u>gei ni</u> shi–kuai qian.
     I lend to you ten–dollar money
     'I'll lend you ten dollars.'
  c. wo jie shi–kuai qian <u>gei ni</u>.
     I lend ten–dollar money to you
     'I'll lend ten dollars to you.'
  d. wo <u>xiang ni</u> jie   shi–kuai qian.
     I facing you borrow ten–dollar money
     'I'll borrow ten dollars from you.'

All important "rent" verbs are given in (97).

(97) a. <u>na</u> 'take from/for'

---

counterpart, *hou* as an agent marker in the passive sentence and found that it arose from exactly the same context.

[8]The generalization given here is only tentative as I have access to only a few speakers of either variety of Mandarin. A large–scale sociolinguistic survey with regard to this usage difference, to the best of my knowledge, has never been conducted so far.

        b.   <u>mai</u> 'buy from/for'
        c.   <u>zu</u> 'rent (as a tenant /as a landlord)'
        d.   <u>fen</u> 'divide from/share in'
        e.   <u>jie</u> 'borrow from/lend to'

2.3.3.2 Verbs of Communication

Verbs of communication fall into three classes according to their syntactic behavior.

(98)   I.   <u>jiao</u>$_1$ 'teach', <u>da (dianhua)</u> 'make (a phone-call),
            <u>xie (xin)</u> 'write (a letter)
     II.   <u>gaosu</u> 'tell', <u>huida</u> 'answer', <u>daying</u> 'promise', <u>wen</u> 'ask',
            <u>qingjiao</u> 'ask', <u>mafan</u> 'trouble', <u>jiao</u>$_2$ 'teach'
     III. <u>jiang</u> 'tell', <u>shuo</u> 'say, speak'

Class I communicative verbs behave like Type I transactional verbs except for two irregularities. First, *jiao$_1$* 'teach' is restricted to the sense in which the theme NP denotes something that can be completely transmitted as a result of teaching, as exemplified by *yi-ge mijue* 'a secret method' in (99). If the theme NP denotes something that cannot be completely transmitted, then *jiao* is used like a Type II transactional verb. *Jiao* in this use will be referred to as *jiao$_2$* 'teach'. The second use is exemplified in (100).

(99) a. wo jiao <u>ta</u> yi-ge mijue.
          I   teach him one-CL secret:method
          'I taught him a secret method.'
      b. wo jiao yi-ge mijue   <u>gei ta</u>.
          I   teach one-CL secret:method to him
          'Same as (a).'

(100) a. wo jiao <u>ta</u> Zhongwen.
          I   teach him Chinese
          'I teach him Chinese.'
      b. *wo jiao Zhongwen <u>gei ta</u>.
          I   teach Chinese to him
          'Same as (a)'

Second, in the case of *da* (*dianhua*) 'make (a phone-call)' and *xie* (*xin*) 'write (a letter)' when the receipient NP marked by *gei* 'to' is fronted, it usually ends in a position between topic/subject and the verb rather than after the verb as is normal with Type I transactional verbs.[9]

(101) a. wo da   yi-ge dianhua   <u>gei ta</u>.
         I make one-CL phone-call to him
         'I will give him a call.'
   b. *wo da   <u>gei ta</u> yi-ge dianhua.
         I make to him one-CL phone-call
         'Same as (a).'
   c. wo <u>gei ta</u> da   yi-ge dianhua.
         I to him make one-CL phone-call
         'Same as (a).'

All the communicative verbs in Class II can occur in the form of : Topic/Subject + V + Animate NP + Inanimate NP, very much like Type II transactional verbs do. Compare (102a) with (94a).

(102) a. <u>wo</u> gaosu <u>ta</u> yi-jian shi.
         I tell him one-CL matter
         'I told him a matter.'
   b. *<u>ta gei wo</u> gaosu yi-jian shi.
         he to me tell   one-CL matter
         'He was told a matter by me.'

However, when we compare (102b) with (94e), we find while the latter is grammatical, the former is not. This strongly suggests that the topic/subject in (102a), namely, *wo* 'I' is not a goal NP and neither is the receipient NP, namely, *ta* 'he' a source NP. Also, the theme

---

[9]Tsao (1988c) suggests that this unusual positioning may be due, at least in part, to the fact that both *da-*(*dianhua*) 'make (a phone-call)' and *xie* (*xin*) 'write (a letter)' are VO compounds and as such they resist being separated by the *gei* phrase, when it is fronted.

NP is by nature an abstract one, which, as we have pointed out previously in connection with transitive verbs that have a clause for object (see (87)), may be derived from a direct quote.

In Class III, we have only two verbs *shuo* 'say, talk' and *jiang* 'speak', which, unlike their English counterparts are not ditransitive verbs at all. Rather they are transitive quatative verbs that we just mentioned. This can be clearly seen by comparing (103) with (87).

(103) a. ta shuo <u>ta yao lai</u>.
        he say he want come
        'He said he wanted to come.'
   b. ta shuo <u>ta yao lai</u> nei-jian shi le
        hes say he want come that-CL matter PART
        'He mentioned the matter that he wanted to come.'
   c. ta shuo-le <u>nei-jian shi</u> le.
        he say-ASP that-CL matter PART
        'He mentioned the matter.'

The receipient of the message can be added, whenever necessary, in the form of a coverb phrase composed of coverb *dui* 'facing' and an NP, as shown in (103d). This coverb phrase, however, cannot occur at any other place, as attested by the ungrammaticality of both (e) and (f) sentences.

(103) d. ta <u>dui wo</u> shuo-le nei-jian shi le.
        he facing me say-ASP that-CL matter PART
        'He mentioned the matter to me.'
   e. *ta shuo-le nei-jian shi <u>dui wo</u> le.
        he say-ASP that-CL matter facing me PART
        'Same as (d).'
   f. *ta shuo-le <u>dui wo</u> nei-jian shi le.
        he say-ASP facing me that-CL matter PART
        'Same as (d).

Both verbs, however, have another use that makes them look like ditransitive verbs. (104a) exemplifies such a use.

(104) a. wo shuo yi-ge gushi gei ta ting.
I say one-CL story for him listen
'(Literally) I'll say a story for him to listen to;
I'll tell him a story.'
b. *wo shuo yi-ge gushi gei ta.
I say one-CL story for him
'Same as (a).'
c. *wo shuo gei ta yi-ge gushi ting.
I say for him one-CL story listen
'Same as (a).'
d. *wo shuo gei ta yi-ge gushi.
I say to him one-CL story
'Same as (a).'
e. wo gei ta shuo yi-ge gushi.
I for him say one-CL story
'I'll tell a story for the benefit of him.'
f. wo wei ta shuo yi-ge gushi.
I for him say one-CL story
'Same as (e).'

In this use, the verb requires another verb like *ting* 'listen' to follow the *gei* phrase. In this pattern, the object of the first verb, namely *yi-ge gushi* 'a story' in this case serves two functions. It is at the same time the object of *shuo* 'say' in the first clause and the topic of the following clause. This being the case, *ting* 'listen', the verb in the second clause, cannot be omitted, and neither can *yi-ge gushi* 'a story' be moved, as attested by the ungrammaticality of (d) and (c) respectively. Shuo 'say' in this use exemplifies a special subtype of telescopic construction that we will take up in Chapter 7.

However, as an action verb, *shuo* 'say' can always take an additional benefactive case when there is a need for it. (104e), where *gei ta* 'for him' is interpreted as a benefactive case, is, therefore, grammatical. That this interpretation of ours is correct is further affirmed by the fact that *gei* in (104e) can be replaced by *wei* 'for, on behalf of' without changing the grammaticality of the sentence, as shown in (104f).

2.4 Passive Sentences

If we interprete passive sentences broadly, then there are at least four ways in

Chinese to express passivity. This can be clearly shown when we examine the various ways that can be properly used to translate a passive sentence in English. They are: (i) the *bei* construction; (ii) sentences with certain passive verbs such as *ai* 'receive' and *shou* 'receive'; (iii) the *shi ....de* construction with the object as the primary topic; and (iv) sentences with middle-voice verbs. These four ways are exemplified by sentences (105) – (108) respectively.

(105) ta bei pian   le.
      he BEI swindle PART
      'He was swindled.'

(106) ta you ai   ma   le.
      he again receive scold PART
      'He was scolded again.'

(107) nei-ben shu shi 1980 nian xie de.
      that-CL book SHI 1980 year write DE
      'The book was written in 1980.'

(108) nei-ben shu chuban le.
      that-CL book publish PART
      'The book has been published.'

In what follows we would like to examine in detail each of the four constructions and find out what they have in common and how they differ. An attempt will also be made in the end to determine the relationship between active and passive sentences in Chinese.

2.4.1 The *Bei* Construction

We are here using the term the *bei* construction in two different senses. In its broad sense, it includes any sentence that can occur in the form:

Patient + Agent Marker + Agent + (Passive Verb) + V + (C)

Since *bei, jiao, rang, gei* and much more restrictedly *you* can all be used as agent marker in this pattern in modern Mandarin, sentences containing them as agent marker should all be included in this broad sense. In its narrow sense, however, it refers to just the type of sentences where *bei* is used as agent marker. In what follows, let us start by concentrating on the *bei* sentence in its narrow sense and move on to other agent markers in our later discussion.

Although often deplored, it is a fact that the *bei* construction in its narrow sense has been used, perhaps rather indiscriminately, to translate passive sentences in English and other European languages. From this observation alone it is clear that the *bei* construction is perceived by the native speakers of Chinese as the closest equivalent of the passive sentence in English. This being the case, let us carefully compare the *bei* construction with the the English passive sentence to see whether we can find out the reason behind this observation.

When we compare an active English sentence such as (109a) with its passive counterpart (109b), we notice that at least three things have taken place.

(109) a. I hit him.
b. He was hit by me.

First, DO in (a) becomes subject in (b). Second, subject in (a) is demoted to an adjunct and is marked by an agent marker *by*. Third, the verb in (b) is marked as passive by turning into a past participle form and being preceded by some form of the verb *be*.

Now let us compare an active Chinese sentence such as (110a) with its passive counterpart, the *bei* sentence such as (110b).

(110) a. wo da ta le.
I hit him PART
'I hit him.'
b. ta bei wo da le.
he BEI me hit PART
'He was hit by me.'

We find that similar things have happened here. First, direct object in (a) becomes subject in (b). Second, subject in (a) is demoted to an adjunct and is marked by an agent marker *bei*. But here the similarity seems to end. There is no sign that the verb is marked as passive in Chinese. This may seem to be a natural consequence of the fact that Chinese verbs lack inflexional change.

However, the fact is that Chinese does have a way of marking its verb as passive, i.e.

by using a passive marking verb. In modern Mandarin, besides the three that we will discuss in the next section, namely, *shou, ai* and *jian,* all roughly translatable as 'receive', *gei* is frequently used for this purpose. Witness the following sentences.

(111) a. ta <u>bei</u> ren   gei da-shang le.
         he by someone GEI hit-wound PART
         'He was wounded by someone.'
      b. ?ta gei ren   gei da-shang le.
         he by someone GEI hit-wound PART
         'Same as (a).'

We have marked (111b) as of questionable grammaticality because we are not sure that it can be used in formal Mandarin. Chao (1968), however, has reported that he has actually heard it said in colloquial speech. We can account for this avoidance phenomenon very nicely by resorting to an often observed principle in Chinese, especially in the formal style. The principle states that the same function word should not be used twice in the same simple sentence and that the closer the two occurrences are, the more strictly the principle is to apply. Chao (1968) uses haplology, a version of this general principle, to explain the collapsing of two *le*'s, i.e. aspectual *-le* and sentence-final *le,* when both occur at the end of a sentence as shown in (112b).

(112) a. wo chi-le ji   le.
         I eat-ASP chicken PART
         'I have eaten the chicken.'
      b. ji   wo chi le.
         chicken I eat ASP/PART
         'Same as (a).'

Chen (1978) extends Chao's principle of haplology to what she calls "distant haplology" to account for the non-occurrence of progressive aspect marker *zai* when it follows a *zai* locative phrase as in (113).

(113) a. ta zai kan shu.
         he ASP read book
         'He is reading a book.'

b. ta zai shufang—li ____ kan shu.
   he at study—LOC ASP read book
   'He is reading a book in the study.'

By following the principle of "distant haplology" we can actually show that there are two *bei*'s in the underlying structure of a *bei* sentence, one of which is deleted in the surface structure. Take (110b) for instance. In our analysis we would posit (110c) as its underlying structure. When the agent phrase is present, it would surface as (110b) with the passive marking *bei* deleted. But, when the agent phrase is not present, the agent NP together with its governing coverb *bei* is deleted, leaving only the passive marking *bei* in the surface as in (110d).

(110) c. ta <u>bei</u> wo <u>bei</u> da le.
          he by me BEI hit PART
          'Same as (110b).'
       d. ta ____ bei da le.
          he by NP BEI hit PART
          'he was hit (by someone).'

Actually because *bei* in (110d) has been traditionally analyzed as a coverb marking an agent, its occurrence in it has baffled many linguists because it constitutes the only exception to an otherwise very general rule in Chinese as well as in many other languages which states that what is governed by a coverb/preposition cannot be deleted. By positing two *bei*'s in the underlying structure, we are not only able to specify exactly the function of *bei* in (110d), but also to unravel a mystery that has puzzled many linguists.[10]

---

[10]This point is clearly revealed when we compare the situation in Taiwanese with that in Mandarin. In Taiwanese, the agent marker in a passive sentence is *hou*, which, as we pointed out in Note 7, was originally derived from the goal marker associated with a "take"—type transactional verb. So far we find a perfect parallel with Mandarin *gei*. However, Taiwanese *hou*, unlike Mandarin *gei* or *bei*, has never developed the function of marking the verb as passive. This being the case, when the agent phrase is an indefinite person, *lang* 'person, someone', it can be blended with *hou* 'to become *hong* as in (ib), but cannot be deleted, leaving *hou* to be followed by the verb directly, as attested by the ungrammaticality of (ic) (cf. (110b) in Mandarin).
(i) a.   i   hou   lang   ma.
          he   by   person scold
          'He was scolded by someone.'
     b.   i   hong   ma.
          he   by:person   scold
          'Same as (a).'

This function of marking the following verb as passive can also be clearly seen when we trace the development of the *bei* construction. Bennett (1981) has argued convincingly that *bei* was originally a full verb meaning 'receive', which took a noun as its object, as shown in (114a). However, since the noun following it was not marked with regard to its syntactic category, misanalysis of constituent structure took place in the manner described in (114b).

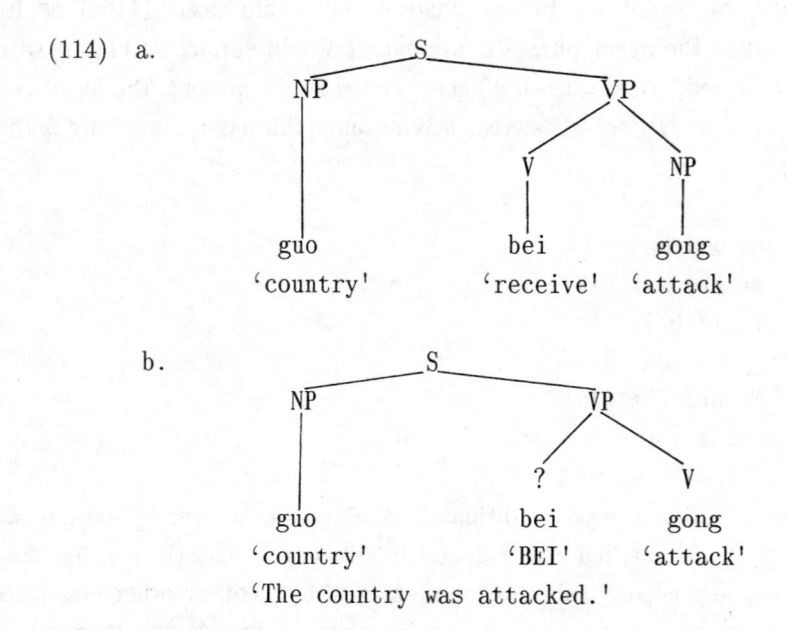

(114) a.
```
           S
      /       \
    NP         VP
    |        /    \
   guo      V      NP
           |       |
          bei     gong
'country' 'receive' 'attack'
```

b.
```
           S
      /       \
    NP         VP
    |        /    \
   guo      ?      V
           |       |
          bei     gong
'country'  'BEI'  'attack'
```
'The country was attacked.'

At this stage, *bei* actually functions as a passive–marking verb, on a par with *jian* shown in the (115) cited by Wang (1980) from *Mencius* (around 4th c B.C.).

(115) Pencheng Gua jian sha.
      Pencheng Gua JIAN kill
      'Pencheng Gua was killed.'

Once this stage was achieved, the insertion of an agent phrase after *bei* would make it a perfect passive structure. The agent insertion, indeed, began not too long after that in the fourth or fifth century as evidenced by the following sentence taken from *Shi Shuo Xin*

---

c. * i   hou   ma.
     he   by   scold
     'Same as (a).'

Yu, a book written in the 5th century.

(116) Liang-zi bei Su Jun hai.
Liang-zi BEI Su Jun harm
'Liang-zi was harmed by Su Jun.'

This account, which we feel to be in the main correct, shows clearly that *bei* was first a passive marking verb before it took up, in addition, the function of a coverb, marking the the following NP as agent. Even in modern Mandarin the function of marking the following verb as passive is still there, though it can only be shown indirectly. So when the need to explicitly mark the verb as passive arises, *gei* is used, as shown in (111).

One of such needs, according to Tsao (1988c), is to disambiguate passive sentences using *jiao* or *rang* as agent marker. This is because *jiao* and *rang* can both be used as telescopic transitive verbs meaning 'ask' and 'let' respectively as shown in (117).

(117) wo jiao ta qu Meiguo.
I ask him go America
'I asked him to go to the U.S.'

So when the NP following the verb is animate and the following verb is transitive, the sentence is subject to two analyses, yielding two different meanings as shown by (118a) and (118b) respectively.

(118) a. wo jiao ta da le.
I by him hit PART
'I was hit by him.'
b. wo jiao ta da le.
I ask him hit PART
'I asked him to hit (something).'
c. wo jiao ta gei da le.
I by him GEI hit PART
'I was hit by him.'

In this connection it is interesting to note that *bei* started out as a passive verb marker and later took on the function of an agent marker, retaining at least in part its original function while *gei* entered the picture of passive sentences first as an agent marker and later took on in addition the function of marking the verb as passive.

Finally, *you* in a much more restricted way than the others, can also be used as an agent marker, as shown in (119).

    (119) congqian   hunyin—de   shi   you fumu
             in:the;past marriage—POSS matter by   parents
             jueding.
             decide
             'In the past, matters related to marriage were to be decided by one's parents.'

As the English translation in (119) suggests, *you* is not a pure agent marker because it takes on the additional meaning that whatever is done is "the agent's duty or prerogative" (Y. Li et al., 1983:176). This explains why its use as agent marker is restricted.

2.4.2 Sentences with Passive Verbs

We have already pointed out that in archaic Chinese passive sentences were created by employing passive marking verbs such as *bei* and *jian* before the main verb of a sentence. Actually even in modern Mandarin, *jian* retains its function in some frozen compounds such as *jian—xiao* 'be laughed at', *jian—ze* 'be blamed (for something)', *jian—qi* 'be deserted' and *jian—liang* 'be forgiven'.

In modern Mandarin, however, the most extensively used passive verb marker is *shou (dao)* 'receive' and next to that *ai* 'adversely receive'. Their uses are exemplified by (120) and (121).

    (120) ta daochu   shou   huanying.
             he everywhere RECEIVE welcome
             'He was welcomed everywhere.'

    (121) ta you   ai   ma   le.
             he again RECEIVE scold PART
             'He was again scolded.'

It is to be noted that in many cases the constituent occurring after these verbs are subject to two analyses. Take (120) for example. *Huanying* 'welcome' can be interpreted as either a noun or a verb and these two analyses can roughly give us the same meaning. This is exactly the situation that Bennett (1981) cited earlier has described for us with regard to *bei* in archaic Chinese. This observation lends support to Bennett's analysis.

Also to be noted is that the topic/subject in this case is semantically a recipient, i.e. *ta* 'he' in (120) is the one who 'receives', and so when the constituent after *shou* 'receive' is interpreted as a verb and it, together with *shou*, is perceived as a passive verb, the recipient NP is then conceived of as a grammatical object which has become topic/subject. This is exactly what happens when an active sentence is turned into a *bei* passive sentence, as we described earlier.

2.4.3 The *Shi ... De* Construction as a Passive Sentence

It is generally agreed that the function of the *shi ...de* construction is to bring into focus the constituent immediately after *shi* in the sentence. Take (122) for instance. Depending on which constituent in (122) is being focused upon, a *shi ...de* sentence can be generated as shown in (123).

(122) ta zuotian   zuo huoche cong Shanghai lai le.
       he yesterday by   train from Shanghai come PART
       'He came from Shanghai yesterday by train.'

(123) a. shi <u>ta</u> zuotian zuo houche cong Shanghai lai de.
          SHI he yesterday by train   from Shanghai come DE
          'It was he that came from Shanghai by train yesterday.'
      b. ta shi <u>zuotian</u>   zuo huoche cong Shanghai lai de.
          he SHI yesterday by train from Shanghai come DE
          'It was yesterday that he came from Shanghai by train.'
      c. ta zuotian   shi <u>zuo huoche</u> cong Shanghai lai de.
          he yesterday SHI by   train   from Shanghai come DE
          'It was by train that he came from Shanghai yesterday.'
      d. ta zuotian   shi <u>cong Shanghai</u> zuo huoche lai de.
          he yesterday SHI from Shanghai by   train   come DE
          'It was from Shanghai that he came by train yesterday.'

As the sentences in (123) show, the *shi ... de* construction is compatible with sentences other than passive ones. It is only when the topic/subject of a *shi ... de* sentence is also interpreted as the direct object of the main verb that it has anything to do with passivity at all. To put it with slight difference, if a passive English sentence which has its focus on a constituent other than its subject is to be translated into Chinese, then an appropriate way to do that is by means of a *shi ... de* construction with the direct object of the verb as topic/subject as shown in the following examples in which the primary stress of the sentence is indicated by underlining.

(124) a. The book was written by Chomsky in 1985.
     b. nei—ben shu shi Chomsky zai 1985 nian xie de.
       that—CL book SHI Chomsky in 1985 year write DE
(125) a. The book was written by Chomsky in 1985.
     b. nei—ben shu shi 1985 nian Chomsky xie de.
       that—CL book SHI 1985 year Chomsky write DE

2.4.4 Sentences with Transitive Verbs in the Middle Voice

What we mean by a sentence with a transitive verb in the middle voice is one that has as its topic/subject the patient phrase of a transitive sentence and that does not contain an agent phrase, as exemplified by (126a).

(126) a. na—ben shu chuban le.
       that—CL book publish PART
       'The book was published.'

Thus in (126a) the verb *chuban* 'publish' is a transitive action verb that has *na—ben shu* 'the book' as the patient NP in its case frame and a human agent, which is here unexpressed. In Chinese when the agent is unexpressed and the patient becomes the topic/subject of the sentence, then the sentence is understood as passive semantically even though syntactically it is not marked as such.

This construction is most appropriate if no adjunct phrase is being focused and there is no implication that the event as described is unfortunate or adverse. If an adjunct is being focused, then *shi ... de* construction as in (b) is to be preferred and if the event is perceived as unfortunate then the *bei* construction is definitely better as in (c), where *chuban* 'publish' is replaced by *daoyin* 'pirate', which imposes an adverse reading on the sentence.

(126) b. na–ben shu shi liushi nian qian chuban de.
        that–CL book SHI sixty year ago publish DE
        'The book was published sixty years ago.'
     c. na–ben shu bei daoyin le.
        that–CL book BEI pirate PART
        'The book was pirated.'

One important note on the comparison of English and Chinese grammar: while English does have a few middle–voice verbs as exemplified by (127) and (128), Chinese, because of its topic orientation, allows almost any transitive verb to appear in the middle voice as shown in (129) to (131).

(127) The house burned down yesterday.

(128) The boat overturned.

(129) nei–ben shu zhao–dao le.
      that–CL book look:for–attain PART
      'The book was found.'

(130) fangzi gai–hao le.
      house build–finish PART
      'The house has been built.'

(131) zhe–zhong cai neng chi ma?
      this–kind vegetable can eat PART
      'Can this kind of vegetable be eaten?'
  Or 'Is this kind of vegetable edible?'

It is intuitively felt that such resultative endings as *dao* 'attain' and *hao* 'finish' in (129) and (130) and such auxiliary verbs as *neng* 'can' in (131) have some effect on our understanding of these sentences as passive, but just what the effect is cannot be pinpointed at this moment. It is an area that awaits further research.

2.4.5 Concluding Remarks Concerning Chinese Passive Sentences

Our comparison of these four constructions involved in expressing passivity in Chinese can be summarized in (132).

(132)

		Bei	Shou	Shi..de	MDV
a.	Object becomes topic/subject	+	+	+	+
b.	Agent phrase appears as an adjunct or is unexpressed	+	−	+	+
c.	Verb marked as passive	+	+	−	−

The table reveals, among other things, the following three generalizations. First, only the *bei* construction has all the attributes that an English passive sentence has. For this reason, it is perceived as the closest Chinese equivalent to the English passive. However, as we pointed out earlier, even today the *bei* construction carries with it the implication that what it describes is some happening adverse to the speaker. To avoid this unnecessary implication and also to take into consideration the informational distribution of a sentence often it is better to use other types of passive sentences.

Second, what is common to all four types of passive sentences is the fact that the patient case has taken up the topic/subject position with the agentive case, if there is one, unexpressed or appearing as an adjunct. This strongly suggests that a passive sentence should be generated in the base as part of the process of subject selection and later on the subject is further topicalized.

Third, one thing that all the previous analyses, to the best of my knowledge, have missed is that in the *bei* construction, the verb is marked passive by *bei* implicitly. The marking can be made explicit through the use of *gei* attached to the verb.

Finally, we would like to make clear that even though all the four constructions are simple declarative sentences, the *shi ... de* construction is not a basic one in the sense that depending on which part of the sentence is being focused on, the construction can involve from zero to two or three topics as exemplified by (133) to (135).

(133)   zero topic
shi ta zuotian   zuo huoche lai de.
SHI he yesterday by train come DE
'It is he that came by train yesterday.'

(134)   single topic
    <u>ta</u> shi zuotian   zuo huoche lai de.
    he SHI yesterday by   train come DE
    'It was yesterday that he came by train.'

(135)   double topic
    <u>ta</u> <u>zuotian</u>   shi zuo huoche lai de.
    he yesterday SHI by   train come DE
    'It was by train that he came yesterday.'

This being the case, *shi* in the *shi ...de* construction should be regarded as a raising predicate which allows topics to be raised. We will present evidence to argue for this position in Chapter 8. The remaining three passive constructions are all basic sentences with only one topic, which is syntactically subject of the clause and semantically the patient case of the main verb.

3 Summary

We can sum up our discussion in this chapter by presenting the major clause pattern that we have identified in the simple one-topic declarative sentence in the following (the number after each pattern refers to the illustrative sentence).

  I. Sentences with State Verbs
    i. Adjectival Sentences
       $T/S + V_S$ (136)
    ii. Naming and Classificatory Sentences
       (a) $T/S + V_C + NP_{Comp}$ (137)
       (b) $T/S + V_N + (zuo) + NP_{Comp}$ (138)
    iii. Possessive and Existential Sentences
       (a) $T/S + V_P + NP_{Def}$ (139)
       (b) $T/S + V_{P/E} + NP_{Ind}$ (140)
       (c) $(T_{Loc}) + V_E + NP_{Ind}$ (141)
    iv. Sentences of Emotive and Mental State
       $T/S_{Pat} + V_E + NP$ (142)

II. Sentences with Action Verbs
   i. Sentences with Intransitive Verbs
      $T/S + V_A +$ (Complement)   (143)
  ii. Sentences with Transitive Verbs
      $T/S + V_A + NP +$ (Complement)   (144)
  iii. Sentences with Ditransitive Verbs
      "Give" Verbs   (145)
      (a) $T/S_{Source} + V_{Give} + NP_{Theme} + gei + NP_{Goal}$
      (b) $T/S_{Source} + V_{Give} + (gei) + NP_{Goal} + NP_{Theme}$
        "Take" Verbs (146)
          $T/S_{Goal} + V_{Take} + NP_{Source} + NP_{Theme}$
        "Rent" Verbs (147)
      (a) $T/S_{Goal} + V_{Rent} + NP_{Source} + NP_{Theme}$
      (b) $T/S + V + NP + gei + NP$

III. Passive Sentences
   i. *Bei* Sentences   (148)
      $T/S_{Pat} + bei + NP_{Agent} + (gei) + V_A +$ (Comp)
  ii. Sentences with Passive Verbs   (149)
      $T/S_{Pat} + shou + V \,(+$ Comp)
  iii. Sentences with Verbs in the Middle Voice
      $T/S_{Pat} + V_A \,(+$ Comp)

(136) ta hen gao.
       he very tall
       'He is very tall.'

(137) ta shi yi-ge xuesheng.
       he be one-CL student
       'He is a student.'

(138) ta jiao (zuo) Lao Wang.
       he call as   Lao Wang
       'He is called Lao Wang.'

(139) ta you nei-ben shu.
       he have that-CL book
       'He has the book.'

(140) ta you yi-ge didi.
       he have that-CL younger:brother
       'He has a younger brother.'

(141) shan-ding-shang you   yi-zuo miao.
       hill-top-LOC   EXIST one-CL temple
       'There is a temple on top of the hill.'

(142) Zhongguoren hen xihuan huar.
       Chinese   very like   flower
       'Chinese like flowers very much.'

(143) ta ku-le   san-ge zhongtou
       he cry-ASP three-CL hour
       'He cried for three hours.'

(144) ta xiu-hao-le   chezi le.
       he repair-finish-ASP car   PART
       'He has finished repairing the car.'

(145) a. ta song yi-ben shu gei wo.
          he give one-CL book to me
          'He gave a book to me.'
       b. ta song (gei) wo yi-ben shu.
          he give (to) me one-CL book
          'He gave me a book.'

(146) ta tou-le   wo wu-kuai   qian.
       he steal-ASP me five-dollar money
       'He stole five dollars from me.'

(147) a. ta zu–le   wo yi–jian fang.
         he rent–ASP me one–CL room
   (i) 'He rented me a room (as a landlord).'
  (ii) 'He rented me a room (as a tenant).'
      b. ta zu gei wo yi–jian fang.
         he rent to me one–CL room
         'Same as (ai).'

(148) Zhang San bei ren   da–si le.
      Zhang San BEI person hit–die PART
      'Zhang San was killed by someone.'

(149) ta daochu   shou   piping.
      he everywhere RECEIVE criticize
      'He was criticized everywhere.'

(150) nei–ben shu chuban le.
      that–CL book publish PART
      'The book has been published.'

CHAPTER FOUR
Sentences with Local Secondary Topics

1 Introductory

In this and the following two chapters we will be concerned with simple sentences that contain two or more topics. This chapter will deal with two constructions, namely, the so-called "double nominative" construction and sentences with non-sentence-initial preverbal temporals and locatives as secondary topics. What they have in common is that they both contain a secondary topic that shows no sign in the surface of having been moved. For lack of a better term, we will simply call them "local secondary topics". As a result of this, even though these two constructions are both subject to two analyses, as shown by (1) and (2), this structural ambiguity has escaped the notice of many Chinese linguists.[1,2]

(1) a. <u>ta</u>　<u>baba</u>　si　le.
　　　Topic Subject
　　　he　father　die PART
　　　'Speaking of him, (his) father died.'

　　b. <u>ta</u>　<u>baba</u>　si　le.
　　　Topic$_1$ Topic$_2$
　　　he　father　　die PART

---

[1]Sentence (1) is actually three-way ambiguous. In addition to the two interpretations given in (1a) and (1b), it may also be analyzed as (i).
(i) <u>ta(-de) baba</u>　si le.
　　Topic/　Subject
　　he-POSS father die PART
　　'His father died.'
In such an analysis, ta(-de) baba 'his father' is an NP in which the possessive marker -de under certain conditions can be deleted.

[2]Japanese, with its distinction between the topic marker wa and the subject marker ga, can reveal the difference much more clearly. Compare (ia) with (ib).
(i) a. zou　　wa hana　ga nagai.
　　　elephant　TM trunk　SM long
　　　'Speaking of the elephant, (its) trunk is long.'
　　b. zou　　wa hana　wa nagai.
　　　elephant　TM trunk　TM long
　　　'Speaking of the elephant, as for (its) trunk (it) is long.'
The difference between (2a) and (2b) can also find its parallel in Japanese in the distinction between ni/de and ni/de-wa.

'Speaking of him, as for his father (he) died.'³

(2) a. <u>ta</u>   zuotian   lai le.
   Topic/Subject
   he   yesterday come PART
   'He came yesterday.'

   b. <u>ta</u>   <u>zuotian</u> lai le.
   Topic₁ Topic₂
   he yesterday come PART
   'Speaking of him, yesterday (he) came.'

In the (a) analyses, both constructions will be considered as a simple single–topic sentence. They differ in that (2a) contains an optional adverbial modifier while (1a) does not. On the other hand, while in (1a) topic and subject are played by the possessor NP and the possessed NP respectively, in (2a) both roles are played by the same NP. In the (b) analyses, both constructions contain two topics. In (1b) the secondary topic is usually the subject of the clause. In (2b), it is the non–sentence–initial preverbal temporal that plays the role of the secondary topic.

It seems that in both analyses, the second element, be it a part of the predicate or a topic, does not change its position in the surface. This lack of change, however, is only apparent. We will argue later on that the element in the (b) analysis has been changed through a process called "secondary topicalization".

We will take up each construction in detail in the following. We will discuss the characteristics of each construction in general and then focus on the constructions in their (b) functions in the end.

2 The So–called "Double Nominative" Construction
2.1 Previous Analyses of the Construction

Of those linguists who have dealt with this construction in some length in the past, the following three, namely, Chao (1968), Tang (1972, 1977) and Teng (1974), are the most representative. Roughly speaking, Chao's analysis represents the American Structuralist

---

³Since English in general does not allow a sentence to have more than one topic, to translate a multiple–topic sentence in Chinese into English is practically impossible. Many of our translations in order to reflect the topical structure of the original Chinese sentences may often sound very unnatural.

approach, while Tang's analysis is done in the framework of the case grammar and Teng's in the spirit of the generative-transformational grammar according to the Aspects model. Because of space limitation only Teng's analysis will be critically reviewed in the following. Interested readers please refer to Tsao (1979, 1980) for criticism of the first two approaches to the construction.

Teng (1974) makes several claims concerning the double nominative construction in Chinese. Let us examine some of his important claims one by one.

1. Teng argues that predicates can consist of an entire sentence; i.e., VP can be rewritten as S. Thus, a sentence containing a double nominative structure such as (3) will have an underlying structure such as (4) in his analysis.

(3) ta duzi e.
he stomach hungry
'(Literally), he (topic), (his) stomach is hungry.'
'He is hungry.'

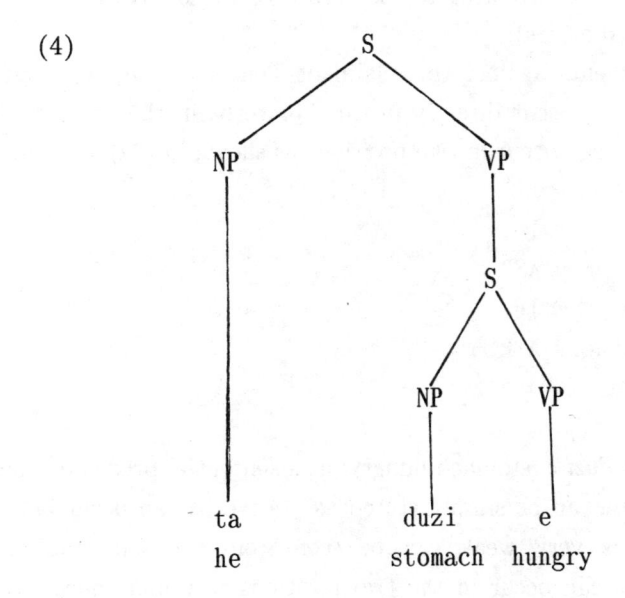

(4)
```
              S
             / \
           NP   VP
           |    |
           |    S
           |   / \
           |  NP  VP
           |  |   |
           ta duzi e
           he stomach hungry
```

The same approach is posited by Wang (1956) and Chao (1968). My general comment about this approach is that it fails to distinguish between topic and subject. The discourse nature of the first nominative can be brought out very clearly if (3) is followed by a possible discourse continuation as in (5):

(5) ta duzi   e,   you jao—bu—dao   dongxi chi, suo—yi
    he stomach hungry also couldn't—find things eat   so
    tang zai chuang—shang shui—jiao.
    lie in bed—LOC   sleep
    'Speaking of him, (his) stomach (was) hungry, (and) (he) couldn't
    find anything to eat, so (he) lay in bed sleeping.'

If we define topic as theme, as it is usually understood, (for a fuller discussion of the criteria for establishing topic in Chinese, see Chapters 2 and 3), then the topic of these sentences is *ta* 'he' because it is the thing that each of the sentences is about. The subject of the first sentence is *duzi* 'stomach' and those of the second and the third, *ta* 'he', which are deleted through a process termed previously as Topic—NP deletion. Such an analysis not only agrees well with the general understanding that topic is what a sentence (or sentences) is (or are) about; it also accords well with the general agreement that subject, as a grammatical term, is always selectionally related to the verb (See E. L. Keenan, 1974, 1976a; Li and Thompson, 1976 for comments).

There are more specific arguments against this claim of Teng's. Teng (op. cit.) argues that Chinese adverbs in general occur directly in front of verbs in the surface and yet, in double nominative sentences, they occur in two positions as shown in (6a) and (6b):

(6) a. ta duzi   you   e   le.
        he stomach again hungry ASP
    b. ta you   duzi e   le.
        he again stomach hungry ASP
        'He is hungry again.'

He then points out that if we regard *duzi e* 'stomach hungry' as a sentential predicate, then the rule of adverb—placing in Chinese can be simply stated as: Adverbs can occur before predicates. That this argument is very weak can be seen from the following two observations: First, not all adverbs can occur in the two positions just mentioned even with the same sentence. Thus, the most common adverb of degree *hen* 'very' can occur only in one position:

(7) a. ta duzi hen e.
   he stomach very hungry
   'He is very hungry.'
   b. *ta hen duzi e.

Since no semantic incompatability is involved in (7), the fact that it is ungrammatical indicates that adverbs are far from a homogeneous class, and that the rule of adverb–placement cannot be simply stated (see Tsao, 1976 and Section 3 of this Chapter for discussion).

More seriously, not all the double nominative constructions exhibit these two possibilities with regard to the position of some adverbs such as *you* 'again' and *ye* 'also', as pointed out by T. C. Tang and Marie–Claude Paris cited by Li and Thompson (1976:487, footnote 9). Thus, in a sentence containing a double nominative construction like (8), only one position is allowed for *you* 'again.'

(8) a. zhe–ke shu, yezi you huang le.
   this–Class tree leaves again yellow ASP
   'This tree (topic), (its) leaves have turned yellow again.'
   b. *zhe–ke shu, you yezi huang le.
   this–Class tree again leaves yellow ASP

Thus, we have no strong evidence to show that what is posited by Teng as the 'sentential predicate' is actually a constituent dominated by a VP node.

2. Teng also claims that since in (6) the adverb you 'again' can occur in two positions while in (9) and (10) it cannot occur between two nominatives, (9) and (10) should not be analyzed as containing a double nominative construction.

(9) *ta you shou teng le.
   he again hand hurt ASP
   'His hand hurts again.'

(10) *ta ye duzi yuan.
   he also belly round
   'His belly is also round!'

I have already pointed out that whether *you* or *ye* can be placed at two different positions or not is not a valid test in distinghishing double nominative constructions from non–double–nominative constructions. From this observation alone I am convinced that Teng is wrong again in this claim. My conviction, however, is further strengthened by the following two examples:

(11) ta shou teng de   hen, zhen   xiang qu kan yisheng.
      he hand hurt PART very really want go see doctor
      'He (topic), (his) hand hurt badly;
      (he) really wanted to see a doctor.'

(12) ta duzi   hen yuan, tui you duan, zhen   nan–kan.
      he stomach very round legs also short really ugly
      'He (topic), (his) stomach is very round, and (his) legs are short;
      (he) is really ugly.'

(11) and (12) demonstrate clearly that given proper context, *shou* 'hand' in *shou teng* 'hand hurt' and *duzi* 'stomach' in *duzi yuan* 'stomach round' can occur as the second nominative in a double nominative construction.

3. Teng claims that (1) will be derived from an underlying structure like (4). (13) below also has the same underlying structure, the possessive marker *–de* being transformationally derived by a late rule called the 'pseudogenitive.'

(13) ta–de   duzi   e.
      he–POSS stomach hungry
      'His stomach is hungry.'

(14), on ther hand, will have (15) as its underlying structure.

(14) ta–de   duzi   hen yuan.
      he–POSS stomach very round
      'His stomach is round.'

(15)
```
           S
          / \
        NP   VP
        /\   /\
       /  \ /  \
   ta-de duzi hen yuan
   his  stomach very round
```

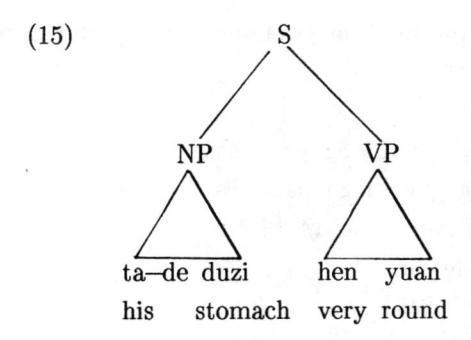

He gives the following evidence. First, he points out that a possessive sentence behaves differently from a pseudo—possessive sentence in conjunction reduction, as shown by (16) and (17) respectively.

(16) a. ta jie—le   Zhang San—de shu; wo jie—le   Li Si—de.
        he borrow—ASP Zhang San's book I borrow—ASP Li Si's
        'He borrowed Zhang San's book; I borrowed Li Si's.'
     b. *ta jie—le Zhang San—de shu; wo jie—le Li Si.

(17) a. ta xue—le   yi—nian—de Zhongwen; wo xue—le   liang—nian.
        he study—ASP one—year's Chinese   I study—ASP two—years
        'He studied Chinese for one year; I studied for two years.'
     b. *ta xue—le yi—nian—de Zhongwen; wo xue—le liang—nian—de.

This shows, according to Teng, that conjunction reduction follows the specification of the real possessive, but precedes the introduction of pseudo— possessive marker. The argument here is quite straightforward and convincing. However, it becomes very doubtful when Teng goes on to argue that this difference provides syntactic evidence for distinguishing the real possessive $-de$ in (14) from the pseduo—possessive $-de$ in (13). After all, the real possessive construction in (16) and the pseudo—possessive construction in (17) are semantically different. For one thing, the possessor in the former case is an animate noun while that in the latter is an inanimate one. But in the case of (13) and (14), the possessor in both cases refers to the same entity and so does the possessed. So if there should be any syntactic difference between (13) and (14), it could not be due to any semantic difference regarding the relation between the two nominatives. However, suspending our semantic objection for a while, let's examine whether (13) and (14) do behave in parallel with (16) and (17) in conjunction reduction. Teng gives the following examples and grammatical judgment:

(18) a. Zhang San—de duzi   hen e;   Li Si ye   shi.
        Zhang San—POSS stomach very hungry Li Si also is
        'Zhang San's stomach is very hungry; so is Li Si.'
     b. *wo—de duzi   hen e;   ni—de ne?
        my   stomach very hungry your PART
        'I am hungry; are you?'
     c. Zhang San—de duzi   hen yuan; Li Si—de ye   shi;.
        Zhang San's stomach very round Li Si's also is
        'Zhang San's stomach is very round; so is Li Si's.'
     d. *Zhang San—de duzi   hen yuan; Li Si ye   shi.
        Zhang San's stomach very round Li Si also is
        'Zhang San's stomach is very round; so is Li Si.'
        (different meaning)

He goes on to explain that, at the stage of deleting identical elements, *de* in (a) is absent. This is supported by the ungrammaticality of (b), in which *de* appears. Since the genuine possessive marker is specified in the underlying structure, it must have been introduced by the stage of conjunction deletion and is not deletable, as indicated by the unacceptable (d).

This argument is extremely weak, as the grammaticality judgment on which the argument is based is far from firm. Speakers disagree with each other as to the grammaticality of the four sentences involved here.[4] That one should not base one's argument on such controversial sentences is self—evident. Besides, by positing (4) as the underlying structure of (3), Teng is ruling out the possibility that *ta—de duzi* 'his stomach' may become a topic when it is in construction with *e* 'hungry'. Actually, such a possibility does exist. Witness the following example:

---

[4]The thirty—one native speakers that I have asked gave the following judgments:
(18)   a. G:19   b. G:18   c. G:23   d. G:13
       U:12   U:13   U:8   U:18

As the results do not show any discenible pattern, I will not comment on them here. Suffice it to point out that even if we go by the rule of majority, most native speakers' grammaticality judgments in (b) still do not agree with Teng's.

(19) ta-de duzi yi e jiu teng, yiding you sheme maobing.
　　　his stomach once hungry then ache must have some trouble
　　　'(literally) His stomach (topic) as soon as (it) (is) hungry,
　　　(it) aches; (it) must have some trouble.'
　　　'As soon as his stomach is empty, it aches;
　　　there must be something wrong with it.'

Likewise, to posit an underlying structure such as (15) for (14) fails to account for sentences such as (12), in which the possessor is the topic instead of the whole possessive construction.

2.2 The Proposed Analysis of The Double Nominative Construction

　　By now an outline should be emerging from our previous discussion of the construction. We have presented arguments to show that the first nominative in the construction is actually a topic while the second is the subject of the particular sentence in which it occurs. Thus, a sentence like (20) will have an analysis like (21).

(20) ta taitai hen piaoliang.
　　　he wife very pretty
　　　'He (topic), (his) wife is very pretty.'

(21) <u>ta,　taitai　hen piaoliang</u>.
　　　TOPIC SUBJECT VP

That the first nominative is actually a topic can be clearly seen if a possible discourse continuation is added to it as in (22).

(22) ta taitai hen piaoliang ernu you cong-ming, zhenshi hao-fuqi.
　　　he wife very pretty children also clever really lucky
　　　'Speaking of him, (his) wife (is) very pretty; (his) children (are)
　　　also clever; (he) is really lucky.'

(22) is what I call a topic chain which consists of three clauses sharing the common primary topic *ta* 'he', for clearly it is what all the three clauses are about, while in the first clause *taitai* 'wife' is clearly the subject of *piaoliang* 'pretty' as is determined by the

selectional restriction. The same analysis can be applied to the second clause, in which the primary topic *ta* 'he' is deleted by a process we refer to as "TOPIC–NP DELETION", while *ernu* 'children' is the subject of the verb *cong–ming* 'clever'. In the third clause, *ta* 'he' serves the double function of topic and subject, but is here deleted by TOPIC–NP DELETION.

Up to this point, in all the examples we have presented, the second nominative in the construction under investigation is always the subject of its clause. There are, however, a number of counterexamples to this generalization. Examine the following sentences.

(23) zhe–ge nühai ya, <u>fuqin</u> bei jiche zhuang–si le.
 this–CL girl PART father BEI motorcycle hit–die PART
 'Speaking of the girl, (her) father was killed by a motorcycle.'

(24) Zhang Jiaoshou ya, <u>shu</u> chuban le, keshi bu chang–xiao.
 Zhang Professor PART book publish PART but not smoothly–sell
 'Speaking of Professor Zhang, (his) book has been published but (it) has not sold well.'

(25) Li Taitai ya, <u>erzi</u> shi qunian bei
 Li Mrs.   PART son SHI last:year BEI
 la–qu   dang   bing   de.
 drag–away serve:as soldier DE
 'Speaking of Mrs. Li, (her) son was drafted by force last year.'

(26) tamen jia, lian <u>wu–sui–de xiaohai</u> ya
 they home including five–year–old's child PART
 dou hui tan gangqin.
 all can play piano
 '(In) their home, even a five–year–old child can play the piano.'

(27) Zhang Taitai <u>nüer</u> bi <u>erzi</u> ya haiyao nenggan.
 Zhang Mrs.   daughter COMP son PART still competent
 'Speaking of Mrs. Zhang, (her) daughter is even more competent than (her) son.'

Each sentence from (23) to (25) involves a kind of passive construction with the possessed NP as the subject of the passive clause. Since we have already concluded in our previous discussion that within a clause the clause-initial subject in any construction in Chinese is at the same time a topic of a certain rank and that what is common to all types of passive constructions is that the patient NP has become a topic, it is only logical that we generalize our characterization of the second nominal in the double nominative construction to that of a topic. Furthermore, since the topic in question is preceded by another topic, which occurs sentence-initially, we will distinguish the two by referring to the first as the primary topic and the second one as the secondary topic.

That this generalization is correct is also affirmed by sentences (26) and (27), which involve a *lian ... dou/ye* construction and a comparative construction respectively. As we will present independent evidence in Chapter 6 to show that only a topic, primary or non-primary, can become the *lian* constituent or a compared constituent, our generalization just revised is in perfect agreement with the generalizations about the *lian ... dou/ye* construction and the comparative construction.

With this new generalization in mind, let us now proceed to examine the possible relation that the first nominative might bear with the second nominative in the construction.

Relationships that are most frequently found are: that of the possessor and the possessed, as in (28) and (29); that of whole and part, as in (30) and (31); and that of class and member, as in (32).

(28) zhe-ge ren, tounao jiandan, sizhi fada.
     this-CL person mind simple four-limbs well-developed
     'Speaking of this person, (his) mind is simple;
     (his) body well-developed.'

(29) Zhongguo, di da, wu buo, renkou duo.
     China land big resources comprehensive population great
     'Speaking of China, (its) land is big;
     (its) resources comprehensive; (its) population great.'

(30) ta-de san-ge haizi (a), yi-ge dang lüshi, yi-ge
     his three-CL children (PART) one-CL serve-as lawyer one-CL

hushi, haiyou yi-ge xue jianzhu.
nurse still one-CL study architecture
'Speaking of his three children, one works as a lawyer;
another is a nurse; (and) the third studies architecture.'

(31) sanshiliu ji   (a), zou   wei shang ji.
     thirty-six alternatives (PART) running-away is best alternative
     '(Of) the thirty-six alternatives (topic),
     running-away is the best.'

(25) yu   (a),   wei-yu xianzai zui gui.
     fish (PART) tuna   now   most expensive
     'Speaking of fish, tuna is now the most expensive.'

These types of the double nominative construction all have paraphrases with some sort of possessive construction. Compare the (a) and (b) sentences in the following examples:

(33) a. zhe-ge nühai yanjing hen da.
        this-CL girl eyes   very big
        'The girl (topic), (her) eyes are very big.'
     b. zhe-ge nühai-de yanjing hen da.
        this-CL girl's eyes   very big
        'The girl's eyes are very big.'

(34) a. wu-ge   pingguo, liang-ge huai-le.
        five-CL apples   two-CL spoil-ASP
        '(Of) the five apples (topic), two are spoiled.'
     b. ?wu-ge pingguo litou-de   liang-ge huai-le.
        five-CL apples among-POSS two-CL   spoil-ASP
        'Two of the five apples are spoiled.'

(35) a. pengyou, jiu-de   hao.
        friends old-Rel. Mar. good
        '(Of) friends (topic), old (ones) are good.'

b. pengyou dangzhong-de jiu-de hao.
   friends among-POSS old-Rel. Mar. good
   'The old friends of all friends are good.'

There are two important differences between (a) and (b) sentences in each pair. First, the truth value of each sentence may be different. (33a) is either about *zhe-ge nühai* 'the girl', the only and primary topic, or about *zhe-ge nühai* 'the girl' and *(ta-de) yanjing* 'her eyes' i.e., with *zhe-ge nühai* 'the girl' as the primary topic and *yanjing* 'eyes' as the secondary topic. (33b), on the other hand, is unambiguous since it can only be about *zhe-ge nühai-de yanjing* 'the girl's eyes'. This difference can be clearly seen when other comment clauses are added, as shown in (36a and b) and (37) for (33a) and (33b) respectively.

(36) a. zhe-ge nühai ya, yanjing hen da, hen piaoliang.
        this-CL girl PART eye very big very beautiful
        'Speaking of the girl, (her) eyes are large and
        (she) is beautiful.'
     b. zhe-ge nühai, yanjing ya hen da, hen
        this-CL girl eye PART very big very
        piaoliang, erduo ya que hen
        beautiful ears PART on:the:contrary very
        xiao, hen nankan.
        small very ugly
        'Speaking of the girl, (her) eyes are large and beautiful but
        her ears are small and ugly.'

(37) zhe-ge nühai-de yanjing ya hen da, hen piaoliang.
     this-CL girl-POSS eye PART very big very beautiful
     'The girl's eyes are large and beautiful.'

Thus, in (36a) we have a topic chain of one topic, i.e. *zhe-ge nühai* 'the girl' with *yanjing hen da* 'eyes are large' as the first comment clause, which is itself a topic-comment structure. In (36b) we have a topic chain of four comment clauses with the first two forming a minor topic chain and the latter two forming another minor topic chain. The first minor topic chain has *yanjing* 'eyes' as its common topic and the second has *erduo* 'ears'. (37), however, is unambiguous. It can only be about *zhe-ge nühai-de yanjing* 'the girl's eyes'.

Second, if a pause particle is to be inserted, then it can be inserted at two different places for each (a) sentence from (33) to (35), as demonstrated in (36a and b) for (33a). In the (b) sentence (33) through (35), there is only one possibility with regard to the insertion of the pause particles, i.e. after the whole possessive phrase, as demonstrated in (37). Since a pause is added at a major break of a sentence, the fact that (a) and (b) sentences in each pair accept pause particles at different places indicates clearly that speakers perceive them differently. More importantly, the perceived difference coincides with the topical difference as we have described it.

The topical difference between (a) and (b) sentences from (33) to (35) constitutes an insurmountable problem for linguists who try to derive one construction from the other. But it may be taken care of by the most recent Government and Binding Theory with its Logical Form component, which, in addition to the Base, has access to the surface structure as well. This topic, however, because of its far-reaching theoretical implication, deserves at least a separate paper-length study and will, therefore, not be discussed in the present volume.

Another less frequently found relationship is that of relevance, as in (38) and (39).[5]

(38) zhe-jian shi (a), wo-de jingyan tai duo le.
this-CL matter (PART) my experience too much ASP
'(With regard to) this matter (topic), my experience is very rich;
i.e., with regard to this matter I have had a great deal of experience.'

(39) liuxue-de shiqing (a), zhengfu zao
studying-abroad-POSS matter (PART) government long-ago
guiding-le banfa.
stipulate-ASP regulation (of procedure)
'(With regard to) the matter of studying abroad (topic),
the government made regulations of procedure long ago.'

---

[5]Actually to look at the construction from a slightly different viewpoint, we can characterize the first nominal in (38) and (39) as delimiting the scope within which the following comment holds true. For more discussion of this "scope-delimiting" function of the first nominal see Section 3.1.1. and Note 14.

Thus in (38) the topic can be optionally preceded by *guanyu, zhiyu,* or *duiyu* 'about, concerning, with regard to, with reference to, etc.' and the sentence can also be paraphrased as (40):

(40)   wo   duiyu   zhe—jian   shi   de   jingyan   tai duo   le
       I   about   this—CL   matter   POSS   experience   too much PART
       'My experience about this matter is very rich.'

As the type of sentences exemplified by (38) and (39) is usually not regarded as "the double nominative construction," we will therefore not go into it here. Suffice it to point out that they present an even greater difficulty for the derivational theory of topic. A subtype of this type of topic requires special mention. This subtype is exemplified by (41) and (42):

(41)   ju   (a),   Taipei zui   hau.
       living   (PART)   Taipei most   good
       'Living (topic), Taipei is best.'

(42)   chi   (a),   zizhucan   zui   pianyi.
       eating   (PART)   buffet   most   inexpensive
       'Eating (topic), buffet is the most inexpensive.'

(41) and (42) can be paraphrased as (43) and (44) respectively.

(43)   zhu—de   difang   (a),   Taipei zui   hao.
       live—Rel   place   (PART)   Taipei most   good
       '(Of all) places to live (topic), Taipei is the best.'

(44)   chi—de   fangshi   (a),   zizhucan   zui   pianyi.'
       eat—Rel   ways   (PART)   buffet   most   inexpensive
       '(Of all) ways to eat (topic), buffet is the most inexpensive.'

This subtype is different from type 3 in that the class term involved (i.e., *difang* 'place' and *fangshi* 'way') is not even mentioned.

2.3 Productive Double Nominative Constructions Versus Verbal Compounds

2.3.1 Teng's View

In a later section of Teng's paper (op. cit.), he takes up the problem of what he calls 'sentence as predicate versus idioms.' I have already given my arguments against the postulation of the sentential predicate if predicate is used in its syntactic sense as Wang (1956), Chao (1968) and Teng are using it.

Teng cites Fraser (1970) in defining an idiom as 'a constituent or series of constituents for which the semantic interpretation is not a compositional function of the formatives of which it is composed.' He thus classifies all the double nominative expressions into two groups as follows (Teng, 1974: 463):

Group A: danzi xiao 'timid' (lit. 'guts [sic] small'), erduo ruan 'gullible' ('ears soft'), xin du 'cruel' ('heart poisonous'), yan hong 'jealous' ('eyes red'), lianpi hou 'brazen-faced' ('face-skin thick')

Group B: duzi e 'hungry' ('stomach hungry'), piqi huai 'bad-tempreed' ('temper bad'), tou teng 'headache' ('head painful'), jixing hao 'good memory' ('memory good'), yao suan 'backache' ('waist sore')

Thus, in his analysis, items in Group A, when not taken in their literal sense, are idioms and those in Group B are sentential predicates. In addition to pointing out that sentential predicates rarely occur lexicalized, Teng gives the following semantic characterization of the two groups (op. cit.: 463):

> Idioms generally characterize personality and temperament by means of physical description in the literal sense. A sentence predicate is characterized by the semantic property of referring to temperament and physical condition, and very rarely physical description...

Nothing beyond this vague semantic characterization of the two groups is given and no reliable syntactic test is provided for distinguishing between them.

2.3.2 The Proposed Analysis

I have already pointed out that what have been regarded by Teng as 'sentence predicates' are not a homogeneous group with regard to their relative position in relation to such adverbs as *you* 'again' and *ye* 'also' as shown in (8). I would, therefore, propose that all the double nominative expressions be reanalyzed as falling into three groups on the basis of their syntactic behavior with regard to the placement of such adverbs as *you* and *ye*.

Group A: Productive Doublt Nominative Expressions

Syntactic characteristic: $Nom_1 + Nom_2 + \begin{Bmatrix} ye \\ you \end{Bmatrix} + V$

Examples:

(45) a. zhe—ke shu yezi ye hen da.
       this—CL tree leaves also very big
       'This tree (topic), (its) leaves are also very big.'
   b. *zhe—ke shu ye yezi hen da.

(46) a. ta duzi ye yuan de hen.
       he stomach also round PART very
       'He (topic), (his) stomach is also very round.'
   b. *ta ye duzi yuan de hen.

Group B. Semi—compounds[6]

Syntactic characteristic: either

$Nom_1 + Nom_2 + \begin{Bmatrix} ye \\ you \end{Bmatrix} + V$

or

$Nom_1 + \begin{Bmatrix} ye \\ you \end{Bmatrix} + Nom_2 + V$

Examples: <u>lianpi hou</u> 'brazen—faced' (lit. 'face—skin thick'), <u>danzi xiao</u> 'timid' (lit. 'gall—bladder small'),[7] <u>erduo ruan</u> 'gullible' (lit. 'ears soft'), <u>duzi da</u> 'pregnant' (lit. 'belly

---

[6]As will be made clear, Group B is on its way to becoming Group C. Since this is the group undergoing change, the membership in the class may differ slightly from speaker to speaker. This fact, however, is expected and does not invalidate the test.

[7]In general, it is true that cross—linguistic translation is a good place to start in finding out whether a certain expression is an idiom or not. That is, if a certain expression in Language A has a lexical counterpart in Language B, then it is an indication that the expression is an idiom. The test, however, is not always reliable. Take the expression *danzi xiao* 'gall—bladder small' for instance. It has a lexical counterpart in English, namely, 'timid'. However, it has not quite lost its literal meaning in Chinese. To the Chinese mind, a timid person may actually have a smaller gall—bladder.

big'), <u>duzi e</u> 'hungry' (lit. 'stomach hungry,') <u>piqi huai</u> 'temper bad,' <u>tou teng</u>₁ 'head ache,' <u>jixing hao</u> 'memory good'

(47) a. ta duzi you e le.
       he stomach again hungry PART
       'He (topic), (his) stomach is hungry.'
    b. ta you duzi e le.

(48) a. ta danzi ye xiao.
       he gall–bladder also small
       'He (topic), (his) gall–bladder is also small;
       i.e., he is also timid.'
    b. ta ye danzi xiao.

Group C: Frozen Compounds

Syntactic characteristic: $Nom_1 + \begin{Bmatrix} ye \\ you \end{Bmatrix} + Nom_2 + V$

Examples: <u>yan hong</u> 'jealous' (lit. 'eyes red'), <u>xin du</u> 'cruel' (lit. 'heart poisonous'), <u>dan xiao</u> 'timid' (lit. 'gall–bladder small'), <u>tou teng</u>₂ 'be troubled by' (lit. 'head ache'), <u>xing ji</u> 'impatient' (lit. 'temperament quick')

(49) a. ta ye yan hong.
       he also jealous
       'He is also jealous.'
    b. *ta yan ye hong.

(50) a. ta ye hen dan xiao.
       he also very timid
       'He is also very timid.'
    b. *ta dan ye hen xiao.

Several points need clarification with regard to this analysis.
First, some of the semi–compounds in Group B can be interpreted literally. When

they are so interpreted they should be regarded as productive double nominative expressions. *Erduo ruan* 'gullible' or 'ears soft' and *duzi da* 'pregnant' or 'belly big' are good examples.

Second, the frozen compounds in Group C are 'frozen' in two senses. First, all the elements in a frozen compound are closely united and cannot be separated. Second, they are modern relics of classical Chinese, as evidenced by their mono–syllabic characteristic. Thus, instead of *dan* 'gall–bladder,' *danzi* is used in modern Chinese and the modern counterpart of *yan* 'eye' is *yanjing*. For this reason, *yan hong* in Group C can only be interpreted as 'jealous' while its modern counterpart *yanjing hong* can only have a literal interpretation and is thus a productive double nominative expression.

Some readers have probably noticed that *tou teng* is listed under both Group B and Group C. This is justified not only because there is a semantic change involved, but also because they behave differently with respect to the placement of adverbs *you* and *ye*. *Tou teng$_1$* 'head ache' patterns with Group B and *tou teng$_2$* 'be troubled by' behaves like a frozen compound. Notice also that there is another interesting change of syntactic property. *Teng* 'ache' is an intransitive verb but when it joins *tou* 'head' to form a compound, the new compound is transitive. Compare (51) and (52).

(51) wo <u>tou teng</u> de bu–de–liao.
     I head ache PART extremely
    '(Lit.) I (topic), (my) head aches extremely.'
    'I have a severe headache.'

(52) ta zheng zai <u>tou teng</u>   zhe–jian shi.
     he right ASP be–troubled–by this–CL matter
    'He is being buried by this matter right now;
    or, this matter is giving him a big headache right now.'

Third, unlike *you* 'again' and *ye* 'also,' *hen* 'very,' the most frequently found adverb of degree in Chinese, can only precede lexicalized verbs (including adjectives) on the surface.[8] Examine the following:

---

[8]T. C. Tang (personal communication) has pointed out to me that *hen* 'very' is a degree adverb while *you* 'again' and *ye* 'also' are conjunctive adverbs and that conjunctive adverbs typically behave differently from other types of adverbs.
    The difference between the two types, as far as we can determine, is that *hen* 'very' should be placed immediately before the verb it modifies while *you* and *ye* are placed between the topic component and the comment component. We will have more to say about the position of *you* and *ye* in Section 3 of this chapter.

(53) a. zhe—ke shu yezi hen da.   (Group A)
       this—CL tree leaves very big
       'This tree (topic), (its) leaves are very big.'
   b. *zhe—ke shu hen yezi da.

(54) a. ta duzi hen e.   (Group B)
       he stomach very hungry
       'He (topic), (his) stomach is very empty.'
   b. *ta hen duzi e.

(55) a. ta hen xingji.   (Group C)
       he very impatient
       'He is very impatient.'
   b. *ta xing hen ji.

This then is one more reliable way of separating frozen compounds from the other two groups. This is also an additional counter-argument against Teng's analysis that places what he calls 'sentence predicates' under a VP node, as we witness that in (54) *hen* 'very' cannot be placed before *duzi e* 'stomach hungry.'

Fourth, by comparing these three groups, it is apparent that Group B is in more than one way the middle stage between Groups A and C. As linguists have just begun to study idioms and the process of idiomatization systematically (see Weinreich, 1969; Fraser, 1970; Chafe, 1970), we will not be able to draw much from previous literature. However, as far as I can determine, two important factors seem to be involved; namely, frequency of use and possibility of syntactic reanalysis. With regard to the first factor, Chao makes the following remark (1968: 370):

> Whether an S—P construction [subject—predicate construction in Chao's analysis, F.T.] is a compound often depends upon frequency of occurrence. Thus *menling bu xiang* 'The doorbell does not ring.' is normally not a compound, and a modal adverb such as *ye* 'also' and *you* 'again' would come between the subject *menling* and the verbal expression *bu xiang*. But when the S—P form is heard often enough, then it begins to acquire the status of a compound and so one hears: *women ye menling bu xiang le*. '(As for) us, the doorbell doesn't ring, either.' (I have changed Chao's Romanization in order to be consistent with the system used in this study.)

John Lyons has gone a step further and offered a possible psychological explanation. He states (1977: 536):

> As soon as any regularly constructed expression is employed on some particular occasion of utterance, it is available for use again by the same person or by others as a ready-made unit which can be incorporated in further utterances; and the more frequently it is used, the more likely it is to solidify as a fixed expression, which native speakers will presumably store in memory, rather than construct afresh on each occasion.

Impressionistic as they are, these remarks do have some intuitive appeal. As a detailed study of the process is certainly beyond the scope of the present study, I will only give a comparison to show how frequency of occurrence can play a role here. Previously, we have classified *duzi yuan* 'stomach round' as a part of a productive double nominative expression and *duzi e* 'belly hungry' as a semi-compound. Even though we do not yet have any solid statistical data, most people that we have asked agree that *duzi e* 'stomach hungry' enjoys a higher frequency of occurrence than *duzi yuan* 'stomach round.' Therefore, other things being equal, the former is more likely to become a compound than the latter.

However, frequency alone cannot explain why some syntactic structures become compounds more easily than others. Syntactic reanalysis can also play an important role here. In other words, what we are claiming here is that at a certain stage of idiomatization and historical change, syntactic structures undergoing change to become compounds must be juxtaposed and must be subject to two possible grammatical analyses which both lead to the same semantic interpretation (for a discussion of how syntactic reanlysis may be related to language change, see Parker, 1976). Take the structure under discussion for instance. A construction such as (56) can be analyzed in two different ways, as in (57) and (58):

(56)   wo duzi   teng.
       I stomach ache
(57)   wo   duzi   teng.
       TOPIC SUBJECT V
(58)   wo   duzi-teng.
       TOPIC and SUB. VERB-COMPOUND

Notice that (57) is the analysis we have posited for Group A productive double nominative expressions and (58) for Group C frozen compounds. Both structures can, of course, lead to the same interpretation in Chinese. Notice also that while (57) is a frequently found Chinese structure type, (58) looks more like the S–V structure type in English. This observation confirms a point that I have argued elsewhere (Tsao, 1978, 1979, 1980); i.e., in Chinese topic and subject are essentially two grammatical notions, while in English both roles are played by what is understood as 'subject' in most cases.

At this stage, what we have just proposed may sound like mere speculation; however, we feel that these are areas that promise great advances in our understanding of idiomatization and syntactic change.

2.3.3 The further Development of Some Idiomatized Verbal Compounds

Actually in the current usage of Mandarin Chinese there are several hundred verbal compounds that were originally derived from the productive double nominative construction. In terms of structure, they fall roughly into three groups. What we have discussed as frozen compounds fall into Group A. Some examples from Groups B and C are given below:

Group B: Nominative (+Nominative) + V (+Adjunct)
a. kou   chi   qingxi
    mouth teeth clear
    'speak clearly'
b. shou nao   bing yong
    hand brain both use
    'using both hands and head'
c. kou   ruo   xuan–he
    mouth like water–fall
    'eloquent'
d. ren   di   sheng–shu
    people place unfamiliar
    'not familiar with either the land or its people'
e. ban   shen bu   sui
    half body not moveable
    'paraplegic'

f. qian-tu si   jin
    future like silk
    'with a bright future'
g. xin-di shan-liang
    heart kind
    'kind-hearted'
h. jing   li   chong-pei
    strength vigor abundant
    'abundant in strength and vigor'
i. shen qing ru   yan
    body light as swallow
    'with a body as light as a swallow'
j. lei   xia ru   yu
    tears fall like rain
    'with tears falling like rain; or, cry profusely'

Group C: Nominative + V + Nominative + V[9]

a. kou   shi xin   fei
    mouth yes heart no
    'insincere'
b. shan   ming shui xiu
    mountain clear water beautiful
    'scenic'
c. mian hong er chi
    face red ear red
    'with both face and ears red with heat or anger'
d. di   guang ren   xi
    land big   population scarce
    'thinly populated'

---

[9]To the extent that our analysis of this type of the frozen verbal compounds is correct, it is an additional strong confirmation of our contention that a topic often extends its domain over several clauses to form a topic chain. It is also an indication that those who have restricted their analyses of the double nominative construction to a single clause have missed a very important fact about the Chinese language.

    e. tou hun nao zhang
       head dizzy brain swollen
       'muddle-headed, confused'
    f. ren jie   di ling
       people outstanding land wonderful
       'being a breeding ground of outstanding people'
    g. wai yuan nei fang
       outside round inside square
       'tactful in his relation with others, but having principles within self'
    h. xin guang ti   pan
       heart broad body fat
       'with a cheerful spirit and a fat body'
    i. chuang ming ji   jing
       window clear desk clean
       '(of a room, etc.) very clean'
    j. er cong mu ming
       ear sharp eye keen
       'clever, smart'

That these are really frozen compounds can be seen by applying the YOU—YE test, as shown in (59) and (60).

    (59) a. ta ye kou-chi-qing-xi.
          he also speak clearly
          'He speaks clearly, too.'
       b. ?ta kou-chi ye qingxi.
       c. *ta kou ye chi-qingxi.

    (60) a. ta ye kou-shi-xin-fei.
          he also insincere
          'He, too, is insincere.'
       b. *ta kou ye shi, xin ye fei.
       c. *ta ye kou-shi, ye xin-fei.

These verbal compounds are mostly state verbs, i.e., predicative adjectives. Many of them, however, have developed further to become attributive adjectives as well, as shown in (61) and (62):

(61) zhe—ge xiao cheng shi—ge shan—ming—shui—xiu—de di—fang.
     this—CL small town is—CL scenic   place
     'This small town is a scenic place.'

(62) shao gen nei—zhong kou—shi—xin—fei—de ren   lai—wang.
     don't with that—kind insincere   people associate
     'Don't associate yourself with that kind of insincere people.'

However, since in Chinese the same *−de* is used as an adjective suffix as well as an adverbial suffix, for an adjective to become an adverb is just one step removed. Therefore, it is small wonder that some of the verbal compounds have also acquired adverbial usage as shown in (63) and (64):

(63) women dan—da—xin—xi—de   shi—guo—le   San—xia.
     we   boldly—but—carefully sail—past—ASP Three Gorges
     'We sailed past the Three Gorges of the Yangtsz River boldly but carefully.'

(64) ta shen—qing—ru—yan—de tiao—qi—lai.
     he agilely   jump—up
     'He jumped up agilely.'

So the path of development can be clearly depicted as (65):

(65) productive double nominative constructions → frozen verbal compounds
     (predicative adjectives) → attributive adjectives—→adverbs

2.4 The Origin Of The Double Nominative Construction

It seems that the construction has been in the language since the time of Archaic Chinese. Witness the following examples:

146

    (66) shi-yi   sheng-ren wei   er bu shi, gong cheng   er bu
           therefore sages   do-work but not store task accomplish but not
           ju.   (Laozi: Dao-de Jing, Chapter 74)
           dwell-on
           'Therefore, the sage does his work without setting any store by it,
           accomplishes his task without dwelling on it.'[10]

    (67) zhi wo zhe   wei wo xin   you.   (The Book of Songs, "Shu-li")
           know me person say I   heart worried
           'Those who knew me said that I was worried.'

    (68) Zou Ji xiu   ba   chi you-yu, shen-ti yi-li.(Zhan-guo-ce,
           "Qi-ce")
           Zou Ji height eight feet and more body   well-shaped
           'Zou Ji (his) height (was) more than eight feet tall,
           and (his) body (was) well-shaped.'

Therefore, historically it is almost impossible to determine when the construction first came into the language, but it is still interesting to speculate on the circumstances that gave rise to it.

In our discussion we will assume that the double nominative construction was originally derived from the non-double-nominative-construction and at the time of its introduction, it must be much more restricted in its use.[11] Such assumptions are made on the ground that the latter construction is far more prevalent than the former universally. We'll also follow the same principle that we set up in our previous discuission of the historical derivation of frozen verbal compounds from productive double nominative constructions, i.e., at a certain stage of historical change, the syntactic structures undergoing change must be juxtaposed and must be subject to two possible grammatical analyses which lead to more or less the same semantic interpretation. Given the assumptions and the principle, we can now go about reconstructing the origin of the

---

    [10]This translation is taken from J.H. Wus *Laotsu's TAO and its Virtue*, Saint John University Press, 1961.

    [11]This should not be taken to imply that topic is derived from subject. As we see it, it is in fact the opposite that actually happened.

construction. Our hypothesis is that the double nominative construction was originally derived from a possessive construction as in (69a), and that the relation betweent the first two nominatives was restricted to that of the inalienable possession.

(69) a. wo—de   wei   tong.
         I—POSS. stomach ache
         'My stomach aches.'

In time, with the possessive marker deleted, this type of sentences can be subject to two structural analyses which had the same interpretation as shown in (69b) and (69c).

(69) b. wo (—de)   wei   tong.[12]
         I—(POSS)   stomach ache
         'My stomach ache.'
     c. wo   wei   tong.
         I (topic) stomach ache
         '(Literally) I (topic), my stomach aches.'
         'I have a stomach ache.'

Although English never gave rise to such a construction, it also occasionally exhibits alternative expressions involving a person as a whole and a part of the person. Compare the (a) and (b) sentences of the following examples:

(70) a. The scene touched her.
     b. The scene touched her heart.

(71) a. He is a little touched.
     b. He is a little touched in his head.

Thus, the (a) and (b) sentences in the above examples are usually regarded as synonymous, but in either case, the (a) sentence is predicated of the person as a whole while the (b)

---

[12]As we don't know the exact forms that were used to indicate the possessive relation in pre—historic Chinese, these modern examples are given just to indicate the relationship between the first two nominatives.

sentences are about a part of the person.

A recent paper by Huang (1980) entitled "On Substance Continuum in Chinese Concept of a Person —An Essay in Language and Metaphysics," discusses the Chinese concept of a person. He states:

> Broadly speaking, a rough consensus among the Pre-chin philosophers on the metaphysics of a person is that a person is constituted of three basic substances: the physical body, the psychophysical *chi's [qi]* and the psychospiritual *hsin* [xin]. (p. 2)

Since *xin* 'heart' is one of the basic constituents of a person, we would expect that, as far as psychological verbs are concerned, it would not make much difference whether these verbs are predicated of a man, his person, or his heart. This expectation is confirmed as can be seen by comparing the (a), (b), and (c) sentences in the following examples:[13]

(72) a. ta hen gaoxing.
       he very happy
    b. ta ren hen gaoxing.
       he person very happy
    c. ta xinli hen gaoxing.
       he heart very happy
       'He is very happy.'

(73) a. ta hen sheng-qi.
       he very angry
    b. ta ren hen sheng-qi.
       he person very angry
    c. ta xinli hen sheng-qi.
       he heart very angry
       'He is very angry.'

(74) a. ta hen jin-zhang.
       he very tense

---

[13]Some of these sentences are taken from Huang (1982).

b. ta ren   hen jin—zhang.
   he person very tense
c. ta xinli hen jin—zhang.
   he heart very tense
   'He is very tense (psychologically).'

This renders some support to our hypothesis that the double nominative construction was originally derived from a construction involving a possessive NP as subject through the Possessive Marker deletion.

There remains one important remark that we would like to make: regardless of whether our hypothesis of the origin of the construction is correct or not, the fact that it has been greatly generalized makes any theory invalid that proposes to derive the construction from an underlying possessive construction of some sort in the synchronic description of Chinese.

3 Non—sentence—initial Preverbal Locatives and Temporals as Topics

Locative expressions in Chinese can occur in three different positions, as exemplified by (75)—(77), while temporal expressions can occur in only two, both preverbal, as exemplified by (78) and (79).

(75) <u>zai Meiguo</u> ta you hen duo pengyou.
     in America he have very many friend
     'In America, he has many friends.'

(76) ta <u>zai Meiguo</u> you hen duo pengyou.
     he in America have very many friend
     (i) 'He has many friends in America.'
     (ii) 'Speaking of him, in America, (he) has many friends.'

(77) nei—fu hua   <u>gua zai qiang—shang</u>.
     that—CL painting hang on wall—LOC
     'The painting was hanging on the wall.'

(78) <u>zuotian</u>   ta mei lai kan wo.
     yesterday he not come see me
     'Yesterday, he didn't come to see me.'

(79) ta zuotian mei lai kan wo.
he yesterday not come see me
(i) 'He didn't come to see me yesterday.'
(ii) 'Speaking of him, yesterday (he) didn't come to see me.'

We already argued in Chapter 3 that postverbal locatives such as the one in (77) should be analyzed as complements. In Chapter 2, we also presented arguments for analyzing sentence-initial temporals and locatives such as those in (75) and (78) as primary topics. That this analysis is very well-motivated can be seen by extending (75) to (75a) and (78) to (78a).

(75) a. zai Meiguo$_i$ ta$_j$ you hen duo pengyou
in America he have very many friend
___$_i$ ___$_j$ changchang da majiang.
often play mahjong
'In America he has many friends;
(there) (he) often plays mahjong.'

(78) a. zuotian$_i$ ta$_j$ mei lai kan wo, ___$_i$ ta$_j$
yesterday he not come see me   he
zuo libai   qu le.
do church:service go PART
'Yesterday he did not come to see me; he went to church.'

It can easily be shown that the locative expression *zai Meiguo* 'in America' in (75a) and the temporal expression *zuotian* 'yesterday' in (78a) has all the grammatical qualities of a primary topic. That is, they occur sentence-initially; they are definite in reference; they extend their domain to more than one clause; and finally, they are in control of coreferential NP deletion or pronominalization in their respective chain.

Semantically, the locative in (75a) provides a physical setting for the two comment clauses and likewise, in (78a) the temporal expression gives a time frame for the two comment clauses in the chain. Logically, as Barry (1975) has pointed out, the locative and the temporal in (75a) and (78a) are "indicators of universe within which events hold true."

We have thus proved beyond any reasonable doubt that sentence–initial temporals and locatives such as those in (75a) and (78a) are primary topics.

The purpose of this section is to show that non–sentence–initial preverbal locatives and temporals such as those in (76) and (79) can in certain context play the role of a topic, albeit a non–primary one. In other words, sentences like (76) and (79) are often, taken in isolation, subject to two structural analyses as reflected in the two translations of each sentence.

However, in order to provide a general background for the understanding of the proposed analysis and our arguments in support of it, we need to digress a little to discuss adverbs in Chinese in general.

3.1 General Remakrs on Chinese Adverbs

This is certainly no place to go into a detailed discussion of adverbs in Chinese. What we would like to do in the following is to concentrate on some aspects that are of immediate concern to our topic at hand. Specifically, we would like to take up two important questions concerning Chinese adverbs, namely, (i) the problem of identifying adverbs in Chinese; and, (ii) the placement of different types of adverbs in a multiple–adverbial construction.

3.1.1 The Problem of Identifying Chinese Adverbs

Just as in many other languages, the adverb in Chinese as a category is an extremely ill–defined cover term for a number different catogories. Tai (1976:393) calls it "a wastebasket for a variety of linguistic entities which bear different semantic relations to different parts of a sentence." This being the case, it is really difficult to set up criteria to identify what adverbs are in Chinese. For instance, Guo (1962) defines an adverb as: "A constituent that is placed before a verb or an adjective, but never before a noun to indicate degree, scope, time, negation etc.". But even with this vagueness, this definition excludes many linguistic entities that other linguists would readily classify as adverbs. Witness (80) and (81).

(80) mingxian-de, ta bu zhidao zhe-jian shi.
      clearly   he not know   this-CL matter
      'Clearly, he was not aware of the matter.'

(81) huang–huang–zhang–zhang–de ta pao–le jin–lai.
    in:a:flurry   he run–ASP enter–come
    'In a flurry, he ran in (toward the speaker).'

Thus, *mingxian–de* 'clearly' and *huang–huang–zhang–zhang–de* 'in a flurry' can both occur before a noun, and yet most linguists would agree to assign them to the catogory of adverbs.

However, rather than make any attempt to fix up the definition so that it can cover all adverbs, which is a task evidently beyond the scope of this section, we would like to take up an area which contributes to the difficulty of defining adverbs in Chinese. This area, which has a great deal to do with the topic of the present section, concerns the ambivalence of some kinds of expression which occur preverbally.

Certain expressions in English also exhibit this ambivalence, as Lyons (1977:474) points out:

> The difference between certain locative adverbials and place–referring nominals is not, in fact, clear–cut in all syntactic positions in English. For example, the demonstrative adverbs 'here' and 'there' and the demonstrative pronouns 'this' and 'that' are equally appropriate as substitutes for 'this place'/'that place' in an utterance like 'This/that place is where we agreed to meet.'

Lyons restricts his comment here on locative expressions. Actually, the same comment is equally applicable to temporal expressions in some contexts. Examine (82).

(82) Yesterday being Sunday, we went to church at about ten.

Chinese temporal and locative expressions in certain positions also exhibit this ambivalence. This is clear when we translate the English sentences mentioned above into Chinese. The problem in Chinese, however, is aggravated by a pronounced tendency to elide the prepositions in many prepositional phrases. This tendency was very strong in archaic Chinese and is still strong in modern standard Chinese. This is exactly the reason, which prompted Wang Li (1956, 1980) to posit a special category of words called "nominals in the relational function" for those nominals that appear to have some adverbial function, i.e., they have the function of a prepositional phrase but the preposition, the governing category, is unexpressed. The following are some of Wang's examples.

(83) Peng-shi zhi zi <u>ban dao</u> er wen yue,
Peng-shi POSS son half way PART ask say
"jun jiang he zhi?"
Lord will where go
'Peng-shi's son <u>during the trip</u> asked, "where is my Lord going?"'
(Mozi, 5th c. B.C.)

(84) <u>shi</u> shu wei da?
matter which be great
'<u>Of all the matters</u>, which is the most important?'
shi qin wei da.
serve parents be great
'To serve one's parents is the most important.'
(Mencius, 4th c. B.C.)

(85) <u>zhe-li</u> bu mai piao.
this-place not sell ticket
(i) '(we) don't sell tickets at this place/here.'
(ii) 'This place does not sell tickets.'
(modern standard Chinese)

(86) <u>san qian kuai qian</u> mai-le yi-jia gangqin.
three thousand dollar money buy-ASP one-CL piano
'(With) three thousand dollars, (we) bought a piano.'
(modern standard Chinese)

Wang (1980:388-394) correctly remarks that omission of preposition in this type of structure was more prevalent in classical Chinese than it is in modern Chinese. He also observes that nominals bearing this function are for the most part locative, temporal and scope-delimiting expressions.[14] Other types of nominals such as instrumentals and

---

[14]A scope-delimiting expression is a term coined by the writer to refer to a prepositional phrase or, more commonly in Chinese, a nominal, which is used as a topic, primary or non-primary, to set a scope within which the following comment is to be interpreted. (84) and (i) below are two examples.
(i) (guanyu) liu-xue-de shi,
(with regard to) study:abroad-Rel. Mar. matter

benefactives do occur, as in (86), but only rarely.

It is the same consideration which prompted Chinese grammarians (Zhu, 1959; Guo, 1960; Chao, 1968 and Lü et al., 1981 among others) to analyze the underlined expressions in (83) − (86) as nouns at the lexical level, which are then said to have the function of adverbial modifiers, or *zhuang yu* to use the termonology employed in mainland China, syntactically. While this approach is able to characterize the expressions involved at both levels, it fails to explain why in Chinese, but not in English, there are so many nominals used to modify verbs (including adjectives). Neither does it explain why most of the expressions having this function are temporals and locatives rather than, say, instrumentals and benefactives. We will attempt to give an explanation later in the section.

3.1.2 Placement of Multiple Adverbials

When there are several adverbial expressions appearing in a row preverbally in a sentence the most information−wise neutral and unmarked order seems to be: temporal (including those of specific time, duration and frequency) > locative > benefactive > manner > instrumental (Chuo, 1987; Li et al., 1983; Zhu, 1959), as exemplified by (87).

```
(87)  nei-ge  lao furen,  qunian     dongtian  shichang
      that-CL old woman   last:year  winter    often
      zai jia-li   wei ta erzi  renzhen-de  yong
      at  home-LOC for her son  earnestly   with
      gouzhen           zhi  maoxianyi.
      hooked:needle knit sweater
      'the old woman often knit sweaters with hooked needles for her
      son at home during the last winter.'
```

The above sentence is taken from Chuo (1987), who also discusses in some detail the placement of some position−wise versatile adverbs such as *you* 'again', *guyi* 'intentionally',

---

```
         zhengfu      zao        guiding-le   banfa        le.
         government   long:ago   stipulate    regulation   PART
```
'With regard to the matter of studying abroad, the government set up regulations long ago.'
For more examples of this kind in Classical Chinese see Wang (1980, Chapter 3, Section 44).

keneng 'probably'[15] and *bu* 'not'. We feel that it is a very valuable approach to discuss these adverbs separately and we will return to the placement of some of these adverbs in the next section.

But before we leave this topic, we would like to raise a very important question that many researchers have taken for granted: Why is there such an order of adverbial placement? More specifically, we would like to know whether it is fortuitous that temporals and locatives precede all others.

3.2 Temporals and Locatives as Non—primary Topics

To the best of my knowledge, the first linguist who specifically analyzed adverbials that occur between the primary topic and the verb as topics is Hocket. He (1958: 201—203) comments:

> Many Chinese comments consist in terms of a topic and comment so that one can have a sentence built up of predications within predications, Chinese— box style. 'Wo *jintian chengli you shi*' freely 'I have business in town today' has topic '*wo*' 'I' and the remainder as comment. '*jintian chengli you shi*' 'There is business in town today' in turn has topic '*jintian*' 'today' and the remainder as comment. '*chengli you shi*' 'There is business in town' consists of topic '*chengli*' 'in town, town's interior' and comment '*you shi*' 'there is business.'[16]

Chao (1968) also recognizes the existence of non—primary temporal and locative topics, although he does not explicitly call them as such. He states (op. cit. p.534):

> If there are both time and place words as subjects [topics in our terms, F. T.], the time word usually though not always precedes the place words, as in *jintian haishang fonglang hen da*. "Today on the sea the wind and waves are high." But the main topic is what decides the main subject [the primary topic, F. T.]. For example, *women jiali jinnian guonian, keshi qunian meiyou.* 'In our house, we celebrate the New Year this year, but last year we didn't.', where the place word *jiali* is the main subject [the primary topic] under which *jianian* and *qunian* are smaller subjects [non—primary topics].[17]

---

[15]Chuo (1987) regards *keneng* as a modal adverb. We will argue in Chapter 8 that *keneng* should be more properly analyzed as a modal auxiliary verb.

[16]The Romanization was in the original in Yale system, which has been changed to be consistent with the system used in this thesis.

[17]Chao's Romanization has also been changed to agree with the presentation here.

Neither Hocket nor Chao, however, gives any specific argument for this analysis. In what follows we would like to present our arguments in its support.

3.2.1 Placement of the Pause Particles

One of the grammatical qualities that the primary topic has is that it can be followed by one of the four pause particles, *a(ya), ba, me,* and *ne.* The same particles can also follow a locative or temporal appearing between the primary topic and the main verb, as exemplified by (88) and (89).

(88) ta <u>zuotian</u> <u>ya</u>   meiyou lai.
he yesterday PART not   come
'Speaking of him, yesterday (he) didn't come.'

(89) ta <u>zai Meiguo</u> <u>ya</u>   you hen duo pengyou.
he in America PART have very many friend
'Speaking of him, in America (he) has many friends.'

Since a pause particle in Chinese occurs between the topic and the comment part of a sentence, (88) and (89) indicate clearly that *zuotian* 'yesterday' in (88) and *zai Meiguo* 'in America' in (89) are perceived by native speakers as belonging to the topic part of the sentence involved.

3.2.2 Definiteness in Reference

Like the primary topic, a temporal or a locative occurring between the primary topic and the main verb is definite in reference in most cases as exemplified by (90).

(90) Li Xiaojie zuotian   chengli you shi.
Li Miss   yesterday town—LOC have business
'Speaking of Miss Li, yesterday in town she had business.'

It is clear that the temporal, *zuotian* 'yesterday' and the locative *chengli* 'in town' in (90) are both definite. There are, however, two minor points that need to be taken care of in this connection. First, if *you* 'EXIST' is analyzed as an indicator showing that the following NP is indefinite but specific, i.e., its reference is identifiable to the speaker but not to the hearer, then we have to allow for cases where the temporal or locative expression involved is indefinite but specific. Compare (91) with (90).

(91) Li Xiaojie <u>you   yi—tian</u> jin   cheng lai kan wo.
      Li Miss   EXIST one—day enter town come see me
      'Speaking of Miss Li, one day (she) came to town to see me.'

Notice that an indefinite, nonspecific temporal or locative is still not allowed as a secondary topic as attested by the ungrammaticality of (92).

(92) *Li Xiaojie <u>yi—tian</u> ya   jin   cheng lai kan wo.[18]
      Li Miss   one—day PART enter town come see me

Notice also that if such an analysis of *you* is adopted, then the referential constraint on the primary topic will have to be laxed to allow for cases of specific NPs as well as temporals and locatives. Compare (90) with (90a), (91) with (91a), and (92) with (92a).

(90) a. <u>you   yi—ge ren</u>   zuotian   cheng—li you shi.
         EXIST one—CL person yesterday town—LOC have business
         'Someone had business in town yesterday.'

(91) a. <u>you   yi—tian</u> Li Xiaojie jin   cheng lai kan wo.
         EXIST one—day Li Miss   enter town come see me
         'One day Miss Li came to town to see me.'

(92) a. *<u>yi—tian</u> Li Xiaojie jin   cheng lai kan wo.
          one—day Li Miss   enter town come see me

As expected, both (90a) and (91a) are grammatical while (92a), in which the indefinite, non—specific temporal secondary topic is fronted to become the primary topic, is not. So when the referential constraint is thus revised, it works for both the primary topic and the secondary topic played by a temporal or a locative. The parallelism remains intact.

---

[18](92) and (92a) in the interpretation under discussion cannot be expressed in English. That is why no translations are given in those two instances.

Second, if the expression involved is a prepositional phrase, then the referential constraint applies to the NP in the phrase rather than to the whole prepositional phrase. This happens only rarely and it happens more often with the locative phrase than with the temporal phrase.

3.2.3 The Constrastive Function

One of the discourse functions of the primary topic is to provide contrast (see Barry, 1975; Tsao, 1979, Chapter 6). This can be clearly seen in the following examples.

(93) ta bu qu; wo qu.
      he not go I go
      '(If) he doesn't want to go, I will.'

(94) fan bu chi le, jiu zai duo he   yi-dian.
      rice not eat PART wine still more drink a-little
      '(As for) rice, we will have no more, but wine, do drink a little more.'

Likewise, secondary topics such as the second nominal in the double nominative construction are often used contrastively as in (95).

(95) ta yanjing zhang de   hen hao-kan,   bizi
      he eye   grow   PART very good-looking nose
      que   bu zhen-me-yang.
      on:the:contrary not so:great.
      'Speaking of him, (his) eyes are very beautiful,
      (but) (his) nose is just so-so.'

Now examine the temporals and locatives occurring in the position in question. They, too, possess this function, as shown in (96) and (97).

(96) ta zai Taiwan you hen duo pengyou, zai zhe-li
      he in Taiwan have very many friend   in this-LOC
      yi-ge ye   meiyou.
      one-CL also not:have
      'In Taiwan he has many friends, (but) in this place he has none.'

(97)　women　jia—li　　<u>jin—nian</u>　guo　　　　nian,
　　　　our　　house—LOC　this—year　celebrate　New:Year
　　　　keshi　<u>qu—nian</u>　　meiyou.[19]
　　　　but　　last—year　not:have
　　　　'(In) our house, (we) celebrate the New Year this year,
　　　　but last year we didn't.'

Thus, it is clear that temporals and locatives occurring in the position under investigation behave like other non—primary topics in having the function of contrastiveness just like the primary topic.

3.2.4 Placement of Adverbs *You* and *Ye*

In Section 2.3.2 of this chapter we used the placement of *you* 'again' and *ye* 'also' as a test to distinguish three constructions, namely, productive double nominative construction, sentences with semi—SP compounds and sentences with frozen SP compounds. The reason that the placement of *you* 'again' and *ye* 'also' can provide such a good test is that both *you* and *ye* can only be placed immediately before a VP. In other words, what precedes *you* and *ye* belongs to the topic component while what follows it belongs to the VP component. This interpretation is in agreement with Chuo's observation (1987) about *you* 'again', which he calls a "repetitive adverb". In his paper he compares sentences such as (a) and (b) in (98) and (99).

(98)　a.　ta—de　　pengyou　<u>you</u>　　<u>zai shang—ge libaitian</u>
　　　　　he—POSS　friend　　again　on　last—CL　Sunday
　　　　　lai　　zhao　ta.
　　　　　come　see　　him
　　　　　'His friend came to see him again last Sunday.'
　　　b.　ta—de　　pengyou　<u>zai shang—ge libaitian</u>　you
　　　　　he—POSS　friend　　on　last—CL　Sunday　　again
　　　　　lai　　zhao　ta.
　　　　　come　see　　him

---

[19](97) appeared earlier in the quotation from Chao that we cited.

'Speaking of him, last Sunday his friend came to see him again.'

(99) a. ta <u>you</u> <u>zai xuexiao—li</u> da—le ren.
he again in school—LOC hit—ASP person
'He hit a person at school again.'
b. ta <u>zai xuexiao—li</u> <u>you</u> da—le ren.
he in school—LOC again hit—ASP person
'Speaking of him, at school (he) hit a person again.'

He observes that the difference between the (a) and (b) sentences in each pair lies in the "shifting of focus". In the (a) sentences the focus is laid on the adverbial following *you* 'again', while in the (b) sentences it is on the verb (1987:137). Since according to our interpretation, only what precedes *you* 'again' can be topic, which normally carries known information, the adverbial in the (a) sentences can not be part of the focus in the respective sentence. The two observations are, therefore, in agreement.

With this observation in mind, let us go back to the temporal and locative in question. Since they can appear both before and after *you* 'again' and *ye* 'also', it is only the temporals and locatives that appear before these two adverbs that are secondary topics, as those in (97b) and (98b). (97a) and (98a), on the other hand, are single—topic sentences with an adverbial modifier. We can easily justify this interpretation by adding another comment clause to (a) and (b) sentences in (99), as in (100 a and b).

(100) a. <u>ta</u>$_i$ you zai xuexiao—li da—le ren,

he again in school—LOC hit—ASP person

suoyi ___$_i$ bu gan huijia.

so not dare go:home

'He hit a person at school again, so (he) dared not go home.'

b. <u>ta</u>$_i$ zai <u>xuexiao—li</u>$_j$ you da—le ren

he in school—LOC again hit—ASP person

suoyi ___$_i$ ___$_j$ bei laoshi chufa le.

so BEI teacher punish PART

'Speaking of him, at school (he) hit a person again,
so (he) (at school) was punished by the teacher.'

3.2.5 Domain and Control Properties

(100b) also shows clearly that temporals and locatives in question can extend their domain to more than one clause, a very important property which we have shown that the primary topic possesses. However, there is a difference. While a secondary topic can extend its domain to more than one clause, it can do that only when the primary topic also does so at the same time. A primary topic is evidently not subject to such a restriction.

Likewise, (100b) shows that the locative or the temporal in question has the control property that a primary topic has, i.e., it is in control of the coreferential NP deletion and pronominalization in the following clauses in the same chain. But again there is a difference. A secondary topic controls the NP deletion and pronominalization only when the primary topic does so at the same time. A primary topic is never subject to such a constraint.

3.2.6 Similarity to Other kinds of Secondary Topics

In the second section of this chapter, we have shown that the possessed NP in the double nominative construction often ends up as a secondary topic as in (101a).

(101) a. ta shuxue hen hao.
he math very good
'Speaking of him, (his) math is very good.'

However, the possessed NP can be, in a proper context, promoted to a primary topic as shown in (101b).

b. shuxue ta hen hao.
math he very good
'Speaking of math, he is very good.'

It has been pointed out that when the possessed NP becomes a primary topic, its meaning is somehow changed. It can now only be interpreted in a generic sense. *Shuxue* in (101b), for instance, can only mean 'speaking of math in general'. It does not denote 'his math' as it is in (101a).

This change of interpretation, however, can be explained in terms of a very general rule of topic scope interpretation, which can be roughly stated as (102).

(102)　　　The primary topic > the secondary topic > the tertiary topic .... where
">" means "has a larger scope than"

Since a possessed NP is by definition only part of the possessor NP, when it becomes the primary topic, it cannot retain its original meaning without conflicting with the topic scope interpretation rule. Only when it takes on the generic sense, is it compatible with the rule just mentioned.

This interpretation rule aside, what is shared by the secondary topic played by the possessed NP and that played by a temporal or locative expression in question is that both can be, in a proper context, promoted to become the primary topic. Compare (103) and (104) with (101).

(103) a. ta$_i$ zuotian$_j$ lai kan wo le, ____$_i$
　　　　he   yesterday come see me PART
　　　　____$_j$ hai dai-zhe taitai yiqi lai.
　　　　　　 more take-ASP wife together come
　　　　'Speaking of him, yesterday (he) came to see me,
　　　　(and) (he) took his wife with him.'

　　b. zuotian$_i$ shi Xingqitian, suoyi ____$_i$ ta
　　　　yesterday be Sunday   so   he
　　　　lai kan wo le.
　　　　come see me PART
　　　　'Yesterday was Sunday, so (yesterday) he came to see me.'

(104) a. ta$_i$ zai Meiguo$_j$ you hen duo shiye,
　　　　he in America have very many enterprises
　　　　____$_i$ ____$_j$ you hen da-de yingxiangli.
　　　　　　　　　　have very big   influence
　　　　'Speaking of him, in America (he) has many enterprises,
　　　　(and) (there) (he) has a great deal of influence.'

　　b. zai Meiguo$_i$ renren dou dei shou
　　　　in America everybody all must abide:by

fa, ____ᵢ ta ye bu liwai.
law   he also no exception
'In America, everybody has to abide by the law,
(and) (there) he is no exception.'

In what follows we would like to give some examples in which the topics, primary and non-primary, are played by various elements that we have identified so far.

(105) a. <u>ta-de yanjing</u> zuotian huai le.
          he-POSS eye-glasses yesterday break PART
          'Speaking of his glasses, yesterday (they) broke.'
      b. <u>zuotian ta-de yanjing</u> huai le.
          yesterday he-POSS eye-glasses break PART
          'Yesterday, his glasses broke.'

(106) a. <u>jintian hai-shang fong lang</u> hen da.[20]
          today sea-LOC wind waves very big
          'Today on the sea the wind and waves are high.'
      b. <u>haishang jintian fong lang</u> hen da.
          sea-LOC today wind waves very big
          'On the sea today the wind and waves are high.'
      c. <u>fong lang jintian hai-shang</u> hen da.
          wind waves today sea-LOC very big
          'Speaking of wind and waves, today on the sea (they) are high.'
      d. <u>fong lang hai-shang jintian</u> hen da.
          wind waves sea-LOC today very big
          'Speaking of wind and waves, on the sea today (they) are high.'

3.3 Summery of Arguments and Ramifications

To sum up, we have found, on the one hand, that temporal and locative expressions occurring between the primary topic and the main verb possess all the qualities of a

---

[20](106a) is also taken from Chao's comment quoted previously.

primary topic except in some cases the qualities involved have further restriction in the case of temporals and locatives. On the other hand, we have also found that the temporal and locative in question and the secondary topic in the double nominative construction have a great deal in common. We have thus proved beyond any reasonable doubt that non-sentence- initial, preverbal locatives and temporals can be non-primary topics.

This conclusion of ours is further supported by the following two observations. First, in our discussion of adverbs in general we have found that universally, locatives and temporals have possessed more nominal quality than other kinds of adverbials. This then explains why they are easier to become topics for, even though topics are not completely restricted to nominals, most of them are, and, other things being equal, the more nominal quality a constituent has, the more likely for it to become a topic. This also accounts for the fact that Chinese allows far more prepositions in a prepositional phrase, especially those expressing time and location, to drop than English does. This is so because Chinese is far more topic-oriented than English.

Second, we have reported the findings of many linguists that the information-wise neutral version of the order of placement of a multi-adverbial construction is: Temporal > locative > benefactive > manner > dative > instrumental and we have raised the question of why temporals and locatives should come first. We are now in a better position to answer the question: Temporals and locatives head the hierarchy because they are, of all adverbials, the easiest to become topics. This observation also implies that other types of adverbial, though not as commonly as temporals and locatives, can become topics as well. This is indeed the case, as can be seen by the following examples.

(107) ta$_i$ weile ta-de haizi$_j$ ya chi-le hen duo
he for   he-POSS child PART eat-ASP very much
ku,   ___$_i$ ___$_j$ zhe ji nian lao-le
suffering   these few year old-ASP
xu   duo.
very much
'Speaking of him, for his children, he underwent much suffering (and) in the past few years (he) has become much older.'

(108) ta wu-kuai qian a mai-le nei-jian da-yi.
he five-dollar money PART buy-ASP that-CL overcoat
'Speaking of him, with five dollars (he) bought the overcoat.'

Thus, by positing certain adverbials, predominantly of them, temporals and locatives, as non—primary topics, we are able to explain these two peculiar phenomena about Chinese adverbials very nicely. These two observations can, in this way, be regarded as indirect supports for our analysis.

CHAPTER FIVE
SENTENCES WITH NON–LOCAL SECONDARY TOPICS

In the last chapter we closely examined two constructions, namely, the double nominative construction and sentences containing non–S–initial preverbal adverbials, especially locatives and temporals. We have presented arguments to show that the second nominal in the double nominative construction and the non–S–initial preverbal locatives and temporals are secondary topics. Since there is no indication that these secondary topics have been moved there, we have termed them "local" secondary topics.

Now there are sentences that contain an element occurring in the same slot but with a correspondence, at least semantically, to a post–verbal element. These sentences are exemplified by the following:

(1) ta (lian)   yi–ge   zi   ye   bu   rende.
    he including   one–CL   character   also not   know
    'He doesn't even know a character.'

(2) ta sheme   shi   dou   gan.
    he whatever   thing   all   do
    'He does all sorts of things.'

(3) ta lian   wuxia   xiaoshuo   dou   nian.
    he including   kongfu   novel   all   read
    'He reads even kongfu novels.'

(4) ta ba fangzi   da–sao   ganjing   le.
    he BA house   sweep   clean   PART
    'He cleaned the house.'

(5) xuesheng–men   gongke   zuo–wan   le.
    students   exercise   do–finish   PART
    'The students have finished their exercise.'

(6) ta da   paiqiu   da   de   hen   hao.
    he play   volleyball play PART very good
    'He plays volleyball very well.'

(7) ta paiqiu   da   de   hen   hao.
    he volleyball play PART very good
    'He plays volleyball very well.'

(1) and (3) involve what is usually known as the *lian...dou/ye* construction. As this construction involves many other constituents than the object NP, we will take it up in the next chapter as a special topic construction. Even though in (2) *lian* cannot appear, we will deal with it in connection with the *lian...dou/ye* construction. We will, of course, explain, in our discussion, why *lian* cannot appear.

(4) exemplifies the *ba* construction, and (5) the object–fronting construction. (6) represents the so-called "verb-copying" construction and (7) a variation of the construction with the first verb omitted. As all three constructions involve the fronting of the object of the verb, they will be carefully examined, and compared and contrasted in the following discussion. Since the *ba* construction is by far the most frequently used expression, we will take it up first, to be followed by the object–fronting construction and the so-called "verb-copying" construction.

1. The *BA* Construction

The *ba* construction in Chinese is probably unique as no similar construction has been found in any other language in the world. It is also the most discussed construction in the Chinese language. Many of the previous treatments were attempts to apply grammatical theories or models such as the American structuralists' theory, transformational grammar theory or case theory to the analysis of this construction. Although many of them bring up important questions and contribute to our understanding of the nature of this construction, none can be said to come close to being able to take care of most of the data. A thorough review will certainly be beyond the scope of this section. To get a general understanding of the problems, interested readers are referred to S. Cheung's article (1973). Many of the more recent treatments will be taken up in the course of our discussion.

The *ba* construction is generally characterized as[1]:

---

[1] In most previous studies, *ba* is treated as a coverb or preposition. These studies also go into varying details in characterizing the V and the Complement. Most of these characterizations are accurate, but very few go beyond the level of what Chomsky (1965)

(8)   Subject ba Object Verb Complement

In other words, the *ba* construction has the effect of taking the direct object of the verb and placing it after *ba*, thus leaving the verb and the complement at the end of the sentence. There are, as far as I can determine, several inadequacies in this representation. The purpose of the present section is to point out these inadequacies and to give an alternative approach that can not only overcome these inadequacies but can also give a better explanation of why it has so many constraints placed upon it and why it should be uniquely found in Chinese.

For the time being, in order not to bias the discussion, I will give a completely neutral representation as follows:

(9) NP_1 ba NP_2 Verb Complement

In what follows I will begin by examining the two NPs involved very closely and by trying to determine how they relate to each other and how they each relate to the other components in the representation.

1.1 The First Noun Phrase (NP_1)

It may seem innocuous enough to characterize the first NP in a *ba* sentence as a subject. After all, there are many *ba* sentences such as (10) in which the first NP is semantically an agent.

(10)   ta   ba   yizi   nong–huai   le
       he   BA chair   make–spoil   PART
       'He spoiled the chair.'

A careful examination of a wider range of data, however, reveals that this description is not general enough and that it should be more appropriately characterized as a topic. To see this we have to digress a little to take up the properties of subject and topic in Chinese.

---

calls "observational adequacy."

1.1.1 The Properties of Subject in Chinese

In our previous discussion of whether there is subject in Chinese and if there is one how we are to identify it, it is concluded that subject in Chinese has the following properties[2]:

(11) a. Subject is always unmarked by preposition.
   b. By position, subject can be identified as the animate NP to the left of the verb; otherwise, the NP immediatelly before the verb.
   c. Subject always bears some selectional relation to the main verb of the sentence.
   d. Subject tends to have a specific reference.
   e. Subject plays an important role in the following coreferential pronominalization or deletion processes:reflexivization, imperativization, and Equi−NP deletion.

1.1.2 The Properties of Topic in Chinese

We have also demonstrated that topic in Chinese can be identified as an NP having the following properties:

(12) a. Topic invariably occupies the S−initial position of the first clause in a topic chain.
   b. Topic can optionally be separated from the rest of the clause in which it overtly occurs by one of the four pause particles: *a (ya), ne, me,* and *ba*.
   c. Topic is always definite or generic.
   d. Topic is a supraclausal notion; it may, and often does, extend its semantic domain to more than one clause.
   e. topic is in control of the pronominalization or deletion of all the coreferential NPs in a topic chain.
   f. Topic, except in clauses where it is also subject, plays no role in such processes as reflexivization, Equi−NP deletion and imperativization.

---

[2]This is natrually just a brief summary. For more detailed discussion, please refer to Chapter 2 and Tsao (1978, 1979).

It is evident from the previous discussion that, while subject and topic should be differentiated and can be thus identified, they are not totally unrelated. In fact, they can be one and the same in sentences such as (13).

(13)   ta   lai   kan   ni   le.
         he   come   see   you   PART
         'He is coming to see you.'

1.1.3 The first NP as Topic

With these properties of subject and topic in mind, we can now go back to the first NP in (10). It is quite clear that the NP in question is both subject and topic as it can be demonstrated to have all those properties of subject and topic we have posited. However, when we turn to other *ba* sentences such as (14) we find that the first NP is a topic but not a subject.

(14)   na   chang   qiu   ba   women   kan–de–lei–si   le.
        that   CL   ball–game   BA   we   see–PART–tire–dead   PART
        'That ball game, we watched it until we were tired to death.'[3]

The first NP in (14), *na chang qiu* 'the ball game' is clearly not the subject as the main verb *kan* 'watch' will selectionally pick *women* 'we' as its subject. In addition, it is *women* 'we' that has the subject properties posited in (11b) and (11d), that is, it is specific in reference and it is an animate NP that occurs to the left of the main verb.[4]

If *na chang qiu* 'the ball game' is not the subject, then what is it? By performing the following test we can clearly see that it is the topic of the sentence.

First, it occurs in the S–initial position and it is definite. It can also be optionally separated from the rest of the sentence by a pause particle as in (15).

---

[3]This English translation is suggested by Dr. Robert B. Kaplan (personal communication). To put it more literally, perhaps the sentence can be translated as, 'The ball game caused us to watch so much that we were tired to death.'

[4]Unlike most subjects, which are unmarked by a preposition, *women* 'we' in (11b) and (11d) is marked by *ba*. It indicates that it is not a straightforward subject. We will have more to say about the properties of the *ba* NP in Section 1.2.

(15) na chang qiu a, ba women kan–de–lei–si le.
'Same as (14)'

It could also be shown to extend its semantic domain over more than one clause by adding another clause to it as in (15):

(16) na   chang   qiu,   zhengzheng   da–le   liu–ge
     that   CL   ball–game   fully   play–ASP   six–CL
     zhongtou,   ba   women   kan–de–lei–si   le.
     hour   BA   we   watch–PART–tire–dead   PART
     'The ball game (topic), it was played for fully six hours, we watched the game so much that it tired us to death.'

All these examples indicate without a doubt that the most general characterization of the first NP in (9) is topic.

1.2 The *Ba* NP (NP$_2$)

1.2.1 Arguments aganist Regarding the *ba* NP as an Object

Mei (1978, 1980) points out the mistake of assuming that the *ba* NP is directly related to the main verb as its object. Below are some examples taken from his 1980 article:

(17) wo chadianr   ba   yaoshi   wang–le   dai   le.
     I almost   BA   key   forget–ASP   bring   PART
     'I almost forgot to bring the key.'

(18) ta ba   bilu   sheng–le   huo.
     he BA   fireplace   build–ASP   fire
     'He fired up the fireplace.'

(19) (ni)   buyao   ba   qiang   kou   duizhe   ren
     (you)   don't   BA   gun   muzzle   point   people
     '(You) don't point your gun at people.'

In (17) the *ba* NP is actually the object of the second verb *dai* 'bring' rather than the main verb *wang* 'forget'. Likewise, in (18) the *ba* NP *bilu* 'fireplace' is the locative NP rather than the object as it can be related to a non—*ba* sentence with a corresponding locative expression as in (20):

(20) ta   zai bilu   sheng—le   huo.
      he   in   fireplace   build—ASP   fire
      'He built a fire in the fireplace.'

In (19) the *ba* NP *qiang kou* 'the muzzle of the gun' is related to the first NP in a possessor—possessed relationship. This is clear when we compare it with a non—*ba* sentence with a corresponding possessive expression as in (21):

(21) ni—de   qiang—kou   buyao   duizhe   ren.
      your   gun—muzzle   don't   point   people
      'Don't point the muzzle of your gun at people.'

These counterexamples show convincingly that it is at least not general enough to regard the *ba* NP as a direct object of the main verb. The next question is then: What is it?

Mei (1978) and Chu (1979) and Li et al. (1984:164) suggest that the *ba* NP should be treated as a topic of some sort. None of them gives much evidence in support of the claim, however. In the following we would like to conduct a full exploration of the semantic and syntactic properties of the *ba* NP and then compare them with the properties of the topic NP to determine whether such a claim can be substantiated.

1.2.2 Semantic and Syntactic Properties of the *ba* NP

Some of the following properties of the *ba* NP have been repeatedly pointed out by previous researchers while others are brought up here for the first time.

1.2.2.1 The Referential Constraint of the *ba* NP

It has been observed by a number of researchers that the *ba* NP must be either definite, generic or, in some restricted situation, specific.

(22) qing   ni   ba   zhouzi   ca—ganjing.
      please   you   BA   table   clean
      'Please clean the table.'

(23) ta ba qian kan–de hen zhong.
 he BA money look–upon very important
 'He regards money as very important.'

Thus, in (22) *zhuozi* 'table' is definite as defined by Hawkins (1978), although it is not explicitly marked. In (23) *qian* 'money' is generic as it refers to money in general, not any particular money such as that I have in my pocket or that you have deposited in the bank.

The *ba* NP, however, can be specific in the sense that its referent is identifiable by the speaker but not by the hearer as in (24):

(24) a. wo ba yi–ben shu diao le.
 I BA one–CL book lose ASP
 'I lost a book.'

When the *ba* NP is specific, however, there seems to be an additional constraint. It seems that in a case like this the first NP (the topic) is restricted to the first person, because changing it to the second or third person seems to make it unacceptable:

(24) b.? ta ba yi–ben shu diao le.
 'He lost a book.'
 c.? ni ba yi–ben shu diao le.
 'You lost a book.'

1.2.2.2 Separability by a Pause Particle

The *ba* NP can be optionally separated from the rest of the sentence by the pause particle *a (ya)*.

(25) wo ba nei–ben shu (a) mai gei Xiao–ming le.
 I BA the–CL book sell to Xiao–ming PART
 'I sold the book to Xiao–ming.'

(26) ta ba nei–zhi bi (ya) nong–duan le.
 he BA the–CL pen make–break PART
 'He broke the pen.'

Two other particles, *ne* and *ba*, however, cannot be used here as both (27a) and (27b) are ungrammatical.

(27) wo ba nei—ben   shu   *a. [ne]   mai gei Xiao—ming le.
                            *b. [ba]

1.2.2.3 Heading a Topic Chain

The *ba* NP can head a topic chain which, of course, is embedded in a larger topic chain headed by a primary topic. Examine the following two sentences:

(28) a. Wang   Xiaojie   ba shu   zhang—le   jia   zai   mai
         Wang   Miss   BA book   raise—ASP   price   then   sell
         gei   women.
         to   us
         'Miss Wang raised the price of the book before she sold it to us.'

(29) a. ta   ba   fangzi   zhengxiu—le   yi   xia,   qi—le—qi
         he   BA   house   repair—ASP   a   little   paint—ASP—paint
         ranhou   zai   mai—chu—qu.
         afterward then   sell—out
         'He had the house repaired, painted, and then sold.'

Thus, (28a) consists of two clauses both of which are about the same topics *Wang Xiaojie* 'Miss Wang', the primary topic and *shu* 'book', the *ba* NP, which occur at the head of the chain. Similarly, in (29a) there are three clauses that make up the chain, each of which is about *ta* 'he', the primary topic and *fangzi* 'the house', the *ba* NP, occurring at the head of the chain. So it is chear that, like the local secondary topics we discussed in the last chapter, the *ba* NP can head a chain only when the primary topic that precedes it also does so.

1.2.2.4 Controlling the Pronominalization and Coreferential NP Deletion Processes

Closely related to the previous property is another property which shows that the *ba* NP is in control of all the pronominalization and coreferential NP deletion in the *ba* topic chain. Examine the (b) and (c) sentences in (28) and (29):

(28) b. Wang Xiaojie ba <u>shu</u>$_i$ zhang–le jia zai ba <u>ta</u>$_i$ mai gei women.
'Same as (28a).'
c. Wang Xiaojie <u>ba shu</u>$_i$ zhang–le jia zai _____$_i$ mai gei women.
'Same as (28a).'

(29) b. ta ba fangzi$_i$ zhengxiu–le yi xia, ba <u>ta</u>$_i$ qi–le–qi, ranhou zai ba <u>ta</u>$_i$ mai–chu–qu.
'Same as (29a).'
c. ta ba fangzi$_i$ zhengxiu–le yi xia, _____$_i$ qi–le–qi, ranhou zai _____$_i$ mai–chu–qu.
'Same as (29a).'

Clearly in both (b) and (c) sentences of (28) and (29), the first *ba* NP is the controller and the later *ba* NP's are victims in the coreferential processes of pronominalization and deletion. On the other hand, that the regular topic is not in control of these processes within the *ba* topic chain is also clear since the (d) and (e) sentences of both (28) and (29) are ungrammatical:

(28) *d. <u>Wang Xiaojie</u>$_j$ ba shu zhang–le jia zai ba <u>ta</u>$_j$ mai gei women.
'Same as (28a).'
*e. <u>Wang Xiaojie</u>$_j$ ba shu zhang–le jia zai _____$_j$ mai gei women.
'Same as (29a).'

(29) *d. <u>ta</u>$_j$ ba fangzi zhengxiu–le yi xia, <u>ba ta</u>$_j$ qi–le–qi, ranhou zai <u>ba ta</u>$_j$ mai–chu–qu.
'Same as (29a).'
*e. <u>ta</u>$_j$ ba fangzi zhengxiu–le yi xia, _____$_j$ qi–le–qi, ranhou zai _____$_j$ mai–chu–qu.
'Same as (29a).'

1.2.2.5 The Properties of the *ba* NP and Those of the Regular Topic NP Compared
To sum up, we have found that the *ba* NP has the following properties:

(30) a. The *ba* NP invariably occupies a position immediately following the primary topic which occurs in the initial position of the first clause in a primary topic + *ba* NP topic chain.
b. The *ba* NP can optionally be separated from the rest of the clause in which it overtly occurs by a pause particle: *a(ya)*.
c. The *ba* NP is mostly definite or generic but it can be specific, especially when the primary topic is in the first person.
d. The *ba* NP has some supraclausal properties as well. It can extend its semantic domain to more than one clause.
e. The *ba* NP is in control of all the pronominalization and coreferential NP deletion processes in a topic chain involving a *ba* NP.

Now if we compare (30) with (12), we find that except in (12f), which is difficult to test in the case of the *ba* construction, the *ba* NP has almost all the properties of the regular topic NP. There are two minor differences. With regard to the referential constraint, the regular topic NP does not allow a specific reading while the *ba* NP, under some special condition, does. As for the property of heading a topic chain, while a *ba* NP can not do so without the primary topic's doing so at the same time, a primary topic can head a chain alone. With so much in common and so little difference, it is justifiable to regard the *ba* NP as a special kind of topic. We will refer to it as the *ba* topic to distinguish it from a primary topic.

1.2.3 Further Similarities Between the Primary Topic NP and the *ba* Topic NP
The similarities between the primary topic NP and the *ba* topic NP do not stop here. More parallels can be seen when we compare the relations that a *ba* NP bears to some other elements in the same clause with those that a topic NP does to other elements in the same clause.

1.2.3.1 The Relations That a Topic NP Bears to Some Other Elements in the Same Clause
As these relations have been carefully examined in our previous discussion the following is a brief summary.

1.2.3.1.1 As a Term of One of the Verbs in the Clause

In the most straightforward case, a topic is either the subject as in (31), the direct object as in (32), or the indirect object as in (33) of the main verb in the same clause:

(31) Zhang San (a),   zuotian   lai   kan wo le.
      Zhang San (PART) yesterday   come see me PART
      'Zhang San (topic), (he) came to see me yesterday.'

(32) zhei–ben shu   (a),   wo yijing   nian–le   san   bian.
      this–CL   book (PART)   I already read–ASP three   times
      'This book (topic), I have already read (it) three times.'

(33) Li Si   (ya),   wo yijing   song–le   yi–fen   li   le.
      Li Si (PART) I already give–ASP   one–CL   present PART
      'Li Si (topic), I have already given (him) a present.'

Sometimes, a topic may bear some grammatical relation to a verb other than the main verb as in (34).

(34) ta (ya),   wo yijing   qu kan–quo   le.
      he (PART) I already go see–ASP   PART
      'He (topic), I already went to see (him).'

1.2.3.1.2 As a Non–term of the Main verb

A topic can be a non–term of the main verb of a clause as exemplified in (35) to (37):

(35) zuotian   (a)   Zhang San lai   kan wo le.
      yesterday (PART)   Zhang San come see me PART.
      'Yesterday (topic), Zhang San came to see me.'

(36) zhuozi–shang   (a),   ta bai–le   yi–pen   hua.
      table–top   (PART)   he place–ASP   one–pot   flower.
      '(On) top of the table (topic), he placed a pot of flowers.'

(37) zhi–jian   shi   (ya),   ta   xie–le   yi–fen   baogao
    this–CL   matter   (PART)   he   write–ASP   one–CL   report
    le.
    PART
    'This matter (topic), he wrote a report (about it).'

Thus, clearly, in (35) *zuotian* 'yesterday', which bears the adverbial relation of time to the main verb, is chosen as a topic of the sentence. In (36), it is the adverbial of place, *zhuozi–shang* '(on) top of the table' that is chosen. In (37), *zhe–jian shi* 'this matter' bears what I previously called 'scope–delimiting relation' to the main verb. NPs of this nature are often chosen as a topic and can be optionally preceded by *guanyu*, or *zhiyu* 'concerning, with regard to, as for, as to etc.'

1.2.3.1.3 Topics that Bear Some Semantic Relationships to the Subject

Semantic relationships that are most frequently found are: that of the possesor and the possessed, as in (38), that of whole and part, as in (39), and that of class and member, as in (40).

(38) nei–ge   ren   (a)   tui   die–duan   le.
    that–CL   person   (PART)   leg   fall–break   PART
    'This man (topic), (his) leg broke (as he fell).'

(39) wu–ge   pingguo   (a)   san–ge   (ta)   chi–le,   liang–ge
    5–CL   apple   (PART)   3–CL   (he)   eat–ASP   2–Cl
    mai–le.
    sell–ASP
    'The five apples (topic), (he) ate three (of them), (and) sold (the remaining) two.'

(40) yu   (a)   weiyu   xianzai   zui   gui.
    fish   (PART)   tuna   now   most   expensive
    'Fish (topic), tuna is now the most expensive.'

There is one more point to be made with regard to this group of sentences: when the verb of the clause is a non-stative one, then the sentence can have an alternative form that has the same propositional meaning, as exemplified by (38a) and (39a). (40) cannot have the alternative form because the main verb *gui* 'expensive' is a stative verb.

(38) a. nei–ge   ren   (a)   die–duan–le   tui   le.
         that–CL person (PART) fall–break–ASP   leg   PART
         'Same as (38).'

(39) a. wu–ge   pingguo   (a),   (ta)   chi–le   san–ge,
         5–CL   apple   (PART) (he)   eat–ASP   3–CL
         mai–le   liang–ge.
         sell–ASP   2–CL
         'Same as (39).'

1.2.3.1.4 Summary

Our previous discussion about the relations that the topic can bear to other elements in the same clause can be briefly summarized as in (41).

(41) a. The topic can be a subject, a direct object, or an indirect object of a verb in the same clause. The verb in question is usually the main verb but occasionally a verb other than the main verb may be involved.
b. The topic can be a non–term of the main verb of the clause. More specifically, the constituents often found are a time adverbial, a locative adverbial, or a 'scope–delimiting' adverbial.
c. The topic sometimes does not bear any direct relationship to the main verb. Rather it bears some semantic relationship to the subject of the verb. The relationships most frequently found are possessor and possessed, whole and part, and class and member.

1.2.3.2 The Relationships that a *ba* NP bears to Other Elements in the Same Clause
1.2.3.2.1 As a Term of One of the Verbs in the Same Clause

Examine the relationships that the *ba* NP bears to the main verb by comparing the following *ba* sentences with their corresponding non–*ba* sentences:

(42) a. ta   he   neibei   jiu,   he–de   chabuduo   zui
       he   drink the–cup   wine   drink–PART   almost   drunk
       le.
       PART
       'He drank the cup of wine (and he was) almost drunk.'
   b. nei   bei   jiu   ba   ta   he–de   chabuduo   zui
      that   cup   wine   BA   he   drink–PART   almost   drunk
      le.
      PART
      'That cup of wine almost made him drunk.'

(43) a. ta   diu–le   nei–zhi   bi   le.
       he   lose–ASP   the–CL   pen   PART
       'He lost the pen.'
   b. ta   ba   nei–zhi   bi   diu   le.
      he   BA   the–CL   pen   lose   PART
      'Same as (a).'

(44) a. wo   song–le   ta   wu–kuai   qian.
       I   give–ASP   he   5–dollar   money
       'I gave him five dollars (as a gift).'
   b.* wo   ba   ta   song–le   wu–kuai   qian.
       I   BA   he   give–ASP   5–dollar   money

(45) a. wo   chadianr   wang–le   dai   yaoshi   le.
       I   almost   forget–ASP   bring   key   PART
       'I almost forgot to bring the key.'
   b. wo   chadianr   ba   yaoshi   wang–le   dai   le.
      I   almost   BA   key   forget–ASP   bring   PART
      'Same as (a).'

It seems evident from the above examples that the *ba* NP can be the subject, the direct object of the main verb as shown in (42) and (43). An indirect object, however, cannot become a *ba* NP as (44) is ungrammatical. (45b), which was earlier cited as (17), clearly indicates that, like the primary topic NP, the *ba* topic NP can be a term of a verb other than the main verb of the clause.

1.2.3.2.2. As a Non-term of the Main Verb of the Clause

Compare the following non-*ba* and *ba* sentences:

(46) a. Zhang San   zuotian   lai   kan   wo   le.
         Zhang San   yesterday   come   see   me   PART
         'Zhang San came to see me yesterday.'
    b.* Zhang San   ba zuotian   lai   kan   wo   le.
         Zhang San   BA yesterday come   see   me   PART

(47) a. ta zai bilu   sheng-le   huo
         he in   fireplace   build-ASP   fire
         'He built a fire in the fireplace.'
    b. ta ba bilu   sheng-le   huo
         he BA fireplace   build-ASP   fire
         'Same as (a).'

(48) a. (guanyu)   nei-jian   shi,   ta   xie-le   yi-fen
         (regarding) the-CL   matter   he   write-ASP   1-CL
         baogao   le.
         report   PART
         'With regard to that matter, he wrote a report (about it).'
    b. ta ba nei-jian shi   xie-le   yi-fen baogao le.
         he BA the-CL matter write-ASP   1-CL   report PART
         'What he did with the matter was write a report (about it).'

A close examination of the related sentences clearly show that the *ba* NP can bear the relation of a locative adverbial or a 'scope-delimiting' adverbial to the main verb of the sentence. A temporal adverbial, however, does not seem to be able to function as a *ba* NP as easily as a locative NP.[5]

---

[5]Note, however, that with a verb which can take a temporal case as its object, *ba* sentences are, of course, possible.
  (i) tamen ba   jiehun-de   riqi   yanhou   le.
       they   <u>ba</u>   marriage's   date   postpone   ASP
       'They postponed their (date of) marriage.'
  (ii) tamen yanhou-le   jiehun-de   riqi.
       they   postpone-ASP   marriage's   date
       'They postponed their (date of) marriage.'

1.2.3.2.3 The *ba* NP that Bears Some Semantic Relationships to the Direct Object of the clause

Cheung (1974) concludes his lengthy review of the treatments of the *ba* construction prior to 1974 by citing some sentences from Thompson (1974) and Hashimoto (1971). He points out that these sentences, which all contain a so-called retained object, are one type of the *ba* sentence that has not been successfully tackled in any of the previous studies. Here are some of his sentences:

(49) ta ba juzi   buo-le   pi
      he BA orange remove-ASP   peel
      'He removed the peel of the orange.'

(50) ni   neng-bu-neng ba nei-ben   shu   jiang yidian   jia?
      you can-not-can   BA the-CL   book lower a-little price
      'Can you reduce the price of that book a little?'

(51) ta ba wuzi   jia-le   wuding.
      he BA house add-ASP   roof
      'He added a roof to the house.'

(52) Zhang San ba men   shang-le   suo.
      Zhang San BA door put-on-ASP   lock
      'Zhang San put a lock on the door.'

(53) ta ba zhimen   ti-le   yi-ge dong
      he BA paper-door kick-ASP   a-CL   hole
      'He kicked a hole in the paper door.'

(54) Zhang San ba hua   jiao-jiao   shui.
      Zhang San BA flower sprinkle-ASP   water
      'Zhang San sprinkled the flower.'

(55) ba Nainai-de   yandai na   yi-gen lai.
      BA Grandma-POSS   pipe   bring a-CL   come
      'Bring one of Grandma's pipes.'

(56) Zhang San ba wu—ge pingguo chi—le   san—ge
      Zhang San BA 5—CL apple   eat—ASP   3—CL
      'Zhang San has eaten three of the five apples.'

If we examine the semantic relationships between the *ba* NP and the so—called retained object, we find that they fall into two categories, one being that of the possessor and the possessed, the other that of the whole and the part. Thus in (49) and (50), the relationship between the *ba* NP and the retained object can be expressed as *juzi—de pi* 'the peel of the orange' and *nei—ben shu—de jia—(qian)* 'the price of the book'. Likewise, in (51) to (53) the relationship in question can be expressed as *wuzi—de wuding* 'the roof of the house', *men—de suo* 'the lock of the door' and *zhimen—de yi—ge dong* 'a hole of the paper door' respectively. (54) requires some explanation. In Chinese, there is a special type of Verb—object compound whose membership includes *bang—mang* 'help', *zhao—xiang* 'take a picture', and *jiao—shui* 'sprinkle water'. With this group of V—O compounds, there are two ways to add an indirect object to it. One way is to use a co—verb like *gei* as in *gei ta bang—mang* 'help with him', *gei ta zhao—xiang* 'take a picture for him' and *gei hua jiao—shui* 'sprinkle some water on the flower'. The other way is to insert the indirect object in its possessive case between the two elements of a V—O compound as *bang ta—de mang* 'help his business', *zhao ta—de xiang* 'take his picture' and *jiao hua—de shui* 'sprinkle flower's water'. We now return to (54). Even though the relationship between the *ba* NP *hua* 'flower' and the retained object *shui* 'water' is not, strictly speaking, semantically oriented, it is, nonetheless, syntactically justified, i.e., *hua* and *shui* can be regarded as having a possessive relation.[6]

In (55) and (56), the relationship between the *ba* NP and the retained object can clearly be seen to be that between the whole and its parts, even though a syntactic paraphrase such as *Nainai—de yandai zhong de yi—gen* 'one of Grandma's pipes' or *wu—ge pingguo zhizhong—de san—ge* ' three out of the five apples' is possible but often feels awkward.

We can thus conclude that the *ba* NP and the so—called retained object, or the direct

---

[6] *Hua* 'flowers' in (54) can also appear as topic of the whole sentence. So instead of (54), we might choose to say (i).

(i) hua,   Zhang San   jiao—le   shui   le.
     flowers Zhang San   sprinkle—ASP   water   PART
     '(As for) the flowers, Zhang San has sprinkled water (on them).'

object of the verb in the clause, can bear the relationships of possessor and possessed or whole and part. We are, however, unable to find examples that show the *ba* NP bearing the relationship of class—member to the retained object.

1.2.3.2.4 Summary

The roles of the *ba* NP in relation to other elements in the same clause can thus be summarized as follows:

(57) a. The *ba* NP can be a subject or a direct object but not an indirect object of a verb in the clause. The verb in question is usually the main verb but occasionally can be a verb other than the main verb.
b. The *ba* NP can be a non—term of the main verb of the clause. The constituents most frequently found are the locative adverbial and the "scope—delimiting" adverbial. It seems more difficult for a temporal adverbial to become the *ba* NP.
c. The *ba* NP sometimes does not bear any direct relationship to the main verb. Rather, it has some semantic relationship to the direct object, which appears in a *ba* construction as a so—called "retained object". The relationships frequently found are possessor and possessed and whole and part.

1.2.3.3 The Roles of the *ba* NP and Those of the primary Topic NP Compared

If we now compare (41) with (57), we find that in (a) both the regular topic NP and the *ba* NP can be the subject or the direct object of a verb in the clause but only the primary topic NP can be an indirect object. In (b), the regular topic NP can be a temporal adverbial, a locative adverbial, or scope—delimiting adverbial of the main verb of the clause but only the latter two can readily become *ba* NPs. Our findings in this section so far largely parallel those reported previously in our examination of the properties of the primary topic NP and the *ba* topic NP. In both cases, we find that the *ba* NP has all the essential properties of the primary topic NP.

A major distinction appears, however, when we compare (42c) with (57c). While the *ba* NP and the primary topic NP can both bear the semantic relationships of possessor—possessed and whole—part to another element in the same clause, the element in question is, nonetheless, different. In the case of the primary NP, it is chiefly the subject of the clause, while in the case of the *ba* NP it is the direct object. This difference gives us some hint as to the different functions that they have. We will return to the point when we take up the meanings and function of the *ba* NP.

1.2.3.4 Three Additional Arguments for Treating the *ba* NP as a Secondary Topic
1.2.3.4.1 Topical Ambiguity with Regard to the *ba* NP

In Chapter Four we pointed out that a double nominative sentence can have two different interpretations, depending on what the topic is, as can be clearly seen by comparing the following (a) sentence with the (b) sentence:

(58) a. zhe—ge   nühai   (a)   yanjing hen   da, hen
        this—CL   girl   (PART)   eyes   very big very
        piaoliang.
        beautiful
        'This girl (topic), (her) eyes are big; (she) is beautiful.'
     b. zhe—ge   nühai—de yanjing   (a)   hen   da, hen
        this—CL   girl's   eyes   (PART)   very big very
        piaoliang.
        beautiful
        'This girl's eyes are very big and very beautiful.'

As the English translations clearly indicate, in (a) it is the girl herself who is said to be beautiful, but in (b), it is the girl's eyes which are said to be beautiful — nothing is said about the girl herself.

Likewise, a *ba* construction can also exhibit this kind of topical ambiguity, depending on what the *ba* NP is. Compare (b) and (c) sentences in the following.

(59) a. ta   na—le   yi—zhang   zhi.
        he   take—ASP   one—CL   paper
        'He took one sheet of paper.'
     b. ta   ba yi—zhang zhi   na—le.
        he   BA one—CL   paper   take—ASP
        'He took one sheet of paper.'
     c. ta   ba zhi   na—le   yi—zhang.
        he   BA paper   take—ASP one—CL
        'From the (stack of) paper, he took one sheet.'

Thus, even though in some sense it can be said that both (b) and (c) sentences are derived from the (a) sentence, they are used to answer (60) and (61) respectively.[7]

(60)　What did he do to the (one) sheet of paper?

(61)　What did he do to the (stack of) paper?

Again we see a parallel property between the primary topic and the *ba* topic. Topical ambiguity with regard to the *ba* NP may yet take another form. Cheung, in his lengthy review referred to earlier (1973), points out that Thompson's article (1973) offers no explanation for cases where two *ba* sentences can be derived from a presumably identical source. Compare (62b) with (62c), both of which are said to have (62a) as their underlying source.

(62)　a.　ta　zai　shujia–shang　　bai–man–le　　shu.
　　　　　he　at　 book–shelf–LOC　put–full–ASP　book
　　　　　'He filled the bookshelf with books.'
　　　b.　ta　ba　shujia　　bai–man–le　　shu.
　　　　　he　BA　bookshelf　put–full–ASP　book
　　　　　'He filled the bookshelf with books.'
　　　c.　ta　ba　shu　　bai–man–le　　shujia.
　　　　　he　BA　book　put–full–ASP　bookshelf.'
　　　　　'He loaded the books onto the bookshelf.'

Thompson could probably have replied by saying that (b) and (c) answer two different questions as in (63) and (64) respectively.

(63) What did he do to the bookshelf?

(64) What did he do to the books?

In addition to this argument, we could add another. We could attach a comment clause to

---

[7]The explanation as well as the examples are taken from Thompson (1973:215–16). She, however, uses them to prove that the structure she posits is correct.

each *ba* topic chain in (62b) and (62c) to show that, since the *ba* NPs are different, the (b) and (c) sentences have different secondary topics, event though they share the same primary topic, *ta* 'he', as is shown in (65) and (66):

(65) ta   ba shujia   bai–man–le   shu,   jiu   haokan   duo
      he   BA bookshelf put–full–ASP   book   then   good–look   much
      le.
      PART
      'He filled the bookshelf with books and (it) looked much better.'

(66) ta   ba shu   bai–man–le   shujia   jiu   zhengqi   duo
      he   BA books   put–full–ASP   bookshelf then   neat   much
      le.
      PART
      'He loaded the books onto the bookshelf and (they) became much neater.'

As the English translations reveal, each added comment in (65) and (66) is about the secondary topic; i.e., *shujia* 'bookself' and *shu* 'books' respectively. This then is another case in support of our proposal to treat the *ba* NP as a topic.[8]

---

[8]Cheung (1973) also mentions that Thompson's account fails to explain why (i) in the following is grammatical while (ii) is not.
  (i)   ta ba qiang ti–le   yi–ge   dong.
           he *ba* wall   kick–ASP   one–CL   hole
           'What he did to the wall was to kick a hole in it.'
  (ii)*   ta ba qiang bu–le   yi–ge   dong.
           he *ba* wall   mend–ASP   one–CL   hole
           'What he did to the wall was to mend a hole in it.'

Several things may be involved when a *ba* sentence is ungrammatical, as we have been trying to show in this paper. By comparing (i) with (ii) we notice that in (i) *qiang–de yi–ge dong* 'a hole in the wall' cannot be made into a topic because it was created, so to speak, after kicking. To put it another way, at the time of kicking the 'patient' or 'receiver' of the action could only be the wall. In (ii), *qiang–de yi–ge done* 'a hole in the wall' is already in existence and is known at least to the speaker, i.e., it is at least specific in reference. Moreover, it was the 'patient' or 'receiver' of the action of *bu* 'mend'. It, therefore, should be made the *ba* NP, rather than *qiang* 'the wall' as shown in (iii) below:
      (iii)   ta ba qiang–de   yi–ge   dong bu–le.
             he *ba* wall's   one–CL   hole mend–ASP
            'What he did to a hole in the wall was to mend it.'

This explanation is similar to what Li (1974) has called "anaphoric" as a feature of the verb that can occur in a *ba*-construction and also the *ba*–NP. Li, however, was concerned with regular *ba* sentences and didn't mention the problem of the 'retained object'.

1.2.3.4.2 The Placement of Two Adverbs *You* and *Ye*

In our previous discussion of the double nominative construction it is reported that the placement of two adverbs *you* 'again' and *ye* 'also' provides a very reliable test for distinguishing a productive double nominative construction as in (67) from a semi-frozen verbal compound as in (68) and a frozen verbal compound as in (69).

(67) a. zhe-ke shu yezi <u>ye</u> hen da.
this-CL tree leaves also very big
'This tree (topic), (its) leaves are also very large.'
b. * zhe-ke shu <u>ye</u> yezi hen da.
this-CL tree also leaves very large

(68) a. ta duzi <u>you</u> e le.
he stomach again hungry PART
'He (topic), (his) stomach is empty again.
b. ta <u>you</u> duzi e le.
he again stomach hungry PART

(69) a. ta ye yan-hong.
he also eye-red
'He (is) also jealous.'
b.* ta yan ye hong.
he eye also red

In my previous studies (1979, 1982), it is claimed that in sentences like (67), *you* and *ye* can only occur between the subject and the VP. In (69), a sentence with a frozen verbal compound such as *yan-hong* 'jealous', *ye* can be placed between *ta*, the topic and the subject of the sentence, and the VP. Since (68), a sentence with a semi-frozen verbal compound like *duzi e* 'hungry' is subject to two analyses, *you* and *ye* can occur at two different places. In one analysis, it has the structure of a productive double nominative construction and so *you* 'again' can occur between *duzi* 'stomach' and *e* 'hungry'. In the other analysis, it is patterned after sentences with a frozen verbal compound; i.e., *duzi e* 'hungry' is regarded as a compound, and *ye* can only occur between *ta* 'he', the subject and the topic, and the VP, *duzi e* as in (68b).

As far as a regular double nominative construction is concerned, it seems accurate to characterize the second nominative as a subject. However, in Chapter 4, we have presented arguments to show that the second nominative in the construction should be more generally characterized as a secondary topic. Given this slight revision, the placement of *you* and *ye* can now be simply stated as:

(70) *you* or *ye* is placed between a topic and the immediately following VP.

With this rule in mind, we can now return to the *ba* construction. When we examine a *ba* sentence with *ye* or *you*, we find, as expected, that they can occur at two different places, with a slight difference in meaning as exemplified in (71a) and (71b).

(71) a. wo ye   ba ta   qing—lai   le.
       I   also   BA him   invite—come   PART
       'I also invited him to come.'
    b. wo ba ta   ye   qing—lai   le.
       I   BA him   also   invite—come   PART
       'He was also invited to come by me.'

Even though, the meanings of the (a) and (b) sentences are slightly different, the fact that *ye* can be placed immediately after *wo* 'I', the primary topic NP, and *ta* 'him', the *ba* NP, strongly indicates that the *ba* NP is also a topic of some sort.

1.2.3.4.3 The "Pseudo—transitive Verbs" and the *ba* Construction

There is one type of *ba* sentence, as exemplified by (72) and (73), for which no linguist, to date, has been able to give a satisfactory explanation.

(72) ta ba ge baba   si   le.
      he BA CL father   die   PART
      'His father died on him.'

(73) ta ba shou—pa   ku—shi   le.
      he BA handkerchief   cry—wet   PART
      'He cried and (as a result of that) his handkerchief got wet.'

Notice for one thing the verb in (72), *si* 'die', in its ordinary usage is an intransitive verb and, likewise, the compound verb in (73), *ku–shi* 'cry–wet', is made up of two verbs, each of which is intransitive. These types of sentences thus pose an insurmountable difficulty for previous analyses, for one of the commonly assumed basic requirements of a *ba* sentence is that the verb must be transitive.

Tang (1980) uses sentences like (74) and (75) to explain how notions like "old" and "new information", "information focus" and "empathy" can be applied to the analysis of Chinese sentences.

(74) a. ta–de   tui   duan   le.
        he–POSS   leg   break   PART
        'His leg broke.'

    b. ta duan–le   tui   le.
       he break–ASP   leg   PART
       'His leg broke.'

(75) a. ta–de   mama   si   le.
        he–POSS   mother die   PART
        'His mother died.'

    b. ta si–le   mama   le.
       he die–ASP   mother PART
       'His mother died.'

Taking a hint from his discussion, I have re–examined some *ba* sentences in the light of how they relate to the non–*ba* sentences of the form of (74) and (75). This examination has led me to the discovery of a very likely path through which sentences like (72) and (73) emerged.

To see this, first examine the following sets of sentences:

(76) a. ta–de   yi–ge   pibao   diu   le.
        he–POSS   1–CL   purse   lose   PART
        'A purse of his (is) lost.'

b. ta yi–ge pibao diu le.
he 1–CL purse lost PART
'He (topic), a purse (of his) (is) lost.'

c. ta diu–le yi–ge pibao le.
he lose–ASP 1–CL purse PART
'He (topic), a purse (of his) (is) lost.'
or 'He lost a purse (of his).'

d. ta ba–ge pibao diu le.
he BA–CL purse lost PART
'He lost a purse of his.'

(77) a. ta–de yi–zhi tui die–duan le.
he–POSS 1–CL leg fall–break PART
'One of his legs broke (as he fell).'

b. ta yi–zhi tui die–duan le.
he 1–CL leg fall–break PART
'He (topic), a leg (of his) broke (as he fell).'

c. ta die–duan–le yi–zhi tui le.
he fall–break–ASP 1–CL leg PART
'Same as (b).'
or 'He broke a leg of his (as he fell).'

d. ta ba yi–zhi tui die–duan le.
he BA 1–CL leg fall–break PART
'He had a leg of his broken (as he fell).'

(78) a. ta–de shoupa ku–shi le.
he–POSS handkerchief cry–wet PART
'His handkerchief got wet (as he cried).'

b. ta shoupa ku–shi le.
he handkerchief cry–wet PART
'He (topic), (his) handkerchief got wet (as he cried).'

c. ta ku–shi–le shoupa le.
he cry–wet–ASP handkerchief PART
'Same as (b).'
or 'He wet his handkerchief (as he cried).'

d. ta ba shoupa   ku–shi   le.
      he BA handkerchief cry–wet PART
      'He got his handkerchief wet (as he cried).'

(79) a. ta–de   baba   si   le.
        he–POSS father die PART
        'His father died.'
     b. ta baba   si   le.
        he father die PART
        'He (topic), (his) father died.'
     c. ta si–le   ge baba   le.⁹
        he die–ASP CL father PART
        'Same as (b).'
     d. ta ba ge baba   si   le.
        he BA CL father die PART
        'He (topic), (his) father died (on him).'

If we compare these sentences first within each set and then across the sets, we find that on the surface the four sentences in each set are similar in distribution. The (a) sentence is one with an NP having a possessive modifier as its topic and subject, which is followed by an intransitive verb. The possessive marker *–de* can be dropped and the possessor NP becomes the topic, giving rise to the (b) sentence, a double nominative construction. Then the possessed NP, which in (b) is the subject and secondary topic, can be , under certanin conditions, moved to the back of the verb, giving us the (c) sentence. And finally the postverbal NP in (c) can be preposed to become a *ba* NP, giving us the (d) sentence, a *ba* construction.

This, however, is where similarity ends. When we compare the verbs in the four sets, we find that they fall into three categories. The verb in (76b), though used intransitively there, is nevertheless capable of being used transitively. Thus, when the possessed NP *yi–ge pibao* 'a purse' is postposed as in (76c), the sentence can be analyzed in two different ways as in (80a) and (80b), with the second being more natural:

---

[9] We will return to the problem of *ge*, which is short for *yi–ge* 'an indefinite marker + a classifier', in (79c and d) in a moment.

(80) a. ta   diu–le   yi-ge   pibao   le.
        Topic V_I Subject

    b. ta   diu–le   yi-ge pibao   le.
        Topic V_T Object

Given the analysis of (80b), it is to be expected that *yi-ge pibao* can be preposed to become a *ba* NP as in (76d).

The verb in (79b), *si* 'die', on the other hand, is an intransitive verb. So (79c) should have only one analysis. A question that immediately arises is: why then should the postverbal subject be capable of becoming a *ba* NP as in (79d)? There are two very likely reasons for this. First, notice that postverbal subject is the possessed NP, which is quite high in the hierarchy of topicality in Chinese, especially when the overall topic is the possessor NP. And since the *ba* NP, as we have been trying to demonstrate, is a topic of some special kind, it is natural, as far as topicality is concerned, for it to become a *ba* NP. Second, it is through the analogy of the change from (76c) to (76d), where a verb capable of transitive interpretation is involved, that an intransitive verb like *si* 'die' can also allow the NP that follows it to be preposed to become a *ba* NP. In other words, the fact that an NP can occur after a verb makes the verb look as if it were transitive. For lack of a better term, I would simply refer to this type of verbs as a "quasi–transitive" verb. Once preposing is allowed in the case of "quasi–transitive" verbs like *si* 'die', it is easy to understand why compound verbs like *die-duan* 'fall–break' in (77c) and *ku-shi* 'cry–wet' in (78c), whose transitivity is even more opaque than *si* 'die', can also allow the NP that follows it to become a *ba* NP.

But how do we know that the *ba* sentences in (77d) actually go through these stages in their derivation. Especially crucial to our hypothesis is the change from (c) to (d), since the process that turns (a) into (b) is still very productive[10] and that which turns (b) into (c) is more or less productive.[11] Implicit in the statement is the fact that the change from (c) to (d) is no longer productive and for that reason it might be very difficult to prove. Fortunately, there is one piece of evidence which strongly suggests this derivation. Tang (1980) comments on the use of *ge*, which is short for *yi-ge*, an indefinite marker with a classifier, in connection with proper nouns in sentences like (81) and (82):

---

[10]See Chapter 4 and Tsao (1982) for a fuller discussion of the circumstances that gave rise to the double nominative construction.

[11]See Tang (1980) for some discussion.

(81) chuang–shang tang–zhe ge Xiaolizi
     bed–LOC   lie–ASP   CL Xiaolizi
     'On the bed (there) lies Xiaolizi.'

(82) zuotian   lai–le   ge Yangdama.
     yesterday come–ASP   CL Yangdama
     'Yesterday, (there) came Yangdama.'

by saying that *ge* (or *wei*, another classifier for persons) is used here because people strongly expect an indefinite noun in the postverbal position of a presentative sentence. Since a proper noun, which is normally definite, is found here, *ge* has to be used to take away some of the shock that people might otherwise have (Tang 1980:7). The same explanation can be given to other intransitive sentences with a post–verbal proper noun as in (79c). This being the case, when the postverbal NP is moved preverbally to become the *ba* NP, it takes the *ge* with it as in (79d).[12] Without incurring such a derivation, it is impossible to explain why the *ba* NP, which is normally required to be definite, would have a *ge*, an indefinite marker in this case, used with a proper noun, which is already definite by itself.

To further confirm my hypothesis, I have examined all the examples given by Hashimoto (1971) and others as compound verbs which are formed by two verbs, both intransitive by themselves, which allow the NP that follows them to be preposed as a *ba* NP. Below are some examples of this type of *ba* sentences.

(83) a. ta ba yanjing   ku–hong   le.
        he BA eyes   cry–red   PART
        'He cried (so much that) his eyes became red.'
     b. ta ku–hong–le   yanjing   le.
        he cry–red–ASP eyes   PART
     c. ta yanjing   ku–hong   le.
        he eyes   cry–red   PART

---

[12]Movement or derivation should be taken in its historical sense here as elsewhere in the paper.

(84) a. ta ba houlong han–ya le.
    he BA throat shout–hoarse PART
    'He shouted (so much that) his throat became hoarse.'
  b. ta han–ya–le houlong le.
    he shout–hoarse–ASP throat PART
  c. ta houlong han–ya le.
    he throat shout–hoarse PART

(85) a. ta ba zuiba xiaowai le.
    he BA mouth laugh–distorted PART
    'He laughed (so much that) his mouth got distorted.'
  b. ta xiao–wai–le zuiba le.
    he laugh–distorted–ASP mouth PART
  c. ta zuiba xiao–wai le.
    He mouth laugh–distorted PART

(86) a. ta ba yizi zuo–ta le.
    he BA chair sit–collapse PART
    'He sat (and as a result) his chair collapsed.'
  b. ta zuo–ta–le yizi le.
    he sit–collapse–ASP chair PART
  c. ta yizi zuo–ta le.
    he chair sit–collapse PART

It is clear from these examples that all the *ba* sentences with this type of verbs can be derived in the same way as (78) and (79), i.e. they can all be said to originate from a double nominative construction.[13]

---

[13]There is one sentence which Hashimoto (1971:40) mentions and attempts to solve by relating it to the causative *shi*–construction. This non–*ba* sentence is given below in (i) and its corresponding *ba* sentence in (ii).
  (i) meimei ku–luan–le wode xin.
    younger sister cry–perplex–ASP my heart
    'Younger sister wept so much that I got very upset.'
  (ii) meimei ba wode xin ku–luan–le.
    younger sister ba my heart cry–perplex–ASP
    'What younger sister did to me was to cry so much that I got upset.'
Hashimoto gives (iii) as the underlying structure of (i):
(iii)

To conclude, the fact that this analysis can account for the emergence of so many *ba* sentences, which otherwise remains a mystery strongly supports the conclusion that we arrived at independently in the earlier sections that the *ba* NP is not just an object of the verb in the clause. It is, more importantly, a topic of some special kind.

1.3 The Meaning and Function of the *Ba* Construction

In our previous discussion, we have demonstrated that there are many similarities between the primary topic and the *ba* NP, and it is on the strength of this that we identify the *ba* NP as a secondary topic of a special kind. There are, however, a few dissimilarities that remain to be explained. A very important one is this: while of all the NPs bearing different grammatical relations to the verb, subject is the highest one in the hierarchy of topic choice, it is the direct object which is the highest in the case of *ba* topic. To explain this important difference and others, we have to go first into the meaning and function of the *ba* construction.

1.3.1 Wang's Theory of "Disposal"

Wang (1945) first proposed the theory of "disposal." According to this theory, a *ba* sentence in the form of X *ba* Y Z, gives us the meaning of X "disposes" of Y in the way described by Z. Evidently, the term "disposal" will have to be stretched considerably in this interpretation. In Wang Li's own words:

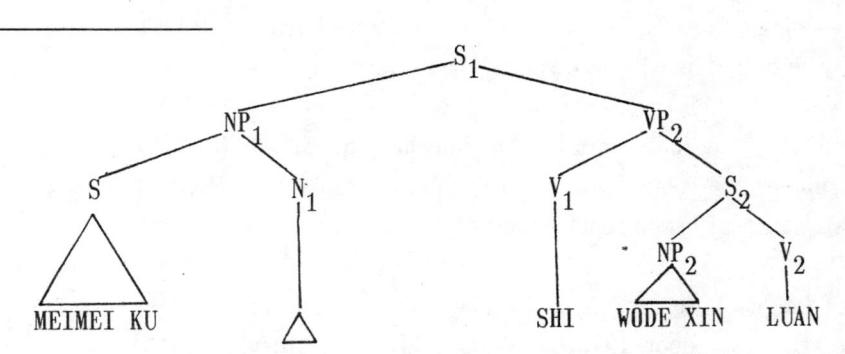

She gives only a very vague semantic justification by saying that the interpretation of (i) is close to causative *shi*-construction with a sentential subject as shown in (iii). Anyone can see that this is a very ad hoc solution for the fact that *ku–luan* 'cry—perplex', which are both intransitive by themselves, has acquired transitivity as a combination. We feel that *ku–luan* 'cry perplex' has become transitive on analogy with *ku–hong* 'cry—red' and *ku–shi* 'cry—wet', when the latter expressions have achieved their status as what we call 'semi–transitive' verbs. Unfortunately, we have no good solid evidence to bring to bear on this point.

The disposal form states how a person is handled, manipulated, or dealt with, how something is disposed of, how an affair is conducted. Since it is especially designed for disposing, the disposal form cannot be used unless the action possesses the quality of disposal. For instance, *wo ai ta*, 'I love him' cannot be restated as *wo ba ta ai*, 'I "take" him and love him.' Again, *tao shu kai hua* 'Peach trees bloomed' cannot be re-stated as *tao shu ba hua kai* 'Peach trees "took" the blooms and bloomed' (Wang Li 1947:160–61;Li's translation 1974:200–01).

Even though many linguists, Lü Shu-xiang (1948), Wang Huan (1959), and Y.R. Chao (1968) among them, have pointed out the inadequacies of Wang's theory, most of them, however, chose to use his term. This fact suggests that most linguists think that Wang's theory has certain merits but is perhaps not general enough. A careful study of their comments on Wang's theory confirms this conclusion. The following are some sentences given by various linguists whose meaning cannot be explained satisfactorily by the "disposal" theory.

(87)   ta   yi-kou-qi   ba   na   san-bai-ge   taijie
he   one-breath   BA   those   300-CL   steps
zou-wan-le.
walk-finish-ASP
'He finished climbing up those three hundred steps in one breath.'

(88)   zhemeyilai,   ta   keyao   ba   ni   hen-tou   le.
so-doing   he   will   BA   you   hate-pierce   PART
'By so doing, he will hate you to the extreme.'

(89)   feiji   kuai   yao   ba   huoche   qudai   le.
airplanes   soon   will   BA   trains   replace   PART
'Airplanes will soon replace trains.'

(90)   ta   ba   gebi-de   Wang   Taitai   dezui   le.
he   BA   next-door-POSS   Wang   Mrs.   offend   PART
'He got Mrs. Wang next door offended.'

(91)   ta   ba   yi-ge   da   hao   jihui
he   BA   one-CL   very   good   opportunity

	cuoguo	le
	miss	PART

'He missed a very good opportunity.'

(92) ta ba damen–de yaoshi diu le.
he BA main–door–POSS key lose PART
'He lost the key to the main door.'

If we examine these sentences carefully, we find that they really present an insurmountable problem for the theory of disposal. Take (90), for instance; here the *ba* NP is *gebi-de Wang Taitai* 'Mrs. Wang next door', but in this sentence, she can hardly be said to be "handled, manipulated, or dealt with". In fact, the most natural reading of the sentence is *ta* 'he', the topic, unintentionally did something and as a result of that he offended Mrs. Wang.

Mei (1978), from which all these sentences are cited, also gave a similar criticism, but on the basis of the criticism, Mei came to the conclusion that the meaning of disposal comes from the verb that is in construction with *ba* in the same sentence. He then went on to demonstrate that the functions of the *ba* construction are two:(i) to mark the *ba* NP as part of the presupposed (old) information; and (ii) to mark the *ba* NP as 'specific' ('definite' in our terms) in reference.[14] We agree fully with his characterization of the functions of *ba*, as we have demonstrated earlier in our effort to establish the *ba* NP as a topic; that is, the *ba* NP has, among others, these two properties. In other words, to say that the *ba* NP is a topic is to say that it is part of the presupposed (old) information, and that its reference is definite.

However, we can not agree with his conclusion—that the meaning of disposal comes from the verb. For one thing, his account fails to explain why we can get the meaning of "disposal" in cases like *ni ba ta zenme le?* 'What did you do to him?', where the verb is completely neutral. For another, his account fails to explain why, in most cases, the *ba* NP actually bears the relation of the direct object to the verb in the same clause.

---

[14]Mei's use of 'specific' is closer to our term 'definite'. He avoids the term 'definite' because he takes it to be a purely syntactic term. He correctly points out that 'specific' (or 'definite' in our term) can only be defined in terms of semantics and pragmatics. For a detailed discussion of his use of 'specific', see Mei (1972). For our use of 'definite' and 'specific' see Tsao (1979, Chapter 5).

1.3.2 Thompson's Analysis

To recapitulate, we find two points especially noteworthy in our discussion of Wang's theory, namely, (i) *ba* does have a meaning close to "disposal", even though to characterize it as "disposal" is probably not general enough, and (ii) most *ba* NPs actually bear the relation of a direct object to the verb in the same clause. With these two points in mind, we find Thompson's characterization of the meaning of the *ba* construction in terms of "transitivity" most appealing.

Thompson (1973) starts out by citing Lyons' definition of transitivity:

> The traditional 'notional' view of transitivity (and the term itself) suggests that the effects of the action expressed by the verb 'pass over' from the 'agent' (or 'actor') to the 'patient' (or 'goal')(Lyons, 1968:350).

Thompson then goes on to say that the notion of transitivity is the one which is expressed in English by the phrase "did something to Y". In other words, transitivity can be conceived of as a three-term formula and the relationship is expressed in Chinese as:

(93)   X   ba   Y   Z

where Z contains a verb and a complement, specifying how Y has been affected. In other words, a *ba* construction is used in answer to the question, *X ba Y zenme le?* 'What did X do to Y?'[15]

This formula fits nicely into our account. Three things are presupposed, namely X, Y and the transitivity relation. Since we have demonstrated that both X and Y are topics, they should represent presupposed information. Furthermore, since Y represents the one that is affected, it is semantically a patient and syntactically a direct object, at least in the typical use of the construction.

There is an important difference between the English and Chinese conception of transitivity. While in English the transitivity relation can be defined solely in terms of the nature of the verb, in Chinese it can be determined only on the basis of the semantic content of the whole phrase, a point that Mei (1978) has so convincingly argued.[16] Compare

---

[15]The English translation suffers a little in that the past tense in it is not as general as the perfective aspect indicated by *—le* in the Chinese original.

[16]Chu (1973, 1976a) has also arrived at a similar conclusion in his comparison of the passive construction in English and Chinese.

(94) with (95) and (96) with (97).

(94) a.* wo ba ta hen le.
I BA he hate PART
b.* What I did to him is to hate him.

(95) a. wo ba ta hen–ji le.
I BA him hate–extreme PART
b.* What I did to him is to hate him to the extreme.'

(96) a.* wo ba ta kanjian le.
I BA he see PART
b.* What I did to him is to see him?

(97) a. wo ba ta kan–yi–kan
I BA he look–to–find–out
b. What I did to him is to take a look at him.

As indicated in (94b) and (95b), the English verb *hate* cannot be used in this particular formula no matter whether it is further modified by the adverbial phrase, 'to the extreme' or not. On the Chinese side, however, while the verb *hen* 'hate' alone cannot occur in a *ba* construction, it can when it is further modified by *ji le* 'to the extreme'. This is exactly the reason why we deliberately use a term Z in (93) without breaking it down to a verb and another component.

Having said this, we have to hasten to add that not even this powerful formula can give us the correct interpretation in all cases. There is another class of *ba* sentences exemplified by (98) and (99) below. These sentences represent what is usually called "the extended use" of the *ba* construction.

(98) nei bei jiu ba ta he–de chabuduo zui
that cup wine BA him drink–PART almost drunk
le.*
PART
'That glass of wine almost made him drunk.'

(99)　na　　chang　qiu　　　　　ba　women　da—de
　　　the　CL　　ball—game　BA　us　　　play—PART
　　　lei—si　　　le.
　　　tire—dead　PART
　　　'That ball game (topic), we played so much that we were tired to death.'

In this extended use of the *ba* construction, the regular topic NP is not an agent and the *ba* NP is not a receiver of an action. Rather, the roles are in this case reversed. This being the case, the interpretive rule of transitivity cannot apply here. Rather, the first term X in this case is a cause and the *ba* construction takes on a causative reading, as *ba* in both (98) and (99) can be replaced by *shi,* the most productive causative particle in Chinese, without any significant change of cognitive meaning.

(98)　a.　nei—bei　　jiu　　　shi　ta　he—de　　　　chabuduo
　　　　　that—CL　wine　SHI　he　drink—PART　almost
　　　　　zui　　　le.
　　　　　drunk　PART
　　　　　'Same as (98).'

(99)　a.　na—chang　qiu　　　　　shi　women　da—de
　　　　　that—CL　　ball—game　SHI　us　　　play—PART
　　　　　lei—si　　　le.
　　　　　tire—dead　PART
　　　　　'Same as (99).'

That a construction for especially marking transitivity should be extended to mean causality may strike some as unusual, but from the perspective of linguistic change, this is anything but unnatural.

First, notice that even though the S—initial NP is higher in topicality than the *ba* NP, they are both topics. And the fact that they have the same status certainly makes switching easier.

Second, Lyons (1977:491, ff.) correctly observes that there are three common schemata for bivalent verbs:

(100) (I)   AFFECT   (AGENT, PATIENT)   (operative)
      (II) PRODUCE (CAUSE, EFFECT)   (factitive)
      (III) PRODUCE (AGENT, EFFECT)   (operative–factitive)

and (I) most closely reflects the traditional notion of transitivity and that many transitive verbs are also causative in that they can be interpreted in terms of (III). With this in mind, we can easily explain why 'kill' in a sentence like *John killed Mary* can have two analyses. On the one hand, it can be analyzed as a transitive verb with *John* as agent and *Mary* as patient; on the other hand, it can also have the analysis of a causative verb as in Scheme (III), CAUSE (John, Mary (DIE)).

In the case of the *ba* construction, we also find the same ambivalence with regard to certain verbs. Compare (101) with (102).

(101) a. ta ba Zhang San ma   le.
          he ba Zhang San scolded PART
          'What he did to Zhang San is to scold him.'
      b.* ta shi   Zhang San ma   le.
          he cause Zhang San scold PART

(102) a. ta ba wo xia–le   yi–tiao
          he ba me scare–ASP one–jump
          'What he did to me was to scare me.'
      b. ta shi   wo xia–le   yi–tiao.
          he cause me scare–ASP one–jump
          'He scared me.'

In (101) *ma* 'scold' is a transitive verb with *ta* 'he' as agent and *Zhang San* as patient and the function of *ba* there is to make this transitivity relation very explicit. Moreover, it is unambiguous as it can have only the transitivity reading. *Xia* 'scare' in (102a), on the other hand, is ambivalent in that it may have the interpretation of (I), a transitive verb or (III), a causative verb. This observation is confirmed by the fact that (102b), which has *shi* in place of *ba*, is grammatical and has almost the same meaning as (102a).

Once casuality reading becomes possible with sentences like (102a), then the door is wide open for sentences like (98) and (99). This is so because the first NPs in (98) and (99) and that of (102a) can all be interpreted as 'cause', whether or not they are animate, and all of them, as we have repeatedly shown, are topics.

A few paragraphs back, we have, following the practice of a number of Chinese grammarians, termed the type of *ba* constructions with a causative reading as "extended" use of *ba*. Now we see that there are good reasons for doing this. For one thing, the extended use is much more restricted in the nature of the verb and the type of NP that can become the S–initial primary topic. For another, this kind of *ba* sentence is far less common than the regular type.[17]

To sum up, one can postulate the following rule for the interpretation of the *ba* clause (or independent sentence):

(103) If the primary topic is capable of being interpreted as the agent of the action denoted by the verb, then assign the transitivity reading to the clause. If not, the clause will be assigned a causality reading.

So far we have demonstrated that the function of *ba* is to mark the NP that immediately follows it as a secondary topic. In terms of the theory of functional sentence perspective, it is, as a topic, part of the theme (old or presupposed) information and in terms of referential function, it is usually definite. To look at the same phenomenon from a different perspective, we can also call the term Z (V + complement) in (93) as comment. In terms of the theory of functional sentence perspective, it is the rheme part of a sentence. As a rheme, any part of it or itself can be focus. This is in complete agreement with the following observation of information exchange in terms of question–answer pairs (the question and answer parts are underlined).

(104) a. ta   zuo–le   shenme   shi   le?
          he   do–ASP   what   thing   PART
          'What did he do?'
       b. ta   mai–le   ta–de   qiche.
          he   sell–ASP his   car
          'He sold his car.'

---

[17]It is based on these two reasons that I don't think it is correct to characterize the *ba* construction as a causative one as Huang (1974) has attempted to prove.

(105) a. ta   ba ta–de qiche zenme le?
         he   BA his   car   what   PART
         'What did he do with his car?'

    b. ta   ba ta–de qiche mai–le?
       he   BA his   car   sell–ASP
       'He had his car sold.'

(106) a. ta   ba ta–de qiche mai–le
         he   BA his   car   sell–ASP
         duo–shao   qian?
         how–much   money
         'How much did he sell his car for?'

    b. ta   ba ta–de qiche mai–le
       he   BA his   car   sell–ASP
       wu–qian   kuai   qian.
       5–thousand dollar   money
       'He had his car sold for five thousand dollars.'

2. The Object Fronting Construction

As mentioned in Chapter 2, a heated debate occurred in mainland China concerning how subject in Chinese is to be identified. Closely related to the issue is the problem of the identification of object when it occurs preverbally as in (107).

(107) ta   nei–ben   shu   hai   mei   kan–wan.
      he   that–CL   book   yet   not   read–finish
      'He hasn't finished reading the book yet.'

One school represented by Li (1969), Wang (1974) and Lü (1947), analyzes *nei–ben shu* 'that book' in (107) as a fronted object. They justify their analysis by arguing that *nei–ben shu* 'that book' is the patient/goal of the main verb *kan* 'read'. Sentences like (107) is thus regarded as an inverted sentence or a variation of the unmarked SVO sentence. The other school represented by Zhang (1953) and The Committee on Syntax, Institute of Linguistics, Chinese National Academy of Sciences(1952–53), analyzes *ta* 'he' in (107) as the major subject, which has the *nei–ben shu hai mei kan–wan* as its predicate, which, in turn, can be analyzed as composed of a subject, *nei–ben shu* 'that book' and a predicate, *hai mei kan—wan* 'not yet finish reading'. It is clear that they base their analysis on position as well as on the notion of "what is being talked about."[18]

The controversy is far from settled. It is, therefore, part of the purpose of the present section to find out the reason that gave rise to the controversy and to suggest how the issue can be resolved. More specifically, we will argue that phrases like *nei—ben shu* 'that book' in (107) is to be treated as object in the clausal level of analysis, but should be treated as a secondary topic in another level, which, for lack of better term, we will call "sentential" or "inter—clausal".

2.1 Topical Qualities of the Fronted Object

The fronted object, just like the *ba* NP we discussed in the last section, has most of the semantic and syntactic properties of the primary topic. First, it occurs at the position immediately following the primary topic, which as we have repeatedly pointed out, appears S—initially. Compare (108a) with (108b).

(108) a. ta_i kan—wan—le   nei—ben   shu,   _____$_i$ jiu
           he   read—finish—ASP   that—CL   book   then
           shui—jiao   le.
           sleep   PART
           'He finished reading the book and then went to bed immediately.'

       b. ta_i nei—ben shu$_j$ kan—wan,   _____$_i$ _____$_j$ jiu   huan
           he   that—CL book   read—finish   then   retun
           gei   wo   le.
           to   me   PART
           'He finished reading the book and then he returned it to me immediately.'

In (108a) only *ta* 'he' is the common topic, while *nei—ben shu* is not and hence it occurs in its usual postverbal position but in (108b) it is one of the two things being talked about and hence it occurs in the position immediately after the primary topic in both clauses.

(108b) also demonstrates clearly that *nei—ben shu* 'that book', the fronted object has the discourse property of extending its domain over more than one clause to form a topic

___

[18]This is also basically Chao's position, as presented in *A Grammar of Spoken Chinese* (1968).

chain. But it can do that only when the primary topic does that at the same time, as the ungrammaticality of (109a) shows. However, if the fronted object is further topicalized to be the primary topic, then no such restriction holds, as the grammaticality of (109b) shows.

(109) a.* ta nei–ben shu$_j$ yi kan–wan, ni ____$_j$ jiu
he that–CL book once read–finish you then
huan gei wo.
return to me
'As soon as he finishes reading the book, you return it to me.'

b. nei–ben shu$_i$ ta yi kan–wan, ____$_i$ ni jiu
that–CL book he once read–finish you then
huan gei wo.
return to me
'Speaking of the book, as soon as he finishes reading it, return it to me.'

Again, (108b) shows unmistakably that the secondary topic *nei–ben shu* 'that book', like the primary topic before it *ta* 'he', is in control of the coreferential NP deletion and pronominalization in the whole topic chain.

Fourthly, just like the primary topic, the fronted object will have to be definite in reference, as an indefinite object NP that is fronted will cause the whole sentence to be ungrammatical. Compare (110) with (111).

(110) a. ta mai–le yi–ben shu.
he buy–ASP one–CL book
'He bought a book.'
b.* ta yi–ben shu mai–le.[19]
he one–CL book buy–ASP

---

[19]
(i) ta yi–ben shu ye mei mai.
he one–CL book also not buy
'He didn't buy even one book.'
Sentences like (i) will be taken as a variation of the *lian .... dou/ye* construction with *lian* 'including' optionally omitted. It will be discussed in full in the next chapter, where we will also argue that *yi–ben shu* 'a book' together with *ye* occurring in the scope of negation functions to indicate genericity, i.e. not even one (of a particular kind).

'Roughly, same as (a).'
c.* yi–ben shu ta mai–le.
one–CL book he buy–ASP
'Roughly, same as (a).'

(111) a. ta mai–le nei–ben shu.
he buy–ASP that–CL book
'He bought the book.'
b. ta nei–ben shu mai–le.
he that–CL book buy–ASP
'Roughly, same as (a).'
c. nei–ben shu ta mai–le.
that–CL book he buy–ASP
'Roughly, same as (a).'

The grammaticality contrast between (110b) and (111b) on the one hand, and (110c) and (111c) on the other clearly demonstrates that only definite object NP can be moved to the preverbal position to become either a fronted object or a primary topic. In a similar vein, (112) shows that a generic object NP, like a definite NP, can be moved to a preverbal position as a fronted object or a primary topic. We are, therefore, justified to conclude that a fronted NP, like a primary topic, is always definite or generic in reference.

(112) a. ta bu chi yü.
he not eat fish
'He doesn't eat fish.'
b. ta yü bu chi.
he fish not eat
'Roughly, same as (a).'
c. yü ta bu chi.
fish he not eat
'Roughly, same as (a).'

Finally, the fronted object, like the primary topic before it, can be separated from the following part of the sentence by one of four pause particles, *a (ya), me, ne, ba*. Compare (a) and (b) in (113).

(113) a. ta nei–ben shu $\begin{Bmatrix} ya \\ me \\ ne \\ ba \end{Bmatrix}$ hai mei kan–wan ne.

he that–CL book PART yet not read–finish PART
'As for him, the book he hasn't finished reading it yet.'

b.* ta hai mei kan–wan nei–ben shu $\begin{Bmatrix} ya \\ me \\ ne \\ ba \end{Bmatrix}$ ne.

he yet not read–finish that–CL book PART PART
'He hasn't finished reading the book yet.'

To sum up, we have found the fronted object NP to possess the following semantic and syntactic properties:

(114) a. It occurs preverbally, following only the primary topic in a clause.
b. It can optionally be separated from the following part of the clause in which it overtly occurs by one of the four pause particles: *a (ya), me, ne,* and *ba.*
c. It is always definite or generic in reference.
d. It has the supra–clausal quality of being extendable to a topic chain provided that the primary topic also does that at the same time.
e. It is in control of the pronominalization and deletion of all the coreferential NPs in a topic chain.

If we compare (114) with (12), we find what the similarities are far too many to be missed. Furthermore, all the minor differences can be attributed to their respective function in the topic chain. It seems that we have proved beyond any reasonable doubt that the fronted NP is indeed a secondary topic.

2.2. Additional Parallelisms

Similarities between the primary topic and the fronted object NP, however, do not stop here. We can give at least two additional parallels.

2.2.1. The Contrastive Function

In addition to sharing the chaining function with the primary topic, as shown in (108b), the fronted object is also similar to the primary topic in being able to be contrasted with a similar constituent in the following clauses. Compare (115a), where the fronted object is the same while the primary topics are being contrasted with (115b), where the primary topic is the same while the fronted objects are being contrasted.

(115) a. ta shuxue$_j$ bu xihuan, wo ___$_j$ ke
he mathematics not like I on:the:contrary
bu taoyan.
not dislike
'He doesn't like mathematics but I don't dislike it.'

b. ta$_i$ Yingwen xihuan, ___$_i$ shuxue
he English like mathematics
que bu xihuan.
on:the:contrary not like
'Speaking of him, English (he) likes but mathematics (he) doesn't.

There is one more thing worth noting here. Even though both constituents can be contrasted, the fronted object, as we have shown in our previous discussion, can have the chaining function only when the primary topic is also identical whereas the primary topic has no such restriction. Therefore, sentences like (115a) will sound better if the identical fronted object is further preposed to become the primary topic as shown in (116).

(116) shuxue$_i$ ta bu xihuan, ___$_i$ wo ke
mathematics he not like I on:the:contrary
bu taoyan.
not dislike
'As for mathematics, he doesn't like it but I don't dislike it.'

2.2.2. Relation with the Retained Object

In our previous discussion of the *ba* construction, we mentioned that the *ba* NP can bear the relation of whole—part or possessor—possessed with another object that is "left behind", so to speak, as a retained object, as shown in (117b). The relation parallels what we have between the first and the second NP in the double nominative construction, as shown in (117a).[20]

(117) a. <u>wu-ge   juzi</u>   <u>liang-ge</u>   lan   le.
          five-CL   orange   two-CL   rot   PART
          '(of) the five oranges, two (of them) rotted.'
      b. ta ba <u>wu-ge   juzi</u>   chi-le   <u>liang-ge</u>.
          he BA five-CL orange   eat-ASP   two-CL
          'What he did to the five oranges is to eat two of them.'

We have also used this parallel to argue that the *ba* NP is a topic of a kind. The same argument also holds here, as witnessed by (117c).[21]

(117) c. ta <u>wu-ge   juzi</u>   chi-le   <u>liang-ge</u>.
          he five-CL   orange   eat-ASP   two-CL
          'Speaking of him, (of) the five oranges (he) ate two.'

From the above discussion it is clear that if the *ba* NP is a topic, the fronted object NP must be one as well.

2.2.3. Summary

At the beginning of our discussion of this construction we mentioned the controversy that occurred in mainland China concerning the proper analysis of sentences like (107). We are now in a better position to explain why there should have arisen such a controversy and to propse our solution.

Those who analyzed the fronted object as a minor subject evidently confuse subject with topic, which as I have repeatedly pointed out in this book and elsewhere(Tsao, 1978, 1979), should be clearly distinguished in Chinese because failure to maintain the distinction hinders us from arriving at many significant generalizations in Chinese. On the other hand,

---

[20]We have previously pointed out that the parallelism is not perfect. In the *ba* construction we are unable to find examples that exhibit the relation of class and member between the *ba* NP and the retained object.

[21]The restriction mentioned in Note 20 also holds in the case object fronting construction. There are no sentences that exhibit the relation of class-member between the fronted object and the retained object.

those who treat the constituent as an object fail to see many of its topical qualities and how it interacts with the primary topic and other types of non—primary topic, an area of study that we will turn to presently.

An obvious solution that we will propose is to treat the constituent as an object in one level of syntactic organization and to treat it as a secondary topic in another level. In other words, we are saying that topic does not stand in contrast with either subject or object. A constituent may be a subject or an object in one level of analysis and yet it may be a topic in another. This view, though not necessarily revolutionary, is of great theoretical consequence but space prevents us from going into it as this point.

2.3. The Fronted Object and its Syntagmatic Relation

Our discussion has led us to see the fronted object as a secondary topic. Assuming that there are no other non—primary topics present, its syntagmatic relation with other elements in the same clause may be illustrated as follows:

(118)　The primary topic + The fronted object + Verb + (Retained object)

We have mentioned the relationship between the fronted object and the retained object in our previous discussion. In what follows we will concentrate on its relationship with the primary topic and the verb.

2.3.1 The Fronted Object and the Primary Topic

At various places in our discussion we have mentioned that the fronted object, being a secondary topic, can, in an appropriate context, be further promoted to be a primary topic. We have just pointed out such a condition in connection with (116).

Another important condition has to do with animacy/inanimacy of the fronted object. If the object is inanimate, as in our examples so far, then it can be freely fronted. But if it is animate as in (119a), then fronting seems to be severely constrained, as (119b) is ungrammatical. However, further fronting to the primary topic seems to improve its grammaticality as (119c) shows.

(119)　a.　　Li Xiaojie　　xihuan　　Zhang Xiansheng.
　　　　　　　Li Miss　　　like　　　Zhang Mr.
　　　　　　'Miss Li likes Mr. Zhang.'

b. Li Xiaojie   Zhang Xiansheng   xihuan.
   Li Miss   Zhang Mr.   like
   (i)* Speaking of Miss Li and Mr. Zhang, (she) likes (him).
   (ii)? Speaking of Mr. Zhang and Miss Li, (he) likes (her).
c.? Zhang Xiansheng   Li Xiaojie   xihuan.
    Zhang Mr.   Li Miss   like
    'As for Mr. Zhang, Miss Li likes (him).'

How are we then to account for this distributional fact? First, note that when both preverbal NPs are animate as in (b), the hearer may have great difficulty in determining which NP serves as agent/actor and which serves as patient/goal as *Zhang Xiansheng* 'Mr. Zhang' can be interpreted as the fronted object (the secondary topic), i.e. patient/goal and *Li Xiaojie* 'Miss Li'. the subject (the primary topic), i.e. agent/actor as given in (i) interpretation. But since, as we have just pointed out, the fronted object, being a secondary topic, can be further topicalized to become the primary topic, *Li Xiaojie* 'Miss Li' can alternatively be interpreted as the fronted object further topicalized and hence should be interpreted as patient/goal with *Zhang Xiansheng* 'Mr. Zhang' interpreted as agent/actor, as shown in the (ii) translation.

But how about (119c)? Aren't there also two preverbal animate NPs that will cause the perceptual confusion that we just mentioned? Why then is it better? The difference in grammaticality between (119b) and (119c) can be attributed to an important perceptual strategy in Chinese, which can be roughly stated as (120):

(120) Interprete the first NP as the primary topic and the first animate NP to the left of the verb as subject.[22]

Given two NPs which can either be animate or inanimate, we have the four possible combinations as set out in (121).

(121) NP_1 NP_2
    a.   inanimate   animate

---

[22]Recall that in Chapter 2 in our discussion of how subject is to be identified in terms of surface position, the second part of the perceptual strategy is used as a criterion. For detail, please see our discussion there.

b. animate   inanimate
c. animate   animate
d. inanimate   inanimate

As combination (d) is not possible, we actually have other three possibilities, which are represented by (a), (b) and (c) sentences in (122) respectively.

(122) a. <u>nei–ben shu</u>   <u>Li Si</u>   xihuan.
       that–CL book   Li Si   like
       'Speaking of the book, Li Si likes (it).'
    b. <u>Li Si</u>   <u>nei–ben shu</u>   xihuan.
       Li Si   that–CL book   like
       'Speaking of Li Si and the book, (he) likes (it).'
    c. <u>Wang Xiaojie</u>   <u>Li Si</u>   xihuan.
       Wang Miss   Li Si   like
       'Speaking of Miss Wang, Li Si likes (her).'

(120) works satisfactorily for us. In (122a), *Li Si* is identified as subject (agent/actor) and secondary topic while *nei–ben shu* 'that book' is taken to be the primary topic and object. In (122b) *Li Si* is identified as the primary topic and subject and *nei–ben shu* 'that book' as the secondary topic (fronted object) and object. (122c) is a crucial case because we have two animate NPs occurring preverbally. According to Huang's (1974) informal survey, about 90 percent of the native speakers asked interprete *Li Si* as subject (agent/actor) and *Wang Xiaojie* 'Miss Wang' as object (patient/goal). Our perceptual strategy can give us that preferred reading. It, however, fails to give us the other reading, which, though not likely, is nevertheless possible. It is exactly because of this that we termed it "perceptual strategy". It gives correct result quickly in most cases, but, unlike a rule, it is not watertight.

2.3.2 The fronted object and the verb

As the name of the construction under discussion indicates, the fronted secondary topic bears the relation of object to the main verb of the sentence. This characterization, however, is not exactly correct. As it turns out, both "object" and "the main verb" need further qualification.

Let us take up the term "verb" first. It is not necessarily the matrix verb. It can be a verb that is embedded within what will be called a "telescopic verb" in Chapter 7. This is exemplified in (123).

(123) a. wo   bi   Zhang San   xie—le   nei—fong   xin.
         I   force   Zhang San   write—ASP   that—CL   letter
         'I forced Zhang San to write that letter.'
      b. wo nei—fong   xin   bi   Zhang San   xie   le.
         I that—CL   letter   force   Zhang San   write PART
         'Roughly, same as (a).'

Bi 'force, compel' is a telescopic verb, a defining characteristic of which is that its object, which immediately follows it, is at the same time the subject of the embedded verb.[23] In addition to 'force', this class includes such verbs as *tsui* 'urge', *qing* 'ask', *bang* 'help', *quan* 'advise' etc. An interesting fact observed by both Huang (1974) and Tang (1977) is that the object can be several verbs away from the matrix verb as long as all the verbs in the path are telescopic verbs. Examine (124).

(124) a. wo   bi   Zhang San   qing   Li Si   bang   Wang Wu
         I   force   Zhang San   ask   Li Si   help   Wang Wu
         xie—le   nei—fong   xin.
         write—ASP   that—CL   letter
         'I forced Zhang San to ask Li Si to help Wang Wu to write the letter.'
      b. wo nei—fong   xin   bi   Zhang San   qing   Li Si   bang
         I that—CL   letter   force   Zhang San   ask   Li Si   help
         Wang Wu xie—le.
         Wang Wu write—ASP
         'Roughly, same as (a).'

A verb that takes a full sentence as its complement, however, does not allow this movement, as the ungrammaticality of (125b) and (126b) shows. Object fronting within the same clause is still allowed, however, as both (125c) and (126c) are both grammatical.

---

[23]For a detailed discussion of the telescopic verb, see Chapter 7.

(125) a.   wo zhidao ta bu xihuan <u>Yingwen</u>.
           I know   he not like English
           'I know that he doesn't like English.'
     b.* wo <u>Yingwen</u> zhidao ta bu xihuan.
           I English   know   he not like
           'Roughly same as (a).'
     c.   wo zhidao ta <u>Yingwen</u> bu xihuan.
           I know   he English   not like
           'Roughly same as (a).'

(126) a.   ta shuo ta yiqian qu-guo <u>Meiguo</u>.
           he say he before go-ASP America
           'He said that he had been to America before.'
     b.* ta <u>Meiguo</u> shuo ta yiqian qu-guo.
           he America   say he before go-ASP
           'Roughly, same as (a).'
     c.   ta shuo ta <u>Meiguo</u> yiqian qu-guo.
           he say he America   before go-ASP
           'Roughly, same as (a).'

All these examples clearly indicate that, as far as object fronting is concered, verbs that take a full sentence as complement block its movement while telescopic verbs allow it to go through.

Likewise, the term object also needs further qualification. Sentential complements, as a rule, do not allow fronting and neither do objects of telescopic verbs, as (127) and (128) clearly show.

(127) a.   wo zhidao <u>ta mingtian bu hui lai</u>.
           I know   he tomorrow not will come
           'I know that he will not come tomorrow.'
     b.* wo <u>ta mingtian bu hui lai</u> zhidao.
           I he tomorrow   not will come know
           'Roughly, same as (a).'

(128) a. wo qing <u>ta</u> ti wo ji xin.
        I ask hime for me mail letter
        'I asked him to mail the letter for me.'
     b.* wo <u>ta</u> qing ti wo ji xin.
        I him ask for me mail letter
        'Roughly, same as (a).'

In Chapter 3 we have argued that ditransitive verbs, on the basis of their semantic and syntactic properties, should be classified into three classes:(a) "give" (outward) verbs such as *song* 'give (as a gift)', *ji* 'send', *jiao* 'hand, hand in' etc.; (b) "take" (inward) verbs such as *ying* 'win', *qiang* 'rob' etc.; and (c) "rent" (bi-directional) verbs such as *zu* 'rent', *jie* 'borrow/lend' and we have pointed out that only in the case of "give" verbs do we have a genuine direct object whereas with a "take" verb, it is not clear at all which of the two postverbal NPs functions as the direct object. Compare (129) with (130).

(129) a. wo song gei ta <u>nei—ben</u> <u>shu</u>.
        I give to him that—CL book
        'I gave him the book.'
     b. wo <u>nei—ben</u> <u>shu</u> song gei ta.
        I that—CL book give to him
        'Roughly, same as (a).'

(130) a. wo fa—le <u>ta</u> wu—kuai qian.
        I fine—ASP him five—CL money
        'I fined him five dollars.'
     b.* wo <u>wu—kuai</u> <u>qian</u> fa—le ta.
        I five—CL money fine—ASP him
        'Roughly, same as (a).'
     c.? wo <u>ta</u> fa—le wu—kuai qian.
        I him fine—ASP five—CL money
        'Roughly, same as (a).'

Since (130c) sounds better than (130b) despite an animate NP being fronted against the constraint we posited earlier, we tend to think that in the case of "take" verbs, the animate NP, rather than the inanimate NP, should be taken as the direct object.[24]

2.4. The Fronted Object and its Paradigmatic Relation

So far in this thesis we have identified, in addition to the fronted object, three other kinds of non−primary topics, namely, the second NP in the double nominative construction, the non−S−initial preverbal locative and temporal and the *ba* NP. Since, like the fronted object, they can all occur in the slot between the primary topic and the verb, they interact with the fronted object in interesting ways.

2.4.1 The Fronted Object and the *ba* NP

An obvious difference between the two is that the *ba* NP is marked while the fronted object is unmarked. Because the *ba* NP is marked by *ba*, a verb that has been on its way to becoming a preposition, it only allows left−dislocation when it is further promoted to become the primary topic, i.e., a pronominal copy has to be left behind. The fronted object, being unmarked, has no such restriction. Compare (a), (b) and (c) with (d) and (e) in (131).

(131)   a.   ta   <u>ba chezi</u>   mai   le.
               he   BA   car   sell   PART
               'What he did to the car was sell (it).'

       b.*   <u>ba chezi</u>   ta   mai   le.
               BA car   he   sell   PART
               'Roughly, same as (a).'

       c.   <u>chezi</u>$_i$ ta   ba   <u>ta</u>$_i$ mai−le.
               car   he   BA   it   sell ASP
               'Speaking of the car, he had it sold.'

       d.   ta   <u>chezi</u>   mai   le.
               he   car   sell   PART
               'Speaking of him and his car, he sold it.'

---

[24]Another piece of confirming evidence is that only the animate one of the two NPs can occur alone as object while the inanimate NP cannot. The contrast is shown in (i) and (ii) below.
    (i)   wo fa−le   ta   le.
              I   fine−ASP   him   PART
              'I have already fined him.'
    (ii)*   wo fa−le   wu−kuai   qian.
              I   fine−ASP   five−CL   money
              'I fined (somebody) five dollars.'

e. <u>chezi</u>　ta　mai　le.
　　car　he　sell　PART
　　'Speaking of the car, he sold it.'

Similarly, raising of the *ba* NP without *ba* out of a complement embedded under a telescopic verb is grammatical as attested by (132d) but to raise *ba* and the NP following it will lead to ungrammaticality, as shown by (132c). Raising of the fronted object in this environment, as we have just pointed out, is always allowed, as shown again in (132e).

(132) a. wo qing Zhang San xie <u>nei–fong</u> <u>xin</u> le.
　　　　 I　ask　Zhang San　write　that–CL　letter　PART
　　　　 'I have asked Zhang San to write the letter.'
　　 b. wo qing Zhang San <u>ba</u> <u>nei–fong</u> <u>xin</u> xie le.
　　　　 I　ask　Zhang San　BA　that–CL　letter　write　PART
　　　　 'Roughly, same as (a).'
　　 c.* wo <u>ba</u> <u>nei–fong</u> <u>xin</u> qing Zhang San xie le.
　　　　 I　BA　that–CL　letter　ask　Zhang San　write　PART
　　　　 'Roughly, same as (a).'
　　 d. wo <u>nei–fong</u> <u>xin</u>$_i$ qing Zhang San ba <u>ta</u>$_i$ xie
　　　　 I　that–CL　letter　ask　Zhang Snn　BA　it　write
　　　　 le.
　　　　 PART
　　　　 'Roughly, same as (a).'
　　 e. wo <u>nei–fong</u> xin qing Zhang San xie le.
　　　　 I　that–CL　letter　ask　Zhang San　write　PART
　　　　 'Roughly, same as (a).'

Semantically, as we have previously pointed out, the *ba* construction in its typical use highlights the transitivity relation between the primary topic and the *ba* NP while no highlighting takes place in the case of object fronting construction. Because of this extra emphasis in transitivity, the roles played by the primary topic and the *ba* NP are fixed so that even when both of them are animate, no ambiguity will ever arise. As a result, the *ba* NP fronting is not subject to animacy constraint. Compare (a) and (b) sentences in (133).

(133) a. Zhang San ba Li Si hen—tou le.
Zhang San BA Li Si hate—pierce PART
'Zhang San hated Li Si to the extreme.'
b.* Zhang San Li Si hen—tou le.
Zhang San Li Si hate—pierce PART
'Roughly, same as (a).'

Finally, the *ba* construction in its extended use has a causative reading but the object fronting construction has never acquired such a reading.

2.4.2 The Fronted Object and the Second NP in the Double Nominative Construction

If the relation between the primary topic and the fronted object is that of possessor and possessed as in (134b), then the sentence is subject to two analyses, i.e. it can be analysed as a double nominative construction or an object fronting construction.

(134) a. ta diu—le pibao.
he lose—ASP purse
'He lost his purse.'
b. ta pibao diu—le.
he purse lost—ASP
(i) 'Roughly, same as (a).' or
(ii) 'Speaking of him, (his) purse (was) lost.'

Of course, normally the verb in a double nominative constrcution is either stative or intransitive and the object fronting construction, as its name implies, occurs with a transitive verb. The two constructions can thus be distinguished but since Chinese freely allows what we previously called "middle—voiced" sentences such as (134b) in the (ii) interpretation, structurally ambiguous cases like (134b) do exist and previously we have utilized this possibility to show how some *ba* sentences such as (77) (repeated here for convenience as (135)) come about whose origin has continued to puzzle many linguists because the compound verb in the sentence is made up of two intransitive verbs.

(135) ta ba yi—zhi tui die—duan le.
he BA one—CL leg fall—break PART
'He had a leg of his broken (as he fell).'

2.4.3 The Fronted Object and the Non–S–initial Preverbal Locative and Temporal

The fronted object interacts with these adverbial secondary topics in interesting ways. Tang (1977) observes that the fronted object should be placed before locatives and temporals.[25] The following is one of his examples.

(136) a. wo gongke   zuotian   yijing   zuo–wan   le.
          I   homework yesterday already   do–finish PART
          'I already finished my homework yesterday.'
    b.?? wo zuotian   gongke   yijing   zuo–wan   le.
          I   yesterday homework already   do–finish PART
          'Roughly, same as (a).'

Since we have argued that both types of constituents can be non–primary topics, we would expect that which constituent should be placed before the other will have to be determined by such discourse factors as domain and so forth. Our expectation is confirmed by the following examples.

(137) a. wo zuotian   gongke   yi   zuo–wan   jiu   qu
          I yesterday   homework once do–finish then go
          shui   le.
          sleep PART
          'Speaking of me, yesterday as soon as I finished my homework I went to bed.'
    b.?? wo gongke   zuotian   yi   zuo–wan   jiu   qu
          I homework   yesterday once do–finish then go
          shui   le.
          sleep PART
          'Roughly, same as (a).'

Because in (137) only *wo* 'I' and *zuotian* 'yesterday' are the shared topics of the two clauses while *gongke* 'homework' is not, they should both be placed before *gongke* 'homework' to

---

[25]Tang calls them adverbials by which he also includes manner adverbs, as is clear from the examples he gives.

facilitate the formation of a topic chain. Since (137b) does not follow this principle, it is of questionable grammaticality.

Having made this point, we have to hasten to admit that taken out of context, sentences do in general sound better with the fronted object preceding a temporal or a locative topic. We do not have very good explanation for it but we suspect that there is a topic hierarchy in Chinese in which the object, being nominal, is higher than the temporal or the locative.

3. The VO—Topicalization Construction
3.1. The Traditional View of the Construction

When an adverbial element of a certain type occurs postverbally as *san—ge zhongtou* 'three hours' in (138), Chinese does not allow the adverbial element to be placed immediately after the direct object as attested by the ungrammaticality of (138a). The grammatical form to be used in this case is (138b).

(138) a.* ta   kan—le   shu   san—ge   zhongtou.
         he   read—ASP   book   three—CL   hour
         'He read (books) for three hours.'
     b. ta   kan—shu   kan—le   san—ge   zhongtou.
         he   read—book read—ASP three—CL hour
         'Same as (a).'

Traditionally this process has been termed "verb—copying" since, judging from the changes in the surface, it seems that a new copy of the verb has appeared between the direct object and the adverbial element (Li and Thompson, 1981; Chu, 1983). As this traditonal view is best represented by Li and Thompson's analysis (1981:442—450), we will briefly summarize their analysis in the following.

Li and Thompson start out by defining "verb—copying" as "a process in which a verb is 'copied' after its direct object when in the presence of certain adverbial elements." This process is schematized in (139).

(139) (subject) <u>verb</u> direct object <u>verb</u> adverbial element

They then further specify the adverbial elements to be of four types:

(i) Quantity adverbial phrase
(140) a.* wo pai–le–shou liang–ci.
 I clap–ASP–hand two–times
 'I clapped my hands twice.'
 b. wo pai–shou pai–le liang–ci.
 I clap–and clap–ASP two–times
 'Same as (a).'

(ii) Complex stative construction[26]
(141) a.* women da lanqiu de dou lei le.
 we play basketball PART all tired PART
 'We played basketball until we were all tired.'
 b. women da lanqiu da de dou lei
 we play basketball play PART all tired
 le.
 PART
 'Same as (a).'

(iii) Locative phrase
(142) a.* baba gua maozi zai yi–jia–shang.
 dad hang hat at clothes–rack–LOC
 'Dad hangs hats on the clothes rack.'
 b. baba gua maozi gua zai yi–jia–shang.
 dad hang hat hang at clothes–rack–LOC
 'Same as (a)

(iv) Directional phrase
(143) a.* women pao–bu dao xuexiao le.
 we run–step to school PART
 'We ran to the school.'

---

[26] 'Complex stative construction" is a term used by Li and Thompson to refer to the kind of complement introduced by the particle *de*. For a fuller discussion see Li and Thompson (1981:623–630) and Chapter 8 of the present volume.

b. women pao—bu pao dao xuexiao le.
   we run—step run to school PART
   'Same as (a).'

Li and Thompson (1981: 444–47) further point out that there are two constraints on the use of this construction. First, with (ii), (iii) and (iv) types of adverbial elements, this process is obligatory but with the (i) type of adverbial elements i.e., the quantity adverbial phrase, the construction is generally not used when the direct object is referential and animate or definite as shown in (144) and (145).

(144) a.* wo kan—le yi—chang dianying wu—ge zhongtou.
         I see—ASP one—CL movie five—CL hour
         'I saw a movie for five hours.'
      b.   wo kan—le ta wu—ge zhongtou.
         I see—ASP him five—CL hour
         'I watched him for five hours.'

(145) a.* ta da—le ren liang—ci.
         he hit—ASP people two—times
       ? 'He hit people twice.'[27]
      b.? ta da—le yi—ge ren liang—ci.[28]
         he hit—ASP one—CL person two—times
         'He hit a person twice.'
      c.   ta da—le na—ge ren liang—ci.
         he hit—ASP that—CL person two—times
         'He hit the person twice.'

Second, the process is triggered only by these four types of adverbial elements. There are other elements occurring after the verb which, however, do not trigger the process.

---

[27](145a) is cited from Li and Thompson (1981:446). They, however, didn't give any English translation in this case.

[28](145b) is also cited from Li and Thompson (1981:446), but the grammatical judgment here is my own.

(146) ta zou–lu hen kuai.
he walk–road very fast
'He walks fast.'

(147) ta zhao ren bang ta.
he seek person help him
'He is looking for someone to help him.'

(148) ta pai–shou jiao–hao.
he clap–hand shout–good
'He clapped his hands (and) shouted his appreciation.'

We will take up these two constraints in our later discussion. Right now let us examine this traditional analysis more closely.

3.2. Inadequacies of the Traditional Analysis

In order to give a neutral representation, the following scheme is used, with the understanding that V_1 and V_2 are in some sense a copy of each other:

(149) $NP_1 + V_1 + NP_2 + V_2 +$ Adverbial Element

There are a number of inadequacies in the traditional analysis. First, by calling it a verb–copying process, it seems to indicate that V_1 is the main verb while V_2 is only a copy of it. This is actually not the case. As we will show presently, V_2 is the main verb and V_1 has been deverbalized. Second, the traditional analysis leaves unspecified whether $V_1 + NP_2$ functions as a unit or not, and if it does, what kind of unit it is and what function it serves. Finally, the traditional analysis fails to offer any explanation as to why (a) and (b) sentences in (150) are felt to be almost synonymous except in one important way.

(150) a. ta xie–zi xie de hen hao.
he write–character write PART very well
'He writes (characters) very well.'

b. xie–zi   ta xie de   hen hao.
    write–character he write PART very well
    'As for writing characters, he does it very well.'

In what follows we would like to present evidence to show that while V$_2$ is a full verb, V$_1$ has been deverbalized. We would also present arguments to support the analysis that V$_1$+NP$_2$ is an NP that functions as a secondary topic.

3.3 Evidence for the Deverbalization of V$_1$

One of the notable grammatical properties of the construction is that V$_1$ in (149) does not take any aspect marker. Aspect markers such as –*le* and –*guo* when they are needed have to be added to V$_2$.

(151) a. ta nian–shu   nian–le   wu–ge   zhongtou.
         he study–book   study–APS five–CL hour
         'He studied for five hours.'
     b.* ta nian–le–shu   nian–le   wu–ge   zhongtou.
         he study–ASP–book study–ASP five–CL hour
         'Same as (a).'
     c.* ta nian–le–shu   nian   wu–ge   zhongtou.
         he study–ASP–book study   five–CL hour
         'Same as (a).'

(152) a. ta zhao–xiang   zhao–guo   liang–ci.
         he take–picture   take–ASP   two–times
         'He has taken pictures twice.'
     b.* ta zhao–guo–xiang   zhao–guo   liang–ci.
         he take–ASP–picture take–ASP   two–times
         'Same as (a).'
     c.* ta zhao–guo–xiang   zhao   liang–ci.
         he take–ASP–picture take   two–times
         'Same as (a).'

The fact that V_1 can no longer take aspect markers is certainly a strong indication that it has become deverbalized. In this connection, observe the following parallel in English deverbalized geundial forms.

(153) a. George denied <u>giving</u> Dick any money.
b. George denied <u>having given</u> Dick any money.

(154) a. After <u>seeing</u> the show, he went home by himself.
b. After <u>having seen</u> the show, he went home by himself.

So it seems that English, in a more restricted way, has lost its aspectual distinction in the gerundial form. Not only that. Actually, the grammatically correct (b) sentences in (153) and (154) are felt to be stylistically less natural than the corresponding (a) sentences.

Our second argument for the deverbalization of V_1 involves another grammatical property of the construction. It has been repeatedly pointed out that in negating the construction a negative particle is placed before V_2 rather than V_1, as is shown in the following two examples.

(155) a. ta   shang—ge   yue   da   qiu   da—le   san—ci.
         he   last—CL   month   play   ball   play—ASP three—times
         'He played ball three times last month.'
  b. ta   shang—ge   yue   da   qiu   <u>mei</u> da   san—ci.
         he   last—CL   month   play   ball   not play   three—times
         'He didn't play ball three times last month.'
  c.* ta   shang—ge   yue   mei   da   qiu   da   san—ci.
         he   last—CL   month   not   play   ball   play   three—times
         'Same as (b).'

(156) a. mama   gua   yifu   gua   zai   yi—jia—shang.
         mother   hang   clothes   hang   at   clothes—rack—LOC
         'Mother hangs clothes on the clothes rack.'
  b. mama   gua   yifu   bu   gua   zai   yi—jia—shang.
         mother   hang   clothes   not   hang   at   clothes—rack—LOC
         'Mother doesn't hang clothes on the clothes rack.'

c.* mama bu   gua   yifu   gua zai
    mother not hang clothes hang at
    yi–jia–shang.
    clothes–rack–LOC
    'Same as (b).'

Now as far as we can determine,the most general rule of negative particle placement is that it is placed, if we disregard certain adverbs which can occur within the scope of negation, right before the verb phrase (see Li and Thompson,1981:417;Chu,1983:150;Li et al.,1984:334;Teng,1985).Since only V_2 is preceded by a negative particle, it seems very clear that V_2 is the main verb of the sentence which retains in full its verbal qualities while V_1 occurs outside the verb phrase and has lost at least some of its verbal qualities.

Finally, there is a group of monosyllabic adverbs such as, *zhi* 'only', *hai* 'still; also, moderately', *cai* 'only' and *zhen* 'really', which occurs before V_2, but not V_1, as the following examples clearly show.

(157) a. ta nian–shu   zhi   nian–le   san   nian.
          he study–book only   study–ASP   three year
          'He only studied for three years.'
      b.* ta zhi   nian–shu   nian–le   san   nian.
          he only   study–book   study–ASP   three year
          'Same as (a).'

(158) a. ta chang–ge   hai   chang   de   bu   cuo.
          he sing–song   moderately   sing   PART   not bad
          'He is not bad at singing.'
      b.* ta hai   chang–ge   chang   de   bu   cuo.
          he moderately   sing–song   sing   PART   not bad'
          'Same as (a).'

Just like the negative particles, these monosyllabic adverbs are normally placed before the verb phrase of the clause. Since they only occur before V_2, rather than V_1, this is yet another strong argument in support of the view that only V_2 is a full verb and that

V_1, occurring as it is outside the verb phrase, has been deverbalized.

3.4. Evidence in Support of the Analysis that $V_1 + NP_2$ Is a Topic NP

In this section evidence will be presented to show that what originated as a verb phrase, i.e., a verb + its object, has become in this construction a topic NP.

3.4.1 The NP in Question and the Primry Topic NP Compared

Previously we have concluded that the primary topic in Chinese has the qualities summarized in (12). Let us now examine whether V_1+NP_2 has the topic properties quoted above. It is clear that (12f) is difficult to test since the NP in question does not interact with any of these processes. So it seems justified to dismiss (12f) as irrelevant in this particular case.

With regard to the properties mentioned in (a) and (b), many researchers may assume right away that the NP in question does not have these properties since, unlike the regular topic, which always heads a sentence, this NP can be preceded by the primary topic. However, contrary to this assumption, this NP, just like all other secondary topics, can head a topic chain, if the primary topic, which precedes it, also does that at the same time. As (159) shows, the primary topic *ta* 'he' and the NP in question *zhao–xiang* 'take–picture' are followed by two comments, marked as C_1 and C_2 resepectively and conjoined by *ye* 'also'. A similar example is found in (160).

(159) ta_i $\underline{zhao–xiang}_j$ $\underline{zhao\ de\ hen\ kuai}_{C_1}$, —$_i$ —$_j$ $\underline{ye}$

he take–picture take PART very quickly also

$\underline{zhao\ de\ hen\ hao}_{C_2}$.

take PART very good

'He takes pictures very quickly and very well.'

(160) ta_i $\underline{xie–zi}_j$ $\underline{xie\ de\ hen\ kuai}_{C_1}$, danshi

he write–character write PART very fast but

$$\underline{\qquad}_i \underline{\qquad}_j \underset{C_2}{\text{xie}} \quad \text{de} \quad \text{bu} \quad \text{zhengqi.}$$
        write PART not neatly
'He writes characters fast but he doesn't write neatly.'

  Also in (160) we can clearly see that both the primary topic *ta* 'he' and the NP in question *zhao—xiang* 'take—picture, are in control of coreferential NP deletion in the topic chain of two clauses sharing the two common topics. The NP in question differs from the primary topic not only in position but also in its ability to extend its domain i.e., its domain can only be equal to or less than that of the primary topic. The former situation is found in the case of (160). The latter situation can be demonstrated by adding one more comment to the original two as in (160a). where the primary topic *ta* 'he' extends its domain to three clauses while the secondary topic has its domain over only the first two.

(160) a. <u>ta</u>$_i$ <u>xie—zi</u>$_j$ xie de hen kuai
    he write—character write PART very fast
    danshi $\underline{\qquad}_i$ $\underline{\qquad}_j$ xie de bu zhengqi, $\underline{\qquad}_i$
    but   write PART not neat
    wo bu neng yong.
    I not can employ
    'He writes characters fast but he doesn't write neatly; I cannot employ him.'

It is clear from the above examples that the NP in question behaves exactly like the primary topic NP as far as controlling coreferential NP deletion is concerned, but differs from the primary topic slightly in being second to it in position and in having more restriction in extending its domain. To sum up our discussion so far, we have found that with regard to (12a, d, e), the NP in question basically possesses these qualities. Furthermore, the minor differences can be accounted for if we assume that the NP in question is a secondary topic.

  But what about (12b)? Does this NP in question also possess this characteristic of the primary topic? Let us put it to test.

(161) a. ta   shuo–hua   shuo   de   hen   qingchu.
         he   speak–speech   speak   PART   very   clearly
         'He speaks very clearly.'

   b. ta   shuo–hua   <u>a</u>   shuo   de   hen   qingchu.
      he   speak–speech   PART   speak   PART   very   clearly
      'Same as (a).'

   c.? ta   shuo–hua   <u>me</u>   shuo   de   hen   qingchu.
       he   speak–speech   PART   speak   PART   very   clearly
       'Same as (a).'

   d.? ta   shuo–hua   <u>ne</u>   shuo   de   hen   qingchu.
       he   speak–speech   PART   speak   PART   very   clearly
       'Same as (a).'

   e.? ta   shuo–hua   <u>ba</u>   shuo   de   hen   qingchu.
       he   speak–speech   PART   speak   PART   very   clearly
       'Same as (a).'

From the above sentences, it is evident that the NP in question can be separated from the following part of the clause by at least the pause particle *a* and its phonetic variant *ya*. But particles *me, ne* and *ba* seem to be less acceptable. As we have pointed out in connection with our discussion with the *ba* secondary topic, since no systematic study has been conducted to investigate the meanings and functions of these four pause particles, we will not be able to explain this difference in distribution between *a (ya)* on the one hand and *me, ne* and *ba* on the other.[29] However, this distributional fact seems to suggest that, as far as this topical quality is concerned, the NP in question is a topic of some kind but is not the primary topic.

Let us now turn to the referential quality of the NP under investigation. Li and Thompson (1981:447) report that the direct object in this construction, i.e., NP_2 in (149), is typically, though not necessarily, nonreferential. This observation, as far as it goes, is correct as can be seen from most of the grammatical sentences cited previously. Let us give

---

[29]To the best of my knowledge, Chao (1968) is the first to mention these pause particles. He, however, did not go into the differences in the use of these particles. In our previous discussion of the *ba* construction, we have found that of the four particles, *a (ya)* is the most unmarked. It can occur anywhere a topic of any kind occurs while the other three, *me, ne* and *ba* seem natural only with the regular topic. The same result is found here in the construction under discussion.

another example.

(162) ta kan–shu kan de hen kuai.
he read–book read PART very fast
'He reads very fast.'

The verb and its object in (162), as in many other cases cited earlier, sometimes function as two separate constituents but at other times as a verbal unit, forming what is usually called a verb–object compound. But the most important fact that concerns us here is that because of this compounding tendency, the object, unless further modified by other modifiers, tends to be interpreted as non–referential. Thus, in (162), *kan–shu*, as a compound, simply means 'reading'. A person may be reading a journal, a magazine or even a newspaper and still be described as *kan–shu* '(literally) read–book'. It is, therefore, clear that *shu*, which literally means 'book' is in this case non–referential.

But here, as we have pointed out, it is the higher NP, i.e., $(V_1+NP_2)_{NP}$, that is our concern. So, instead of being concerned with the referential quality of NP_2, the object, we should be concerned with the question of how this typical referential characteristic of NP_2 contribute to the referential quality of the higher NP as a whole. In fact, a careful examination reveals that this lack of referentiality of NP_2 helps make the higher NP generic in interpretation. In (162), for example, we are not talking about the reading of any specific book or the reading of all the books in the world. Here we are talking about reading in its most general sense.

Sometimes, NP_2, the object, can be not only referential but also definite as in (163).

(163) ta pa na–zuo shan pa–le wu–ci.
he climb that–CL mountain climb–ASP five–times
'He has climbed that mountain five times.'

When this happens, NP_2, the object, has the effect of making the higher NP definite in the sense that now we are talking about some specific person's climbing that specific mountain rather than any other mountain. Thus, as far as the NP under discussion is concerned, it is either generic or definite in reference. It has, therefore, the referential property of a topic as described in (12c).

To summarize, we have demonstrated that the NP under investigation has, except for (12f), which is difficult to put to test in this case, basically all the properties mentioned in (12a) through (12e). Some further restrictions, as we have pointed out, are readily accountable if we assume that it, together with the *ba* NP, the fronted object, the non-S-initial preverbal locative and temporal, is a secondary topic. Our evidences, however, are not restricted to these. We have at least two others that lend support to it.

3.4.2 Two Additional Arguments for Treating $V_1 + NP_2$ as a Secondary Topic

The first argument has to do with the fact that the NP in question can be further promoted to be the primary topic.

Previously we have pointed out that all the secondary topics that we have posited can all be further promoted to become the primary topics as shown in the (b) sentences in (164) to (167).

(164) a. ta <u>yanjing</u> bu ling.
he eyes not good
'He (topic), (his) eyes are bad.
b. <u>yanjing</u>, ta bu ling.
eyes he not good
'As for eyes, he is bad.'

(165) a. ta <u>zuotian</u> mei lai.
he yesterday not come
'speaking of him, he didn't come yesterday.'
b. <u>zuotian,</u> ta mei lai.
yesterday he not come
'Speaking of yesterday, he didn't come.'

(166) a. women ba <u>Zhang San</u> da-shang le.
we BA Zhang San hit-hurt PART
'We had Zhang San wounded.'
b. <u>Zhang San,</u> women ba ta da-shang le.
Zhang San we BA him hit-hurt PART
'As for Zhang San, we had him wounded.'

(167) a. ta <u>fan</u> bu chi.
he meal not eat
'He won't eat his meal.'
b. <u>fan</u>, ta bu chi.
meal he not eat
'As for the meal, he won't eat it.'

The NP in question i.e., V_1+NP_2 in (149) behaves exactly like all other secondary topics in occurring between the primary topic and the main verb of the clause and in being able to be further promoted to become the primary topic, as shown in (168).

(168) a. tamen <u>pao—bu</u> dou pao de hen kuai.
they run—step all run PART very fast
'They all run very fast.'
b. <u>pao—bu</u>, tamen dou pao de hen kuai.
run—step they all run PART very fast
'As for running, they all run fast.'

Our second argument has to do with the fact that the NP in question can be explicitly contrasted. As we have pointed out in our previous discussion, all topics, be they primary or secondary, can be contrasted, as shown in the following (c) and (d) sentences in (164) to (167).[30]

(164) c. ta <u>yanjing</u> bu ling, <u>bizi</u> que hen hao.
he eyes not good nose on:the:contrary very good
'He (topic), (his) eyes are poor, but (his) nose is very good.'
d. <u>yanjing</u>, ta bu ling, <u>bizi</u> que hen hao.
eyes he not good nose on:the:contrary very good
'As for eyes, he is poor, but as for nose, he is very good.'

---

[30]For a discussion of the contrastive function of the primary topic see Tsao (1979, Chapter 6).

(165) c. ta_i zuotian mei lai, ______j jintian
he yesterday not come today
que lai le.
on:the:contrary come PART.
'Speaking of him, though yesterday he didn't come, he did today.'

d. zuotian ta_i mei lai, jintian ______i
yesterday he not come today
que lai le.
on:the:contrary come PART.
'As for yesterday he didn't come; as for today, he did.'

(166) c. women ba Zhang San bushi ba Li Si da–shang le.
we BA Zhang San not BA Li Si hit–hurt PART
'We had Zhang San, not Li Si, wounded.'

d. Zhang San bushi Li Si, women ba ta da–shang le.
Zhang San not Li Si we BA him hit–hurt PART
'Zhang San, rather than Li Si, we had him wounded.'

(167) c. ta fan bu chi, jiao haishi yao shui.
he meal not eat snap still want sleep
'He won't eat his meal but will sleep some more.'

d. fan ta bu chi, jiao haishi yao shui.
meal he not eat snap still want sleep
'As for the meal, he won't eat it, but as for his sleep, he will have some more.'

The NP in question, being a topic, can also be contrasted no matter whether it is the primary or the secondary topic in the particular sentence. This is demonstrated in (168c and d).

(168) c. tamen pao–bu dou pao de hen kuai,
they run–step all run PART very fast
xie–zi que xie de hen

236

    write—character on:the:contrary write PART very
    man.
    slowly
    'They (topic) all run fast, but all write (Chinese characters) slowly.'
 d. <u>pao—bu</u> tamen dou pao de hen kuai,
   run—step they all run PART very fast
   <u>xie—zi</u> que   xie de hen
   write—character on:the:contrary write PART very
   man.
   slowly
   'As far running, they all run fast, but as for writing Chinese characters, they all do it slowly.'

 It is thus very clear that the NP in question functions exactly like all other secondary topics in being able to be promoted to be the primary topic and in being able to be contrasted. It is on the strength of this pattern congruity that we have argued to posit it as a secondary topic as well.

3.4.3 Summary

 To sum up our discussion in the previous two sections, we have demonstrated in the first section that the NP in question in (149) has almost all the grammatical properties of the primary topic. It is on the strength of this similarity that we proposed to posit the NP as a topic. At the same time, based on the positional difference and other grammatical differences that exist between the two topics, we have termed it a secondary topic.

 In the second section, we further compared the NP in question with all other types of secondary topics that we have established so far in Chinese in its ability to be further promoted to become the primary topic and its ability to be contrasted. Our comparison shows that the NP in question behaves exactly like all other types of secondary topics. This pattern congruity renders further support to our analysis of treating the NP consisting of $V_1 + NP_2$ as a secondary topic.

 To stop to take a look at the process as a whole, we feel that on the basis of our findings that V_1 has been deverbalized and that it has been moved, together with its object, out of the VP to become a secondary topic, it is inappropriate to term the process verb—copying. Instead, we would propose to call it verb—object topicalization. Realizing that it is a topicalization process will also enable us to explain why a verb needs to be inserted. When $V_1 + NP_2$ are moved out, the V node under VP is empty. Since in Chinese there is a very important structural constraint which stipulates that a non-nominal sentence, i.e. a verbal one, must have a verb, a verb has to be inserted.[31] As Chinese has no dummy verb such as *do* in English, the original verb is the only alternative, for by so doing the selectional compatibility between the verb and the post-verbal adverbial is ensured.[32]

3.5 Differences Between these Five Types of Secondary Topics

Now that we have proved beyond any reasonable doubt that the noun phrase consisting of V_1+NP_2 is itself a secondary topic, our next concern is to find out what difference there is between the four types of secondary topics that we have posited, since they, being all secondary topics, stand, from the point of view of sentence pattern, in contrast with each other.

The most important feature that distinguishes these five types of secondary topics is that the relation between the primary topic and the secondary topic is different in each case. In the double nominative construction, the relation between the two topics is usually that of possessor and possessed, whole and part or class and member (see also Tsao, 1982; Chao, 1968 for discussion). The locative and temperal that are secondary topics often function to further delimit the scope of the following comment already delimited by the primary topic. The two topics, otherwise do not bear very close relation. In the *ba* construction, the relation is usually that of agent (the primary topic) and patient (the secondary topic) except in its extended causative use (Chu, 1983; Tsao, 1987a). In the case where we have an unmarked, preverbal object in an SOV construction, the relation between the primary and the secondary topic seems to be quite open-ended. An important thing to remember is that the verb is a two-place predicate and the primary topic is its subject while the secondary topic its object. Finally, there is the so-called 'verb-copying' construction. Again, the relation between the two topics seems to be quite open-ended. All we can do to characterize it is that the primary topic is usually the subject while the secondary topic consists of its verb, now deverbalized, and the object of the verb.

At the first glance, it may seem that the five types are in complementary

---

[31] In functional terms, this means that a sentence cannot be all topics without a proper comment.

[32] The last observation is in part due to Mr. Tien-wei Xie, who is a linguistics student at the University of Pittsburgh.

distribution. This is not entirely true. Overlaps between the five types are found occasionally. This is especially true with regard to the three nonlocal secondary topics discussed in this chapter, where only transitive verbs are involved and where, in one way or another, the object has been moved to a preverbal position. Because of these functional similarities existing between the latter three constructions, overlaps more easily arise.

We have already reported on the similarity and difference between the object–fronting construction and the *ba* construction in our previous discussion. Now let us add VO–topicalization to the picture to see how the three interact with each other.

Since all three constructions involve moving the object to a preverbal position, one can easily predict that there may be cases where all three processes may lead to sentences that have very similar meanings. (169) below is such a case.

(169) a. ta gua–maozi gua zai qiang–shang.
he hang–hat hang at wall–LOC
'As for him and as for hanging hats, he hangs them on the wall.'
b. ta maozi gua zai qiang–shang.
he hat hang at wall–LOC
(i) 'As for him and as for hats, he hangs them on the wall.'
(ii) 'As for him and as for the hat, he hangs (hung) it on the wall.'
c. ta ba maozi gua zai qiang–shang.
he BA hat hang at wall–LOC
(i) 'He hangs his hats on the wall.'
(ii) 'He had his hat hung on the wall.'

In (169) *maozi* 'hat' in the phrase *gua–maozi* 'hang–hat' is nonreferential. But once *maozi* 'hat' is isolated from its verb to become a topic, as in (169b) and (169c), then it becomes generic or definite in reference. This difference in interpretation is reflected in the English translations.

If now we specify *maozi* 'hat' as definite, as in (170), what will happen?

(170) a.? ta gua na–ding maozi gua zai qiang–shang.
he hang that–CL hat hang at wall–LOC
'As for him and as for hanging the hat, he hangs it on the wall.'
b. ta na–ding maozi gua zai qiang–shang.
he that–CL hat hang at wall–LOC

	(i)	'As for him and as for that hat, he hangs it on the wall.'
	(ii)	'As for him and as for that hat, he hung it on the wall.'

c. ta   ba   na–ding   maozi   gua   zai   qiang–shang.
he   BA   that–CL   hat   hang   at   wall–LOC

(i) 'He hangs that hat on the wall.'
(ii) 'He had that hat hung on the wall.'

As (170a) shows, the verb + object phrase topicalization produces a sentence whose grammatical status is dubious. If it is grammatical at all, it has only the habitual reading. However, *ba* topicalization and the unmarked object topicalization are both permitted and the resulting sentences have both habitual and perfected readings, as reflected in the English translations. So, it seems that when the object NP is definite, the (verb + object) NP topicalization is severely constrained.[33]

3.6 The VO Topicalization and Its Syntagmatic Relation

Let us now go back to (149) and examine again this construction as a whole.

(149) $NP_1 + V_1 + NP_2 + V_2$ + Adverbial element

In the analysis proposed, NP_1 is the primary topic, $V_1 + NP_2$ is the secondary topic. These two topics are then followed by V_2, the main verb and then one of the four kinds of adverbial elements. Given this analysis, there are at least two questions that can legitimately be raised: (i) Instead of positing two separate topics, can we regard $NP_1 + V_1 + NP_2$ to be just a topic, as Chow (1989) has argued?; (ii) What is the reason that triggers this process of *verb + object* phrase topicalization?

Our answer to the first question is no. There are two strong reasons for this position both of which were implicit in some of the examples we gave earlier. Thus, in (160a) repeated below, we found that the primary topic *ta* 'he' and the secondary topic *xie-zi* 'write-character' each has its domain extended over a topic chain (with the secondary topic chain embedded in the primary topic chain, of course) and each is in control of the pronominalization or coreferential NP deletion process in its own chain.

---

[33]See Section 3.6 of this chapter for an explanation of this constraint.

(160) a. ta$_i$ xie–zi$_j$ xie   de   hen   kuai,   danshi
         he   write–character write PART very   fast   but
         —$_i$ —$_j$ xie   de   bu   zhengqi,——$_i$ wo bu   neng
                      write PART not   neat   I   not able
         yong
         employ
         'He writes Chinese characters fast but not neatly; I can't employ him.'

Similar examples abound. Space consideration permits us to give just one more.

(171) ta$_i$ xie–shi$_j$ xie   de   bu   zemeyang,   keshi ————$_i$
         he   write–poetry write PART not   so–well   but
         ping–shi   que   ping   de   hen
         criticize–poetry on:the:contrary criticize PART very
         hao.
         well
         'He can't write good poetry but he can write very good poetic critique.'

In (171) we have a topic chain of two comments and the only shared topic in this case is *ta* 'he', not *ta xie–shi* 'he writes–poetry'. This example also shows that the secondary topic can be put in contrast while the primary topic is held identical. Thus, in (171) what is common to both comment clauses is the primary topic *ta* 'he' while the two different secondary topics, i.e., *xie–shi* 'write–poetry' and *ping–shi* 'criticize–poetry' are being contrasted. This is yet another reason why the primary topic should be separated from the secondary one.

In this connection, let us recall (168a and b):

(168) a. tamen pao–bu   dou pao de   hen   kuai.
         they   run–step   all run PART very   fast
         'They all run very fast.'
      b. pao–bu,   tamen dou pao de   hen   kuai.
         run–step   they   all run PART very   fast
         'As for running, they all run very fast.'

Thus, when the need arises, the secondary topic can be further promoted to become the primary topic and the primary topic, if there is one, will then be demoted to be the secondary one. Since their roles can be interchanged, they should be treated as two separate topics.

It is thus important to know that the same sequence of morphemes *subject + verb + object* as *ta kai–che* 'he drive–car' can be subject to two different analyses depending on the clause type in which it occurs. Compare (172) with (173).

(172)   ta   kai–che   kai–le   wu–ge   zhongtou.
          he   drive–car   drive–ASP   five–CL   hour
          'As for him and as for driving, he did it for five hours.'

(173)   ta   kai–che   bu   xing.
          he   drive–car   not   do
          'It won't do for him to drive.'

In (172) *ta kai–che* 'he drive–car' is composed of a primary topic *ta* 'he' and a secondary topic, *kai–che* 'drive–car' while in (173) the whole phrase *ta kai–che* 'he drive–car' functions as a unit serving the role of subject in the sentence. As sentential nominalization is not our concern at this point, we will not go into the justification of positing a sentential subject in (173). Suffice it to point out that the same sequence can also function as an object as in (174).[34]

(174)   wo   bu   fandui   <u>ta</u>   <u>kai–che</u>.
          I   not   object   he   drive–car
          'I don't object to his driving.'

Let us turn now to the second question. The answer here is far less straightforward. However, by comparing this construction with the *ba* construction and the SOV construction, we find that they all perform essentially the same function — that is, moving what originated as a postverbal element to a preverbal position to become a secondary topic and thus leaving only one element in the postverbal position. In terms of the

---

[34] For discussion of sentential subjects and objects see Chapter 8.

functional sentence perspective theory, the topics, representing old, presupposed information, belong to the theme part of a sentence, while the verb and the postverbal adverbial element in the construction under investigation, representing new information, belongs to the rheme part of a sentence. Since in Chinese we have as many as three processes performing this function, it is clear that the principle of making the rheme part of a sentence as simple as possible is a very important one.

By taking this perspective, we are also able to offer an explanation for an otherwise quite puzzling phenomenon. Earlier when we introduced Li and Thompson's analysis, we mentioned a constraint which says to the effect that in case where the adverbial element is a quantifying adverbial phrase, $V_1 + NP_2$ phrase topicalization is not required if NP_2 is referential and animate or definite, as shown in (144) repeated below:

(144) a.* wo   kan—le   yi—chang dianying wu—ge   zhongtou.
          I   see—ASP   one—CL   movie   five—CL hour
          'I saw a movie for five hours.'
      b. wo   kan—le   ta   wu—ge   zhongtou.
          I   see—ASP   him   five—CL   hour
          'I watched him for five hours.'

While I have little doubt that this is the reminant of a historical change, the question remains: Why are only NPs that are referential and animate or definite not affected? A plausible answer that we would like to suggest is as follows. Since referential NPs that are animate or definite are quite high in the hierarchy of topicality, they are most likely to be taken as old, presupposed information and least likely to be taken as focus, which carries the newest information in the rheme part of the sentence. For this reason, a referential NP that is animate or definite, even though it occurs postverbally, is not likely to rival with the postverbal adverbial element for the position of focus. Because of this non—rivalry, the NP is tolerated to occur postverbally i.e., in the rheme part of a sentence.[35]

This theme—rheme distinction can also provide a functional explanation as to why the negative particles occur, in general, between the secondary topic and the main verb i.e., V_2 in this construction. Since a topic, be it primary or secondary, usually represents

---

[35]For a similar explanation, see Ernst (1986).

presupposed information, it is normally not negated.[36] So, it is only natural for it to be placed outside the scope of normal negation.

To sum up, our discussion of this construction and its comparison with other double topic constructions have led us to the conclusion that in Chinese there is a strong tendency of moving constituents representing old information to the preverbal position, making the rheme part as simple as possbile so as to make it very clear what the new information being conveyed is.

Recently, within the Government and Binding school of generative grammar, three attempts have been made to take care of this very general phenomenon in Chinese (Huang, 1982, 1984; Li, 1985 and Ernst, 1986). Huang posited a phrase structure condition, which stipulates that within a given sentence in Chinese, the head (the verb or VP) may branch to the left only once, and only on the lowest level of expansion (1984:54). In other words, by positing such a PSC, Huang is claiming that only one element can occur post-verbally. Counterexamples abound for this claim of Huang's. Li (1985), to take care of these counterexamples, has evoked other mechanisms but as Ernst (1986) has pointed out, Li's account is not only ad hoc but, more importantly, too restrictive. It fails to take care of grammatical sentences such as (144b) and (145c). To take care of these counter-examples, Ernst has to posit a pragmatic-based principle called "Chinese Information Principle", which says:

> The ideal of Chinese is to keep the new, asserted information of each clause as
> focused as possible by isolating it after the verb.

One cannot miss the similarity of his principle with my statement given in the paragraphs above.

3.7 The Residual Problem

Recall that at the beginning of this section we cited Li and Thompson (1981), who report that there are four types of complement structure that trigger what they call "verb-copying" process. The four types are: (i) quantity adverbial phrase, (ii) complex stative construction, (iii) locative phrase, and (iv) directional phrase. A closer examination reveals that type (ii) does not pattern with the other three. It differs in the following respects.

First, only the complex stative construction is capable of functioning as the main predicate as shown by its ability to be questioned using V-not-V form. Compare (a) with

---

[36]See Chu (1983:232) for a similar explanation for the negation fact reported here.

244

(b), (c) and (d) in (175).

(175) a.   ta   pao–bu   pao   de   kuai–bu–kuai?
          he   run–step   run   PART fast–not–fast
          'Does he run fast?'

b.*   ta   pao–bu   pao–le   wu–ge   zhongtou   bu   wu–ge
       he   run–step   run–ASP   five–CL   hour   not   five–CL
       zhongtou?
       hour
       'Did he run for five hours?'

c.*   ta   gua   maozi   gua   zai–bu–zai   yi–jia–shang?
       he   hang   hats   hang   at–not–at   clothes–rack–LOC
       'Did he hang his hats at the clothes–rack?'

d.*   ta   pao–bu   pao   dao–bu–dao   xuexiao?
       he   run–step   run   to–not–to   school
       'Did he run to the school?'

On the other hand, the V_2 in the Type (ii) construction alone cannot have any aspect marker attached to it and neither can it be put in the V–not–V question form. Witness the contrast between the (a) sentences and (b), (c), and (d) sentences in (176) and (177).

(176) a.*   ta   yijing   pao–bu   pao–le   de   hen   lei
       he   already   run–step   run–ASP   PART   very   tired
       ma?
       PART
       'Has he already run (himself) tired?'

b.   ta   pao–bu   pao–le   wu–ge   zhongtou.
          he   run–step   run–ASP   five–CL   hour
          'He ran for five hours.'

c.   ta   shui–jiao   shui–guo   diban   ma?
          he   sleep–sleep   sleep–ASP   floor   PART
          'Has he ever slept on the floor before?'

d.   ta   pao–bu   pao–dao–le   xuexiao.
          he   run–step   run–to–ASP   school
          'He ran to the school.'

(177) a.* ta pao–bu pao–bu–pao de hen lei?
he run–step run–not–run PART very tired
'Did he run himself tired?'
b. ta pao–bu you–mei–you pao wu–ge zhongtou?
he run–step have–not–have run five–CL hour
'Has he run for five hours?'
c. ta gua–maozi gua–bu–gua zai qiang–shang?
he hang–hats hang–not–hang at wall–LOC
'Does he hang (his) hats on the wall?'
d. ta pao–bu pao–bu–pao dao xuexiao?
he run–step run–not–run to school
'Does he run to the school?'

The inability to be questioned using V–not–V form and to take an aspect marker strongly indicates that V_2 in Type (ii) construction is not a matrix verb. This is hardly unexpected given that we have shown in this construction the main predicate is the constituent following V_2.

Furthermore, the four pause particles *a(ya), me, ne,* and *ba* can be placed after *de* in Type (ii) construction but cannot be placed after V_2 in Types (i), (iii) and (iv) constructions or after *zai* 'at' and *dao* 'to' in Types (iii) and (iv) respectively, as shown in (178).

(178) a. ta pao–bu pao de ya hen kuai.
he run–step run PART PART very fast
'He runs very fast.'
b.* ta pao–bu pao–le ya wu–ge zhongtou.
he run–step run–ASP PART five–CL hour
'He ran for five hours.'
c.* ta gua–maozi gua ya zai qiang–shang.
he hang–hats hang PART on wall–LOC
'He hangs (his) hats on the wall.'
d.* ta gua–maozi gua zai ya qiang–shang.
he hang–hats hang on PART wall–LOC

     'Same as (c).'
  e.* ta pao–bu pao ya dao xuexiao.
     he run–step run PART to school
     'He ran to the school.'
  f.* ta pao–bu pao dao ya xuexiao.
     he run–step run to PART school
     'Same as (e).'

Likewise, as will be argued in Chapter 8, in the surface structure only topics, primary or non–primary, are allowed to occur before a class of important clause connectives such as *suiran* 'although', *yinwei* 'because', as a consequence of the rule of topic–raising.[37] The effect of the rule is shown in (179).

 (179) a. <u>suiran</u> ta zuotian shengbing, ta haishi lai le.
     though he yesterday get:sick he still come PART
    'Although he was sick yesterday, he came.'
   b. ta <u>suiran</u> zuotian shengbing, ta haishi lai le.
     he though yesterday get:sick he still come PART
    'Same as (a).'
   c. ta zuotian <u>suiran</u> shengbing, ta haishi lai le.
     he yesterday though get:sick he still come PART
    'Same as (a).'

Now observe the following examples involving the complex stative construction.

 (180) a. <u>suiran</u> ta zhao–xiang zhao de hen man, keshi
     though he take–picture take PART very slow but
     que   hen hao.
     on:the:contrary very good
    'Although it takes him a long time to take a picture, he does it well.'
   b. ta <u>suiran</u> zhao–xiang zhao de hen man, keshi
     he though take–picture take PART very slow but

---

[37]This is necessarily a much simplified account. For a fuller discussion, see Chapter 8.

    que   hen hao.
    on:the:contrary   very good
    'Roughly, same as (a).'
  c. ta zhao–xiang <u>suiran</u> zhao de hen man, keshi
    he take–picture though take PART very slow but
    que   hen hao.
    on:the:contrary   very good
    'Roughly, same as (a).'
  d. ta zhao–xiang zhao de <u>suiran</u> hen man, keshi
    he take–picture take PART though very slow but
    que   hen hao.
    on:the:contrary   very good
    'Roughly, same as (a).'

(180d) seems to present some problem as *zhao + de* 'take + PART' do not form a constituent, let alone a topic. This can be clearly seen by its inability to be preposed to become a primary topic, as shown by the ungrammatical (181c).

 (181) a. ta zhao–xiang zhao de hen man.
      he take–picture take PART very slow
      'It takes him a long time to take a picture.'
    b. zhao–xiang ta zhao de hen man.
      take–picture he take PART very slow
      'Roughly, same as (a).'
    c.* zhao de ta zhao–xiang hen man.
      take PART he take–picture very slow

This apparent counterexample and the three facts that we have observed can be explained if we assume that *ta zhao–xiang zhao de* is an NP and a topic itself. In fact both Chu (1978) and Tai (1986) have presented evidence to argue that *de* in this construction has the nominalizing function, i.e., it turns the sentence before it into a noun clause, very much like the *de* in the "be–headed" relative clause such as *jiao shu–de* 'literally, people who teach; teacher.'[38] As we will have much more to say about this construction in Chapter 8, we will simply point out at this point that we find their arguments convincing and that their conclusion is independently affirmed by our own evidence. In addition, we have urther discovered that the structure marked by *de* is a topic itself containing within it two topics, as *ta* 'he' and *zhao—xiang* 'take—picture' in (180), which can be further raised by the Topic—raising rule.

---

[38]For a detailed discussion of the "be—headed" relative clause, see Chapter 8.

CHAPTER SIX
SENTENCES WITH SPECIAL TOPICS

In the three previous chapters we have identified the primary topic as well as various non-primary topics, secondary, tertiary and so forth. In this chapter we will explore two special constructions in the light of our findings. These two constructions are the *lian... dou/ye* construction and the comparative construction, as exemplified by (1) and (2) respectively.

(1) ta lian   Xingqitian dou qu shangban.
    he including Sunday   all go work
    'He goes to work even on Sunday.'

(2) ta Xingqiwu bi   Xingqiyi you kong.
    he Friday   COMP Monday have leisure
    'He has more free time on Friday than on Monday.'

These two constructions differ from those that we have discussed so far in that both involve a constituent that has a topic of some rank. To be more specific, the *lian* constituent such as *Xingqitian* 'Sunday' in (1) has to be a topic, primary or non-primary while in a comparative construction not only do the constituents being compared such as *Xingqiwu* 'Friday' and *Xingqiyi* 'Monday' in (2) have to be topics, they must both be topics of an equal rank, i.e., they must both be primary, secondary, or tertiary topics. It is in this way that these constituents are called special topics.

In what follows we will present ample evidence to substantiate our claim and we will also go into discussion of various syntactic and semantic phenomena related to these two constructions.

1. The *Lian...Dou/Ye* Construction
1.1. A Brief Review of Some Previous Analyses

Various Chinese linguists have in the past touched upon the *lian* construction. In my book (Tsao, 1979), *A Functional Study of Topic in Chinese: The First Step towards Discourse Analysis,* I mistakenly took the constituent that occurs after *lian* in this construction as a focus and briefly discussed how it can be distinguished from a regular topic NP when they both occur in the sentence—initial position. Tang (1977) compares what he calls *lian* movement rule with topicalization and object—fronting rules. His conclusion is that they are basically three different rules, even though they do have some grammatical properties in common. By far the most detailed analysis of the construction was done by Paris (1977). In her paper she has found several important generalizations that have been neglected in the previous discussion. Finally, Li and Thompson (1981) in their grammar briefly summarizes the important properties that this construction has been found to possess.

There are, of course, other people who have touched upon this construction before but I think the four sources that I just mentioned are representative and only those four will be reviewed in the following. As Li and Thompson's discussion, though brief, was the most general, we will naturally begin with it.

1.1.1. Li and Thompson's Analysis

Li and Thompson's grammar (1981) devotes only two pages to the discussion of this construction. Their succinct discussion will be briefly summarized and then commented upon. They characterize the construction in the following terms:

> The *lian....dou/ye* construction singles out one part of the sentence with the meaning of 'even'. It is formed by putting the particle *lian* before the element being singled out. This element must occur at some point in the sentence before *dou* (or *ye,* which is interchangeable with *dou*), but not necessarily immediately before it (p.338).

They further point out that if the *lian* constituent is not the subject/topic itself, then, the *lian* phrase can occur in two different places without any change of meaning, as exemplified by (a) and (b) in (3).

(3) a. wo   lian   ta dou bu xihuan.
       I   including him all not like
       'I don't even like him.'
    b. lian   ta wo dou bu xihuan.
       including him I all not like
       'Same as (a).'[1]

---

[1] As we will argue later on, (3a) and (3b) do not mean exactly the same. In (3a) the

Finally, they point out that the *lian* constituent can be a verb phrase or a coverb phrase as exemplified by (4) and (5).

(4) ta <u>lian   da-zi</u>   dou bu hui.
    he including hit-character all not know:how
    'He doesn't even know how to type.'

(5) ta <u>lian   gen ta nüer</u>   dou bu shuo-hua.
    he including with his daughter all not speak-speech
    'He doesn't even speak to his daughter.'

This characterization of theirs is quite neutral and, as far as it goes, quite accurate. There are, however, two points that need clarification. First, it is, strictly speaking, not accurate to describe the *lian* constituent in (4) as a verb phrase. We have ample evidence to show what originated as a VP is here nominalized and functions like an NP. Examine the following parallel examples.

(6) a. ta bu xihuan <u>da-zi</u>.
       he not like hit-character
       'He doesn't like typing.'
    b. ta <u>da-zi</u>   bu xihuan.
       he hit-character not like
       'As for him and as for typing, he doesn't like it.'
    c. ta <u>lian   da-zi</u>   dou bu xihuan.
       he including hit-character all not like
       'He doesn't even like typing.'
    d. <u>da-zi</u>   ta bu xihuan.
       hit-character he not like
       'As for typing, he doesn't like it.'
    e. <u>lian   da-zi</u>   ta dou bu xihuan.
       including hit-character he all not like
       'As for typing, he doesn't even like it.'

---

lian phrase is a secondary topic while in (3b) it is a primary topic. In other words, the same phrase has more topical prominence in (3b) than in (3a).

It is clear from (6a) that *da—zi* 'typing' is here the object of the transitive verb *xihuan* 'like' and is therefore an NP. Furthermore, like many object NPs, it can occur between the primary topic and the main verb to become a secondary topic as in (6b). And as a secondary topic, it can be further promoted to become the primary topic as in (6d). Note also that it is only when the phrase occurs as a topic, primary or secondary, will it be possible for it to be preceded by *lian* 'including' in a *lian* construction. Holding back our judgement for a moment as to whether the *lian* constituent should be treated as a topic NP, we can, on the basis of the evidence presented so far at least see that *da—zi* 'typing' in (4) as well as in (6c)and (6e) is definitely an NP.

Our sceond comment has to do with the statement that the construction "singles out one part of the sentence with the meaning 'even'" in the passage just quoted. The statement is not quite accurate as far as the main verb of a sentence is concerned. Compare (7b) with (7c).

(7) a. ta xihuan daishu.
    he like   algebra.
    'He likes algebra.'
  b. ta lian   daishu dou xihuan
    he including algebra all like
    'He even likes algebra .'
  c.*ta lian   xihuan dou daishu.
    he including like all algebra.
  d.*ta lian   xihuan daishu dou
    he including like algebra all

Unlike the object, the main verb of the sentence cannot be freely singled out to be the *lian* constituent and neither can the whole VP as shown by (c) and (d) sentences respectively.[2] It is only in certain constructions, as in (8), that a constituent which is in some sense a verb can be placed in the slot.

---

[2]The main verb in an English sentence can be qualified by "even" when the verb is stressed, as in (i):
  (i) He even LIKES Li Si.

(8) ta <u>lian   shui</u> dou mei shui.
    he including sleep all not sleep.
    'He didn't even sleep at all.'

We will, in a later section, give an explanation as to why this should be so.

1.1.2. Paris' Analysis

   Paris (1977) gives a rather extensive discussion of this construction. She starts out by pointing out the inadequacies of what she calls "traditional analyses" of the construction as represented by Guo, Yi-zhou (1957), Ding, Sheng-shu et al. (1961) etc. Then she takes up the syntax of the construction by providing arguments against the treatment of *lian* as a preposition. She also points out that Hagege's proposal (1975) that *lian* be treated as a focalizer cannot be correct even on his own terms. Furthermore, she argues that the *lian* constituent cannot be transformationally derived. We will discuss her arguments in connection with Tang's analysis.

   At this point, it suffices to point out that her finding that all types of the *lian* constituent are either the regular noun phrase or other types of constituents having a great deal of nominal quality is in the main correct. We will take up this issue in some detail later on, too.

   In the latter half of her paper, Paris characterizes the semantics of the construction. Her proposal is to treat *lian* as a quasi-quantifier and *dou/ye* as quantifiers. The interaction of these two provides us with the meaning of 'even'. We will postpone until later on the examination of the details of her arguments. Right now let us simply point out that even though she has gone farther than any previous attempt in her characterization of the semantic function of the construction, her proposal to treat *lian* as a quasi-quantifier is apparently quite ad hoc because it is the sole member of this category in Chinese grammar. More importantly, because she fails to see the parallel existing between the *lian* constituent and other types of NPs that we have characterized as secondary topics such as the *ba* NP in the *ba* construction as in (9a), the fronted object NP as in (10a), the second NP in the double nominative construction and the fronted VP in the so-called verb-copying construction as in (11a) and (12a) respectively, she is unable to reveal the true nature of the *lian* constituent. Compare the (a) and (b) sentences in the following.

(9) a. ta ba <u>Zhang San</u> qing-lai   le.
    he BA Zhang San invite-come PART
    'He invited Zhang San to come.'
  b. ta <u>lian   Zhang San</u> ye   qing-lai   le.
    he including Zhang San also invite-come PART
    'He even invited Zhang San to come.'

(10) a. ta <u>qiu</u> da-po   le.
    he ball hit-break PART
    'He broke the ball.'
  b. ta <u>lian   qiu</u> dou da-po   le.
    he including ball all hit-break PART
    'He even broke the ball.'

(11) a. ta <u>bizi</u> hen   haokan.
    he nose very good-looking
    'He (topic), his nose is very handsome.'
  b. ta <u>lian   bizi</u> dou hen   haokan.
    he including nose all very good-looking
    'As for him, even his nose is handsome.'

(12) a. ta <u>zhao-xiang</u>   zhao de   hen hao.
    he take-picture take PART very well
    'As for him and as for taking pictures, he is very good.'
  b. ta <u>lian   zhao-xiang</u> dou zhao de   hen hao.
    he including take-picture all take PART very well
    'As for him, even taking pictures he does it well.'

1.1.3. Tsao's Previous Analysis

Actually such an oversight was not committed by Paris alone, Tsao (1979) was misled by the stress associated with the *lian* constituent into analyzing the *lian* constituent, as in (13), as a focus and thus failed to see its true nature.

(13) <u>lian   Si-shu</u>   tamen ye   mai de hen duo.
     including Four-books they also sell PART very many
     'Even Fourbooks, they sold a great many of them.'

As a matter of fact, in the same book (Tsao, 1979) I already found out that topics can be stressed when they are contrastive. Since the meaning of *lian* in conjunction with *dou/ye* requires that the *lian* constituent to be always, explicitly or implicitly, in contrast, the fact that there is always a stress associated with it is therefore no argument against treating it as a topic.[3]

1.1.4. Tang's Analysis

Tang (1977) proposes to treat the *lian* constituent as an NP that has been moved to the slot by a fronting transformation. He, however, doesn't give a formal rule to account for the movement. As Paris (1977) has already presented two convincing reasons against such a derivational theory, we'll simply summarize her arguments below, adding any comment as we think fit.

First, there are cases where the *lian* constituent has no underlying source. (14a) and (15a) could not be derived from (14b) and (15b) respectively since (14b) and (15b) are both ungrammatical.

(14) a. Wei.....lian   yao qu ban-kai ta ye   tai bu
        Wei   including want to move   it also raise not
        qi   shou lai.
        up   hand PART
        '...even if she wanted to move it, Wei could not raise her hand.'
     b.*Wei tai bu qi shou lai yao qu ban-kai ta.
        Wei raise not up hand PART want to move   it
(15) a. ta lian   yi-ci   ye   mei lai.
        he including one-time also not come
        'He did not come even once.'
     b.*ta mei lai yi-ci.
        he not come one-time

---

[3] For a more detailed discussion of the relationship between the *lian* topic and stress, see Section 1.5.

Second, and more importantly, *lian* movement transformation sometimes produces a drastic change in the meaning of a sentence. Compare (16a) with (16b).

(16) a. Li Si mei he   yi-bei cha.
        Li Si not drink one-cup tea
        'Li Si didn't drink a cup of tea.'
     b. Li Si lian   yi-bei cha ye   mei he.
        Li Si including one-cup tea also not drink
        'Li Si didn't drink any tea at all.'

While (16a) normally means that *Li Si* drank some tea but the quantity was not up to one cup, (16b) means that he didn't have any tea at all.

One special feature of Tang's analysis is that he actually goes into a comparison of the *lian* fronting, topicalization and object fronting rules. He, however, concludes that the former, though having some properties in common with the latter two, is an independent rule. Even though there are many problems with Tang's approach to the construction, he should be given the credit of seeing that the *lian* constituent is in some way related to a primary topic as produced by topicalization in his framework and to a secondary topic as produced by his object fronting rule.[4]

1.2. The Nominal Nature of the *Lian* Constituent

One of the greatest constroversies in the past discussion of this construction has to do with the nature of the element that occurs after *lain*. In order not to bias the reader we have up to this point used "constituent" to refer to it and will continue to do so until we can positively identify what it is.

Paris' paper referred to earlier (1977) contains a section exclusively devoted to this topic. Since her arguments are in general quite convincing, we will present a summery of her discussion in the following, adding our comment whenever necessary.

Paris (1977:55) first gives a quite exhaustive list of the kinds of elements that can occur as a *lian* constituent. According to her, the *lian* constituent can be :(i) regular NPs as in (17) and (18); (ii) VPs as in (19) and (20); (iii) PPs as in (21) and (22); (iv) time

---

[4]The primary topic and the secondary topic are, of course, not Tang's terms but mine.

adverbials as in (23); (v) whole or reduced subordinate clauses as in (24) and (25); (vi) predicate nominals as in (26) and (27); and (vii) the first part of a reduplicate VP as in (28).

(17) <u>lian   ta</u> ye ting—bu—dong   wo—de
     including he also listen—not—understand my
     hua. (topic/subject).
     word
     'Even he doesn't understand my words.'

(18) ta <u>lian   wo—de hua</u> ye ting—bu—dong.(object NP)
     he including my   word also listen—not—understand
     'He didn't even understand my words.'

(19) renmen sihu <u>lian   duzi   e</u>   dou wangji le.(VP)
     people seem including stomach hungry all forget PART
     'People seem to have forgotten that they were hungry.'

(20) ta <u>lian   chang—ge</u> dou bu hui. (VP)
     he including sing—song all not know:how
     'He doesn't even know how to sing.'

(21) ta zai shenme difang dou bu chi, <u>lian   zai</u>
     he at any   place all not eat including at
     <u>fanguan</u>   dou bu chi.(PP)
     restaurant all not eat
     'He doesn't eat anywhere, even in restaurants.'

(22) Zhang Taitai zhen   bu hao; ta <u>lian dui</u>
     Zhang Mrs.   really not good she including to
     <u>ta—de nüer</u>   dou bu shuo yi—ju hua. (PP)
     her   daughter all not say one—CL word
     'Mrs. Zhang is really unpleasant; she doesn't even speak to her daughter.'

(23) ta <u>lian   Xingqitian</u> ye lai mafan wo.(time adv.)
    he including Sunday   also come trouble me
    'Even on Sunday he came to bother me.'

(24) <u>lian   ni zai women xuexiao-li jiaoshu</u>, wo dou
    including you at our   school-LOC teach   I all
    tongyi. (subordinate clause)
    agree
    'I even agree that you teach in our school.'

(25) <u>lian   jiaoshou zuo yanjiang de   shihou</u>, Li Si dou
    including professor make speech DE   moment Li Si all
    bu-ting-de shuohua.
    incessantly talk
    'Even when the professor makes a speech, Li Si doesn't stop talking.'

(26) ta xue Zhongwen <u>lian   san-ge yue</u> dou mei
    he study Chinese including three-CL month all not
    xue-man. (predicate nominal)
    study-full
    'He didn't even complete three months of Chinese.'

(27) <u>lian   san-ge yue de Zhongwen</u>, ta dou mei
    including three-CL month DE Chinese   he all not
    xue-man.(predicate nominal)
    study-full
    'Same as (26).'

(28) ta lian   <u>xie-zi</u>   dou xie de tebie
    he including.write-character all write PART especially
    hao. (the first part of a reduplicate VP)
    well
    'Even his calligraphy is outstanding.'

Paris (1977:56) then goes on to show that those elements that are not regular NPs have all exhibited some nominal qualities. First, Paris points out, whatever *lian* is, it cannot precede real VPs as shown in (29); nor can it precede manner or reason adverbials as shown in (30) and (31).[5]

(29) *Zhang San <u>lian   qu-le   youju</u>.
     Zhang San including go-ASP post-office

(30) *Li Si <u>lian   hen xiaoxin</u> dou fan-le   san-ci
     Li Si including very careful all commit-ASP three-CL
     cuowu.
     mistake

(31) *ta <u>lian   weile nüpengyou</u> dou bu lai shang-ke.
     he including for girl-friend all not come take-lesson

She then examines all the elements that can occur after *lian* in this construction one by one.

<u>(i) Nominalized VPs and Nominal Clauses</u>

Previously in Section 1.1 in our comment on Li and Thompson's characterization of this construction we have demonstrated that it is a misnormer to call *da-zi* 'hit character' in (6) a VP. Because it has many grammatical properties specific to the NP, it should be more properly called "nominalized VP". The same argument applies to *chang-ge* 'sing-song' in (20) and *duzi e* 'stomach hungry' in (19). In addition, Paris (1977) points out that both VPs can be replaced by ordinary NPs as in (32) and (33).

(32) renmen sihu wangji-le <u>nei-jian shi</u>.
     people seem forget-ASP that-CL matter
     'People seem to have forgotten the matter.'

---

[5]It seems to be incorrect to say that "the reason adverbial" cannot appear as the *lian* constituent. Withess the following counterexample, which is perfectly grammatical.
(i) ta lian   <u>weile pengyou</u>   dou keyi bu   lai
    he including for   friend   all can   not come
    shang-ke,   hekuang   shi weile ziji-de   haizi.
    have-class let:alone be   for   his:own   child
    'Even for his friend, he can cut classes, let alone for his own child.'

(33) ta bu hui <u>nei-ge zi</u>.
   he not know that-CL character
   'He doesn't know that character.'

Likewise, the clause in (24), *ni zai women xuexiao-li jiaoshu* 'you teach in our school', functions like an NP as it is replaceable by a regular NP. Compare (24) with (34).

(34) wo tongyi <u>zhe-jian shi</u>.
   I agree this-CL matter.
   'I agree to the matter.'

(ii) <u>Adverbial Subordinate Clauses</u>

In (25) the clause *jiaoshou zuo yanjiang de shihou* 'the time when the professor was making a speech' is a time clause so it seems to be an adverbial clause in function, but in form, as Paris (1977:56) points out, it is a complex NP whose head noun is determined by a whole S. Its syntactic structure reads as [$_{NP}$(S de) NP]

(iii) <u>Time Adverbials</u>

Unlike other adverbial phrases, time adverbials behave in many ways like nominals: they cannot be preceded by negative markers as shown in (35); they can function as object of *shi* in a pseudo-cleft construction as in (36); and they can conjoin like NPs with *gen* 'and' as in (37).

(35) *ta $\begin{Bmatrix}\text{mei}\\\text{bu}\end{Bmatrix}$ Xingqitian lai.
   he not Sunday come
   'He $\begin{Bmatrix}\text{didn't}\\\text{doesn't}\end{Bmatrix}$ come on Sunday.'

(36) ta lai de na yi tian shi Xingqitian.
   he come DE that one day be Sunday
   'The day that he came is Sunday.'

(37) Xingqitian gen Xingqiwu bu tong.
    Sunday   and Friday not same
    'Sunday and Friday are different.'

(iv) Prepositional Phrases

Paris (1977:57) observes that PPs containing inanimate NPs, like subject and object NPs, are deleted under relativization and it is on the basis of this observation that she argues that PPs possess nominal quality. This observation of hers, unfortunately, is at best inconclusive as it is made solely on the basis of the behavior of the *ba* phrase under relativization. Let's examine her examples, reproduced here as (38) and (39).

(38) ta ba yifu   xi-wan   le.
    he BA clothes wash-finish PART.
    'He has finished washing the clothes.'

(39) ta φ xi-wan   (-le) de   yifu   zai
    he   wash-finish PART Rel.Mar. clothes at
    chuang-shang.
    bed-LOC
    'The clothes that he has finished washing are on the bed.'

Her observation is called to doubt for three reasons. First, it is not exactly clear whether *ba* should be called a preposition.[6] Second, besides (38), (39) can have (40) below as its underlying source, where *yifu* 'clothes' is clearly an object NP.

(40) ta xi-wan   yifu   le.
    he wash-finish clothes PART
    'He has washed the clothes.'

Third, this phenomenon is peculiar to the *ba* phrase. Other prepositional phrases do not exhibit such a characteristic. Compare (39) with (41).

---

[6]In Tsao (1987a), *ba* in the *ba* construction is regarded as a secondary topic marker. It is not clear, however, whether it should at the same time be regarded as a preposition or not.

(41) a. wo <u>zai nei-ge daxue</u> nian-le yi-nian shu.
I at that-CL university study-ASP one-year study
'I studied at that university for a year.'
b. wo <u>zai nar</u> nian-le yi-nian shu de
I at there study-ASP one-year study Rel. Mar.
nei-ge daxue....
that-CL university
'the university where I studied for a year....'
c.*wo <u>nar</u> nian-le yi-nian shu de nei-ge
I there study-ASP one-year study Rel.Mar. that-CL
daxue.....
university
'Same as (b).'

This does not mean, however, that her conclusion is necessarily incorrect. On the contrary, we have other pieces of evidence to show that it is correct. A prepositional phrase by definition has two constituents:a preposition and a noun phrase.[7] However, under certain as yet unclear conditions, the preposition can be deleted without changing its grammaticality, reducing a prepositional phrase to a noun phrase. Compare (a) and (b) sentences in the following examples.

(42) a. <u>zai jia-li</u> ta bu tan gongshi. (PP)
at home-LOC he not talk business
'At home he doesn't talk about business.'
b. <u>jia-li</u> ta bu tan gongshi. (NP)
home-LOC he not talk business
'Same as (a).'

(43) a. <u>zai na-ge shihou</u> Taibei hai meiyou dian. (PP)
at that-CL time Taipei yet not-have electricity
'At that time, there was no eletricity in Taipei.'

---

[7]Wang Li (1956, 1980) refers to this type of adverbials without a preposition as *guanxi yu* 'relational phrases'.

b. na-ge shihou Taibei hai mei-you dian. (NP)
   that-CL time   Taipei yet not-have eletricity
   'Same as (a).'

It seems that in becoming a topic, the preposition in a prepositional phrase is often deleted. The same phenomenon is observed when many prepositional phrases are placed in the *ba* or *lian* constituent, as exemplified by (44b) and (44c) respectively.

(44) a. ta zai biru   sheng-le huo.
        he at fireplace build-ASP fire
        'He built a fire at the fireplace.'
     b. ta ba biru   sheng-le huo.
        he BA fireplace build-ASP fire
        '(Roughly) same as (a).'
     c. ta lian   biru   dou sheng-le huo.
        he including fireplace all build-ASP fire
        'He built a fire even in the fireplace.'

(v) The First Part of a Reduplicate VP

In (28) *xie-zi* 'write character' has lost must of verbal quality. Li (1975:880) points out that *xie* 'write' in this construction cannnot be preceded by a modal verb, or a negative marker; nor can it be suffixed by an aspectual marker. Examine (45), (46) and (47).

(45) *ta hui xie-zi   xie de tebie   hao.
      he will write-character write PART expecially well

(46) *ta mei xie-zi   xie de tebie   hao.
      he not write-character write PART expecially well

(47) *ta xie-le zi   xie de tebie   hao.
      he write-ASP character write PART especially well

Paris (1977:57) further points out that, like NPs, *xie-zi* 'write-character' can be placed in the initial position of a sentence and functions like a regular topic as shown in (48).

(48) <u>xie-zi</u>, Zhang San xie de tebie hao.
write—character Zhang San write PART especially well
'As for calligraphy, Zhang San is very good at it.'

Actually we have, on the basis of this observation and many others, pointed out in chapter 4 that the V+O constituent that occurs at the front part of this construction is a secondary topic, which like other types of secondary topics, can all be promoted to become the primary topic as in (48).

This last statement provides us with a very good transition to the next section where we will present many arguments to show that the *lian* constituent is not only an NP or its equivalent but also, depending on where it occurs in the sentence, a secondary topic or a primary topic.

1.3. Arguments for Treating the *Lian* Constituent as a Topic

1.3.1. The Roles Played by the Primary Topic and Those Played by the *Lian* Constituent Compared

In Tsao (1979) it is found that the primary topic can play one of the following roles in a sentence. It can be the subject, the object, the time adverbial, the locative adverbial, the scope—delimiting phrases.[8] In the case of the so-called "double nominative construction", it does not play any syntactic role directly. Rather, it bears the semantic relation of possessor—possessed, whole—part or class—member to the second nominal, which is the subject of the clause. To this list, we have added the following two in our previous discussion. The V+O phrase occurring in the first part of a verb—copying construction and the *ba* phrase in the *ba* construction can both occur as the secondary or the primary topic of the sentence. With only one exception, in each and every case where a topic, be it primary or secondary, is possible, there is a corresponding *lian* construction with the topic as the *lian* constituent. Examine the following parallel cases.

---

[8] I used to call it "relational adverb", but now I think the term should be more properly defined as in Note 7. The phrases used in this function should be called "scope—delimiting phrases" because they delimit the scope of the following comment and for that reason, they can be optionally preceded by *guanyu*, *zhiyu* and *duiyu* all of which can be translated as "with regard to", "concerning" or simply "about" in English.

(49) a. <u>wo</u> bu xihuan ta. (subject)
    I not like   him
    'I don't like hime.'
  b. <u>lian   wo</u> ye bu xihuan ta.
    including I also not like   him
    'Even I don't like him.'

(50) a. <u>ta</u>, wo bu xihuan. (object)
    he   I   not like
    'As for him, I don't like him.'
  b. <u>lian   ta</u>, wo ye bu xihuan.
    including him I also not like
    'Even him, I don't like.'

(51) a. <u>zuotian</u>   ni gege   lai kan ni.(time adverbial)
    yesterday your elder brother come see you
    'Yesterday, your elder brother came to see you.'
  b. <u>lian   zuotian</u> ni gege   ye lai kan
    including yesterday your elder brother also come see
    ni.
    you
    'Even yesterday, your elder brother came to see you.'

(52) a. <u>chuang-dixia</u> bai-man-le   wuxia xiaoshuo. (place adv.)
    bed-under   place-full-ASP kongfu novel
    'Under the bed were packed with kongfu novels.'
  b. <u>lian   chuang-dixia</u> dou bai-man-le   wuxia
    including bed-under   all place-full-ASP kongfu
    xiaoshuo.
    novel
    'Even under the bed were packed with kongfu novels.'

(53) a. <u>zhei-jian shi</u>, ta xie-le yi-fen baogao.(scope-delimiting phrase)
    this-CL matter he write one-CL report
    '(Concerning) this matter, he wrote a report.'

b. <u>lian   zhe-jian shi</u>   ta ye xie-le   yi-fen
   including this-CL matter he also write-ASP one-CL
   baogao.
   report
   'Even (with regard to) this matter, he wrote a report.'

(54) a. <u>Xiaohua</u>, <u>yanjing</u> hen hao-kan. (possessor-possessed)
       Xiaohua   eye   very good-looking
       'Xiaohua (topic), her eyes are beautiful.'
   b. <u>lian   Xiaohua</u> yanjing dou hen hao-kan.
      including Xiaohua   eye   all very good-looking
      'Even Xiaohua has beautiful eyes.'

(55) a. <u>na   wu-ge pingguo</u>, <u>liang-ge</u> lan-le. (whole-part)
       those 5-CL   apple   2-CL   rot-ASP
       '(Of) those five apples, two rotted.'
   b.?<u>lian   na wu-ge pingguo</u> ye liang-ge lan-le.[9]
      including those 5-CL   apple   also 2-CL   rot-ASP
      'Even those five apples, two of them rotted.'

(56) a. <u>yifu</u>,   xin-de   hao. (Class-member)
       clothes new-ones good
       'Speaking of clothes, new ones are good.'
   b. <u>lian   yifu</u>   ye xin-de hao.[10]
      including clothes also new-ones good
      'Even clothes, new ones are good.'

---

[9]As indicated by the question mark, (55b) sounds strange. The exact reason, however, is not clear. I suspect that its marginal grammaticality may be due to pragmatic consideration. As I will point out later on *lian X dou/ye (y)* construction means 'even X (y)' where X is pragmatically the least expected member of a certain set that (y). Pragmatically, it is quite difficult to imagine a situation in which *wu-ge pingguo* 'five apples' is the least expected member of a set that has the property of *liang-ge lan le* 'two rotted'. It is, I believe, this difficulty that makes (55b) less acceptable.

[10]For some reason that is yet unclear to me, it is more natural to use *yeshi* rather than *ye* alone in (56b).

(57) a. wo <u>ba Zhang San</u> jiao lai le. (*ba*–NP as the secondary topic)
     I BA Zhang San call come PART
     'I had Zhang San summoned.'
   b. wo <u>lian   Zhang San</u> ye jiao lai le.
     I including Zhang San also call come PART
     'I even had Zhang San summoned.'
   c. <u>Zhang San</u> a, wo <u>ba ta</u> jiao lai le.
     Zhang San PART I BA him call come PART
     'Zhang San (topic), I had him summoned here.'
   d. <u>lian   Zhang San</u> a, wo dou <u>ba ta</u> jiao lai le.
     including Zhang San PART I all BA him call come PART
     'Even Zhang San, I had him summoned.'

(58) a. ta <u>zuo–wen</u>   zuo de hen kuai.
     he write–composition write PART very fast
     'He is quick at writing compositions.'
   b. ta <u>lian   zuo–wen</u>   dou zuo de hen
     he including write–composition all write PART very
     kuai.
     fast
     'He is quick at even writing compositions.'
   c. <u>zuo–wen</u>   a, ta zuo de hen kuai.
     write–composition PART he write PART very fast
     'Speaking of writing compositions, he is very quick.'
   d. <u>lian   zuo–wen</u>   a, ta dou zuo de
     including write–compositions PART he all write PART
     hen kuai.
     very fast
     'Even writing compositions, he is very quick at it.'

The parallelism here is simply too striking to be missed. The parallelism, however, does not stop here. If we turn our attention to cases where certain constituents cannot become topics, we find striking parallels as well. We mentioned earlier that according to

Paris (1977) only manner adverbials cannot become *lian* constituents.[11] The same constraint is found in the case of the primary topic. Compare (b) and (c) sentences in the following.

(59) a. ta <u>hen kuai-de</u> zou-guo-le na-ge difang.
       he very quickly walk-pass-ASP that-CL place
       'He walked past the place very quickly.'
   b.*<u>hen kuai-de</u> a, ta zou-guo-le na-ge difang.
       very quickly PART he walk-pass-ASP that-CL place
   c.*<u>lian   hen kuai-de</u>, ta dou zou-guo-le na-ge
       including very quickly   he all walk-pass-ASP that-CL
       difang.
       place

In addition, for any post-verbal constituent such as object to become a topic it is necessary that the constituent be moved to a pre-verbal position. Likewise, it is necessary for any post-verbal constituent to be moved to a pre-verbal position before it can become a *lian* constituent. Examine the following sentences.

(60) a. ta zuotian   qing <u>Zhang San</u> le.
       he yesterday invite Zhang San   PART
       'He invited Zhang San yesterday.'
   b.*ta zuotian   qing <u>Zhang San</u> a, le.
       he yesterday invite Zhang San PART PART
   c.*ta zuotian   dou qing <u>lian   Zhang San</u> le.
       he yesterday   all invite including Zhang San PART

1.3.2. The Grammatical Qualities of the Primary Topic and Those of the *Lian* Constituent Compared

In Chapter 2, we have, after a careful and detailed examination of all the grammatical qualities that topic may have, come up with the following list:

---

[11]Paris also includes the reason adverbial here, but as pointed out in Note 5 it is probably a mistake.

(61) a. Topic invariably occupies the clause-initial position of the first clause in a topic chain.
b. Topic can optionally be separated from the rest of the clause, in which it overtly occurs, by one of the following four pause particles: *a (ya), ne, me* and *ba*.
c. Topic is always definite or generic in reference.
d. Topic can have the supraclausal function of extending its semantic domain to more than one clause.
e. Topic is in control of the pronominalization or deletion of all the coreferential NPs in a topic chain.
f. Topic, except in clauses in which it is also subject, plays no role in such processes as reflexivization, passivization, Equi-NP deletion and imperativization.

(61f) involves quite a few processes, the test of all of which will certainly take us far afield. We will therefore only take reflexivization as an example.

(62) a. Li Si a,   Zhang San xihuan ta. (object NP as topic)
        Li Si PART Zhang San like   him
        'Li Si (topic), Zhang San likes him.'
    b.*Li Si$_i$ a,   Zhang San xihuan ta-ziji$_i$.
        Li Si PART Zhang San like   he-self
    c. lian   Li Si a,   Zhang San dou xihuan ta.
        including Li Si PART Zhang San all like   him
        'Even Li Si, Zhang San likes him.'
    d.*lian   Li Si$_i$ a,   Zhang San dou xihuan ta-ziji$_i$.
        including Li Si PART Zhang San all like   he-self

If we compare (a) with (c) and (b) with (d) in (62), it is quite apparent that neither the primary topic nor the *lian* topic plays any role in reflexivization.

Likewise, it can be easily demonstrated that (61a) is true for the *lian* constituent, even though, due to its meaning, the *lian* constituent is seldom found to head a topic chain. Examine (63) and (64).

(63) lian Xingqitian_i ta dou qu shangban, ____i ta
    including Sunday he all go work   he
    dou bu xiuxi.
    all not rest
    'Even Sunday, he went to work and didn't rest.'

(64) lian qiang—shang_i dou xi de hen ganjing, ____i
    including wall—LOC all wash PART very clean
    dou qi—le haoji bian.
    all paint—ASP several times
    'Even the wall was washed clean and painted several times.'

A close examination of (63) and (64) reveals that the *lian* phrase heads a topic chain of two comments in both cases and the *lian* constituent is in control of the NP coreferential pronominalization or deletion in the chain. (61a, d and e) evidently hold true for the *lian* constituent.

Furthermore, the sentences in (65) clearly show, whether the *lian* consitituent occurs in the initial position of the highest sentence or not, it can be separated by one of the pause particles.

(65) a. lian ta { ya / me / ne / ?ba } shuxue dou bu xihuan.[12]
        including him PART math all not like
        'Even he doesn't like math.'

    b. ta lian shuxue { ya / me / ne / ?ba } dou bu xihuan.
        he including math PART all not like
        'He doesn't even like math.'

---

[12] As no linguists have up to date taken up a serious study of the meaning and use of these pause particles, their meaning and use remain unclear. We are, therefore, unable to account for why *ba* is less acceptable in this particular context.

c. lian shuxue $\begin{Bmatrix} ya \\ me \\ ne \\ ?ba \end{Bmatrix}$ ta dou bu xihuan.

    including math   PART he all not like
    'Even math, he doesn't like it.'

It is clear, then, that as far as the behavior described in (61b) is concerned, the *lian* constituent parallels the primary topic.

In an affirmative *lian* sentence, the *lian* constituent always has a definite or generic reference, as demonstrated by (66a) and (66b). An indefinite, non-generic NP cannot occur there without causing ungrammaticality as (66c) shows.

(66) a. <u>lian   nei-ge ren</u>   dou zuo-de-liao, hekuang
        including that-CL preson all do-PART-able not-to-say
    shi ni.
    be you
    'Even that man can do it, not to say you.'
  b. <u>lian   ren</u> dou zuo-de-liao, hekuang shi shen.
    including human all do-PART-able not-to-say be god
    'Even humans can do it, not to say gods.'
  c.*<u>lian   yi-ge ren</u> dou-zuo-de-liao.[13]
    including a-CL man all-do-PART-able
    *'Even a man can do it.'

Thus, (61c) holds true for the *lian* constituent in the affirmative sentence. In the negative sentence, the situation is more complicated. Examine the following sentences.

(67) a. <u>lian   nei-ge zi</u>   ta dou bu hui.
      including that-CL character he all not know
      'He doesn't even know that character.'

---

[13]"A man" in the English translation of (66c) is to be taken in its non-specific, non-generic sense.

b. <u>lian</u>   Zhongguo zi   ta dou bu hui.
   including Chinese   character he all not know
   'He doesn't even know Chinese characters.'
c. <u>lian</u>   yi–ge zi   ta dou bu hui.
   including a–CL   character he all not know
   (i) *'He doesn't even know a character (i.e., a non–specific character).
   (ii) 'He doesn't even know a character.(= He doesn't know any character at all.)

(67c) is ungrammatical when *yi–ge zi* 'a character' is taken in its non–specific, non–generic sense as shown in translation (i). It is grammatical only when taken in the sense of (ii), where the *lian* constituent interacting with negation to produce a univeral reading. We will attempt to give an explanation as to why this is so in our later discussion.

To sum up our discussion in this section, the *lian* constituent is found to possess the following grammatical properties:

(68) a. The *lian* constituent invariably occupies the clause–initial position of the first clause in a *lian* topic chain.
b. The *lian* constituent can optionally be separated from the rest of the clause, in which it overtly occurs by one of following three pause particles:*a (ya), ne* and *me*.
c. The *lian* constituent is always definite or generic in reference.
d. The *lian* constituent can extend its semantic domain to more than one clause.
e. The *lian* constituent is in control of the pronominalization or deletion of all the coreferential NPs in a *lian* topic chain.
f. At least in the case of reflexivization, the *lian* constituent except in clauses in which it is also subject, plays no role in it.

If we compare (68) with (61), we find that the similarities are again too many and too close to miss. There is, however, one great difference. The *lian* constituent, unlike the primary topic, does not always show up in the clause–initial position of the highest clause. When this happens, it is not the primary topic but it still has many of the topical properties and it occurs in a slot parallel to the *ba* phrase in a *ba* sentence, the second nominative in a double nominative construction, the fronted object, and the V+O phrase in the so-called verb reduplication clause. As we have pointed out in chapters 4 and 5, these constituents are secondary topics. Since the *lian* phrase can occur in the same slot, it must be in these cases, a secondary topic as well.

1.3.3 An Additional Argument

Previously in connection with our comment on Li and Thompson's analysis, we mentioned that the main verb and the verb phrase are the two constituents that cannot be moved freely to the *lian* slot. Now that we have found that the *lian* phrase is actually a topic, primary or secondary, we can offer a very good explanation why this is so.

Our explanation, simply stated, is this: any topicalization is blocked if, as a result of the process, what is left behind cannot be its comment. With this in mind, let us take up (7) (repeated here as (69)) again.

(69) a. ta   xihuan daishu.
        he   like   algebra
        'He likes algebra.'
     b. ta <u>lian   daishu</u> dou xihuan.
        he including algebra all like
        'He even likes algebra.'
     c.*ta <u>lian   xihuan</u> dou daishu.
        he including like   all algebra
     d.*ta <u>lian   xihuan daishu</u> dou.
        he including like   algebra all

(69c) and (69d) are ungrammatical because when the verb *xihuan* 'like' or the verb phrase *xihuan daishu* 'like algebra' is fronted, what is left behind does not form a comment at all.

We hope we have by now proved beyond any reasonable doubt that the *lian* constituent is indeed a topic. There, however, remains two important questions for us to answer:(i) It is a well-known fact that topic, representing normally old information, does not usually bear a stress. If it is true, then why should the *lian* constituent, being a topic as we have argued, always bear a stress? (ii) Why of all adverbs are only *dou* 'all' and *ye* 'also' allowed in this construction? Let us take up the second question first.

1.4. The Function of *Dou* and *Ye* in this Construction

To answer the second question, we have to study the meaning of the *lian* construction first. Semantically, we have pointed out that *lian* X *dou/ye* in Chinese means the same as "even X" in English. Following Fraser's (1971) analysis of *even* in English, we might break down the meaning of the *lian...dou/ye* construction into three components, one assertion and two presuppositions. Thus in saying (70a or b), the speaker asserts (71a) and pragmatically presupposes (71b and c).[14]

(70) a. Zhang San <u>lian   Li Si</u> ye   bu renshi.
     Zhang San including Li Si also not know
     'Zhang San doesn't even know Li Si.'

   b. <u>lian   Li Si</u> Zhang San ye   bu renshi.
     including Li Si Zhang San also not know
     'Same as (a).'

(71) a. Zhang San does not know Li Si.
   b. Zhang San does not know other people.
   c. The speaker would not expect, or would not expect the hearer to expect, Zhang San not to know Li Si.

To put it plainly, (70) means that there is a group of people whom *Zhang San* doesn't know and of this group *Li Si* is the one that the speaker least expects or would least expect the hearer to expect, *Zhang San* not to know. This being the case, the speaker will have to have some means to indicate what that group is. So in Chinese the function of *lian* in the *lian* X *dou/ye* construction is to indicate to the hearer that the whole group of which X is a member is the group whose identity is in question.

But why are *dou* 'all' and *ye* chosen for this purpose? To understand how this works, we have to investigate the function of *dou* 'all' and *ye* 'also' first. According to Li and Thompson (1981) and Hou (1983), *dou* 'all' is unique among all adverbs in Chinese in that

---

[14]In Fraser's original analysis, (71a) is also regarded as a presupposition. Following Heringer's suggestion (personal communication), however, I feel that assertion is better because the truth value of (71a) changes when (70) is put in the affirmative as in (i).
(i) Zhang San   lian   Li Si   ye   renshi.
    Zhang San   including   Li Si   also   know
    'Zhang San even knows Li Si.'

it can only refer to NPs that precede it to indicate totality, as shown in (72a).

(72) a. zhei-xie haizi women dou xihuan.
    these   child we   all like
    (i)   'We all like all the children.'
    (ii) 'We all like the children.'
    (iii) 'We like all the children.'

However, if one of eligible NPs is stressed, then the scope of *dou* is automatically applied to that NP as shown in (72b).

(72) b. zhei-xie haizi   women dou xihuan.
        (with stress)
        these   child   we   all like
        'We like all these children.'

On the other hand, *ye* 'also', as pointed out by Paris (1977:62), can have its scope both to the right and to the left, as reflected in the two translations in (73).

(73) ta ye   chang-ge.
     he also sing-song
     (i) 'He, too, sang.'
     (ii) '(Besides doing something else), he sang also.'

However, if a constituent in the same clause as *ye* bears a contrastive stress, then the domain of *ye* is automatically directed to it. Since in the case of the *lian* construction, the *lian* constitiuent always bears a contrastive stress, the scope of *ye*, like that of *dou*, will always correctly be assigned to it. This is a very important reason why *dou* 'all' and *ye* 'also' are chosen for this construction. Another important reason has to do with their meanings, i.e. roughly 'all' and 'also' respectively. Notice that previously in our analysis of the meaning of (70), we stated that part of the meaning of (70) is that there is a group of people whom Zhang San doesn't know and this group includes Li Si. Now one way to indicate this group is to say that there are other people besides Li Si that Zhang San doesn't know. Another way is to say, more explicitly, that there is a group, all the members of which Zhang San doesn't know and this group includes Li Si. In the first way, *ye* 'also' is used and in the second, the most natural choice in Chinese is *dou* 'all', being the most prevalent universal quantifier in the language.

With this explanation in mind, we can now turn to a related question that we raised earlier: Why in a negative *lian* sentence, an indefinite *lian* constituent like *yi-ge zi* 'one character' in (67c) can only have the negative universal interpretation, i.e. NOT (ANY)=NO?

The answer is quite straightforward. Previously, we said that *lian* X *dou/ye* construction expresses the idea that we are dealing with a set in which X is, for some reason, the least expected member. So in order to be able to identify the set, we need to first establish the reference of X. Since the X in (67c), i.e. *yi-ge zi* 'one character' is in one interpretation non-generic, non-specific, it does not meet the requirement. (67c) with this interpretation of *yi-ge zi* 'one character', therefore, does not make any sense. On the other hand, in the interpretation as indicated in (ii), it is permissible, because it has a negated generic reading. The actual operation can be systematically represented as:

NOT (EVEN ONE (y)) = ALL (NOT (y))

1.5. The *Lian* Topic and Stress

Returning now to the first question, i.e., since topic is normally unstressed, why should the *lian* topic always bear a stress? To answer this question, we have to first correct a commonly held wrong assumption—topic is always unstressed. Tsao (1979:225-227) points out one of the discourse functions that topic can serve is to place two or more things in the topic slots for contrast as in (74). In our previous discussion of secondary topics we have at various places pointed out that they also have this function. Take object fronting construction for instance. The fronted object is often contrasted with a similar constituent in the following clause, as shown in (75). Topics in this function are always stressed.

(74) <u>didi</u>   hen   xiaoqi, <u>gege</u>   que
     younger brother very stingy   older brother on:the:contrary
     hen dafang.
     very generous
     'While the younger brother is quite stingy, his older brother is very generous.'

(75) wo$_i$ <u>fan</u> bu chi le; ____$_i$ <u>jiu</u> zai he   yixie.
    I   rice not eat PART   wine more drink some
    'As for me, rice, I will have no more; wine, (I) will drink some more.'

The *lian* constituent, being a topic, can, of course, be explicitly contrasted as in (76).

(76) a. budan   <u>bieren-de   hua</u>   ta ting bu
       not-only other-people's speech he listen not
       dong,   <u>lian   wo-de hua</u>   ta dou
       understand including my speech he all
       ting   bu dong.
       listen not understand
       'Not only can he not understand other people's speech,
       he cannot understand even my speech.'
    b. ta$_i$ <u>lian   wo-de hua</u>   dou ting   bu dong, ____$_i$
       he including my speech all listen not understand
       <u>bieren-de   hua</u>   gengjia ting   bu   dong.
       other-people's speech even-more listen not   understand
       'He doesn't even understand my speech; other people's speech will
       be even more difficult for him to understand.'

More importantly, the *lian* NP, as we have pointed out, refers to the least expected member of a certain set; it, therefore, always carries a contrast and a surprised overtone. For this reason, the *lian* NP always bears a stress. The stress should, therefore, not prevent us from considering it as a special topic.

1.6. Summary

We have in the previous sections examined the past treatments of the construction including that of Tsao's (1979). We have found that even though many of them have made significant contributions to our understanding of the construction, none of them have offered a satisfactory generalization as to what can be the *lian* constituent. A few researchers including Tsao (1979) were misled, by the fact that the *lian* constituent always carries a contrastive stress, into analyzing it as a focus construction. In the course of our discussion, we have presented new evidence to show that the *lian* constituent is always a topic, primary or non-primary, and the stress that is associated with it is due to the implicit or explicit contrast associated with the *lian* constituent.

We have also pointed out that semantically the *lian* constituent in conjunction with the following *dou* or *ye* is to identify the ad hoc class of things in which the entity designated by the *lian* constituent is the least expected member. Furthermore, we attempted to explain, semantically and syntactically, why *ye* 'also' and *dou* 'all', of all adverbs, are selected, so to speak, to be in construction with *lian* 'including'.

2. The Comparative Constructions
2.1. Introduction

Tai (1969) observes that coordinate conjunction reduction in Chinese is possible in the subject position but not possible in the object position as exemplified by (77) and (78) below respectively.

(77) a. <u>ta</u> ti-le   qiu, <u>ta</u> ye da-le   ren.
        he kick-ASP ball he also hit-ASP man
        'He kicked the ball and he hit the man.'
     b. ta ti-le   qiu, _____ ye da-le   ren.
        he kick-ASP ball   also hit-ASP man
        'He kicked the ball and hit the man.'

(78) a. wo mai-le <u>li</u>, ni chi-le <u>li</u>.
        I buy-ASP pear you eat-ASP pear
        'I bought the pear and you ate the pear.'
     b.*wo mai-le, ni chi-le, li.
        I buy-ASP you eat-ASP pear
        'I bought and you ate, the pear.'

Earlier, we have further observed that the ungrammatical (78b) can be made grammatical if the shared object NP is topicalized as in (78c).

(78) c. li,   wo mai—le,   ni chi—le.
       pear I buy—ASP you eat—ASP
       'The pear (topic), I bought (and) you ate.'

Generalizing these two observations, Tsao (1979) concludes that coordinate conjunction reduction is allowed in Chinese only in the topic position (notice that in this case subject is in Tsao's framework also topic).

In a more general way it will be argued in this section that the compared constituents in a comparative construction in Chinese are topics of some kind. But to see this, it is necessary to examine Li and Thompson's (1981) analysis, for they claim that the first of the two compared constituents is restricted only to the topic/subject of the sentence. This claim of theirs, as will be shown presently, is on the right track but is not general enough. The primary purpose of the present section is to show that by incorporating some recent findings in the study of non—primary topics in Chinese (see Chapters 4 and 5; Chu, 1979) it is now possible to make a correct generalization that the compared constituents in a comparative construction must not only be topics, primary or non—primary, but also topics of an equal rank, i.e., both must be primary, secondary, or tertiary etc. This generalization will also enable us to propose a universally valid parameter in accounting for syntactic differences in comparison between languages like Chinese, Japanese, and Korean on the one hand and languages like English on the other.

2.2. Li and Thompson's Analysis

Li and Thompson (1981) contains a very succint account of the comparative constructions in Chinese. They started out by giving a schema of the comparative structure as in (79):

(79)   X Comparison word Y (Adverbial) Dimension

The dimension along which X and Y are being compared can be: (a) superiority, i.e. X is more than Y; (b) inferiority, i.e. X is less than Y; or, (c) equality, i.e., X is the same as Y. The comparative morphemes are in each case, (a) superiority: *bi* (literally 'compare with') as in (80); (b) inferiority: *mei (you)* 'not'...*(neme)*; *buru* (literally 'not as')...*(neme)*, as in (81) and, (c) equality: *gen....yiyang* (literally 'the same as'), as in (82).

(80) ta bi   ni gao.
    he Compare you tall
    'He is taller than you.'

(81) ta {mei(you) / buru} ni (neme) gao.
    he {not / not:as} you that tall
    'He is not as tall as you.'

(82) ta gen ni yiyang gao.
    he with you same tall
    'He is as tall as you (are).'

Since superiority comparison is by far the most common and since what is structurally true of the *bi* comparison is in general also true of the other two types of comparison (Li and Thompson, 1981; Li 1973; Fu, 1977), we will concentrate on the *bi* comparison in the following discussion.

After giving the general schema, Li and Thompson pointed out that "the verb phrase that signals the dimension along which the two items are being compared must be capable of being quantified or measured" (p.568). In syntactic terms this means that exactly those verbs that can occur with *hen* 'very' can occur in verb phrases expressing dimension in a comparative structure. These include (1) non-activity verbs, of which there are two types: (a) transitive—for instance, *xihuan* 'like', *ai* 'love', *hen* 'hate', and (b) intransitive—such as *hao* 'good' and *shufu* 'comfortable'; (2) verb phrases containing measurable adverbs, such as *zao* 'early', *wan* 'late', *chang* 'often'. This characterization is factually correct but terminology-wise inconsistent. One wonders whether it is the verb or the adverb that really matters. This terminological confusion can be avoided if the whole 'verb phrase', or in functional terms, the complete 'comment clause' is taken to be the unit involoved.[15]

---

[15] As Chu (1983: 235) correctly remarks, sometimes the dimension of comparison is expressed by a comment clause like *liqi da* 'strength big' as in (i) and (ii) below.

(i) gege   gen   wo yiyang liqi   da.
     elder brother with   I   same   strength big
     'My elder brother is as physically strong as I am.'

(ii) gege   meiyou   wo neme   liqi   da.
     elder brother not   I   that   strength big
     'My elder brother is not as physically strong as I am.'

Please also refer to our later discussion of compared constituents deletion in 2.4.1.

Their characterization of X and Y in (79), however, is far more inadequate. Their generalization about X and Y is that "X must be the subject or the topic of the verb phrase that expresses the dimension, and Y must be understood as the standard of comparison" (p.569). There are three important inadequacies with regard to this generalization. First, while it is true that objects in general seem difficult to be X and Y in the schema, as attested by sentences in (83) cited from them, there are cases where it is possible for objects to be compared constituents as shown by the grammaticality of (84).

(83) a.*wo xihuan gou bi mao.
      I like dog COMP cat
      'I like dogs more than (I do) cats.'
    b.*wo gou bi mao xihuan.
      I dog COMP cat like
      'Same as (a).'

(84) ta lanqiu bi paiqiu da—de hao.
     he basketball COMP volleyball play—PART good
     'He plays basketball better than (he does) volleyball.'

Second, they claim, as an implication of the generalization just cited, that coverb phrases cannot be compared. But this is far too restrictive, as attested by the following counterexamples.

(85) ta dui ni bi dui wo hao.
     he to you COMP to me nice
     'He is nicer to you than (he is) to me.'

(86) yong shou bi yong kuaizi chifan fangbian.
     with hand COMP with chopsticks eat convenient
     'It is more convenient to eat with hands than (it is) with chopsticks.'

Third, their explanation why sentences like (87) are grammatical in Chinese is not convincing at all.

>   (87) a. ta bi   zuotian   shufu.
>   he COMP yesterday feel—good
>   'He feels better than he did yesterday.'

Their exact explanation goes like this (p.571):

> In this sentence where X is *wo* 'I' and Y is *zuotian* 'yesterday', although *wo* 'I' is the subject of the verb *shufu* 'feel—good', we are, of course, not directly comparing *wo* 'I' and *zuotian* 'yesterday'. Rather, what we understand from this sentence is that 'I today' am feeling better than 'I yesterday'. That is, speaking of Mandarin must sometimes infer what makes sense from a comparative sentence in which X and Y are not directly comparable.

That this explanation is highly unsatisfactory can be clearly shown when we compare (87a) with (87b), where both X and Y are spelt out.

>   (87) b. ta jintian bi   zuotian   shufu.
>   he to—day COMP yesterday feel—good
>   'Same as (a).'

From the previous explanation, one would take (87a) and (87b) to be synonymous and in some sense (87a) can be said to be derived from (87b) through some kind of deletion process. However, (87b) does not seem to be compatible with Li and Thompson's generalization about X and Y i.e., X must be subject or topic. From my understanding of their grammar, *jintian* 'today', occurring after subject/topic, which is in this case *ta* 'he', is itself neither a subject nor a topic. This, then is another genuine counterexample to their generalization. Furthermore, as we will show later on, their reference to the pragmatic principle of making inference is completely unnecessary and can be replaced by two principles of compared constituent deletion.

2.3. The Proposal

To recapitulate, we have found Li and Thompson's analysis to be factually correct in its characterization of the comparative dimension but is far too restrictive in its characterization of the compared constituents X and Y.

In what follows, we would like to give our proposal, which can not only take care of all the inadequacies of Li and Thompson's analysis, but can also capture many significant generalizations about the comparative structures in Chinese, which researchers have hitherto been unable to make.

Our proposal is simply that the compared constituents, X and Y in schema (79), must be topics of an equal rank, i.e., they must both be primary topics, secondary topics, or tertiary topics etc., and the dimension of comparison must be expressed by a comment clause containing a verb or an adverb capable of being modified by *hen* 'very'. What is meant by topics of different ranks should be very clear by now and no further illustration is necessary.

2.3.1. Topic Qualities of The Compared Constituents

Before we examine the topic qualities that the compared constituents have, we have to make two points clear. First, as far as all the qualities listed in (61) are concerned, they fall roughly into two categories: discoursal and inherent qualities. Disregarding (61f), which space consideration prevents us from putting the processes to test, (61a, b, d, and e) are discoursal qualities in that each has to do with the relationship of one constituent with another, while (61c) stands alone in that it denotes a quality inherent in the constituent itself.

Second, as a general rule in Chinese when two topics A and B are placed parallelly at the beginning of a clause, then, as far as the discoursal qualities are concerned, either A alone is taken as a topic or else (A and B) together as a unit is regarded as a topic, as (88a and b) below show. B alone is never taken to be a topic, as evidenced by the ungrammaticality of (88c and d).

(88) a. $\underline{\text{Zhang San}_i \text{ gen Li Si}_j}$ yiqi   kan dianying
Zhang San with Li Si together see movie
ranhou ___$_{i,j}$ chi xiaoye.
then   eat mid—night—snack
'Zhang San and Li Si went to a movie together and then he
(or they) had mid—night snack.'
b. $\underline{\text{Zhang San}_i}$ gen   Li Si yiqi   kan dianying
Zhang San with Li Si together see movie

ranhou ta-ziji$_i$ chi xiaoye.

then he-self eat mid-night-snack

'Zhang San and Li Si went to a movie together and then he himself had mid-night snack.'

c.*Zhang San gen <u>Li Si</u>$_k$ yiqi   kan dianying

Zhang San with Li Si together see movie

ranhou _____$_k$ chi xiaoye.

then   eat mid-night-snack

*'Zhang San and Li Si went to a movie and then he (Li Si) had mid-night snack.'

d.*Zhang San gen <u>Li Si</u>$_k$ yiqi   kan dianying

Zhang San with Li Si together see movie

ranhou ta-ziji$_k$ chi xiaoye.

then   he-self eat mid-night-snack.

*'Zhang San and Li Si went to a movie and then he (Li Si) himself had mid-night snack.'

On the basis of these two observations, we would then predict that the two compared constituents X and Y, if they are indeed topics, then either X alone or X and Y together as a unit will have all the discoursal qualities listed in (61) while X and Y should each have the inherent quality indicated in (61c). This prediction is borne out by the following examples.

(89) a. <u>Zhang San$_i$ bi   Li Si$_j$</u> congming, _____$_{i,j}$

Zhang San COMP Li Si clever

ken   xia   gongfu.

willing spend time

'Zhang San is more clever than Li Si and (he) is willing to spend time (doing it)' (i)

'Zhang San is more clever and more willing to spend time (doing it) than Li Si.'(j)

b.*Zhang San bi <u>Li Si</u>$_k$ congming, ___$_k$
   Zhang San COMP Li Si clever
   ken   xia gongfu.
   willing spend time
   *'Zhang San is more clever than Li Si and (he) is willing to spend time (doing it).'(k)

(90) a. <u>Zhang San</u>$_i$ bi Li Si congming, <u>ta</u>$_i$ shi ge
     Zhang San COMP Li Si clever   he is CL
     hao renxuan.
     good candidate
     'Zhang San is more clever than Li Si and he is a good candidate.'
   b.*Zhang San bi <u>Li Si</u>$_j$ congming, <u>ta</u>$_j$ shi ge
     Zhang San COMP Li Si clever   he is CL
     hao renxuan.
     good candidate
     *'Zhang San is more clever than Li Si and he is a good candidate.' (j)

(91) a. <u>Zhang San</u>$_i$ $\begin{Bmatrix} a \\ me \\ ne \\ ba \end{Bmatrix}$ bi Li Si congming, ___$_i$
     Zhang San PART COMP Li Si clever
     ken   xia gongfu.
     willing spend time
     'Zhang San is more clever than Li Si and (he) is willing to spend time (doing it).'
   b. <u>Zhang San bi Li Si</u>$_j$ $\begin{Bmatrix} a \\ me \\ ne \\ ba \end{Bmatrix}$ congming, ___$_j$
     Zhang San COMP Li Si PART clever
     ken   xia gongfu.
     willing spend time

'Zhang San is more clever and more willing to spend time (doing it) than Li Si.'

(92) a. Zhang San$_i$ a   bi   Li Si congming, ta$_i$ shi

   Zhang San PART COMP Li Si clever   he is

   ge hao renxuan.

   CL good candidate

   'Zhang San is more clever than Li Si and he is a good candidate.'

   b.?Zhang San$_i$ bi   Li Si a   congming, ta$_i$ shi

   Zhang San COMP Li Si PART clever   he is

   ge hao renxuan.

   CL good candidate

   'Zhang San is more clever than Li Si and he is a good candidate.'

   c.*Zhang San bi Li Si$_j$ a   congming, ta$_j$ shi

   Zhang San COMP Li Si   PART clever   he is

   ge hao   renxuan.

   CL good candidate

   *'Zhang San is more clever than Li Si and he (Li Si) is a good candidate.'

From (89a) and (90a), we know that either the NP *Zhang San* alone or the larger NP comprising *Zhang San* and *Li Si* possesses all the qualities denoted by (61a), (61d) and (61e), i.e., either NP occupies the inital position of the first clause in a topic chain, is supraclausal and is in control of pronominalization or deletion of all the coreferential NPs in the topic chain. The NP *Li Si*, however, does not have any of these qualities, as attested by the ungrammaticality of (89b) and (90b).

The fact that both (91a) and (91b) are grammatical further indicates that either the NP *Zhang San* or the larger NP consisting of *Zhang San* and *Li Si* has the topic quality of being separable from the rest of the sentence by one of the four pause particles, *a (ya), me, ne,* and *ba.* Now let's compare (92a) with (92b). The fact that (92a) is grammatical while (92b) is not indicates that the pause particle should be placed immediately after the topic NP. This principle in conjunction with the fact that (92c) is ungrammatical indicates unambiguously that the NP Li Si does not possess this topic quality.

It remains now for us to prove that the compared constituents i.e. X and Y in (79), both have the referential quality of being definite or generic. To see this, examine the following sentences.

(93) na–zhang zhuozi bi zhe–ba yizi gao.
     that–CL table COMP this–CL chair tall
     'That table is taller than this chair.'

(94) zhuozi bi yizi gao.
     table COMP chair tall
     'Tables are taller than chairs.'

(95) a.*zhuozi bi na–ba yizi gao.
        table COMP that–CL chair tall
        *'Tables are taller than that chair.'[16]
     b.*nei–zhang zhuozi bi yizi gao.
        that–CL table COMP chair tall
        *'That table is taller than chairs.'
     c.*yi–zhang zhuozi bi na–ba yizi gao.
        one–CL table COMP that–CL chair tall
        *'A table is taller than that chair.'
     d.*nei–zhang zhuozi bi yi–ba yizi gao.
        that–CL table COMP a–CL chair tall
        *'That table is taller than a chair.'

As (93) and (94) show, when both X and Y are definite or generic, a comparative sentence is grammatical. All other combinations, as shown in (a) through (d) in (95), result in an ungrammatical sentence.

It is then safe to conclude that not only must both X and Y be definite or generic, they must possess the same referential quality, i.e., if one of them is definite, the other

---

[16]It is interesting to note that while (95a) is ungramatical, (i) below is gramatical.
(i) renhe zhuozi dou bi na–ba yizi gao.
    any table all COMP that–CL chair tall
    'Any talbe is taller than that chair.'
This fact seems to indicate that within the category of "generic" a further distinction between "general" as represented by (95a) and "random", as represented by (i) is necessary.

must be definite as well.

2.3.2. Parallelism Between the Compared Constituent and the Primary Topic

It seems clear that whatever can be a primary topic can also be a compared constituent. Recall that this is Li and Thompson's characterization of X in schema (79). So, a few illustrative examples will suffice.

(96) a. <u>ta</u> nenggan.
      he competent
      'He is competent.'
   b. <u>ta</u> bi <u>wo</u> nenggan.
      he COMP I competent
      'He is more competent than I am.'

(97) a. <u>ta</u> jixing hao.
      he memory good
      'He, (his) memory is good.'
   b. <u>ta</u> bi <u>wo</u> jixing hao.
      he COMP I memory good.
      'As for him and me, (his) memory is better than mine.'

(98) a. <u>ta xie de   shu</u> hen duo.
      he write Rel.Mar. book very many
      'The books that he has written are many.' i.e.,
      'He has written many books.'
   b. <u>ta xie de   shu</u> bi <u>wo kan de</u>
      he write Rel. Mar. book COMP I read Rel. Mar.
      shu duo.
      book many
      'The books that he has written are more than the books that I have read.' i.e., 'He has written more books than I have read.'

(99) a. <u>wu-li</u>   re.
      house-inside hot
      'It is hot in the house.'

b. <u>wu-li</u>   bi <u>wu-wai</u>   re.
      house-inside COMP house-outside hot
      'It is hotter in the house than (it is) outside.'

(100) a. <u>zai jia chi</u> pianyi.
         at home eat inexpensive
         'It is inexpensive to eat at home.'
      b. <u>zai jia chi</u> bi <u>zai fanguan chi</u> pianyi.
         at home eat COMP at restaurant eat inexpensive
         'It is more inexpensive to eat at home than to eat in a restaurant.'

(101) a. <u>ta lai Taibei</u> fangpian.
         he come Taipei convenient
         'It is convenient for him to come to Taipei.'
      b. <u>ta lai Taibei</u> bi <u>wo qu Xianggang</u> fangpian.
         he come Taipei COMP I go Hong Kong convenient
         'It is more convenient for him to come to Taipei than (it is) for me to go to Hong Kong.'

Thus, a simple NP (96), a simple NP serving as the first nominal in a double nominative construction (97), a complex NP containing a relative clause (98), a locative NP (99), a nominalized VP (100), or a nominal clause (101) can all be a primary topic and at the same time be a compared constituent. The parallelism is simply too striking to be missed.

2.3.3 Parallelism Between the Compared Constituent and the Secondary Topic

In a similar vein, what we have established as secondary topics can all become compared constituents. Witness the following parallelism.

(102) a. ta <u>yanjing</u> zhang de piaoliang.
         he eye   grow PART beautiful
         'He (topic), (his) eyes are beautiful.'

b. <u>ta</u> <u>yanjing</u> bi <u>bizi</u> zhang de   piaoliang.

   he eye   COMP nose grow PART beautiful
   'He (topic), (his) eyes are more beautiful than (his) nose.'

(103)a. <u>tamen dixong</u> <u>laosan</u>   hen nenggan.

   they brothers the-third very competent
   'Speaking of the brothers, the third is very able.'

b. <u>tamen dixong</u>   <u>laosan</u>   bi <u>laoda</u>   nenggan.

   they brothers the-third COMP the-eldest competent
   'Speaking of the brothers, the third is more able than the eldest.'

(104)a. <u>ta</u> <u>lanqiu</u>   da   de   hao.

   he basketball play PART well
   'He plays basketball well'

b. <u>ta</u> <u>lanqiu</u>   bi   <u>paiqiu</u>   da de hao.

   he basketball COMP volleyball play PART well
   'He plays basketball better than (he does) volleyball.'

(105)a. <u>ta</u> ba <u>qian</u> kan   de   zhong.

   he BA money regard PART important
   'He regards money as very important.'

b. <u>ta</u> ba <u>qian</u> bi (ba) <u>shengming</u> kan   de

   he BA money COMP (BA) life   regard PART
   zhong.
   important
   'He regards money as more important than (he does) life.'

(106)a. <u>ta</u> <u>shuo Yingyu</u> shuo de   hao.

   he speak English speak PART well
   'He speaks English well.'

    b. ta shuo Yingyu bi shuo Fayu shuo de

       he speak English COMP speak French speak PART
       hao.
       well
       'He speaks English better than (he does) French.'

(107) a. ta jintian hen shufu.

       he today   very feel-good
       'He feels better today than (he did) yesterday.'

    b. ta jintian bi zuotian shufu.

       he today COMP yesterday feel-good
       'He feels better today than (he did) yesterday.'

(108) a. ta dui ni hao.

       he to you nice
       'He is nice to you.'

    b. ta dui ni bi dui wo hao.

       he to you COMP to me nice
       'He is nicer to you than (he is) to me.'

Thus, except for the manner adverb and some multifunctional adverbs such as *ye, dou, you, hai,* any constituent that can occur in the slot inbetween the primary topic and the main verb, be it the seccond nominal in a double nominative construction (102, 103), fronted object NP (104), the *ba* NP in a *ba* construction (105), the fronted VO constituent in a so-called "verb-copying" construction (106), a temporal NP (107), or a coverb phrase (108), can be a secondary topic and at the same time be a compared constituent.

    In this connection, it is appropriate to comment on a commonly-held but erroneous assumption that direct objects cannot be compared in Chinese. It is correct that a direct object in its postverbal position cannot be a compared constituent. This phenomenon was first pointed out by Hashimoto (1971) and her celebrated example is the failure in Chinese to translate the following English sentence.

(109)   I love truth more than (I love) my teacher.

The Chinese translation of this famous quotation, according to Hashimoto, is clearly (112), as both (110) and (111) are ungrammatical.

(110) *wo ai   zhenli bi   wo-de laoshi.
      I love truth COMP I-POSS teacher

(111) *wo zhenli bi   wo-de laoshi ai.
      I truth COMP I-POSS teacher love

(112) wo ai wo-de laoshi, wo geng   ai   zhenli.
      I love I-POSS teacher I even-more love truth
      'I love my teacher but I love truth even more.'

We have already noticed that the compared constituents cannot occur post-verbally. So (110) is automatically ruled out. But (111) with the compared constituents fronted remains ungrammatical. The fact requires some explanation, to which we will return presently. As for (112), even though it is perfect Chinese, it is not, strictly speaking, a comparative construction. Furthermore, as reflected in the translation, an undesirable semantic addition is introduced in the Chinese version. In an effort to find a semantically faithful translation, Fu (1977), Li and Thompson (1981), and Chu (1983) have all hit upon (113), which employs the so-called "verb-copying" construction.

(113) <u>wo ai   zhenli</u> bi <u>ai   wo-de laoshi</u> ai   de
      I love truth   COMP love I-POSS teacher love PART
      duo.
      much
      'Same as (109).'

(113), as a matter of fact, cannot not be put in a *ba* construction.[17] In other cases where the *ba* construction is possible as in (105) previously cited then direct objects can be fronted to become compared constituents. Examples like (105) and (113) indicate

---

[17]Some linguists have claimed that the reason *ai* 'love' cannot be put in the *ba* construction is because it is not an action verb. However, as we will argue later on, the fact that it is monosyllabic is perhaps a more important reason.

unmistakably that as far as direct objects are concerned, if they can be fronted in a topicalization process, then they can also become compared constituents.

There are three pieces of supportive evidence in the form of constraints associated with these topicalization processes. First, in the case of topicalizing the VO constituent in the so-called "verb-copying" construction, a very important constraint as it is applied to the comparative structure is that the two verbs involoved should be identical, for otherwise there is no way of determining which verb should be "copied". On the basis of this constraint we would predict that comparing direct objects by means of VO topicalization is possible just in cases where the verbs involved are identical. Such a prediction is borne out by the following two examples.

(114) a. He speaks English better than (he does) French.
     b. ta <u>shuo</u> Yingyu bi ta <u>shuo</u> Fayu <u>shuo</u>
        he speak English COMP he speak French speak
        de hao.
        PART well
        'Same as (a).'

(115) a. He speaks English better than he writes French.
     b.*ta <u>shuo</u> Yingyu bi ta <u>xie</u> Fayu <u>shuo</u>
       he speak English COMP he write French speak
       de hao.
       PART well
     c.*ta <u>shuo</u> Yingyu bi ta <u>xie</u> Fayu <u>xie</u>
       he speak English COMP he write French write
       de hao.
       PART well

Another piece of confirming evidence comes from object-fronting topicalization. In both Chapter 1 and Chapter 5 we have observed that this process is subject to a surface structure constraint which states that this process is blocked just in cases where the output of the rule would create a situation where it is impossible to distinguish the roles played by the two preverbal NPs. Examine the following examples.

(116) a. wo xihuan Zhang San.
        I like Zhang San
        'I like Zhang San.'

b.*wo Zhang San xihuan.
   I Zhang San like
   (i) 'I like Zhang San.' or (ii)'Zhang San likes me.'

(117) a. wo xihuan mao.
         I like   cat
         'I like cats.'
      b.?wo mao xihuan.
         I cat like
         'I like cats.' or less likely, 'Cats like me.'

(118) a. wo xihuan daishu.
         I like   algebra
         'I like algebra.'
      b. wo daishu xihuan.
         I algebra like
         'I like algebra.'

(116b) is ungrammatical i.e., object fronting is blocked, because with two preverbal NPs both human, there is no way of knowing which is the actor and which is the patient as reflected in the two possible readings of the sentence.[18] (117b) is better than (116b) because with the two preverbal NPs one human and the other just animate, the probability of a confusion of the roles of the actor and the patient is far less. In other words, it is far less likely for cats to like me than for me to like cats, even though the possibility is there. (118b), as expected is grammatical because it is only possible for me to like algebra but not for algebra to like me.

On the basis of this constraint one would predict that comparison of the two objects by means of the object fronting topicalization process is possible only when they are both inanimate. Such a prediction is borne out by the following (c) sentences from (116) through (118).

---

[18]Actually the picture is even more complicated than described. Recall that in our previous discussion of the object fronting construction we also mentioned that there is a perceptual strategy to the effect that when there are two animate NPs to the left of the verb, the first NP to the left of the verb, as Zhang San in (116b), is to be taken as subject. In other words, in (116b) (ii) interpretation is far more likely than (i) even though (i) cannot be ruled out completely.

(116) c.*wo Zhang San bi   Li Si xihuan.
        I Zhang San COMP Li Si like
        'I like Zhang San more than (I do) Li Si.' or
        'Zhang San likes me more than Li Si does.'

(117) c.?wo mao bi   gou xihuan.[19]
        I cat COMP dog like
        'I like cats more than (I do) dogs.' or less likely,
        'Cats like me more than dogs do.'

(118) c. wo daishu bi   jihe   xihuan.
        I algebra COMP geometry like
        'I like algebra more than geometry.'

There is another constraint at work in this process. The same constraint has been found to be at work in the case of *ba* NP topicalization (see Wang, 1980; Chu, 1983; Tsao, 1987 and Chapter 5 among others). Simply stated, it says that the *ba* NP topicalization is blocked just in cases where the output of the rule would yield a monosyllabic VP at the end of a sentence. Compare (b) and (c) sentences in (119).

(119) a. wo hen   daishu.
        I hate algebra
        'I hate algebra.'
     b.*wo ba daishu hen.
        I BA algebra hate
        'Same as (a).'
     c. wo ba daishu hen—tou   le.
        I BA algebra hate—through PART
        'I hate algebra extremely.'

---

[19](117c) appeared earlier in our discussion of Li and Thompson's anlaysis as (83b), which they regard as ungrammatical. My own intuition, as shown in the marking of (117c), differs from theirs slightly. This slight difference in grammaticality judgment, however, does not in any way affect our argument here.

The same constraint is found in the case of direct object topicalization, as is evident by comparing (120) with (121).

(120) a. wo ai   daishu.
        I love algebra
        'I love algebra.'
     b.*<u>wo</u> <u>daishu</u>   ai.
        I algebra love
        'Same as (a).'

(121) a. wo xihuan daishu.
        I like   algebra
        'I like algebra.'
     b. <u>wo</u> <u>daishu</u>   xihuan.
        I algebra like
        'Same as (a).'

The same constraint, as expected, is at work in the case of topicalized direct objects serving as compared constituents. Compare (120c) with (121c).

(120) c.*<u>wo</u> <u>daishu</u>   bi   <u>jihe</u>   ai.
        I algebra COMP geometry love
        'I love algebra more than (I do) geometry.'

(121) c. <u>wo</u> <u>daishu</u>   bi   <u>jihe</u>   xihuan.
        I algebra COMP geometry like
        'I like algebra more than (I do) geometry.'

With these two constraints in mind, let us return to (111). It is clear that (111) is ungrammatical because it violates both of the constraints involved in object fronting topicalization in that one of the objects is human, being *wo-de laoshi* 'my teacher' and the verb phrase left at the end of the sentence after object fronting, namely, *ai* 'love', is monosyllabic.

We have thus demonstrated unmistakably that the constraints at work in the topicalization processes of the *ba* NP fronting, object NP fronting and VO constituent fronting are also at work when direct objects are fronted to become compared constituents. In so doing, we have also cleared away a popular myth that in Chinese direct objects cannot be compared.

To sum up our discussion in this section, we have shown that these topicalized direct object NPs that become the compared constituents are indeed what we call secondary topics. These together with other types of secondary topics such as locative, temporal and reason adverbials that occur in the position between the primary topic and the verb can all become the compared constituents. To put it another way, the compared constituents X and Y that occur after the primary topic are indeed secondary topics of one kind or another.

So far in order to simplify presentation, we have restricted ourselves in this section to the primary and secondary topics. It is perfectly possible, however, for a sentence to have a tertiary or even a quaternary topic. It is also possible, though not likely, for tertiary topics to become compared constituents. Witness the following sentence.

(122) tamen jia   san-ge haizi   doushi yanjing bi
 their family three-CL children all   eye   COMP
 bizi zhang de   piaoliang.
 nose grow PART beautiful
 'Speaking of the three children in their family, (their) eyes are all more beautiful than (their) noses.'

2.4. Principles of Compared Constituents Deletion
2.4.1. The Primary Principle

Like many languages in the world, Chinese allows many constituents in a comparative structure to be deleted. The most general principle is:

(123) Any compared topic, primary or non-primary, can be deleted if it is identical to another topic of an equal rank. Only forward deletion, however, is allowed.

For illustrative purpose, let us restrict ourselves to sentences with one to three topics.

2.4.1.1. Single—Topic Comparison

Since there is only one topic in the sentence, this must be the place where comparison occurs, and since two things being compared must be different, there is no room for deletion here, as (124) clearly shows.

(124) <u>ta</u> bi <u>wo</u> hui shuo—hua.
      he COMP I   can speak—speech
      'He can speak better than I.'

2.4.1.2. Double—Topic Comparison

Since there are two topics involved, and since both of them cannot be the same, only three possible situations can arise, each of which is represented by a sentence in the following.

(125) <u>ta Yingwen</u> bi <u>wo Fawen</u> hao de duo.

   he English COMP I French good PART much
   'Speaking of him and speaking of me, (his) English is much better than (my) French.'

(126) a. <u>ta</u>$_i$ <u>zui</u> bi ____$_i$ <u>yanjing</u> zhang de piaoliang.
         he mouth COMP   eye   grow PART beautiful
         'Speaking of him, (his) mouth is more beautiful than (his) eyes.'
     b.* ____$_i$ <u>zui</u> bi <u>ta</u>$_i$ <u>yanjing</u> zhang de piaoliang.
             mouth COMP he   eye   grow PART beautiful
         'Same as (a).'

(127) a. <u>ta jixing</u>$_j$ bi <u>wo</u> ____$_j$ hao de duo
         he memory COMP I   good PART much
         'Speaking of him and speaking of me, (his) memory is much better than mine.'

In (125) both the primary and the secondary topics are different. Since both of them are different, no identical topic deletion can take place. The principle has no effect here. In (126a), however, the primary topics are the same while the secondary topics differ. The principle applies to delete the second occurence of the primary topic, namely, ta_i 'he'.

Furthermore, since (126b) is ungrammatical, it is clear that backward deletion is not allowed. (127), on the other hand, represents a situation where the primary topics differ while the secondary topics are the same. The principle applies again to delete the second occurrence of the secondary topic, namely, *jixing* 'memory'. (127a), however, has a variation as shown in (128a), which requires some explanation, for some linguists (see, Fu, 1977) have, we believe, erroneously regard it as a case of forward deletion.

(128) a. <u>ta</u> bi <u>wo</u> jixing hao de duo.
        he COMP I memory good PART much
        'He is much better than I in memory.'

As shown in the analyses of both (127a) and (128a), we regard (127a) as a double–topic comparative sentence with a simple comment, namely *hao de duo* and (128a) as a single–topic comparative sentence with a complex comment in the form of *jixing hao de duo*.[20]

We have two pieces of supportive evidence. First, in (127a), it is possible to insert a pause particle immediately after *wo* 'I', as shown in (127b), indicating that *jixing* 'memory' is regarded as part of the topic complex while in (128a) it is not possible to place a pause particle immediately after *jixing* 'memory' as shown by the ungrammatical (128b), indicating that *jixing* is not regarded as part of the topic complex but rather as part of the comment clause.

(127) b. ta jixing bi wo a hao de duo.
        he memory COMP I PART good PART much
        'Same as (a).'

(128) b.*ta bi wo jixing a hao de duo.
        he COMP I memory PART good PART much
        'Same as (a).'

---

[20]Please refer to Note 15, where we pointed out the necessity of allowing for complex comment in Chinese.

Second, if we were to follow the suggestion made by some linguists by analyzing (128a) as a case of backward deletion, i.e., *jixing* 'memory' is a secondary topic in control of the deletion of the first occurrence of it, then we would run into an insurmountable difficulty of explaining why backward deletion is allowed in this case while it is disallowed in others such as (126b).

2.4.1.3. Triple—Topic Comparison

Comparative sentences involving three topics are, as we said earlier, not very common, but they are theoretically interesting in that the principle of deletion plays a far more important role in this situation. Depending on the number of compared constituents that are the same, i.e., from 0 to 2 in the case of triple—topic comparative sentences, we can predict precisely what number of possible structural variations there can be. The following is such an example.

(129) (With none of the three topics identical)
ta zuotian zai xuexiao bi   wo jintian zai jiali
he yesterday at   school COMP I   today   at home
gaoxing.[21]
happy
'He was happier at school yesterday than I am at home today.'

(130) (With one of the three topics identical)
a. ta_i zuotian   zai xuexiao bi ____$_i$ jintian
   he yesterday at school COMP   today
   zai jiali gaoxing.
   at home   happy
   'He was happier at school yesterday than (he) is at home today.'
b. ta $zuotian_j$ zai xuexiao bi wo ____$_j$ zai jiali
   he yesterday at school   COMP I   at home

---

[21]Hashimote (1971: 34) gives sentences like (129) as examples where "more than one pair of 'compared' constituents may occur within the same sentence".

>   gaoxing.
>   happy
>   'He was happier at school yesterday than I was at home.'
> c. ta zuotian <u>zai xuexiao</u>$_k$ bi wo jintian ____$_k$
>   he yesterday at   school   COMP I today
>   gaoxing.
>   happy
>   'He was happier at school yesterday than I am today.'

(131) (With two of the three topics identical)
> a. <u>ta</u>$_i$ <u>zuotian</u>$_j$ zai xuexiao bi ____$_i$ ____$_j$
>   he yesterday at   school COMP
>   zai jiali gaoxing.
>   at home happy
>   'He was happier at school yesterday than (he) was at home.'
> b. <u>ta</u>$_i$ zuotian <u>zai xuexiao</u>$_k$ bi ____$_i$ jintian
>   he   yesterday at   school   COMP   today
>   ____$_k$ gaoxing
>   happy
>   'He was happier at school yesterday than (he) is today.'
> c. ta <u>zuotian</u>$_j$ <u>zai xuexiao</u>$_k$ bi wo ____$_j$ ____$_k$
>   he yesterday at   school   COMP I
>   gaoxing.
>   happy
>   'He was happier at school yesterday than I was.'

Like the situation found in double-topic comparison, often there are options of placing certain elements in the topic or in the comment. Instead of (130c), for example, one can say (132).

(132) <u>ta</u> bi <u>wo</u> zuotian   zai xuexiao gaoxing.
      he COMP I yesterday at school   happy
      'Same as (130c).'

(132), however, as we have argued, should be treated as a single—topic comparison with a complex comment.

2.4.2. Deletion of Identical Elements in a Compared Constituent

In our previous discussion of the deletion of the identical compared constituents involving VO topicalization in the so—called "verb—copying" construction, we deliberately left out some variations to simplify presentation. The full range of variations can now be shown in the following.

(133) a. ta zhaoxiang   zhao de bi   wo   zhaoxiang
       he take—picture take PART COMP I   take—picture
       zhao de   hao.
       take PART good
       'He is better than I in taking pictures.'
   b. ta zhao—xiang   zhao de   bi   wo hao.
       he take—picture take PART COMP I   good
       'Same as (a).'
   c. <u>ta</u> <u>zhao—xiang</u>   bi <u>wo</u> <u>zhao—xiang</u>   zhao de   hao.
       he take—picture COMP I   take—picture take PART good
       'Same as (a).'
   d. <u>ta</u> <u>zhaoxiang</u>$_j$ bi <u>wo</u> _____$_j$ zhao de   hao.
       he take—picture COMP I   take PART good
       'Same as (a).'
   e. <u>ta</u> bi <u>wo</u> zhaoxiang   zhao de   hao.
       he COMP I   take—picture take PART good
       'Same as (a).'

So far we have said some thing about (133c), (133d) and (133e), but we have not dealt with (133b) yet. The problem here is whether we should, on analogy with (131c), a triple—topic comparative sentence, regard *zhao de* in (133a) and (133b) as a tertiary topic or not.

Recall that in our previous discussion of the VO fronting construction, we have presented evidence to show that in a sentence like (133 a and b), *zhao de* do not form a topic. We have also argued that *de* is a nominalizer which turns the whole structure before it into an NP and that this NP is a topic containing two topics within it, which can be raised if necessary. Given this analysis, all we need to do to take care of (131b) is to posit a second principle of deletion to be called "Identical Elements in a Compared Constituent Deletion", which can be simply stated as (134).

(134) Any element within a compared constituent can be deleted if it is identical with an element in a previous compared constituent.

There is independent evidence that such a principle is needed. Compare (a) and (b) sentences in (135) and (136).

(135) a. <u>ta qi   jiaotache shang xuexiao</u> bi   <u>wo qi</u>
       he ride bicycle   go   school COMP I ride
       <u>jiaotache shang xuexiao</u> fangbian.
       bicycle   go   school   convenient
       'It is more convenient for him to go to school by bicycle than it is for me.'

   b. <u>ta qi   jiaotache shang xuexiao</u> bi   <u>wo   </u>
       he ride bicycle   go   school COMP I
       fangbian.
       convenient
       'Same as (a).'

(136) a. <u>zhe-ge fangjian-de hua</u>   bi   <u>nei-ge</u>
       this-CL room-POSS   picture COMP that-CL
       <u>fangjian-de hua</u>   haokan.
       room-POSS   picture beautiful
       'The pictures in this room are more beautiful than the pictures in that room.'

   b. <u>zhe-ge fangjian-de   hua</u>   bi   <u>nei-ge fangjian-de   </u>
       this-CL room-POSS   picture COMP that-CL room-POSS
       haokan.
       beautiful
       'The pictures in this room are more beautiful than (those) in that room.'

Thus, the elements that are shared by the two nominalized clauses in (135a), namely, *qi jiaotache shang xuexiao* 'go to school by bicycle' are no longer repeated in (135b). Likewise, in (136a) the shared element in the two compared topics is the possessed NP *hua* 'pictures' and it is, therefore, deleted in (136b).

Returning now to (133a), we find that the sentence, from which all other sentences are derived, is itself subject to two analyses. In one analysis, *ta zhao-xiang zhao de* and *wo zhao-xing zhao de* are both topics and therefore can be compard as in (133a). Given this analysis, (133b) can be generated by applying the rule of Identical Elements in a Compared Constituent Deletion. In the second analysis, (133a) contains one or two raised topics. If only one topic is raised, than (133e) is derived. If two topics are both raised, then (133c) can be generated. If the rule of Identical Compared Constituents Deletion applies, than (133d) is derived.

2.4.3. Two Minor Deletion Principles

In order to account for all the deletion phenomena in the comparative constructions, two more minor deletion principles are required. one of them would be called "Present—time Deletion" while the other would be termed "The Second Compared Constituent Genitive Deletion".

2.4.3.1. Present—time Deletion Principle

Simply put, this principle states that topical constituents referring to the present time can be deleted. Examine the following sentences.

(137) ta_j ___$_i$ bi ___$_j$ gangcai lianse
      he   COMP   a-while-ago face-color
      hao duo le
      good much PART
      'He looks much better than (he did) a while ago.'

(138) wo_j ___$_i$ bi ___$_j$ zuotian shufu.
      I   COMP   yesterday feel-good
      'I feel better today than (I did) yesterday.'

(139) ta$_j$ ___$_i$ bi ___$_j$ qunian shenti hao
     he   COMP   last-year health good
     duo le.
     much PART
     'His health is much better this year than (it was) last year.'

Thus in (137) through (139), the deleted NP_j in each case is understood to be the primary topic according to the primary principle of compared constituents deletion that we just discussed, but the deleted NP_i is in each case understood to be a time constituent related to the present, i.e., *xianzai* 'now' in (137), *jintian* 'today' in (138) and *jinnian* 'this year' in (139).

There is an independent constraint which interacts with this deletion principle, however. The constraint states that only the NP referring to the present time that occurs to the left of *bi* can be deleted. That this is indeed true can be seen by comparing (137) with (140b).

(140) a. ta <u>gangcai</u> bi <u>xianzai</u> lianse hao
        he a-while-ago COMP now   face-color good
        duo le.
        much PART
        'He looked much better a while ago than (he) does now.'
    b.*ta gangcai bi _____ lianse hao
        he a-while-ago COMP   face-color good
        duo le.
        much PART
        'Same as (a).'

2.4.3.2. The Second Compared Constituent Genitive Deletion Principle

Genitive marker deletion works quite extensively in Chinese. However, up to now it has not been systematically studied. For this reason, it is not easy to characterize it precisely at this point. As far as we can determine, there seem to be three principles involved. Even though we will try to charactize all three of them, only one of them applies within the domain of the compared constituents and for this reason it will be referred to as "The Second Compared Constituent Genitive Deletion principle".

The first and perhaps the most general principle of the genitive marker deletion is this: The genitive marker *-de* can be freely deleted if the possessor NP bears one of the following two relationships to the possessed NP: (i) the possessed NP denotes a certain kinship relation between the two; (ii) the possessor NP denotes a group of which the possessed NP is a member. This principle works across the board, i.e., it is not restricted to any position in a sentence. However, the deletion seems to be obligatory in the topic position while optional in others. Compare (141b) with (142b).

(141) a. women _____-POSS jia   you   wu-ge ren.
         we   family EXIST five-CL people
         'There are five people in our family.'
     b.?women-de jia   you   wu-ge   ren.
        we-POSS family EXIST five-CL people
        'Same as (a).'

(142) a. ta dao women _____-POSS xuexiao lai kan wo.
         he came we   school to see me.
         'He came to our school to see me.'
     b. ta dao   women-de xuexiao lai kan wo.
        he come we-POSS school to see me
        'Same as (a).'

The second principle states that any NP with an internal possessive relationship can have the possessor NP separated and promoted to become an independent topic NP, a process which Tang (1972), following Fillmore (1968), calls "adnominal NP promotion".

(143) a. ta-de   toufa hen chang, hen piaoliang.
         she-POSS hair very long   very beautiful
         'Her hair is very long and beautiful.'
     b. ta   _____-POSS toufa hen chang, hen   piaoliang.
        she   hair very long   very beautiful
        'She (topic), (her) hair is very long, (and) (she) is very beautiful.'

Thus the genitive marker *−de* can be deleted only when the possessor NP becomes an independent topic as in (143b), where the topic chain is about *ta* 'she', rather than about *ta−de toufa* 'her hair' as it is the case in (143a).

As we said earlier, only the third principle bears directly upon the genitive marker deletion within the compared constituents. This principle can be characterized as: when a possessive NP occurs as the second of a paired compared constituents and the possessed NP is identical with that of the first compared constituent, then the possessive marker can be optionally deleted after the possessed NP is deleted by the rule of Identical Elements in a Compared Constituent Deletion. Compare (a) and (b) sentences in the following.

(144) a. ta−de   toufa bi   wo−de   chang.
        he−POSS hair COMP I−POSS long
        'Her hair is longer than mine.'

   b. ta−de   toufa bi   wo− _____POSS chang.
        he−POSS hair COMP I   long
        'Same as (a).'

As can be expected, Principle 2 and Principle 3 of the genitive marker deletion interact in comparative constructions in an interesting way. Compare (145a) with (145b).

(145) a. ta <u>shenti</u>$_i$ bi wo ____$_i$ hao, you ken
        he body   COMP I   good also willing
        yongkong,   jianglai   yiding   hen you
        work−hard   in−the−future certainly very have
        chengjiu.
        achievement
        'He (topic), his health is better than mine; (he) is willing to work hard ; (he) will certainly achieve a great deal in the future.'

   b. ta−de   shenti bi wo− _____POSS hao, ganmao−le,
        he−POSS body   COMP I   good catch−cold−ASP
        xiuxi liang tian jiu hao le.
        rest two   days then well PART

'His health is better than mine; when (he) catches cold, (he)only has to take a rest for two days and (he) is well again.'

In (145a), where the primary topic is clearly *ta* 'he', the gentive marker *-de* is deleted as result of "adnominal NP promotion", and the second occurrence of *shenti* 'boby' in the same clause is deleted by the primary principle of Identical Compared Topic Deletion. In (145b), on the other hand, the whole NP consisting of the possessor NP and the possessed NP, i.e. *ta-de shenti* 'his body', is the primary topic, and the genitive marker associated with *wo* 'I' is deleted by The Second Compared Constituent Genitive Deletion principle that we have just discussed.

With these principles of deletion, we can now give a very explicit account for cases which Li and Thompson (1981:571), as cited earlier, claim to be only capable of being explained in terms of pragmatic inference.

(146) wo$_i$ ____$_p$ bi ____$_i$ zuotian shufu.
     I   COMP   yesterday feel—good
    'I feel better (today) than I did yesterday.'

(147) women—de xin gen Nainai— ____POSS yiyang.
    we—POSS heart with Grandma's   same
    'Our heart is the same as Grandma's.'

It should be perfectly clear by now that ____$_p$ in (146) is deleted through the principle of Present—time Compared Constituent Deletion while the second occurrence of *wo* 'I' is deldeted through the primary principle of Idenitical Compared Constituents Deletion. In (147), on the other hand, the genitive marker *-de* is deleted by the principle of The Second Compared Constituent Genitive Deletion.

2.5. Summary and Implications
2.5.1. Summary of Major Findings

To sum up, we have found Li and Thompson's (1981) characterization that the first of paired compared constituents must be topic/ subject to be far too restrictive and presented evidence to argue that both compared constituents in a pair must be topics, primary or non—primary, of an equal rank, and there could be as many pairs as there are topics in a sentence.

These important findings also lead us to the discovery of four principles of deletion, namely, Identical Compared Constituents Deletion, Present-time Deletion, The Second Compared Constituent Genitive Deletion and finally, Identical Elements in a Compared Constituent Deletion, which jointly account for the elliptical phenomena in the comparative structure without recourse to pragmatic inference as is required in Li and Thompson's analysis.

2.5.2. Theoretical Implications
2.5.2.1. Are There Sentential Sources Underlying Comparison?

Whatever your theoretical orientation, it is generally agreed that there are two sentences underlying a comparative sentence in English.[22] This view is, we think, completely justified because even in the surface structure, it is always possible to give two finite clauses, with one located on each side of *than*. This shows the wisdom of traditional grammarians in treating *than* as a conjunction.[23] Chinese, on the other hand, has no comparative conjunction equivalent to *than* in English. Chinese *bi* is evidently a "coverb", and so it is much more difficult to argue for the position that in Chinese, as it is in English, there are two sentences underlying a comparative sentence.

We will not give a full review here of the arguments for or against deriving a comparative sentence from an underlying structure containing two sentences in Chinese, partly because doing so will take us too far afield and partly because some of the arguments are so closely tied to their respective underlying grammatical theories that makes it very difficult to give an objective evaluation.[24] Suffice it to say that most researchers think it desirable to have an underlying structure containing two sentences (Fu, 1977; Hashimoto, 1966, 1971; Cheng, 1966). Our own analysis is compatible with such a proposal if we assume that except for cases of conjoined topics, each sentence has only one topic for each rank.

---

[22] For a pretty thorough review up to 1977, see Fu (1977).

[23] There are indications, however, that *than* in English may be undergoing change. Notice that in (i) below, *me* rather than *I* is far more common in current English.
  (i) John can run faster than *me*.

[24] For a review of some important works, see Fu (1977).

2.5.2.2. Topical Comparison vs. Sentential Comparison

The fact that only topics of an equal rank can be compared is a surface structure constraint that exists in Chinese. English, being a non-topic-prominent language, evidently lacks such a surface constraint. Such a difference goes a long way in explaining many syntactic differences existing in English and Chinese in doing comparison. In the following we will give just a few noticeable ones.

First, as we mentioned earlier, it is rather easy in English to compare two objects but the comparison of two objects in Chinese is subject to many constraints associated with such topicalization processes as object fronting, *ba* NP fronting, and VO constituent fronting, which, in one way or another, all involve moving the object to a preverbal position. Actually, not only objects themselves, but also any constituents associated with the objects, as exemplified by (148a) and (149a) in English, will have to be turned into topics of some form in Chinese before they can be compared, as (148b) and (149b) show.

(148) a. John bought <u>more books</u> than I did.
b. Yuehan mai de   shu bi   wo mai de
   John buy Rel. Mar. book COMP I buy Rel. Mar.
   duo.
   many
   '(Literally) the books that John bought are more than the books that I bought.'

(149) a. John bought <u>more books in Taipei</u> than in <u>Tainan</u>.
b. Yuehan zai Taibei mai de   shu' bi
   John in Taipei buy Rel. Mar. book COMP
   zai Tainan mai de   duo
   in Tainan buy Rel. Mar. many
   '(Literally) the books that John bought in Taipei are more than the books that he bought in Tainan.'

Second, our analysis accounts naturally for the fact that while it is possible to translate (150) into Chinese using a comparative sentence , it is impossible to do so with (151).

(150)   He speaks English better than (he does) French.

(151)   He speaks English better than he writes French.

Third, it explains in a natural way why English always has the *than* clause attached to the end of a comparative sentence while in Chinese X *bi* Y phrase always occurs preverbally.

Fourth, it gives a natural account for the phenomenon that two adjectives, as a rule, can be compared only when there happen to be corresponding abstract nouns related to them such as *shendu* ' depth' is related to *shen* 'deep' and *kuandu* 'width' is to *kuan* 'wide'. Otherwise, comparison of two adjectives using a comparative sentence is impossible. Witness (152) and (153).

(152) a. The river is <u>wider</u> than it is <u>deep</u>.
    b. zhei-tiao he   de   kuandu bi   shendu da.
       this-CL   river POSS width COMP depth great
       '(Literally) the width of this river is greater than its depth.'

(153) a. John is more talkative than tactful.
    b. Yuehan ai   shuo-hua danshi shuo-hua mei jiqiao.
       John   love talking but   talking no tact
       '(Literally) John loves talking but he doesn't talk with tact.'

Since the single distinction between topical comparison and non-topical comparison can explain naturally so many syntactic differences in comparison between Chinese, a topic-prominent language and English, a non-topic-prominent language, we will hypothesize further that such a distinction is a universally valid parameter in accounting for syntactic behavior in comparison.

Such a hypothesis, of course, can only be confirmed (or disconfirmed) by in-depth studies of comparison in such topic-prominent languages as Lisu, Lahu, Japanese and Korean on the one hand, and such non-topic-prominent languages as French, Spanish, Norwegian, and Turkish on the other. But judging from the convincing correlation that we have demonstrated between topic-prominency in general and syntactic behavior in comparison, this is a promising path worth persuing.

PART III

COMPOUND AND COMPLEX SENTENCES

CHAPTER SEVEN
TELESCOPIC SENTENCES
COMPOUND SENTENCES
AND
CLAUSE CONNECTIVES

Up to now we have discussed in great detail the basic clause types of all Chinese sentences. We have found that the single string that runs through all these clause types is topic, primary and non-primary. We are now in a position to take up the matter of how these basic clause types are put together to form compound sentences.

Things, however, are not as simple and straightforward as our previous statement sounds. For one thing, Chinese is well-known for its lack of grammatical markings and as a result, clauses often run together without clear-cut boundary to form what has been loosely termed "serial verb constructions", as exemplified by (1).

(1) ta   sheng bing   le,   mei   weikou,   zuoshi
    he   get   sick   PART   have:not appetite do-business
    bu   qijing.
    not   vigorous
    'He was sick, lost his appetite and didn't work vigorously.'

For another, the use of clause connectives, as we have previously pointed out, is often syntactically optional. And even when they do occur they do not necessarily occur at the beginning position of a clause. In fact they can occur at various positions in a clause and no linguists, to the best of my knowledge, have been able to give an explicit account of their distribution.

This chapter will therefore begin with an in-depth exploration of the so-called "serial verb constructions" in Chinese. It will then be followed by a careful examination of compound sentences and clause connectives, when these are used, to join them together.

1 The So-called "Serial Verb Constructions"

Compared to other more commonly found constructions such as the passive and the comparative, etc., serial verb constructions have only recently been seriously studied. Maybe because of their recent introduction and maybe because of their telescopic nature, a great deal of controversy and confusion has arisen.[1] We will therefore begin our discussion by clearing away some terminological confusion and by setting up criteria to define and classify the constructions in a linguistically significant and well-justified way. Then we will attempt to give an adequate description of each type of the constructions.

1.1 Previous Treatments of Chinese Serial Verb Constructions

Up to date, only Li and Thompson (1981) and Chu (1983) have treated the construction in enough detail for comparison. We will therefore begin by giving a summary of their treatments and then give our comments as comparison is being made.

1.1.1 Li and Thompson's Treatment

Li and Thompson described various types of the serial verb construction in several papers (1974, 1975, 1978a and 1978b) and these descriptions culminated in a long chapter entitled "Serial Verb Constructions" in their *Mandarin Chinese grammar* (1981:594-622).

Li and Thompson in this latter work define the serial verb construction as "a sentence that contains two or more verb phrases or clauses juxtaposed without any marker indicating what the relationship is between them" (1981:594), and they schematize it as:

(2)   (NP)   V   (NP)   (NP)   V   (NP)

As Chinese is very well-known for its meagerness in syntactic marking, it can be expected that there are many consturctions that can fit this definition. Realizing this, Li and Thompson go a step further in classifying, on the basis of meaning relation that holds between the two verbs, the sentences that fit this definition into four types.

Their characterization of these four types is briefly summarized in the following with some illustrative examples cited from them.

1.1.1.1 Two or More Separate Events

The first type is called "Two or More Separate Evants" by Li and Thompson and the events are said to be related in one or more of the following four ways:

---

[1] For a discussion of the terminological confusion in Chinese in mainland China, see Deng, 1982.

(3) a. Consecutive: One event occurs after the other
    b. Purpose: The first event is done for the purpose of achieving the second.
    c. Alternating: The subject alternates between two actions
    d. Circumstance: The first verb phrase describes the circumstances under which the event in the second verb phrase or clause occurs.

Some illustrative examples follow:

(4) wo mai piao jin-qu.
    I buy ticket enter-go
    'I bought a ticket and went in', or 'I bought a bicket to go in.'

(5) wo didi   kai-che   chu-shi   le.
    my younger-brother drive-car exit-affair PART
    'My younger brother had an accident while driving.'

(6) ta nian-shu xin hen zhuan.
    he study-book heart very engrossed
    'When he is studying, he is very engrossed.'

(7) he   dian   jiu zhuang-zhuang   danzi.
    drink a-little wine strengthen-strengthen gall-bladder
    'Drink a little wine, and it will give you courage.' , or
    'Drink a little wine to give yourself courage.' , or
    'Get some courage by drinking a little wine.'

They further comment that the meanings of the individual verb phrases determine which of the semantic relationships in (3a) — (3d) are possible, and the speech context determines which of these interpretations is most likely (1981:597).

This is also the type that was exclusively treated in an earlier paper (1974). One noticeable change occurred when we compare the two treatments. In the early version, the two verbs are said to share the same subject. That requirement is dropped in the later version. We'll come back to this point in our comment.

1.1.1.2 The Pivotal Construction

Li and Thompson, following Chao (1968), call this type of the serial verb construction the pivotal construction. The defining characteristic of the construction is that it contains a noun phrase that is simultaneously the subject of the second verb and the direct object of the first verb (1981:607).

Li and Thompson further divide this type of the serial verb construction into two groups, roughly depending on whether the second part of the sentence is factive or non–factive.[2]

Group I: Non–factive

(8) wo quan   ta nian yi.
    I advise him study medicine
    'I advise him to study medicine.'

(9) wo qing   nimen qu chi bingqilin.
    I invite you   go eat ice–cream
    'I invite you all to go have some ice–cream.'

Group II: Factive

(10) xiao haizi xiao ta shi yi–ge da pangzi.
     small child laugh him be one–CL big fatso
     'The children laughed at him for being a big fatso.'

(11) ta piping   wo bu yonggong.
     he criticise me not industrious
     'He criticised me for not being industrious.'

1.1.1.3. Descriptive Clauses

The type of serial verb construction called by Li and Thompson the "descriptive clause" involves a transitive verb whose direct object is "described" by a following clause, as schematized in (12):

---

[2]They didn't use these two terms. Instead, they chose to give more detailed explanation.

```
                    describes
                  ┌─────┬──┐
    (12)  NP  V   NP  (NP)  V  (NP)
```

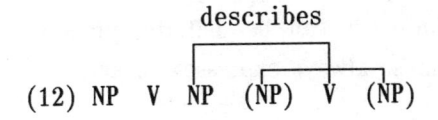

This type can be further divided into two subtypes which are termed "realis" and "irrealis" descriptive clauses respectively.

1.1.1.3.1. Realis Descriptive Clauses

This type of descriptive clauses has the following properties: (i) The direct object of the first verb is always indefinite, and (ii) the second clause provides an incidental description of this indefinite direct object. The following are some of their examples.

(13) ta you yi-ge meimei   hen xihuan kan dianying.
     he exist one-CL younger-sister very like   see movie
     'He has a younger sister who likes to see movies.'

(14) wo da-po-le   yi-ge chabei hen zhiqian.
     I hit-broken-ASP   one-CL tea-cup very valuable
     'I broke a teacup that is very valuable.'[3]

They comment that the function of this type of descriptive clauses is to introduce a new reference into the conversation and add some information about it. For this reason they regard it as a type of presentative sentences. They term it the "realis" descriptive clause because the description provided by the second clause is realized; it is in the here-and-now of the "real world", as opposed to the irrealis descriptive clause which adds hypothetical or projected information about the noun phrase of the first clause (1981:612).

1.1.1.3.2. Irrealis Descriptive Clauses

This subtype is different from the previous one in that the second verb phrase names an unrealized (irrealis) activity involving the direct object of the first verb, as mentioned in

---

[3]A more literal translation that reflects the structure of the Chinese original in (13) and (14) should be (i) and (ii) respectively.
  (i)   He has a younger sister (and she) likes to see movies.
  (ii)   I broke a teacup (and it) is very valuable.

the previous paragraph. In addition, there are two important differences. First, the direct object of the first verb is not necessarily indefinite; it can be definite, indefinite or non-referential. Second, the verb of the irrealis clause always expresses an activity. The following are some of their examples.

(15) women zhong nei-zhong cai   chi.
     we   raise that-kind vegetable eat
     'We raise that kind of vegetable to eat.'

(16) gei zhei-ge ren   pai   yi-ge shijian chongxin jiancha.
     give this-CL person arrange one-CL time   repeat   examine
     'Schedule a retest for this person.' or '(more literally),
     Arrange a time for this person to be re-examined.'

1.1.1.4 One VP/Clause Is the Subject or Direct Object of Another

As we will argue later on that this type should not be included in the serial verb construction, we will not go into the detail of Li and Thompson's discussion. We will simply note that in one subtype the meaning of the first verb allows it to be followed by a direct object that is a clause as in (17) and (18):

(17) ta fouren [$_S$ta zuo-cuo le].
     he deny   he do-wrong PART
     'He denies that he was wrong.'

(18) wo kongpa [$_S$ni   laibuji].
     I fear   you can-not-make-it-in-time
     'I am afraid you can't make it in time.'

In the other subtype, the meaning of the second verb allows it to occur with a clause as its subject. (19) and (20) are two examples.

(19) [$_S$da sheng nian kewen]$_S$ keyi bangzhu fayin.
         big voice read lesson   can help   pronunciation
     'Reading the lesson aloud can help one's pronunciation.'

(20) [$_S$wu-ge ren zuo yi-jia motoche]$_S$ zhen weixian
    five-CL person sit one-CL motorcycle real dangerous
    'It's really dangerous for five people to ride one motorcycle.'

1.1.2 Chu's Treatment

Chu (1983:270) defines the serial verb construction as one where more than one verb occurs one after another with or without anything intervening between them but where no verb phrase or clause can be identified as subordinated to another. On the basis of this definition, he identifies three types of serial verb constructions.

1.1.2.1 Loosely Bounded Clauses

The first type of serial verb constructions, one that is termed "Two or More Separate Events" by Li and Thompson, is called "Loosely Bounded Clauses" by Chu, who characterizes it as follows, "The shared noun is the initial noun in the first clause and can also be interpreted as the initial noun of the second clause." (1983:275) Some of his examples are cited below:

(21) yinhang jiu-dian   kai men, kaishi yingye.
     bank   nine-o'clock open door begin business
     'The bank opens at nine o'clock (and) starts business.'

(22) zhei-ge xiaohai shuo-hua   kou-chi   bu qingchu.
     this-CL child   say-speech mouth-tooth not clear
     '(When) this child talks, his pronunciation is not clear.'

He comments that the semantic relationship between the two clauses seems to depend on the lexical meanings of the verb phrases and the circumstances under which the events occur. Though he admits that most of the relations seem to fall into the four types that Li and Thompson have described, i.e. consecutive, purpose, alternating, and circumstance, he contends that it is by no means impossible to conceive of other relations (p. 277). Examine the following example cited from him:

(23) women zhei—liang chezi mai gei ni, bu zhuan qian.
    we   this—CL   car sell to you not make money
    'We sell this car to you (and) will not make money (on it).'

The most reasonable relation between the two clauses, according to Chu, is one of result.

He also adds that he purposely avoided the term "subject" because the shared noun is not always subject. In (22) the shared noun *zhei—ge Xiaohai* 'this child' is clearly the topic of the second clause (1983:277).

1.1.2.2 The Pivotal Construction

Chu, also following Chao (1968), defines this type of serial verb construction as one "with two verbs, one after the other, with an intervening noun which semantically is the direct object of the first verb and the subject of the second." (p.271) In the following we also cite some examples from him.

(24) wo qing ta bangmang.
    I ask him help
    'I ask him to help.'

(25) dajia   dou zai deng ni lai.
    everybody all ASP wait you come
    'Everybody is waiting for you to come.'

(26) women gongxi   ni de   jiang.
    we   congratulate you receive award
    'We congratulate you on receiving the award.'

Chu also notes that there are constructions which look like the pivotal ones but are actually not. (27) is such an example.

(27) tamen dou shuo wo bu dui.
    they all say I not right
    'They all said that I was wrong.'

In (27) *wo* 'I' cannot be the recipient of *shuo* 'say' while *ni* 'you' in (26) can.[4] This difference is reflected in the potential phonological pause. A pause may occur after the pivotal noun in (26) but such a pause is more appropriate before the corresponding noun in a sentence like (27).

1.1.2.3 The "Elaborative" Clause

Chu distinguishes this type of serial verb construction from the other two by saying that this type can have one or more than one noun between the verbs and that if there is only one such noun, it must be syntactically related to the second verb, usually its subject; if there are two nouns, the first one must be related, usually the object of the second verb (1983:273). The following are two of his examples.

```
(28) wo cong tushuguan jie-le     yi-ben shu bu haokan.
     I   from library   borrow-ASP one-CL book not good-reading
     'I borrowed a book from the library which was not interesting
     (i.e. but the book was not interesting).'

(29) wo chuban-le    yi-ben shu hen duo ren   yao mai.
     I  publish-ASP one-CL book very many people want buy
     'I published a book which many people wanted to buy
     (i.e. and many people wanted to buy it).'
```

Chu also notes that the noun involved is always indefinite and it means that the preceding verb introduces it into the discourse for the first time and the rest of the sentence goes on to elaborate on it. This is the reason why the clause is called "elaborative" (1983:274). From this description it is clear that his "elaborative clause" is equivalent to what Li and Thompson (op. cit.) have termed the "realis descriptive clause".

1.1.3. Summary and Comments

The chart given in (30) sums up the terminological correspondence between Li and

---

[4]Shuo in (27) can have a simple noun as its object as in (i) below, though in that case, it means 'criticize' rather than 'say'.
```
(i)  ni    lao    shuo      wo.
     you   always criticize  me
     'You are always criticizing me.'
```

Thompson's and Chu's analysis of various types of serial verb constructions. At this point, in order not to bias the reader, we will simply call each type by a number. We will have more to say about the ways these constructions can best be treated and what we think they should be called in the next section.

(30)

	Li and Thompson	Chu
Type 1	Two or more separate events	Loosely Bounded clauses
Type 2	Pivotal Constructions	The pivotal construction
Type 3	A realis Descriptive clauses	Elaborative clauses
	B irrealis	No mention
Type 4	One VP/clause is the subject or direct object of another	Not discussed as a serial verb construction

We have already mentioned that we agree with Chu in not treating Type 4 as a serial verb construction. We do this for two reasons. First, taking a hint from Chu, who, as cited in 1.1.2.2, mentions that the potential phonological pause can be utilized to distinguish Type 4 constructions from Those of Type 2, we find that this test can actually be extended to distinguish Type 4 from the other three types. This is so because, as is implicit in Chu's analysis and as we will argue in the next section, the other three types all involve at least a shared NP, one that plays a role in both of the two adjacent clauses. But there is no such NP in the Type 4 construction. Also related to this is the observation that only Type 4 allows adverbial elements to go between the first verb and the following NP. Compare *xiwang* 'hope', a Type 4 verb with *qing* 'invite', a Type 2 verb in (31) and (32).[5]

(31) a. <u>xiwang dajia</u>   duo ti   yijian.
        hope   everyone more bring:forth opinion
        '(We) hope that everyone will bring forth more of their opinions.'

_____

[5]The observation and the examples are taken from a book entitled *Grammar and Rhetoric* published by Beijing Daxue Zhongwen Xi (Department of Chinese, Beijing University) (1980:26).

b. jinhou   xiwang dajia   duo ti   yijian.
      from:now:on hope   everyone more bring:forth opinion
      'From now on (we) hope that everyone will bring forth more of their
       opinions.'
   c. xiwang jinhou   dajia   duo ti   yijian.
      hope   from:now:on everyone more bring:forth opinion
      '(We) hope that from now on everyone will bring forth more of their
       opinions.'
   d. xiwang dajia   jinhou   duo ti   yijian.
      hope   everyone from:now:on more bring:forth opinion
      '(We) hope that everyone, from now on, will bring forth more of
       their opinions.'

(32) a. qing   dajia   duo ti   yijian.
        invite everyone more bring:forth opinion
        '(We) invite everyone to bring forth more of their opinions.'
     b. jinhou   qing   dajia   duo ti   yijian.
        from:now:on invite everyone more bring:forth opinion
        'From now on (we) invite everyone to bring forth more of their
         opinions.'
     c.*qing   jinhou   dajia   duo ti   yijian.
        invite from:now:on everyone more bring:forth opinion
     d. qing   dajia   jinhou   duo ti   yijian.
        invite everyone from:now:on more bring:forth opinion
        '(We) invite everyone from now on to bring forth more of their
         opinions.'

Our second reason has to do with the fact that Chinese has very little syntactic marking. This fact implies that in doing Chinese linguistics, linguists often have to depend on reliable discoursal or semantic information. Since, according to Li and Thompson's characterization of Type 4, whether or not a certain string of words functions as either sentential subject or object can be determined by the meaning of the verb involved, we feel sure to infer from this that they would attribute it as part of speaker-hearer knowledge of the language. If this is so, we would think that there is sufficient justification to treat it under embedded structure as Chu does (1983:242-247).

Another thing that strikes us in Li and Thompson's treatment is the heterogeneity of criteria with which each type is established. If one examines their account closely, one finds that sometimes semantic criteria are used, sometimes, syntactic and at other times, functional. After reading their analysis one cannot but wonder just what it is that ties all these structures together.

Turning now to Chu's analysis, we find that he is not as complete as Li and Thompson. He does not deal with Type 3B, one that was termed by Li and Thompson as "irrealis descriptive clauses". Though he is more consistent than Li and Thompson in the criteria used in setting up the types, he is not completely consistent either. In the next section we will present evidence to show that his avoidance of topic might have prevented him from arriving at some of the generalizations that we find in these constructions.

1.2. The Proposed Analysis

It should be clear from our previous comments that as a working definition, we would define the serial verb construction as a sentence that contains two or more verb phrases or clauses juxtaposed without any formal marker indicating what the relationship is, and that the two adjacent clauses will have to be understood as having a shared NP between them. This working definition will naturally rule out Type 4 construction as this construction does not require there to be a shared NP between the two clauses.

1.2.1. Type 1:The Plain Topic Chain

We mentioned earlier that Li and Thompson in their early treatment of this construction made it a requirement that the two verb phrases or clauses share the same subject (1974:96). This requirement was rightly dropped in the later analysis (1981), indicating that they have come to the realization that the shared NP is not subject in all cases.

Chu (1983) actually uses a circumlocution, "the initial noun", in designating the shared element in this type of structure. He notes, however, that he deliberately uses the term because, even though the shared noun is in most cases subject, in some cases it should be more appropriately called topic (1983:277).

This terminological avoidance and circumlocution can be made unnecessary if we realize that the initial NP is actually the primary topic, which, as we have argued repeatedly, should be made to subsume subject occuring in the initial position but not vice versa.

Let us examine some examples here.

(33) ta zuo xiti   jingshen bu jizhong.
     he do exercises spirit   not concentrated
     '(When) he is doing his exercises, he is not attentive.'

(34) zhei–ge ren   wo hen taoyan, ni qing ta zou ba.
     this–CL person I very dislike you ask him leave PART
     'This person, I don't like (him) at all; please ask him to leave.'

Thus, in the second clause of (33), *ta* 'he', the shared NP, is actually the first NP in a double nominative construction with *jingshen* 'spirit', the possessed noun, as the second NP. Since the first Np in this consturction has been analyzed as topic by many linguists (Li and Thompson, 1976, 1981; Chu, 1983; Tsao 1979, 1981 among others) and since no convincing counterproposal has appeared recently, I think it is justifiable to assume that it is topic that is involved here. (34) is even more striking. Here the initial NP, *zhei–ge ren* 'this person' is clearly the direct object in both clauses.[6] No subject seems to be involved here. Rather, the direct object in both clauses has been moved to the clause–initial position to become topic. So to summarize, since the initial NP, which is shared by both clauses, can be subject, the first NP in a double nominative construction, and an S–initial fronted direct object, the only general enough term for it is topic, which, as I have repeatedly pointed out, can bear all these different relations to each individual clause in which it occurs but which is fronted to the clause–initial position to designate the thing being talked about.

But if there is still lingering doubt about the initial NP in (33) being topic, let us put it to test to see how much topic quality it has.

In Chapter two we have demonstrated that a Chinese topic has the following qualities (see also Li and Thompson, 1981, Tang, 1979 for similar lists):

---

[6]The second clause in (34) is actually a complex one which we will term later on as "telescopic–pivotal construction". It contains two clauses with *ta* 'him' simultaneously serving as direct object of the preceding verb and the topic–subject of the following clause. However, in order not to complicate the argument here, we will temporarily regard the whole construction as a simple clause.

(35) a. Topic invariably occupies the initial position of the first clause in a topic chain.
b. Topic can optionally be separated from the rest of the clause, in which it overtly occurs by one of the four pause particles *a (ya), ne, me* and *ba*.
c. Topic is always definite or generic.
d. Topic is a supraclausal notion; it may, and often does, extend its semantic domain to more than one clause.
e. Topic is in control of the pronominalization or deletion of all the coreferential NPs in a topic chain.
f. Topic, except in clauses in which it is also subject, plays no role in such processes as pro+*ziji* reflexivization and imperativization.

Even without examination, it is clear that the initial NP in all the sentences of this type possesses the qualities described in (35a) and (35d) for it is part of our difinition of this type of serial verb construction. The NP in question is also true of (35b), because any one of the four pause particles can be inserted immediately after the initial NP in (33), as shown in (33a), and the resultant sentence is still grammatical.

(33) a. ta $\begin{Bmatrix} a \\ ne \\ me \\ ba \end{Bmatrix}$ zuo xiti jingshen bu jizhong.

he PART do exercises spirit not concentrated
'(when) he is doing his exercises, he is not attentive.'

The initial NP in this construction must be definite as in (33), or generic as in (33b) below because a non-generic, indefinite NP occurring in that position will result in an ungrammatical sentence, as witnessed by (33c).

(33) b. yi-nianji xuesheng zuo xiti   jingshen bu jizhong.
    first-grade student do exercise spirit not concentrated
    '(When) first-grade students are doing their exercises, they are not attentive.'
   c.*yi-ge xuesheng zuo xiti jinshen bu jizhong.
     one-CL sutdent do exercise spirit not concentrated
     ?'(When) a student is doing his exercise, he is not attentive.'

So the initial NP in this construction also has the quality described in (35c).

It is also evident that the initial NP of this construction is in control of the pronominalization or deletion of all the clause–initial NPs in this construction, as is clearly reflected in the translations of all the examples. Conversely, if, as shown in (36), the deleted or pronominalized element of the second clause is not understood to be coreferential to the initial NP of the first clause, then the sentence is unacceptable.

(36) * ta$_i$ changchang da tade taitai$_j$ _____$_j$ chu–qi.
      he   often   beat his wife   vent–anger

It is clear then that the initial NP of this construction also has the quality described in (35e).

Since to examine the role the initial NP of this construction played in each of the processes listed in (35f) would take us afar, and since in the case of (33) it would not be discriminative anyway, we would invite the reader to try them out with other examples.

Now that we have proved that the initial NP of this construction possesses all the topic qualities described in (35a)–(35e), we can safely conclude that it is a topic and the two or more clauses that follow it form a topic chain.

If this is clear, then it is easy to understand why the semantic relations between any two clauses in a chain can vary so much. I have pointed out elsewhere (1980) that the topic chain, taken in its broad sense of including a chain of one clause, is the basic sentence form in Chinese, and since all the clauses are related to the topic as comments, they are felt to be related to each other and the semantic relation between them can be left unspecified if the speaker feels no need to make it explicit. But for ease of reference, we would refer to the type of topic chains unmarked by connectives as the "plain topic chain" to distinguish it from the marked topic chain.

1.2.2. Type 2:Telescopic Construction

Li and Thompson (1981) and Chu (1983), both following Chao (1968), have termed this type of serial verb construction the pivotal construction and they have both defined it as a structure which can be schematized as follows:

(37) NP V₁ NP V₂ (NP)
       └──┘ └──┘
        DO   SUBJ

In what follows we would like to demonstrate that the role the shared NP plays in the following clause is not subject in all cases. Rather, it should be more appropriately analyzed as topic.

Let us start by examining some example sentences.

(38) wo mingling ta qu.
     I order   him go
     'I ordered him to go.'

(39) ta xiao   wo jingshen guofen jinzhang.
     he laugh—at I spirit   too   tense
     'He laughed at me for being too nervous.'

(40) ta piping   wo xin   bu zhuan.
     he criticise me heart not engrossed
     'He criticised me for not being attentive.'

It is clear from our previous discussion that only in (38) do we have a shared NP that bears the relation of subject to the following verb. The shared NPs in (39) and (40) play the role of topic in their following clauses respectively. Since in our framework, topic subsumes subject when it occurs in the clause—initial position, we could generalize by stating that in the pivotal construction the shared NP serves as direct object in the preceding clause and as topic in the following clause. In other words, there is certain overlap between the two adjacent clauses. And from now on we would refer to any structure with some telescoping occurring between two adjacent clauses as "telescopic construction". As we will argue later there are two other distinguishable types of such construction, we would refer to this type as "telescopic—pivotal" construction.

There is one more question that we would like to answer, i.e., why do so many linguists take the relationship of the shared NP to the following verb to be that of subject? It is not surprising that Chao should call it subject as he does not distinguish topic from subject. But why should linguists like Li and Thompson, and Chu, who both argue, as we have shown, that Chinese has both topic and subject, also take the same position?

To see the reason for this oversight, we have to examine the nature of the verbs that can occur in this type of telescopic construction. Of all the three treatments we have mentioned, only Chao gives a list of many typical verbs of this class (1968:126). For ease of discussion the whole list is reproduced below:

jiao 'cause, tell'; *shi* 'cause'; *rang* 'let'; *zhun, xu, zhunxu* 'permit'; *yao* 'want'; *qing* 'request, invite'; *quan* 'persuade, advise'; *cui* 'urge, hurry'; *bi* 'compel'; *yin* 'induce'; *gudong* 'incite'; *songyong* 'incite'; *ren* 'recognize'; *suan, ju, suanju* 'elect'; *pai* 'dispatch'; *bang(zhe)* 'help'; *pei(zhe)* 'keep company'; *dai(zhe)* 'take along'; *ling(zhe)* 'lead'; *fu(zhe)* 'support'; *song* 'send'; *yue* 'make an agreement with'; *zhao* 'get(someone) to ...'; *guai* 'blame'; *pa* 'be arfaid'; *xihuan* 'like'; *maiyuan* 'complain'; *jinzhi* 'prohibit'.

We will exclude from discussion two groups of verbs. First, the verb *shi* 'cause' is a very productive causative verb in modern Mandarin. It can be used in a number of contexts and for that reason should be separately treated. Second, all those verbs with an optional *zhe* 'continuative aspect marker' should be excluded as well because the possible cooccurrence with *zhe* indicates that each of these verbs expresses an action or state subordinate to that expressed by the second verb.

With these verbs excluded, the remaining verbs fall into three main categories.

The verbs in category A include: *rang* 'let'; *zhun, xu, zhunxu* 'permit'; *yao* 'want'; *qing* 'request'; *quan* 'persuade, advise'; *cui* 'urge, hurry'; *bi* 'compel'; *song* 'dispatch'; pai 'dispatch'; *jinzhi* 'prohibit'; *yin* 'induce'; *gudong* 'incite'; and *songyong* 'incite' *zhao* 'get someone to....'.[7] They are all "directive" verbs as every one of them is related to the imperative sentences. This can be demonstrated with their possible cooccurrence with *bie* 'don't', a verb that marks a negative imperative, unless it is ruled out because of semantic incompatibility between the verb and *bie* 'don't', as it is the case with *jinzhi* 'prohibit' in (41d).

---

[7] A number of verbs, of course, have other uses. *Rang*, for instance, can also be used as a passive marker. *Zhao* is another case. While occurring in this construction it is a Category A verb, it can also be used in the Type 3B telescoped—descriptive construction, meaning 'look for someone to do something for someone or oneself.'

(41) ta   a. yao   wo bie   qu.
         b. qing
         c. quan
        *d. jinzhi
     he   a. want   me don't go
         b. request
         c. advise
         d. prohibit
     'He wanted/requested/advised/*prohibited me not go.'

All of these verbs can occur in the frame schematized in (42).

(42) $NP_1 + V_A + NP_2 + V_{action}\ (+NP_3)$

This category of verbs is, as expected, very similar to the category of verbs that is used in turning English imperative sentences into indirect speech, and that explains why the verb following the shared NP must be an action verb.

Category B is more restricted in its membership and all the members have to do with "role-setting" i.e. electing, appointing etc. The members include: *xuan, ju, xuanju* 'elect'; *ren* 'recognize'; and *pai* 'dispatch'. All of them can occur in the frame:

(43) $NP_1 + V_B + NP_2 + \begin{Bmatrix} zuo \\ \underline{dang} \\ wei \end{Bmatrix} + NP_3$

Some examples follow:

(44) tamen xuan Li Xiaojie dang   zhuxi.
     they elect Li Miss   serve chairperson
     'They elected Miss Li as chairperson.'

(45) ta ren   Li Shou-xin zuo   yizi.
     he recognize Li Shou-xin serve foster-son
     'He adopted Li Shou-xin as his foster son.'

It should be noted that this category is not only more restricted in its membership but also in the verbs that can follow it. They are limited to *zuo, dang* and *wei*, all translatable as 'acting as, serving as' in English.

Category C verbs include: *piping* 'criticise'; *maiyuan* 'complain'; *guai* 'complain'; *pa* 'be afraid'; *xihuan* 'like'; and *gongxi* 'congratulate'. They are all verbs that express one's attitude or feeling towards someone or something. They can occur in the frame:

(46) $NP_1 + V_C + NP_2 + V + (NP_3)$

Some illustrative examples follow:

(47) wo xihuan ta you qian.
     I like him have money
    'I like him having a lot of money.'

(48) ta pengyou guai ta jingshen bu jizhong.
     he friend complain him spirit not concentrated
    'His friend complained about his not being attentive.'

Again we find that while it is justifiable to call the shared NP in (47) the subject of the second clause, it is clear that the role played by the shared NP in the second clause of (48) is that of topic. And again our previous argument applies here: only topic is a category general enough to designate the role played by the shared NP in the second clause.

From our previous discussion of the three categories of verbs that can occur in the so-called pivotal construction we can see that even though all the categories of verbs have one feature in common, namely, that they can all be followed by an object NP which is capable of being interpreted as playing a role in the following clause, yet the role it plays is not restricted to that of subject. In the case of Category A and Category B verbs, it is justifiable to call the shared NP subject of the following clause as subject is defined in terms of subject–verb selectional restrictions. However, the same argument does not hold in the case of Category C verbs, where in many cases the shared NP plays the role of topic in the second clause.

Now we are in a better position to explain why so many linguists have taken the shared NP to be the subject of the second clause. This is because in most cases of the so-called pivotal construction, the shared NP can be so identified. However, as we have pointed out, this is not true in all cases and the only general enough term for the role of the shared NP in the second clause remains to be topic.

1.2.3. Type 3

Li and Thompson (1981:611) characterize this type of serial verb construction as one occurring in the following frame:

$$
(49)\quad NP \quad V_1 \quad \overset{\text{describes}}{NP} \quad (NP) \quad V_2 \quad (NP)
$$

They further distinguish between what they call the realis descriptive clause and the irrealis descriptive clause. Chu (1983), on the other hand, concentrates on the first type and calls it the elaborative clause. We will take up each type in turn in the following discussion.

1.2.3.1. Type 3A: Telescopic-Presentative Construction

Let us begin by re-examining (28) and (29) cited again here as (50) and (51) for ease of reference.

(50) wo cong tushuguan jie—le   yi—ben shu, bu haokan.
     I from library   borrow—ASP one—CL book not good—reading
     'I checked out a book from the library (but) (it) is not interesting.'

(51) wo chuban—le   yi—ben shu, hen duo ren   yao mai.
     I publish—ASP one—CL book very many people want buy
     'I published a book (and) many people wanted to buy (it).'

Chu states that in regard to sentences like (50), where there is only one NP between the first and the second verb, the shared NP usually plays the role of subject of the second verb, but that, with respect to sentences like (51) where two NPs occur between the two verbs, the first of the two NPs usually plays the role of direct object of the second verb. Such an unnecessarily complex description can be simplified if we realize that in a marked word order, object can precede subject to become the primary topic and in an unmarked word order, subject coincides with the primary topic as the initial element in a clause. With this understanding, we can now see that the shared NP is actually the topic of the second clause in both (50) and (51).

That this analysis is correct can be further confirmed by the fact that the shared NP is in some cases the first NP of a double nominative construction and it can be the initial NP that leads a topic chain. Examine (50a) and (51a), which are expanded versions of (50) and (51) respectively.

(50) a. wo cong tushuguan jie—le   yi—ben shu, wenzi
        I from library   borrow—ASP one—CL book language
        shenao, gushi pingchang, bu haokan.
        abstruse story trite   not good—reading
        'I borrowed a book from the library whose language is abstruse
        and whose story is trite; (it)(is) not interesting.'

(51) a. wo chuban—le   yi—ben shu, yinshua jingmei,
        I publish—ASP one—CL book printing exquisite
        jiaqian gongdao, hen duo ren   yao mai.
        price   reasonable very many people want buy
        'I published a book, exquisitely printed and reasonably priced
        (and) many people wanted to buy it.'

There is one thing which seems to go against our treating the shared NP as topic of the second clause. We have pointed out in (35c) that topic is always definite or generic, but as can be readily seen in (50) and (51), the shared NP is evidently non—generic and indefinite. Actually, the fact that it is indefinite may turn out to be a very strong argument for analyzing it as topic of the second clause, if we understand that the function of this type of serial verb construction is to introduce a new topic into the discourse. Li and Thompson (1981:611) correctly characterize it as a type of presentative sentences whose function is to introduce an indefinite NP into a discourse as topic.

Another confirming fact is that a coreferential NP or a pronominal copy may occur immediately after the indefinite shared NP, especially when the NP is followed by a long topic chain or is separated from its comments by some inserted elements as in (52) and (53), respectively.

(52) ta you yi–ge meimei,   ta chuanzhuo shimao,
    he has one–CL younger–sister she wearing   stylish
    sixiang yanghua,   hen xihuan kan dianying.
    thinking westernized very like   watch movies
    'He has a younger sister; she is fashionable in dress,
    (and) westernized in thought, (and) is very fond of movies.'

(53) ta–de dayi you yi–ge hei   dian, zhei–ge hei
    his   coat has one–CL black spot this–CL black
    dian, shuo ye qiguai, zeme   xi   dou xi–bu–diao.
    spot say also strange however wash all wash–not–off
    'His coat has a black spot, (and) this spot, strange to say,
    however (one) washes (it), (it) won't come off.'

The fact that a coreferential definite NP or pronominal copy can be used immediately after the indefinite shared NP strongly supports the analysis that posits an underlying definite NP, which following the general rule of discourse coreferential NP deletion in Chinese, is deleted in most cases.[8,9]

---

[8] In Tsao,1979,I touched upon this analysis but didn't really argue for it.

[9] At the Second International Conference on Sinology (Academia Sinica, Taipei, 1986), in the discussion that followed the presentation of my paper "Serial Verb Constructions in Chinese" on which this section is based, both Prof. Mei Kuang and Prof. Tang Ting–chi raised the question that since the NP involved here is indefinite while a topic is usually definite, it is questionable whether the NP can be regared as topic. Prof. Mei further pointed out a possible objection in that since the indefinite NP involved serves the discourse function of introducting a topic, it should not be treated in a sentence grammar. This later question is a very complex one which requires at least a paper–length discussion. I hope that I can take it up sometime in the future. But briefly my position is that it depends on whether the discourse function is syntacticized in the language or not. In the case in question I think most linguists would agree that it is in Chinese. Returning to the first question, I can, in addition to the evidence presented, cite a similar difficulty in English grammer which, to the best of my knowledge, has not yet been resolved. Thus, English relative pronouns are regarded as "definite", but it can refer to an antecedent that is indefinite as in (i):
(i) I know a man who dislikes Chinese food.
Furthermore, as will be discussed in Chatper 8 (See also Tsao, 1986), this is a case where the English relative clause, instead of its normal identifying function, serves the function of an assertive clause, very much like a comment clause in Chinese and, not surprisingly, is translated as such, as shown in (ii):
(ii)   wo renshi yi–ge   ren,   (ta) bu xihuan Zhongguo cai
       I   know a–CL   person   he   not like   Chinese   food

Since the presentative construction has so much in common with this type of serial verb construction in function, one naturally wonders whether the presentative construction can be treated as a serial verb construction. In what follows we would like to explore this possibility by examining all types of presentative constructions more closely.

Li and Thompson (1981:509–19) correctly points out that there are two types of verbs that can appear in a presentative sentence.[10] One type is what they call "existential" and "positional" verbs such as *you* 'exist, have', *shi* 'be', *zuo* 'sit', *tang* 'lie', *piao* 'float' etc. The other is what they call "verbs of motion", such as *chulai* 'come out', *tao* 'escape', *dao* 'arrive' or *lai* 'come'.

The first type of verbs can appear in the structures represented by the following two schemata:

(54) a. existential verb + presented NP + <u>zai</u> 'at' + locus + (VP)
     b. (<u>zai</u> 'at') + locus + existential verb + presented NP + (VP)

(55a) and (55b) below exemplify these two schemata respectively:

(55) a. you   yi-ge ren   zai waimian jiao   men.
       EXIST one-CL person at   outside knock-at door
       'There was a person (and he) was knocking at the door outside.'
     b. (zai) waimian you   yi-ge ren   jao   men.
       at   outside EXIST one-CL person knock-at door
       'Outside there was a person (and he) was knocking at the door.'

Li and Thompson (1981:511) state that there is a difference between (55a) and (55b) in that the latter but not the former has a sentence-initial locus that should be treated as a topic. This statement is in the main correct. But their claim that only (55b) but not (55a) should be analyzed as a serial verb construction seems to be ill-considered. We have evidence to show that *zai* 'at' in (54a) should be treated as a verb. Compare (56) with (57):

Notic that in (ii) the optional *ta* 'he' in the comment clause is definite. Interesting enough, according to Quick et al. (1972:959), this is the only environment in which in colloquial British English the nominative case relative pronoun can be optionally deleted.

[10] See also Chapter 3 of our discussion of presentive verbs.

(56) you   yi–ge ren   zai waimian.
    Exist one–CL person at   outside
    'There is a person outside.'

(57)*you   yi–ge ren   cong waimian.
    Exist one–CL person from outside

Since *zai waimain* 'at outside' in (56) can be the center of predication while *cong waimian* 'from outside' in (57) cannot, it seems reasonable to assume that *zai* 'at' in this construction is a full verb while *cong* should be regarded as coverb or preposition.[11] If this is the case, then (54a), just like (54b), should be treated as a serial verb construction.

Turning now to the verbs of motion, we find that they occur in one of the three forms represented by (58):

(58) a. existential verb + presented NP + (CV + locative) + V_m + (VP)

   b. (CV) + locative + existential verb + presented NP + V_m + (VP)

   c. locative + V_m + presented NP + (VP)

(59a, b, and c) exemplify these schemata respectively.

(59) a. you   san–ge ren   (cong qianmian) lai le.
        exist three–CL person from front   come PART
        'Three people are coming (in the front).'
    b. (cong) qianmian you   san–ge   ren   lai le.
        from front   exist three–CL person come PART
        'In the front, (there) came three persons.'
    c. qianmian lai–le   san–ge   ren,   dashengde zhengchao–zhe.
        front   come–ASP three–CL person loudly   quarrel–ASP

---

[11]Both Chang (1979) and Chu (1983) give several other tests that can be used to determine how much verbal quality an element has. Most of the tests involve the addition of aspect markers such as *zai*, *–zhe*, *–le*, *–guo*, *–qilai* and verbal reduplication. Many of these aspect markers cannot be used with *zai* 'exist' and *cong* 'from' because of semantic incompatibility.

'In front (there) came three persons, loudly quarreling
(with each other).'

Making allowance for the possible occurrence of a locative coverb phrase which intervenes between the presented NP and the verb of motion as in (a), we can clearly see that the presented NP in (a) and (b) should be treated as the shared NP in a telescopic construction. It is less clear that the presented NP in (c) should be so treated as well. However, as (59c) shows, it can be so treated if the optional VP does occur. So it seems that the solution is clear. In the case of (c), if the optional VP does occur then the sentence should be analyzed as a telescopic construction with a presented function. If it does not occur, then it is a simple sentence with its subject occurring postverbally, just like a weather expression, or *you* 'exist' and *shi* 'be' sentences when they are the only verb in the sentence. These sentences also often have the presentative function even though the presented NP is picked up and commented upon in a separate sentence that follows it. In other words, whether the presented NP is picked up in the same sentence is a matter of discourse strategy.

Since all sentences containing a telescopic structure of this type have the presentative function, we will refer to them as "telescopic-presentative" sentences. There is, however, one great difference in the relationship between the shared NP and the preceding verb among the three subtypes of the telescopic-presentative construction. In the case of *you* 'exist' and other transitive verbs the shared NP is evidently the object of the first verb. In the case of *shi* 'be', it is a nominative complement while in the case of a simple sentence with a motion verb, it is a postposed subject. This being the case we need to modify our definition of telescopic-presentative construction by simply referring to a postverbal NP, rather than specifying that it is the direct object. Whether it is a direct object, a nominative complement, or a subject will, of course, depend on the particular verb that precedes it. So it seems clear that what is important here is not the role that it plays in the first clause but rather that the presented NP should occur postverbally.

So far we have discussed only what Li and Thompson call "realis descriptive clause" in which the shared NP is always indefinite. Our next question is naturally: "What about the 'irrealis descriptive clause'"?

1.2.3.2. Type 3B: Telescopic-Descriptive Construction

Li and Thompson (1981:618) state that there are three differences between the two types of what they call "descriptive clauses". First, the direct object of the first verb in an irrealis clause is not necessarily an indefinite noun phrase; it can be definite, indefinite, or non-referential. Second, the verb of the inrrealis clause always expresses an activity. Finally, the irrealis descriptive clause always expresses an unrealized event. Some examples follow:

(60) women zhong <u>nei zhong cai</u> chi.
    we raise that kind vegetable eat
    'We raise that kind of vegetable to eat.'

(61) wo you <u>yifu</u> xi.
    I have clothes wash
    'I have clothes to wash.'

(62) <u>wo</u> you qian mai shu.
    I have money buy book
    'I have money for buying books.'

(63) <u>gei zhei-ge ren</u> pai <u>yi-ge shijian</u> chongxin jiancha.
    for this-CL person arrange a-CL time again examine
    'Arrange a time for this person to be re-examined.'

(64) a. ta song <u>gei wo</u> <u>nei-ben shu</u> kan.
        he give to me that-CL book read
        'He gave me that book to read.'
     b. ta song <u>nei-ben shu</u> <u>gei wo</u> kan.
        he give that-CL book to me read
        'He gave that book to me to read.'

Li and Thompson's characterization of this type of telescopic construction as presented in 1.1.1.3.2 is in the main correct. They, however, do not explore the structural relationship between the two clauses and the role of the shared NP in each of them. Since we have defined a telescopic construction as one with at least one shared NP between two clauses, we will first go into the structural aspect of the construction.

From the examples just given it is not difficult to see that the shared NP is the direct object of the preceding verb in all cases with a possible exception of (64a and b) where the first verb has two objects, direct and indirect, which occur after it. The question here is whether the indirect object NP also plays a role in the second clause. We will return to this question presently.

Turning now to the relation between the shared NP and the second verb, we find that it spans a wide range of possibilities. In (60) and (61), it is the direct object of the second verb. In (62), it seems to bear the relation of an instrumental adverb to the verb while in (63) the shared NP plays the role of a temporal adverb in the second clause. Taking all these possibilities into consideration, a candidate for the role that the shared NP plays in the second clause strongly suggests itself and that is topic (see Tsao, 1978, 1979 and Chapter 2 of the present volume for a discussion of all the possible relations that a topic can bear to the main verb in the same clause). In addition, the shared NP always occurs at the initial position of the second clause, which, as we have repeatedly pointed out, is the position for topic. Analyzing it as topic of the second clause has the additional advantage of making this type of telescopic construction in line with the others.

There is one thing which distinguishes this type from the others. In the interpretation of this type of telescopic construction an animate agent is always involved.[12] On the basis of the data that we have gathered, the principle seems to be this: If there is an NP in the first clause marked by *gei* as a benefactive as *zhei-ge ren* 'this person' in (63) or as the indirect object as *wo* 'me' in (64), then it is interpreted as the agent in the second clause. If there is no such phrase marked by *gei*, then the topic–subject is so interpreted, as *women* 'we', *wo* 'I' in (60), (61) and (62) respectively. (Those NPs involved in this interpreation are double underlined in the example sentences.)

Actually we have evidence to suggest that this animate NP should also be marked by *gei* in the underlying structure. One piece of syntactic evidence has to do with the occurrence of *gei* phrase immediately before the second verb when no *gei* phrase occurs in the first clause. If the *gei* object NP is coreferential with the topic–subject then *ziji* 'self', the reflexive pronoun, is used. Compare (65) and (66) with (60).

(65) women zhong nei zhong cai   gei ziji chi.
     we   raise that kind vegetable for self eat
     'We raise that kind of vegetable for ourselves to eat.'

---

[12]This is in line with Li and Thompson's characterization that the second clause of this type of telescopic construction expresses an activity.

```
(66) women zhong nei  zhong cai      gei Zhang San chi.
     we    raise that kind  vegetable for Zhang San eat
     'We raise that kind of vegetable for Zhang San to eat.'¹³
```

The *gei* coverb phrase, however, cannot be added when there is an overt *gei* phrase present in the first clause. Compare (67) with (63).

```
(67) ?gei zhei-ge ren     pai      yi-ge shijian gei ta
      for this-CL person arrange  a-CL  time    for him
      chongxin jiancha.
      again    examine
     ?'Arrange a time for this person for him to be re-examined.'
```

But when one of the *gei* phrases is deleted, be it the first or the second, the sentence is again grammatical as (63) and (68) show.

```
(68) pai      yi-ge shijian gei zhei-ge ren     chongxin jiancha.
     arrange a-CL  time    for this-CL person again     examine
     'Arrange a time for this person to be re-examined.'
```

This fact, coupled with the unacceptability of the English translation in (67), strongly suggests that redundancy is the reason here for the ungrammaticality of (67). This also gives us a hint that in the underlying representation there is always a *gei* phrase in sentences of this type. The *gei* phrase is obligatorily deleted when there is another coreferential *gei* phrase in the first clause, but otherwise it is either reflexivized or deleted when the *gei* object NP is coreferential with the topic-subject.

As this type of serial verb construction contains at least one shared NP which plays a role in either of the two adjacent clauses, it should be regarded as a type of telescopic construction, but unlike the other two types of telescopic construction that we disscussed

---

[13]We notice that in the translation of this type of telescopic construction, English often employs the infinitive construction and just as *gei* is used in Chinese to mark the clause subject of this kind, *for* is used in English. We will return to this correspondence in the later section of the chapter.

earlier, the second clause of this type has the function of describing the shared object NP of the first clause. We will, therefore, term it telescopic-descriptive construction.

1.3. Summary and Implications
1.3.1 Summary

Our findings can be summarized in Chart 1.

TYPE / FEATURE	Plain Topic Chain	Telescopic Construction - Pivotal	Telescopic Construction - Presentative	Telescopic Construction - Descriptive
The roles of the shared NPs in the first clause	topic	Do	Do, Nominative complement, or Subject	1. Do 2. Subject, IO or Benefactive ph
The roles of the shared NPs in the second clause	topic	topic	topic	1. topic 2. topic (clause subject)
Refereatial quality of the shared NPs	definite	definite	in definite (in the first clause)	indefinite, definitite or non-referential (in the first cl)

In all, we recognize two major types of serial verb constructions in Chinese, namely, the plain topic chain and the telescopic construction. These two types differ in three important ways. First, in the former the shared NP plays the role of topic in both clauses while in the latter the shared NP is topic of second clause only. Second, because of this difference in the role the shared NP plays in the first clause, the referential requirement is also different. In the case of the plain topic chain, the shared NP is definite or generic while in the case of the telescopic construction, the referential requirement differs among the three different types. Finally, also as a consequence of the first difference, the shared NP plays a double role only in the case of the telescopic construction. In a strict sense, the shared NP in the plain topic chain dose not play a role in the first clause because its absence dose not in any way affect the completness of the first clause while the opposite is true in the telescopic construction. And it is because of this syntactic overlap in the second type that we have termed it the telescopic construction.

We have thus found a well-motivated way of defining what the serial verb construction is in Chinese. We have argued that not only will it be necessary for there to be several unmarked VPs occuring in succession, but that the two adjacent VPs will have to have a shared NP between them and the shared NP always plays the role of topic in the second clause.

We have also seen in the course of our discussion what important function is served by topic in the analysis of Chinese. We have found that even though subject, as defined by the selectional restriction between it and the verb, can be identified from time to time, its role in the analysis of Chinese is much more restricted than that of topic, a conclusion that I have arrived at independently time and again in my previous research. At least we have seen in several places in our previous discussion that the failure to utilize the notion of topic may prevent us from getting at significant generlizations.

Our analysis of the telescopic construction should also by itself be of some interest. We have touched upon areas such as the structural relation between the two clauses in the case of the telescopic—descriptive construction, which have hitherto received very little attention from Chinese linguists.

1.3.2. Implications for Universal Grammatical Theory

One important conclusion that we have arrived at is that topic plays a crucial role in the analysis of the serial verb constructions in Chinese. On the basis of such compelling evidence, one would hypothesize that it should also play an important role in the analysis of similar construction in other languages. There is some evidence to support such a hypothesis. In the past literature, the serial verb construction has been discussed with reference to such African languages as Yoruba, Ijo, Ewe, and Twi and there seems to be a general understanding that it is subject that is involved. Welmers (1973: 367) goes as far as to assert that serialization.....seems to involve actions that can be associated with each other only if they are performed by the same subject. Recently, there is a growing awareness that it is topic that plays an important role here (Philip Davis personal communication). We need more in—depth studies of similar construction in other languages to see whether there is indeed such a common base in the serial verb construction.

Another implication has to do with the telescopic—descriptive construction. In our discussion we have argued that the subject of the second clause in this construction is marked by *gei* in the underlying structure. It is of great interest to note that the corresponding benefactive—dative marker *for* is also used in the corresponding construction in English, as in (69) and (70).

(69)   We raised the vegetagble <u>for Zhang San to eat</u>.[14]

---

[14](69) appeared earlier as the English translation given for (66).

(70) I brought a basket <u>for you to carry the food in</u>.

Such a close correspondence may prompt us to come to a hasty conclusion that certainly in English and in Chinese, and possibly in many other languages, the secondary clause subject is marked by a preposition or its equivalent. Such a generalization, however, should be taken with great reserve since the similarity between the two languages does not go far beyond that.

A closer examination reveals that this use of *gei* in Chinese is much more restricted than its English counterpart. *Gei* as a subject marker only marks an agent in the active sentence and a patient in the passive sentence in this construction. The English counterpart *for* has a considerably wider distribution. It marks all kinds of subject in the infinitive clause. It is the marker of an agentive subject in (69) and (70), a patient subject in (71) and a dummy subject in (72).

(71) Schedule a session <u>for him to be examined</u>.

(72) To call it a serial verb construction it is necessary <u>for there to be at least two verb phrases in a row</u>.

As (72) also shows, *for,* in yet another way, is more general than *gei*. *For* can be used to mark any infinitive in almost any position in a sentence, be it subject, or adjunct, or object, but *gei* in Chinese is restricted to only the telescopic–descriptive construction. This is yet another support for the theory that English is a subject–prominent language while Chinese is a topic–prominent language.

2. COMPOUND SENTENCES AND CLAUSE CONNECTIVES
2.1. Compound Sentences and Clause Connectives Defined

Previously in the discussion of the first type of the so–called "serial verb construction," as exemplified by (73), formerly cited as (41),

(73) we   mao   piao   jin qu.
     I   buy   ticket   enter–go
    (i) 'I bought a ticket and went in.' or
    (ii) 'I bought a ticket to go in.'

we mentioned Li and Thompson's (1981) contention that this type of serial verb construction is used to express only four types of meaning relation, namely, (a) consecutive, (b) purpose, (c) alternating and (d) circumstance. We also mentioned Chu's (1983) comment that Li and Thompson's characterization is too restrictive. That Chu's criticism is fully justified is confirmed by the following examples.

(74) a. ta   zuotian   sheng bing meiyou   lai.
        he yesterday get   sick not: have come
    (i) 'He was sick yesterday and he didn't come.'
    (ii) 'Because he was sick yesterday, he didn't come.'

(75) a. ta qiche chushi   si   le.
        he car   have: an: accident die PART
    (i) 'He had a car accident and he died.' or
    (ii) 'He had a car accident and, as a result, he died.'

From examples like (74a), (75a) and many others previously cited, it is clear that causal relation and that of consequence are actually quite frequent. Furthermore, the relation between the two clauses in (74a) and (75a) can be made explicit by adding clause connectives as in (74b) and (75b).

(74) b. yinwei ta zuotian   sheng bing suoyi meiyou   lai.
        because he yesterday get   sick so   not: have come
    'Becaus he was sick yesterday, he didn't come.'

(75) b. ta qiche chushi   jieguo si   le.
        he car   have: an: accident result die PART
    'He had a car accident and, as a result, he died.'

In our discussion we have also pointed out that sentences like those in (73) – (75) are topic chains, marked or unmarked, and that because the clauses in a chain share a common topic (or common topics), they are felt to be semantically and syntactically related and thus no clause connectives are required syntactically.[15] Of course, when a speaker wants to

---

[15] See also Tsao (1982) for a similar point.

make the meaning relation very explicit, he can then add clause connectives such as *yinwei* 'because', *suoyi* 'so' and *jieguo* 'result'. For ease of reference, those marked by clause connectives are termed "marked topic chains" and those not involving the use of clause connectives "plain (or unmarked) topic chains". They are all instances of compound sentences.

Though most of compound sentences in Chinese are of the form that we have just described, it is not necessary for the two clauses in a compound sentence to form a chain. They can each be a chain (including, of course, a chain of one clause) as exemplified in (76) and (77).

(76) a. ni   bu   qu   wo   qu.
        you   not go   I   go
        'If you won't go, I will.'
     b. <u>ruguo</u> ni   bu   qu   wo   qu.
        if   you not go   I   will
        'Same as (a).'

(77) a. laoshi   zuotian   sheng bing meiyou lai,   women tiqian
        teacher   yesterday get   sick not: have come we   earlier
        fang-xue.
        leave-school
        'Because the teacher was sick (and) didn't come to work, we left school earlier.'
     b. <u>yinwei</u>   laoshi   zuotian   sheng   bing   meiyou   lai
        because   teacher   yesterday get   sick   not: have come
        women   tiqian   fang-xue.
        we   earlier   leave-school
        'Same as (a).'

To sum up, what has been defined as compound sentences consists of four types, as represented in (78).

(78)

	plain	marked
one single topic chain	(74a)	(74b)
two separate topic chains	(77a)	(77b)

Examples like (74a) and (75a) also indicate strongly that it is futile to pursue the distinction between a coordinate compound sentence, i.e., one formed by two independent clause, and a subordinate complex sentence, i.e., one formed by a main clause and an adverbial clause, as Chinese makes no formal distinction between then in many cases. They will, therefore, all be called compound sentences in the present study. In fact, we have much evidence to show that what is traditionally called adverbial clauses should be more properly analyzed as topics, an analysis that we will go into presently.

Let us now turn to clause connectives. So far we have been using the term broadly and we will continue to use it as a general cover term until we can characterize their syntactic properties more precisely. For our present purpose, we will broadly define clause connectives as any constituent that is neither a noun nor a verb (including adjectives), occurring in the first or the second clause to mark the semantic relation between the two, as the underlined parts in (74b), (75b), (79) and (80) show.

(79) ta yi   chi-wan   zaofan   jiu   zou   le.
     he once eat-finish   breakfast then leave PART
     'As soon as he finished breakfast, he left.'

(80) zhe-jian dayi   wo yue   kan,   yue   xihuan.
     this-CL   overcoat I   the: more look   the: more like
     'Speaking of the overcoat, the more I look at it, the more I like it.'

2.2 Traditional Classification of Clause Connectives

The broad definition we just gave is in agreement with most studies of Chinese clause connectives that we are aware of (Chao, 1968; Chu, 1983; Deng, 1980; Guo, 1960; Li and Thompson, 1981; Lu, 1977; Lu et al., 1981 and Wang, 1955). Most of them also adopt a four-way classification of clause connectives, as shematized in (81).

(81)   EXAMPLES   CATEGORY
    a. <u>erqie</u> 'and, also'; <u>suoyi</u> 'so'   conjunction proper
    b. <u>budan</u> 'not only'; <u>yinwei</u> 'because'   adverbial conjunction
    c. <u>hai</u> 'still'; <u>que</u> 'on the contrary'   adverbial connective
    d. ....<u>yue</u> ....<u>yue</u> 'the more...the   repetitive correlative
       more....'   connective

Aside from the fact that the same morpheme is used in the two clauses, Class (d), as far as syntactic behavior is concerned, dose not differ from Class (c). For that reason, it can be grouped together with the latter. Classes (a) and (c) are quite straightforward in that the former class occurs only at the initial position of the second clause as shown in (82), while the latter class never occurs at the initial position of a clause no matter whether it appears at the first or the second clause as shown in (83).

(82) a. ta   zuotion   mei lai, <u>suoyi</u> ta bu zhidao laoshi
        he   yesterday not come so   he not know teacher
        jiao dao   nali.
        teach up: to what: place
        'Since he didn't come yesterday, he dosen't know how far the teacher has covered.'
    b.*ta   zuotian   mei lai, ta <u>suoyi</u> bu zhidao laoshi
        he   yesterday not come he so   not know   teacher
        jiao dao   nali.
        teach up: to what: place
        'Same as (a).'

(83) a. wo quan—le   ta ban—tian, ta <u>que</u>   lian
        I persuade—ASP him half—day he on: the: contrary including
        yiju   hua   ye mei ting—jin—qu.
        one—sentence speech   also not listen—into
        'I persuaded him for a long time but he didn't even take in one word.'

b.*wo quan-le   ta ban-tian, que   ta lian
   I persuade-ASP him half-day on:the contrary he including
   yi-ju   hua   ye mei ting-jin-qu.
   one-sentence speech also not listen-into
   'Same as (a).'

Class (b) connectives, on the other hand, exhibit much more variability as far as their position in the clause is concerned, as shown in (84).

(84) a. yinwei nei-bu   dianying ta mei kan-guo, suoyi bu
        because that-CL movie   he not see-ASP so   not
        zhidao hao-bu-hao.
        know   good-not-good
        'Because he hasn't seen the movie before, he doesn't know whether it is good or not.'
     b. nei-bu   dianying yinwei ta mei kan-guo, suoyi bu
        that-CL movie   because he not see-ASP so   not
        zhidao hao-bu-hao.
        know   good-not-good
        'Roughly, same as (a).'
     c. nei-bu   dianying ta yinwei mei kan-guo, suoyi bu
        that-CL movie   he because not see-ASP so   not
        zhidao hao-bu-hao
        know   good-not-good
        'Roughly, same as (a).'

Notice that Class (b) connectives, as exemplified by *yinwei* 'because' in (84), sometimes behave like a conjunction proper in being able to occur clause-initially, and sometimes behave like an adverb in occurring in a position between the primary topic and the main verb of the clause. This being the case, most traditional grammarians call the class "adverbial conjunction" to show its hybrid nature.

Actually, this observation of the surface word order is misleading. As we will present ample evidence to argue, Class (b) connectives are conjunctions proper like those in Class (a). Their surface positional variation is actually due to its interaction with topics of various ranks and will be accounted for in a later section by the rule of topic-raising. But before we embark on that, we have to take up adverbial clauses in general.

2.3. Clauses of Condition, Time, Concession & Reason as Topics

Haiman (1978) convincingly argues on morpho-syntactic and semantic grounds that the conditional clause in many languages, English, Chinese, Japanese and Hua, a Papuan language, among them, should be treated as a topic. Chao (1968), whom Haiman cited for support, actually argues that in Chinese, time, concessional, and reason clauses, just like conditional ones, should all be analyzed as topics, though terminology-wise he prefers to call it subject.[16] He gives three convincing reasons for his analysis (see Sections 2.3.1., 2.3.2., and 2.3.3. for detail). In addition, my own research of the topic phenomenon in Chinese in the past has yielded a couple more. These arguments will be presented in the following sections one by one.

2.3.1. Placement of Pause Particles

It is a well-known fact that four pause particles can be optionally placed after the topic as in (85b) — (85e) These particles mean different things but the difference between them is so subtle that it is very difficult to bring it out in a simple sentence like (85).

(85) a. Zhang San shu nian-wan le.
       Zhang San book study-finish PART
       'Speaking of Zhang San, (he) has finished his study.'
    b. Zhang San ⎡me shu nain-wan le.
    c.   ⎢ne
    d.   ⎨ba
    e.   ⎣a
       Zhang San PART book study-finish PART
       'Same as (a).'

---

[16]Chao (1968) and Lü et al. (1981) both call the sentence-initial constituent "subject". But it is very clear from the examples and analyses they give that what they call "subject" is in my framework the primary topic. For a detailed comment on Chao's analysis of "subject" see Tsao, 1979 Chapter 2.

Now notice the close parallel between pause particles after conditional clauses and those after the topic.

(86) a. yaoshi xia—qi   yu   lai, zanmen jiu   bie
      if   fall—ASP rain ASP   we   then don't
      chuqu   le.
      go—out PART
      'If it starts to rain, we'd better not go out.'
   b. yaoshi xia—qi   yu   lai me, rang we   kan
      if   fall—ASP rain ASP PART let   me   see
      zenme   ban.
      how   do
      'If it starts to rain (hesitation), let me see what shall we do.'
   c. yaoshi xia—qi   yu   lai ne, na   bu   yaojin.
      if   fall—ASP rain ASP PART that not matter
      'If it is (a question of) starting to rain, that won't matter.'
   d. yaoshi xia—qi   yu   lai ba, zanmen zuo
      if   fall—ASP rain ASP PART we   take
      che   ba.
      car   PART
      'If it is (the alternative of) starting to rain, we will take a car.'
   e. yaoshi xia—qi   yu   lai a,   na   jiu
      if   fall—ASP rain ASP PART that then
      zaogao le.
      mess   PART
      'If it should start to rain, that would be a mess.'

Sentences in (86) and the interpretations given are all cited from Chao (1968: 118).Because the functions of these four particles have so far received scanty attention, their meanings are somehow unclear and not every one will agree with Chao on some of the interpretations, but the fact remains that syntactically conditional clauses, just like topic, can be followed by one of the four pause particles. As a matter of fact, not only the conditional clause but also the other three types of clause can each be followed by a pause particle as shown by sentences (87) – (89).

(87) ta   lai   de   shihou (a),   jiao ta   deng
     he   come   Rel. Mar. time   PART   ask   him   wait
     yi–xia.
     a–while
     'When he comes, ask him to wait a while.'

(88) suiran   ta   bu   yonggong   (me), zong–suan
     although he   not   work: hard PART   after–all
     kao–jige   le.
     pass: test PART
     'Although he didn't study hard, he, after all, passed the test.'

(89) yinwei   ta   meiyou   qian   (ne), suoyi bu
     because   he   not: have   money PART   so   not
     neng lai.
     can   come
     'Because he didn't have any money. he couldn't come.'

2.3.2. Optional Occurrence of Some General Words as Head NPs

As many of these clause are translatable into English adverbial clauses, many grammarians have analyzed them as adverbial clauses in Chinese as well. But they should be more appropriately analyzed as complex NPs containing a relative clause at least in the underlying structure since general head NPs such as those listed in (90) can all optionally occur.

(90) .....de hua   'the case that.....', 'the event that ......'
     .....de shihou   'the time that....'
     .....de na yi
          tian   'the day that...'
     .....zhi hou   'the time after....'[17]

---

[17] *Zhi* is the Classical Chinese counterpart of Modern Chinese *de*. *Zhihou* 'after' and *zhiqian* 'before' are clearly reminants of Classical Chinese. In the same context, *yihou*

.....zhi qian 'the time before....'

.....de { yuanyin / yuangu / liyou } 'the reason that....'

Now witness the following examples.

(91) a. yaoshi ta ken jiaru, women jiu keyi
     if   he willing join we   then can
    zucheng yi dui le.
    form   a team PART
    'If he is willing to join us, we can form a team.'

b. yaoshi ta ken jiaru de hua, women jiu
   if   he willing join Rel. Mar. case we   then
   keyi zucheng yi dui le.
   can form   a team PART
   '(In) the event that he is willing to join us,
   we can form a team.'

(92) a. ta lai kan wo, shou shi kongkong de.
    he come see me hand be empty   PART
    'When he came to see me, (his) hands were empty.'

b. ta lai kan wo de shihou, shou shi kongkong de.[18]
   he come see me Rel. Mar. time hand be empty   PART
   'Same as (a).'

(93) a. wei-le que shao lüfei, ta mei neng lai
    because lack   travel-expense he not can come
    'Because he didn't have enough travel expenses, he couldn't come.'

'after' and *yiqian* 'before' can be used. The origin of the latter two, however, is less apparent.

[18](92b) can sometimes be preceded by *dang* 'at', which will be analyzed as a preposition having the whole NP as its object. The presence of *dang* 'at', however, does not affect our argument that the whole time expression is a topic. This is because in Chinese a prepositional phrase can, in a more restricted way, be a topic as well.

b. wei-le que-shao lüfei de yuangu,
because lack travel-expenses Rel. Mar. reason
ta mei neng lai.
he not can come
'Same as (a).'

So far we have not mentioned the Chinese equivalent of the English adverbial clause of place. An important reason for this is that the Chinese counterpart in this case is always realized with a head NP such as *-de difang* 'the place that.....' or *-de na-ge chengshi* 'the city where ....' Here we have even stronger reason for analyzing it as a complex NP containing a relative clause with a head.

Examine the sentences in (94).

(94) a. dajia yonggong de difang, ni bu neng
everybody study REL place you not can
dasheng shuohua.
loudly speak
'Where everybody is studying, you must not talk loudly.'
b.*dajia yonggong, ni bu neng dasheng shuohua.
everybody study you not can loudly speak
'Same as (a).'[19]

2.3.3. The Position of the Clause in Question

One of the grammatical characteristics of the primary topic is that it almost always occurs in the initial position of the sentence in which it overtly occurs as in (95a). Occasionally, it can occur sentence-finally as in (95b). When this happens, it is interpreted as an afterthought.

(95) a. na-zhong zhi, yi-zhang wu fen qian.
that-kind paper a-sheet five cent money
'That kind of paper, (it) five cents a sheet.'

---

[19](94b) can be grammatical if it means either (i) 'When everybody is studying you must not talk loudly' or (ii) 'If everybody is studying, you must not talk loudly.'

b. yi-zhang wu fen qian, na-zhong   zhi.
      a-sheet   five cent money that-kind paper
      'A sheet is five cents, that kind of paper.'

Again the type of clause in question most frequently occurs in the initial position of a sentence as in (96a) and (97a). Occasionally, it may occur sentence-finally as in (96b) and (97b). When this happens, it is, like a sentence-final primary topic, interpreted as an afterthought.

(96) a. ruguo ni bu xiang qu, ni keyi bu qu.
        if   you not want go you can not go
        'If you don't want to go, you don't have to.'
     b. ni keyi bu qu, reguo ni bu xiang qu.
        you can not go if   you not want go
        'you don't have to go, if you don't want to.'

(97) a. suiran tianqi hen   huai, wo haishi yao   qu.
        though weather very bad   I still want go
        'Though the weather is very bad, I still want to go.'
     b. wo haishi yao qu, suiran tianqi hen   huai.
        I still want go though weather very bad
        'I still want to go, though the weather is very bad.'

2.3.4. Referential Constraint of the Clause in Question

Another grammatical characteristic of the primary topic is that it is referentially definite, generic or at least specific in the case of existential topic. Compare the (a), (b), (c) and (d) sentences in (98).

(98) a. <u>na-ge   ren</u>   zai men-qian mai   shuazi.
        that-CL person   in door-front sell brush
        'That man, (he) is selling brushes in front of the door.'
     b. <u>you yi-ge ren</u> zai menqian   mai shuazi
        exit one-Cl person   in door-front sell brush
        'There is a man selling brushes in front of the door.'

c. *<u>yi-ge ren</u> zai men-qian mai shuazi.
   one-CL person in door-front sell brush
d. <u>xiangxia ren</u> xihuan zai men-qian mai shuazi,
   country people love in door-front sell brush
   'Country people love to sell brushes in front of the door.'

Now examine the close parallel we have with regard to the clause in question.

(99) a. <u>shang-ci wo qu kan ta de shihou</u>, ta
        last-time I go see him Rel. Mar time he
        ganghao bu zai jia.
        happen not at home
        'Last time (when) I went to see him, he happened to be out.'
     b. <u>you yi-ci wo qu kan ta de shihou</u>, ta
        exit one-time I go see him Rel. Mar. time he
        ganghao bu zai jia.
        happen not at home
        'Once (when) I went to see him, he happened to be out.'
     c. *<u>yi-ci wo qu kan ta de shihou</u>, ta ganghao
        one-time I go see him Rel. Mar. time he happen
        bu zai jia.
        not at home
     d. <u>mei-yi-ci wo qu kan ta de shihou</u>, ta dou
        every-time I go see him Rrl. Mar. time he all
        bu zai jia.
        not at home
        'Every time (when) I go to see him, he is out.'

2.3.5. The Clause in question as the *Ba* NP, *Lian* NP and the Compared NP

We have previously pointed out that the *ba* NP in the *ba* construction, the *lian* constituent in the *lian* construction and the *bi* constituent in the comparative structure, as exemplified in (100a), (101a), and (102a), are all topics.

(100) a. ta <u>ba na-zhong zhi</u> na-le   yi zhang
         he BA that-kind paper take-ASP a sheet
         'He took a sheet of paper of that kind.'

(101) a. <u>lian   wo</u> ta dou bu   zhende.
         including me he all not recognize
         'Even me, he couldn't recognize.'

(102) a. ta <u>Yingyu</u> bi <u>Fayu</u> shuo de hao.
         he English COMP French speak DE well
         'He speaks English better than French.'

Now compare the (b) sentences in (100) through (102) with their (a) counterparts respectively.

(100) b. wo de   <u>ba ta nain-shu de   difang</u> dasao-ganjing.
         I have: to BA he study-book-Rel. Mar. place sweep-ganjing.
         'I have to clean the place where he studies.'

(101) b. <u>lian   jiaoshou yanjiang de   shihou</u>, ta
         including professor lecture Rel. Mar. time   he
         dou zai jianghua.
         all ASP speak
         'Even when the professor was giving a lecture, he was talking.'

(102) b. <u>ta zai jia de   shihou</u> bi <u>zai xuexiao de</u>
         he at home Rel. Mar. time   COMP at school Rel. Mar.
         <u>shihou</u> hua shuo de shao.
         time   word say DE little
         'He talks less when he is home than when he is at school.'

Since the type of clause in question can be the *ba* NP, the *lian* constituent or the compared constituent, it is a topic as well.

2.3.6. Parallel Between a Phrase Topic and the Clause in Question

We have also pointed out that temporal, locative and reason phrases, as exemplified in the (a) sentences of (103) through (105), can all be topics.

(103) a. <u>shang-ge Xingqitian</u>, ta dai-zhe haizi qu
    last-CL Sunday   he take-ASP child go
    gongyuan wan.
    park   play
    'Last Sunday, he took along his child to the park to play.'

(104) a. <u>na-ge difang</u>, bu neng shuohua.
    that-CL place not can talk
    '(At) that place, (you) must not talk.'

(105) a. <u>weile haizi de jiauyu</u>,   ta chi-le
    for child POSS education he suffer-ASP
    duoshao ku.
    much   hardship
    'For his children's education, he suffered much hardship.'

Now examine the close parallel between a temporal phrase and temporal clause, a locative phrase and a locative clause etc. by comparing the (b) sentences in (103) through (105) with their (a) counterparts respectively.

(103) b. <u>bu xia-yu de shihou</u>, ta dai-zhe haizi
    not fall-rain Rel. Mar. time he take-ASP child
    qu gongyuan wan.
    go park   play
    'When it is not raining, he takes along his child to the park to play.'

(104) b. <u>gege nian-shu de difang</u>, bu neng shuohua.
    older-brother study Rel. Mar. place not can talk
    '(At) the place where my older brother studies, (you) must not talk.'

(105) b. weile   rang haizi shang daxue,   ta
   in: order: that let child go   university he
   chi—le   duoshao ku.
   suffer—ASP much   hardship
   'In order that his child may go to college, he suffered much hardship.'

It is clear from the close parallelism that we have demonstrated that if temporal, locative and reason phrases can be topics, then temporal locative and reason clauses can also be.

 To summarize, we have presented six compelling arguments in support of the claim first made by Chao (1968) that the Chinese clauses translatable into English as temporal, locative, concessive, reason or conditional clause should in Chinese be more appropriately analyzed as topics.

2.3.7. An Apparent Counterexample

 There seems to be a group of sentences that counters our analysis of treating these clauses as topics. Examine the following examples.

(106) a. $\underline{ta}_i$ zou chuqu de   shihou, _____$_i$ faxian deng
   he walk out Rel. Mar. time   find   light
   hai   meiyou guan.
   still not   shut—off
   'When he walked out, he found that the lights were not yet shut off.'
  b.*$\underline{\text{ta zou chuqu de}\quad\quad\text{shihou}}_i$, _____$_i$ faxian deng
   he walk out   Rel. Mar. time   find   light
   hai   meiyou guan.
   still not   shut—off

(107) a. $\underline{wo}_i$ yinwei meiyou   shijian suoyi _____$_i$
   I   because not: have time   so

mei mai liwu.
not buy gift
'Because I didn't have time, I didn't buy a gift.'

b.*wo yinwei meiyou shijian$_i$ suoyi _____$_i$

I because not:have time   so

mei mai liwu.
not buy gift

It is clear that in (106) and (107) it is the topic of the clause in question, namely, *ta* 'he' in (106) and *wo* 'I' in (107), rather than the whole clause, namely, *ta zou chuqu de shihou* 'when he walked out' or *wo yinwei meiyou shijian* 'because I didn't have time' that is the topic of each sentence because only the former is in control of identical topic deletion in the topic chain.

This apparent incongruity in the identification of topic can be fully resolved if we assume that there is a rule of topic—raising, whose effect is to relate sentences like (107c) to sentences like (107a).

(107) c. yinwei wo$_i$ meiyou shijian, suoyi wo$_i$ mei mai liwu.

because I not:have time   so   I   not buy gift

'Same as (a).'

The rule has the additional advantage of explaining why clause connectives such as *yinwei* 'because', *suiran* 'although' and many others can occur after topics. One may, however, raise the question of the validity of the rule because it violates Ross' Complex NP constraint in that some constituents contained in a complex NP such as *ta zou chugu de shihou* '(at) the time he walked out' are moved out of it by the rule. Such a difficulty, however, is only apparent. To begin with, it is not exactly clear even today how such a constraint, if there is one, is to be formulated (see Huang, 1984 and Xu, 1986 for two different views). More importantly, Chao (1968), on the basis of phonological evidence, has pointed out that *-de shihou* 'time that', *-de hua* 'case that' and many others can be regarded as enclitics (p.120). When this happens, we would argue that the NP in question is no longer "complex" as Ross (1967) defines it and the raising of constituents out of it will not constitute any violation of the constraint.

2.4 Topic—raising and the Placement of Clause Connectives
2.4.1 Previous Discussion of the Placement of Clause Connectives

As far as I know, no grammarians up to date have been able to give a precise description of the positions that Group (b) connectives can occur. Take a recent example. Lü et al. (1981) characterize the position of *suiran* 'although' and others like it as being able to occur "before or after the subject" (p. 454).[20] This statement can be exemplified by the sentences in (108) and (109).

(108) a. suiran *ta* bu xihuan na—jian dongxi, keshi haishi mai le.
      though he not like   that—CL thing but   still   buy PART
      'Even though he didn't like the thing, (he) still bought it.'
   b. *ta* suiran bu xihuan na—jian dongxi, keshi haishi mai le.
      he though not like   that—CL thing but   still   buy PART
      'Same as (a).'

(109) a. yinwei *wo* meiyou   qian, suoyi mei chuqu.
      because I not:have money so   not out:go
      'Because I had no money, I didn't go out.'
   b. *wo* yinwei   meiyou   qian, suoyi mei chuqu.
      I because not:have money so   not out:go
      'Same as (a).'

While the description, as stated by Lü et al., seems to be able to take care of examples like (108) and (109), it can easily be shown that it is so imprecise that there is no way to prove whether it is correct or not. To begin with, most grammarians, with the exception of Li and Thompson (1981), Lü et al. (1981) and Chao (1968), take the notion of subject in Chinese for granted. As a result, one does not know whether sentences like (110) are accounted for by their descriptions or not simply because one does not know whether *na—jian shi* in (110) is to be regarded as the subject or not.

---

[20] Li and Thompson describe it as being able to occur either in the sentence—initial position or after the subject or topic (1981:635). One serious problem with this description is, among other things, that where the subject and the topic are not the same, one is completely at a loss. See Note 21 for further discussion.

(110) <u>na-jian shi</u>　　suiran <u>ni</u> mei gen ta shuo, ta
　　　 that-CL matter though you not to him tell he
　　　 haishi zhidao le.[21]
　　　 still know PART
　　　 'With regard to the matter, even though you didn't tell him,
　　　 he knew it anyway.'

Even for grammarians like Lü et al. (1981), Li and Thompson (1981) and Chao (1968) who define subject and/or topic clearly, the term "after" in the description still begs the question. If it is taken to mean "immediately after", then it is falsified by sentences like (111) and (112) and if it doesn't mean that, then it doesn't mean anything at all because there can be indefinitely many positions after "subject".

(111) <u>Xiao Zhang zuotian</u>　　suiran bu shufu,　　keshi
　　　 Xiao Zhang yesterday though not feel:well but
　　　 haishi qu shangban le.
　　　 still go work PART
　　　 'Although yesterday Xiao Zhang didn't feel well, he still went
　　　 to work.'

(112) <u>Xiao Zhang na-ben shu</u>　yinwei　mei nian-guo,
　　　 Xiao Zhang that-CL book because not read-ASP
　　　 suoyi bu zhidao hao bu hao.
　　　 so not know good not good
　　　 'Because Xiao Zhang has never read the book, he does not know
　　　 whether it is good or not.'

The problem presented by sentences like (111) and (112) is quite clear. What is involved is more than subject and/or topic as they are usually understood. We need a term that can cover all the elements that can occur immediately after what we call "the primary

---

[21]The problem that (110) creates for Li and Thompson is that if we take *na-jian shi* 'that matter' to be topic and *ni* 'you' to be subject, then their statement that the clause connective can occur "after the subject or topic" is tautologous because in (110) it occurs between the topic and the subject.

topic". As we have argued on independent grounds that various constituents that can occur in that position should be called "the secondary topic" in counterdistinction with the primary topic, the solution suggests itself. We will assume that in the underlying structure Class (b) connectives, just like those in Class (a), occur in the clause—initial COMP (complementizer) position and because various clause topics can be raised to become sentential topics, the clause connectors thus appear in positions after these various topics in the surface structure.

2.4.2 The Rule of Topic—Raising

Following Huang's (1982) suggestion, we will present a multi—topic clause in Chinese as (113).[22]

(113) $[_{\bar{S}}\text{COMP}[_S\text{Topic}_1[_S\text{Topic}_2....]]]]$

Now assuming that only two clauses, each with no more than two topics, are involved and that such connectives as *suiran* 'although', *yinwei* 'because' and ... *de shihou* 'time that, when' are placed in COMP (complementizer), then the rule of topic—raising can be roughly formulated as (114).

(114) Topic—Raising (optional)

Part (a)
$[_{\bar{S}}\text{COMP}[_S\text{Topic}_{a1}[_S\text{Topic}_{a2}[_S.....]]]] +$
$[_{\bar{S}}\text{COMP}[_S\text{Topic}_{b1}[_S\text{Topic}_{b2}[_S.....]]]] \rightarrow$
$[_{\bar{S}}\text{Topic}_i + \text{Topic}_j[_{\bar{S}}\text{COMP}[_S e_i[_S e_j[_S.....]]]] +$
$[_{\bar{S}}\text{COMP}[_S e_i[_S e_j[_S.....]]]]]$

Tp=Topic

---

[22]Huang (1982:89) actually proposes two possible representations as shown in (i) and (ii) below:
   (i) $[_{\bar{S}}\text{COMP}[_S\text{Topic}[_S\text{Topic}[_S.....]]]]$
  (ii) $[_{\bar{\bar{S}}}\text{COMP}[_{\bar{S}}\text{Topic}[_{\bar{S}}\text{Topic}[_S.....]]]]$

However, he is not quite determinate as to which one is the correct representation. We have arbitrarily chosen (i) merely as a matter of convenience.

Condition: Both (i) Tp_{a1} and Tp_{b1} have the same referential index;
and (ii) Tp_{a2} and Tp_{b2} have the same referential index.

Part (b)
$[_{\bar{S}}COMP[_S Topic_{a1}[_S Topic_{a2}[_S .....]]]] +$
$[_{\bar{S}}COMP[_S Topic_{b1}[_S Topic_{b2}[_S .....]]]] \rightarrow$
$[_{\bar{S}} Topic_i + Topic_j [_{\bar{S}}COMP[_S e_i[_S e_j[_S .....]]]] +$
$[_{\bar{S}}COMP[_S e_i[_S Topic_{b2}[_S .....]]]]]$

Tp=Topic

Condition: Both (i) Tp_{a1} and Tp_{b1} have the same referential index;
and (ii) Tp_{a2} and Tp_{b2} have contrastive stress.

Part (c)
$[_{\bar{S}}COMP[_S Topic_{a1}[_S Topic_{a2}[_S .....]]]] +$
$[_{\bar{S}}COMP[_S Topic_{b1}[_S Topic_{b2}[_S .....]]]] \rightarrow$
$[_{\bar{S}} Topic_i [_{\bar{S}}COMP[_S e_i[_S Topic_{a2}[_S .....]]]] +$
$[_{\bar{S}}COMP[_S Topic_{b1}[_S Topic_{b2}[_S .....]]]]]$

Condition: Both Tp_{a1} and Tp_{b1} have contrastive stress.

Postponing our discussion of the justification of the rule until the next section, here we will take up five additional points in connection with the rule. First, the rule is in three parts because the conditions are all different and the outputs are different as well. Part (b) is necessitated by sentences like (115) and (116) and part (c) by sentences like (117).

(115) <u>ta erduo</u> suiran zhang de bu zemeyang, <u>yanjing</u> que
he ears though grow DE not so:great eyes   on:the:contrary
zhang de hen hao.
grow DE very well

'Speaking of him, even though his ears are not really great, his eyes are beautiful.'

(116) <u>Xiao Zhang</u> <u>ping-shi</u>   suiran ping   de hen hao,
Xiao Zhang criticize-poetry though criticize DE very well
<u>xie-shi</u>   que   xie de bu zemeyang.
write-poetry on:the:contrary write DE not so:great
'Speaking of Xiao Zhang, although he is quite good at poetic criticism, he is not so good at writing poetry.'

(117) <u>wo</u> suiran mei ba Xiao Zhang —de dizhi   gaosu ta, <u>ta</u>
I   though not BA Xiao Zhang POSS address tell him he
haishi ba ta zhaodao le.
still BA him find   PART
'Although I didn't tell him Xiao Zhang's address, he still had him found.'

The fact that both referential identity and contrastive stress should play a part in conditioning the rule is anything but surprising. Tsao (1979, Chapter 6) has found that with regard to the subsequent discourse, topic has either the "chaining function", i.e., clauses sharing the same topic are put together into a topic chain, or the "contrastive function", i.e., it is a fixed slot in a clause in which two elements, each occurring in that slot in two successive clauses, can be contrasted. The two conditioning factors are, therefore, a genuine reflection of these two functions of topic.

However, the role that phonological stress plays in a syntactic rule and how a grammatical theory should handle that is still very unclear at present. This is so because both in Chomsky's Standard Theory and more recent Extended Standard Theory syntax has been assumed as independent or autonomous. It therefore follows that phonology should play no role in syntactic rules and yet as Baker (1978) has clearly demonstrated, stress or the lack of it, is clearly needed in a syntactic rule in English which is termed "Auxiliary Shift" by him and which is formulated as follows:

(118) $\quad$ NP $-$ Adv. $-\begin{Bmatrix} M \\ \text{have} \\ \text{be} \end{Bmatrix}$ Tns $-$ X

$\qquad\qquad\qquad\qquad\quad$ <−stress>
$\qquad\qquad\quad$ 1 $\qquad$ 2 $\qquad\quad$ 3 $\qquad\quad$ 4
$\implies$ 1, $\quad$ 3+2, $\quad$ 0, $\quad$ 4

This rule is needed to account for the syntactic facts demonstrated by the following sentences, where stressed words are capitalized.

(119) $\quad$ a. Fritz probably WILL be working when you arrive.
$\qquad\quad$ b.*Fritz WILL probably be working when you arrive.

(120) $\quad$ a. John has admired Sue only since last year, but Bill ALWAYS has.
$\qquad\quad$ b.*John has admired Sue only since last year, but Bill has ALWAYS.

Since, as I just stated, not much is known about the role of phonological stress in a grammatical theory envisaged by Chomsky and his followers, the transformational rule formulated in (114) should be regarded as very tentative and I have chosen to follow the model only eclectically. In other words, I am taking the grammatical model provided by Chomsky in spirit, not in letter.

Second, the raised topics should be Chomsky−adjoined to the $\overline{S}_1$ so that they are the left sisters of S_1 and S_2. In this way the raised topics c−command their traces or pronominal copies. And if we make the further assumption that the raised topics and their traces or pronominal copies are coindexed, then the traces of the raised topics or their pronominal copies are properly bound according to G−B theory.[23]

Third, *dang* 'at' can occur at the beginning of a clause containing ... *de shihou* 'time that; when' and *zai* 'at' can occur clause−initially in a locative clause with the connective ... *de difang* 'place that; where'. When this happens, topic−raising is blocked, as attested by the ungrammaticality of (121 b).

---

[23]C−command: A C−commands B if and only if the first branching node dominating A also dominates B and A does not itself dominate B (van Riemsdijk, H. and Williams, E., 1986, p. 142).

Proper−binding: An anaphor (including trace) must be properly bound (i.e., coindexed and C−commanded) by its antecedent (including moved phrases) (van Riemsdijk and Williams, op. cit., p. 143).

(121) a. dang wo diyi ci kan–dao ta de   shihou, wo
         at I first time see him Rel. Mar. time   I
         shi chi–le   yi jing.
         SHI suffer–ASP one surprise
         'When I first saw him, I indeed was shocked.'
    b.*wo dang diyi ci kan–dao ta de shihou, wo
         I at   first time see him REL time   I
         shi chi–le   yi jing.
         SHI suffer–ASP one surprise

Since *dang* 'at' and *zai* 'at' are both prepositions, this means that when the NP is governed by a preposition, raising is blocked.

Fourth, in our rule we assume that in each clause there are no more than two topics. Even though in theory there can be indefinitely many topics, in actuality, topics that are raised seldom exceed two. Also topics that are governed by a marker like *ba, lian* or *dui* 'to, toward' seem to resist raising, suggesting that these markers, which are all evolved from verbs, haven't lost all their verbal qualities yet.

Finally, the rule is optional in Modern Chinese, as along with sentences such as (122) and (123), which are to be expected according to the rule, we have grammatical sentences like (124), where the condition is met but the rule does not apply.

(122) yinwei ni meiyou   lai, dajia–de   xingzhi
      because you not:have come everybody–POSS interest
      dou cha   le.
      all decrease PART
      'Because you didn't come, people's interest decreased.'

(123) ni yinwei meiyou   lai, suoyi bu zhidao
      you because not:have come so   not know
      dangshi–de   qingxing.
      that–time–POSS situation
      'Because you didn't come, you don't know the situation at that time.'

(124) yinwei <u>ni</u> meiyou lai, suoyi <u>ni</u> bu zhidao
because you not:have come so you not know
dangshi-de qingxing.
that-time-POSS situation
'Same as (123).'

Although many native speakers that I have checked feel that (123) is to be preferred over (124), none regard (124) as ungrammatical (see Chao, 1968:114, for a similar comment). The situation in Classical Chinese, as far as we can make out, is very much the same. Examine the following sentences in Classical Chinese.[24]

(125) zong <u>shang</u> bu sha wo, <u>wo</u> du bu
even:if superior not kill me I alone not
kui yu xin hu? (−Same Topic, −Raising)
feel:ashamed at heart PART
'Even if my superior will not kill me, how can I not feel ashamed at heart?'
("The Biographies of Zhang Er and Chen Yu," *Historical Records*)

(126) zong <u>wo</u> bu wang, <u>zi</u> ning bu lai? (+Contrastive Topic)
even:though I not go you willing not come
'Even though I do not go (to see you), why don't you come?'
("Songs of Cheng," *Book of Poetry*)

(127) qie <u>yu</u> zong bu de da zang, <u>yu</u>
moreover I even:if not receive grand funeral I
si yu daolu hu? (+Same Topic, +Raising)
die on road PART

---

[24]By citing examples from various periods of Classical Chinese, no claim is being made that Classical Chinese, as it is usually understood, is a stationary language of no change. Nothing can be farther from the truth as Wang Li has admirably shown in his monumental work, *Hanyu Shi Gao* (The History of the Chinese Language). The assumption we are making is simply that there is as yet no evidence to shown that there was a change with regard to the rule of Topic-raising occurring some time in the long history of Classical Chiness.

'Moreover, even if I will not receive a grand funeral (as a nobleman), will I die on the roadside (without a proper burial)?'
("Zi-han," *Analects*)

(128) wu₁ shi₂   sui   neng jiyi,   ___₁ ___₂ yi wei zhi
      I   that:time though can remember   also not know
      qi yan zhi bei   ye. (+Same Topics, +Raising)
      his words POSS sadness PART
      'Even though at that time I was able to remember (them), I, too,
      was not able to know the sadness of his words.'
      (Han Yu, "Ji Shi-er Lang Wen")

(129) Lao-pu_i   sui qi   Jiangjun_j sui gui,   ___j
      Old-servant though debased General   though eminent
      ningke yi   shi   duo   hu? (+Contrastive Topic, +Raising)
      how:can with power snatch PART
      'Even though I, Old Servant, is debased and you, General, is eminent,
      how can you snatch it away from me with your power?'
      ("The Biography of Marquis Wei Chi," *Historical Records*)

On the basis of these examples and many others we can find, it is clear that although clause connectives themselves, like many nouns and verbs, have become disyllabic, e.g. *sui* → *suiran* 'though', their interaction with topics, both primary and non-primary, as captured by the rule of Topic-raising, remains intact.

2.4.3 Justifications for the Rule of Topic-Raising

Apart from the most important justification that such a rule is needed to account for the distribution of this class of clause connectives in Modern and Classical Chinese, we can give the following additional reasons in support of the rule.

First, recently Mei (1987) has argued convincingly that the (b) sentences in (130) and (131) are derived from (a) sentences through topicalization and then the (c) sentences are further derived from the (b) sentences through a rule of what he calls "Topic-raising"[25]

---

[25]Mei's argument is roughly that since we have independent reasons to assume that in Chinese there is also a distinction between tensed and non-tensed sentences and yet the NP movement rule as exemplified by (130c) does not follow the tensed sentence condition

(130) a. kanqilai Xiao Zhang hui ying.
　　　　seem　　 Xiao Zhang will win
　　　　'It seems that Xiao Zhang will win.'
　　b. kanqilai <u>Xiao Zhang</u> hui yin.
　　　　　　　　　topic
　　　　seem　　 Xiao Zhang will win
　　　　'Same as (a).'
　　c. Xiao Zhang kanqilai hui ying.
　　　　Xiao Zhang seem　　 will win
　　　　'Xiao Zhang seems to be winning.'[26]

(131) a. keneng　 ta hui lai.
　　　　possible he will come
　　　　'It is possible that he will come.'
　　b. keneng　 <u>ta</u>　 hui lai.
　　　　　　　　 topic
　　　　possible he　　 will come
　　　　'It is possible that he will come.'
　　c. ta keneng　 hui lai.
　　　　he possible will come
　　　　'He is likely to come.'

　　Although Mei does not mention it, it is actually possible to raise more than one topic from the embedded clause. This, we believe, constitutes another argument for his rule of Topic—raising. Compare sentences in (132) and (133) with those in (130) and (131) respectively.

(TSC) posited by Chomsky (van Riemsdijk and Williams, 1986: 118). He therefore argues that the subject in the tensed S first moved to the topic position and is subsequently raised. Since his argument is couched in the most recent G—B Theory of Transformational Grammar, it will take us too far afield to review it here.

　　[26]It is certainly an idiosyncratic property of the English verb "possible" that it disallows "subject—raising".

(132) a. kanqilai Xiao Zhang hui ying na–chang qiu.
　　　　seem　 Xiao Zhang will win　that–CL ball:game
　　　　'It seems that Xiao Zhang will win the game.'
　　b. kanqilai na–chang qiu　　　Xiao Zhang hui ying.

　　　　seem　 that–CL ball:game Xiao Zhang will win
　　　　'Same as (a).'
　　c. na–chang qiu　　　Xiao Zhang kanqilai hui ying.
　　　　that–CL ball:game Xiao Zhang seem　　will win
　　　　'As for that game, Xiao Zhang seems to be winning it.[27]
　　d. na–chang qiu　　　kanqilai Xiao Zhang hui ying.[28]
　　　　that–CL ball:game seem　　Xiao Zhang will win
　　　　'As for that game, it seems that Xiao Zhang will win it.'

(133) a. keneng　 ta mingtian hui lai.
　　　　possible he tomorrow will come
　　　　'It is possible that he will come tomorrow.'
　　b. keneng　 mingtian ta hui lai.

　　　　possible tomorrow he will come
　　　　'It is possible that tomorrow he will come.'
　　c. mingtian ta keneng　 hui lai.

　　　　tomorrow he possible will come
　　　　'Tomorrow he may come.'
　　d. mingtian keneng　 ta hui lai.
　　　　tomorrow possible he will come
　　　　'Tomorrow it is possible that he will come.'

It is clear from the above examples that not only the primary topic but also the

---

[27]We realize that the English translation in (132c) with its reading of imminent future does not mean exactly the same as that of (132a). But structure–wise, it is the closest that we can find in English. It is therefore used.

[28]There are several other possibilities besides (132c) and (132d), which space consideration prevents us from spelling out here. The same comment also applies to (133).

secondary topic are involved in the raising rule, exactly like the situation that we have in the case of topic—raising rule interacting with clause connectives. Also like the latter rule, the rule of topic—raising interacting with *keneng*—verbs is optional as attested by all the (b) sentences in (130) through (133). Furthermore, as in the case of our Topic—raising rule, Mei's rule raises topic(s) from an embedded clause dominated by an NP. With so many characteristics in common, one naturally wonders whether the two rules can be collapsed. Actually, if we make a further assumption, as many grammarians have done, that in the case of *keneng* verbs the COMP in the embedded S is empty, then the two rules are easily collapsible. The only difficulty seems to be that the two rules interact and the rule involving an empty COMP feeds into the other rule as attested by the following sentences.

(134) a. <u>mingtian</u> jishi <u>ta</u> keneng bu hui ying,
tomorrow even:if he possible not will win
women ye dei zhunbei kai qingzhu hui.
we also need prepare hold celebration party
'Tomorrow even if he may not win, we will still need to prepare for the celebration party.'
b. jishi <u>mingtian</u> <u>ta</u> keneng bu hui ying,
even:if tomorrow he possible not will win
women ye dei zhunbei kai qingzhu hui.
we also need prepare hold celebration party
'Even if tomorrow he may not win, we will still need to prepare for the celebration party.'

Since the exact formulation of the rules remains to be done, we will not pursue the possibility any further. Suffice it to point out that a very similar rule, if not the same, of Topic—raising is needed for the grammar of Modern Chinese.

Second, as specified in (114), our rule of Topic—raising affects only the placement of the clause connectives in the first clause. It has no effect on the relative position in the surface structure of such clause connectives as *danshi* 'but', *buguo* 'but' *erqie* 'and', *yaoburan* 'otherwise' and *fouze* 'otherwise', which occur in the second clause. If we make the same assumption that we made previously with regard to clause connectives that occur in the first clause that they also occur in the deep structure in the COMP position in the second $\bar{S}$, then since in Chinese there is no other rule that can move any element in the $\bar{S}_2$ beyond COMP, these clause connectives should remain in the initial position of the second clause in the surface structure. Witness (135).

(135) a. <u>Xiao Zhang</u>$_1$ suiran hen youqian, danshi _____$_1$ hen xiaoqi.
Xiao Zhang though very rich but very stingy
'Although Xiao Zhang is very rich, he is very stingy.'
b. *<u>Xiao Zhang</u>$_1$ suiran hen youqian, _____$_1$ danshi hen xiaoqi.
'Same as (a).'
c. <u>Xiao Zhang</u>$_1$ suiran hen youqian, danshi <u>ta</u>$_1$ hen xiaoqi.
'Same as (a).'
d. *<u>Xiao Zhang</u>$_1$ suiran hen youqian, <u>ta</u>$_1$ danshi hen xiaoqi.
'Same as (a).'

Our rule of Topic—raising will also explain a similar phenomenon that happens with clause connectives such as *yinwei* 'because' when they, instead of occurring in the first clause as they normally do, actually occur in the second clause expressing an afterthought. Compare (136) with (135).

(136) a. <u>Xiao Zhang</u>$_1$ zuotian mei lai, yinwei _____$_1$ sheng bing le.
Xiao Zhang yesterday not come because get sick PART
'Xiao Zhang didn't come yesterday because he was sick.'
b. *<u>Xiao Zhang</u>$_1$ zuotian mei lai, _____$_1$ yinwei sheng bing le.
'Same as (a).'
c. <u>Xiao Zhang</u>$_1$ zuotian mei lai, yinwei <u>ta</u>$_1$ sheng bing le.
'Same as (a).'
d. *<u>Xiao Zhang</u>$_1$ zuotian mei lai, <u>ta</u>$_1$ yinwei sheng bing le.
'Same as (a).'

In the most recent G—B theory, the ungrammatical sentences in (130) and (131) can all be filtered out because the topic traces or pronominal copies in them are not properly bound. That is, though they are all coindexed with their antecedent *Xiao Zhang,* none of them are c—commanded by their antecedent.

Third, the Topic—raising rule captures very nicely a very important distinction between a clause topic and a sentence topic. While a clause topic has its domain within a clause, a sentence topic has its domain over a whole sentence or a topic chain as it is defined in Tsao (1979). A sentence topic which is a quantifier phrase will be, after being raised, in a position of C-commanding other QPs contained in the following comment clauses. Li (1983) in accounting for the different scope interpretations of quantifier phrases such as *meitian* 'every day' and *bushao ren* 'quite a few people' in (137a) and (138a), has argued convincingly that the difference is due to whether the quantifier phrase in question is a topic or not and that (137a) and (138a) can be structurally represented as (137b) and (138b) respectively.

(137) a. meitian   (you)   bushao   ren   shang jiaotang.
          every-day there:be quite:a:few people go   church
          'During any given one day, quite a few people go to church.'

   b.
                        S
                   ╱   ╲
               TOPIC   S
                △   ╱   ╲
             meitian   (you) bushao ren (meitian)
                          shang jiaotang.

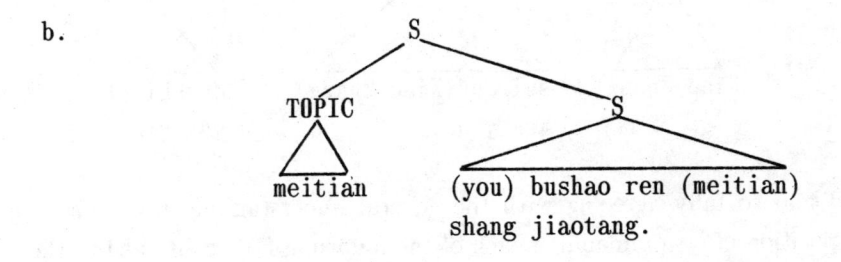

(138) a. (you)   bushao   ren   meitian   shang jiaotang.
          there:be quite:a:few people every:day go   church
          'there are quite a few people who go to church every day.'

   b.
                        S
                   ╱   ╲
               TOPIC   S
                △   ╱   ╲
            (you) bushao   (bushao ren) meitian shang
               ren   jiaotang.

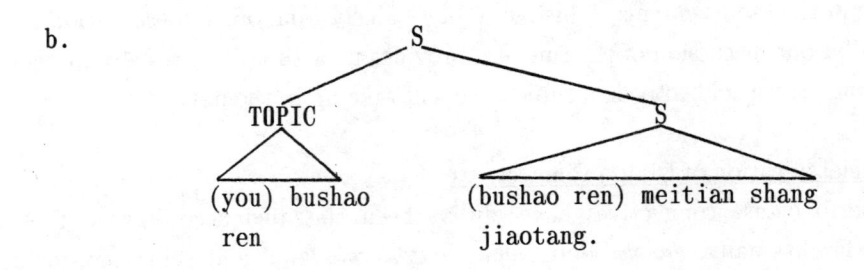

Generalizing Li's representation, we would propose (64) as a general structure of a topic chain.

(139)

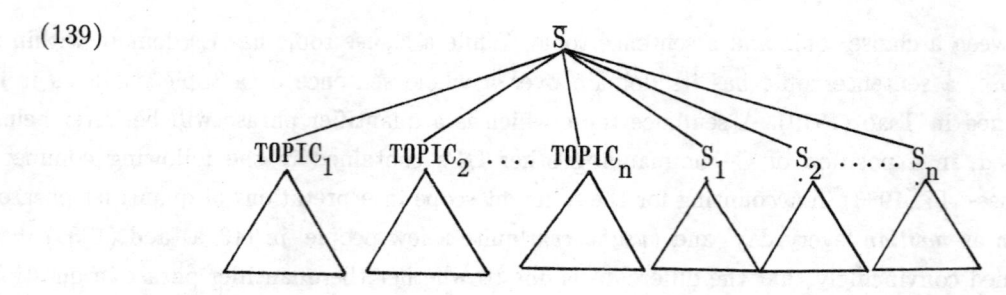

```
                              S̄
        ┌──────┬──────┬──────┬──────┬──────┐
     TOPIC₁  TOPIC₂ .. TOPICₙ   S₁     S₂ ..... Sₙ
       △      △        △       △      △        △
```

Adopting this general schema, we can now represent (135a) as (140).

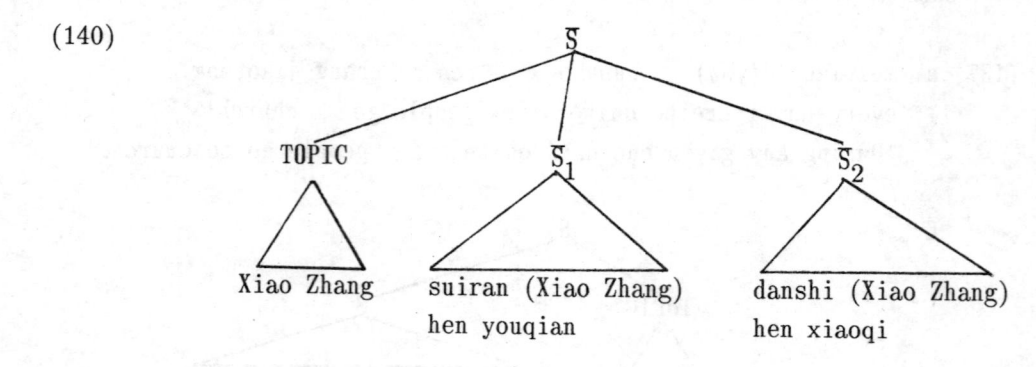

(140)

```
                    S̄
         ┌──────────┼──────────┐
       TOPIC        S₁          S₂
         △          △           △
      Xiao Zhang  suiran (Xiao Zhang)  danshi (Xiao Zhang)
                  hen youqian          hen xiaoqi
```

In addition to fully agreeing with the general understanding that a sentence topic stands in a position of c–commanding each of the following QPs contained in the comment clauses and thus has a wider scope interpretation than other QPs, we can give at least one more supportive evidence to show that this structural representation as an output of our Toipc–raising rule is not far off the track. It is a well–known fact in phonology that a sentence topic is capable of receiving an assignment as a tonic unit in itself on a par with any clause in the same sentence. This fact follows nicely from our representation.

Finally, our discussion of the rule also provides us with a linguistically motivated way of classifying clause connectives, a subject we will take up in the next section.

2.5. A Reclassification of Clause Connectives

Hitherto clause connectives have always been classified according to their surface positions. Traditionally, *danshi* 'but', *buguo* 'but', *erqie* 'and' and *suoyi* 'so', for examples are classified as "pure conjunctions" because they invariably occur at the initial position of the second clause. Adverbials, mostly monosyllabic, such as *ye* 'also', *hai* 'still' *cai* 'then' and *jiu* 'then' etc. are classified as "adverbs" because they occur in the position usually occupied by other kinds of adverbs and they never occur at the beginning of the clause unless the topic(s) is/are deleted. The third group, which is the largest, contains such connectives as *suiran* 'although', *yinwei* 'because', *ruguo* 'if', *zongshi* 'even if'. They are classified as "adverbial connectives" because they can occur in the position usually occupied by a pure conjunction, i.e. clause—initially, or in the position normally occupied by an adverb.

With the introduction of our rule of Topic—raising we can now see clearly that the third group, instead of being regarded as a hybrid, should be more properly identified with the first group as "conjunctions" because in the deep structure they both occur in the clause—initial position. The fact that members of the third group can sometimes occur in other positions while those of the first cannot is readily accounted for by the rule of Topic—raising. Connectives such as *...de shihou* 'time that, when' and *...de difang* 'place that, where' should be regarded as "conjunctive particles". They are so called because they occur clause—finally and they are phonetically reduced, but, on the other hand, they behave like conjunctions in having the function of bringing two clauses together semantically and in allowing the clause they introduce to have the topic(s) raised out of it.

The second group of connectives containing such adverbs as *ye* 'also', *hai* 'still, yet', *cai* 'then' and *que* 'on the contrary' is basically adverb, which has the derived (secondary) function of connecting clauses. This analysis is justified on the ground that the members of the group never occur in the COMP in the deep structure and hence can not have any interaction with the rule of Topic—raising and that semantically they are basically adverbs of inclusion or evaluation (for an account of the tendency of some types of adverbs to be used as clause connectives, see Chu, 1983:61—63). Therefore, even though this group of connectives may sometimes appear in the same position as *suiran* 'although' and *yinwei* 'because' in the surface structure, they are there through two different paths. For the group of adverbs in question, it is there in the deep structure, but for the group containing *yinwei* 'because', it ends up there as a result of the rule of topic—raising.

Likewise, repetitive correlative connectives such as *yue... yue...* 'the more ... the more ...' and *yi mian (bian) ...yi mian (bian) ...*' while ...' should also be analyzed as adverbs because they can never occur clause—initially in the deep structure.

The following chart gives a summary comparison between our schema of classification and that of the traditional one.

(141)   Examples   Traditional   Tsao's
   a. <u>erqie</u> 'but also', <u>suoyi</u>   True Conjunction   Conjunction
      'so'
   b. <u>budan</u> 'not only', <u>yinwei</u> Adverbial–Con-   Conjunction
      'because'   junction
   c. <u>hai</u> 'still', <u>que</u> 'on the Adverbial–   Adverbial–
      contrary'   Connective   Connective
   d. <u>yue</u> ... <u>yue</u> ... 'the   Correlative–   Adverbial–
      more ... the more ...'   Connective   Connective

In other words, in our analysis if we characterize the connectives occurring in the first clause as [+ Forward Linking] and those occurring in the second as [−Forward Linking] and those that occur in the deep structure in the COMP as [+Conjunction] and those that do not occur in the COMP as [−Conjunction] then all the clause connectives in Chinese fall neatly into the following four cells as shown in (142).[29]

(142)

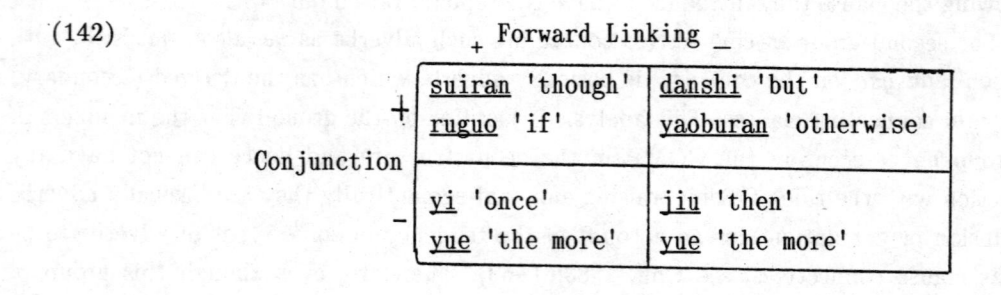

	+ Forward Linking −	
+ Conjunction	<u>suiran</u> 'though' <u>ruguo</u> 'if'	<u>danshi</u> 'but' <u>yaoburan</u> 'otherwise'
−	<u>yi</u> 'once' <u>yue</u> 'the more'	<u>jiu</u> 'then' <u>yue</u> 'the more'

---

[29]The feature [±Forward Linking] is adopted from Li and Thompson (1981: 632ff).

CHAPTER EIGHT
COMPLEX SENTENCES

1. Compound vs. Complex Sentences

In the last chapter we went into different types of compound sentences. One thing to be noted is that we depart from traditional view in treating what is traditionally called "adverbial clauses" not as subordinate clauses, hence falling out of the realm of complex sentences, which will be dealt with in the present chapter. Consistent with our previous view, we will define a complex sentence in Chinese as one that contains a main clause and an embedded clause. Clause embedding, in our view, consists mainly of two types: nominalized clauses as subject or object and relativization. The former will be taken up in Sections 2 and 3 and the latter in Section 4. In the final section, a special structure, which is traditionally called descriptive/resultative complement construction will be scrutinized. This special construction has recently become the subject matter of a heated debate among Chinese linguists. There are roughly two opposing views concerning the proper analysis of the "complement". We will examine arguments for each side closely and then give what our theory has to say about them. An account that is both consistent with our theory and the relevant data involving this construction will finally be proposed.

2. Sentences with Raising Predicates

Before we take up clause—embedding, we have to take care of a very important type of sentences that lies between simple and complex sentences, i.e., what looks like a simple sentence in the surface is actually derived from a complex one containing an embedded clause. The simpleness of the structure in the surface is the direct result of having certain topics, primary and non—primary, raised from the embedded clause.

2.1. Two Groups of Raising Predicates

We have come across some of the raising predicates in our previous discussion of the rule of Topic—raising in Chapter 7. To recapitulate, there we cited Mei (1989) in regarding *kan—qi—lai* 'look like', *nan* 'difficult' and *rongyi* 'easy'/etc. as predicates that subcategorize a sentence in the deep structure as shown in (1). All the surface variations, as shown in (2a) through (2i) are then derived via the rule of Topic—raising.

(1) [$_S$[$_{VP}$ kan–qi–lai[$_S$ ta mingtian hui ying na–chang
       look–like   he tomorrow will win that–CL
   qiu]]][1]
   ball:game

(2) a. kan–qi–lai   ta mingtian hui   ying   na–chang qiu.
       look–like   he tomorrow will   win   that–CL   ball:game
       'It looks like that he will win the ball game tomorrow.'
   b. <u>ta</u> kan–qi–lai   mingtian hui   ying   na–chang qiu.
      he look–like   tomorrow will   win   that–CL   ball:game
      'Roughly same as (a).'
   c. <u>ta</u> <u>maingtian</u> kin–qi–lai hui ying na–chang qiu.
      he tomorrow   look–like   will win   that–CL   ball:game
      'Roughly same as (a).'
   d. <u>na–chang qiu</u>   kan–qi–lai   ta mingtian hui   ying.
      that–CL ball:game   look–like   he tomorrow will win
      'Roughly same as (a).'
   e. <u>na–chang qiu</u>   <u>ta</u> kan–qi–lai   mingtian hui   ying.
      that–CL ball:game   he look–like   tomorrow will win
      'Roughly same as (a).'
   f. <u>ta</u> <u>na–chang qiu</u>   kan–qi–lai   mingtian hui   ying.
      he that–CL ball:game   look–like   tomorrow will win
      'Roughly same as (a).'
   g. <u>ta</u> <u>na–chang qiu</u>   <u>mingtian</u>   kan–qi–lai hui   ying.
      he that–CL ball:game   tomorrow   look–like   will win
      'Roughly same as (a).'
   h. <u>ta</u> <u>mingtian</u> <u>na–chang qiu</u>   kan–qi–lai hui   ying.
      he tomorrow   that–CL ball:game look–like   will win
      'Roughly same as (a).'
   i. <u>mingtian</u> <u>ta</u> <u>na–chang qiu</u>   kan–qi–lai hui   ying.
      tomorrow   he that–CL ball:game look–like   will win
      'Roughly same as (a).'

---

[1]Actually, the modal auxiliary *hui* 'will' predicating a future event will be analyzed as a raising predicate as well. So there is ground for positing another S within the inner S in (1). But to simplify presentation here we will temporarily disregard it.

Raising predicates like *kan—qi—lai* 'look—like' can be further differentiated into two groups.

Group (A): *kan—qi—lai* 'look—like', *hao—xiang* 'seem', *sihu* 'seem' and *kongpa* 'be afraid'[2], *qia—qiao* 'happen (to)'

Group (B): *nan* 'difficult', *rongyi* 'easy', *hao* 'good, appropriate' and *heshi* 'appropriate', *qia—dang* 'appropriate, proper'

Those in (A) can occur in the S—initial position while those in (B) can occur in the S—final position. Sentences (2a), cited earlier, and those in (3) exemplify the first group and those in (4) show the typical distribution of sentences containing a verb in the second group.

(3) a. hao—xiang ta bu xiang lai.
    seem he not want come.
    'It seems that he doesn't want to come.'

   b.* ta bu xiang lai hao—xiang.
    he not want come seem

   c. <u>ta</u> hao—xiang bu xiang lai.
    he seem not want come
    'Roughly, same as (a).'

(4) a. ta zuo zhe—jian shi he-shi.
    he do this—CL job appropriate
    'It is appropriate for him to do the job.'

   b.* heshi ta zuo zhe—jian shi.
    appropriate he do this—CL job

   c. <u>ta</u> heshi zuo zhe—jian shi.
    he appropriate do this—CL job
    'Roughly, same as (a).'

---

[2]*Kongpa* 'be afraid' is semantically rather similar to the English parenthetical verb 'be afraid', as can be seen in (i) and (ii) below, although *kongpa* in Chinese patterns with other raising predicates.

(i) <u>kongpa</u> ta yi—ge ren zuo—bu—liao nei—jian shi.
    afraid he one—CL person do—not—finish that—CL matter
    'I am afraid that he alone won't be able to handle the matter.'

(ii) nei—jian shi kongpa ta yi—ge ren zuo—bu—liao.
    that—CL matter afraid he one—CL person do—not—finish
    'Speaking of the matter, I'm afraid, he won't be able to handle it alone.'

d. zhe–jian shi   ta   heshi   zuo.
    this–CL   job   he   appropriate   do
    'Roughly, same as (a).'

e. ta   zhe–jian shi   heshi   zuo.³
    he   this–CL   job   appropriate   do
    'Roughly, same as (a).'

To the best of my knowledge, no satisfactory explanation has been put forth as to why Group A verbs can occur S–initially while Group B cannot. We suspect that has to do with the fact that those in Group (A) are verbs while those in Group (B) are adjectives. The distinction is very clear as only those in Group (B) can be used attributively. The contrast can be clearly brought out by comparing the grammatical (5) and (6), which contain Group (B) verbs, with the ungrammatical (7) and (8), where Group (A) verbs are used attributively.

(5) hen   nan   –de   shi
     very   difficult   Adj. Mar.   matter
     'Very difficult matters'

(6) heshi   –de   ren
     appropriate   Adj. Mar.   person
     'An appropriate person'

(7)* kan–qi–lai   –de   shi
     look–like   Adj. Mar.   matter

(8)* hao–xiang   –de   cuowu
     seem   Adj. Mar.   mistake

There is, however, an important observation which seems to counter our claim that

---

³There is another possible variation in (4), as shown in (i).
(i)   zhe–jian shi   ta   zuo   heshi.
      this–CL   matter   he   do   appropriate
(i), however, involves only topicalization. It does not involve raising, as there is no indication that either *zhe–jian shi* 'this matter' or *ta* 'he' has been raised out of the sentence boundaries.

Group (A) words are verbs. Thus, it has often been observed that while Group (B) words can regularly occur in an V–not–V question, as shown in (9), Group (A) words cannot, as shown by the ungrammatical (10).

(9)   ta   lai   heshi–bu–heshi?
       he   come   appropriate–not–appropriate
       'Is it appropriate for him to come?'

(10)*   hao–xiang–bu–hao–xiang   yao   xia   yu?
        seem–not–smme   will   fall   rain
        ?'Does it seem that it's going to rain?'

Likewise, the negative particle *bu* 'not' can occur only with those of Group (B). Compare (11) with (12), which is ungrammatical.

(11)   ta   lai   bu   heshi.
       he   come   not   appropriate
       'It is not appropriate for him to come.'

(12)*   bu   hao–xiang   yao   xia   yu.
        not   seem   will   fall   rain
        'It doesn't seem that it's going to rain.'

In this case, there is probably a good semantic explanation for it. Notice that the verbs in Group (A) all indicate "uncertainty" on the part of the speaker, not the subject/topic of the sentence. In other words, they are directly tied to the speech act of assertion. For this reason, they are not fit to be questioned or negated. Our explanation receives further confirmation when we examine the syntactic distribution of the corresponding verbs in English. Observe the following range of facts concerning *seem* and *be afraid*.

(13)   a.   I am afraid that he won't be able to come today.
       b.*   I am not afraid that he won't be able to come today.
       c.*   Am I afraid that he won't be able to come today?

(14) a. It seems that John is happy.
b.? It doesn't seem that John is happy.
c.? Does it seem that John is happy?
d. John seems to be happy.
e. John doesn't seem to be happy.
f. Does John seem to be happy?

(14e) and (14f) seem to be counterexamples to our theory that *seem* cannot be questioned nor negated. But actually they are not. Semantically, it is quite clear that what is questioned or negated is not the verb *seem* but rather the embedded verb *happy*. The fact that negation and question appear with the main verb probably has to do with a strong tendency in English for the main verb to attract these elements.

2.2. Modal Auxiliary Verbs

Quite similar to *kan–qi–lai* 'seem, look–like' in distribution is *keneng* 'possible', which is usually regarded as a modal auxiliary verb. Compare the sentences in (15) with those in (2).

(15) a. keneng   ta   mingtian   hui   ying   na–chang   qiu.
     possible   he   tomorrow   will   win   that–CL   ball:game
     'It is possible that he will win the ball game tomorrow.'
b. ta keneng mingtian hui ying na–chang qiu.
c. ta mingtian kengeng hui ying na–chang qiu.
d. na–chang qiu keneng ta mingtian hui ying.
e. na–chang qiu ta keneng mingtian hui ying.
f. ta na–chang qiu keneng mingtian hui ying.
g. ta na–chang qiu mingtian keneng hui ying.
h. ta mingtian na–chang qiu keneng hui ying.
i. mingtian ta na–chang qiu keneng hui ying.

Due to this perfect parallelism, it follows that if *kan–qi–lai* 'look–like' is a raising predicate, then *keneng* 'possible' should also be analyzed as one as well. Furthermore, *keneng* can be negated by *bu* and can appear in a V–not–V question, as shown in (16) and (17).

(16) ta   mingtian   bu   keneng   ying   na—chang   qiu.⁴
      he   tomorrow   not   possible   win   that—CL   ball:game
      'It is impossible for him to win the game tomorrow.'

(17) ta   mingtian   keneng—bu—keneng   ying   na—chang   qiu?
      he   tomorrow   possible—not—possible   win   that—CL   ball:game
      'Is it possible for him to win the ball game tomorrow?'

Finally, *keneng* 'possible', just like *kan—qi—lai* 'look—like', is a one—place predicate which takes an abstract event or situation as its argument. So there is ample reason to posit *keneng* as a verb that subcategories a sentence in the underlying structure.

Chinese modal auxiliary verbs, however, have not been, to the best of my knowledge, systematically examined from this perspective. In what follows we will therefore look at the most important ones from this point of view. As our previous examination of *keneng* suggests that the syntactic behavior of Chinese modal auxiliaries seems to be closely tied to their meaning, we will take up the semantics of modal auxiliaries first.

2.2.1 The Semantics of Modal Auxiliaries

In an interesting paper, Tiee (1985) classifies Chinese modal auxiliaries on semantic ground into three types, namely, epistemic, deontic and dynamic. Our study shows that this classification is not only semantically sound, but also has important syntactic correlates, the latter of which Tiee failed to see. In what follows, we will take up the meaning of the modal auxiliaries first, and then go on to explore their syntactic behavior.

2.2.1.1. Epistemic Modality

An epistemic modal, according to Halliday (1970:327—29), expresses the speaker's assessment of the probability of what he is saying or the extent to which he regards it as self—evident. It relates to an inference by the speaker and is mainly concerned with possibility and probability. It, therefore, is the modality of propositions, rather than actions, states or events. *Keneng* 'possible', *hen keneng* 'probable', *hui* 'future—predictive',

---

[4]It is certainly an idiosyncracy in English grammar that the verb 'possible' while it itself is a raising predicate, its negative counterpart, i.e. 'impossible' is not. It is also to be noted that while we employ the same term "raising predicate", its significance in English and Chinese is different. In English, the constituent that is raised is always subject while in Chinese, various topics can be raised. So it should be more accurate to refer to them as "subject—raising predicates" and "topics—raising predicates" respectively.

and *gai*, *yinggai*, and *yingdang* '(it) ought to be the case that...' belong to this class. In syntactic terms, this means an epistemic modal auxiliary is a one—place predicate taking a whole proposition as its complement, just as what we have done in our analysis of *keneng* 'possible'. Some more examples involving another modal of this class, *yinggai* '(it) ought to be the case that ...' follow.

(18) a. yinggai ta mingtian hui ying na—chang qiu.
       should he tomorrow will win that—CL ball:game
       'It ought to be the case that he will win the ball game tomorrow.'
   b. <u>ta</u> yinggai mingtian hui ying na—chang qiu.
   c. ta <u>mingtian</u> yinggai hui ying na—chang qiu.
   d. <u>na—chang qiu</u> yinggai ta mingtian hui ying.
   e. <u>na—chang qiu ta</u> yinggai mingtian hui ying.
   f. <u>ta na—chang qiu mingtian</u> yinggai hui ying.
   g. <u>ta na—chang qiu mingtian</u> yinggai hui ying.
   h. <u>ta mingtian na—chang qiu</u> yinggai hui ying.
   i. <u>mingtian ta na—chang qiu</u> yinggai hui ying.

2.2.1.2. Deontic Modality

Tiee defines deontic modality as what "gives permission, makes a promise or threat, or lays an obligation upon the subject of a sentence." (1985:92) It is an act rather than a proposition. Translated into syntactic terms, it means that a deontic modal auxiliary subcategorizes an argument as subject and a VP.

According to the meaning they denote, deontic modals fall into three categories: (i) permission: *neng* 'can', *nenggou* 'can, may', *keyi* 'may'; (ii) necessity: *yao* 'must, have to', *bixu*, *bidei*, *xuyao*, *dei* '(it) is necessary for someone to ...' and (iii) moral obligation: *yinggai*, *yingdang*, *gai* 'should, ought to'. Examine the following examples involving *yinggai* expressing moral obligation.

(19) a.* yinggai ni mingtian nian na—ben shu.
        should you tomorrow read that—CL book
        'You should read the book tomorrow.'
    b. ni yinggai mingtian nian na—ben shu.
        you should tomorrow read that—CL book
        'Same as (a).'

c. ni   mingtian   yinggai   nian   na–ben   shu.
   you   tomorrow   should   read   that–CL   book
   'Tomorrow you should read the book.'

d. mingtian   ni   yinggai   nian   na–ben   shu.
   tomorrow   you   should   read   that–CL   book
   'Same as (c).'

e.* na–ben   shu   yinggai   ni   mingtian   nian.
    that–CL   book   should   you   tomorrow   read
    Same as (a).'

f. na–ben   shu   ni   yinggai   mingtian   nian.
   that–CL   book   you   should   tomorrow   read
   'As for the book, you should read (it) tomorrow.'

By comparing (19) with (18), we can easily discern two important distinctions. First, we see that deontic *yinggai* differs from epistemic *yinggai* in that the former subcategorizes an agent and a VP while the latter has the whole clause as its argument. This difference is the single most important feature that distinguishes the two classes of modals.

The other distinction is that deontic *yinggai*, unlike epistemic *yinggai*, is clearly not a raising predicate for although *mingtian* 'tomorrow', a time adverbial, can occur both before and after *yinggai*, as shown in (19b) on the one hand and (19c and d) on the other, the positional difference results in a change of meaning as reflected in the different translations in (b) and (c). More crucially, by comparing (18d) with (19e), we see that while epistemic *yinggai* allows the object of the main verb to become the matrix topic, a similar movement is disallowed in the case of deontic *yinggai* as (19e) is ungrammatical. This clearly indicates that deontic *yinggai*, unlike epistemic *yinggai*, is not a raising predicate. Cases such as (19f) where the object of the main verb can appear in S–initial position should, therefore, be regarded as the result of regular topicalization.

2.2.1.3. Dynamic Modality

What we here refer to as dynamic modality is roughly equivalent to what are often called "neng–yuan dongci" by Chinese linguists. Such dynamic (nengyuan) modals deal with ability, will and desire. Accoring to Tiee, "they are related directly to the subject of a sentence, and denotes the feeling or ability of the subject. They are often subject–oriented but they can also be used in a neutral or a circumstantial possibility or necessity." (1985:94). Such modal auxiliary verbs as *hui* 'be able to, can', *neng* 'can, be able to', *yao* 'will, want to', *yuanyi* 'wish to, be willing to', *ken* 'be willing to, consent to', and *gan* 'dare' belong to this class.

Examine the following examples.

(20) a.* hui ta shuo Yingyu.
        can he speak English
        'He can speak English.'
    b. ta hui shuo Yingyu.
        he can speak English
        'Same as (a).'
    c. Yingyu, ta hui shuo.
        English he can speak
        'As for English, he can speak (it).'

(21) a.* neng ta chu-guo.
        can he exit-country
        'He can go abroad.'
    b. ta neng chu-guo.
        he can exit-country
        'Same as (a).'

(22) a.* neng zhe-jian jiaoshi zuo wu-bai-ge ren.
        can this-CL classroom sit five-hundred-CL people
        'This classroom can sit five hundred people.'
    b. zhe-jian jiaoshi neng zuo wu-bai-ge
        this-CL classroom can sit five-hundred-CL
        ren.
        people
        'Same as (a).'

We find in (20)–(22) that both *hui* 'be able to, can' and *neng* 'can, be able to' cannot take a proposition as its complement as (20a), (21a) and (22a) are all ungrammatical. Also in most cases dynamic modal auxiliaries, just like deontic ones, will take an animate agent as its subject as shown in (20b) and (21b). But, unlike deontic modals, some dynamic modal auxiliaries can take an inanimate subject, as shown in (22b), to denote circumstantial possibility, capacity, or necessity.

2.2.2 The Syntax of Modal Auxiliaries

So far we have shown what distinguishes the epistemic modal from the other two classes is that it alone subcategorizes a sentence in the underlying structure. This can be demonstrated by its ability to occur at the beginning of a sentence in the surface, as shown by (18a) and (15a). There is, however, one notable exception to this generalization. Epistemic *hui* 'future–predictive' cannot occur in that position, as (23a) is ungrammatical. Sentences in (23) give the distribution of epistemic *hui*.

(23) a.* hui ta mingtian ying na–chang qiu.
          will he tomorrow win that–CL ball:game
          'He will win the ball game tomorrow.'
    b.* <u>mingtian</u> hui ta ying na–chang qiu.
    c.* <u>na–chang qiu</u> hui ta mingtian ying.
    d.* <u>na–chang qiu mingtian</u> hui ta ying.
    e.? <u>ta</u> hui mingtian ying na–chang qiu.[5]
    f. <u>ta</u> mingtian hui ying na–chang qiu.
    g. <u>mingtian ta</u> hui ying na–chang qiu.
    h. <u>na–chang qiu ta</u> mingtian hui ying.
    i. <u>ta mingtian na–chang qiu</u> hui ying.
    j. <u>mingtian na–chang qiu ta</u> hui ying.

Two things stand out when we compare (23) with (18) or (15). First, as we have just noted, epistemic *hui* cannot appear in the S–initial position. Second, topic–raising is allowed as long as the embedded agentive subject, *ta* 'he' in (24), is raised.[6] This is quite

---

[5] We don't have very good explanation why (23e), where *mingtian* 'tomorrow' is not raised, does not sound as good as (23f) or (23g), where it is raised. We suspect that it may have something to do with the fact that *hui* 'will' can also serve as a focus verb, almost on a par with *shi* 'BE', in bringing focus to the constituent immediately following it. Since *hui* 'will' already makes a strong assertion about a future event, to put *mingtian* 'tomorrow' in focus as in (23e) may seem out of place.

[6] *Hui* 'will', however, can also take a sentence where there is underlyingly no agent–subject, as shown in (ia).
(i) a. yiding hui <u>mingtian fasheng nei–jian shi</u>
      certainly will tomorrow happen that–CL incident
In such a situation, the requirement that agent be raised before all others is, of course, irrelevant and all topics can be freely raised, as shown in (b), (c) and (d) below.

clear when we compare the ungrammatical (b), (c) and (d) in (24) with all other grammatical sentences.

These two distributional characteristics can be satisfactorily accounted for if we assume that epistemic *hui* is historically derived from the more basic dynamic *hui* 'be able to, can', which, you may recall, requires an animate subject, and that the evolution is not quite complete, with the result that epistemic *hui*, as it is used today, is caught "mid-stream", so to speak, in that it retains the requirement that there be an animate matrix subject when there is one but at the same time allows other topics to be raised.

However, regardless of whether this hypothesis is correct or not, the fact remains that this *hui* is not yet a full-fledged epistemic modal. This hybrid nature of epistemic *hui* further explains why it always precedes deontic or dynamic modals but follows epistemic *keneng* 'possible' or *yinggai* 'should' in the surface linear order when two or three modals occur in a cluster. The sequence can be systematically represented by the following diagram.

(24)
1	2	3
keneng 'possible'	hui 'future-predictive'	a. deontic keyi 'may' bidei 'must' yinggai 'should, ought to'
yinggai 'should'		b. dynamic hui 'be able to, can' neng 'can, be able to' ken 'be willing to' yuanyi 'be willing to' yao 'want to, will' keyi 'can'

---

b. **mingtian** yiding hui fasheng nei-jian shi.
   tomorrow certainly will happen that-CL incident
   'Roughly, tomorrow such an incident will certainly happen.'

c. **nei-jian shi** yiding hui (zai) mingtian fasheng.
   that-CL incident certainly will on tomorrow happen
   'Roughly, the incident will certainly happen tomorrow.'

d. **mingtian nei-jian shi** yiding hui fasheng.
   tomorrow that-CL incident certainly will happen
   'Roughly, speaking of tomorrow, the incident will certainly happen then.'

That this account is correct is confirmed when we examine all the examples given by Chao in which modals appear in a cluster as shown in (25).

(25)   a.   <u>hui</u> <u>yao</u> 'will want to' (2, 3b)
          b.   <u>hui</u> <u>neng</u> 'will be able to' (2, 3b)
          c.   <u>hui</u> <u>ken</u> 'will be willing to' (2, 3b)
          d.   <u>keneng</u> <u>hui</u>   'possibly will' (1, 2)
                            'may be able to' (1, 3b)
          e.   <u>yinggai</u> <u>keyi</u>   'ought to be permitted to' (1, 3a)
                            'ought to be able to' (1, 3b)
          f.   <u>yinggai</u> <u>hui</u> <u>ken</u> 'ought to be possible to be willing to' (1, 2, 3b)
          g.   bu <u>hui</u> bu <u>gan</u> bu <u>yuanyi</u> 'will not be afraid to be unwilling to' (2, 3b, 3b)

It can be easily affirmed that none of the clusters in any of their interpretations violates the principle that we have posited.

2.2.3. Summary

To sum up, we have posited, on the basis of meaning and syntactic distribution, three classes of modal auxiliaries in Chinese. The epistemic modal is a one–place predicate, having a clause as its complement. In the case of *keneng* 'possible, may' and *yinggai* 'logical should', various topics, primary and nonprimary, can be raised to the matrix clause while in the case of *hui* 'future–predictive', a restriction is imposed that the agentive subject, if there is one, must be raised before other topics can be raised. A deontic modal, on the other hand, subcategorizes an agentive subject and a VP. While this is also true with most dynamic modals, some of them such as *neng* 'can, be able to' and *yao* 'will' have uses that do not require an agentive subject.

Therefore, in terms of structure, only epistemic *keneng*, *yinggai* and *hui* are raising predicates. The rest are not. We have discussed them altogether in the previous section just for the sake of convenience.

Actually, epistemic *hui* 'future–predictive', because it has a strong assertive force concerning an event in the future and because it allows various topics, which usually represent old, known information, to be raised, has further developed into a focus indicator on a par with the most productive marker *shi*. Compare the (a) and (b) sentences in (27)–(29).[7]

---

[7] I owe this insight and the examples from (27)–(29) to Cheng (1983).

(26) wo mingtian zai gongyuan–li jian ta.
    I tomorrow in park–LOC   see him
    'I will see him in the park TOMORROW.' (Capitalization indicates stress.)

(27) a. wo <u>hui</u> mingtian zai gongyuan–li jian ta.
       I will tomorrow in park–LOC   see him
       'I will see him in the park TOMORROW.'
    b. wo <u>shi</u> mingtian zai gongyuan–li jian ta.
       I BE   tomorrow in park–LOC   see him
       'It is tomorrow that I will see him in the park.'

(28) a. wo mingtian <u>hui</u> zai gongyuan–li jian ta.
       I tomorrow will in park–LOC   see him
       'Tomorrow I will see him IN THE PARK'
    b. wo mingtian <u>shi</u> zai gongyuan–li jian ta.
       I tomorrow BE   in park–LOC   see him
       'It is in the park that I will see him tomorrow.'

(29) a. wo mingtian zai gongyuan–li <u>hui</u> <u>jian</u> <u>ta</u>.
       I tomorrow in park–LOC   will see him
       I will <u>see</u> <u>him</u> in the park tomorrow.'
    b. wo mingtian zai gongyuan–li <u>shi</u> jian ta.
       I tomorrow in park–LOC   BE see him
       'It is to see him that I will be in the park tomorrow.'

This parallelism also strongly suggests that *shi* in the *shi* ... *de* construction should be analyzed as raising predicate, a task we will turn to in the next section.

2.3. <u>Shi</u> in the <u>Shi</u> ... <u>De</u> Construction

But just what do we mean by the *shi* ... *de* construction? Before we can define the construction satisfactorily, we have to examine several different uses of *shi* in Chinese.

2.3.1. Different Uses of *Shi*

We have already touched upon some uses of *shi* in our previous discussion of simple one–topic sentences. They can be briefly recapitulated as follows:

(i)   equative *shi*
(30) na–ge   ren   shi   Zhang San.
      that–CL person be   Zhang San
      'That person is Zhang San.'

(ii) classificatory *shi*
(31) Zhang San shi Zhongguoren.
      Zhang San be   Chinese
      'Zhang San is Chinese.'
(32) ta shi jiao–shu–de.
      he be   teach–book–Rel. Mar.
      'He is one who teaches (i.e. a teacher).'

(iii) existential *shi*
(33) damen–de   zheng duimian   shi yi–ke   shu.
      gate–POSS right opposite be   one–CL   tree
      'Right opposite the gate is a tree.'

The difference between an equative and a classificatory sentence is that in the former the two arguments can be interchanged without affecting the cognitive meaning of the sentence while in the latter they cannot. In (32) we have what will be termed a "be–headed" relative clause serving as a noun. This is rather prominent construction in Chinese and will be taken up in connection with our discussion of relativization in Section 3.4. of this chapter. (33) exemplifies a rather special use of *shi* in an existential construction, which we briefly touched upon in Chapter 3.

There are other uses that we haven't touched upon yet.[8] They will be exemplified by the following sentences.

(34) hua   shi hong de.
      flower BE   red   PART
      'Flowers ARE red.' (Capitalization indicates stress.)

---

[8]We mentioned briefly in our previous discussion of Chinese passive sentences (Chapter 4) that certain English passive sentences should be more appropriately rendered as *shi ... de* sentences in Chinese whose structure will be closely examined in this section.

(35) a. ta   shi cong   Shanghai lai   de   nei–ge   ren.
        he   BE from   Shanghai come   Rel. Mar. that–CL   person
        'He is the man who came from Shanghai.'
    b. ta   shi cong   Shanghai lai   de.
        he   BE from   Shanghai come   PART
        (i) 'Same as (a).'
        (ii) 'It is from Shanghai that he came.'

(36) a. wo   xiang mai de   (dongxi) shi   na–ben   zidian.
        I   want buy Rel. Mar. thing   BE   that–CL   dictionary
        'What I want to buy is that dictionary.'
    b. na–ben   zidian   shi wo xiang mai de
        that–CL   dictionary   BE   I   want   buy Rel. Mar.
        (dongxi).
        thing
        (i) 'That dictionary is what I want to buy.'
        (ii) 'Speaking of the dictionary, it is I who wants to buy it.'

(37) a. ta   zuotian   zai   Taibei   mai–le   na–ben   shu.
        he   yesterday at   Taipei   buy–ASP   that–CL   book
        'He bought the book in Taipei yesterday.'
    b. <u>shi</u> ta   zuotian   zai   Taibei   mai–le   na–ben   shu.
        BE   he   yesterday   at   Taipei   buy–ASP   that–CL   book
        'It was he who bought the book in Taipei yesterday.'
    c. ta   <u>shi</u>   zuotian   zai   Taibei   mai–le   na–ben   shu
        he   BE   yesterday   at   Taipei   buy–ASP   that–CL   book
        de.
        PART
        'It was yesterday that he bought the book in Taipei.'
    d. ta   zuotian   <u>shi</u>   zai   Taibei   mai–le   na–ben   shu
        he   yesterday BE   at   Taipei   buy–ASP   that–CL   book
        de.
        PART
        'It was in Taipei that he bought the book yesterday.'

e. ta   zuotian   zai   Taibei   shi   mai–le   na–ben   shu
    he   yesterday   at   Taipei   BE   buy–ASP   that–CL   book
    de.
    PART
    (i) 'He did buy the book when he was in Taipei yesterday.'
    (ii) 'It was that book that he bought in Taipei yesterday.'

f.* ta   zuotian   zai   Taibei   mai–le   shi   na–ben   shu.
    he   yesterday   at   Taipei   buy–ASP BE   that–CL   book

g. na–ben   shu   shi   ta   zuotian   zai   Taibei   mai
    that–CL   book   BE   he   yesterday   at   Taipei   buy
    de.
    PART
    'Speaking of the book, it was he who bought it in Taipei yesterday.'

h. na–ben   shu   ta   shi   zuotian   zai   Taibei   mai
    that–CL   book   he   BE   yesterday   at   Taipei   buy
    de.
    PART
    'Speaking of the book it was yesterday that he bought it in Taipei.'

i. na–ben   shu   ta   zuotian   shi   zai   Taibei   mai
    that–CL   book   he   yesterday   BE   at   Taipei   buy
    de.
    PART
    'Speaking of the book, it was in Taipei that he bought it yesterday.'

j. na–ben   shu   ta   zuotian   zai   Taibei   shi   mai–le.
    that–CL   book   he   yesterday   at   Taipei   BE   buy–ASP
    'Speaking of the book, he did buy it in Taipei yesterday.'

Sentence (b) through (d) and (f) through (j) in (37) exemplify what is known as cleft sentences. By comparing a cleft sentence with a non–cleft sentence such as (37a), it can be clearly seen that the former is marked by the presence of *shi* and in most cases also by the presence of *de* at the end of the sentence, the proper analysis of both of which has long been a matter of controversy. As far as information structure of the sentence is concerned, *shi* is usually regarded as having the function of marking the immediately following constituent as information focus, except for the case of verb + object, as in (37e), which is ambiguous in the interpretation of focus as shown in the (i) and (ii) readings.

Similar in function but very different in structure is a sentence type known as pseudo—cleft construction, as exemplified by sentences in (35) and (36). Like the cleft sentence, it also isolates a constituent as information focus. But that constituent has to be an NP and *shi* in this case functions as an equative verb, linking two referentially equivalent NPs. This characteristic can be clearly seen by comparing the (a) and (b) sentences in both (35) and (36).

Also notice that both (b) sentences in (35) and (36) are ambiguous, being subject to two readings, one pseudo—cleft and the other cleft. This might be the reason which has prompted some linguists to propose to derive the cleft sentence from the pseudo—cleft one and eventually from the equative sentence with *shi* as its main verb (see Zhu, 1978 for example). This position is clearly untenable as the cleft construction is used in a much wider context and there is no indication whatsoever that the pre—*shi* part and the post—*shi* part are indeed NPs except in the restricted cases shown in (35b) and (36b). This does not mean that historically this could not have been the case. In fact, we feel that this restricted context could very well be the context from which *shi* began to develop its focusing function (see Wang, 1988 for argument for this position).

(34) represents yet another related but different use of *shi*. In this construction what occurs after *shi* is an adjectival verb, which is then followed by *de*. This *de* is either a sentence—final particle as in the case of the cleft sentence or, more likely, as we will argue later on, a relative clause marker whose head noun has been deleted as in the case of (32). Judging from the surface, this construction does look like the cleft construction, but this formal similarity is misleading. We have three pieces of evidence to show that they are two distinct constructions.

First, while *shi* in a cleft sentence can often be omitted without changing the meaning of the sentence significantly, as can be seen by comparing (a) and (b) sentences in (38), in the case of sentences like (34) *shi* cannot be deleted without causing ungrammaticality, as shown in (39).

(38) a. ta shi zuotian lai de.
    he BE yesterday come PART
    'It was yesterday that he came.'
   b. ta ZUOTIAN lai de.(Capitalization indicates stress.)
    he yesterday come PART
    'Roughly, same as (a).'

(39)* hua   hong   de.
     flower red   DE
     'same as (34).'

Second, sentences like (34) are close in meaning to sentences with classificatory *shi*. Thus, according to native speakers' interpretation, (34) is roughly paraphrasable as (40), in which *de* behaves like a relative clause marker in being followed by a head noun.

(40) hua   shi   hong   de   dongxi.
     flower BE   red   Rel. Mar. thing
     'Roughly, same as (34).'

(40) should be more accurately translated as 'The flower belongs to a category of things which is red.' A cleft sentence such as (37b) or (37d), on the other hand, cannot be so interpreted.

Finally, cleft *shi* can occur with sentences like (34), as shown in (41).

(41) shi   hua   shi   hong   de.
     BE   flower be   red   PART
     'It is flowers which ARE red.'

(41), though stylistically odd because of containing two *shi*s in such a short sentence, is nevertheless grammatical while no other *shi* can be added to a cleft sentence like (38a), as attested by the ungrammaticality of (38c).

(38) c.* shi   ta   shi   zuotian   lai   de.
         BE   he   BE   yesterday come   PART

Cheng (1983) has a very convincing explanation why a cleft sentence like (38a) does not allow two occurrences of *shi*. He has explained this by positing the principle of unified focus, which requires a cleft sentence to have a single unified focus. This principle not only explains why (38c) is ungrammatical, it also shows that sentences such as (34) are not cleft sentences since they allow cleft *shi* to occur in them.

2.3.2. Meaning of *Shi* and *De* in the Cleft Construction

Earlier we have said that in a cleft sentence *shi* and *de* often cooccur. This statement implies that they do not cooccur all the time. In fact, we have pointed out that *shi* in this use can be omitted if the function of specifying the focus is replaced by stress as shown in (38b). Likewise, *de* can be deleted especially when the event described happens in the future. Compare (a) and (b) sentences in the following.

(42) a. ta   shi   mingtian   dasuan   dao   zhe–li   lai   de.
        he   BE   tomorrow   plan   reach here   come   PART
        'It is tomorrow that he plans to come here.'
    b. ta   shi   mingtian   dasuan   dao   zhe–li   lai.
        he   BE   tomorrow   plan   reach here   come
        'Roughly, same as (a).'

(42a) and (42b) can be said to be cognitively synonymous with a slight difference in the speaker's attitude towards the future event described.

We will go into this attitudinal distinction in a moment. For the time being, let us point out that on the basis of the distribution of these two elements we can come to two conclusions. On the one hand, since they do not always occur together we can safely infer that they probably mean two different things. On the other hand, as they frequently cooccur, we have to conclude that their meanings must be highly compatible, even mutually reinforcing.

Let us begin with *shi*. There are roughly two main approaches to the analysis of *shi*. One is to treat it as a verb (Paris, 1979; Cheng, 1983 and Huang, 1988b among others). The other is to treat it as a focus marker (see Teng, 1979 for example)[9]. The latter approach faces two insurmontable difficulties. First, it is unable to explain the verbal qualities that *shi* possesses. It can, for example, appear in an V–not–V question and can be negated by *bu* 'not', as shown respectively in (43) and (44).

(43) a. ta   shi–bu–shi   zuotian   cong   Taibei   lai   de?
        he   BE–not–BE   yesterday from   Taipei   come   PART
        'Is it yesterday that he came from Taipei?'

---

[9]Cheng (1983) also contains a succinct comparison of his and Teng's approaches.

	b.*	ta	shi	zuotian	cong	Taibei	lai–bu–lai	de.
		he	BE	yesterday	from	Taipei	come–not–come	PART
		'Same as (a).'						

(44)	a.	ta	bu	shi	zuotian	cong	Taibei	lai	de.
		he	not	BE	yesterday	from	Taipei	come	PART
		'It was not yesterday that he came from Taipei.'							
	b.*	ta	Shi	zuotian	cong	Taibei	bu	lai	de.
		he	BE	yesterday	from	Taipei	not	come	PART
		'Same as (a).'							

Second, it cannot explain why as a focus marker it cannot occur postverbally, as shown by the ungrammaticality of (37f).

Since it possesses some verbal qualities and since in every one of its other uses it is clearly a verb, we will posit it as a verb. However, in terms of meaning, it clearly does not have the concrete meaning that an ordinary verb such as *pao* 'run' or *xie* 'write' has. Perhaps, it will be wise to regard it as a *xuhua–le de dongci* (grammaticalized verb), whose function is to mark a constituent within its scope as focus[10].

How about *de*? We have so far temporarily marked it as a sentential particle. But is it really one? Let us look at it more closely.

When a *shi* ... *de* sentence denotes a past event, then *de* is required, as shown in the ungrammaticality of (45b).

(45)	a.	ta	shi	qunian	lai	Meiguo	de.
		he	BE	last:year	come	U. S.	PART
		'It was last year that he came to the U.S.'					
	b.*	ta	shi	qunian	lai	Meiguo.
		he	BE	last:year	come	U. S.
		'Same as (a).'					

This cooccurrence dependency has prompted Teng (1979), following Dragunov (1952), to posit it as a past–tense marker. That this characterization is not general enough is clearly

---

[10]For a detailed discussion of the scope interpretation in a *shi* ... *de* construction, see Cheng (1983).

seen by the following counterexamples taken from Paris (1979).

>   (46) ta   shi mei—tian   qu kan dianying   de.
>   he   BE   every—day   go see movie   PART
>   'It is every day that he goes to the movies.'

>   (47) ta   shi mingtian hui   qu kan dianying   de.
>   he   BE   tomorrow will go see movies   PART
>   'It is tomorrow that he will go to the movies.'

(46) and (47) show clearly that both future and habitual activities can cooccur with *de* in this construction.

While both Chu (1979, 1983, 1985) and Paris (1979) agree that what precedes *de* represents some sort of presupposition, neither of them goes a step further to specify what it means. Cheng (1983), on the other hand, claims that *de* is an aspectual—modal particle, which, in contrast with *—le*, denotes an "unchanged situation." This paper of Cheng has made great contribution to our understanding of the focus devices in Chinese and we will continue to draw from his insights in our later discussion, but we feel very hesitant in ascribing the function of marking "unchanged situation" to a particle that frequently cooccurs with a past verb. We feel that it would make more sense if we treat it as an aspectual—modal particle, showing the speaker's attitude towards the proposition expressed in the sentence. This observation in conjunction with the finding that "expectation" on the part of the speaker plays a very significant part in the interpretation of Chinese sentences (for example, see Tsao, 1976, Chu, 1983), we would propose to describe its meaning as denoting a presupposition on the part of the speaker that some event happened, regularly happens or will happen, as expected, i.e., there has been or will be no change in the expectation of the speaker.

That we are probably not too far off the track can be clearly seen by comparing the following (a) and (b) sentences containing *le* and *de* respectively.

>   (48) a. ni   shi shenme shihou   lai   de?
>   you BE   what   time   come   PART
>   'When did you come?'

      b. ni   shenme   shihou   lai   le?
          you   what   time   come PART
          'When did you come? (I'm surprised that you are here.)'

As shown in the translation, (48a) is an ordinary question, inquiring about the time with the event of "his coming here" taken as something expected, but (48b), in direct contrast, lacks such an expectation. It shows that the speaker has no prior expectation of "his coming here".

With this meaning in mind, let us go back to the two sentences in (42). (42a), the one with *de*, carries the meaning that "his coming here" is a scheduled or prearranged event. The main assertion is about the time. (42b), on the other hand, is a confirmation of someone's assertion and does not carry the expectation that we just described.

2.3.3. The Structure of the *Shi ... De* Construction

Unlike our previous discussion of the meaning of *de*, where difference is the rule, most linguists agree that *de* in this construction is a sentence–final particle. Chao (1968), however, reported that in some dialects the construction has a variant form in which *de* is preposed to the position immediately preceding the final NP, as shown in (49b).

(49) a. ta   shi   Jiuyue   sheng   haizi   <u>de</u>.
           she   BE   September bear   child   PART
          'It was in September that she gave birth to a child.'
      b. ta   shi   Jiuyue   sheng   de   haizi.
           she   BE   September bear   PART child
          'Same as (a).'

Since this variant form is allowed only in some Northern dialects, we will take it to be derived. In other words, in a dialect where both forms exist, sentences like (49b) will be derived from sentences like (49a).

Let us now turn our attention to *shi*. We have pointed out the untenability of analyzing *shi* as a focus marker. The alternative is to treat it as a verb and earlier we have proposed to analyze it as a raising predicate that allows various topics to be raised. Let us now examine in detail what evidence we have in support of this proposal.

First, like epistemic modal auxiliaries *keneng* 'possible' and *yinggai* 'should', it can occur at the beginning of a sentence, as shown in (50).

(50) shi   ta   zuotian   mai—le   nei—ben   shu.
      BE   he   yesterday   buy—ASP   that—CL   book
      'It was he who bought the book yesterday.'

Second, *Shi* 'BE' can both precede and follow epistemic modals while it always precedes other modals such as *hui* 'be able to, can' and *yuanyi* 'be willing to'. Compare (51) with (52).

(51) a. na—ben   shu   keneng   ta   shi   zuotian   mai   de.
         that—CL   book   possible he   BE   yesterday   buy   PART
         'Speaking of the book it is possible that it was yesterday that he bought (it).'

     b. na—ben   shu   ta   shi   keneng   zai   zuotian   mai
         that—CL   book   he   BE   possible on   yesterday buy
         de.
         PART
         'Speaking of the book, it IS possible that he bought it yesterday.'

(52) a. ta   shi   hui   zuo—fan.
         she   BE   can   cook—meal
         'She does know how to cook.'

     b.* ta   hui   shi   zuo—fan.
         she   can   BE   cook—meal

This range of facts follows naturally from our analysis that both epistemic modals and *shi* in this construction are raising predicates which subcategorize a clause while dynamic modals such as *hui* 'can, be able to' and *yuanyi* 'be willing to' are not.

Third, all those unmarked topics, primary or non—primary, that we have posited, can all precede *shi*.[11] This can be clearly seen in all the grammatical sentences with *shi* in (37).

---

[11]As a rule of thumb, only topics unmarked by coverbs can be raised. But there are cases where even marked topics can be raised. Examine the following two sentences.

(i)   ta   ba qian   shi   kan   de   bi   shengming   hai   zhong.
      he   BA money   BE   regard   DE   COMP   life   even   important
      'Roughly, he did regard money as even more important than life.'

(ii) ta   dui ni   bi   dui wo   shi   hao   de   duo   le.
      he   to you   COMP to me   BE   good   DE   much   PART

(37f), in our account, is ungrammatical because the verb with its aspect marker is raised in violation of the Topic-raising rule. Some more examples follow.

(53) a. ta   yanjing   hen   piaoliang.
       he   eye   very   beautiful
       'Speaking of him, his eyes are beautiful.'

   b. shi ta   yanjing   hen   piaoliang.
      BE   he   eye   very   beautiful
      'It is he whose eyes are beautiful.'

   c. ta   shi   yanjing   hen   piaoliang.
      he   BE   eye   very   beautiful
      'Speaking of him, it is (his) eyes that are beautiful.'

   d. ta   yanjing   shi   hen   piaoliang.
      he   eye   BE   very   beautiful
      'Speaking of him, (his) eyes ARE very beautiful.'

   e. yanjing   shi   ta   hen   piaoliang.
      eye   BE   he   very   beautiful
      'Speaking of eyes, it is his that are beautiful.'

   f. yanjing   ta   shi   hen   piaoliang.
      eye   he   BE   very   beautiful
      'Speaking of eyes, his ARE very beautiful.'

(54) a. ta   da   lanqiu   da   de   hen   hao.
       he   play   basketball   play   PART   very   good
       'He plays basketball very well.'

   b. shi ta   da   lanqiu   da   de   hen   hao.
      BE   he   play   basketball   play   PART   very   good
      'It is he who plays basketball very well.'

   c. ta   shi   da   lanqiu   da   de   hen   hao.
      he   BE   play   basketball   play   PART   very   good
      'Speaking of him, it is playing basketball that he does very well.'

   d. ta   da   lanqiu   shi   da   de   hen   hao.
      he   play   basketball   BE   play   PART   very   good
      'As for him, playing basketball he does do it well.'

'He does treat you much better than me.'

e. da   lanqiu   shi ta da   de   hen hao.
   play basketball   BE he play PART very good
   'Speaking of playing basketball, it is he who does it very well.'

f. da   lanqiu   ta shi da   de   hen hao.
   play basketball   he BE play   PART very good
   'Speaking of playing basketball, he does do it very well.'

Our fourth argument has to do with clause conjunctions such as *suiran* 'although' and *yinwei* 'because'. Previously, we have argued that such conjunctions are generated in the COMP (complementizer) position in the deep structure. The NP's and PP's that precede them in the surface structure are actually placed there as a result of the rule of Topic–raising. If this is correct, and we have every reason to believe that it is, then the fact that *shi* can only occur after such conjunctions as *suiran* 'although' can receive a very natural explanation — *shi*, being a verb, can only follow these conjunctions, even though both of them can be preceded by various topics as a result of the rule of Topic–raising. The following examples illustrate the complex interaction between clause conjunctions, *shi* and various topics.

(55) a. suiran   women shi   zuotian   cai   renshi de
        though   we   BE   yesterday only know   PART
        que   haoxiang   shi lao pengyou le.
        on:the:contrary seem   be   old friend   PART
        'Although we knew each other only yesterday, it seems that we are old friends.'

     b. women suiran   shi   zuotian   cai   renshi de
        we   though   BE   yesterday only know   PART
        que   haoxiang   shi lao pengyou le.
        on:the:contrary seem   be   old friend   PART
        'Roughly, same as (a).'

     c.* women shi   zuotian   suiran   cai   renshi de
        we   BE   yesterday though   only know   PART
        que   haoxiang   shi lao pengyou le.
        on:the:contrary seem   be   old friend   PART
        'Roughly, same as (a).'

Conversely, since manner adverbs and non-copied verbs, as we have argued, cannot be topics and consequently can never be raised, it follows that they can never precede *shi*. That this is in fact true is confirmed by the following sentences.

(56) a. ta congcongmangmang-de zou-chuqu.
he hurriedly walk-out
'He walked out hurriedly.'

b. ta *shi* congcongmangmang-de zou-chuqu.
he BE hurriedly walk-out
'It was hurriedly that the walked out.'

c.* ta congcongmangmang-de *shi* zou-chuqu.
he hurriedly BE walk-out

(57) a. ta chi-guo fan le, keshi mei chi-bao.
he eat-ASP meal PART but not eat-full
'Although he ate the meal, he did not eat enough.'

b.* ta chi-guo *shi* fan le, keshi mei chi-bao.
he eat-ASP BE meal PART but not eat-full
'He ate the MEAL, but he didn't have enough.'

c. ta chi *shi* chi-guo fan le, keshi mei chi-bao.
he eat BE eat-ASP meal PART but not eat-full
'Though he did have the meal, he didn't have enough.'

A word of explanation about (57) is in order here. (57c) exemplifies a special construction known as a concession clause, involving verb-copying and the use of *shi*. The point we are making by invoking such a construction is simply that in this construction *shi* can appear before the verb and its object only when it is preceded by a topicalized copy of the verb, as can be clearly seen by comparing (b) and (c) sentences above.

Likewise, we have pointed out that neither the telescopic verb nor the NP that occurs between the two verbs in this construction can be topicalized. They, therefore, cannot be followed by *shi*, as shown in (58).

(58) a. ta mama bi ta jiehun.
her mother force her get:married
'Her mother forced her to get married.'

b. ta   mama   shi   bi   ta   jiehun.
   her   mother BE   force   her   get:married
   'Her mother did force her to get married.'
c.* ta   mama   bi   shi   ta   jiehun.
    her mother force BE   her   get:married
    'It was her that her mother forced to get married.'
d.* ta   mama   bi   ta   shi   jiehun.
    her mother force her   BE   get:married
    'It was to get married that her mother forced her.'

Finally, we have repeatedly pointed out that *shi* cannot occur postverbally. This observation, in our account, follows as a natural consequence of two facts. First, no topics occur postverbally and hence no postverbal constituents, unless they have been fronted to become topics first, can be raised to precede *shi*. Second, *shi* being a raising predicate will have a larger scope than the other verb unless the latter is also a raising predicate and hence in terms of surface linear sequence, cleft *shi* can only precede the other verb.

To sum up, we have presented six arguments supporting the analysis of positing cleft *shi* as a raising predicate subcategorizing a sentence in the deep structure and allowing various topics in the embedded sentence to be raised to precede it via the rule of Topic–raising.

2.3.4. Summary

In this section we first distinguish between the cleft construction from the pseudo–cleft one. In a pseudo–cleft sentence, *shi* is an equative verb linking two NP's which are referentially equivalent, as *ta* 'he' and *cong Shanghai lai de na–ge ren* 'the one who came from Shanghai' are in (35a). In cases where the head NP is deleted as in (35b) the relative clause marker *de* may be re–interpreted as a nominalizer but the equivalent relation of the two NP's flanking the verb *shi* 'be' remains unchanged. In the case of the cleft construction as in (37), *de* is a modal particle, indicating that the whole sentence, excepting the part marked by *shi* as focus, represents a situation expected by the speaker while *shi* is a grammaticalized verb whose function is to mark a constituent in its scope, usually the one immediately following it, as focus. Structure–wise, *shi* in this construction, like *keneng* 'possible' is a raising predicate that allows various topics contained in the embedded sentence it subcategorizes to be raised. By positing *shi* as a verb that takes a sentence as its complement and by positing a rule of Topic–raising, which is independently needed in Chinese grammar, we can account for a wide range of facts related to the cleft construction. This account is also in perfect agreement with Cheng's (1983) finding that focusing is often accompanied by topicalization. In this particular case topics, which represent unfocused information, are raised out of the scope of *shi*, thereby facilitating the identification of the focused elements.

3. Sentences with Sentential Subjects and Objects

A sentence can be embedded in another sentence and function as the subject or object of the main verb of the embedding (matrix) sentence. When this happens the whole sentence is a complex one and the embedded sentence is called the sentential subject or object of the matrix verb.

In what follows, we would examine very closely sentential subjects and objects in Chinese. As we have pointed out earlier, whether a sentential subject or object can occur in a sentence or not is determined by the matrix verb. To study the distribution and interpretation of this type of complex sentences we have to look into these verbs very carefully.

3.1. Sentential Subjects
3.1.1. Verbs that Take Sentential Subjects

Verbs that take snetential subjects, taken in its broad sense, embrace all one—place verbs that subcategorize a sentential complement. They include all the raising predicates that we have discussed as well as non—raising predicates, i.e., those that do not allow topics contained in the embedded clause to be raised. Since we have explored the former group in some detail, we will take up the latter group here and bring in a comparison later.

Verbs that take sentential subjects in its latter sense are rare. Below are some examples.

(59) ni   guang   shuo   nei—ge   <u>mei—yong</u>.
     you   merely   say   that—CL   useless
     'That you merely say it is of no use.'

(60) ta   ren   name   hao   que   si   de
     he   person   so   good   on:the:contrary   die   PART

> name zao zhen <u>kexi</u>.
> so young really pitiful
> 'It is a real pity that he is such a nice person and that he died so young.'

(61) ta mingtian bu lai bu <u>yaojin</u>.
he tomorrow not come not important
'It is not important that he won't come tomorrow.'

The sentential subject itself can be in the form of a statement as in (59) — (61) or a question, a V–not–V question as well as a WH–question, as shown in (62) and (63) respectively.

(62) ta mingtian lai–bu–lai mei guanxi.
he tomorrow come–not–come not matter
'It doesn't matter whether he comes tomorrow or not.'

(63) shei mingtian bu lai mei guanxi.
who tomorrow not come not matter
'Who does it not matter that won't come tomorrow?'

3.1.2. Raising vs. Non–raising Predicates

In the underlying structure, both raising and non–raising predicates look alike. It is just that in the derivation some predicates allow topics to be raised and others don't. And this accounts for the surface differences in word order. Compare (64) with (65).

(64) a. Zhang San mingtian mai–bu–mai shu <u>mei guanxi</u>.
Zhang San tomorrow buy–not–buy book not matter
'It doesn't matter whether tomorrow Zhang San will buy the book or not.'
b.* Zhang San <u>mei guanxi</u> mingtian mai–bu–mai shu.
Zhang San not matter tomorrow buy–not–buy book
'Roughly, same as (a).'

(65) a. Zhang San   mingtian   qu mai shu   <u>bu</u>   <u>heshi</u>.
        Zhang San   tomorrow   go buy book   not   appropriate
        'It is not appropriate for Zhang San to buy the book tomorrow.'
    b. Zhang San   <u>bu</u>   <u>heshi</u>   mingtian   qu mai   shu.
        Zhang San   not   appropriate   tomorrow   go buy   book
        'Roughly, same as (a).'[12]
    c. Zhang San   mingtian   <u>bu</u>   <u>heshi</u>   qu mai   shu.
        Zhang San   tomorrow   not   appropriate   go buy   book
        'Roughly, same as (a).'
    d. shu,   Zhang San   mingtian   <u>bu</u>   <u>heshi</u>   qu mai.
        book   Zhang San   tomorrow   not   appropriate   go buy
        'Roughly, same as (a).'
    e. mingtian   Zhang San   shu   <u>bu</u>   <u>heshi</u>   qu mai.
        tomorrow   Zhang San   book   not   appropriate   go buy
        'Roughly, same as (a).'

Two points are worth noting here. First, (65d) looks like a case of so—called "tough—movement" in English, as can be shown by comparing it with (66).

(66) a. It is difficult to buy the book.
    b. The book is difficult to buy.

But closer examination reveals significant differences. For one thing, in English only the object of the embedded verb is allowed to be raised by the rule of tough—movement. But in Chinese, all topics, primary and non—primary, are raisable with a raising predicate. For another, the verbs that allow tough—movement in English are more restricted than the ones that allow topic—raising in Chinese. *Heshi* 'appropriate' and *keneng* 'possible', for instance, are raising predicates in Chinese but their English counterparts cannot undergo tough—movement. Both restrictions in English are to be expected in view of the fact that English, as we have repeatedly shown, is far less topic—oriented than Chinese.

     It is also of interest to find out why both English and Chinese allow topics to be raised out of sentential complement. As yet there is very little discussion of this

---

     [12]Since in English 'inappropriate' is not a raising predicate, sentences (65b) − (65e) cannot be appropriately translated.

phenomenon in the literature, not to say consensus. But we feel that our study of the discourse functions of topics may throw some light on this knotty problem. Roughly, our hypothesis is that it is unwieldy to have a sentential subject, being an abstract idea in the form of a clause, as a sentential topic. We have some evidence in support of this hypothesis. First, since both tough–movement and topic–raising rules are optional, they are more likely to have to do with discourse than with syntax proper and it is common sense knowledge that in our daily discourse, though we often exchange ideas which are abstract, we almost never begin our utterences with abstract ideas. Furthermore, in our previous discussion of a related rule of topic–raising in connection with placement of such clause conjunctions as *yinwei* 'because' and *suiran* 'although' we have come across a very similar observation that abstract ideas in the form of a clause are less likely to be topics, though in the latter case we are dealing with abstract ideas such as "the time that ....", "the plact that ..." or "the reason that ...". (see Chapter 7 for details). This need for concrete topics, preferably human, becomes even clearer when we consider the fact that Chinese topics, chiefly the primary topic and more restrictedly the secondary topic, are frequently called upon to serve the chaining function of bringing several clauses together on the basis of sharing the same topic(s).

3.2. Sentential Objects
3.2.1. The Form of the Sentential Object

Unlike English where sentential objects are headed by a rich array of complementizers such as *that* (in the case of a statement), a WH–word like *whether, what, how* (in the case of a question), a *for ... to* (in the case of an infinitive) and POSS–ING (in the case of a gerund), Chinese, as a rule, does not use any complementizers to introduce its sentential objects.[13] Rather, Chinese sentential objects have forms that are no different from ordinary statements or questions, as exemplified by the following sentences.[14]

---

[13] Both Huang (1984) and Cheng (1985) have noticed that Mandarin, in colloquial speech at least, has an emerging complementizer for nominal clauses in the form of *shuo* 'say', as shown in (i).

(i) ta   tiyi   (shuo) women mei–ge   ren   juan   wu–kuai
     he   propose   say   we   every–CL   person donate five–dollar
     qian.
     money
     'He proposed (that) everyone of us donate five dollars.'

[14] Because there is no difference in form between a direct and an indirect statement and question, sometimes it is difficult to tell in writing whether it is a direct question or not when the matrix verb is a verb of locution, as shown in (i) below.

(i) a. ta   wen wo, "Zhang San   da–le   shei?"
         he   ask me   Zhang San   hit–ASP   who

(67) wo zhidao <u>ta mingtian hui lai</u>.
    I know   he tomorrow will come
    'I know that he'll come tomorrow.'

(68) ta bu zhidao <u>Li Si da—shang—le   shei</u>.
    he not know   Li Si hit—wound—ASP   who
    'He doesn't know whom Li Si hit and wounded.'

(69) ta bu zhidao <u>mingtian yao—bu—yao   kai—hui</u>.
    he not know   tomorrow need—not—need   attend—meeting
    'He doesn't know whether he needs to attend a meeting or not tomorrow.

Thus, the sentential objects in sentences (67) through (69) are a statement, a WH—question and a V—not—V question respectively. As can be expected there are co—occurrence restrictions between the type of sentential object and the verb, which we will take up in connection with our discussion of the classification of verbs that can take a sentential object.

Another interesting phenomenon that has attracted a number of researchers is that the sentential object can in many cases be followed, or replaced, by an abstract noun in apposition to it. In English, there are some nouns used in this function such as *the fact, the rumor* etc., but they are rather restricted in number. Chinese, on the other hand, has a rich array of such nouns. Listed in (70) are most of the common ones.

(70) a. <u>shiqing</u> or <u>shi</u> 'matter'   b. <u>shishi</u> 'fact'
    c. <u>wenti</u> 'problem, question'   d. <u>yiwen</u> 'question'
    e. <u>xiaoxi</u> 'news'   f. <u>yijian</u> 'opinion'
    g. <u>jihua</u> 'plan'   h. <u>hua</u> 'speech, word'
    i. <u>yaoyan</u> 'rumor'

These appositives can be optionally preceded by such determiners as *zhe, zhei* 'this' and *na*,

---

          'He asked me, "Who(m) did Zhang San hit?"'
  b. ta wen wo Zhang San   da—le   shei.
    he ask me Zhang San   hit—ASP who
    'He asked me who(m) Zhang San hit.'
In actual speech, the two are distinguished by having a pause before a direct question and by saying it with a rising intonation.

nei 'that' and an appropriate classifier. Examine the following examples.

(71) a. wo zhidao ni   yao   lai.
         I know   you   will come
         'I know that you are coming.'
     b. wo zhidao ni   yao   lai   de (na–jian) shi.
         I know   you   will come DE that–CL   matter
         'I know of the matter of your coming.'
     c. wo zhidao ni   yao   lai   de jihua.
         I know   you   will come DE plan
         'I know of your plan to come here.'
     d. wo zhidao ni   yao   lai   de chuanyan.
         I know   you   will come DE rumor
         'I know of the rumor that you are coming here.'
     e. wo zhidao ni   yao   lai   de mimi.
         I know   you   will come DE secret
         'I know of the secret of your coming here.'

(72) a. ta shuo–guo ta xiang dao zhe–li lai.
         he say–ASP he want   to   here   come
         'He mentioned that he would like to come here.'
     b. ta shuo–guo ta xiang dao zhe–li lai de
         he say–ASP he want   to   here   come DE
         (na–zhong)   hua.
         that–CL   speech
         'Roughly, same as (a).'
     c. ta shuo–guo ta xiang dao zhe–li lai de shi.
         he say–ASP he want   to   here   come DE matter
         'He mentioned the matter of his coming here.'

Some of these verbs can be associated with many more appositive nouns than others, as can be seen by comparing (71) with (72), but every verb forms a close tie with only one appositive noun that is most closely associated with its meaning. So when the verb with its sentential object occurs without the following appositive, it is interpreted in that sense. This is demonstrated by the (b) paraphrases of both (71) and (72).

There are, however, two verbs that do not have any appositives associated with them. They are *renwei* 'think, regard' and *yiwei* 'think or think incorrectly', as shown in (73).

(73) a. ni   renwei zhe–jian shi   gai   zenme chuli?
        you   think   this–CL   matter should how   handle
        'How do you think the matter should be handled?'
    b.* ni   renwei zhe–jian shi   gai   zenme chuli
        you   think   this–CL   matter should how   handle
        de yijian?
        DE opinion
        'Roughly, same as (a).'

Another interesting phenomenon in connection with the use of these appositives is that when the sentential object occurs postverbally, the use of these appositives is optional, as we have just shown, but when the sentential object occurs preverbally as when it occurs as a *ba* or *bei* NP in a *ba* or *bei* construction, then their occurrence is obligatory, as witnessed by the ungrammaticality of (74d).

(74) a. renren   dou ting–dao ni   yao   lai.
        everybody all hear   you want come
        'Everybody heard that you would like to come.'
    b. renren   dou ting–dao ni   yao   lai   de xiaoxi.
       everybody   all hear   you want come DE news
       'Everybody heard of the news that you would like to come.'
    c. ni   yao   lai   de xiaoxi bei ren   chuan–chuqu
       you want come DE news   BEI people spread–out
       le.
       PART
       'The news that you would like to come was spread out.'
    d.* ni   yao   lai   bei ren   chuan–chuqu le.
        you want come BEI people spread–out   PART
        'Roughly, same as (c).'

The reason for this requirement is not yet totally clear. We feel, however, that it definitely has to do with ease of perception. Earlier we have pointed out that the use of the sentential object is determined by the matrix verb. In terms of actual perception of sentences like (74a), a hearer, having heard the matrix verb, *tingdao* 'hear', will naturally come to expect there to be a sentential object following close behind, but a person, being exposed to (74d) will have no such advantage, for what follows *bei* is usually not a nominal clause. In the latter case, therefore, a hearer will need the help of the appositive to determine that it is a preposed sentential object.[15]

A comparable situation can be found in English. The complementizer *that* heading a sentential object in its postverbal position is optional, as can be seen by comparing (75a) with (75b), but the same complementizer, when occurring in a preverbal position as in a passive sentence, becomes necessary, as shown in (76).

(75) a. Everyone knows that he is coming here tomorrow.
b. Everyone knows he is coming here tomorrow.

(76) a. That he is coming here tomorrow is known to everyone.[16]
b.* He is coming here tomorrow is known to everyone.

Thus, even though different elements are involved in Chinese and English, we have basically the same phenomenon and the same explanation will also account for the English data.

The third point of interest in connection with the sentential object is that in some cases the clause may, due to different rules of Indentical NP deletion, some obligatory and some optional, actually end up as a VP in the surface structure. Compare (77a) with (77b).

(77) a. wo$_i$ xiwang ____$_i$ neng qu.
I hope can go
'I hope that I can go.'
b. wo xiwang ni neng qu.
I hope you can go
'I hope that you can go.'

---

[15] Please also see Li et al. (1984: 262—264) for a similar but more elaborate explanation for this phenomenon.

[16] The same principle can also be applied to account for the obligatory presence of complementizer 'that' in the case of unextraposed sentential subject, as shown in (i).
(i) a. That he was coming here surprised everyone.
b.* He was coming here surprised everyone.

As these deletion rules are determined to a great extent by the meaning of the matrix verb, we will discuss them in connection with the classification of verbs that take sentential objects.

3.2.2. Verbs that Take Sentential Objects

Having made clear the formal aspects of the sentential object, we will now proceed to examine the relation between the verb and the sentential object that it subcategories.

3.2.2.1 Major Classes of Matrix Verbs

Verbs that take sentential objects fall into four classes: verbs of locution, verbs of cognition, verbs of imagination and verbs of inquiry. The first three classes can take both statement and question as object while the last one can only take question. In this section we will give all the important verbs of each class. We will take up the interpretation of sentences containing these verbs and their sentential objects in the next.[17]

3.2.2.1.1. Verbs of Locution

Verbs in the class can be further divided into two.

Type A: Say–type verbs

These verbs take no unmarked indirect object and most of them can also take *shuo* 'say' when they take a direct question. Important say–type verbs are given below.

(78) a. shuo 'speak, say'   b. jiang 'speak'
      c. shuoming 'explain'   d. biaoming 'reveal'
      e. gaobai 'confess'   f. tiqi 'bring up'
      g. tidao 'mention'   h. xuanbu 'announce'
      i. baogao 'report'   j. baozheng 'guarantee'
      k. toulu 'reveal'

Type B: Tell–type verbs

These verbs take a statement as direct object and in addition, an unmarked indirect object. They include:

---

[17] The discussion in this and the following section is largely based on Li et al. (1984).

(79) a. gaosu 'tell'   b. tongzhi 'notify'
      c. huida 'answer'   d. jinggao 'warn'
      e. tixing 'remind'

3.2.2.1.2. Verbs of Cognition

These verbs are also known as "factive verbs" because they take sentential objects that denote matters presupposed to be facts.[18] The following verbs belong to this class.

(80) a. zhidao 'know'   b. jide 'remember'
      c. wangle 'forget'   d. wangji 'forget'
      e. fajue 'discover'   f. kan–qingchu 'see clearly'
      g. mingbai 'understand'   h. xiangqi 'recollect'
      i. renchu 'know, make out'   j. liaodao 'predict correctly'
      k. tihuidao 'know through experience'   l. xiangdao 'think of'
      m. caidao 'guess correctly'   n. kanchu 'perceive'
      o. kanjian 'see'   p. tingjian 'hear'
      q. fajue 'discover'   r. faxian 'discover'
      s. dongde 'understand'   t. huiyi 'recollect'

3.2.2.1.3. Verbs of Imagination

Contrary to that of the previous class, the objects of these verbs are not facts, but ideas, plans, hopes or misconceptions that are created by an act of imagination. Verbs of imagination can be further divided into verbs of judgment, thinking–feeling, approval, and hope–fear.

A. Verbs of Judgement

(81) a. jueding 'decide'   b. renwei 'regard as'
      c. duanding 'decide'   d. panding 'judge'
      e. guji 'estimate'   f. cai 'guess'
      g. caixiang 'guess'   h. kan 'think'

---

[18]In addition to verbs of cognition, factive verbs include some verbs of emotion such as *houhui* 'regret', *qikuai* 'feel strange' etc. See Section 3.2.2.2.1. for more discussion of factivity.

i. xiangxin 'believe' j. huaiyi 'doubt'
k. chengren 'recognize' l. yiwei 'assume; assume incorrectly'

B. Verbs of Approval
(82) a. zancheng 'approve' b. tongyi 'agree'
c. fandui 'oppose' d. piping 'criticise'
e. pa 'be afraid' f. tiyi 'propose'
g. jianyi 'propose, suggest' h. zhuzhang 'advocate'
i. huanying 'welcome' j. zuzhi 'prevent'
k. fangai 'prevent' l. qiangdiao 'emphasize'
m. guanxin 'be concerned about"

C. Verbs of Thinking—Feeling
(83) a. xiang 'think' b. kaolü 'consider'
c. wangle 'forget' d. wangji 'forget'
e. dongde 'know how to' f. jide 'remember'
g. gandao 'feel' h. ganjue 'feel'
i. mengdao 'dream of'

D. Verbs of Hope—Fear
(84) a. xiwang 'hope' b. pan 'hope'
c. panwang 'hope' d. baozheng 'garantee'
e. pa 'fear' f. haipa 'fear'
g. danxin 'worry' h. jingtan 'marvel, wonder'
i. bimian 'avoid' j. xihuan 'like'
k. taoyan 'dislike'

Of these four classes, verbs of judgment and thinking—feeling can take a V—not—V question as their object, while verbs of approval and hope—fear cannot. This contrast is shown in (85).

(85) a. ni juede ta hui—bu—hui hui—lai?
you feel he will—not—will come—back
'Do you feel that he will come back?'

b.* ni   zancheng ta hui–bu–hui   hui–lai?
   you   approve   he will–not–will come–back
   'Do you approve of his coming back or not?'

3.2.2.1.4. Verbs of Inquiry

As its name implies, verbs of this class can take only questions as their objects. This class can be further divided into two sub–classes, ask–type verbs and test–type verbs, depending on whether they can take an indirect object (ask–type) or not (test–type). Below we give all the important verbs in each type.

(86)   Ask–type Verbs
    a. <u>wen</u> 'ask'   b. <u>panwen</u> 'interrogate'
    c. <u>diaocha</u> 'investigate'   d. <u>qingwen</u> 'ask politely'
    e. <u>zhuijiu</u> 'seek a final answer'

(87)   Test–type Verbs
    a. <u>cai</u> 'guess'   b. <u>xiang zhidao</u> 'want to know'
    c. <u>taolun</u> 'discuss'   d. <u>yanjiu</u> 'study'
    e. <u>yao zhidao</u> 'want to know'   f. <u>tantao</u> 'inquire'
    g. <u>kaolü</u> 'deliberate'   h. <u>shiyan</u> 'test'

3.2.2.2. The Interpretation of the Sentential Object

There are several complicated issues involved in the interpretation of the sentential object. Below we will take up three important ones, namely, (1) factive vs. non–factive interpretation, (2) direct vs. indirect interrogative interpretation, and finally (3) the interpretation of the subject in the sentential object clause.

3.2.2.2.1. Factive Sentential Objects

We have pointed out that verbs of cognition are factive verbs. This is so because a verb of cognition presupposes the proposition expressed by its sentential object to be true, no matter whether the matrix verb is affirmative or negative, as shown in (88).

(88) a. ta zhidao Roulan yijing   jie–hun   le.
       he know   Roulan already   get–married   PART
       'He knew that Roulan had already got married.'

b. ta   bu   zhidao   Roulan   yijing   jie—hun   le.
   he   not   know   Roulan   already   get—married   PART
   'He didn't know that Roulan had already got married.'

Thus, in both (88 a and b), the sentential object "Roulan had already got married" is assumed to be true by the speaker no matter whether the matrix verb *zhidao* 'know' is negated or not.

Another class of factive verbs has to do with one's feelings, and following Lien (1986) will be called 'emotive factives', the most important members of which are given in (89).

(89) a. <u>hen gaoxing</u> 'very glad'   b. <u>hen rongxing</u> 'honored'
     c. <u>houhui</u> 'regret'   d. <u>baoqian</u> 'sorry'

The two sentences in (90), one affirmative and the other negative, exemplify the use of *houhui* 'regret' as a factive verb.[19]

(90) a. ta   houhui   mei   qu   kai—hui.
       he   regret   not   go   attend—meeting
       'He regretted that he didn't attend the meeting.'
    b. ta   bu   houhui   mei   qu   kai—hui.
       he   not   regret   not   go   attend—meeting
       'He didn't regret that he didn't attend the meeting.'

Thus in (90), whether he regretted or not, the fact remains that he didn't attend the meeting.

Actually, not all verbs of cognition are equally strong in their factive interpretation. The contrast can be clearly brought out if we compare (88) with (91), especially when the matrix verb is negated.

---

[19]It is interesting to note that Chinese requires *houhui* 'regret' be followed in some cases by *bu gai* 'not should' in its sentential object while English does not. This contrast can be seen by comparing (i) with its English translation.
(i) ta   houhui   (ta)   <u>bu   gai</u>   gen   Li Xiaojie   jiehun.
    he   regret   he   not   should   with   Li Miss   marry
    'He regretted that he married Miss Li.'

(91) a. ta   faxian   Roulan yijing   jie–hun   le.
       he   discover   Roulan already get–married   PART
       'He discovered that Roulan had already got married.'
    b. ta mei faxian   Roulan yijing   jie–hun   le.
       he not discover Roulan already get–married   PART
       'He didn't discover that Roulan had already got married.'

(91b), as compared to (88b), does not necessarily presuppose the proposition that "Roulan had already got married" to be true. This can be seen by the fact that the truth can be cancelled by a following statement, as shown in (91c).

    c. ta mei faxian   Roulan   yijing   jie–hun.
       he not discover Roulan   already get–married
       shishi–shang,   ta lian   Roulan   dou mei zhao–dao.
       in–fact   he including Roulan   all not find
       'He didn't discover that Roulan had already got married. In fact, he didn't even find Roulan.'

So, as far as factive presupposition is concerned, there is good reason to subdivide verbs of cognition into two: factive vs. semifactive, as represented by *zhidao* 'know' and *faxian* 'discover' respectively.

3.2.2.2.2. Direct vs. Indirect Interrogatives

It seems self–evident that if the matrix verb is in a question form, then the whole sentence is interpreted as a question, as shown in (92a) and if the question form appears in the sentential object, then it is interpreted as an indirect question, as shown in (92b).

(92) a. ni   zhidao–bu–zhidao   ta   hui   lai?
       you   know–not–know   he   will   come
       'Do you know that he will come?'
    b. ni   bu   zhidao   ta   hui–bu–hui   lai.
       you not   know   he   will–not–will   come
       'You don't know whether he will come or not.'

Things, however, are not as straightforward as that. There are at least two situations that require closer examination. They are represented by the following two sentences.

(93)   ni   zhidao   ta   mingtian   yao   lai   ma?
you   know   he   tomorrow   will   come   PART
(i) 'Do you know that he will come tomorrow?'
(ii) 'Do you know whether he will come tomorrow?'

(94)   ni   renwei   ta   mingtian   yao   lai   ma?
you   think   he   tomorrow   will   come   PART
'Do you think that he will come tomorrow?'

First, notice that when the matrix verb is a cognitive verb, then a sentence involving a final question particle is ambiguous between two readings, as shown in the two translations in (93). One may wish to attribute this ambiguity to the different scope interpretations of the final particle *ma*, i.e., whether it has its scope over the matrix sentence, the embedded sentence alone or both. However, for reason that is not totally clear at the moment, the second possibility — that the embedded sentence alone is questioned — is ruled out.[20] However, when the form is embedded in a verb of imagination, such as *renwei* 'think' as in (94), the sentence is unambiguous, as it can only have the interpretation that the matrix sentence alone is questioned.

This interpretation is further affirmed when we replace the particle *ma* question by the V–not–V question, as shown in (95) and (96).

(95)   a.   ni   zhidao–bu–zhidao   ta   mingtian   yao   lai?
you   know–not–know   he   tomorrow   will   come
'Same as (93i).'

---

[20] We suspect that the impossibility of questioning a sentential object embedded under a verb of cognition in this case as well as in (95c) may be due to a semantic clash between what is presupposed by the matrix verb and what is meant by the embedded clauses, i.e., it is not congruent for the same speaker to say that he knows of something that he is questioning. That this interpretation is probably correct is affirmed by the fact that a negative cognitive verb can take a question as its object. Compare (95c) with (i) below.
(i)   ni   bu   zhidao   ta   mingtian   yao–bu–yao   lai.
you   not   know   he   tomorrow   will–not–will   come
'You don't know whether he will come tomorrow or not.'

  b. ni zhidao–bu–zhidao ta mingtian yao–bu–yao lai?
    you know–not–know he tomorrow will–not–will come
    'Same as (93ii).'
  c.* ni zhidao ta mingtian yao–bu–yao lai?
    you know he tomorrow will–not–will come

(96) a. ni renwei ta mingtian yao–bu–yao lai?
    you think he tomorrow will–not–will come
    'Same as (94).'
  b.* ni renwei–bu–renwei ta mingtian yao–bu–yao lai?
    you think–not–think he tomorrow will–not–will come
 * 'Do you think whether he will come tomorrow?'
  c.* ni renwei–bu–renwei ta mingtian yao lai?
    you think–not–think he tomorrow will come

We can clearly see from these examples that verbs of imagination behave differently from verbs of cognition in allowing a question that occurs syntactically in the sentential object to go up to the matrix sentence in interpretation.[21] Verbs of locution and inquiry pattern with verbs of cognition in this respect, as readers can determine for themselves by putting some of the verbs in these two classes to test.

  WH–questions also follow the same principle of interpretation except when a WH–word occurs in a sentential object embedded under a matrix question whose main verb is a verb of imagination. In that case, the WH–word is interpreted as an indefinite determiner. Compare (97) with (98), especially the (b) and (c) sentences.

(97) a. ni zhidao <u>shei</u> yao lai.
    you know who will come
    'You know who will come.'
  b. ni zhidao–bu–zhidao <u>shei</u> yao lai?
    you know–not–know who will come
    'Do you know who will come?'
  c. <u>shei</u> zhidao <u>shei</u> yao lai?
    who know who will come
    'Who knows who will come?'

---

  [21]Tang (1988:301–302) has come to a similar conclusion although he has posited fewer verbs and he calls them "verbs of conjecture."

(98) a. ni   renwei ta   gai   chi   dian   sheme yao?
       you   think   he   should eat   a:little what   medicine
       'What medicine do you think he should take a little?'

   b. ni   renwei–bu–renwei   ta   gai   chi   dian   sheme
      you   think–not–think   he   should take   a:little some
      yao?
      medicine
      'Do you think that he should take some medicine or not?'

   c. sheme ren   renwei ni   gai   chi   dian   sheme
      what person think   you   should eat   a:little some
      yao?
      medicine
      'Who thinks that you should take some medicine?'

3.2.2.2.3. The Interpretation of Subject in the Sentential Object

In our previous attempt to identify subject in Chinese, we have discussed the verb *xiang* 'want' as an Equi-verb. In this use of *xiang* 'want' the deleted subject of the embedded clause is always interpreted as coreferential with the matrix subject, as shown in (99).

(99) a. ta$_i$ xiang   ____$_i$ qu.
        he   want   go
        'He wants to go.'

   b. ta$_i$ xiang   ziji$_i$ qu.
      he   want   self   go
      'He wants to go himself.'

   c. ta$_i$ xiang   ta–ziji$_i$ qu.
      he   want   he–self   go
      'Same as (b).'

There are other verbs that behave like *xiang* 'want'. They include *dasuan* 'intend', *jihua* 'plan' and *kaolü* 'consider'. As they share the common characteristic that their matrix subject expresses an intention to do something himself, they will be called "verbs of self-intention". These verbs can be followed by a zero (a deleted NP), *ziji* 'self' or pro+*ziji* 'pro+self', as shown in (99) (a), (b) and (c). In a sentence like this, the zero or the pro-form is interpreted as coreferential with the matrix subject. But a pronoun, identical in form with the matrix subject, cannot occur in that position no matter whether it is intended to be coreferential with the matrix subject or not, as (99d) is ungrammatical in both interpretations. Likewise, a full NP cannot occur in that position unless it is preceded by either *rang* 'let' or (*jiao* 'make'), as shown by (99e) and (99f) respectively.

    d.   <u>ta</u> xiang <u>ta</u> qu.
         he   want he go
  *   i   i   (i)
  *   i   j   (ii)
      (i) 'He wants himself to go.'
      (ii) 'He wants him to go.'
    e.* ta xiang Lao Wang qu.
         he want   Lao Wang go
      'He wants Lao Wang to go.'
    f.   ta xiang rang Lao Wang qu.
         he want   let   Lao Wang go
      'He wants to let Lao Wang go.'

Things seem to be nice and neat up to this point but it ceases to be so when we go beyond this small group of verbs. For this reason, the generalizations that we are to make with regard to the interpretation of the subject of the sentential object should be taken as highly tentative. As far as we can make out, verbs of thinking-feeling (e.g., *renwei* 'think') and verbs of hope-fear (e.g., *xiwang* 'hope') behave differently from verbs of cognition (e.g., *zhidao* 'know'), judgment (e.g., *xiangxin* 'believe') and approval (e.g., *zancheng* 'approve'). In the following discussion, we will take up the interpretation of the embedded subject when it is in one of the following four forms: (i) a zero, (ii) a pronoun of the same form as the matrix subject, (iii) *ziji* 'self' form and (iv) pro+*ziji*.

    With verbs of thinking-feeling or hope-fear as represented by *renwei* 'think' and *xiwang* 'hope', the situation is like the following.

    When the embedded subject is a zero, the non-realized NP can be interpreted as coreferential with the matrix subject, as shown in (100) or as coreferential with an NP mentioned previously in the discourse, as shown in (101).

(100) ta$_i$ xiwang ____$_i$ neng qu
      he   hope   can go
      'He hopes that he can go.'

(101) A: ni xiang ta neng–bu–neng qu?
        you think he can–not–can go
        'Do you think he can go?'
    B: wo bu zhidao. wo xiwang ____ neng qu.
        I not know I hope can go
        'I don't know. I hope he can.'

In the case of a pronoun identical in form with the matrix subject, the embedded subject cannot be construed as referring back to the matrix subject but rather to someone else. This is shown in (102) (a) and (b) respectively.

(102)   ta xiwang ta neng qu.
    a.* i   i
    b.   i   j
    a. 'He hopes that he can go.'
    b. 'He hopes that he (someone else) can go.'

By using the form of *ziji* 'self' or pro+*ziji* 'pro+self'', the embedded subject is interpreted as referring back to the matrix subject. These two cases are exemplified in (103) and (104) respectively.

(103)   ta xiwang ziji neng qu.
    a.   i   i
    b.* i   j
    a. 'He hopes that he himself can go.'
    b. 'He (i) hopes that he himself (j) can go.'

(104)   ta xiwang ta–ziji neng qu.
    a.   i   i
    b.* i   j
    a. 'Same as (103a).'
    b. 'Same as (103b).'

With verbs of cognition, judgment and approval, the picture is different. When the embedded subject is a zero, it cannot be construed as coreferential with the matrix subject. The only possible controller of this unrealized NP is a previously mentioned coreferential NP. Compare (105) with (106).

(105)   ta   xiangxin   _____   bubi   qu.
        he   believe   no:need   go
   a.* i   i
   b.   i   j
   a.   'He believes that he himself need not go.'
   b.   'He believes that he (someone else) need not go.'

(106)   A: ni   xiang   ta   you–mei–you   biyao   qu?
           you   think   he   have–not–have   need   go
           'Do you think there is a need for him to go?'
        B: wo   xiangxin   _____   bubi   qu.
           I   believe   no:need   go
           'I believe (he) need not go.'

The situation is just the reverse when a pronoun, identical in form with the matrix subject appears in the slot. In this case, it is possible, though not necessary, to construe it as coreferential with the matrix subject. This is shown in (107), where both interpretations result in grammatical sentences.

(107)   ta   xiangxin   ta   bubi   qu.
   a.   i   i
   b.   i   j
   a.   'He believes that he need not go.'
   b.   'He believes that he (someone else) need not go.'

When either *ziji* or pro–*ziji* is used, as in (108) and (109), the embedded subject is always interpreted as coreferential with the matrix subject. Compare the (a) and (b) sentences in (108) and (109).

(108)   ta xiangxin   ziji   bubi   qu.
         he believe   self   no:need   go
   a.   i   i
   b.*   i   j
   a. 'He (i) believes that he himself need not go.'
   b. 'He (i) believes that he himself (j) need not go.'

(109)   ta xiangxin   ta-ziji   bubi   qu.
   a.   i   i
   b.*   i   j
   a. 'Same as (108a).'
   b. 'Same as (108b).'

Our discussion of the interpretation of the embedded subject in construction with the three classes of verbs can be summarized in the following chart.

matrix verb / embedded subject	verbs of self-intention (e.g., xiang 'want')	verbs of hope-fear, thinking-feeling (e.g., xiwang 'hope')	verbs of cognition, judgment & approval (e.g., zhidao 'know', xiangxin 'believe')
zero	always coreferential with matrix subj.	can be coreferential with matrix subj.	cannot be coreferential with matrix subj.
identical pronoun	—	cannot be coreferential with matrix subj.	can be coreferential with matrix subj.
ziji	always coreferential	always coreferential	always coreferential
pro + ziji	always coreferential	always coreferential	always coreferential

The Interpretation of the Embedded Subject

426

This discussion, though far from being conclusive, has far-reaching implication for the study of Chinese grammar. Despite the reservation that we have with regard to our findings, one thing is very clear when we compare the situation we are describing with the comparable situation in English. And that is: Chinese allows far more interaction between syntax and discourse. In English, for instance, the subject of an embedded finite clause can never be deleted but this is clearly not the case in Chinese, as our discussion has clearly shown. Furthermore, this is by no means an isolated case. In our discussion throughout the book we have time and again come across similar observations. Looking at the phenomenon under discussion this way, it can then be construed as yet another substantiation of our claim that Chinese is far more discourse-oriented than English.

4. Relativization

Like English and many other languages, Chinese allows a sentence to be embedded within a noun phrase as a modifier of the head NP, as shown in (110). This process is known as relativization and the clause that is so embedded is called a relative clause.

(110) a. nei-ge   ren   xihuan   nei-ben   shu.
         that-CL person   like   that-CL   book
         'The man likes the book.'

   b. xihuan   nei-ben   shu   de   nei-ge   ren
      like   that-CL   book   Rel. Mar.   that-CL   person
      lai-le.
      come-ASP
      'The man who likes the book has come.'

   c. nei-ge   ren   xihuan   de   nei-ben   shu
      that-CL person   like   Rel. Mar.   that-CL   book
      lai-le.
      come-ASP
      'The book that the man likes has come.'

Thus, functionally in (110b) the relative clause *xihuan nei-ben shu de* 'who likes the book' modifies *ren* 'person'. To put it another way, it further restricts the reference of *ren* so as to help the hearer identify the exact referent that the speaker has in mind. Formally, the head NP is always understood to play a role in the relative clause. In (110b), it is the subject and in (110c), it is the object. When this happens, the head NP is either deleted or pronominalized, depending on the role that it plays in the relative clause.[22]

This is, of course, just a general discussion. We will go into the details of relative clause formation and its function very shortly. As English relativization has been extensively discussed, the process and function of Chinese relativization can be best approached by comparing them with those in English. The following two sections will, therefore, be devoted to these two aspects of Chinese relative clauses.

4.1. Formal Characteristics
4.1.1. Word Order

One striking contrast between the relative clause in English and Chinese is its position with regard to its head. In Chinese the relative clause precedes its head in the surface structure, while in English the relative clause follows its head.[23] Compare (111) and (112), where the relative clause is underlined and the head is italicized.

(111)   *The man* who came to see you yesterday is Mr. Wang.

(112)   zuotian   lai   kan   ni   de   *nei–ge   ren* shi
        yesterday come   see   you   Rel. Mar. that–CL   man   be
        Wang Xiansheng.
        Wang Mr.
        'The man who came to see you yesterday is Mr. Wang.'

While this positional difference is quite straightforward, it turns out to have other far-reaching implications. These points will be taken up in the relevant sections. Right now, we would like to concentrate on a minor variation in Chinese. The variation in question is that the determiner–quantifier–classifier phrase (DQC) can occur in the two positions as shown in (113a) and (113b). The DQC phrase is underlined.

(113) a. ni   yao   de   nei   san–ben   shu   zai
          you   want Rel. Mar. those three–CL   book   at

---

[22]In our previous attempt to identify subject and topic in Chinese, we have gone into various situations with regard to this process. See Chapter 2 for discussion.

[23]I am fully aware that there are linguists who argue that the relative clause in Chinese should follow its head in the deep structure. See among others Tai (1973) and Tang (1979).

                wo jia—li.
                my house—LOC
                'The three books you want are at my place.'
        b. <u>nei   san—ben</u> ni   yao   de   shu   zai
            those three—CL   you want Rel. Mar. book at
            wo jia—li.
            my house—LOC
            'Same as (113a).'

    Chao (1968) characterizes the relative clause in (113a) (where the DQC follows it) as "restrictive" in function, and that in (113b) (where the DQC precedes it) as "descriptive" in function. Hashimoto (1971) follows Chao's characterization. However, Tang (1979), on the basis of most native speakers' judgment in Taiwan, comes to the conclusion that no such distinction is systematically observed and claims that no hard and fast rules exist to account for this positional difference. Huang (1982:68–69), on the other hand, claims that the semantic distinction does exist, no matter how subtle it is, and it shows up as a grammatical distinction when a relative clause occurs within a noun phrase used in apposition to a proper name, as shown by the contrast between (114a) and (114b).

    (114) a.   Niuyue,   zhei—ge   renren   dou   xiaode   de
                    New York this—CL   everyone all   know   Rel. Mar.
                    chengshi....
                    city
                    'This city, New York, which everyone knows....'
           b.?   Niuyue,   renren   dou   xiaode   de   zhei—ge
                    New York everyone all   know   Rel. Mar. this—CL
                    chengshi....
                    city
                    'Same as (a).'

While I agree with Huang in his judgment that (114a) is better than (114b), I do not find (114b) to be completely ungrammatical as he claims. So it seems to me that such a subtle distinction should best be taken care of as a stylistic preference rather than a systematic syntactic difference.

4.1.2. Relative Pronouns

It has been correctly pointed out by Paris (1976) that only English has relative pronouns. She characterizes them as morphemes which stand for nouns and vary morphologically in accordance with the function of the noun which is relativized in the relative clause and which are also sensitive to the [± HUMAN] feature of that noun.

(115)　The man $\left\{\begin{array}{l}\text{that}\\ \text{who}\\ *\text{whom}\end{array}\right\}$ is wearing a hat ....

(116)　The man $\left(\left\{\begin{array}{l}\text{whom}\\ \text{that}\end{array}\right\}\right)$ John saw ....

(117)　The book $\left(\left\{\begin{array}{l}\text{which}\\ \text{that}\end{array}\right\}\right)$ John likes ....

It is also well-known that when a relative pronoun is in the objective case, it can be optionally deleted, as indicated by the parentheses in (116) and (117). The best explanation for the deletion, as far as I can determine, is the one given by Bever and Langendoen (1971) that we referred to in Chapter 1. In their paper they convincingly argue that there are two very important perceptual strategies in English, which, informally stated, say that: (a) when we come across a noun phrase followed by a finite verb phrase, then mark the noun phrase as the beginning of a sentence (or clause); and (b) when the finite verb phrase in question is intransitive, then mark it as the end of the sentence (or clause), or if it is transitive or a linking verb phrase, then mark the noun phrase following the verb phrase as the end. Given these two strategies and the fact that the objective-case relative pronoun is followed by the subject nominal and the finite verb phrase of the relative clause, then the demarcation of the relative clause can be made without the presence of the relative pronoun. That is why its presence, in the objective case, is optional.

This explanation also shows clearly that the relative pronoun, like adverbial connectives such as 'when', 'where' etc. has the connective function — it helps the demarcation of the main clause and the relative clause. At the same time, it serves the function of narrowing down the possible role that the relativized NP plays in the relative clause.

Chinese, on the other hand, has no relative pronouns that serve these two functions. Rather, the first function is served by the relative clause marker *de*, while the second function is served by the empty NP slot or the resumptive pronoun in the relative clause.

4.1.3. Topicality

In Chapter two where we examined the role played by subject and topic in various syntactic processes, we reported on Keenan and Comrie's Accessibility Hierarchy (AH), which they claim to be universally utilized in the formation of relative clauses. AH, you may recall, can be summarized as (118).

(118) AH: SU > DO > IO > OBL > GEN > O COMP
where > =   is more accessible than
SU =   subject; DO =direct object; IO =indirect object;
OBL =   major oblique case NP (NPs that express arguments of the main predicate, as 'the chest' in 'John put the money in the chest,' rather than ones having a more adverbial function like 'that day' in 'John left on that day');
GEN =   genitive (or possessor) NP (e.g., 'the man' in 'John took the man's hat');
O COMP = object of comparison (e.g., 'the man' in 'John is taller than the man')

As far as Chinese relative clause formation is concerned, they observe, on the basis of data provided by Sanders and Tai (1972), that the pronominalization and deletion of relativized NP in the relative clause follows the hierarchy shown in (119).

(119)   SU   DO   IO   OBL   GEN O COMP
           −   +/−   +   +   +   +
key: − means that no pronoun is retained; +/− means that in some cases the pronoun is retained and in others it is not; + means that pronominalization is obligatory.

As we have commented on the hierarchy extensively in our earlier discussion, there is no need to repeat ourselves. Our examination of the coreferential NP deletion or pronominalization process and other related phenomena in Chinese relative clause formation, however, has led us to a different conclusion that it is actually topicality rather than accessibility that is involved, i.e., if an NP can be topicalized, then it can also be relativized.

Earlier we have presented a number of arguments in support of this conclusion. They need not be repeated here. However, our later discussion of the topical structure in Chinese has unearthed at least one more argument for it. In our discussion of the comparative structure like (120):

(120) X bi   Y you–qian.
       X COMP Y have–money
       'X is richer than Y.'

we have pointed out that X and Y must be topics of an equal rank and that, as far as discourse quality of topic is concerned, it is the first topic NP X or the larger NP containing both X and Y that has it. Y alone has very little, if any, such quality.

Now if relativization is indeed closely related to topicalization as we have claimed, then one would expect X in (120) to be much more relativizable than Y. That this is indeed the case can be seen by comparing (b) and (d) with (c) in (121).

(121) a.   Xiaoming   bi   ta   gao   san   cun.
            Xiaoming   COMP he   tall   three inch
            'Xiaoming is taller than he by three inches.'
       b.   _____   bi   ta   gao   san   cun   de   ren
                       COMP he   tall   three inch   Rel. Mar. person
            shi Xiaoming.
            be   Xiaoming
            'The one who is taller than he by three inches is Xiaoming.'
       c.?? Xiaoming   bi   ta   gao   san   cun   de
            Xiaoming   COMP he   tall   three inch   Rel. Mar.
            ren   shi   ta.
            person be   he
       ??   'The one who Xiaoming is taller than by three inches is he.'
       d.   _____   bi   Xiaoming   ai   san   cun   de
                       COMP Xiaoming   short three inch   Rel. Mar.
            ren   shi   ta.
            person be   he
            'The one who is shorter than Xiaoming is he.'

This is another strong proof that topicalization and relativization are indeed closely related processes.

In this connection, it is of some interest to note that Bresnan (1982) in her attempt to set up a universal model in the framework of lexical–functional grammar has also posited the discourse function of relativization of an NP as topicalization.

4.1.4. Head NPs

In Chinese when the head NP of a relative clause refers to any of the general categories such as *dongxi* 'things' or *ren* 'person/people,' then it can often be deleted, resulting in what I would call a 'beheaded' relative clause, as in (122) and (123).

(122) women   jinnian   dongtian   chi   de   (dongxi)   dou
       we   this–year   winter   eat   Rel. Mar. thing   all
       you   de.
       have   PART
       'We have all the food for this winter.'

(123) gangcai   da   dianhua   lai   de   (ren)
       just:now   make   phone–call   come   Rel. Mar. person
       shi   shei?
       be   who
       'Who was the person that just called?'

Li and Thompson (1981) have a rather general discussion on this type of relative clauses. Their findings can be summarized as follows:

(124) To be well–formed, a beheaded relative clause must contain a verb with at least one of its participants unspecified. The missing participant can be either the subject or the direct object or both, but never the indirect object.

Some examples follow:

(125) nimen   mei–you   wo   xihuan   de.
       you   not–have   I   like   Rel. Mar.
       'You don't have what I like.'

(126)   la   che   de   hen   nan   guo   rizi.
        pull   rickshaw Rel. Mar. very   hard   pass   day
        'A rickshaw puller (lit. a person who pulls a rickshaw) has a hard life.'

(127)   mai   de   buru   zu   de   hao.
        buy   Rel. Mar. not:as   rent   Rel. Mar. good
        'Things bought are not as good as things rented.'

As the translation in (125) shows, in English the only thing that comes close to this usage is 'what', but 'what' is much more restricted in its reference.

Examples like (126) and (127), which are common in Chinese, indicate another important use of the beheaded relative clause as a referring expression. We will have more to say when we take up functional characteristics.

Another relevant observation about the head noun in Chinese relative clause is made by Tang (1977, 1979). A few head NPs such as *shengyin* 'sound', *qiwei* 'odor', etc., may have no syntactically identical NP in the relative clause, as examples in (128) and (129) show:

(128)   wo wen–dao   you   dongxi   shao–jiao   de   weidao.
        I smell   EXIST   thing   burn   DE   odor
    *   'I smelt the odor that something was burnt.' (=I smelt something burnt; or, I smelt the odor of something burnt.)

(129)   ta ting–dao   you   ren   tan   gangqin   de   shengyin.
        he hear   EXIST   person   play   piano   DE   sound
    *   'He heard the sound that someone was playing the piano.' (= He heard someone playing the piano; He heard the sound of someone playing the piano.)

As the translations in (128) and (129) show, English will have to use a construction other than the relative clause in expressing the same idea. Actually, in Chinese we also have some evidence to show that *de* in (128) and (129) is not a relative clause marker. Rather, it behaves like the appositive marker *de* that we discussed earlier in connection with sentential object, as exemplified in (130b).

(130) a. wo   ting–dao   you   ren   yao   lai.
         I   hear   EXIST   person will come
         'I heard that someone is coming.'
      b. wo   ting–dao   you   ren   yao   lai   de xiaoxi.
         I   hear   EXIST   person will come DE news
         'I heard the news that someone is coming.'

By comparing (130b) with (128) or (129), we can clearly see the semantic and syntactic parallel existing between the clause in question and the NP that follows it.

Another piece of evidence that we have is that in (128) or (129) *weidao* 'odor' or *shengyin* 'sound' can be omitted without changing the meaning of the sentence, as (128a) and (129a) show.

(128) a. wo   wen–dao   you   dongxi   shao–jiao.
         I   smell   EXIST   thing   burnt
         'I smelt something burnt.'

(129) a. ta   ting–dao   you   ren   tan   gangqin.
         he   hear   EXIST   person play   piano
         'He heard someone playing the piano.'

This exactly parallels the situation that we have found existing between a sentential object and its appositive NP, as exemplified in (a) and (b) in (130). In any case, since there are good reasons to doubt whether *qiwei* 'odor' and *shengyin* 'sound' in (128) and (129) are head nouns of a relative clause, we have *de* in both of them marked as 'DE' rather than as a relative clause marker.

4.1.5. Adverbial Phrases within the Relative Clause

In both Chinese and English adverbial phrases of place, time, and reason in a relative clause can be deleted if they are coreferential with ones in the main clause. Compare the following Chinese examples with their English translations.

(131) zhe   shi   Li Xiaojie   nian–shu   de   difang.
      this be   Li Miss   study–book   Rel. Mar.   place
      'This is the place (that/where) Miss Li studies.'

(132) na   shi   wo fuqin   qushi   de   na–yi   nian.
      that be   my father   die   Rel. Mar. that–CL   year
      'That was the year (that/in which/when) my father died.'

(133) na   jiu   shi   Zhang San   chi–dao   de
      that exactly   be   Zhang San   late–arrive   Rel. Mar.
      liyou.
      reason
      'That was the exact reason (that/why) Zhang San was late.'

With the coreferential instrumental phrase in the relative clause, the picture is different. In English the instrumental preposition cannot be deleted. Compare the (a) and (b) sentences in (134).

(134) a.*   That was the knife (that) he chopped the meat.
      b.   That was the knife (that) he chopped the meat with.

In Chinese, the instrumental coverb *yong* with its object can be deleted altogether as indicated in (135a).[24] To have the instrumental coverb with or without its object would both result in ungrammaticality, as indicated by (135b). If *yong*, the instrumental coverb is used, then, to make the sentence grammatical another verb *lai* 'come' indicating purpose will have to be added after it. When this happens, the resumptive pronoun can be optionally inserted between the two verbs, as shown in (135c).

(135) a.   nei   shi   ta qie   rou   de   daozi.
            that   be   he chop meat   Rel. Mar.   knife
            'That was the knife (that) he chopped the meat with.'
      b.*   nei   shi   ta yong (ta)   qie   rou   de
            that   be   he with it   chop   meat   Rel. Mar.

---

[24] I have here deliberately avoided the term preposition as a designation for *yong* for the obvious reason that its grammatical status in Modern Mandarin is rather uncertain, as will be seen in our discussion of its behavior in relativization.

daozi.
knife
'Same as (a).'

c. nei   shi   ta   yong (ta)   lai   qie   rou   de
   that   be   he   use   it   to   chop   meat   Rel. Mar.
   daozi.
   knife
   'That was the knife (that) he used to chop the meat with.'

4.1.6. Relative Clause Stacking

When a relative clause is used to modify any NP contained in another relative clause, we have what is called a "stacked relative clause." When this happens, the relative clause will end up in English in either a self—embedded structure as in (136) or a right—branching structure as in (137).

(136)   The girl that the boy that the cow chased kissed blushed.

(137)   The policeman who caught the thief who stole the watch that I bought last week is here.

In Chinese, the resulting configuration is somewhat different. The stacked relatives will form either a self—embedded structure as in (138) or a left—branching one as in (139).

(138)   zhuo—dao—(le)   tou—(le)   wo   shangxingqi   mai—(le)
        catch—(ASP)   steal—(ASP)   I   last:week   buy—(ASP)
        de   shoubiao   de   xiaotou   de
        Rel. Mar.   watch   Rel. Mar.   thief   Rel. Mar.
        jingyuan   zai   zheli.
        policeman   at   here
        'Same as (137).'[25]

---

[25]Please note that the self—embedded structure in Chinese in this case corresponds to a right—branching one in English.

(139)	chunjuan	shi	dajia	xihuan	chi	de	yong
	egg–roll	be	everybody	like	eat	Rel. Mar.	use
	mianfen	zuo	de	shiwu.		
	flour	make	Rel. Mar.	food		

'Egg roll is a kind of food that is made of flour that everybody likes to eat.'

Now it is generally agreed that a right–branching structure is easier to perceive than a left–branching structure, which in turn is easier than a self–embedded structure.[26] By comparing English stacked relatives with Chinese ones, it is easy to see that Chinese stacked relatives are more complex, since both have the self–embedded structure, but Chinese has, in addition, a left–branching structure while English has a right–branching one. Also notice that while both (136) and (138) exhibit a self–embedded structure, (138) is in some sense more complex because the relativized NPs are chopped away rather than pronominalized in the form of a relative pronoun as in the case of (136). We can, therefore, justifiably conclude that Chinese stacked relative clauses present a more complex structure than do their English counterparts. This is perhaps the reason why stacked relatives almost never occur in Chinese while they show up occasionally in English.

4.2 Functional Characteristics

In the previous section, we have mentioned that formally, Chinese does not maintain a distinction between a restrictive relative clause and a non–restrictive one. In this section we will pursue the question that since Chinese has no non–restrictive relative clauses, then, how are the ideas expressed as a non–restrictive clause in another language such as English expressed in Chinese.

To answer the question presupposes that we have in our Universal Grammar an explicit description of the function that relative clauses, restrictive and non–restrictive serve. Since, to the best of my knowledge, nothing of the sort has been attempted, and since English relative clauses have been extensively studied, we will again go into the uses of English relative clauses first so as to provide a basis for the description of Chinese relatives later.

4.2.1. Uses of English Relative Clauses

The well–known distinction in English between restrictive and non–restrictive

---

[26] See Chomsky (1965: 12–15) and Larkin and Shook (1978) for discussion.

relative clauses can be demonstrated by comparing (140) with (141).

(140)   The soldiers $\begin{Bmatrix} \text{that} \\ \text{who} \end{Bmatrix}$ were brave ran forward.

(141)   The soldiers, who were brave, ran forward.

Lyons (1977:761) characterizes the restrictive function of the relative clause in the following terms:
> Restrictive relative clauses ... are used, characteristically, to provide descriptive information which is intended to enable the addressee to identify the referent of the expression within which they are embedded.

Thus, only the relative clause in (140) has the function of further "narrowing down" the referent of its head to the extent that the addressee will be able to determine which soldiers of all the soldiers in question ran forward. (141), on the other hand, says that all the soldiers in question ran forward and that these soldiers were, moreover, brave.

This distinction in English is marked by intonational, morphological, and punctuational differences. Intonationally, the nonrestrictive relative clause, like the one in (141), forms an intonation unit by itself while a restrictive relative, like the one in (140), does not. Morphologically, the relative pronoun 'that' is in most cases avoided in the non-restrictive relative clause while it is freely used in the restrictive relative. In punctuation, a comma is used to separate a non-restrictive relative from its head as (141) clearly shows, where as no comma normally appears between a restrictive relative and its head, as shown in (140).

Within the category of non-restrictive relative clauses, there seems to be reason to suggest a further distinction, one between what we would call "parenthetical" relatives and "continuative" relatives. The two types are represented by (142) and (143) respectively.

(142)   May Smith, who is in the corner, wants to meet you. (parenthetical)

(143)   He gave the letter to the clerk, who then copied it. (continuative)

As (142) shows, a parenthetical non-restrictive relative, as its name implies, gives information that is incidental and parenthetical in nature while a continuative clause, as shown by (143), gives a proposition that is stronger in its assertive force and is, therefore, more readily paraphrasable by an independent clause conjoined to the main clause, as exemplified by (144).

(144)   He gave the letter to the clerk and he then copied it.

Looking at it in this light, then, the so–called "sentence relative clause", which points back not to an NP but to a whole clause or sentence (or even a sequence of sentences), falls under the continuative relative clause. This type with its possible paraphrase is exemplified by (145).

(145)   He admires Mrs. Brown a. {which surprises me.}
　　　　　　　　　　　　　　　　　 b. {which I find strange.}
　　　　a = 'and it surprises me that he does.'
　　　　b = 'and I find it strange that he does.'

Let us now turn back to the restrictive relative. Our previous discussion may have given the impression that it is completely homogeneous. This is not so, especially if we go by the formal criterion of the presence or absence of a comma between its head and the relative. What I am saying is that there is some incongruity between what can be formally established as the restrictive relative and what can be functionally identified as such.

A case in point is a type which usually involves an indefinite NP as its head as in (146) and (147).

(146)   There is a man (who) lives in China.

(147)   I have a friend who loves anything Chinese.

(146) is an existential sentence with a restrictive relative clause embedded in it, and yet if we go back to Lyons' characterization of the restrictive relative clause, we can clearly see that the relative clause actually has more of an assertive function than an identifying function. Compare the (a) and (b) sentences in (148) and (149).[27]

(148)   a.   Something keeps upsetting me.
　　　　b.   There's something (that) keeps upsetting me.

---

[27](148) and (149) are cited from Quirk et al. (1972: 959).

(149) a. I'd like you to meet some people.
b. There's some people (that) I'd like you to meet.

It is quite clear that in both (148b) and (149b) it is the relative clause, rather than the main clause, that carries the important part of the message. No wonder that in the colloquial speech this is the only case where the relative pronoun, though in the subjective case, can be omitted (see Quirk et al., 1972: 959).

Practically the same comment can be given to the function of the relative clause in (147): i.e., the information provided by the relative clause seems to be more important than, or at least as important as, that provided by the main clause. (147), however, is not an existential sentence and therefore the relative pronoun 'who' in it cannot be deleted.

4.2.2. Uses of Chinese Relative Clauses

Speaking of the functions of Chinese relative clauses, the first question that arises is whether in modern Chinese there is the non—restrictive relative clause. We have already pointed out that speakers do not see the positional difference of the DQC phrase, i.e., whether it is pre—relative or post—relative, as correlated with the difference between restrictiveness and non—restrictiveness.

Tang (1979b), who agrees with us on this count, argues, however, that in Chinese there is the non—restrictive relative clause which in most cases occurs after the head but sometimes can occur before it. Below are three of his examples (1979b: 257):

(150) na   yi—ge   ren,   liu   huzi   de,   shi   wo waigong.
      that   one—CL   person sport   beard   DE   be   my grandpa
      'The man, who sports a beard, is my grandpa.'

(151) zhe   yi—ben   zidian,   wo zuotian   zai   Taibei   mai
      this   one—CL   dictionary   I   yesterday in   Taipei   buy
      de,   feichang   shiyong.
      DE   very   useful
      'This dictionary, which I bought in Taipei yesterday, is very useful.'

(152) juyou   wu—qian   nian   youjiu   lishi   de Zhongguo...
      have   five—thousand year   long   history   DE China
      'China, which has a long history of five thousand years ...'

Most speakers that I have asked pointed out that sentences like (150) and (151) are usually found in translation or Westernized writing, or else the relative clause occurs as an afterthought. If this characterization is correct, then the status of this style of relative clause in modern Chinese grammar is best left unresolved, as it is still undergoing changes. In (152) we have a case where a pre–head relative clause is clearly used non–restrictively since the head *Zhongguo* 'China' is a proper noun which, under normal circumstances, is uniquely identifiable. However, such usage of the relative clause is, as many researchers have already pointed out (Wang 1955, Chu 1979, Tsai, 1972 etc.), probably due to the influence of English and other European languages. As far as I can determine, however, such usage is still largely restricted to the cases where the head is either a proper noun or a pronoun; in other words, when the relative is "inherently" non–restrictive (Quirk et al., 1972: 858–9), where it is not likely to cause any confusion about its function.

Turning now to the question of how Chinese handles these sentences that contain non–restrictive relative clauses, I find that there is a consensus among the researchers just cited that instead of using a corresponding relative clause in Chinese, the relative should be recast as a comment clause in a topic chain. (153) and (154) are two such examples given by Chu (1979) and Yu (1981), respectively.

(153) a. This city, which has a population of two million ....
      b.? you   liangbaiwan   renkou   de ben   shi ....
          have   two–million   population   DE this   city
      c. ben   shi,   you   renkou   liangbaiwan ....
          this   city   have   population two–million

(154) a.? xianshen   yu   gemingde   zhuanglie   da
          devoted   to   revolutionary   grandiose   great
          ye   de ta,   zaoyi   jiang   shengsi
          enterprise DE he   long:ago   JIANG   life
          zhi–zhi–du–wai.
          not:care:about
          'He, who is devoted to the grandiose enterprise of revolution, ceased to care about his own life long ago.'
      b. ta,   xianshen   yu   gemingde   zhuanglie   da
          he   devoted   to   revolutionary   grandiose   great

ye   zaoyi   jiang   shengsi   zhi–zhi–du–wai.
enterprise   long:ago   JIANG   life   not:care:about
'Same as (a).'²⁸

In this connection, it is appropriate to go back to the type of restrictive relative clause involving an indefinite NP as head, as in (146) and (147) cited earlier. The corresponding Chinese construction has been discussed in Chapter 7, where we compared Li and Thompson's (1981) and Chu's (1983) studies with ours. Li and Thompson call it "realis descriptive clause," while Chu terms it "elaborative clause".

As we pointed out earlier, Li and Thompson regard this construction as a type of descriptive clause which they schematize as (155).

$$(155) \quad NP \quad V_1 \quad \overset{describes}{\overbrace{NP \quad (NP)}} \quad V_2 \quad (NP)$$

They further characterize it as having the following properties: (1) the direct object of the first verb is always indefinite, and (2) the second clause provides an incidental description of this NP.²⁹ They also regard this construction as a type of presentative sentence whose function in discourse "is to present or introduce a noun phrase to be described" (1981:611). This type is termed "realis" because the description provided by the clause is always "realized", i.e., it is here and now of the "real world". Below are two such examples cited from their study.

(156)   wo   peng–dao–le   yi–ge   waiguoren,   hui   shuo
        I   meet–arrive–ASP   one–CL   foreigner   know:how   speak

---

²⁸To reflect the organization of the Chinese sentences, (153c) should be rendered as (i) and (154b), as (ii).
   (i)   This city (topic), (it) has a population of two million ....
   (ii)   He (topic) is devoted to the grandiose enterprise of revolution (and) ceased to care about his own life long ago.

²⁹I suspect the impression that the comment clause is giving only "incidental description" might be induced by the English translation, which, as I have pointed out, can only use a non–identifying relative clause, very similar in function to a continuative or parenthetical relative.

    Zhongguohua.
    Chinese
    'I met a foreigner who can speak Chinese.'

(157) ta chao—le yi—ge cai, hen hao chi.
   he fry—ASP one—CL dish very good eat
   'She fried a dish which was very good to eat.'

  Chu (1983:255) further claims that the event or situation expressed by the second clause precedes that expressed by the first clause. As we have given a detailed comparison of the two approaches previously, I would go directly to the conclusion here. I think Li and Thompson are on the right track in regarding the first clause of this construction as a presentative construction. However, I do find their characterization of the second clause as providing "an incidental description" far too restrictive. Like all presentative constructions, the first clause here presents or introduces an NP as *topic* which can then start a topic chain of usually more than one comment. This function can be best illustrated by providing a natural continuation in the form of another comment clause added to each of the two examples in (155) and (156) cited from Li and Thompson.

(156) a. wo peng—dao—le yi—ge waiguoren, hui   shuo
     I meet—arrive—ASP one—CL foreigner know:how speak
     Zhongguohua, hai hui   chang Jingxi.[30]
     Chinese   more know:how sing Peking:opera
     'I met a foreigner who can speak Chinese and who can sing Peking opera as well.'

(157) a. ta chao—le yi—ge cai, hen hao chi, women
     he fry—ASP one—CL dish very good eat we
     bu—dao san fenzhong jiu chi—guang le.
     not—up:to three minute then eat—up   PART

---

  [30]The longer the topic chain, the more awkward is its English translation in this case. This is so because a topic chain in Chinese can have a number of comment clauses following a topic but an English sentence of this type does not seem to tolerate more than two conjoined relative clauses.

'She fried a dish (which) was very tasty and (which) we finished in less than three minutes.'

To summarize, the discussion of restrictive vs. non-restrictive function of relative clauses in both English and Chinese in these two sections has led us to the conclusion that while in English, except for some cases involving an indefinite NP as head, the distinction can in general be maintained, in Chinese the non-restrictive relative clause seems to have a marginal grammatical status and most people would prefer to render an English non-restrictive relative as a comment clause in a topic chain. In the case of non-identifying relative involving an indefinite head NP, the Chinese corresponding structure for the head NP in question is a presented NP topic, introduced by a presentative construction and to be commented upon by the following clauses.

4.2.3. Referring Function

Because of the special allowance in Chinese to delete the head of a relative clause when it is a general noun such as *ren* 'people' or *dongxi* 'thing' the resulting beheaded relative clause has a special referring function which is lacking in English. In English there are in general two ways to refer to a class of objects. If there is a name in the language that already refers to it, then the name is normally used. If there is no such name, then an ad hoc phrase or clause can be used to refer to it. However, because of the existence of the beheaded relative clause such as *jiao shu de* 'teacher' (literally, one who teaches books), *zuo maimai de* 'business person' (literally, one who does business), *zhong tian de* 'farmer' (literally, one who plants the field), etc., it seems that Chinese has three ways of naming a category, each of which has its basically different referring function. Compare the expressions in (158).

(158) a. jiaoshi 'teacher'
b. jiao shu de 'one who teaches books'
c. jiao   Xiaohua   dili   de   na-ge   ren
teach   Xiaohua   geography   Rel. Mar.   that-CL   person
'The person who teaches Xiaohua geography'

It seems clear that as a referring expression (a) is more fixed, and hence more formal and more elegant stylistically, than (b), which in turn is more fixed than (c).

5. The So-called *DE* Complement Construction
5.1. General Characteristics

The so-called *de* complement construction is one of the most controversial structures in Chinese. The construction is exemplified by the following sentences.

(159)   ta   pao   de   hen   kuai.
        he   run   DE   very   fast
        'He runs very fast.'

(160)   ta   pao   de   hen   lei.
        he   run   DE   very   tired
        'He was very tired from running.'

(161)   ta   pao   de   quan   shen   shi   han.
        he   run   DE   whole   body   be   perspiration
        'He ran so much that he was sweating all over.'

Most researchers agree, however, that (159) is different from (160) and (161). In (159) the so-called complement *hen kuai* 'very fast' gives a description of the way that the main verb *pao* 'run' is executed while sentences (160) and (161) state a situation that happens as a result of his running. The difference has prompted many linguists to term the first type "descriptive complement" and the second type "resultative complement". Another important difference is that while in the surface structure both types can be in the form of a verb phrase, only the second type can be in the form of a clause as well.

A feature common to both types is that when the first verb is a transitive one with an object, the verb has to be reduplicated before particle *de* is attached to it to form a so-called "verb-copying" construction that we discussed in Chapter 5. Thus, if, instead of using *pao* 'run' intransitively, we use the transitive equivalent *pao bu* 'run step', then (159) will have to be stated as (162), and (160) as (163).

(162)   ta pao   bu   pao   de   hen   kuai.
        he run   step   run   DE   very   fast
        'Roughly, same as (159).'

(163)　ta　pao　bu　　pao　de　hen　　lei
　　　　he　run　step　run　DE　very　tired
　　　'Roughly, same as (160).'

To sum up, the construction can be schematically represented as (164).

(164)　　NP$_1$ + Verb$_1$ + (Object + Verb$_1$) + de + $\begin{cases} \text{phrase} \\ \text{clause} \end{cases}$

5.2. Two Different Analyses in the Past

Now with these structural features in mind we can take up the controversy concerning its proper analysis. There are basically two hypotheses with the major difference lying in the assignment of the main verb of the sentence. The first hypothesis contends that the final verb, i.e. *kuai* 'fast' in (159) or *lei* 'tired' in (160), is the main predicate and in the case of a "descriptive complement" as in (159), the general analysis is to regard all the elements preceding *de* as forming a relative clause of a special kind with an abstract head NP such as *sudu* 'speed' or *yangzi* 'manner' usually deleted in the surface.[31]

The second hypothesis maintains that the penultimate verb, i.e. the verb occurring immediately before *de* as *pao* 'run' in both (159) and (160), is the main verb and that the elements occurring after *de* should be treated as adverbial complement.

These two analyses will be referred to as final–verb hypothesis and penultimate–verb hypothesis respectively. We will go into the distributional facts for and against each hypothesis in the following sections. After a careful examination of these facts, we will propose a third analysis, which is compatible with our framework and which can account for most, if not all, of the distributional facts involving this construction.

5.2.1. The Final–verb Hypothesis

Various linguists (Chao, 1968; Tai, 1973, 1986; Tang, 1977; Chu, 1983 and C–R Huang and Mangione, 1985) have in the past argued in one way or another for this analysis. They have produced a number of arguments which we will summarize in the following. Since we are here more interested in getting the distributional facts, we will

---

[31] The proponents of the final–verb hypothesis do not have a uniform analysis with regard to the "resultative complement". Chao (1968), who proposes the analysis we have just mentioned, does not give any explicit account of the resultative complement. Tai (1986), on the other hand, has posited an abstract verb 'cause' as the predicate for the matrix clause.

present the argument without citing the source and we will, immediately after the presentation, give our comment. Also, since in general the two hypotheses are somewhat complementary in the sense what is in favor of one hypothesis will, by implication, go against the other, each of the following arguments, unless otherwise stated, should be taken in this light.

First, as we pointed out earlier in our discussion of the deletion phenomena in the comparative structure, there can be a pause or pause particle occurring after *de*, as it is the case after other kinds of topic. Examine (165).

(165) a. ta pao de a/me hen man.
he run DE PART very slow
'Speaking of the way he runs, it is slow.'

a. ta pao de _____ hen man.
he run DE (pause) very slow
'Same as (a).'

Please note in this connection that clause connectives such as *yinwei* 'because' and *suiran* 'although' can occur in the same position, as shown in (165c). Likewise, *shi*, the focus verb, can also occur there, as shown in (165d).

(165) c. ta pao de suiran hen man, keshi buzi
he run DE although very slow but stride
que hen da.
on:the:contrary very big
'Although he runs slowly, his strides are big.'

d. ta pao de shi hen man.
he run DE BE very slow
'Speaking of his running, it IS slow.'(Capitalization indicates stress.)

Since we have presented ample evidence to show that what occurs immediately before a pause particle, a clause connective like *suiran* 'although' and the focus verb *shi* is a raised topic, the three observations just given strongly support the hypothesis that the constituent ending in *de* is a topic and by implication what occurs after it is the main predicate.

Second, a V—not—V question starts after *de* and not with the verb before *de*, as shown in (166)

(166) a. ni   zou   de kuai—bu—kuai?
you   walk DE fast—not—fast
'Speaking of (the speed of) your walking, is it fast or not? = Do you walk fast?'
b.* ni   zou—bu—zou   de kuai?
you   walk—not—walk   DE fast
'Same as (a).'
c. ni   zou—de—kuai—zou—bu—kuai?
you   walk—DE—fast—walk—not—fast
* (i) 'Same as (a).'
(ii) 'Can you walk fast?'

(166c), if taken in the sense of (166a) is ungrammatical but taken in its potential mode, i.e. with *de* interpreted as 'can' and *bu* as 'cannot', it is then grammatical. Since it is generally assumed that it is the main verb of a sentence that can take the V—not—V form, the distributional fact observed in (166) can then be taken as another support for the final—verb hypothesis.[32]

Third, the verb immediately precedes *de* in this construction can never take any aspect marker. Take *zuo* 'do' for instance.

(167) a. ta   zuo   nei—jian   shi   zuo   de   hen   hao.
he   do   that—CL   job   do   DE   very   good
'He did the job very well.'

---

[32]This assumption has been challenged by J. Huang (1988a) whose argument hinges crucially on examples like (i).
(i) ni   renwei   ta   zuotian   you—mei—you   lai?
you   think   he   yesterday   have—not—have   come
'Do you think he came yesterday?'
As we have explained that *renwei* 'think' is a verb of imagination that typically behaves differently from other verbs in allowing the V—not—V question to occur in the embedded clause in syntax but to interprete it as having a larger scope as if it occurred in the matrix clause. This being the case, (i), in our opinion, does not constitute a genuine counterexample to the generalization.

b. ta zuo nei–jian shi zuo $\left\{\begin{matrix} *\text{zhe} \\ *\text{guo} \\ *\text{le} \\ *\text{qilai} \end{matrix}\right\}$ de hen hao.

he do that–CL job do ASP PART very good

Normally, *zuo* 'do' is compatible with all the aspect markers but as (167b) shows, it is incompatible with none of them when occurring in this construction. This fact strongly suggests that the verb in question is not the main verb of the construction. In order to be completely convincing, of course, one has to show that the final verb in this construction can take some of the aspect markers. Unfortunately, this cannot be done because the final verb in this construction is always a state verb, which, as we showed in Chapter 3, does not, as a rule, take any aspect marker.

Fourthly, negation of the construction is usually done by inserting *bu*, the most general negative marker, before the final verb, as shown in (168a). The same marker, however, cannot occur before the penultimate verb, as shown by the ungrammatical (168b).

(168) a. nei–jian shi ta zuo de bu kuai.
that–CL job he do DE not fast
'Speaking of the job, the way he did it was not fast.'
b.* nei–jian shi ta bu zuo de kuai.
that–CL job he not do DE fast
'Same as (a).'

Since normally negation occurs before the main verb of a sentence in Chinese, the fact that it can occur before the final verb, but not before the penultimate verb, in this construction indicates that the final verb is the main verb of this type of sentence. Furthermore, this distributional fact also agrees well with the analysis which takes what goes before the final verb as topic/subject. This is so because by placing the negation marker before the final verb the part of the sentence that goes before it will fall outside the scope of negation and is thus taken as old, presupposed information normally represented by the topic/subject of a sentence.

However, to do the penultimate–verb hypothesis justice, it has to be pointed out that the penultimate verb can be negated by placing negative elements such as *meiyou* 'not–EXIST' or *bushi* 'not–the–case' before it, as shown in (c) and (d) in (168).

(168) c. nei–jian   shi   ta   mei–you   zuo   de   hen   kuai.
       that–CL   job   he   not–EXIST   do   DE   very   fast
       'It is not the case that he did the job very fast.'
   d. nei–jian   shi   ta   bu–shi   zuo   de   hen   kuai.
       that–CL   job   he   not–BE   do   DE   very   fast
       'Roughly, same as (c).'

Negation in this case, however, is marked in the sense that the whole proposition is negated, as shown in the English translation.[33] Nevertheless, the fact that the penultimate verb can also be negated strongly suggests that the penultimate verb may be regarded as the verb of the construction under certain as yet unclear conditions.

Finally, the final verb phrase serves the same funciton as the main predicate in other sentence types does in answering a question while the penultimate verb does not. Examine the following question and answer pairs.

(169) A: ni   zuotian   dao   nar   qu   le?
       you   yesterday   to   where   go   PART
       'Where did you go yesterday?'
   B: (wo)   dao   Taibei   qu   le.
       I   to   Taipei   go   PART
       'I went to Taipei.'

(170) A: Lao Li   nian   shu   nian   de   zhemeyang?
       Lao Li   study   book   study   DE   how
       'How is Lao Li's study going?'
   B: (nian   de)   bu   tai   hao.
       study   De   not   too   good
       'Not too good.'

(171) A: ni–de   gongzuo   zhemeyang?
       your   work   how
       'How is your work?'

---

[33]For a similar observation, see Chu (1983).

>
> B: (zuo de) hen youyisi.
> work DE very interesting
> 'I am interested (in my work as a result of doing it).'

(169) shows that in giving answer to a normal question the predicate of the sentence must be retained. (170) and (171) show that the final verb, rather than the penultimate verb, is the part that must be retained. Furthermore, the penultimate verb can be omitted not only when it is a repetition of a part of question as in (170), but also when it is not such a repetition as in (171). This, then, is another clear indication that the fianl verb, rather than the penultimate verb, is the main verb of the construction.

5.2.2. The Penultimate—verb Hypothesis

There are also quite a few adherents to this hypothesis (see, Mei, 1978; Paris, 1979; Zhu, 1982; Ross, 1984; Li, 1985 and Huang, 1982, 1988a). They have altogether produced a number of arguments in support of this hypothesis. They will be briefly presented in the following with our comments.

To begin with, a pause or pause particle can also occur in front of the penultimate verb as it is the case with the final verb. This is shown in (172).

> (172) a. ta pao bu *ya* pao de hen kuai.
> he run step PART run DE very fast
> 'He runs fast.'
> b. ta pao bu _____ pao de hen kuai.
> he run step (pause) run DE very fast
> 'Same as (a).'

Likewise, *shi* 'BE' and other raising predicates can occur in the place, as shown in the following sentences.

> (173) a. ta pao bu *shi* pao de hen kuai.
> he run step BE run DE very fast
> 'He did run very fast.'

> (174) a. ta pao bu *keneng* pao de hen kuai.
> he run step possible run DE very fast

'It is possible that he runs fast.'

Clause conjunctions such as *yinwei* 'because' and *suiran* 'although' can also occur there, as witnessed by (175a).

(175) a. ta pao bu <u>suiran</u> pao de hen kuai, buzi
       he run step although run DE very fast step
       que   bu—gou   da.
       on:the:contrary   not—enough   big
       'Although he runs fast, his strides are not big enough.'

These three observations strongly suggest that what occurs after the penultimate verb in the construction can be taken as the main predicate as well.

There is, however, a distributional fact with regard to these grammatical words which presents a serious problem for both hypotheses. This can be demonstrated by the following sentences.

(172) c. ta <u>ya</u> pao bu pao de hen kuai.
       he PART run step PART DE very fast
       'Roughly, same as (172a).'

(173) b. ta <u>shi</u> pao bu pao de hen kuai.
       he BE run step run DE very fast
       'Roughly, same as (173a).'

(174) b. ta <u>keneng</u> pao bu pao de hen kuai.
       he possible run step run DE very fast
       'Roughly same as (174a).'

(175) a. ta <u>suiran</u> pao bu pao de hen kuai, buzi
       he although run step run DE very fast step
       que   bu—gou   da.
       on:the:contrary   not—enough   big
       'Roughly, same as (175a).'

This distributional fact indicates that in addition to the penultimate and the final verb, the first verb can be taken as the main predicate as well. Any hypothesis, to be general enough, should take this into account.

The second argument, due originally to Paris (1979), involves some twelve grammatical qualities which she claims to be sensitive to the distinction between a sentential subject/object (S+0) and the constituent that precedes *de* in this construction (S+*de*). Her attempt here is to show that since S+*de* does not function like a sentential subject/object, it is not an NP and *de* cannot be a nominalizer, as the final—verb hypothesis has claimed. Space consideration forbids us from going into all her tests. We will, however, briefly summarize some of her important arguments and then give our comments.

First, she contends that, as shown in (176b), a sentential object can occur independently as a separate sentence while a S+*de* clause cannot, as the ungrammaticality of (177b) shows.

(176) a. wo tingshuo ta bu yao gen ni shuohua.
          I hear he not want with you speak
          'I heard that he would not talk to you.'

     b. ta bu yao gen ni shuohua.
          he not want with you speak
          'He would not talk to you.'

(177) a. ta chang de hen hao.
          he sing DE very good
          'Roughly, he sings well.'

     b.* ta chang de.
           he sing DE

Strictly speaking, this argument is valid only in showing that subordination is overtly marked by *de* in the case of S+*de* clause, while in the case of S+0 it is not overtly marked at all. This is so because if we take intonation into consideration, then neither S+0 nor S+*de* can occur independently.

Second, when the verb is transitive, then verb reduplication must take place in an S+*de*, as we showed earlier in (162) and (163), but the same verb contained in an S+0 clause cannot undergo the same process, as the ungrammatical (178b) clearly shows.

(178) a. ni   zhei–yang   zuo   shi   hen   huangtang.
         you   this–way   do   things very   absurd
         'It is very absurd that you should do things this way.'
   b.* ni   zhei–yang   zuo   shi   zuo   hen   huangtang.
         you   this–way   do   things do   very   absurd
         'Same as (a).'

While this observation is certainly valid, the explanation for it is by no means straightforward. We have briefly touched upon it in our previous discussion of the so–called "verb–copying" construction, and we will go back to this point in connection with our proposed analysis of the construction in question.

Third, the matrix verb in a complex sentence containing a sentential subject (S+0) cannot be reduplicated (as shown in (179b)) while the final verb in the construction under discussion can (as shown in (180b)).

(179) a. ta mei neng lai   kan ni   zhen   qiguai.
         he not able come see you really strange
         'It is strange that he could not come to see you.'
   b.* ta mei neng lai   kan ni   qiqikuaikuai.
         he not able come see you strange
         'Roughly, Same as (a).'

(180) a. ta zhongshi   chuan de   hen   qiguai.
         he always   dress DE   very strange
         'Roughly, he always dresses strangely.'
   b. ta zhongshi   chuan de qiqiguaiguai   de
         he always   dress DE strange   PART
         'Practically, same as (a).'

We have, however, good reason to doubt the validity of this argument. Observe that *qiguai* 'strange' is about the only verb which can show up in both clause types. This fact suggests that it must be different senses of *qiguai* 'strange' that determine this distribution. In fact, close inspection reveals that $qiguai_1$, as used in (179), is an attitudinal verb, like *kexi* 'piteous' and *huangtang* 'absurd' cited earlier, which indicates the speaker's attitude towards the proposition he is making, while $qiguai_2$, as used in (180), is a descriptive state verb. Since only descriptive verbs, as we stated in Chapter 3, can undergo reduplication, the ungrammaticality of (179b) is expected. Now that we have found that this distinction is attributable to the meaning difference between two classes of verbs, it follows that it has nothing to do with the point that the argument is intended, i.e., that the S+*de* clause is not a nominalized constituent.

Whe have gone into some length in making this point because we feel that quite a few of her other arguments can be criticized in a similar manner.[34]

Her fourth argument involves relativization. As she points out, the subject NP and the object NP contained in a sentential subject cannot be relativized, as shown in (181).

(181) a. zhei—ge   haizi   kan   nei—bu   dianying   zhen   qiguai.
          this—CL   child   see   that—CL   movie   really strange
          'It is really strange that the child should be seeing that movie.'
     b.* kan   nei—bu   dianying   zhen   qiguai   de
          see   that—CL   movie   really strange   Rel. Mar.
          nei—ge   haizi ....
          that—CL   child
       * 'The child who it is strange that should be seeing that movie ....'

---

[34]For instance, her argument called "Movement to Sentence—initial Position' which can be exemplified by (i) and (ii) below, is called to doubt because the fact that *qiguai* 'strange' in (ia), but not in (iia), can be moved to the S—initial position, as in (ib), has more to do with its being an attitudinal verb than with the fact that what originally precedes it is a sentential subject. In fact, we feel that *qiguai* 'strange' in (ib) is a sentence itself, as it is often utterred as an independent intonation unit. What follows it is another sentence which explains this remark of the speaker. This interpretation is shown in the English translation.
(i)   a. ta mei neng lai   kan ni   zhen   qiguai.
          he not able come see you really strange
          'It is really strange that he was not able to come see you.'
      b. qiguai   ta mei neng lai   kan ni.
          strange   he not able come see you
          'How strange! He was not able to come see you.'
(ii) a. ta zongshi   chuan de hen   qiguai.
          he always   dress DE very strange
          'Roughly, he is always dressed up strangely.'
      b.* qiguai   ta zongshi   chuan de.
          strange   he always   dress DE

456

  c.*   nei–ge   haizi   kan   zhen   qiguai   de
     that–CL   child   see   really   strange   Rel. Mar.
     nei–bu   dianying
     that–CL   movie
   * 'The movie which it is strange that the child should be seeing ....'

In contrast, the subject or object NP contained in an S+*de* clause can be relativized, as shown in (182).

 (182)   a.   laoshi   jiang   kewen   jiang   de   hen   qingchu.
      teacher   explain   texts   explain   DE   very   clear
      'Roughly, the teacher explained the texts very clearly.'
    b.   jiang   kewen   jiang   de   hen   qingchu   de
      explain   texts   explain   DE   very   clear   Rel. Mar.
      nei–wei   laoshi ....
      that–CL   teacher
      'Roughly, the teacher who explained the texts very clearly ....'
    c.   laoshi   jiang   de   hen   qingchu   de
      teacher   explain   DE   very   clear   Rel. Mar.
      nei–xie   kewen ....
      those   texts
      'Roughly, the texts that the teacher explained very clearly ....'

  Now it is generally assumed that the subject and the object contained in a sentential subject cannot be relativized since it is in violation of a universal constraint called "sentential subject constraint" (see Ross, 1967). If the S+*de* part of the construction, so the argument goes, is indeed a nominalized NP, then we would expect the same constraint at work here. So the fact that it is not is evidence against regarding S+*de* clause as a nominalized subject.

  This argument, as far as it goes, is valid, but as we have pointed out earlier, the–final verb hypothesis claims that the S+*de* portion of the construction has an underlying structure of a complex NP, a relative clause with its head, to be exact. That is underlyingly, it is in the form of [NP, S]$_{NP}$ in which the head NP is an astract noun such as *yangzi* 'manner' or *sudu* 'speed' similar to an English adverbial clause 'the manner in which ....'. This being the case, it is similar in structure to adverbial clauses of time, place and condition, which, as we have argued, should be in the form of a relative clause whose head NP is accliticized.

We have also argued that these adverbial clauses are functionally topics, which allow topics contained in them, be it the subject, the object or other constituents, to be raised. The raising process does not violate the Complex NP Constraint (Ross. 1967) because the head NP of the relative has been accliticized, thereby reducing the complex NP to a simple one. On the basis of this structural and functional similarity between an adverbial clause and the descriptive complement clause under discussion, we have good reason to posit the same function and a very similar structure to the S+*de* clause, the only difference being that in the latter case the head NP is deleted in the surface, rather than accliticized. The posited structure and function coupled with the relativization principle we set up earlier, i.e., what is topicalizable is also relativizable, should be able to account for the relativization phenomena observed in connection with the S+*de* clause.

The third argument, which was given by Huang (1988a), goes like this. In Chinese, Huang points out, an overt pronoun cannot occur as the possessive of an NP C—commanding its antecedent (as in (183) and (184)) but can be the possessive of the subject NP of an adverbial clause or sentential subject (as in (185) and (186)).

(183) * ta–de$_i$ meimei hen taoyan Zhang San$_i$.
his sister very dislike Zhang San
'His sister dislikes Zhang San very much.'

(184) * tade$_i$ meimei shuo Zhang San$_i$ hui–lai–le.
his sister say Zhang San return–ASP
'His sister said that Zhang San has returned.'

(185) ta–de$_i$ meimei yi hui dao jia, Zhang San$_i$
his sister once return to home Zhang San
jiu shengqi.
then anger
'As soon as his sister arrived home, Zhang San became angry.'

(186) ta–de$_i$ meimei mei de jiang shi Zhang San$_i$
his sister not receive prize make Zhang San
hen shiwang.
very disappointed
'That his sister did not get the prize disappointed Zhang San.'

As Huang pointed out, the difference between (183) – (184) on the one hand, and (185) – (186) on the other can be attributed to the relative height of the pronoun in relation to its antecedent. In (183) – (184), the NP immediately contains the pronoun *ta–de* 'his' C–commands its antecedent while in (185) – (186) the pronoun is one–step further embedded, as the NP immediately containing the pronoun *ta–de* 'his' C–commands only the rest of the sentential subject or adverbial clause, but does not C–command the antecedent *Zhang San*. He further points out that given this analysis, the fact that (187) is un–grammatical in the two interpretations given where *ta–de* 'his' is interpreted as coreferential with *Zhang San*, would argue against treating what goes before *de* as a subject since in this analysis the structure of (187) parallels that of (186), but while (186) is grammatical, (187) is not.

(187) * ta–de$_i$ meimei qi de Zhang San$_i$ zhi fadou.
his sister anger DE Zhang San straight tremble
(i) 'His sister causes Zhang San to be so angry that he trembled all over (with anger).'
(ii) 'His sister was so angry that Zhang San trembled all over (with fear).'

This argument, however, is not as strong as Huang would like it to be. Although most native speakers that I have checked agree with Huang in his interpretation, there are quite a few whose grammatical judgment is unfirm, and there are speakers who feel that *ta–de* 'his' in (187) can be coreferential to *Zhang San*.[35] This result is, perhaps, what is to be expected. For one thing, the interpretation of a pronoun or a zero in Chinese is very often affected by such discourse factors as highlighting a referent or showing contrast. So until these factors are better understood, pronominal interpretation in sentences taken in

---

[35]Of the twenty native speakers that I have asked, most of them students at National Tsing Hua University, slightly over one third (7) showed obvious sign of hesitation. One fifth of them (4) said both interpretations are possible. My own judgment is not firm in this case.

isolation used as a syntactic argument should be taken with great reservation. For another, as we will argue later, sentences like (187) in isolation are subject to at least two analyses and this structural ambiguity may actually contribute to the difficulty of the interpretation of the pronoun.

5.3. Our Proposed Analysis

Now we have carefully considered important arguments for both hypothses, it seems very clear that the solution cannot be a simple one. This is necessitated by the observation that both hypothese are correct up to a point and yet neither is totally correct. Thus, it seems that we are in a bind. Fortunately, our previous analyses of related structure suggest a possible way out of this difficult situation. But before we give our proposal we need to go into the difference between the resultative complement and the descriptive complement.

5.3.1. Differences Between the Two Types of Complement

The two types of complement differ in a number of ways. First, only sentences with a descriptive complement can have a paraphrase in the form of a relative clause with such heads as *yangzi* 'manner' or *sudu* 'speed', as shown in (188) and (189).

(188) a. ta zou de hen man.
he walk DE very slow
'Speaking of the way he walks, it is slow.'
b. ta zou de sudu hen man.
he walk Rel. Mar. speed very slow
'The speed in which he walks is slow.'

(189) a. ta xiao de hen tian.
he smile DE very sweet
'Speaking of the way he smiles, it is sweet.'
b. ta xiao de yangzi hen tian.
he smile Rel. Mar. manner very sweet
'The way he smiles is very sweet.'

Sentences with a resultative complement do not have such a paraphrase, as the ungrammaticality of (190b) shows.

(190) a.   ta   zou   de   hen   lei.
           he   walk   DE   very   tired.
           'He was tired from walking.'

    b.*   ta   zou   de   sudu/yangzi   hen   lei.
          he   walk   Rel. Mar.   speed/manner   very   tired.
          'Roughly, same as (a).'

Second, only the resultative complement contains a topic in the underlying structure. The topic can be deleted by the rule of Identical Topic NP deletion if it is coreferential with a previous topic in the same topic chain, as shown in (191). If it is not coreferential with a previous topic, then it is retained, as shown in (192).

(191) ta_i pao   de   _____$_i$ hen   lei.
        he   run   DE   very   tired
        'He was tired from running.'

(192)   ta   ku   de   wo   xinli   hen   nanguo.
        he   cry   DE   I   heart   very   sad
        'He cried so much that I felt very sad.'

The descriptive complement, on the other hand, is not construed as having a topic. This is shown in (193).

(193) a.* ta_i tiao   de   _____$_i$ hen   gao.
           he   jump   DE   very   high
           'He jumped very high.'
     b.   ta   tiao   de   hen   gao.
          he   jump   DE   very   high
          'Same as (a).'

The usual claim with regard to this deletion process is that complement subject is deleted by the rule of Equi–NP deletion (see Mei, 1978 for an explicit account of this). That this characterization is not general enough can be seen by the following examples, where it is clear that the controller and the victim in this deletion process are both topics.

Examine (194) and (195).

(194)　ta$_i$　ku　de　____$_i$　yanjing　dou　hong　le.
　　　　he　cry　DE　　　　eye　all　red　PART
　　　'He cried so much that his eyes were red.'

(195)　nei–guo　niurou$_i$　ta　dun　de　____$_i$　tai　lan　le.
　　　　that–pan　beef　he　stew　DE　　　　too　soft　PART
　　　'Speaking of the pan of beef, he stewed it so long that it became too soft.'

Since what is deleted (i.e. the victim) in (194) is clearly the first nominal in a so–called "double nominative" construction, which, as we have repeatedly pointed out, should be analyzed as topic and since in cases like (195) where the controller NP is a topicalized object, the only category broad enough to characterize either the controller or the victim is topic. Of course, when the complement topic is not identical with the matrix topic, as in (192), no deletion will take place.

In this connection, we would like to comment on a point made by Mei (1978). In discussing the deletion process, he maintains that in accordance with the controller, the process can be further divided into two: subject–controlled deletion, as shown in (191) and object–controlled deletion, as shown in (196) and (197).

(196)　ta　ba　men$_i$　qi　de　____$_i$　hen　hong.
　　　　he　BA　door　paint　DE　　　　very　red
　　　'He had the door painted very red.'

(197)　ta　ba　nei–ge　laotour$_i$　qi　de　____$_i$　chadianr
　　　　he　BA　that–CL　old–man　anger　DE　　　　almost
　　　　hun–guoqu　le.
　　　　faint–away　PART
　　　'He angered the old man so much that the old man almost fainted.'

We have already pointed out that as a controller "subject" is not a general enough category. Rather, what is involved is a topic. If that is true, then how can we explain counterexamples like (196) and (197)? Actually, instead of being counterexamples, they turn out to be additional support for our generalization. To see this, first notice that the controller of deletion in both cases are the *ba* NP and we have argued that the *ba* NP is also a topic. Actually, not only *ba* NP, but the fronted NP, another non–primary topic according to our previous analysis, can be the controller. Examine (198), which is another way of saying (195).

(198)   ta <u>nei–guo   niurou</u>$_i$ dun   de   _____$_i$ tai   lan   le.
        he that–pan   beef   stew   DE   too   soft   PART
        'Speaking of him and the pan of beef, (he) stewed (it) so long that (it) became too soft.'

From these examples it seems very clear that what is important for them to be controller is not whether they are subjects or objects, but rather that they should be topics, primary or non–primary. This is yet another instance which shows what an important role topic plays in Chinese grammar.

If this characterization is basically correct, then it follows that in the case of the resultative complement there is always a clause underlying it even though in the surface it may end up as a verb phrase while the descriptive complement, on the other hand, is always in the form of a verb phrase, in its deep structure as well as the surface structure.

The third difference between the two types of complement structure is that only in the case of the descriptive complement do we have a related structure with the same form appearing preverbally. Compare (199) with (200).

(199)   a.   ta   nei–jian   shi   zuo   de   hen   kuai.
             he   that–CL   job   do   DE   very quickly
             'He did the job very quickly.'
        b.   ta   hen   kuai–de   zuo–le   nei–jian   shi.
             he   very   quickly   do–ASP   that–CL   job
             'Roughly, same as (a).'

(200)   a.   ta   chang   de   hen   lei.
             he   sing   DE   very   tired
             'He sang so much that he became very tired.'

b.*   ta   hen   lei–de   chang.[36]
     he   very   tired   sing
     'Roughly, same as (a).'

Finally, as pointed out by Hashimoto (1972), the resultative complement exhibits a close parallel with the extent complement marked by *dao* 'reach' while the descriptive complement does not. Compare (201) with (202).

(201) a.   Zhang San   he   jiu   he   de zui   le.
       Zhang San   drink   wine   drink   DE drunk   PART
       'Zhang San drank so much that he got drunk.'
     b.   Zhang San   he   jiu   he   dao bu–xing–ren–shi.
       Zhang San   drink   wine   drink   DAO unconscious
       'Zhang San drank to the extent of becoming unconscious.'

(202) a.   ta   yun   qiu   yun   de hen   kuai.
       he   dribble   ball   dribble   DE very   fast
       'Roughly, he dribbles fast.'
     b.*   ta   yun   qiu   yun   dao hen   kuai.
       he   dribble   ball   dribble   DAO very   fast

These differences strongly suggest that despite their surface similarity in some cases, it is a mistake to posit basically the same structure for them underlyingly.[37]

---

[36]Sentence (200b) is grammatical in the interpretation that 'He sang tiredly.'

[37]This does not mean in every case of the so–called "*de* complement" construction we can make a clear distinction between the two types. There are cases where such a sentence is compatible with both interpretations. (i) below exemplifies such a case.
     (i)   ta   tou   lan   tou   de hen   zhun.
         he   shoot   basket   shoot   DE very   accurate
       a. 'His (way of) shooting is accurate.'
       b. 'He is accurate in shooting.'
That it is possible to have a descriptive interpretation, as shown in (a), is confirmed by the fact that *zhun(que)* 'accurate' can appear as preverbal modifier, as shown in (ii).
     (ii)   ta   hen   zhunque–de   tou–zhe   lan.
         he   very   accurately   shoot–ASP   basket
       'He was shooting very accurately.'
On the other hand, the fact that we can say (iii)
     (iii)   ta   hen   zhun.
         he   very   accurate
       'He is very accurate.'

5.3.2. Deep Structures for the Descriptive and the Resultative Complements

The differences discussed in the last section also suggest that the descriptive complement is a verb phrase and the resultative complement is a clause in the deep structure. Sentences (159), (160), and (161) given at the beginning of Section 5 will therefore have (203), (204) and (205) as their deep structures respectively.

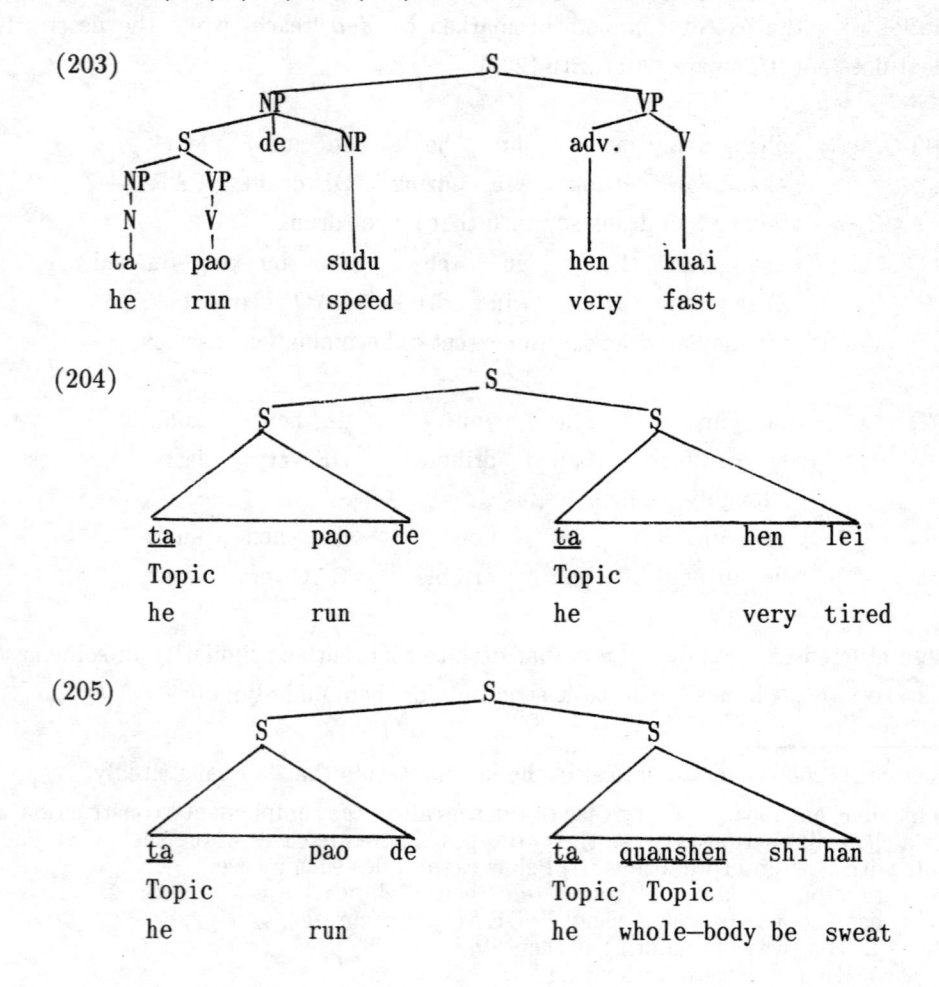

(203)
```
              S
         ┌────┴────┐
         NP        VP
      ┌──┼──┐    ┌──┴──┐
      S  de NP  adv.   V
     ┌┴┐     │    │    │
     NP VP   │    │    │
     │  │    │    │    │
     N  V    │    │    │
     │  │    │    │    │
     ta pao sudu  hen kuai
     he run speed very fast
```

(204)
```
                S
         ┌──────┴──────┐
         S             S
       ╱─┼─╲         ╱─┼─╲
      ta pao de    ta  hen lei
     Topic        Topic
      he  run      he  very tired
```

(205)
```
                S
         ┌──────┴──────┐
         S             S
       ╱─┼─╲         ╱──┼──╲
      ta pao de    ta quanshen shi han
     Topic        Topic Topic
      he  run      he  whole—body be sweat
```

---

indicates that the sentence can also have the (ib) interpretation, a resultative reading. This fact alone does not refute our contention that the two types can, in principle, be distinguished.

Three important points can be made concerning the deep structures that we have just posited. First, the most important different between (203), on the one hand, and (204) and (205) on the other is that while (203) represents a more typical topic-comment structure of Chinese with the topic being complex in containing a relative clause whose head may be deleted as it bears an adverbial relation of manner to the main verb in the relative clause, (204) and (205) on the other hand, look more like a coordinate structure containing two clauses with *de* marking the relation between the two. This structural difference parallels that of the two types of adverbial clauses that we have posited, namely, the adverbial clause of time, place and condition on the one hand and that of concession on the other so that the rules that are required to generate the two types of adverbial clauses can be readily extended to generate these two types of "complement" structures under discussion.

Second, given the structures, the Identical Topic Deletion rule can apply only to the resultative complement structure, deleting identical topics in it and thus resulting in a structural convergence with the descriptive complement in some cases.

Finally, as the topics in a clause marked by *de* are either dominated by an NP or an S, they can be optionally raised by the Topic-raising rule that we discussed in detail in the previous chapter. Thus, in both (206) and (207) the (a) sentences represent the base form and all other sentences represent cases where one or more than one topic has been raised.

(206) a. ta   pao bu   pao de (ya) hen   man.
         he   run step run DE PART very   slow
         'Speaking of the speed in which he runs, it is slow.'

   b. <u>ta</u> (ya) pao bu   pao de hen   man.
      he PART run step run DE very slow
      'Speaking of him, he runs very slowly.'

   c. <u>ta</u> <u>pao</u> <u>bu</u>   (ya)   pao de hen   man.
      he run   step   PART   run DE very slow
      'Speaking of him running, he runs very slowly.'

(207) a. ta   pao bu   pao de (ya) hen   lei.
         he   run step run DE PART very   tired
         'He got tired from running.'

   b. <u>ta</u> (ya) pao bu   pao de hen   lei.
      he PART run step run DE very tired
      'Speaking of him, he was tired from running.'

       c. ta pao bu   (ya) pao de hen lei.
          he run step   PART run DE very tired
          'Speaking of him running, he got tired from it.'

When the whole construction, be it a simple topic–comment structure with a complex topic as in (208) or a topic chain of two clauses as in (209), is further embedded as a complement of the focus verb *shi*, then topic raising can likewise occur. Compare (208) with (206), and (209) with (207).

(208) a. ta pao bu   pao de (ya) shi hen man.
         he run step   run DE PART BE very slow
         'As for his running, he does run very slowly.'
     b. ta (ya) shi pao bu   pao de hen man.
         he PART BE run step   run DE very slow
         'Speaking of him, he does run very slowly.'
     c. ta pao bu   (ya) shi pao de hen man.
         he run step   PART BE run DE very slow
         'As for him running, he does run very slowly.'

(209) a. ta pao bu   pao de (ya) shi hen lei.
         he run step   run DE PART BE very tired
         'Speaking of him running, he did get very tired from it.'
     b. ta (ya) shi pao bu   pao de hen lei.
         he PART BE run step   run DE very tired
         'Speaking of him, it was from running that he got very tired.'
     c. ta pao bu   (ya) shi pao de hen lei.
         he run step   PART BE run DE very tired
         'Speaking of him running, it was from doing it that he got very tired.'

5.4 Residual Problems

There are three questions that remain to be answered. First, if as we have argued, the resultative complement is underlyingly always a clause, why then should it allow the V–not–V form of questioning when the verb is bare, i.e. not in construction with any topic, as in (160)?

Although we don't have much hard evidence for it, we feel that we can give a very plausible explanation for this phenomenon. But before we get to that, first notice that it is not true to say that whenever the rule of Identical Topic NP deletion applies then the V–not–V question form can be used as this is ruled out by the impossibility of using the V–not–V form of question with sentences like (161). So by comparing sentences that allow the V–not–V form with those that do not, it is clear that this form is allowed only when the verb is totally bare. This being the case, we may hypothesize that when the verb is in such a state it may trigger structural re–analysis whose effect is to blot out the second clause and to join the bare verb with the previous clause as its main verb on analogy with sentences containing the descriptive complement, as shown in (159) and (203). Semantically, this is necessitated by finding a new topic for the bare verb, now completely detached, to attach itself to. Structurally, this is facilitated by having a parallel in the case of the descriptive complement structure.

A parallel case of re–analysis can be found in English. Compare the following related sentences.

(210)   a.   It seems that John is intelligent.
          b.   John seems to be intelligent.
          c.   John seems intelligent.

The usual analysis of (210c) is to posit (210a) as an underlying source and then to derive (210b) from it via the rule of Subject–raising and finally to derive (210c) by further applying the rule of "to–be" deletion. However, once this stage is reached, the verb, i.e. *intelligent* is completely bare and its relationship with its subject has become very opaque. It is in this case that the sentence undergoes re–analysis to become similar in pattern to link–verb sentences like (211).

(211) John becomes intelligent.

Once reanalysis takes place, to return to our question of the resultative construction, then it will be perceived as patterning with the descriptive complement construction.[38] This explains why in both V–not–V question and in negation, the two types of complement behave the same.

---

[38]Another condition favorable to the re–analysis hypothesis is the observation we have just made in Note 37 that there are cases where sentences with *de* complement are subject to both analyses.

Our second question is: why both types of complement structure allow two kinds of negation, one with *bu* and the other with *mei(you)* or *shi*, as shown in (168) and (169) as well as two types of V–not–V question, one with the final verb and the other with one of the preceding verbs, using such forms as *you–mei–you* or *shi–bu–shi*, as shown in (212).

(212) a. ta zou de hen lei.
he walk DE very tired
'He was tired from walking.'
b. ta zou de lei–bu–lei?
he walk DE tired–not–tired
'Was he tired from walking?'
c. ta you–mei–you zou de hen lei?
he have–not–have walk DE very tired
'Is it the case that he was very tired from walking?'
d. ta shi–bu–shi zou de hen lei?
he BE–not–BE walk DE very tired
'Roughly, same as (c).'

Before we can answer this question, we would like to point out that there are basically two types of questions in Chinese. If the question is about the main verb, then a simple V–not–V question will be asked, as shown in (213) and (214).

(213) a. ta hen nenggan.
he very competent
'He is very competent.'
b. ta nenggan–bu–nenggan?
he competent–not–competent
'Is he competent?'

(214) a. ta lai–le.
he come–ASP
'He came.'
b. ta lai–le meiyou?
he come–ASP have:not
'Did he come?'

       c. ta you–mei–you lai?
          he have–not–have come
          'Same as (b).'

However, if the question involves more than a single verb, as for instance a proposition, then question forms exemplfied in either (215c) or (215d) can be used.

(215) a. ta yiqian lai–guo zhe–li san ci.
         he before come–ASP here three times
         'He has been here three times before.'
     b. ta yiqian lai–guo zhe–li san ci mei–you?
         he before come–ASP here three times have–not
         'Has he been here three times before?'
     c. ta you–mei–you yiqian lai–guo zheli san ci?
         he have–not–have before come–ASP here three times
         'Is it the case that he has been here three times before?'
     d. ta shi–bu–shi yiqian lai–guo zhe–li san ci?
         he BE–not–BE before come–ASP here three times
         'Roughly, same as (c).'

What is especially noticeable in the examples is that we are positing two *you* questions, one alternating with such aspect markers as *–le* or *–guo*, as in (214 b and c) or (215b) and the other having a larger scope as in (215c). This use of *you–mei–you* can be replaced by *shi–bu–shi*, as shown in (215d).

If this is basically correct, then we can easily see why a multi–topic construction such as (216) can have the two types of question, depending on whether the component which is questioned is simple or complex.

(216) a. ta ba di sao–ganjing–le.
         he BA floor sweep–clean–ASP
         'He had the floor swept clean.'
     b. ta ba di sao–ganjing–le mei–you?
         he BA floor sweep–clean–ASP have–not
         'Did he have the floor swept clean?'

    c. ta   you–mei–you   ba   di   sao–ganjing?
        he   have–not–have   BA floor sweep–clean
        'Same as (b).'

    d. ta   you–mei–you   ba   di   sao–ganjing–le?
        he   have–not–have   BA floor sweep–clean–ASP
        'Is it the case that he had the floor swept clean?'

    e. ta   shi–bu–shi   ba   di   sao–ganjing–le?
        he   BE–not–BE   BA floor sweep–clean–ASP
        'Roughly, same as (d).'

Basically, the same principle applies in the case of negation, although in this case, because it has closer interaction with semantic presupposition, the distribution of *mei–you* 'have–not' is even more restricted.

Now if this is understood, then it can be easily seen why both types of complement structure allow two types of question and negation. This is so because a sentence like (206) or (207) can receive several analyses and depending on whether the comment part is simple or complex, a question and negation of narrow or wide scope can be used.

Our final question has to do with the marker *de*. Again if two different structures underlie these two types of complement constructions as we have argued, then why do they share the same marker *de*?

As it is used in modern Mandarin, there is clearly only one *de* in pronunciation. Most writers choose " 得 " as a character to represent it. The etymon chosen, however, varies among linguists. Chao (1968) and Mei (1978) use "的", while Gao (1971) writes it as " 得 ". Historically, different writers showed different preference. Dialectally, the picture, as far as I can determine, is also unclear. As is clear from our previous discussion, the same *de* is used in the following three situations represented by the following three sentences.

  (217) a. jiao–shu   de (nominalization)
              teach–book–Rel. Mar.
              'one who teaches; teacher'

        b. ta   tiao   de   hen   mei.
            he   dance DE   very beautiful
            'Roughly, the way he dances is very beautiful.'

       c. ta   tiao de hen   lei.
          he   dance DE very tired
          'Roughly, he was very tired from dancihg.'

In Taiwanese, a separate morpheme is used in each case[39] while in Cantonese and Wu dialects (Chen, 1979) the same morpheme is used for the latter two situations. So without a cross–dialectal study of many more dialects and an in–depth historical study of its development, anything we say at this moment is no more than hypothesis.

Simply put, our hypothesis is that before the two types of complement construction converged, the *de* in them should have been two different but perhaps homophonous, or at least very similarly pronounced, morphemes representable in Chinese character by "的" and "得" respectively. Later, due to the structural convergence that we have outlined, the two constructions were perceived as so closely related that the same morpheme began to be used to indicate the relation between the "complement" and what goes before it.

This is, then, the hypothesis, which, we believe, can best account for all the data that we have known and is at the same time compatible with our theory of Chinese grammar. Its confirmation (or disconfirmation), will, of course, await further research.

---

[39]This statement about Taiwanese is a simplification. We are counting only the most widely used morphemes in each case, i.e., *e*, as a relative clause marker, *tioh* for marking a descriptive complement and *kah* for a resultative complement. For a fuller description of all the particles used in all three cases, see Cheng et al. (1989: 162ff.).

APPENDIX I

KEY TO THE SYMBOLS USED IN THE TRANSCRIPTION

//   The double obliques indicate the point at which a current speaker's talk is overlapped by the talk of another.

=   The equal signs indicate 'latching'; i.e., no interval between the end of the prior and the start of the next piece of talk.

(0.0)   Numbers in parentheses indicate elapsed time in seconds.

: :   Colon(s) indicate that the prior syllable is prolonged. Multiple colons indicate a more prolonged syllable.

APPENDIX II

(1) cengjing shi lishi—shang zui guanghui—de
    once   was history—in most glorious

    quanwang   Ali, jinnianlai   shengli hou,
    boxing—chompion   recent—years victory after

    zongshi shuo yao tuisiu, dan zong
    always said want retire but always

    wei tuixiu, jieguo bai   zai chu—chudao—de
    not retire result beated in green—handed

    Shibinkesi shouxia, benlai   keyi guangrong
    Spinx   hands   originally could gloriously

    tuixiu de, que—budao   luocheng zheyang
    retire PART little—expect become   such

    yi—ge xiachang.
    a—CL end

(2) er ni bu   hui xiangxin naxie chuangshuo de,
    but you not will believe those legends   PART

    zhen xiang wo ye   hen nan   xiangxin
    just like I also very difficult believe

    ta   yiyang, yinwei women quan shi you
    them   because we   all are have

    zhishi   you lixing you   duli   sikao
    knowledge have reason have independent thinking

    nengli de   xiandai ren,   women
    ability Rel. Mar. modern people we

    tingqu—le zhe yi—lei—de chuangshuo, liji
    heard—ASP this kind   legends   immediately

    hui zhichen   ta—de huangmiu, ta—de
    will point—out its   absurdity its

    wuji   lai. dan renhe huangmiu
    unreliability PART but any   absurd

    wuji—de   chuangyan dou ceng bei
    unreliable legends   all once by

    yi—dai   yi—dai   —li geng—duo—de
    one—generation one—generation LOC even—more

```
renmen xiangxin-guo, buran     ta bu  hui
people believe-ASP   otherwise it not will

xiang fong yiyang-de yanchuang, geng bu  hui
like  wind           spread     even not will

chuang dao women-de er-zhong.
spread to   our     ear-LOC
```

BIBLIOGRAPHY

Bach, Emmon. 1974. Syntactic theory. New York: Holt, Rinehart and Winston.

Baker, Carl L. 1978. Introduction to generative-transformational syntax. Englewood Cliffs, N.J.: Prentice-Hall, Inc.

Bambase, Aya. 1982. Issues in the analysis of serial verb constructions. Journal of West African Languages 12, 2:3-21.

Barry, Roberta. 1975. Topic in Chinese: an overlap of meaning, grammar, and discourse function. Papers from the parasession on functionalism. Grossman R. et al. (eds.), Chicago: Chicago Linguistic Society.

Bei Jing Daxue Zhongwen Xi (Department of Chinese, University of Beijing). 1980. Yufa xiuci (Grammar and rhetoric).

Bennett, Paul A. 1981. The evolution of passive and disposal sentences. JCL 9, 1:63-90.

Bever, T.G. and D.T. Langendoen. 1971. A dynamic model of the evolution of language. Linguistic Inquiry 2:433-463.

Chafe, Wallace. 1970. Meaning and the structure of language. Chicago University Press.

Chafe, Wallace. 1972. Discourse structure and human knowledge. Language comprehension and the acquisition of knowledge. ed. by R. O. Freedle and J. B. Carroll. Washington: V. H. Winston.

Chafe, Wallace. 1976. Givenness, contrastiveness, definiteness, subjects, topics, and points of view. Subject and topic. ed. by C. Li. New York: Academic Press.

Chan, Stephen W. 1974. Asymmetry in temporal and sequential clauses in Chinese. JCL 2,3:340-353.

Chang, Roland (張強仁). 1977. Co-verbs in spoken Chinese. Taipei: Jeng Chung Book Company.

Chao, Y. R. (趙元任). 1948. Mandarin primer. Cambridge, MA: Harvard University Press.

Chao, Y. R. (趙元任). 1968. A grammar of spoken Chinese. Berkeley and Los Angeles: University of California Press.

Chen, Chung-Yu (陳重瑜). 1978. The two aspect markers hidden in certain locatives. Cheng, R., Y. Li and T. Tang eds. Proceedings of Symposium on Chinese Linguistics, 1977 Linguistic Institute of the Linguistic Society of America. Taipei: Student Book. pp. 233-242.

Chen, Chung-Yu (陳重瑜). 1979. Predicative complements. JCL 7, 1:44-64.

Chen, Ji-Ying (陳紀瀅). 1978. Use more full stops and less exclamation marks. Taipei: Central Daily News. Sept. 18, 1978. p.10.

Cheng, Robert L. (鄭良偉). 1967. Universe-scope relations and Mandarin noun phrases. Project on Linguistic Analysis, Ohio State University, Series 2, No.3, pp.1–182.

Cheng, Robert L. (鄭良偉). 1983. Focus device in Mandarin Chinese. Studies in Chinese syntax and semantics. Tang, T., Cheng, L. and Li, Y. (eds.) Taipei: Student Book.

Cheng, Robert L. (鄭良偉). 1985. A comparison of Taiwanese, Taiwan Mandarin, and Peking Mandarin. Language 61, 2:352–377.

Cheng, Robert L. (鄭良偉). et al. 1989. Mandarin function words and their Taiwanese equivalents. Taipei: The Crane Publishing Co. (in Chinese)

Cheung, Hung-Nin Samuel (張洪年). 1973. A comparative study in Chinese grammars: the *ba*-construction. JCL 1, 3:343–82.

Chomsky, Noam. 1964. Current issues in linguistic theory. The structure of language: readings in the philosophy of language. ed. by Fodor, J.A. and Kats, I.J. Englewood Cliffs, N.J.: Prentice–Hall.

Chomsky, Noam. 1965. Aspects of the theory of syntax. MIT Press.

Chomsky, Noam. 1971. Deep structure, surface structure and semantic interpretation. Semantics. ed. by Steinberg, D. and Jacobovits, L. Cambridge University Press.

Chomsky, Noam. 1977. On WH-movement. Culicover, D. W., et al. eds. Formal Syntax. New York: Academic Press, pp. 71–132.

Chow, Fa-Kao (周法高). 1961. A historical grammar of Ancient Chinese. part 1: Syntax (Chapters 1–4). The institute of History and Philosophy, Academia Sinica special publications, No.39.

Chow, James C. (周見賢). 1989. Proposition as topic: an exploration of S V O V C sentences in Chinese. Studies in English literature and linguistics 15:101–114.

Chu, Chauncey C. (屈承熹). 1970. The structrue of *Shr* and *You* in Mandarin Chinese. Unpublished doctoral dissertation. University of Texas at Austin.

Chu, Chauncey C. (屈承熹) 1973. The passive construction: Chinese and English. JCL 1: 437–470.

Chu, Chauncey C. (屈承熹) 1976a. Some semantic aspects of action verbs. Lingua 40: 43–54.

Chu, Chauncey C. (屈承熹) 1976b. 'Conceptual wholeness' and the 'retained' object. JCL 4, 1:14–23.

Chu, Chauncey C. (屈承熹). 1979a. Hanyu-de cixu he cixu bianqian-zhong-de wenti. (Problems in Mandarin word order and word order change) in Papers in linguistics: theory, application, and Chinese grammar. Taipei: The Crane Publishing Co. (in Chinese)

Chu, Chauncey C. (屈承熹). 1979b. A study of translation from a linguistic point of view. Papers in linguistics: theory, applicatoin, and Chinese grammar. Taipei: The Crane Publishing Co. (in Chinese)

Chu, Chauncey C. (屈承熹). 1979c. The function of the *shi...de* construction in Chinese. Papers in theoretical, applied linguistics and Chinese grammar. Taipei: The Crane Publishing Co.

Chu, Chauncey C. (屈承熹). 1983. A reference grammar of Mandarin Chinese for English speakers. New York: Peter Lang.

Chu, Chauncey C. (屈承熹). 1985. Ambiguity in Mandarin verb phrases: cases with *le* and *shi...de*. In Kim, N. and Tiee, H. eds. Studies in East Asian linguistics. pp.1–23.

Chung, Sandra. 1976. On the subject of two passives in Indonesian. Subject and topic. ed. by C. Li. New York: Academic Press.

Chuo, Fred Ping-lang (卓平郎). 1987. Chinese multiple adverbials. Chinese-Western encounter: Studies in linguistics and literature. ed. by Bramkamp, A. et al. Taipei: Chinese Materials Publication Center, pp.127–160.

Cinque, Guglielmo. 1977. The movement nature of left dislocation. Linguistic Inquiry 8, 397–412.

CKIP (中文詞知識庫小組) 1989. Quoyu-de cilei fenxi (An analysis of parts of speech in Mandarin Chinese). Rev. ed. Taipei: Computer Center, Academia Sinica.

Clark, H. H. and E. V. Clark. 1977. Psychology and language: an introduction to psycholinguistics. New York: Harcourt Brace Jovanovich, Inc.

Deng, Fu-Nan (鄧福南). 1982. Lian-dong-shi ji jian-yu-shi wenti—jian tan fuza weiyu wenti. Hanyu yufa zhuanti shi jiang (Ten lectures on special topics in Chinese grammar). Changsha: Hunan Jiaoyu Chubanshe. pp.78–100.

Deng, Fu-Nan (鄧福南). 1982. Danju he fuju-de huafen (The demarkation of simple and compound sentences). Hanyu yufa zhuanti shi jiang (Ten lectures on special topics in Chinese grammar). pp.149–166. Hunan Jiaoyu Chubanshe.

Ding, Sheng-shu (丁聲樹). et al. 1961. Xiandai Hanyu yufa jianghua (Talks on Modern Chinese grammar). Yuwen huibian 12. Peking: Zhongguo Yuwen Xueshe.

Dragunov, A. A. (龍果夫). 1952. Issledovanija po grammatike Sovremennogo Kitajskogo jazyka: Chasti rechi. Moscow: Academija Nauk. (Grammatical Studies of Modern Chinese (Chinese translation), Peking: Kexue Chuban She. 1958.)

Ernst, Thomas. 1986. (In)definiteness and Chinese verb complements. Paper presented at 1986 Chinese Language Teachers Association Annual Meeeting. Nov. 21–23, Dallas, Texas.

Fillmore, Charles J. 1968. The case for case. Bach, Emmon and Robert T. Harms (eds.), Universals in linguistics theory. New York: Holt, Rinehart, and Winston.

Fraser, Bruce. 1970. Idioms within a transformational grammar. Foundation of Language 6:22–42.

Fraser, Bruce. 1971. An analysis of *even* in English. Studies in linguistic semantics. Fillmore, C. and T. Langendoen (eds.), 151–180. New York: Holt, Rinehart, and Winston.

Fu, Yi–Chin (傅一勤). 1977. Comparative structures in English & Mandarin Chinese. Unpublished Ph.D. dissertation. The Univ. of Michigan.

Givon, T. (ed.) 1979. Syntax & Semantics vol. 12. Discourse & syntax. New York: Academic Press.

Gao, Ming–Kai (高明凱). 1971. Hanyu yufa lunji (Papers in Chinese grammar). Hong Kong: Chongwen Shuju.

Gary, J. O. and E. L. Keenan. 1977. On collapsing grammatical relations in universal grammar. Syntax and semantics. vol. 8: grammatical relations. ed. by Cole, P. and J. M. Sadock. New York: Academic Press.

Guo, Yi–Zhou. 1960. Fuci, jieci, lianci (Adverbs, prepositions, and conjunctions). Shanghai: Shanghai Educational Press. (Also in Yuwen huibian, Book II, Peking: Zhongguo Yuwen Xuehui, 1967).

Gundel, Jeanette K. 1974. The role of topic and comment in linguistic theory. Unpublished doctoral dissertation, University of Texas at Austin.

Gundel, Jeanette K. 1975. Left dislocation and the role of topic–comment in linguistic theory. Ohio State University working papers in linguistics. No.18. pp.72–131.

Hagege, Claude. 1975. La probleme linguistique des prepositions et la solution Chinoise (Avec un essai de typologie a travers plusieurs groupes de languages). Louvain: Peeters.

Haiman, John. 1978. Conditionals are topics. Language, 54:564–89.

Halliday, M. A. K. 1967. Notes on transitivity and theme in English. Journal of Linguistics 3:37–81, 199–244; 4:179–216.

Halliday, M. A. K. 1970a. Language structure and language function. New horizons in linguistics. ed. by John Lyons. Harmondsworth: Penguin Books.

Halliday, M. A. K. 1970b. Functional diversity in language as seen from a consideration of modal and mood in English. Foundations of Language 6:322–65.

Holliday, M. A. K. 1985. An introduction to functional grammar. London: Edward Arnold.

Harris, Z. 1951. Methods in structural linguistics. Chicago: University of Chicago Press.

Hashimoto, Anne Y.(橋木余靄芹)1966. Embedding structures in Mandarin. Unpublished Ph.D. dissertation, Ohio State University.

Hashimoto, Anne-Yue. (橋木余靄芹) 1971a. Descriptive adverbials and the passive construction. Unicorn 7:84–93. Also in Teng, S–H. (ed.) 1985.

Hashimoto, Anne Yue. (橋木余靄芹) 1971b. Mandarin syntactic structures. Unicorn 8 (Chinese Linguistics Project and Seminar). Pinceton University.

Hashimoto, M. 1969. Observations on the passive construction. Unicorn 5:59–71. Also in Teng, S–H. (ed.) 1985.

Hawkinson, A. K. and L. M. Hyman. 1974. Hierarchies of natural topic in Shona. Studies in African Linguistics 5,2:147–170.

Hawkins, J. A. 1978. Definiteness and indefiniteness: A study in reference and grammaticality prediction. London: Croom Helm.

Henne, Henry, O. B. Rongen and L. J. Hansen. 1977. A handbook on Chinese language structure. Oslo: Universitetsforlaget, University of Oslo.

Hinds, John V. 1973. Japanese discourse structure: some discourse constraints on sentence structure. Unpublished doctoral dissertation, University of Buffalo.

Hockett, Charles F. 1958. A course in modern linguistics. New York: Macmillan.

Hou, John Y. (侯炎堯). 1983. Totality in Chinese: the syntax and semantics of *dou*. Tang, T., R. Cheng and Y. Li eds., Studies in Chinese syntax and semantics, pp.253–272. Taipei: Student Book.

Hou, John Y.(侯炎堯). 1985. A constrastive study of Chinese and English relative clauses. Paper presented at the First International Conference of Teaching Chinese to Speakers of Other Languages. Peking, China. (in Chinese)

Householder, Fred W. and Robert L. Cheng. 1967. Universe-scope relations in Chinese and Japanese. Unpublished manuscript, University of York.

Huang, Chu–Ren (黃居仁). and Mangione, L. 1985. A reanalysis of *de:* adjuncts and subordinate clauses. Proceedings of the 4th West Coast Conferece on Formal Linguistics.

Huang. Chu–Ren (黃居仁). 1989. Mandarin Chinese NP *de*- a comparative study of current grammatical theories. Institute of History and Philology special publications No.93. Taipei: Academia Sinica.

Huang, C–T. James (黃正德). 1974. Constraints on transformations: a study of Chinese movement transformations. Unpublished M.A. thesis. National Taiwan Normal University.

Huang, C–T. James (黃正德). 1982. Logical relations in Chinese and the theory of grammar. Ph.D. dissertation. Cambridge, Massachusetts: MIT.

Huang, C–T. James (黃正德). 1984a. On the distribution and reference of empty pronouns. Linguistic Inquiry 15,4:531–74.

Huang, C–T. James. (黃正德) 1984b. Phrase structure, lexical integrity, and Chinese compounds. JCLTA 19,2:53–78.

Huang, C–T. James (黃正德). 1988a. *Wo pao de Kuai* and Chinese phrase structure. Language 64,2:274–311.

Huang, C–T. James (黃正德). 1988b. Two kinds of transitive and intransitive verbs in Chinese. Paper presented at the Second-International Conference on Teaching Chinese to Speakers of Other Languages. Taipei, Taiwan Dec. 27–31. To appear in the the Proceedings.

Haung, Lilian M. (黃美金). 1984. Serial verbs in transition. In Studies in English literature and linguistics, an annual publication by the Department of English, National Taiwan Normal Unversity. pp. 148–162.

Huang, Liu Ping (黃六平). 1983. Hanyu wenyan yufa gangyao (Outline of grammar of Classical Chinese). Taipei: Hanjing Wenhua Shiye Co. (First ed., 1973).

Huang, Shuan–Fan (黃宣範). 1966. Subject and object in Chinese. Project on Linguistic Analysis. Series 1. No.13. pp.25–103.

Huang, Shuan–Fan (黃宣範) 1974. Mandarin causatives. JCL 2, 3:355–69.

Huang, Shuan–Fan (黃宣範). 1982. Chinese concepts of a person– an essay on language and metaphysics. JCL 10,1:86–107.

Huang, Shuan–Fan (黃宣範). 1983. On the (almost perfect) identity of speech and thought: evidence from Chinese dialects in Chu. C, Coblin, W. S. and Tsao, F. eds. Papers from the Fourteenth International Conference on Sino–Tibetan Languages and Linguistics. Taipei: Student Book, 171–186.

Huang, Y–H. (黃運驊) 1984. 'Reflexives in Chinese', Studies in English Literature and Linguistics 10, 163–188.

Jespersen, Otto. 1958. The Philosophy of grammar. London: Allen and Unwin. (First published in 1924).

Johnson, D. E. 1974a. On the role of grammatical relations in linguistic theory. Papers from the Tenth Regional Meeting of the Chicago Linguistic Society. pp.269–283.

Johnson, D. E. 1974b. Toward a theory of relationally–based grammar. Unpublished doctoral dissertation, University of Illinois at Urbana.

Justus, Carol. 1976. Relativization and topicalization in Hittite. Li, C. N. (ed.) Subject and topic. New York: Academic Press, pp.215–45.

Kaplan, R. M. and J. Bresnan. 1982. Lexical functional grammar: a formal system for grammatical representation. Bresnan, J. (ed.) The mental representation of grammatical relations. Cambridge, Mass.: MIT Press.

Keenan, E. L. 1974. The functional principle: generalizing the notion subject of. Papers from the Tenth Regional Meeting of the Chicago Linguistic Society. 298–309.

Keenan, E. L. 1976a. Toward a universal definition of 'subject'. Subject and topic. ed. by C. Li. New York: Academic Press.

Keenan, E. L. 1976b. Remarkable subjects in Malagasy. Subject and topic. ed. by C. Li. New York: Academic Press.

Keenan, E. L. and Bernard Comrie. 1977. Noun phrase accessibility and universal grammar. Linguistic Inquiry 8:63–99.

Keenan, E. O. and B. Schieffelin. 1976a. Topic as a discourse notion: a study of topic in the conversation of children and adults. Subject and topic. ed. by C. Li. New York: Academic Press.

Keenan, E. O. and B. Schiefflin. 1976b. Foregrounding referents: a reconsideration of left dislocation in discourse. Proceedings of the Second meeting of the Berkeley Linguistics Society, 240–257.

Kim, Nam-Kil and Henry H. Tiee (鐵宏業). (eds.) 1985. Studies in East Asian linguistics. Department of East Asian languages & Culture. U.S.C.

Kuno, Susumu. 1971. The position of locatives in existential sentences. Linguistic Inquiry 2:333–378.

Kuno, Susumu. 1972. Functional sentence perspective; a case study from Japanese and English. Linguistic Inquiry 3:269–320.

Kuno, Susumu. 1976. Subject, theme, and speaker's empathy—a re-examination of relativization phenomena. Li, C. N. (ed.) pp. 419–44.

Larkin, G and R. Shook. 1978. Interlanguage, the monitor and the sentence combining. Paper presented at the Los Angeles Second Language Research Forum.

Leech, Geoffrey. 1974. Semantics. Harmonsworth, Middlesex, England: Penguin Books.

Li, A. Y-H. (李豔惠). 1985. Abstract case in Chinese. Unpublished Ph.D. dissertation. Los Angeles: USC.

Li, Charles N. (李訥). 1975. Synchrony vs. diachrony in language structure. Language 51, 4:873–886.

Li, Charles N. (李訥). 1976. Subject and topic. New York: Academic Press.

Li, Charles N. (李訥) and Sandra A. Thompson. 1973. Serial verb constructions in Mandarin Chinese: subordination or coordination? You take the high node and I'll take the low node. pp. 96–103. Chicago Linguistic Society.

Li, Charles N. (李訥) and Sandra A. Thompson. 1974. Chinese as a topic—prominent language. Unpublished paper presented at the Seventh International Conference on Sino—Tibetan Languages and Linguistics, Atlanta, Georgia.

Li, Charles N. (李訥) and Sandra A. Thompson. 1975. The 'paratactic relative clause' in Mandarin Chinese. Asian studies on the Pacific coast. Honolulu: University of Hawaii, Department of East Asian Languages, pp. 1—8.

Li, Charles N. (李訥) and Sandra A. Thompson. 1976. Subject and topic: a new typology of language. Li, C. (ed.), Subject and topic. New York: Academic Press.

Li, Charles N. (李訥) and Sandra A. Thompson. 1978a. An exploration of Mandarin Chinese. In Lehmann, W. (ed.) Syntactic typology. Austin: University of Texas Press, pp. 223—266.

Li, Charles N. (李訥) and Sandra A. Thompson 1978b. Grammatical relations in languages without grammatical signals. In Dressler, W. (ed.) Proceedings of the XIIth International Congress of Linguistics. Innsbruck: Innsbrucker Beitrage Zur Sprachwissenschaft, Universitat Innsbruck.

Li, Charles N. (李訥) and Sandra A. Thompson. 1979. Third—person anaphora and zero—anaphora in Chinese discourse. In Givon, Talmy (ed.) Discourse and syntax. Syntax and semantics, Vol. 12. New York: Academic Press, pp. 311—335.

Li, Charles N. (李訥) and Sandra A. Thompson. 1981. Mandarin Chinese: A functional reference grammar. Berkeley and Los Angeles: University of California Press.

Li, Frances C. 1977. Communicative function in Chinese syntax. JCLTA 12, 2.

Li, Jing Xi (黎錦熙). 1969. Xin zhu Guoyu yufa (Chinese grammar) Taipei: Commercial Press.

Li, Lin—Ding (李臨定). 1963. *Dai de zi de buyu ju* (Complement sentences with *de*) Zhongguo Yuwen 1963. 5:396—410.

Li, Ming—Kuang (黎明光). 1973. A transformational approach to comparative constructions. Unpublished master thesis. Taipei, Taiwan: The English Research Institute, National Taiwan Normal University.

Li, Ying—Che (李英哲). 1971. An investigation of case in Chinese grammar. Seton Hall University Press.

Li, Ying—Che (李英哲). 1972. Problems of subject, object, etc. in Chinese. C. Tang, J. Tung, and A. Wu, (eds.), Papers in linguistics in honor of A. A. Hill. Taipei: Rainbow Bridge Book Co.

Li, Ying—Che (李英哲). 1974. What does 'disposal' mean?— Features of the verb and noun in Chinese. JCL 2, 2:200—18.

Li, Ying—Che (李英哲). 1983. Aspects of Quantification and Negation in Chinese. Tang, T., R. Cheng and Y. Li (eds.) Studies in Chinese syntax and semantics: universe and scope: presupposition and quantification in Chinese. Taipei: Student Book Co., pp.227—240.

Li, Ying—Che (李英哲), R. L. Cheng (鄭良偉), L. Foster, S. H. Ho (賀尙賢), J. Y. Hou (侯炎堯) & M. Yip. 1983. Mandarin Chinese: A practical reference grammar for students and teachers. Vol. 1. Taipei: The Crane Publishing Co.

Lien, Chin—Fa (連金發). 1986. Complement—taking predicates revisited—a case study of factives. Paper presented at 1986 Annual Conference of Chinese Language Teachers Association.

Lin, Helen T. 1981. Essential grammar for modern Chinese. Boston: Cheng & Tsui.

Lin, R—W. (林若望). 1989. On Adjunct extraction of *weisheme* and *zeme*. Unpublished M.A. thesis, National Tsing Hua University.

Lin, Shuang—Fu (林雙福). 1974. Locative construction and *ba*-construction in Mandarin. JCLTA 9, 2:66—83.

Lu, Charles A. 1977. On two topic markers in Chinese. JCLTA 12, 3.

Lü, Ji—Ping (呂冀平). 1955. Zhuyu he binyu—de wenti (Problems concerning subject and object in Chinese). Yuwen Huibian 9:10—20.

Lü, Ji—Ping (呂冀平). 1956. Duiyu zhuyu—de dingyi ji qi zai Hanyu—zhong—de yingyong shangque (A discussion on Wang's article, The definition of subject and its application in Chinese). Yuwen Huibian 9:204—213.

Lü, Shu—Xiang (呂叔湘). 1948. Zhongguo wenfa yaolue (Essentials of Chinese grammar). Shanghai: Commercial Press.

Lü, Shu—Xiang (呂叔湘). 1955a. Hanyu yufa lunwenji (Essays on Chinese grammar). Peking: Kexue Chubanshe.

Lü, Shu—Xiang (呂叔湘). 1955b. *Ba* zi yongfade yanjiu (On the uses of *ba*). Hanyu yufa lunwen ji.

Lü, Shu—Xizng (呂叔湘) and others. 1981. Xiandai Hanyu babai ci (Eight hundred function words in Modern Chinese). Peking: Commercial Press.

Lü, Y. E. (呂施玉惠). 1975. Word order, transformation, and communicative function in Mandarin Chinese, Unpublished doctoral dissertation, Cornell University.

Lyons, John. 1986. Introduction to theoretical linguistics. Cambridge: Cambridge University Press.

Lyons, John. 1977. Semantics. vols. 1 and 2. Cambridge: Cambridge University Press.

Ma, Jian–Zhong (馬建忠). 1935. Mashi wentong (Ma's grammar). Shanghai: Commercial Press. First appeared in 1898.

Mei, Kuang (梅廣). 1972. Studies in the transformational grammar of Modern Standard Chinese. Ph.D. dissertation, Harvard University.

Mei, Kuang (梅廣). 1978a. The *ba*–sentences in Modern Chinese. Bulletin of the College of Fine Arts, National Taiwan University 27:145–180.

Mei, Kuang (梅廣). 1978b. Guoyu yufa zhong de dongcizu buyu (On the VP complement in Mandarin Chinese). Papers in honor of Professor Chu Wan–li on his 70th birthday. Taipei: Lianjing, pp. 511–36.

Mei, Kuang (梅廣). 1980. Is Modern Chinese really an SOV language? In Tang, T–C, F. Tsao and Y. Li (eds.) Papers from the 1979 Asian and Pacific Conference on Linguistics and Language Teaching, 175–197. Taipei: Student Book Co.

Mei, Kuang (梅廣). 1987a. Raising sturcture in Chinese. Paper presented at the Symposium on Modern Grammatical Theories and Chinese Syntax, July 30, 1987, Tsing Hua University, Hsin–chu, Taiwan.

Mei, Kuang (梅廣). 1987b. Shi lun dongci chongfu (On verb reduplication). Paper Presented at the Second International Conference in Sinology. To appear in the Proceedings.

Nesfield, J. C. 1961. Outline of English grammar. Revised edition. London: Macmillian Co.

Paris, Marie–Claude (白梅麗). 1976. Relative clause formation in English and Mandarin Chinese and Ross' Constraints: a contrastive approach. Proceedings of the 2nd International Conference of the English Contrastive projects, University of Bucharest Press.

Paris, Marie–Claude (白梅麗). 1979a. Some aspects of the syntax and semantics of the *lian...ye/dou* construction in Mandarin. Cahiers de Linguistique–Asie Orientale 5:47–70, Paris.

Paris, Marie–Claude (白梅麗). 1979b. Nominalization in Mandarin Chinese. Department de Recherches Linguistiques, Universite Paris VII.

Parker, Frank. 1976. Language change and the passive voice. Language 52:449–460.

Perlmutter, D. and P. M. Postal. 1974. Some gerneral laws of grammar. Unpublished handout, Linguistic Institute of LSA, University of Massachusetts.

Postal, P. M. 1976. Avoiding reference to subject. Linguistic Inquiry 7, 1:551–81.

Quirk, R., S.Greenbaum, B. Leech, and J. Svartrik. 1972. A grammar of contemporary English. London: Longman

Ross, John R. 1967. Constraints on variables in syntax. Unpublished Ph.D. dissertation, MIT (Reproduced by the Indiana Linguistic Club).

Ross, John R. 1970. Gapping and order of constituents. In M. Bierwisch and K. E. Heidolph, (eds.) Progress in linguistics. The Hague and Paris.

Ross, Claudia. 1983. On the function of Mandarin *de.* JCL 11, 2:214–246.

Ross, Claude. 1984. Adverbial modification in Mandarin. JCL 12, 2:207–234.

Sanders, G. and James H–Y Tai (戴浩一). 1972. Immediate dominance and identity deletion. Foundations of Language 8:161–198.

Sankoff, B. and P. Brown. 1976. The origins of syntax in discourse. Language 52:631–666.

Schachter, Jacquelyn. 1974. An error in error analysis. Language Learning 24, 2:205–14.

Schachter, Jacquelyn and Marianne Celce–Murcia. 1977. Some reservations concerning error analysis. TESOL Quarterly, 11, 4:441–52.

Schacter, Paul. 1976. The subject in Philippine languages: Topic, actor, actor–topic, or none of the above. Li, C. N. (ed.) Subject and topic. New York: Academic Press, pp. 493–518.

Schachter, Paul. 1979. 'Reference–related and role–related properties of subjects.' In Syntax and Semantics, Vol. 12:281–308. New York: Academic Press.

Schane, Sanford A. 1971. The phoneme revisited. Lg. 47:503–521.

Shi, Dingxu. (石定栩). 1989. Topic chain as a syntactic category in Chinese. JCL 17, 2:223–262.

Shimizu, Midori. 1976. Relational grammar and promotional rules in Japanese. Papers from the 11th Regional Meeting of the Chicago Linguistic Society, 529–535.

Shulman, H. G. 1970. Encoding and retention of semantic and phonemic information in short–term memory. Journal of Verbal Learning and Verbal Behavior, 9:499–508.

Shuman, H. G. 1972. Semantic confusion errors in short–term memory. Journal of Verbal Learning and Verbal Behavior, 11:221–227.

Sibley, Jean E. 1980. Topicalization in spontaneous Chinese monoloque: an empirical study. Unpublished M.A. thesis, Hong Kong University.

Simon, Harry F. 1958. Some remarks on the structure of the verb complex in standard Chinese. Bulletin of the School of Oriental and African Studies. 21:553–577.

Stockwell, R. D., P. Schachter, and B. H. Partee. 1973. The major syntactic structures of English. New York: Holt, Rinehart and Winston.

Tai, James H–Y. (戴浩一). 1969. Coordination reduction. Unpublished Ph.D. dissertation, Indiana University (Reproduced by the Indiana Linguistic Club).

Tai, James H–Y. (戴浩一). 1973a. A derivational constraint on adverbial placement in Mandarin Chinese. JCL 1,3:397–413.

Tai, James H–Y. (戴浩一). 1973b. Chinese as a SOV language. Papers from the 9th Chicago Linguistic Society Meeting. Chicago Linguistic Society, pp. 659–71.

Tai, James H–Y. (戴浩一). 1975. On two functions of place adverbials in Mandarin Chinese. JCL 3, 2/3:154–179.

Tai, James H–Y. (戴浩一). 1976. Semantics and syntax of inner and outer locatives. Brown, R. L. et al. (eds.) Proceedings of the 1976 Mid–American Linguistics conference. Minneapolis, Minnesota: University of Minnesota, pp. 393–401.

Tai, James H–Y. (戴浩一). 1978. Anaphoric constraints in Mandarin Chinese narrative discourse. In Hinds, John. (ed) Anaphora in discourse. Edmonton, Alberta: Linguistic Research, pp. 279–338.

Tai, James H– Y. (戴浩一). 1986. Adverbial modification and implicature in Mandarin Chinese (On how *pao de hen kuai* is different from *pao de hen lei*). Paper presented at 1986 Annual Meeting of Chinese Language Teachers Association, Dallas, Texas, Nov. 21–23.

Tang, Ting–Chi (湯廷池). 1972. A case grammar of spoken Chinese. Taipei: Hai Guo Book Co.

Tang, Ting–Chi (湯廷池). 1975. A case grammar classification of Chinese verbs. Taipei: Hai Guo Book Co.

Tang, Ting–Chi (湯廷池). 1977a. A contrastive study of Chinese and English relativization. Yingyu jiaxue lunji (Papers in teaching English as a second language). Taipei: Student Book Co.

Tang, Ting–Chi (湯廷池). 1977b. Studies in transformational grammar of Chinese Vol. I: movement transformations. Taipei: Student Book Co.

Tang, Ting–Chi (湯廷池). 1979a. Existential sentences, pseudo–cleft sentences and relative clauses: a contrastive analysis between English, Chinese, and Japanese. Guoyu yufa yanjiu lunji (Studies in Chinese syntax). Taipei: Student Book Co.

Tang, Ting–Chi (湯廷池). 1979b. Relative clauses in Chinese. Guoyu yufa yanjiu lunji (Studies in Chinese syntax). Taipei: Student Book Co.

Tang, Ting–Chi (湯廷池). 1979c. Double–object constructions in Chinese. Guoyu yufa yanjiu lunji (Studies in Chinese syntax). Taipei: Student Book Co.

Tang, Ting–Chi (湯廷池). 1979d. On the two uses of the auxiliary verb *hui*. Guoyu yufa yanjiu lunji (Studies inChinese syntax). Taipei: Student Book Co., pp.1–6.

Tang, Ting–Chi (湯廷池). 1979e. On the demarkation of subject and topic. Guoyu yufa yanjiu lunji (Studies in Chinese syntax). Taipei: Student Book Co., pp.73–80.

Tang, Ting–Chi (湯廷池) 1980. Objectives and methodology in linguistic analysis: syntax, semantics & pragmatics. In Tang, T–C, F. Tsao and Y. Li (eds.) Papers from the 1979 Asian and Pacific Conference on Linguistics and Language Teaching. Taipei:

Student Book Co., pp.1–10.

Tang, Ting–Chi (湯廷池). 1988. Hanyu cifa jufa lunji (Studies in Chinese morphology and syntax). Taipei: Student Book Co.

Teng, Shou–Hsin (鄧守信). 1974a. Double nominatives in Chinese. Language 50:455–473.

Teng, Shou–Hsin (鄧守信). 1974b. Negation in Chinese. JCL 2, 2:125–140.

Teng, Shou–Hsin (鄧守信). 1975. A semantic study of transitivity relations in Chinese. Berkeley and Los Angeles: University of California Press.

Teng, Shou–Hsin (鄧守信). 1979. Remarks on cleft sentences in Chinese. JCL 7, 1:101–114. (Also in Teng, S. (ed), Readings in Chinese transformational syntax, pp.157–168).

Teng, Shou–Hsin (鄧守信) (ed.) 1985. Readings in Chinese transformational syntax. Taipei: The Crane Publishing Co.

Thompson, Sandra A. 1971. The deep structrue of relative clauses. Fillmore, C. J. and D. T. Langedoen (eds.), Studies in linguistic semantics. New York: Holt, Rinehart and Winston.

Thompson, Sandra A. 1973a. Resultative verb compounds in Mandarin Chinese: a case for lexical rules. Language 49, 2:361–379.

Thompson, Sandra A. 1973b. Transitivity and some problems with *ba* construction in Mandarin Chinese. JCL 1, 2:208–221.

Tiee, Henry H. (鐵宏業). 1985. Modality in Chinese. Kim, N. and H. Tiee (eds.) pp.84–96.

Tiee, Henry H. (鐵宏業). 1986. A reference grammar of Chinese sentences. Tucson: University of Arizona Press.

Tsai, S. G. (蔡濯堂,筆名思果). 1972. A study of translation. Hong Kong: You Lian Publishing Co. (in Chinese).

Tsang, Chui Lim. 1981. A semantic study of modal auxiliary verbs in Chinese. Unpublished Ph. D. dissertation, Stanford University.

Tsao, Feng–Fu (曹逢甫). 1976. Expectation in Chinese: a functional analysis of two adverbs. Proceedings of the Second Annual Meeting of the Berkeley Linguistic Society, pp.360–74.

Tsao, Feng–Fu (曹逢甫). 1978a. Anglicization of Chinese morphology and syntax in the past two hundred years. Studies in English literature and linguistics, 44–54. Taipei; Department of English, National Taiwan Normal University.

Tsao, Feng–Fu (曹逢甫). 1978b. Subject and topic in Chinese. In Cheng, R., Y. Li and T–C Tang (eds.) Proceedings of Symposium on Chinese Linguistics, 1977 Linguistic Institue of the Linguistic Society of America, 165–96. Taipei: Student Book Co.

Tsao, Feng-Fu (曹逢甫). 1979. A functional study of topic in Chinese: The first step towards discourse analysis. Taipei: Student Book Co.

Tsao, Feng-Fu (曹逢甫). 1980. Sentences in English and Chinese: An exploration of some basic syntactic differences. Li, P. J., G. Chen, M. Tien and F. Tsao (eds.) Papers in honor of Professor Lin Yu-Keng on her seventieth birthday. Taipei: Wen Shin Publishing Co. (Chinese version in Tang, T. et al. (eds.) 1980. Papers from the 1979 Asian and Pacific Conference on Linguistics and Language Teaching).

Tsao, Feng-Fu (曹逢甫). 1982. The double nominative construction in Mandarin Chinese. Tsing Hua Journal of Chinese studies 14:275-97.

Tsao, Feng-Fu (曹逢甫). 1983. Linguistics and written discourse in particular languages: contrastive studies: English and Chinese (Mardarin). Kaplan, R. (ed.) Annual Review of Applied Linguistics, 1982. Rowley, MA: Newbury House, pp.99-117.

Tsao, Feng-Fu (曹逢甫). 1986. Relativization in Chinese and English: A contrastive study of form and function. JCLTA 11, 3:13-47.

Tsao, Feng-Fu (曹逢甫). 1987a. A topic-comment approach to the *ba* construction. JCL 15, 1:1-54.

Tsao, Feng-Fu (曹逢甫). 1987b. On the so-called 'verb-copying' construction in Chinese. JCLTA 22, 2:13-44.

Tsao, Feng-Fu (曹逢甫). 1988a. The functions of Mandarin *gei* and Taiwanese *hou* in the double object and passive constructions. In Cheng, R. L. and S. Huang (eds.) The structure of Taiwanese: a modern synthesis. Taipei: Crane Publishing Co., pp.165-208.

Tsao, Feng-Fu (曹逢甫). 1988b. Cong zhuti-pinglun-de guandian tan Zhongwende juxing (Chinese sentence patterns: a topic-comment approach). Paper presented at the Second International Conference on Teaching Chinese to Speakers of Other Languages. Dec. 27-31. Taipei, Taiwan. To appear in the Proceedings.

Tsao, Feng-Fu (曹逢甫). 1989a. Topics and the *lian...dou/ye* construction revisited. in Tai, James H-Y. and F. Hsueh, (eds.) Functionalism and Chinese grammar. Chinese Language Teachers Association Monograph No.1, pp.248-278.

Tsao, Feng-Fu (曹逢甫). 1989b. Comparison in Chinese: A topic-comment approach. Tsing Hua Journal of Chinese Studies. New series 19, 1:151-190.

Tsao, Feng-Fu (曹逢甫). 1989c. The topical function of preverbal locatives and temporals in Chinese. Paper presented at 1989 International Conference on Sino-Tibetan Languages and Linguistics, Oct. 5-8, University of Hawaii, Honolulu, Hawaii.

Tsao, Feng-Fu (曹逢甫). Forthcoming a. Serial verb cosntructions in Chinese. To appear in the Proceedings of the Second International Conference on Sinology. Taipei: Academia Sinica.

Tsao, Feng-Fu (曹逢甫). Forthcoming b. Topics and clause connectives in Chinese. To appear in Papers in memory of Prof. F. K. Li. Taipei: Institute of History and Philology, Academia Sinica.

Tse, John K-P. (謝國平). 1986. Zero-pronominalization in Mandarin Chinese: planned vs. unplanned discourse. Studies in English Literature and Linguistics, an annual publication of the Department of English, National Taiwan Normal University, pp. 99-117.

Van Riemskijk, Henk and Williams, Edwin. 1986. Introduction to the theory of grammar. The MIT Press.

Wang, Fred Fang-Yu, Henry C. Fenn, and Pao-Ch'en Lee. 1953. Chinese dialogues. New Haven, Conn.: Yale University Press.

Wang, Huan (王還). 1963. *Ba*-sentences and *bei*-sentences. Translated into English in Project on Linguistic Analysis. Wang, W. S-Y. (ed.) No.4. Columbus: Ohio State University, Department of Linguistics.

Wang, Li (王力). 1945. Zhongguo yufa lilun. (Theory of Chinese Grammar) Shanghai: Commercial Press.

Wang, Li (王力). 1956. Zhuyu-de dingyi ji qi zai Hanyu-zhong-de yingyong. (A Definition of subject and its application in Chinese). Yuwen huibian 9, 169-180. Peking: Zhongguo Yuwen Xuexshe.

Wang, Li (王力). 1974. Zhongguo yufa gangyao (Outline of Chinese grammar). Taipei: The Horizon Publishing Co. (First printed in Shanghai in 1946).

Wang, Li (王力). 1983. Hanyu shi gao (A history of the Chinese language). Rev. (ed.) Peking: Zhonghua.

Wang, Peter J-T. 1980. Anti-monosyllabicity in Chinese sentence structures. In Li, P., G. Chen, M. Tien F. Tsao eds., Papers in honor of Prof. Lin Yu-k'eng on her seventieth birthday. Taipei: Wen Shin Publishing Co., pp.43-51.

Wang, William S-Y.(王世元)1964. Some syntactic rules for Mandarin. Proceedings of the 9th International Congress of Linguistics, 191-202.

Wang, Xiao-Xing. 1988. Chinese copulas and the development of *shi*. Unpublished M.A. paper, University of Pittsburgh.

Weinreich, Uriel. 1969. Problems in the analysis of idioms. Jaan Puhvel. (ed.), Substance and structure of language. Berkeley and Los Angeles: University of California Press.

Welmers, W. E. 1973. African language structures. Berkeley and Los Angeles: University of California Press.

Xing, Gong–Wan (邢公畹). 1956. Lun Hanyu zaojufa–shang–de zhuyu he binyu (On subject and object in the syntax of Chinese). Yuwen huibian 9:41–47.

Xu, Lie–Jiong (徐烈炯). 1985–1986. Toward a lexical–thematic theory of control. Linguistic Review 5:345–376.

Xu, Lie–Jiong (徐烈炯). 1986. Free empty category. Linguistic Inquiry 18, 1:75–93.

Xu, Lie–Jiong (徐烈炯). and D. T. Langendoen. 1985. Topic structures in Chinese. Language 61, 1:1–27.

Ying, Ming. 1978. Punctuation marks and teaching of the national language. Central Daily News, Oct. 8, p.10.

Yu, K. C. (余光中). 1972. Cremation of the crane: an anthology of lyrical and critical essays. Taipei: Chu Wenxue Publishing Co. (in Chinese).

Yu, K. C. (余光中). 1981. On the watershed: a collection of critical essays. Taipei: Chun Wenxue Publishing Co. (in Chinese).

Yuwen huibian (語文彙編). 1969. Vol. 9. Peking: Zhong Hua Book Co.

Zhang, Qi–Chun (張其春). 1955a. Guoyu–de da xiao zhuyu (The major and minor subject in Chinese). Zhongguo yuwen yanjiu cankao ziliao xuanji (A selected collection of papers on the Chinese language), (ed.) by Shu Zhong, Peking: Zhong Hua Book Co.

Zhang, Qi–Chun (張其春). 1955b. Zhuyu he weiyu–de guanxi (The relation between subject and predicate in Chinese). Yu–wen huibian 9:48–52.

Zhang, Zhi–Gong 張志公. 1953. Hanyu yufa changshi (General knowledge about Chinese grammar). Zhongguo Qingnian Chubanshe (Chinese Youth Publishing Co.).

Zhongguo Kexue Yuan, Yuyan Yanjiusuo, Yufaxiaozu (中國科學院語言研究所語法小組). 1952–53. Yufa jianghua (Talks on Chinese grammar). Zhongguo Yuwen, Dec., 1952 and Jan., 1953.

Zhu, De–Xi (朱德熙). 1959. Dingyu he zhuangyu (Adjectival and adverbial modifiers). Shanghai: Shanghai Education Press (Also in Yuwen huibian Book II. Peking: Zhongguo Yuwen Xuehui.).

Zhu, De– Xi (朱德熙). 1978. *De* zi jiegou he panduanju (The *de* construction and the classificatory sentence). Zhongguo Yuwen, 1978 (Also in Xiandai Hanyu yanjiu (現代漢語研究). Peking: Commercial Press).

Index

A

Accessibility Hierarchy	可近階層	30,430
adnominal dative promotion	與格領屬名詞組提昇	8,9
adjective (see also state verb)	形容詞	68,70,71,145,151,154
adjectival (sentence)	形容 (句)	70,72
adverb	副詞	4,12,13,100,124,125
		139,145,151,280,283
		291,339,348,375
adverbial	副語	30,145,152,154,155,160
		164,260,264,322,346,
		348,349,351,352,374
of manner (=manner adverbial)	狀態副語	154,164,259,264,353,403
of place (see locative adverbial)	處所副語	264
of reason (=reason adverbial)	理由副語	259,297
of time (see temporal adverbial)	時間副語	44,260,385
scope-delimiting	範圍限制副語	153,179,180,182,185,264
		265
adverbial clause	副詞子句	260,346,349,351,457
of concession	讓步副詞子句	349-376
of condition (=conditional adverbial clause)	條件副詞子句	349-376
of place (=locative adverbial clause)	處所副詞子句	349-376
of reason (=reason adverbial clause)	理由副詞子句	349-376
of time (=temporal adverbial	時間副詞子句	349-376

clause)		
adverse passive	不利的被動	21,114,115,116
Auxiliary verb (see modal auxiliary verb)	助動詞(情貌助動詞)	

B

Ba construction	把字句	33,80,168-205,264,411
extended use of --	引伸用法	201-204
meaning of --	意義	197-205
function of --	功用	33,197-205
Ba (object) NP	把字賓語名詞組	80,172-190,219,355,356 411
baoqian	抱歉	417
Bei construction	被字句	106-112,411
bivalent (=two-place)	二元的	202
bixu	必須	384
budan	不但	347

C

cai	才	49,50,374
C-command	C 統制	365
case	格	5,8,9,10,15,17,20,79,100 103,114,116
agentive	施事格	116,117
dative	與格	8,9
goal	目標格	79,96,99,109,117
locative	處所格	116,117
patient	受事格	79,114,116,117
source	來源格	103,117,131
Case grammar	格語法	9,79,123

Case marking	格的標誌	5,20
Chinese Information Principle	漢語訊息原則	243
Chinese sentence	漢語的句子	6-17,19,62,107,313
Chao's definition	趙的定義	6,7
Tang's characterization	湯的描述	7
Teng's characterization	鄧的描述	11
Wang's definition	王的定義	7,17
Chinese subject(=subject in chinese)	漢語的主語	20-53,54,60,61,461
Chinese topic (=topic in chinese)	漢語的主題	53-65,325
Clause connective	子（分）句聯接語	64,343,346,360,374
adverbial --	副詞性的	30,100,145,346,349,351 353,375
conjunction (proper)	連詞	15,16,279,309,347,348 375,376
forward-linking	前向接連的	376
repetitive correlative	重複關連	375-376
cleft sentences (=*Shi...de* construction)	分裂句（=是...的結構）	
comparison	比較	30,256,279-283,294,297 300-302,310,311,314,356
dimension of --	----種類	279,280,283
word(morpheme)	比較詞	279,280
compared constituent	比較項	131,283-297,355,356
Compared Constituents Deletion	比較詞刪除	297,303,304,309
complementary distrubution	互補分佈	237-238
complex sentence	繁句	1,65,70,78,95,96,346 377-471
complex stative construction (=de complement construction)	複雜狀態結搆 （="得"字補語句）	223
complementizer (COMP)	補語（子句）連詞	362-364,371,375,376,402
Compound	複合詞	65,343

directional verb compound (DVC)	方向複合詞	84-86
frozen (verbal) compound	凝固複合詞	138-145
idiomatized verbal compound	成語化動詞複合詞	142-145
resultative verb compound (RVC)	結果複合動詞	84,93
semi-compound	半複合詞	137-141
verb-object compound(=VO compound)	動賓複合詞	25,93,103
compound sentences	複句	64,78,96,313,343-376
conjunction reduction	聯結刪略	15,16,127,278,279
Coreferential NP Deletion	同指名詞組刪除	40,46,48,239

D

danshi	但是	371,374
de complement construction	"得"字補語句	445-471
descriptive --	描述 ----	87,316,317,321,324,332 337,338,445-471
resultative --	結果 ----	84,87,93,115,445-471
definite	有定的	25,26,40,53,56,59,74,83 150,156,269,271,272,287 318,326,333,334,338,341 354
deletion	刪除	12,16,124,128,149,150 161,269,270,272,282,286 299,300,302-308,326,334 359,413,426
backward	逆向	299,300
forward	順向	297,299
dei	得	384
direct object	直接賓語	20,30,33,43,100,107,114 291-293,296,297,316,317 318,320,325,328
discourse-oriented languages	言談取向語	40,47,48,50,51,426

Discourse Theme Deletion	言談話題刪除	48-50
disposal theory	(把字句) 處置論	197-199
distant haplology	非緊鄰同音脫落	108,109
dou		274-276
double nominative construction	"雙主語" 結構	8-14,17,121-149,158,159
		161,164,253,272,289,291
		325,333,371,461

E

embedded clause	包孕子句	96,324,369,371
		405-425
empathy	關心	191
English sentence	英語的句子	1,5,6,25,59,81,106
Chomsky's characterization	喬姆斯基的描述	2
Jespersen's definition	葉氏的定義	2,7
Nesfield's definition	納氏的定義	1
English subject	英語的主語	60,61
(=subject in English)		
English topic	英語的主題	60
(=topic in English)		
Equi-NP Deletion	Equi-名詞組刪略	40,41,43,48,53,54,56
		59,269
existential (sentence)	存在句	59,70,78,335,391

F

factive (verb)	事實 (動詞)	316,414,416-418
focus (see information)	焦點 (見information條)	
functional sentence perspective	句子的功能分佈觀	242

G

G-B theory	管轄約束理論	243,365,369,372
generic	通指	269,271,272,276,287
		326,332,354
genetive (marker) deletion	領屬標誌刪除	305-308

H

Head NP	中心名詞組	30,351,432-434
hierarchy of topicality	主題屬性階層	430
hen	很	12,139,280,282
heshi	合適	379-381
hao-xiang	好像	379
houhui	後悔	417
hui	會	85,378,381,383,384
		385-390

I

Identical Elements in a Compared Constituent Deletion	在比較項中相同 成份刪除	302,303,304,309
imperativization	祈使化	27,28,53,54,56,59,60
		269
information	訊息	37,38,60,67,80,116,273
		317,323
focus	焦點訊息	38,113,114,115,116,122
		166,191,249,254,278
		393-399
new	新訊息	38,191
old	舊訊息	191,199,273
instrumental (adverb)	工具副詞	154,339

interrogative (question)	疑問句	418-421
direct question	直接問句	418-421
indirect question	間接問句	418-421
V-not-V question	正反問句	243-245,381,382,396
		418-419,447,448,468
wh question	wh 問句	420-421
particle question	助詞問句	419-420

J

jiu	就	64,132,133,158,374

K

kan-qi-lai	看起來	377-379
ken	肯	386
keneng	可能	155,371,382,383,388,389
		451
keyi	可以	384,388,389
kongpa	恐怕	379

L

left-branching	左分枝(的)	436
lian constituent	連字成份	131,249-256,263,264
		267-273,276-278,355,356
lian...dou/ye construction	連字句	131,249-278
lian phrase (=*lian* constituent)	連字詞組	131,256-273,276,277,278
lian topic	連字主題詞	269,272,276-277,355,356
locative	處所詞	87,89,90,92,94,99,100
		108,121,149-165,264,289
		297,337,357,358,365

M

middle-voiced (sentence)	中態（句）	74, 94, 106, 114, 115
modal auxiliary verb	情態助動詞	70, 155, 382, 390
modality	情態	95, 383-387
deontic modality	義務情態	384-385
dynamic modality	能願情態	385-386
epistemic modality	認知情態	383-384
multiple-topic (sentence)	多主題的	121-311, 362

N

nan	難	24, 73, 123, 377-380
neng	能	50, 115, 385, 386, 388
non-term	（動詞的）非必要論元	25, 178-179
new information (see information)	新訊息（見訊息條）	

O

object fronting construction	賓語提前句	80, 205-222
Oblique (case)	斜位	21, 30
observational adequacy	觀察上的妥當性	168
old information (see information)	舊訊息（見訊息條）	
one-place (predicate)	一元(述語)	384
one-topic (sentecne)	單一主題（句）	67, 120, 391

P

parameter	參數	279, 311
passive sentence	被動句	105-117, 118, 269

passivization	被動化	53,269,270,272
pause particles	停頓動詞	54-56,134,156,170
		174-175,177,186,208-209
		231,245,270,285-286,326
		349-350,451,452,465-466
perceptual strategy	理解策略	3,5
Phrase Structure Condition (PSC)	詞組結構條件	243
pivotal construction	承軸結構	40,300,316,327,328,331
Present-time Deletion	現在時刪除	304,309
presupposed	預設的	38,199,200,243
presupposition	預設	274,470
pronominalization	代名化	27,30,31,33,47,48,51,53
		56,80,150,161,239,327
		427
proper binding	適切的約束	365
pseudo-cleft construction	準分裂句	260,394
pseudo-transitive verb	準及物動詞	190-197

Q

quantifier phrase (QP)	量化詞詞組	373,374

R

raising predicate	(主題)提昇動詞	117,377-405,406-408
referential property	指稱屬性	
of relative clauses	關係子句的指稱屬性	30
of subject	主語的指稱屬性	25-26
of topic	主題的指稱屬性	53,55
reflexivization	反身(代名)化	27,28,53,54,56,59,60
		136
relative clause	關係子句	30,34,35,37,38,351,353

		426-444
non-restrictive	非限定的關係子句	437-444
restrictive	限定的關係子句	38,344,437-444
stacking	關係子句的堆疊	436-437
relative pronoun	關係代名詞	429-430
relativization	關係子句化	29,30,33,426-444
renwei	認爲	411,414,420-421
retained object	保留賓語	183,184,185,201,210
		211,212
right-branching	右分枝的	436,437
rongyi	容易	377,379

S

selectional (restriction)	互選的(限制)	53,129,130,331,341,342
sentence	句子	
in Chinese	漢語的句子	6-17,343,345,358,360
		362,371,376
in English	英語的句子	1-6,331,342
of emotive and mental state	感情與心理狀態句	79,80
with an action verb	行動動詞句	68,80,92,105
with a special topic	特殊主題句	249-311
sentence-oriented (languages)	句子取向(語)	19
sentential comparison	句子式比較	310-311
sentential object	賓語子句	309-311,408-426,433
sentential subject	主語子句	405-408
serial verb constructions	系列動詞結構	38,313,314,316,318,319
		320,321,322,324,327,332
		333,335,336,340,341,342
		343,344
Shi...de construction	是...的結構	113,114,116,117,390-405

		451
(=cleft sentence)	(=分裂句)	
suoyi	所以	45,52,62,160,162,344,374
		376
speaker and hearer deletion	說化者與聽話者刪除	50-53
specific	有指的	53,54,156,157,173,354
structure reanalysis	結構重分析	467
subcategorization	次類畫分	385,405
subject	主語	1,2,3,6,7,11,12,17,19
		20-29,35,39-43,51-55
		59-64,69,73,79,80,95,99
		107,111,113,114,116,117
in English	英語的主語	60,61
in Chinese	漢語的主語	20-53,54,60,61,170,360
		361
subject-prominent (languages)	主語明顯(語)	19

T

telescopic sentence	套疊句	215,327-342,403
telescopic-descriptive	套疊-描述句	337-340,341,342
telescopic-pivotal	套疊-承軸句	328-332,341
telescopic-presentative	套疊-引介句	332-337,341
temporal	時間詞	122,149,150-156,182
		339,357,358
temporal clause	時間子句	
(=adverbial clause of time)		
Tensed Sentence Condition	帶時式句條件	368-369
(TSC)		
term	(動詞的)必要論元	178,180-182
theme-rheme distinction	(句中)舊--新訊息區分	242
transitivity	施受關係	80,200-205

topic	主題	
contrastive function of	對比功能	158-159,210-211,234
		255,276,277,364
general properties	一般特質	53
in English		
in Chinese		170,325,360,361
primary	大主題	74,80,83,106,161,162
		313,324,333,348,353
		354,361,368,370
non-primary	非大主題	155,163,165,212,249
		313,368
secondary	次主題	33,121,161,162,343,362
		371
tertiary	參主題	162,249
topic-raising	主題提昇	349,360,362,365,368,369
		371,372,375
topic-prominent languages	主題明顯語	19,20,311
topical ambiguity	主題歧義	186-188
topical comparison	主題組比較	310-311
topicality	主題性	430-432
topic chain	主題串	39,40,43-50,54,56,63,64
		67,78,81,326,327,333
		341,344,345,359,365,373
		443
plain	不帶連接語的主題串	40,324-327,341,345-346
marked	帶連接語的主題串	345,346

V

verb	動詞	
action verb	行動動詞	60,68,80,84,88,92,95
		105,115

ditransitive verb	雙賓動詞	96,100,104
intransitive verb	不及物動詞	90,94
in the middle voice	中態動詞	114
of approval	贊成動詞	415,425
of cognition (=factive verb)	認知 (=事實) 動詞	78,414,425
of conjecture	猜臆動詞	420
of communication	溝通動詞	96,102
of emotive and mental state	感情與心理狀態動詞	79,80
of hope-fear	希望--恐懼動詞	415,425
of imagination	想像動詞	414
of inquiry	探詢動詞	416
of judgment	判斷動詞	414,425
of location	姿置動詞	77,88,89,90,91,95
of locution	言語動詞	408,413-414
of motion	移位動詞	77,88,90,91,92
of thinking and feeling	感思動詞	415,425
of self-intention	自我企圖動詞	421-422,425
of transaction	交易動詞	96
of vocal action	動聲動詞	88
passive verb	受動詞	106,111,112,113
quality verb	性質動詞	70,72
state verb	狀態動詞	68,69,70,90
transitive action verb	及物行動動詞	80,95,114
verb-copying construction	動詞重複句	80,445,454
VO-topicalization construction (=verb-copying construction)	動賓主題提前句	222-248,302-303

X

xiang	想	14,40,45,83,101,421-422 425
xiangxin	相信	422,424,425

| *xiwang* | 希望 | 422,423,425 |

Y

yao	要	42,96,385,388
ye	也	13,14,137,138,139,159 274-276
yinggai	應該	384,385,388
you	有	59,74-76,78,156,157
you	又	13,14,137,138,139,154 159
yuan (yi)	願(意)	14,62,386,388
yong	用	154,435-436
yue...yue...	越...越...	375,376

Z

| *zancheng* | 贊成 | 415 |
| *zhidao* | 知道 | 414,416,417,419,420 |

國立中央圖書館出版品預行編目資料

```
國語的句子與子句結構 = Sentence and clause
structure in Chinese : a functional perspec-
tive / 曹逢甫著 -- 初版 -- 臺北市：臺灣學生，民
79
 22,505 面 ； 26公分 -- （現代語言學論叢  乙類；
14）
 參考書目：面 476-491 含索引
  ISBN 957-15-0089-5（精裝）-- ISBN 957-
15-0090-9（平裝）
 1.中國語言 - 文法
802.63
```

國語的句子與子句結構

著作者：曹　　逢　　甫
出版者：臺　灣　學　生　書　局
本書局登
記證字號：行政院新聞局局版臺業字第一一〇〇號
發行人：丁　　文　　治
發行所：臺　灣　學　生　書　局
　　　　臺北市和平東路一段一九八號
　　　　郵政劃撥帳號〇〇〇二四六六一八號
　　　　電　話：3 6‧3 4 1 5 6
　　　　FAX:(02)3636334
印刷所：淵　明　印　刷　廠
　　　　地　址：永和市成功路一段43巷五號
　　　　電　話：9 2 8 7 1 4 5
香港總經銷：藝　文　圖　書　公　司
　　　　地址：九龍又一村達之路三十號地下
　　　　　後座　電話：3 8 0 5 8 0 7

定價 精裝新台幣四六〇元
　　　平裝新台幣四〇〇元

中華民國七十九年四月初版

80254　版權所有‧翻印必究
ISBN 957-15-0089-5（平裝）
ISBN 957-15-0090-9（精裝）

MONOGRAPHS ON MODERN LINGUISTICS

Edited by

Ting-chi Tang

National Tsing Hua University

ASSOCIATE EDITORIAL BOARD

1. Jin-nan Lai (Tamkang University)
2. Yu-hwei E. Lii (National Taiwan Normal University)
3. Kuang Mei (National Taiwan University)
4. Chien Ching Mo (National Chengchi University)
5. Tsai-fa Cheng (University of Wisconsin)
6. Jeffrey C. Tung (National Taiwan Normal University)

現代語言學論叢編輯委員會

總 編 纂：湯 廷 池 （國立清華大學）
編輯委員：施 玉 惠 （國立師範大學）
　　　　　梅　　廣 （國立臺灣大學）
　　　　　莫 建 清 （國立政治大學）
　　　　　董 昭 輝 （國立師範大學）
　　　　　鄭 再 發 （美國威斯康辛大學）
　　　　　賴 金 男 （私立淡江大學）
　　　　　　（姓氏以筆劃多寡為序）

現代語言學論叢書目

甲類① 湯廷池著：國語變形語法研究第一集：移位變形
② 鄭良偉
　 鄭謝淑娟著：臺灣福建話的語音結構及標音法
③ 湯廷池著：英語教學論集
④ 孫志文著：語文教學改革芻議
⑤ 湯廷池著：國語語法研究論集
⑥ 鄭良偉著：臺灣與國語字音對應規律的研究
⑦ 董昭輝著：從「現在完成式」談起
⑧ 鄧守信著：漢語及物性關係的語意研究研究
⑨ 溫知新
　 楊福綿編：中國語言學名詞滙編
⑩ 薛鳳生著：國語音系解析
⑪ 鄭良偉著：從國語看臺語的發音
⑫ 湯廷池著：漢語詞法句法論集
⑬ 湯廷池著：漢語詞法句法續集

乙類① 鄧守信著：漢語主賓位的語意研究（英文本）
② 溫知新等十七人著：中國語言學會議論集（英文本）
③ 曹逢甫著：主題在國語中的功能研究（英文本）
④ 湯廷池等十八人著：1979年亞太地區語言教學研討會論集
⑤ 莫建清著：立陶宛語語法試論（英文本）
⑥ 鄭謝淑娟著：臺灣福建話形容詞的研究（英文本）
⑦ 曹逢甫等十四人著：第十四屆國際漢藏語言學會論文集（英文本）
⑧ 湯廷池等十人著：漢語句法、語意學論集（英文本）
⑨ 顧百里著：國語在臺灣之演變（英文本）
⑩ 顧百里著：白話文歐化語法之研究（英文本）
⑪ 李梅都著：漢語的照應與刪闕（英文本）
⑫ 黃美金著：「態」之探究（英文本）
⑬ 坂本英子著：從華語看日本漢語的發音
⑭ 曹逢甫著：國語的句子與子句結構